P9-CAA-685

INSPECTOR ALLEYN CALLS

A MYSTERY GUILD LOST CLASSICS OMNIBUS

INSPECTOR ALLEYN CALLS

OVERTURE TO DEATH

DEATH AT THE BAR

FINAL CURTAIN

NGAIO MARSH

Mystery Guild
Garden City, New York

OVERTURE TO DEATH
Copyright © 1939 by Ngaio Marsh

DEATH AT THE BAR
Copyright © 1940, renewed © 1967 by Ngaio Marsh

FINAL CURTAIN
Copyright © 1947, renewed © 1975 by Ngaio Marsh

All rights reserved.

This edition published by arrangement with
Harold Ober Associates.

The characters and events in this book are fictitious.
Any similarity to real persons, living or dead, is coincidental.

ISBN 978-1-61523-306-9

Manufactured in the United States of America

CONTENTS

Ngaio MARSH

Overture to Death

For
The Sunday Morning Party:
G. M. L. Lester
Dundas and Cecil Walker
Norman and Miles Stacpoole Batchelor
and
MY FATHER

CAST OF CHARACTERS

JOCELYN JERNIGHAM of Pen Cuckoo
HENRY JERNIGHAM, his son
ELEANOR PRENTICE, his cousin
TAYLOR, his butler
WALTER COPELAND, B.A. Oxon., Rector of Winton St. Giles
DINAH COPELAND, his daughter
IDRIS CAMPANULA, of the Red House, Chipping
DR. WILLIAM TEMPLETT, of Chippingwood
SELIA ROSS, of Duck Cottage, Cloudyfold
SUPERINTENDENT BLANDISH,
of the Great Chipping Constabulary
SERGEANT ROPER, of the Great Chipping Constabulary
MRS. BIGGINS
GEORGIE BIGGINS, her son
GIBSON, Miss Campanula's chauffeur
GLADYS WRIGHT, of the Y.P.F.C.
SAUL TRANTER, poacher
CHIEF DETECTIVE-INSPECTOR ALLEYN, of the Criminal Investigation Department
DETECTIVE-INSPECTOR FOX, his assistant
DETECTIVE-SERGEANT BAILEY, his finger-print expert
DETECTIVE-SERGEANT THOMPSON, his camera expert
NIGEL BATHGATE, journalist, his Watson

CONTENTS

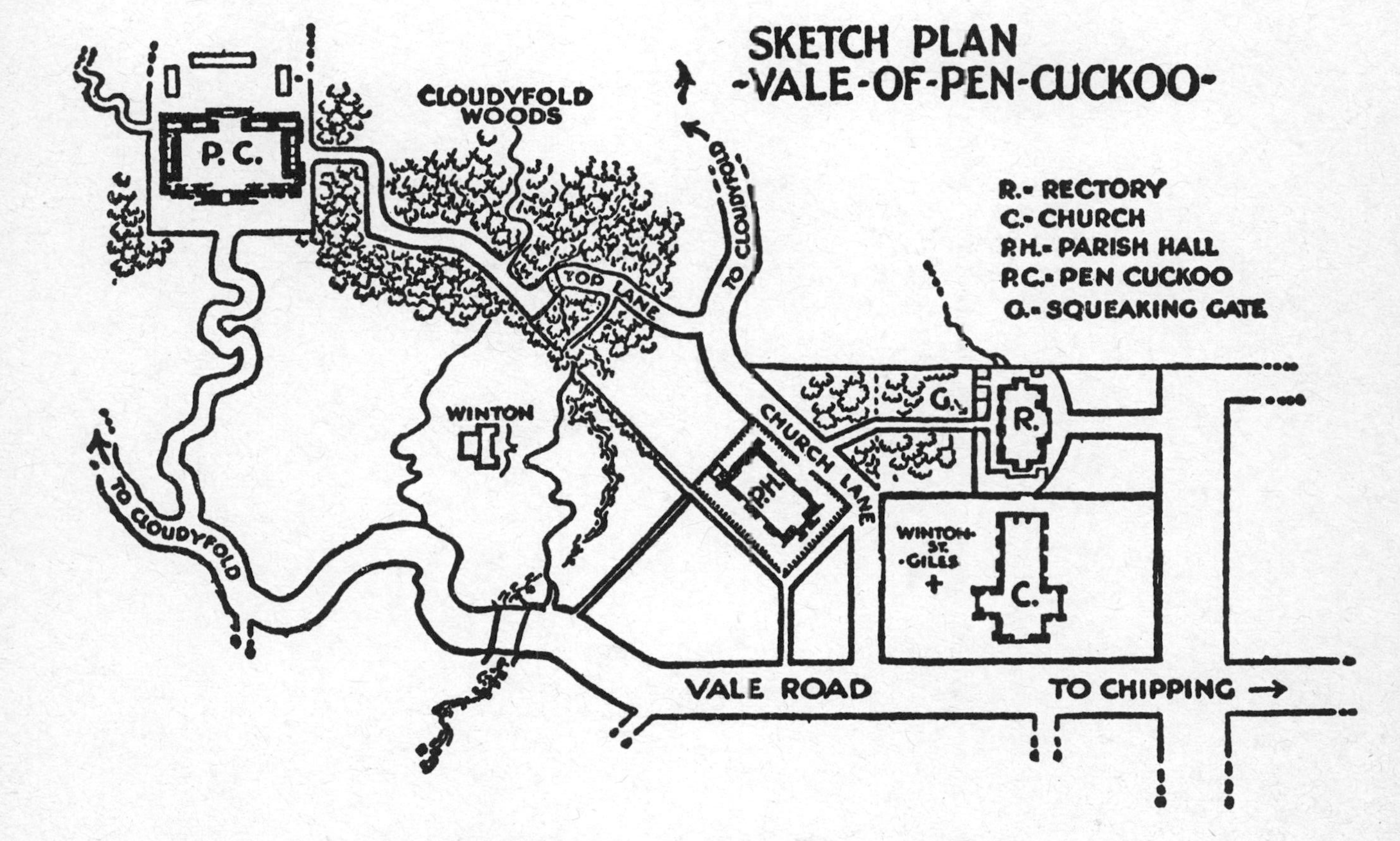
SKETCH PLAN
-VALE-OF-PEN-CUCKOO-
R.- RECTORY
C.- CHURCH
P.H.- PARISH HALL
P.C.- PEN CUCKOO
G.- SQUEAKING GATE
P.C.
CLOUDYFOLD WOODS
TOP LANE
TO CLOUDYFOLD
TO CLOUDYFOLD
WINTON
CHURCH LANE
P.H.
G.
R.
WINTON-ST.-GILES
C.
VALE ROAD
TO CHIPPING →

CHAPTER ONE

They Meet at Pen Cuckoo

i

JOCELYN JERNIGHAM was a good name. The seventh Jocelyn thought so as he stood at his study window and looked down the vale of Pen Cuckoo towards that precise spot where the spire of Salisbury Cathedral could be seen through field-glasses on a clear day.

"Here I stand," he said, without turning his head, "and here my forebears have stood, generation after generation, and looked over their own tilth and tillage. Seven Jocelyn Jernighams."

"I'm never quite sure," said his son Henry Jocelyn, "what tilth and tillage are. What precisely, father, is a tilth?"

"There's no feeling for that sort of thing," said Jocelyn, angrily, "among the present generation. Cheap sneers and clever talk that mean nothing."

"But I assure you I like words to mean something. That is why I ask you to define a tilth. And you say, 'the present generation.' You mean my generation, don't you? But I'm twenty-three. There is a newer generation than mine. If I marry Dinah——"

"You quibble deliberately in order to lead our conversation back to this absurd suggestion. If I had known——"

Henry uttered an impatient noise and moved away from the fireplace. He joined his father in the window and he too looked down into the darkling vale of Pen Cuckoo. He saw an austere landscape, adamant beneath drifts of winter mist. The naked trees slept soundly, the fields were dumb with cold; the few stone cottages, with their comfortable signals of blue smoke, were the only waking things in all the valley.

"I too love Pen Cuckoo," said Henry, and he added, with that tinge of irony which Jocelyn, who did not understand it, found so irritating: "I have all the pride of prospective ownership. But I refuse to be bully-ragged by Pen Cuckoo. I refuse to play the part of a Victorian young gentleman with a touch of Cophetua thrown in. I refuse to allow this conversation to run along the lines of ancient lineage. The proud father and self-willed heir stuff simply doesn't fit. We are not discussing a possible misalliance. Dinah is not a blushing maid of inferior station. She is part of the country, rooted equally with us. If we are going to talk about her in county terms, I can strike a suitable attitude and say there have been Copelands at the rectory for as many generations as there have been Jernighams at Pen Cuckoo."

"You are both much too young——" began Jocelyn.

"No, really, sir, that won't do. What you mean is that Dinah is too poor. If it had been somebody smarter and richer, you and my dear cousin Eleanor wouldn't have talked about youth. Don't let's pretend."

"And don't you talk to me like a damned sententious young puppy, Henry, because I won't have it."

"I'm sorry," said Henry, "I know I'm being tiresome."

"You're being extremely tiresome. Very well, I'll speak as plainly as you like. Pen Cuckoo means more to me and should mean more to you, than anything else in life. You know as well as I do that we're damned hard up. There are all sorts of things that should be done to the place. Those cottages up at Cloudyfold! Winton! Rumbold tells me that Winton'll leak like a basket if we don't fix up the roof. The point is——"

"I can't afford to make a poor marriage?"

"If you choose to put it like that."

"How else can one put it?"

"Very well, then."

"Well, since we must speak in terms of hard cash, which I assure you I don't enjoy, Dinah won't always be the poor parson's one ewe lamb."

"What d'you mean?" asked Jocelyn, uneasily, but with a certain air of pricking up his ears.

"I thought everybody knew Miss Campanula has left all her filthy lucre, or most of it, to the rector. Don't pretend, father; you must have heard that piece of gossip. The cook and housemaid witnessed the will and the housemaid overheard Miss C. bawling about it to her lawyer. Dinah doesn't want the money and nor do I—much—but that's what'll happen to it eventually."

"Servant's gossip," muttered the squire. "Most distasteful. Anyway, it may not—she may change her mind. It's *now* we're so damned hard-up."

"Let me find a job of work," Henry said.

"Your job of work is here."

"What! with a perfectly good agent who looks upon me as a sort of impediment in his agricultural speech?"

"Nonsense!"

"Look here, father," said Henry gently, "how much of this has been inspired by Eleanor?"

"Eleanor is as anxious as I am that you shouldn't make a bloody fool of yourself. If your mother had been alive——"

"No, no," cried Henry, "let us not put ideas into the minds of the dead. That is so grossly unfair. Let's recognise Eleanor's hand in this. Eleanor has been too clever by half. I didn't mean to tell you about Dinah until I was sure that she loved me. I am not sure. The scene, which Eleanor so conveniently overheard yesterday at the rectory, was purely tentative." He broke off, turned away from his father, and pressed his cheek against the window pane.

"It is intolerable," said Henry, "that Eleanor should have spoilt the memory of my first—my first approach to Dinah. To stand in the hall, as she must have done, and to listen! To come clucking back to you like a vulgar hen, agog with her news! As if Dinah was a housemaid with a follower. No, it's too much!"

"You've never been fair to Eleanor. She's done her best to take your mother's place."

"For God's sake," said Henry violently, "don't use that detestable phrase! Cousin Eleanor has never taken my mother's place. She is an aging spinster cousin of the worst type. It was not particularly kind of her to come to Pen Cuckoo. Indeed, it was her golden opportunity. She left the Cromwell Road for the glories of 'county.' It was the great moment of her life. She's a vulgarian."

"On her mother's side," said Jocelyn, "she's a Jernigham."

"Oh, my dear father!" said Henry, and burst out laughing.

Jocelyn glared at his son, turned purple in the face, and began to stammer.

"You may laugh, but Eleanor—Eleanor—in bringing this information—unavoidably overheard—no question of eavesdropping—only doing what she believed to be her duty."

"I'm sure she told you that."

"She did and I agreed with her. I am most strongly opposed to this affair with Dinah, and I am most relieved to hear that so far it is, as you put it, purely tentative."

"If Dinah loves me," said Henry, setting the Jernigham jaw, "I shall marry her. And that's flat. If Eleanor wasn't here to jog at your pride, father, you would at least try to see my side. But Eleanor won't let you. She dramatises herself as the first lady of the district. The squiress. The chatelaine of Pen Cuckoo. She sees Dinah as a sort of rival. What's more, I believe she's genuinely jealous of Dinah. It's the jealousy of a woman of her age and disposition, a jealousy rooted in sex."

"Disgusting balderdash!" said Jocelyn, angrily, but he looked uncomfortable.

"No!" cried Henry. "No, it's not. I'm not talking highbrow pornography. You must have seen what Eleanor is. She's an avid woman. She was in love with you until she found it was a hopeless proposition. Now she and her girl friend the Campanula are rivals for the rector. Dinah says all old maids always fall in love with her father. Everybody sees it. It's a recognised phenomenon with women of Eleanor's and Idris Campanula's type. Have you heard her on the subject of Dr. Templett and Selia Ross? She's nosed out a scandal there. The next thing that happens will be Eleanor feeling it her duty to warn poor Mrs. Templett that her husband is too fond of the widow. That is, if Idris Campanula doesn't get in first. Women like Eleanor and Miss Campanula are pathological. Dinah says——"

"Do you and Dinah discuss my cousin's attachment, which I don't admit, for the rector? If you do, I consider it shows an extraordinary lack of manners and taste."

"Dinah and I," said Henry, "discuss everything."

"And this is modern love-making!"

"Don't let's start abusing each other's generations, Father. We've never done that. You've been so extraordinarily understanding in so many ways. It's Eleanor!" said Henry. "It's Eleanor, Eleanor, Eleanor who is to blame for this!"

The door at the far end of the room was opened and against the lamplit hall beyond appeared a woman's figure.

"Did I hear you call me, Henry?" asked a quiet voice.

ii

Miss Eleanor Prentice came into the room. She reached out a thin hand and switched on the lights.

"It's past five o'clock," said Miss Prentice. "Almost time for our little meeting. I asked them all for half-past five."

She walked with small mimbling steps towards the cherrywood

table which, Henry noticed, had been moved from the wall into the centre of the study. Miss Prentice began to place pencils and sheets of paper at intervals round the table. As she did this she produced, from between her thin closed lips, a dreary flat humming which irritated Henry almost beyond endurance. More to stop this noise than because he wanted to know the answer, Henry asked:

"What meeting, Cousin Eleanor?"

"Have you forgotten, dear? The entertainment committee. The rector and Dinah, Dr. Templett, Idris Campanula, and ourselves. We are counting on you. And on Dinah, of course."

She uttered this last phrase with additional sweetness. Henry thought, "She knows we've been talking about Dinah." As she fiddled with her pieces of paper Henry watched her with that peculiar intensity that people sometimes lavish on a particularly loathed individual.

Eleanor Prentice was a thin, colourless woman of perhaps forty-nine years. She disseminated the odour of sanctity to an extent that Henry found intolerable. Her perpetual half-smile suggested that she was of a gentle and sweet disposition. This faint smile caused many people to overlook the strength of her face, and that was a mistake, for its strength was considerable. Miss Prentice was indeed a Jernigham. Henry suddenly thought that it was rather hard on Jocelyn that both his cousin and his son should look so much more like the family portraits than he did. Henry and Eleanor had each got the nose and jaw proper to the family. The squire had inherited his mother's round chin and indeterminate nose. Miss Prentice's prominent grey eyes stared coldly upon the world through rimless pince-nez. The squire's blue eyes, even when inspired by his frequent twists of ineffectual temper, looked vulnerable and slightly surprised. Henry, still watching her, thought it strange that he himself should resemble this woman whom he disliked so cordially. Without a taste incommon, with violently opposed views on almost all ethical issues, and with a profound mutual distrust, they yet shared a certain hard determination which each recognised in the other. In Henry this quality was tempered by courtesy and by a generous mind. She was merely polite and long-suffering. It was typical of her that although she had evidently overheard Henry's angry reiteration of her name, she accepted his silence and did not ask again why he had called her. Probably, he thought, because she had stood outside the door listening. She now began to pull forward the chairs.

"I think we must give the rector your arm-chair, Jocelyn," she said. "Henry, dear, would you mind? It's rather heavy."

Henry and Jocelyn helped her with the chair and, at her instruction, threw more logs of wood on the fire. These arrangements completed, Miss Prentice settled herself at the table.

"I think your study is almost my favourite corner of Pen Cuckoo, Jocelyn," she said brightly.

The squire muttered something, and Henry said, "But you are very fond of every corner of the house, aren't you, Cousin Eleanor?"

"Yes," she said softly. "Ever since my childhood days when I used to spend my holidays here (you remember, Jocelyn?) I've loved the dear old home."

"Estate agents," Henry said, "have cast a permanent opprobrium on the word 'home.' It has come to mean nothing. It is a pity that when I marry, Cousin Eleanor, I shall not be able to take my wife to Winton. I can't afford to mend the roof, you know."

Jocelyn cleared his throat, darted an angry glance at his son, and returned to the window.

"Winton is the dower-house, of course," murmured Miss Prentice.

"As you already know," Henry continued, "I have begun to pay my addresses to Dinah Copeland. From what you overheard at the rectory do you think it likely that she will accept me?"

He saw her eyes narrow but she smiled a little more widely, showing her prominent and unlovely teeth. "She's like a French Caricature of an English spinster," thought Henry.

"I'm quite sure, dear," said Miss Prentice, "that you do not think I willingly overheard your little talk with Dinah. Far from it. I was very distressed when I caught the few words that——"

"That you repeated to father? I'm sure you were."

"I thought it my duty to speak to your father, Henry."

"Why?"

"Because I think, dear, that you two young people are in need of a little wise guidance."

"Do you like Dinah?" asked Henry abruptly.

"She has many excellent qualities, I am sure," said Miss Prentice.

"I asked you if you liked her, Cousin Eleanor."

"I like her for those qualities. I am afraid, dear, that I think it better not to go any further just at the moment."

"I agree," said Jocelyn from the window. "Henry, I won't have any more of this. These people will be here in a moment. There's the rectory car, now, coming round Cloudyfold bend. They'll be here in five minutes. You'd better tell us what it's all about, Eleanor."

Miss Prentice seated herself at the foot of the table.

"It's the Y.P.F.C.," she said. "We badly want funds and the rector suggested that perhaps we might get up a little play. You remember, Jocelyn. It was the night we dined there."

"I remember something about it," said the squire.

"Just among ourselves," continued Miss Prentice, "I know you've always loved acting, Jocelyn, and you're so good at it. So natural. Do you remember *Ici on Parle Français* in the old days? I've talked it all over with the rector and he agrees it's a splendid idea. Dr. Templett is *very* good at theatricals, especially in funny parts, and dear Idris Campanula, of course, is all enthusiasm."

"Good Lord!" ejaculated Henry and his father together.

"What on earth is *she* going to do in the play?" asked Jocelyn.

"Now, Jocelyn, we mustn't be uncharitable," said Miss Prentice, with a cold glint of satisfaction in her eye. "I dare say poor Idris would make quite a success of a small part."

"I'm too old," said Jocelyn.

"What nonsense, dear. Of course you're not. We'll find something that suits you."

"I'm damned if I'll make love to the Campanula," said the squire, ungallantly. Eleanor assumed her usual expression for the reception of bad language, but it was coloured by that glint of complacency.

"Please, Jocelyn," she said.

"What's Dinah going to do?" asked Henry.

"Well, as dear Dinah is almost a professional——"

"She *is* a professional," said Henry.

"Such a pity, yes," said Miss Prentice.

"Why?"

"I'm old-fashioned enough to think that the stage is not a very nice profession for a gentlewoman, Henry. But of course Dinah must act in our little piece. If she isn't too grand for such humble efforts."

Henry opened his mouth and shut it again. The squire said, "Here they are."

There was the sound of a car pulling up on the gravel drive outside, and two cheerful toots on an out-of-date klaxon.

"I'll go and bring them in," offered Henry.

iii

Henry went out through the hall. When he opened the great front door the upland air laid its cold hand on his face. He smelt frost, dank earth, and dead leaves. The light from the house showed him three figures climbing out of a small car. The rector, his daughter Dinah, and a tall woman in a shapeless fur coat—Idris Campanula. Henry produced the right welcoming noises and ushered them into the house. Taylor, the butler, appeared, and laid expert hands on the rector's shabby overcoat. Henry, his eyes on Dinah, dealt with Miss Campanula's furs. The hall rang with Miss Campanula's conversation. She was a large arrogant spinster with a firm bust, a high-coloured complexion, coarse grey hair, and enormous bony hands. Her clothes were hideous but expensive, for Miss Campanula was extremely wealthy. She was supposed to be Eleanor Prentice's great friend. Their alliance was based on mutual antipathies and interests. Each adored scandal and each cloaked her passion in a mantle of conscious rectitude. Neither trusted the other an inch, but there was no doubt that they enjoyed each other's company. In conversation their technique varied widely. Eleanor never relinquished her air of charity and when she struck, the blow always fell obliquely. But Idris was one of those women who pride themselves on their outspokenness. Repeatedly did she announce that she was a downright sort of person. She was particularly fond of saying that she called a spade a spade, and in her more daring moments would add that her cousin, General Campanula, had once told her that she went further than that and called it a "B. shovel." She cultivated an air of bluff forthrightness that should have deceived nobody, but actually passed as true currency among the simpler of her acquaintances. The truth was that she reserved to herself the right of broad speech, but would have been livid with rage if anybody had replied in kind.

The rector, a widower whose classic handsomeness made him the prey of such women, was, so Dinah had told Henry, secretly terrified of both these ladies who loomed so large in parochial affairs. Eleanor Prentice had a sort of coy bedside manner with the rector. She spoke to him in a dove-smooth voice and frequently uttered little musical laughs. Idris Campanula was bluff and proprietary, called him "my dear man" and watched him with an intensity that made him blink, and aroused in his daughter a conflicting fury of disgust and compassion.

Henry laid aside the fur coat and hurried to Dinah. He had known Dinah all his life, but while he was at Oxford and later, when he did a course with a volunteer air-reserve unit, he had seen little of her. When he returned to Pen Cuckoo, Dinah had finished her dramatic course, and had managed to get into the tail end of a small repertory company where she remained for six weeks. The small repertory company then fell to pieces and Dinah returned home, an actress. Three weeks ago he had met her unexpectedly on the hills above Cloudyfold, and with that encounter came love. He had felt as if he saw her for the first time. The bewildering rapture of discovery was still upon him. To meet her gaze, to speak to her, to stand near her, launched him upon a flood of bliss. His sleep was tinged with the colour of his love and when he woke he found her already waiting in his thought. "She is my whole desire," he said to himself. And, because he was not quite certain that she loved him in return, he had been afraid to declare himself until yesterday, in the shabby, charming old drawing-room at the rectory, when Dinah had looked so transparently into his eyes that he began to speak of love. And then, through the open door, he had seen Eleanor, a still figure, in the dark hall beyond. Dinah saw Eleanor a moment later and, without a word to Henry, went out and welcomed her. Henry himself had rushed out of the rectory and driven home to Pen Cuckoo in a white rage. He had not spoken to Dinah since then, and now he looked anxiously at her. Her wide grey eyes smiled at him.

"Dinah?"

"Henry?"

"When can I see you?"

"You see me now," said Dinah.

"Alone. Please?"

"I don't know. Is anything wrong?"

"Eleanor."

"Oh, Lord!" said Dinah.

"I must talk to you. Above Cloudyfold where we met that morning? To-morrow, before breakfast. Dinah, will you?"

"All right," said Dinah. "If I can."

Idris Campanula's conversation flowed in upon their consciousness. Henry was suddenly aware that she had asked him some sort of question.

"I'm so sorry," he began. "I'm afraid I——"

"Now, Henry," she interrupted, "where are we to go? You're forgetting your duties, gossiping there with Dinah." And she laughed her loud rocketting bray.

"The study, please," said Henry. "Will you lead the way?"

She marched into the study, shook hands with Jocelyn and exchanged pecks with Eleanor Prentice.

"Where's Dr. Templett?" she asked.

"He hasn't arrived yet," answered Miss Prentice. "We must always make allowances for our medical men, mustn't we?"

"He's up beyond Cloudyfold," said the rector. "Old Mrs. Thrinne is much worse. The third Cain boy has managed to run a nail through his big toe. I met Templett in the village and he told me. He said I was to ask you not to wait."

"Beyond Cloudyfold?" asked Miss Prentice sweetly. Henry saw her exchange a glance with Miss Campanula.

"Mrs. Ross doesn't have tea till five," said Miss Campanula, "which *I* consider a silly ostentation. We certainly will *not* wait for Dr. Templett. Ha!"

"Templett didn't say anything about going to Mrs. Ross's," said the rector, innocently, "though to be sure it is on his way."

"My dear good man," said Miss Campanula, "if you weren't a saint—however! I only hope he doesn't try and get her into our play."

"Idris dear," said Miss Prentice. "May I?"

She collected their attention and then said very quietly:

"I think we are all agreed, aren't we, that this little experiment is to be just among ourselves? I have got several little plays here for five and six people and I fancy Dinah has found some too."

"Six," said Miss Campanula very firmly. "Five characters won't do, Eleanor. We've three ladies and three men. And if the rector——"

"No," said the rector, "I shall not appear. If there's any help I can give behind the scenes, I shall be only too delighted, but I really don't want to appear."

"Three ladies and three men, then," said Miss Campanula. "Six."

"Certainly no more," said Miss Prentice.

"Well," said the squire, "if Mrs. Ross is very good at acting, and I must say she's an uncommonly attractive little thing——"

"No, Jocelyn," said Miss Prentice.

"She is very attractive," said Henry.

"She's got a good figure," said Dinah. "Has she had any experience?"

"My dear child," said Miss Campanula loudly, "she's as common as dirt and we certainly don't want her. I may say that I myself have seen Eleanor's plays and I fully approve of *Simple Susan*. There are six characters: three men and three ladies. There is no change of scene, and the theme is suitable."

"It's rather old," said Dinah dubiously.

"My dear child," repeated Miss Campanula, "if you think we're going to do one of your modern questionable problem-plays you're very greatly mistaken."

"I think some of the modern pieces are really *not* quite suitable," agreed Miss Prentice gently.

Henry and Dinah smiled.

"And as for Mrs. Selia Ross," said Miss Campanula, "I believe in calling a spade a spade and I have no hesitation in saying I think we'll be doing a Christian service to poor Mrs. Templett, who we all know is too much an invalid to look after herself, if we give Dr. Templett something to think about besides——"

"Come," said the rector desperately, "aren't we jumping our fences before we meet them? We haven't appointed a chairman yet and so far nobody has suggested that Mrs. Ross be asked to take part."

"They'd better not," said Miss Campanula.

The door was thrown open by Taylor, who announced:

"Mrs. Ross and Dr. Templett, sir."

"What!" exclaimed the squire involuntarily.

An extremely well-dressed woman and a short rubicund man walked into the room.

"Hullo! Hullo!" shouted Dr. Templett. "I've brought Mrs. Ross along by sheer force. She's a perfectly magnificent actress and I tell her she's got to come off her high horse and show us all how to set about it. I know you'll be delighted."

CHAPTER TWO

Six Parts and Seven Actors

i

It was Henry who rescued the situation when it was on the verge of becoming a scene. Neither Miss Campanula nor Miss Prentice made the slightest attempt at cordiality. The squire uttered incoherent noises, shouted "What!" and broke out into uncomfortable social laughter. Dinah greeted Mrs. Ross with nervous civility. The rector blinked and followed his daughter's example. But on Henry the presence of Dinah acted like a particularly strong stimulant and filled him with a vague desire to be nice to the entire population of the world. He shook Mrs. Ross warmly by the hand, complimented Dr. Templett on his idea, and suggested, with a beaming smile, that they should at once elect a chairman and decide on a play.

The squire, Dinah, and the rector confusedly supported Henry. Miss Campanula gave a ringing sniff. Miss Prentice, smiling a little more widely than usual, said:

"I'm afraid we are short of one chair. We expected to be only seven. Henry dear, you will have to get one from the dining-room. I'm so sorry to bother you."

"I'll share Dinah's chair," said Henry happily.

"Please don't get one for me," said Mrs. Ross. "Billy can perch on my arm."

She settled herself composedly in a chair on the rector's left and Dr. Templett at once sat on the arm. Miss Prentice had already made sure of her place on the rector's right hand and Miss Campanula, defeated, uttered a short laugh and marched to the far end of the table.

"I don't know whether this is where I am bidden, Eleanor," she said, "but the meeting seems to be delightfully informal, so this is where I shall sit. Ha!"

Henry, his father, and Dinah took the remaining chairs.

From the old chandelier a strong light was cast down on the eight faces round the table; on the squire, pink with embarrassment; on Miss Prentice, smiling; on Miss Campanula, like an angry mare, breathing hard through her nostrils; on Henry's dark Jernigham features; on Dinah's crisp and vivid beauty; on the rector's coin-sharp priestliness and on Dr. Templett's hearty undistinguished normality. It shone on Selia Ross. She was a straw-coloured woman of perhaps thirty-eight. She was not beautiful but she was exquisitely neat. Her hair curved back from her forehead in pale waves. The thick white skin of her face was beautifully made-up and her clothes were admirable. There was a kind of sharpness about her so that she nearly looked haggard. Her eyes were pale and you would have guessed that the lashes were white when left to themselves. Almost every human being bears some sort of resemblance to an animal and Mrs. Ross was a little like a ferret. But for all that she had a quality that arrested the attention of many women and most men. She had a trick of widening her eyes, and looking slantways. Though she gave the impression of fineness she was in reality so determined that any sensibilities she possessed were held in the vice of her will. She was a coarse-grained woman but she seemed fragile. Her manner was gay and good-natured, but though she went out of her way to do kindnesses, her tongue was quietly malicious. It was clear to all women who met her that her chief interest was men. Dinah watched her now and could not help admiring the cool assurance with which she met her frigid reception. It was impossible to guess whether Mrs. Ross was determined not to show her hurts or was merely so insensitive that she felt none. "She *has* got a cheek," thought Dinah. She looked at Henry and saw her own thoughts reflected in his face. Henry's rather startlingly fierce eyes were fixed on Mrs. Ross and in them Dinah read both awareness and appraisal. He turned his head, met Dinah's glance, and at once his expression changed into one of such vivid tenderness that her heart turned over. She was drowned in a wave of emotion and was brought back to the world by the sound of Miss Prentice's voice.

"——to elect a chairman for our little meeting. I should like to propose the rector."

"Second that," said Miss Campanula, in her deepest voice.

"There you are, Copeland," said the squire, "everybody says 'Aye' and away we go." He laughed loudly and cast a terrified glance at his cousin.

The rector looked amiably round the table. With the exception of Henry, of all the company he seemed the least embarrassed by the arrival of Mrs. Ross. If Mr. Copeland had been given a round gentle face with unremarkable features and kind shortsighted eyes it would have been a perfect expression of his temperament. But ironical nature had made him magnificently with a head so beautiful that to most observers it seemed that his character must also be on a grand scale. With that head he might have gone far and become an important dignitary of the church, but he was unambitious and sincere, and he loved Pen Cuckoo. He was quite content to live at the rectory as his forebears had lived, to deal with parish affairs, to give what spiritual and bodily comfort he could to his people, and to fend off the advances of Idris Campanula and Eleanor Prentice. He knew very well that both these ladies bitterly resented the presence of Mrs. Ross, and that he was in for one of those hideously boring situations when he felt exactly as if he was holding down with his thumb the cork of a bottle filled with seething ginger-pop.

He said, "Thank you very much. I don't feel that my duties as chairman will be very heavy as we have only met to settle the date and nature of this entertainment, and when that is decided all I shall have to do is to hand everything over to the kind people who take part. Perhaps I should explain a little about the object we have in mind. The Young People's Friendly Circle, which has done such splendid work in Pen Cuckoo and the neighbouring parishes, is badly in need of funds. Miss Prentice as president and Miss Campanula as secretary, will tell you all about that. What we want more than anything else is a new piano. The present instrument was given by your father, wasn't it, squire?"

"Yes," said Jocelyn. "I remember quite well. It was when I was about twelve. It wasn't new then. I can imagine it's pretty well a dead horse."

"We had a tuner up from Great Chipping," said Miss Campanula, "and he says he can't do anything more with it. I blame the scouts. Ever since the eldest Cain boy was made scout-master they have gone from bad to worse. He's got no idea of discipline, that young man. On Saturday I found Georgie Biggins tramping up and down the keyboard in his boots and whanging the wires inside with the end of his pole. 'If I were your scout-master,' I said, 'I'd give you a beating that you'd not forget in a twelvemonth.' His reply was grossly impertinent. I told the eldest Cain that if he couldn't control his boys himself he'd better hand them over to someone who could."

"Dear me, yes," said the rector hurriedly. "Young barbarians they are sometimes. Well now, the piano is of course not the sole property of the Y.P.F.C. It was a gift to the parish. But I have suggested that, as they use it a great deal, perhaps it would be well to devote whatever funds result from this entertainment to a piano fund, rather than to a general Y.P.F.C. fund. I don't know what you all think about this."

"How much would a new piano cost?" asked Dr. Templett.

"There's a very good instrument at Preece's in Great Chipping," said the rector. "The price is £50."

"We can't hope to make that at our show, can we?" asked Dinah.

"I tell you what," said the squire. "I'll make up the difference. The piano seems to be a Pen Cuckoo affair."

There was a general gratified murmur.

"Damned good of you, squire," said Dr. Templett. "Very generous."

"Very good indeed," agreed the rector.

Miss Prentice, without moving, seemed to preen herself. Henry saw Miss Campanula look at her friend and was startled by the singularly venomous glint in her eye. He thought, "She's jealous of Eleanor taking reflected glory from father's offer." And suddenly he was appalled by the thought of these two aging women united in so profound a dissonance.

"Perhaps," said the rector, "we had better have a formal motion."

They had a formal motion. The rector hurried them on. A date was fixed three weeks ahead for the performance in the parish hall. Miss Prentice who seemed to have become a secretary by virtue of her seat on the rector's right hand, made quantities of notes. And all the time each of these eight people knew very well that they merely moved in a circle round the true matter of their meeting. What Miss Prentice called "the nature of our little entertainment" had yet to be determined. Every now and then someone would steal a covert glance at the small pile of modern plays in front of Dinah, and the larger pile of elderly French's acting editions in front of Miss Prentice. And while they discussed prices of admission, and dates, through each of their minds raced their secret thoughts.

ii

The rector thought, "I cannot believe it of Templett. A medical man with an invalid wife! Besides, there's his professional position. But what persuaded him to bring her here? He must have known how they would talk. I wish Miss Campanula wouldn't look at me like that. She wants to see me alone again. I wish I'd never said confession was recognised by the Church, but how could I not? I wish she wouldn't confess. I wish that I didn't get the impression that she and Miss Prentice merely use the confessional as a means of informing against each other. Six parts and seven people. Oh, dear!"

The squire thought, "Eleanor's quite right, I was good in *Ici on Parle Français*. Funny how some people take to the stage naturally. Now, if Dinah and Henry try to suggest one of those modern things, as likely as not there will be nothing that suits me. What I'd like is one of those charming not-so-young men in a Marie Tempest comedy. Mrs. Ross could play the Marie Tempest part. Eleanor and old Idris wouldn't have that at any price. I wonder if it's true that they don't really kiss on the stage because of the grease paint. Still, at rehearsals . . . I wonder if it's true about Templett and Mrs. Ross. I'm as young as ever I was. What the devil am I going to do about Henry and Dinah Copeland? Dinah's a pretty girl. Hard, though. Modern. If only the Copelands were a bit better off it wouldn't matter. I suppose they'll talk about me, both of them. Henry will say something clever. Blast and damn Eleanor! Why the devil couldn't she hold her tongue, and then I shouldn't have had to deal with it. Six parts and seven people. Why shouldn't she be in it, after all? I suppose Templett would want the charming not-so-young part and they'd turn me into some bloody comic old dodderer."

Eleanor Prentice thought, "If I take care and manage this well it will look as if it's Idris who is making all the trouble and he will think her uncharitable. Six parts and seven people. Idris is determined to stop that Ross woman at all costs. I can see one of Idris's tantrums coming. That's all to the good. I shall be forty-nine next month. Idris is more than forty-nine. Dinah should work in the parish. I wonder what goes on among actors and actresses. Dressing and undressing behind the scenes and travelling about together. If I could find out that Dinah had—— If I married, Jocelyn would make me an allowance. To see that woman look at Templett like that and he at her! Dinah and Henry! I can't bear it. I can't endure it. Never show you're hurt. I want to look at him, but I mustn't. Henry might be watching. Henry knows. A parish priest should be married. His head is like an angel's head. No. Not an angel's. A Greek god. Prostrate before Thy throne to lie and gaze and gaze on Thee. Oh, God, let him love me!"

Henry thought, "To-morrow morning if it's fine I shall meet Dinah above Cloudyfold and tell her that I love her. Why shouldn't Templett have his Selia Ross in the play? Six parts and seven people to the devil! Let's find a new play. I'm in love for the first time.

I've crossed the border into a strange country and never again will there be a moment quite like this. To-morrow morning, if it's fine, Dinah and I will meet up on Cloudyfold."

Dinah thought, "To-morrow morning, if it's fine, Henry will be waiting for me above Cloudyfold and I think he will tell me he loves me. There will be nobody in the whole wide world but Henry and me."

Templett thought, "I'll have to be careful. I suppose I was a fool to suggest her coming, but after she said she was so keen on acting it seemed the only thing to do. If those two starved spinsters get their teeth into us it'll be all up with the practice. I wish to God I was made differently. I wish to God my wife wasn't what she is. Perhaps it'd be all the same if she wasn't. Selia's got me. It's like an infection. I'm eaten up with it."

Selia Ross thought, "So far so good. I've got here. I can manage the squire easily enough, but he's got his eye on me already. The boy's in love with the girl, but he's a man and I think he'll be generous. He's no fool, though, and I rather fancy he's summed me up. Attractive, with those light grey eyes and black lashes. It might be amusing to take him from her. I doubt if I could. He's past the age when they fall for women a good deal older than themselves. I feel equal to the whole lot of them. It was fun coming in with Billy and seeing those two frost-bitten old virgins with their eyes popping out of their heads. They know I'm too much for them with my good common streak of hard sense and determination. They're both trying to see if Billy's arm is touching my shoulders. The Campanula is staring quite openly and the Poor Relation's looking out of the corner of her eyes. I'll lean back a little. There! Now have a good look. It's a bore about Billy's professional reputation and having to be so careful. I want like hell to show them all he's mine. I've never felt like this about any other man, never. It's as if we'd engulfed each other. I suppose it's love. I won't have him in their bogus schoolroom play without me. He might have a love scene with the girl. I couldn't stand that. Seven people and six parts. Now, then!"

And Idris Campanula thought, "If I could in decency lay my hands on that straw-coloured wanton I'd shake the very life out of her. The infamous brazen effrontery! To force her way into Pen Cuckoo, without an invitation, under the protection of that man! I always suspected Dr. Templett of that sort of thing. If Eleanor had the gumption of a rabbit she'd have forbidden them the house. Sitting on the arm of her chair! A fine excuse! He's practically got his arm around her. I'll look straight at them and let her see what I think of her. There! She's smiling. She knows, and she doesn't care. It amounts to living in open sin with him. The rector *can't* let it pass. It's an open insult to me, making me sit at the same table with them. Every hand against me. I've no friends. They only want my money. Eleanor's as bad as the rest. She's tried to poison the rector's mind against me. She's jealous of me. The play was *my* idea and now she's talking as if it was hers. The rector must be warned. I'll ask him to hear my confession on Friday. I'll confess the unkind thoughts I've had of Eleanor Prentice and before he can stop me I'll tell him what they were and then perhaps he'll begin to see through Eleanor. Then I'll say I've been uncharitable about Mrs. Ross and Dr. Templett. I'll say I'm an outspoken woman and believe in looking facts in the face. He *must* prefer me to Eleanor. I ought to have married. With my ability and my money and my brains I'd make a success of it. I'd do the Rectory up and get rid of that impertinent old maid. Dinah could go back to the stage as soon as she liked, or if Eleanor's gossip is true, she could marry Henry Jernigham. Eleanor wouldn't care much for that. She'll fight tooth and nail before she sees another chatelaine at Pen Cuckoo. I'll back Eleanor up as far as Dr. Templett and his common little light-of-love are concerned, but if she tries to come between me and Walter Copeland she'll regret it. Now then, I'll speak."

And bringing her large, ugly hand down sharply on the table she said:

"May I have a word?"

"Please do," said Mr. Copeland nervously.

"As secretary," began Miss Campanula loudly, "I have discussed this matter with the Y.P.F.C. members individually. They plan an entertainment of their own later on in the year and they are *most* anxious that this little affair should be arranged *entirely* by ourselves. Just five or six, they said, of the people who are really interested in the Circle. They mentioned you, of course, rector, and the squire, as patron, and you Eleanor, naturally, as president. They said they hoped Dinah would not feel that our humble efforts were beneath her dignity and that she would grace our little performance. And you, Henry, they particularly mentioned you."

"Thank you," said Henry solemnly. Miss Campanula darted a suspicious glance at him and went on:

"They seem to think they'd like to see me making an exhibition of myself with all the rest of you. Of course, I don't pretend to histrionic talent——"

"*Of course* you must have a part, Idris," said Miss Prentice. "We depend upon you."

"Thank you, Eleanor," said Miss Campanula; and between the two ladies there flashed the signal of an alliance.

"That makes five, doesn't it?" asked Miss Prentice sweetly.

"Five," said Miss Campanula.

"Six, with Dr. Templett," said Henry.

"We should be very glad to have Dr. Templett," rejoined Miss Prentice, with so cunningly balanced an inflection that her rejection of Mrs. Ross was implicit in every syllable.

"Well, a G.P.'s an awkward sort of fellow when it comes to rehearsals," said Dr. Templett. "Never know when an urgent case may not crop up. Still, if you don't mind risking it I'd like to take a part."

"We'll certainly risk it," said the rector. There was a murmur of assent followed by a deadly little silence. The rector drew in his breath, looked at his daughter who gave him a heartening nod, and said:

"Now, before we go any further with the number of performers, I think we should decide on the form of the entertainment. If it is going to be a play, so much will depend upon the piece chosen. Has anybody any suggestion?"

"I move," said Miss Campanula, "that we do a play, and I suggest *Simple Susan* as a suitable piece."

"I should like to second that," said Miss Prentice.

"What sort of play is it?" asked Dr. Templett. "I haven't heard of it. Is it new?"

"It's a contemporary of *East Lynne* and *The Silver King* I should think," said Dinah.

Henry and Dr. Templett laughed. Miss Campanula thrust out her bosom, turned scarlet in the face, and said:

"In my humble opinion, Dinah, it is none the worse for that."

"It's so amusing," said Miss Prentice. "You remember it, Jocelyn, don't you? There's that little bit where Lord Sylvester pretends to be his own tailor and proposes to Lady Maude, thinking she's her own lady's maid. Such an original notion and so ludicrous."

"It has thrown generations of audiences into convulsions," agreed Henry.

"Henry," said the squire.

"Sorry, Father. But honestly, as a dramatic device——"

"*Simple Susan*," said Miss Campanula hotly, "may be old-fashioned in the sense that it contains no disgusting innuendoes. It does not depend on vulgarity for its fun, and that's more than can be said for most of your modern comedies."

"How far does Lord Sylvester go——" began Dinah.

"Dinah!" said the rector quietly.

"All right, Daddy. Sorry. I only——"

"How old is Lord Sylvester?" interrupted the squire suddenly.

"Oh, about forty-five or fifty," murmured Miss Prentice.

"Why not do the *Private Secretary*?" inquired Henry.

"I never thought *The Private Secretary* a very nice play," said Miss Prentice. "I expect I'm prejudiced." And she gave the rector a reverent smile.

"I agree," said Miss Campanula. "I always thought it in the worst of taste. I may be old-fashioned but I don't like jokes about the cloth."

"I don't think *The Private Secretary* ever did us much harm," said the rector mildly. "But aren't we wandering from the point? Miss Campanula has moved that we do a play called *Simple Susan*. Miss Prentice has seconded her. Has anybody else a suggestion to make?"

"Yes," said Selia Ross, "I have."

CHAPTER THREE

They Choose a Play

i

IF MRS. ROSS had taken a ticking bomb from her handbag and placed it on the table, the effect could have been scarcely more devastating. What she did produce was a small green book. Seven pairs of eyes followed the movements of her thin, scarlet-tipped hands. Seven pairs of eyes fastened, as if mesmerised, on the black letters of the book cover. Mrs. Ross folded her hands over the book and addressed the meeting.

"I do hope you'll all forgive me for making my suggestion," she said, "but it's the result of a rather odd coincidence. I'd no idea of your meeting until Dr. Templett called in this afternoon, but I happened to be reading this play and when he appeared the first thing I said was, 'Some time or other we simply *must* do this thing.' Didn't I, Billy? I mean, it's absolutely marvellous. All the time I was reading it I kept thinking how perfect it would be for some of you to do it in aid of one of the local charities. There are two parts in it that would be simply ideal for Miss Prentice and Miss Campanula. The Duchess and her sister. The scene they have with General Talbot is one of the best in the play. It simply couldn't be funnier and you'd be magnificent as the General, Mr. Jernigham."

She paused composedly and looked sideways at the squire. Nobody spoke, though Miss Campanula wetted her lips. Selia Ross waited for a moment, smiling frankly, and then she said:

"Of course I didn't realise you had already chosen a play. Naturally I wouldn't have dreamt of coming if I had known. It's all this man's fault." She gave Dr. Templett a sort of comradely jog with her elbow. "He bullied me into it. I ought to have apologised and crept away at once, but I just couldn't resist telling you about my discovery." She opened her eyes a little wider and turned them on the rector. "Perhaps if I left it with you, Mr. Copeland, the committee might just like to glance at it before they quite decide. *Please* don't think I want a part in it or anything frightful like that. It's just that it *is* so good and I'd be delighted to lend it."

"That's very kind of you," said the rector.

"It's not a bit kind. I'm being thoroughly selfish. I just long to see you all doing it and I'm secretly hoping you won't be able to resist it. It's so difficult to find modern plays that aren't offensive," continued Mrs. Ross, with an air of great frankness, "but this really is charming."

"But what is the play?" asked Henry, who had been craning his neck in a useless attempt to read the title.

"*Shop Windows*, by Jacob Hunt."

"Good Lord!" ejaculated Dinah. "Of course! I never thought of it. It's the very thing."

"Have you read it?" asked Mrs. Ross, with a friendly glance at her.

"I saw the London production," said Dinah. "You're quite right, it would be grand. But what about the royalties? Hunt charges the earth for amateur rights, and anyway he'd probably refuse them to us."

"I was coming to that," said Mrs. Ross. "If you should decide to do it I'd like to stand the royalties if you'd let me."

There was another silence, broken by the rector.

"Now, that's very generous indeed," he said.

"No, honestly it's not. I've told you I'm longing to see it done."

"How many characters are there?" asked the squire suddenly.

"Let me see, I think there are six." She opened the play and counted prettily on her fingers.

"Five, six—no, there seem to be seven! Stupid of me."

"Ha!" said Miss Campanula.

"But I'm sure you could find a seventh. What about the Moorton people?"

"What about you?" asked Dr. Templett.

"No, no!" said Mrs. Ross quickly. "I don't come into the picture. Don't be silly."

"It's a damn' good play," said Henry. "I saw the London show too, Dinah. D'you think we could do it?"

"I don't see why not. The situations would carry it through. The three character parts are really the stars."

"Which are they?" demanded the squire.

"The General and the Duchess and her sister," said Mrs. Ross.

"They don't come on till the second act," continued Dinah, "but from then on they carry the show."

"May I have a look at it?" asked the squire.

Mrs. Ross opened the book and passed it across to him.

"Do read the opening of the act," she said, "and then go on to page forty-eight."

"May I speak?" demanded Miss Campanula loudly.

"Please!" said the rector hurriedly. "Please do. Ah—order!"

ii

Miss Campanula gripped the edge of the table with her large hands and spoke at some length. She said that she didn't know how everybody else was feeling but that she herself was somewhat bewildered. She was surprised to learn that such eminent authorities as Dinah and Henry and Mrs. Ross considered poor Pen Cuckoo capable of producing a modern play that met with their approval. She thought that perhaps this clever play might be a little too clever for poor Pen Cuckoo and the Young People's Friendly Circle. She asked the meeting if it did not think it would make a great mistake if it was over-ambitious. "I must confess," she said, with an angry laugh, "that I had a much simpler plan in mind. I did not propose to fly as high as West End successes and I don't mind saying I think we would be in a fair way to making fools of ourselves. And that's that."

"But, Miss Campanula," objected Dinah, "it's such a mistake to think that because the cast is not very experienced it will be better in a bad play than in a good one."

"I'm sorry you think *Simple Susan* a bad play, Dinah," said Miss Prentice sweetly.

"Well, I think it's very dated and I'm afraid I think it's rather silly," said Dinah doggedly.

Miss Prentice gave a silvery laugh in which Miss Campanula joined.

"I agree with Dinah," said Henry quickly.

"Suppose we all read both plays," suggested the rector.

"I have read *Shop Windows*," said Dr. Templett. "I must say I don't see how we could do better."

"We seem to be at a disadvantage, Eleanor," said Miss Campanula unpleasantly, and Miss Prentice laughed again. So, astonishingly, did the squire. He broke out in a loud choking snort. They all turned to look at him. Tears coursed each other down his cheeks and he dabbed at them absent-mindedly with the back of his hand.

His shoulders quivered, his brows were raised in an ecstasy of merriment, and his cheeks were purple. He was lost in the second act of Mrs. Ross's play.

"Oh! Lord!" he said, "this is funny."

"Jocelyn!" cried Miss Prentice.

"Eh?" said the squire, and he turned a page, read half-a-dozen lines, laid the book on the table and gave himself up to paroxysms of unbridled laughter.

"Jocelyn!" repeated Miss Prentice. "Really!"

"What?" gasped the squire. "Eh? All right, I'm quite willing. Damn' good! When do we begin?"

"Hi!" said Henry. "Steady, Father! The meeting hasn't decided on the play."

"Well, we'd better decide on this," said the squire, and he leant towards Selia Ross. "When he starts telling her he's got the garter," he said, "and she thinks he's talking about the other affair! And then when she says she won't take no for an answer. Oh, Lord!"

"It's heavenly, isn't it?" agreed Mrs. Ross, and she and Henry and Dinah suddenly burst out laughing at the recollection of this scene, and for a minute or two they all reminded each other of the exquisite facetiæ in the second act of *Shop Windows*. The rector listened with a nervous smile; Miss Prentice and Miss Campanula with tightly-set lips. At last the squire looked round the table with brimming eyes and asked what they were all waiting for.

"I'll move we do *Shop Windows*," he said. "That in order?"

"I'll second it," said Dr. Templett.

"No doubt I am in error," said Miss Campanula, "but I was under the impression that my poor suggestion was before the meeting, seconded by Miss Prentice."

The rector was obliged to put this motion to the meeting.

"It is moved by Miss Campanula," he said unhappily, "and seconded by Miss Prentice, that *Simple Susan* be the play chosen for production. Those in favour——"

"Aye," said Miss Campanula and Miss Prentice.

"And the contrary?"

"No," said the rest of the meeting with perfect good humour.

"Thank you," said Miss Campanula. "*Thank you*. Now we know where we are."

"You wait till you start learning your parts in this thing," said Jocelyn cheerfully, "and you won't know whether you're on your heads or your heels. There's an awful lot of us three, isn't there?" he continued, turning the pages. "I suppose Eleanor will do the Duchess and Miss Campanula will be the other one—Mrs. Thing or whoever she is! Gertrude! That the idea?"

"That was my idea," said Mrs. Ross.

"If I may be allowed to speak," said Miss Campanula, "I should like to say that it is just within the bounds of possibility that it may not be ours."

"Perhaps, Jernigham," said the rector, "you had better put your motion."

But of course the squire's motion was carried. Miss Campanula and Miss Prentice did not open their lips. Their thoughts were alike in confusion and intensity. Both seethed under the insult done to *Simple Susan*, each longed to rise and, with a few well-chosen words, withdraw from the meeting. Each was checked by a sensible reluctance to cut off her nose to spite her face. It was obvious that *Shop Windows* would be performed whether they stayed in or flounced out. Unless all the others were barefaced liars, it seemed that there were two outstandingly good parts ready for them to snap up. They hung off and on, ruffled their plumage, and secretly examined each other's face.

iii

Meanwhile with the enthusiasm that all Jernighams brought to a new project Jocelyn and his son began to cast the play. Almost a century ago there had been what Eleanor, when cornered, called an "incident" in the family history. The Mrs. Jernigham of that time was a plain silly woman and barren into the bargain. Her Jocelyn, the fourth of that name, had lived openly with a very beautiful and accomplished actress and had succeeded in getting the world to pretend that his son by her was his lawful scion, and had jockeyed his wife into bringing the boy up as her own. By this piece of effrontery he brought to Pen Cuckoo a dram of mummery, and ever since those days most of the Jernighams had had a passion for theatricals. It was as if the lovely actress had touched up the family portraits with a stick of rouge. Jocelyn and Henry had both played in the O.U.D.S. They both had the trick of moving about a stage as if they grew out of the boards, and they both instinctively bridged that colossal gap between the stage and the front row of the stalls. Jocelyn thought himself a better actor than he was, but Henry did not realise how good he might be. Even Miss Prentice, a Jernigham, as the squire had pointed out, on her mother's side, had not escaped that dram of player's blood. Although she knew nothing about theatre, mistrusted and disliked the very notion of the stage as a career for gentle people, and had no sort of judgment for the merit of a play, yet in amateur theatricals she was surprisingly composed and perfectly audible, and she loved acting. She knew now that Idris Campanula expected her to refuse to take part in *Shop Windows*, and more than half her inclination was so to refuse. "What," she thought. "To have my own play put aside for something chosen by that woman! To have to look on while they parcel out the parts!" But even as she pondered on the words with which she would offer her resignation, she pictured Lady Appleby of Moorton Grange accepting the part that Jocelyn said was so good. And what was more, the rector would think Eleanor herself uncharitable. That decided her. She waited for a pause in the chatter round Jocelyn, and then she turned to the rector.

"May I say just one little word?" she asked.

"Yes, yes, of course," said Mr. Copeland. "Please, everybody. Order!"

"It's only this," said Miss Prentice, avoiding the eye of Miss Campanula. "I do hope nobody will think I am going to be disappointed or hurt about my little play. I expect it *is* rather out-of-date, and I am only too pleased to think that you have found one that is more suitable. If there is anything that I can do to help, I shall be only too glad. Of course."

She received, and revelled in, the rector's beaming smile, and met Idris Campanula's glare with a smile of her own. Then she saw Selia Ross watching her out of the corners of her eyes and suddenly she knew that Selia Ross understood her.

"That's perfectly splendid," exclaimed Mr. Copeland. "I think it is no more than we expected of Miss Prentice's generosity, but we are none the less grateful." And he added confusedly, "A very graceful gesture."

Miss Prentice preened and Miss Campanula glowered. The others, vaguely aware that something was expected of them, made small appreciative noises.

"Now, how about casting the play?" said Dr. Templett.

iv

There was no doubt that the play had been well chosen. With the exception of one character, it practically cast itself. The squire was to play the General; Miss Prentice, the Duchess; Miss Campanula, of whom everybody felt extremely frightened, was cast for Mrs. Arbuthnot, a good character part. Miss Campanula, when offered this part, replied ambiguously:

"Who knows?" she asked darkly. "Obviously, it is not for me to say."

"But you will do it, Idris?" murmured Miss Prentice.

"I have but one comment," rejoined Miss Campanula. "Wait and see." She laughed shortly, and the rector, in a hurry, wrote her name down opposite the part. Dinah and Henry were given the two young lovers, and Dr. Templett said he would undertake the French Ambassador. He began to read some of the lines in violently broken English. There remained the part of Hélène, a mysterious lady who had lost her memory, and who turned up in the middle of the first act at a country house-party.

"Obviously, Selia," said Dr. Templett, "you must be Hélène."

"No, *no*," said Mrs. Ross, "that isn't a bit what I meant. Now do be quiet, Billy, or they'll all think I came here with an ulterior motive."

With the possible exception of the squire, that was precisely what they all did think, but not even Miss Campanula had the courage to say so. Having accepted Mrs. Ross's play they could do nothing but offer her the part, which, as far as lines went, was not a long one. Perhaps only Dinah realised quite how good Hélène was. Mrs. Ross protested and demurred.

"If you are quite sure you want me," she said, and looked sideways at the squire. Jocelyn, who had glanced through the play and found that the General had a love-scene with Hélène, said heartily that they wanted her very much indeed. Henry and Dinah, conscious of their own love-scenes, agreed, and the rector formally asked Mrs. Ross if she would take the part. She accepted with the prettiest air in the world. Miss Prentice managed to maintain her gentle smile and Miss Campanula's behaviour merely became a degree more darkly ominous. The rector put on his glasses and read his notes.

"To sum up," he said loudly. "We propose to do this play in the Parish Hall on Saturday 27th, three weeks from to-night. The proceeds are to be devoted to the piano-fund and the balance of the sum needed will be made up most generously by Mr. Jocelyn Jernigham. The committee and members of the Y.P.F.C. will organise the sale of tickets and will make themselves responsible for the—what is the correct expression, Dinah?"

"The front of the house, Daddy."

"For the front of the house, yes. Do you think we can leave these affairs to your young folk, Miss Campanula? I know you can answer for them."

"My dear man," said Miss Campanula, "I can't answer for the behaviour of thirty village louts and maidens, but they usually do what I tell them to. Ha!"

Everybody laughed sycophantly.

"My *friend*," added Miss Campanula, with a ghastly smile, "my *friend* Miss Prentice is president. No doubt, if they pay no attention to me, they will do anything in the world for her."

"Dear Idris!" murmured Miss Prentice.

"Who's going to produce the play?" asked Henry. "I think Dinah ought to. She's a professional."

"Hear, hear!" said Dr. Templett, Selia Ross and the squire. Miss Prentice added rather a tepid little, "Of course, yes." Miss Campanula said nothing. Dinah grinned shyly and looked into her lap. She was elected producer. Dinah had not passed the early stages of theatrical experience when the tyro lards his conversation with professional phrases. She accepted her honours with an air of great seriousness and called her first rehearsal for Tuesday night, November 9th.

"I'll get all your sides typed by then," she explained. "I'm sure Gladys Wright will do them, because she's learning and wants experience. I'll give her a proper part so that she gets the cues right. We'll have a reading and if there's time I'll set positions for the first act."

"Dear me," said Miss Prentice, "this sounds very alarming. I'm afraid, Dinah dear, that you will find us all very amateurish."

"Oh, no!" cried Dinah gaily. "I know it's going to be marvellous." She looked uncertainly at her father and added, "I should like to say, thank you all very much for asking me to produce. I do hope I'll manage it all right."

"Well, you know a dashed sight more about it than any of us," said Selia Ross bluntly.

But somehow Dinah didn't quite want Mrs. Ross so frankly on her side. She was aware in herself of a strong antagonism to Mrs. Ross and this discovery surprised and confused her, because she believed herself to be a rebel. As a rebel, she should have applauded Selia Ross. To Dinah, Miss Prentice and Miss Campanula were the hated symbols of all that was mean, stupid, and antediluvian. Selia Ross had deliberately given battle to these two ladies and had won the first round. Why, then, could Dinah not welcome her as an ally after her own heart? She supposed it was because, in her own heart, she mistrusted and disliked Mrs. Ross. This feeling was entirely instinctive and it upset and bewildered her. It was as if some dictator in her blood refused an allegiance that she should have welcomed. She could not reply with the correct comradely smile. She felt her face turning pink with embarrassment and she said hurriedly:

"What about music? We'll want an overture and an entr'acte."

And with those words Dinah unconsciously rang up the curtain on a theme that was to engulf Pen Cuckoo and turn *Shop Windows* from polite comedy into outlandish shameless melodrama.

CHAPTER FOUR

Cue For Music

i

As SOON as Dinah had spoken those fatal words everybody round the table in the study at Pen Cuckoo thought of Rachmaninoff's Prelude in C. sharp Minor, and with the exception of Miss Campanula, everybody's heart sank into his or her boots. For the Prelude was Miss Campanula's speciality. In Pen Cuckoo she had the sole rights in this composition. She played it at all church concerts, she played it on her own piano after her own dinner parties, and, unless her hostess was particularly courageous, she played it after other people's dinner parties, too. Whenever there was any question of music sounding at Pen Cuckoo, Miss Campanula offered her services, and the three pretentious chords would boom out once again: "Pom, *pom*, POM." And then down would go Miss Campanula's foot on the left pedal and the next passage would follow in a series of woolly but determined jerks. She even played it as a voluntary when Mr. Withers, the organist; went on his holidays and Miss Campanula took his place. She had had her photograph taken, seated at the instrument, with the Prelude on the rack. Each of her friends had received a copy at Christmas. The rector's was framed, and he had not known quite what to do with it. Until three years ago when Eleanor Prentice had come to live at Pen Cuckoo, Idris Campanula and her Prelude had had it all their own way. But Miss Prentice also belonged to a generation when girls learnt the pianoforte from their governesses, and she, too, liked to be expected to perform. Her *pièce de resistance* was Ethelbert Nevin's Venetian Suite, which she rendered with muffled insecurity, the chords of the accompaniment never quite synchronising with the saccharine notes of the melody. Between the two ladies the battle had raged at parish entertainments, Sunday School services, and private parties. They only united in deploring the radio and in falsely pretending that music was a bond between them.

So that when Dinah in her flurry asked, "What about music?" Miss Campanula and Miss Prentice both became alert.

Miss Prentice said, "Yes, of course. Now, couldn't we manage that amongst ourselves somehow? It's *so* much pleasanter, isn't it, if we keep to our own small circle?"

"I am afraid my poor wits are rather confused," began Miss Campanula. "Everything seems to have been decided out of hand. You must correct me if I'm wrong, but it appears that several of the characters in this delightful comedy—by the way, is it a comedy?"

"Yes," said Henry.

"Thank you. It appears that some of the characters do not appear until somewhere in the second act. I don't know which of the characters, naturally, as I have not yet looked between the covers."

With hasty mumbled apologies they handed the play to Miss Campanula. She said:

"Oh, thank you. Don't let me be selfish. I'm a patient body."

When Idris Campanula alluded to herself jocularly as a "body" it usually meant that she was in a temper. They all said, "No, no! Please have it." She drew her pince-nez out from her bosom by a patent extension and slung them across her nose. She opened the play and amidst dead silence she began to inspect it. First she read the cast of characters. She checked each one with a large bony forefinger, and paused to look round the table until she found the person who had been cast for it. Her expression, which was forbidding, did not change. She then applied herself to the first page of the dialogue. Still everybody waited. The silence was broken only by the sound of Miss Campanula turning a page. Henry began to feel desperate. It seemed almost as if they would continue to sit dumbly round the table until Miss Campanula reached the end of the play. He gave Dinah a cigarette and lit one himself. Miss Campanula raised her eyes and watched them until the match was blown out, and then returned to her reading. She had reached the fourth page of the first act. Mrs. Ross looked up at Dr. Templett who bent his head and whispered. Again Miss Campanula raised her eyes and stared at the offenders. The squire cleared his throat and said:

"Read the middle bit of Act II. Page forty-eight, it begins. Funniest thing I've come across for ages. It'll make you laugh like anything."

Miss Campanula did not reply, but she turned to Act II. Dinah, Henry, Dr. Templett, and Jocelyn waited with anxious smiles for her to give some evidence of amusement, but her lips remained firmly pursed, her brows raised, and her eyes fishy. Presently she looked up.

"I've reached the end of the scene," she said. "Was that the funny one?"

"Don't you think it's funny?" asked the squire.

"My object was to find out if there was anybody free to play the entr'acte," said Miss Campanula coldly. "I gather that there is. I *gather* that the Arbuthnot individual does not make her first appearance until halfway through the second act."

"Didn't somebody say that Miss Arbuthnot and the Duchess appeared together?" asked Miss Prentice to the accompaniment, every one felt, of the Venetian Suite.

"Possibly," said Miss Campanula. "Do I understand that I am expected to take this Mrs. Arbuthnot upon myself?"

"If you will," rejoined the rector. "And we hope very much indeed that you will."

"I wanted to be quite clear. I dare say I'm making a great to-do about nothing but I'm a person that likes to know where she is. Now I *gather*, and you must correct me if I'm wrong, that if I do this part there is no just cause or impediment," and here Miss Campanula threw a jocular glance at the rector, "why I should not take a little more upon myself and seat myself at the instrument. You *may* have other plans. You *may* wish to hire Mr. Joe Hopkins and his friends from Great Chipping, though on a Saturday night I gather they are rather more independable and tipsy than usual. *If* you have other plans then no more need be said. If not, I place myself at the committee's disposal."

"Well, that seems a most excellent offer," the poor rector began. "If Miss Campanula——"

"May I?" interrupted Miss Prentice sweetly. "May I say that I think it very kind of dear Idris to offer herself, but may I add that I do also think we are a little too inclined to take advantage of her generosity. She will have all the young folk to manage and she has a large part to learn. I do feel that we should be a little selfish if we also expected her to play for us on that dreadful old piano. Now, as the new instrument is to be in part, as my cousin says, a Pen Cuckoo affair, I think the very least I can do is to offer to relieve poor Idris of this unwelcome task. If you think my little efforts will pass muster I shall be very pleased to play the overture and entr'acte."

"Very thoughtful of you, Eleanor, but I am quite capable——"

"Of course you are, Idris, but at the same time——"

They both stopped short. The antagonism that had sprung up between them was so obvious and so disproportionate that the others were aghast. The rector abruptly brought his palm down on the table and then, as if ashamed of a gesture that betrayed his thoughts, clasped his hands together and looked straight before him.

He said, "I think this matter can be decided later."

The two women glanced quickly at him and were silent.

"That is all, I believe," said Mr. Copeland. "Thank you, everybody."

ii

The meeting broke up. Henry went to Dinah who had moved over to the fire.

"Ructions!" he said under his breath.

"Awful!" agreed Dinah. "You'd hardly believe it possible, would you?"

They smiled secretly and when the others crowded about Dinah, asking if they could have their parts before Monday, what sort of clothes would be needed, and whether she thought they would be all right, neither she nor Henry minded very much. It did not matter to them that they were unable to speak to each other, for their thoughts went forward to the morning, and their hearts trembled with happiness. They were isolated by their youth, two scathless figures. It would have seemed impossible to them that their love for each other could hold any reflection, however faint, of the emotions that drew Dr. Templett to Selia Ross, or those two ageing women to the rector. They would not have believed that there was a reverse side to love, or that the twin-opposites of love lay dormant in their own hearts. Nor were they to guess that never again, as long as they lived, would they know the rapturous expectancy that now pressed them.

Miss Prentice and Miss Campanula carefully avoided each other. Miss Prentice had seized her opportunity and had cornered Mr. Copeland. She could be heard offering flowers from the Pen Cuckoo greenhouses for a special service next Sunday. Miss Campanula had tackled Jocelyn about some enormity committed on her property by the local fox-hounds. Dr. Templett, a keen follower of hounds, was lugged into the controversy. Mrs. Ross was therefore left alone. She stood a little to one side, completely relaxed, her head slanted, a half-smile on her lips. The squire looked over Idris Campanula's shoulder, and caught that half-smile.

"Can't have that sort of thing," he said vaguely. "I'll have a word with Appleby. Will you forgive me? I just want——"

He escaped thankfully and joined Mrs. Ross. She welcomed him with an air that flattered him. Her eyes brightened and her smile was intimate. It was years since any woman had smiled in that way at Jocelyn, and he responded with Edwardian gallantry. His hand went to his moustache and his eye brightened.

"You know, you're a very alarming person," said Jocelyn.

"Now what precisely do you mean by that?" asked Mrs. Ross.

He was delighted. This was the way a conversation with a pretty woman ought to start. Forgotten phrases returned to his lips, waggishly nonsensical phrases that one uttered with just the right air of significance. One laughed a good deal and let her know one noticed how damned well-turned-out she was.

"I see that we have a most important scene together," said Jocelyn, "and I shall insist on a private rehearsal."

"I don't know that I shall agree to that," said Selia Ross.

"Oh, come now, it's perfectly safe."

"Why?"

"Because you are to be the very charming lady who has lost her memory. Ha, ha ha! Damn' convenient, what!" shouted Jocelyn, wondering if this remark was as daring as it sounded. Mrs. Ross laughed very heartily and the squire glanced in a gratified manner round the room, and encountered the astonished gaze of his son.

"This'll show Henry," thought Jocelyn. "These modern pups don't know how to flirt with an attractive woman." But there was an unmistakably sardonic glint in Henry's eye, and the squire, slightly shaken, turned back to Mrs. Ross. She still looked roguishly expectant and he thought, "Anyway, if Henry's noticed *her*, he'll know I'm doing pretty well." And then Dr. Templett managed to escape Miss Campanula and joined them.

"Well, Selia," he said, "if you're ready I think I'd better take you home."

"Doesn't like me talking to her!" thought the squire in triumph. "The little man's jealous."

When Mrs. Ross silently gave him her hand, he deliberately squeezed it.

"*Au revoir*," he said. "This is your first visit to Pen Cuckoo, isn't it? Don't let it be the last."

"I shouldn't be here at all," she answered. "There have been no official calls, you know."

Jocelyn made a slightly silly gesture and bowed.

"We'll waive all that sort of nonsense," he said. "Ha, ha, ha!"

Mrs. Ross turned to say good-bye to Eleanor Prentice.

"I have just told your cousin," she said, "that I've no business here. We haven't exchanged calls, have we?"

If Miss Prentice was at all taken aback, she did not show it. She gave her musical laugh and said, "I'm afraid I am very remiss about these things."

"Miss Campanula hasn't called on me either," said Mrs. Ross. "You must come together. Good-bye."

"Good-bye, everybody," said Mrs. Ross.

"I'll see you to your car," said the squire. "Henry!"

Henry hastened to the door. Jocelyn escorted Mrs. Ross out of the room and, as Dr. Templett followed them, the rector shouted after them:

"Just a minute, Templett. About the youngest Cain."

"Oh, yes. Silly little fool! Look here, rector——"

"I'll come out with you," said the rector.

Henry followed and shut the door behind them.

"Well!" said Miss Campanula. "Well!"

"*Isn't it?*" said Miss Prentice. "*Isn't it?*"

iii

Dinah, left alone with them, knew that the battle of the music was postponed in order that the two ladies might unite in abuse of Mrs. Ross. That it was postponed and not abandoned was evident in their manner, which reminded Dinah of stewed fruit on the turn. Its sweetness was impregnated by acidity.

"Of course, Eleanor," said Miss Campanula, "I can't for the life of me see why you didn't show her the door. I should have refused to receive her. I should!"

"I was simply dumbfounded," said Miss Prentice. "When Taylor announced them, I really couldn't believe my senses. I am deeply disappointed in Dr. Templett."

"Disappointed! The greatest piece of brazen effrontery I have ever encountered. He shan't have my lumbago! I can promise him that."

"I really should have thought he'd have known better," continued Miss Prentice. "It isn't as if we don't know who he is. He should be a gentleman. I always thought he took up medicine as a *vocation*. After all, there have been Templetts at Chippingwood for——"

"For as long as there have been Jernighams at Pen Cuckoo," said Miss Campanula. "But, of course, you wouldn't know that."

This was an oblique hit. It reminded Miss Prentice that she was a new-comer and not, strictly speaking, a Jernigham of Pen Cuckoo. Miss Campanula followed it up by saying, "I suppose in your position you could do nothing but receive her; but I must say I was astonished that you leapt at her play as you did."

"I did not leap, Idris," said Miss Prentice. "I hope I took the dignified course. It was obvious that everybody but you and me was in favour of her play."

"Well, it's a jolly good play," said Dinah.

"So we have been told," said Miss Campanula. "Repeatedly."

"I was helpless," continued Miss Prentice. "What could I do? One can do nothing against sheer common persistence. Of course she has triumphed."

"She's gone off now, taking every man in the room with her," said Miss Campanula. "Ha!"

"Ah, well," added Miss Prentice, "I suppose it's always the case when one deals with people who are *not quite*. Did you hear what she said about our not calling?"

"I was within an ace of telling her that I understood she received men only."

"But, Miss Campanula," said Dinah, "we don't know there's anything more than friendship between them, do we? And even if there is, it's their business."

"Dinah, *dear*!" said Miss Prentice.

"As a priest's daughter, Dinah——" began Miss Campanula.

"As a priest's daughter," said Dinah, "I've got a sort of idea charity is supposed to be a virtue. And, anyway, I think when you talk about a parson's family it's better not to call him a priest. It sounds so scandalous, somehow."

There was a dead silence. At last Miss Campanula rose to her feet.

"I fancy my car is waiting for me, Eleanor," she said. "So I shall make my adieux. I am afraid we are neither of us intelligent enough to appreciate modern humour. Good-night."

"Aren't we driving you home?" asked Dinah.

"Thank you, Dinah, no. I ordered my car for six, and it is already half-past. Good-night."

CHAPTER FIVE

Above Cloudyfold

i

THE NEXT morning was fine. Henry woke at six and looked out of his window at a clear, cold sky with paling stars. In another hour it would begin to get light. Henry, wide awake, his mind sharp with anticipation, leapt back into bed and sat with the blankets caught between his chin and his knees, hugging himself. A fine winter's dawn with a light frost and then the thin, pale sunlight. Down in the stables they would soon be moving about with lanthorns to the sound of clanking pails, shrill whistling, and boots on cobblestones. Hounds met up at Moorton Park to-day, and Jocelyn's two mounts would be taken over by his groom to wait for his arrival by car. Henry spared a moment to regret his own decision to give up hunting. He had loved it so much: the sound, the smell, the sight of the hunt. It had all seemed so perfectly splendid until one day, quite suddenly as if a new pair of eyes had been put into his head, he had seen a mob of well-fed expensive people, with red faces, astraddle shiny quadrupeds, all whooping ceremoniously after a very small creature which later on was torn to pieces while the lucky ones sat on their horses and looked on, well satisfied. To his violent annoyance, he had found that he could not rid himself of this unlovely picture and, as it made him feel slightly sick, he had given up everything but drag-hunting. Jocelyn had been greatly upset and had instantly accused Henry of pacifism. Henry had just left off being a pacifist, however, and assured his father that if England was invaded he would strike a shrewd blow before he would see Cousin Eleanor raped by a foreign mercenary. Hugging his knees, he chuckled at the memory of Jocelyn's face. Then he gave himself four minutes to revise the conversation he had planned to have with Dinah. He found that the thought of Dinah sent his heart pounding, just as it used to pound in the old days before he took his first fence. "I suppose I'm hunting again," he thought, and this primitive idea gave him a curiously exalted sensation. He jumped out of bed, bathed, shaved and dressed by lamplight, then he stole downstairs out into the dawn.

It's a fine thing to be abroad on Dorset hills on a clear winter's dawn. Henry went round the west wing of Pen Cuckoo. The gravel crunched under his shoes and the dim box-borders smelt friendly in a garden that was oddly remote. Familiar things seemed mysterious as if the experience of the night had made strangers of them. The field was rimed with silver, the spinney on the far side was a company of naked trees locked in a deep sleep from which the sound of footsteps among the dead leaves and twigs could not awaken them. The hillside smelt of cold earth and frosty stones. As Henry climbed steeply upwards, it was as if he left the night behind him down in Pen Cuckoo. On Cloudyfold, the dim shapes took on some resolute form and became rocks, bushes and posts, expectant of the day. The clamour of far-away cock-crows rose vaguely from the valley like the overlapping echoes of dreams, and with this sound came the human smell of woodsmoke.

Henry reached the top of Cloudyfold and looked down the vale of Pen Cuckoo. His breath made a small cold mist in front of his face, his fingers were cold and his eyes watered, but he felt like a god as he surveyed his own little world. Half-way down, and almost sheer beneath him, was the house he had left. He looked down into the chimney-tops, already wreathed in thin drifts of blue. The servants were up and about. Farther down, and still drenched in shadow, were the roofs of Winton. Henry wondered if they really leaked badly and if he and Dinah could ever afford to repair them. Beyond Winton his father's land spread out into low hills and came to an end at Selwood Brook. Here, half-screened by trees, he could see the stone façade of Chippingwood which Dr. Templett had inherited from his elder brother who had died in the Great War. And separated from Chippingwood by the hamlet of Chipping was Miss Campanula's Georgian mansion, on the skirts of the village but not of it. Farther away, and only just visible over the downlands that separated it from the Vale, was Great Chipping, the largest town in that part of Dorset. Half-way up the slope, below Winton and Pen Cuckoo, was the church, Winton St. Giles, with the rectory hidden behind it. Dinah would strike straight through their home copse and come up the ridge of Cloudyfold. If she came! Please God, make it happen, said Henry's thoughts as they used to do when he was a little boy. He crossed the brow of the hill. Below him, on the far side, was Moorton Park Road and Cloudyfold Village, and there, tucked into a bend in the road, Duck Cottage, with its scarlet door and window frames, newly done up by Mrs. Ross. Henry wondered why Selia Ross had decided to live in a place like Cloudyfold. She seemed to him so thoroughly urban. For a minute or two he thought of her, still snugly asleep in her renovated cottage, dreaming perhaps of Dr. Templett. Farther away over the brow of a hill was the Cain's farm, where Dr. Templett must drive to minister to the youngest Cain's big toe.

"They're all down there," thought Henry, "tucked up in their warm houses, fast asleep; and none of them knows I'm up here in the cold dawn waiting for Dinah Copeland."

He felt a faint warmth on the back of his neck. The stivered grass was washed with colour, and before him his own attenuated shadow appeared. He turned to the east and saw the sun. Quite near at hand he heard his name called, and there, coming over the brow of Cloudyfold, was Dinah, dressed in blue with a scarlet handkerchief round her neck.

Henry could make no answering call. His voice stuck in his throat. He raised his arm, and the shadow before him sent a long blue pointer over the grass. Dinah made an answering gesture. Because he could not stand dumbly and smile until she came up with him, he lit a cigarette, making a long business of it, his hands cupped over his face. He could hear her footsteps on the frozen hill, and his own heart thumped with them. When he looked up she was beside him.

"Good-morning," said Henry.

"I've no breath left," said Dinah; "but good-morning to you, Henry. Your cigarette smells like heaven."

He gave her one.

"It's grand up here," said Dinah. "I'm glad I came. You wouldn't believe you could be hot, would you? But I am. My hands and face are icy and the rest of me's like a hot-cross bun."

"I'm glad you came, too," said Henry. There was a short silence. Henry set the Jernigham jaw, fixed his gaze on Miss Campanula's chimneys, and said, "Do you feel at all shy?"

"Yes," said Dinah. "If I start talking I shall go on and on talking, rather badly. That's a sure sign I'm shy."

"It takes me differently. I can hardly speak. I expect I'm turning purple, and my top lip seems to be twitching."

"It'll go off in a minute," said Dinah. "Henry, what would you do if you suddenly knew you had dominion over all you survey? That sounds Biblical. I mean, suppose you could alter the minds—and that means the destinies—of all the people living down there—what would you do?"

"Put it into Cousin Eleanor's heart to be a missionary in Polynesia."

"Or into Miss Campanula's to start a nudist circle in Chipping."

"Or my father might go surrealist."

"No, but honestly, what would you do?" Dinah insisted.

"I don't know. I suppose I would try and simplify them. People seem to me to be much too busy and complicated."

"Make them kinder?"

"Well, that might do it, certainly."

"It would do it. If Miss Campanula and your Cousin Eleanor left off being jealous of each other, and if Dr. Templett was sorrier for his wife, and if Mrs. Ross minded more about upsetting other people's apple-carts, we wouldn't have any more scenes like the one last night."

"Perhaps not," Henry agreed. "But you wouldn't stop them falling in love, if you can call whatever they feel for each other, falling in love. I'm in love with you, as I suppose you know. It makes me feel all noble minded and generous and kind; but, just the same, if I had a harem of invalid wives, they wouldn't stop me telling you I loved you, Dinah. Dinah, I love you so desperately."

"Do you, Henry?"

"You'd never believe how desperately. This is all wrong. I'd thought out the way I'd tell you. First we were to have a nice conversation and then, when we'd got to the right place, I was going to tell you."

"All elegant like?"

"Yes. But it's too much for me."

"It's too much for me, too," said Dinah.

They faced each other, two solitary figures. All their lives they were to remember this moment, and yet they did not see each other's face very clearly, for their sight was blurred by the agitation in their hearts.

"Oh, Dinah," said Henry. "Darling, darling Dinah, I do love you so much."

He reached out his hand blindly and touched her arm. It was a curious tentative gesture. Dinah cried out: "Henry, my dear."

She raised his hand to her cold cheek.

"Oh, God!" said Henry, and pulled her into his arms.

Jocelyn's groom, hacking quietly along the road to Cloudyfold, looked up and saw two figures locked together against the wintry sky.

ii

"We must come back to earth," said Dinah. "There's the church clock. It must be eight."

"I'll kiss you eight times to wind up the spell," said Henry. He kissed her eyes, her cheeks, the tips of her ears, and he kissed her twice on the mouth.

"There!" he muttered. "The spell's wound up."

"Don't!" cried Dinah.

"What, my darling?"

"Don't quote from Macbeth. It couldn't be more unlucky!"

"Who says so?"

"In the theatre everybody says so."

"I cock a snook at them! We're not in the theatre: we're on top of the world."

"All the same, I'm crossing my thumbs."

"When shall we be married?"

"Married?" Dinah caught her breath, and Henry's pure happiness was threaded with a sort of wonder when he saw that she was no longer lost in bliss.

"What is it?" he said. "What has happened? Does it frighten you to think of our marriage?"

"It's only that we *have* come back to earth," Dinah said sombrely. "I don't know when we'll be married. You see, something pretty difficult has happened."

"Good Lord, darling, what are you going to falter in my ear? Not a family curse, or dozens of blood relations stark ravers in lunatic asylums?"

"Not quite. It's your Cousin Eleanor."

"Eleanor!" cried Henry. "She scarcely exists."

"Wait till you hear. I've got to tell you now. I'll tell you as we go down."

"Say first that you're as happy as I am."

"I couldn't be happier."

"I love you, Dinah."

"I love you, Henry."

"The world is ours," said Henry. "Let us go down and take it."

iii

They followed the shoulder of the hill by a path that led down to the rectory garden. Dinah went in front, and their conversation led to repeated halts.

"I'm afraid," Dinah began, "that I don't much care for your Cousin Eleanor."

"You astonish me, darling," said Henry. "For myself, I regard her as a prize bitch."

"That's all right, then. I couldn't mention this before you'd declared yourself, because it's all about us."

"You mean the day before yesterday when she lurked outside your drawing-room door? Dinah, if she hadn't been there, what would you have done?"

This led to a prolonged halt.

"The thing is," said Dinah presently, "she must have told your father."

"So she did."

"He's spoken to you?"

"He has."

"Oh, Henry!"

"That sounds as if you were settling a quotation. Yes, we had a grand interview. 'What is this I hear, sir, of your attentions to Miss Dinah Copeland?' 'Forgive me, sir, but I refuse to answer you.' 'Do you defy me, Henry?' 'With all respect, sir, I do!' That sort of thing."

"He doesn't want it?"

"Eleanor has told him he doesn't, blast her goggling eyes!"

"Why? Because I'm the poor parson's daughter, or because I'm on the stage, or just because he hates the sight of me?"

"I don't think he hates the sight of you."

"I suppose he wants you to marry a proud heiress."

"I suppose he does. It doesn't matter a tuppenny button, my sweet Dinah, what he wants."

"But it does. You haven't heard. Miss Prentice came to see Daddy last night."

Henry stopped dead and stared at her.

"She said—she said——"

"Go on."

"She told him we were meeting, and that you were keeping it

from your father, but he'd found out and was terribly upset and felt we'd both been very underhand and—oh, she must have been absolutely foul! She must have sort of hinted that we were——" Dinah boggled at this and fell silent.

"That we were living in roaring sin?" Henry suggested.

"Yes."

"My God, the minds of these women! Surely the rector didn't pay any attention."

"She's so loathesomely plausible. Do you remember the autumn day, weeks ago, soon after I came back, when you drove me to Moorton Bridge and we picnicked and didn't come back till the evening?"

"Every second of it."

"She'd found out about that. There was no reason why the whole world shouldn't know, but I hadn't told Daddy about it. It had been such a glowing, marvellous day that I didn't want to talk about it."

"Me, too."

"Well, now, you see, it looks all fishy and dubious, and Daddy feels I have been behaving in an underhand manner. When Miss Prentice had gone he took me into his study. He was wearing his beretta, a sure sign that he's feeling his responsibilities. He spoke more in sorrow than in anger, which is always rather toxic, and the worst of it is, he really was upset. He got more and more feudal and said we'd always been—I forget what—almost fiefs or vassals of this-man's-man of the Jernighams, and had never done anything disloyal, and here was I behaving like a housemaid having clandestine assignations with you. On and on and on; and Henry, my dear darling, ridiculous though it sounds, I began to feel shabby and common."

"He didn't believe——"

"No, of course he didn't believe that. But, all the same, you know he's frightfully muddled about sex."

"They all are," said Henry, with youthful gloom. "And with Eleanor and Idris hurling their inhibitions in his teeth——"

"I know. Well, anyway, the upshot was, he forbade me to see you alone. I said I wouldn't promise. It was the first really deadly row we've ever had. I fancy he prayed about it for hours after I'd gone to bed. It's very vexing to lie in bed knowing somebody in the room below is praying away like mad about you. And, you see, I adore the man. At one moment I thought I would say my own prayers, but the only thing I could think of was the old Commination Service. You know: 'Cursed is he that smiteth his neighbour secretly. Amen.' "

"One for Eleanor," said Henry appreciatively.

"That's what I thought, but I didn't say it. But what I've been trying to come to is this: I can't bear to upset Daddy permanently, and I'm afraid that's just what would happen. No, please wait, Henry. You see, I'm only nineteen, and he can forbid the bans—and, what's more, he'd do it."

"But why?" said Henry. "Why? Why? Why?"

"Because he thinks that we shouldn't oppose your father and because, secretly, he's got a social inferiority complex. He's a snob, poor sweet. He thinks if he smiled on us it would look as if he was all agog to make a grand match for me, and was going behind the squire's back to do it."

"Absolutely drivelling bilge!"

"I know, but that's how it goes. It's just one of those things. And it's all due to Miss Prentice. Honestly, Henry, I think she's positively evil. *Why* should she mind about us?"

"Jealousy," said Henry. "She's starved and twisted and a bit dotty. I dare say it's physiological as well as psychological. I imagine she thinks you'll sort of dethrone her when you're my wife. And, as likely, as not, she's jealous of your father's affection for you."

They shook their heads wisely.

"Daddy's terrified of her," said Dinah, "*and* of Miss Campanula. They *will* ask him to hear their confessions, and when they go away he's a perfect wreck."

"I'm not surprised, if they tell the truth. I expect what they really do is to try to inform against the rest of the district. Listen to me, Dinah. I refuse to have our love for each other messed up by Eleanor. You're mine. I'll tell your father I've asked you to marry me, and I'll tell mine. I'll *make* them see reason; and if Eleanor comes creeping in—my God, I'll, I'll, I'll——"

"Henry," said Dinah, "how magnificent!"

Henry grinned.

"It'd be more magnificent," he said, "if she wasn't just an unhappy, warped, middle-aged spinster."

"It must be awful to be like that," agreed Dinah. "I hope it never happens to me."

"You!"

There was another halt.

"Henry," said Dinah suddenly. "Let's ask them to call an armistice until after the play."

"But we must see each other like this. Alone."

"I shall die if we can't; but all the same I feel, somehow, if we said we'd wait until then, that Daddy might sort of begin to understand. We'll meet at rehearsals, and we won't pretend we're not in love, but I'll promise him I won't meet you alone. It'll be—it'll be kind of dignified. Henry, *do* you see?"

"I suppose so," said Henry unwillingly.

"It'd stop those hateful old women talking."

"My dear, nothing would stop them talking."

"Please, darling Henry."

"Oh, Dinah."

"Please."

"All right. It's insufferable, though, that Eleanor should be able to spoil a really miraculous thing like Us."

"Insufferable."

"She's so completely insignificant."

Dinah shook her head.

"All the same," she said, "she's a bad enemy. She creeps and creeps, and she's simply brimful of poison. She'll drop some of it into our cup of happiness if she can."

"Not if I know it," said Henry.

CHAPTER SIX

Rehearsal

i

THE REHEARSALS were not going any too well. For all Dinah's efforts, she hadn't been able to get very much concerted work out of her company. For one thing, with the exception of Selia Ross and Henry, they would *not* learn their lines. Dr. Templett even took a sort of pride in it. He was forever talking about his experiences in amateur productions when he was a medical student.

"I never knew what I was going to say," he said cheerfully. "I'm capable of saying almost anything. It was always all right on the night. A bit of cheek goes a long way. One can bluff it out with a gag or two. The great thing is not to be nervous."

He himself was not at all nervous. He uttered such lines of the French Ambassador's as he remembered, in a high-pitched voice, made a great many grimaces, waved his hands in a foreign manner, and was never still for an instant.

"I leave it to the spur of the moment," he told them. "It's wonderful what a difference it makes when you're all made-up, with funny clothes on. I never know where I ought to be. You can't do it in cold blood."

"But, Dr. Templett, you've got to," Dinah lamented. "How can we get the timing right or the positions, if at one rehearsal you're on the prompt and at the next on the o.p.?"

"Don't you worry," said Dr. Templett. "We'll be all right. Eet vill be—'ow you say?—so, so charmante."

Off-stage he continually spoke his lamentable broken English, and when he dried up, as he did incessantly, he interpolated his: " 'ow you say?"

"If I forget," he said to the rector, who was prompting, "I'll just walk over your side and say, ' 'ow you say?' like that, and then you'll know."

Selia Ross and he had an irritating trick of turning up late for rehearsals. Apparently the youngest Cain's big toe still needed Dr. Templett's attention, and he explained that he picked up Mrs. Ross and brought her to rehearsal on his way back from Cloudyfold. They would walk in with singularly complacent smiles, half an hour late, while Dinah was reading both their parts and trying to play her own. Sometimes she got her father to read their bits, but the rector intoned them so carefully and slowly that everybody else was thrown into a state of deadly confusion.

Miss Campanula, in a different way, was equally troublesome. She refused to give up her typewritten part. She carried it about with her and read each of her speeches in an undertone during the preceding dialogue, so that whenever she was on the stage the others spoke through a distressing mutter. When her cue came she seldom failed to say, "Oh. Now it's me," before she began. She would often rattle off her lines without any inflexion, and apparently without the slightest regard for their meaning. She was forever telling Dinah that she was open to correction, but she received all suggestions in huffy grandeur, and they made not the smallest difference to her performance. Worse than all these peculiarities were Miss Campanula's attempts at characterization. She made all sorts of clumsy and ineffective movements over which she herself seemed to have little control. She continually shifted her weight from one large foot to the other, rather in the manner of a penguin. She wandered about the stage and she made embarrassing grimaces. In addition to all this, she had developed a frightful cold in her nose, and rehearsals were made hideous by her catarrhal difficulties.

Jocelyn was the type of amateur performer who learns his lines from the prompter. Unlike Miss Campanula, he did not hold his part in his hand. Indeed, he had lost it irrevocably immediately after the first rehearsal. He said that it did not matter, as he had already memorized his lines. This was a lie. He merely had a vague idea of their sense. His performance reminded Dinah of divine service, as he was obliged to repeat all his lines, like responses, after the rector. However, in spite of this defect, the squire had an instinctive sense of theatre. He did not fidget or gesticulate. With Dr. Templett tearing about the stage like a wasp, this was particularly refreshing.

Miss Prentice did not know her part either, but she was a cunning bluffer. She had a long scene in which she held a newspaper open in her hands. Dinah discovered that Miss Prentice had pinned several of her sides to the sheets of the *Times*. Others were left in handy places about the stage. When, in spite of these manœuvres, she dried up, Miss Prentice stared in a gently reproachful manner at the person who spoke after her, so that everybody thought it was her *vis-à-vis* who was at fault.

Mrs. Ross had learnt her part. Her clear, hard voice had plenty of edge. Once there, she worked, tried to follow Dinah's suggestions, and was very good-humoured and obliging. If ever anything was wanted, Mrs. Ross would get it. She brought down to the Parish Hall her cushions, her cocktail glasses and her bridge table. Dinah found herself depending more and more on Mrs. Ross for "hand props" and odds and ends of furniture. But, for all that, she did not like Mrs. Ross, whose peals of laughter at all Dr. Templett's regrettable antics were extremely irritating. The determined rudeness with which Miss Prentice and Miss Campanula met all Mrs. Ross's advances forced Dinah into making friendly gestures which she continually regretted. She saw, with something like horror, that her father had innocently succumbed to Mrs. Ross's charm, and to her sudden interest in his church. This, more than anything else she did, inflamed Miss Campanula and Eleanor Prentice against Selia Ross. Dinah felt that her rehearsals were shot through and through with a mass of ugly suppressions. To complete her discomfort, the squire's attitude towards Mrs. Ross, being ripe with Edwardian naughtiness, obviously irritated Henry and the two ladies almost to breaking point.

Henry had learnt his part and shaped well. He and Dinah were the only members of the cast who gave any evidence of team work. The others scarcely even so much as looked at each other, and treated their speeches as if they were a string of interrupted recitations.

ii

The battle of the music had raged for three weeks. Miss Prentice and Miss Campanula, together and alternately, had pretended to altruistic motives, accused each other of selfishness, sulked, denied all desire to perform on the piano, given up their parts, relented, and offered their services anew. In the end Dinah, with her father's moral support behind her, seized upon a moment when Miss Campanula had said she'd no wish to play on an instrument with five dumb notes in the treble and six in the bass.

"All right, Miss Campanula," said Dinah, "we'll have it like that.

Miss Prentice has kindly volunteered, and I shall appoint her as pianist. As you've got the additional responsibility of the Y.P.F.C. girls in the front of the house, it really does seem the best idea."

After that Miss Campanula was barely civil to anybody but the rector and the squire.

Five days before the performance, Eleanor Prentice developed a condition which Miss Campanula called "a Place" on the index finger of the left hand. Everybody noticed it. Miss Campanula did not fail to point out that it would probably be much worse on the night of the performance.

"You'd better take care of that Place on your finger, Eleanor," she said. "It's gathering, and to me it looks very nasty. Your blood must be out of order."

Miss Prentice denied this with an air of martyrdom, but there was no doubt that the Place grew increasingly ugly. Three days before the performance it was hidden by an obviously professional bandage, and everybody knew that she had consulted Dr. Templett. A rumour sprang up that Miss Campanula had begun to practise her Prelude every morning after breakfast.

Dinah had a private conversation with Dr. Templett.

"What about Miss Prentice's finger? Will she be able to play the piano?"

"I've told her she'd better give up all idea of it," he said. "There's a good deal of inflammation, and it's very painful. It'll hurt like the devil if she attempts to use it, and it's not at all advisable that she should."

"What did she say?"

Dr. Templett grinned.

"She said she wouldn't disappoint her audience, and that she could rearrange the fingering of her piece. It's the 'Venetian Suite,' as usual, of course?"

"It is," said Dinah grimly. " 'Dawn' and 'On the Canal' for the overture, and the 'Nocturne' for the entr'acte. She'll never give way."

"Selia says she wouldn't mind betting old Idris has put poison in her girl friend's gloves like the Borgias," said Dr. Templett, and added: "Good Lord, I oughtn't to have repeated that! It's the sort of thing that's quoted against you in a place like this."

"I won't repeat it," said Dinah.

She asked Miss Prentice if she would rather not appear at the piano.

"How thoughtful of you, Dinah, my dear," rejoined Miss Prentice, with her holiest smile. "But I shall do my little best. You may depend upon me."

"But, Miss Prentice, your finger!"

"Ever so much better," said Eleanor in a voice that somehow suggested that there was something slightly improper in mentioning her finger.

"They are waiting to print the programmes. Your name——"

"Please don't worry, dear. My name may appear in safety. Shall we just not say any more about it, but consider it settled?"

"Very well," said Dinah uneasily. "It's very heroic of you."

"Silly child!" said Eleanor playfully.

iii

And now, on Thursday, November the 25th, two nights before the performance, Dinah stood beside the paraffin heater in the aisle of the parish hall, and with dismay in her heart prepared to watch the opening scenes in which she herself did not appear. There was to be no music at the dress rehearsal.

"Just to give my silly old finger time to get *quite* well," said Miss Prentice.

But Henry had told Dinah that both he and his father had seen Eleanor turn so white after knocking her finger against a chair that they thought she was going to faint.

"You won't stop her," said Henry. "If she has to play the bass with her feet, she'll do it."

Dinah gloomily agreed.

She had made them up for the dress rehearsal and had attempted to create a professional atmosphere in a building that reeked of parochial endeavour. Even now her father's unmistakably clerical voice could be heard beyond the green serge curtain, crying obediently:

"Beginners, please."

In front of Dinah, six privileged Friendly Young Girls, who were to sell programmes and act as ushers at the performance, sat in a giggling row to watch the dress rehearsal. Dr. Templett and Henry were their chief interest. Dr. Templett was aware of this and repeatedly looked round the curtain. He had insisted on making himself up, and looked as if he had pressed his face against a gridiron and then garnished his chin with the hearth-brush. Just as Dinah was about to ring up the curtain, his head again bobbed round the corner.

"Vy do you, 'ow you say, gargle so mooch?" he asked the helpers. A renewed paroxysm broke out.

"Dr. Templett!" shouted Dinah. "Clear stage, *please*."

"Ten thousand pardons, Mademoiselle," said Dr. Templett. "I vaneesh." He made a comic face and disappeared.

"All ready behind, Daddy?" shouted Dinah.

"I think so," said the rector's voice doubtfully.

"Positions, everybody. House lights, please." Dinah was obliged to execute this last order herself, as the house lights switch was in the auditorium. She turned it off and the six onlookers yelped maddeningly.

"Ssh, please! Curtain!"

"Just a minute," said the rector dimly.

The curtain rose in a series of uneven jerks, and the squire, who should have been at the telephone, was discovered gesticulating violently to someone in the wings. He started, glared into the house, and finally took up his position.

"Where's that telephone bell?" demanded Dinah.

"Oh, dear!" said the rector's voice dismally. He could be heard scuffling about in the prompt-corner and presently an unmistakable bicycle bell pealed. But Jocelyn had already lifted the receiver and, although the bell, which was supposed to summon him to the telephone, continued to ring off-stage, he embarked firmly on his opening lines:

"Hallo! Hallo! Well, who is it?"

The dress rehearsal had begun.

Actors say that a good dress rehearsal means a bad performance. Dinah hoped desperately that the reverse would prove true. Everything seemed to go wrong. She suspected that there were terrific rows in the dressing-rooms, but as she herself had no change to make, she stayed in front whenever she was not actually on the stage. Before the entrance of the two ladies in the second act, Henry came down and joined her.

"Frightful, isn't it?" he asked.

"It's the end," said Dinah.

"My poor darling, it's pretty bad luck for you. Perhaps it'll pull through to-morrow."

"I don't see how—— Dr. Templett!" roared Dinah. "What are you doing? You ought to be up by the fireplace. Go back, please."

Miss Prentice suddenly walked straight across the stage, in front of Jocelyn, Selia Ross and Dr. Templett, and out at the opposite door.

"Miss Prentice!"

But she had gone, and could be heard in angry conversation with Georgie Biggins, the call-boy, and Miss Campanula.

"You're a very naughty little boy, and I shall ask the rector to forbid you to attend the performance."

"You deserve a sound whipping," said Miss Campanula's voice. "And if I had my way——"

The squire and Dr. Templett stopped short and stared into the wings.

"What is it?" Dinah demanded.

Georgie Biggins was thrust on the stage. He had painted his nose carmine, and Miss Prentice's hat for the third act was on his head. He had a water pistol in his hand. The girls in the front row screamed delightedly.

"Georgie," said Dinah with more than a suspicion of tears in her voice, "take that hat off and go home."

"I never——" began Georgie.

"Do what I tell you."

"Yaas, Miss."

Miss Prentice's arm shot through the door. The hat was removed. Dr. Templett took Georgie Biggins by the slack of his pants and dropped him over the footlights.

"Gatcha!" said Georgie and bolted to the back of the hall.

"Go on, please," said poor Dinah.

Somehow or another they got through. Dinah took them back over the scenes that had been outstandingly bad. This annoyed and bored them all very much, but she was adamant.

"It'll be all right on the night," said Dr. Templett.

"Saturday's the night," said Dinah, "and it won't."

At midnight she sat down in the third bench and said she supposed they had better stop. They all assembled in one of the Sunday School rooms behind the stage and gathered round a heater, while Mrs. Ross gave them a very good supper. She had insisted on making this gesture and had provided beer, whisky, coffee and sandwiches. Miss Campanula and Miss Prentice had both offered to make themselves responsible for this supper, and were furious that Mrs. Ross had got in first.

Dinah was astounded to learn from their conversation that they thought they had done quite well. The squire was delighted with himself; Dr. Templett still retained his character as a Frenchman;

and Selia Ross said repeatedly that she thought both of them had been marvellous. The other two ladies spoke only to Mr. Copeland, and each waited until she could speak alone. Dinah saw that her father was bewildered and troubled.

"Oh, Lord!" thought Dinah. "What's brewing now?" She wished that her father was a stronger character, that he would bully or frighten those two venomous women into holding their tongues. And suddenly, with a cold pang, she thought: "If he should lose his head and marry one of them!"

Henry brought her a cup of black coffee.

"I've put some whisky in it," he said. "You're as pale as a star, and you look frightened. What is it?"

"Nothing. I'm just tired."

Henry bent his dark head and whispered:

"Dinah?"

"Yes."

"I'll talk to father on Saturday night when he's flushed with his dubious triumphs. Did you get my letter?"

Dinah's hand floated to her breast.

"Darling," whispered Henry. "Yours, too. We can't wait any longer. After to-morrow?"

"After to-morrow," murmured Dinah.

CHAPTER SEVEN

Vignettes

i

"I HAVE sinned," said Miss Prentice, "in thought, word and deed by my fault, by my own fault, by my most grievous fault. Especially I accuse myself that since that last confession, which was a month ago, I have sinned against my neighbour. I have harboured evil suspicions of those with whom I have come in contact, accusing them in my heart of adultery, unfaithfulness and disobedience to their parents. I have judged my sister-woman in my heart and condemned her. I have listened many times to evil reports of a woman, and because I could not in truth say that I did not believe them——"

"Do not seek to excuse rather than to condemn yourself," said the rector from behind the Norman confessional that his bishop allowed him to use. "Condemn only your own erring heart. You have encouraged and connived at scandal. Go on."

There was a brief silence.

"I accuse myself that I have committed sins of omission, not performing what I believed to be my bounden Christian duty to the sick, not warning one whom I believe to be in danger of great unhappiness."

The rector heard Miss Prentice turn a page of the note-book where she wrote her confessions. "I know what she's getting at," he thought miserably. But because he was a sincere and humble man, he prayed: "Oh, God, give me the strength of mind to tackle this woman. Amen."

Miss Prentice cleared her throat in a subdued manner and began again. "I have consorted with a woman whom I believe to be of evil nature, knowing that by doing so I may have seemed to connive at sin."

"Our Lord consorted with sinners and was sinless. Judge not that you be not judged. The sin of another should excite only compassion in your heart. Go on."

"I have had angry and bitter thoughts of two young people who have injured someone who is——"

"Stop!" said the rector. "Do not accuse others. Accuse only yourself. Examine your conscience. Be sure that you have come here with a contrite and humble heart. If it holds any uncharitable thoughts, repent and confess them. Do not try to justify your anger by relating the cause. God will judge how greatly you have been tempted."

He waited. There was no response at all from his penitent. The church, beyond the confessional, seemed to listen with him for the next whisper.

"My daughter, I am waiting," said the rector, and was horrified when he was answered by a harsh, angry sobbing.

ii

In spite of her cold, Miss Campanula was happy. She was about to make her confession, and she felt at peace with the world and quite youthful and exalted. The terrible black mood that had come upon her when she woke up that morning had vanished completely She even felt fairly good-humoured when she thought of Eleanor playing her "Venetian Suite" at the performance to-morrow evening. With that Place on her finger, Eleanor was likely enough to make a hash of the music, and then everybody would think it was a pity that she, Idris Campanula, had not been chosen. That thought gave her a happy, warm feeling. Nowadays she was never sure what her mood would be. It changed in the most curious fashion from something like ecstasy to a dreadful irritation that came upon her with such violence and with so little provocation that it quite frightened her. It was as if, like the people in the New Testament, she had a devil in her, a beast that could send her thoughts black and make her tremble with anger. She had confessed these fits of rage to Father Copeland (she and Eleanor called him that when they spoke of him together), and he had been kind and had prayed for her. He had also, rather to her surprise, suggested that she should see a doctor. But there was nothing wrong with her health, she reflected, except lumbago and the natural processes attached to getting a little bit older. She pushed that thought away quickly, as it was inclined to make her depressed, and when she was depressed the beast took advantage of her.

Her chauffeur drove her to church, but she was a few minutes early, so she decided that she would look in at the parish hall and see if the committee of the Y.P.F.C. had begun to get it ready for tomorrow night. The decorating, of course, would all be done in the morning under her supervision; but there were floors to be swept, forms shifted and tables moved. Perhaps Eleanor would be there—or even Father Copeland on his way to church. Another wave of ecstasy swept over her. She knew why she was so happy. He would perhaps be at Pen Cuckoo for this ridiculous "run through for words" at five o'clock; but, better than that, it was Reading Circle night in the rectory dining-room, and her turn to preside. After it was over she would look in at the study, and Father Copeland would be there alone and would talk to her for a little.

Telling her chauffeur to wait, she marched up the gravelled path to the hall.

It was locked. This was irritating. She supposed those young people imagined they had done enough for one day. You might depend upon it, they had made off, leaving half the work for tomorrow. She was just going away again when dimly, from within, she heard the sound of strumming. Someone was playing chopsticks very badly, with the loud pedal on. Miss Campanula felt a sudden desire to know who had remained inside the hall to strum. She rattled the doors. The maddening noise stopped immediately.

"Who's in there?" shouted Miss Campanula, in a cold-infected voice, and rattled again.

There was no answer.

"The back door!" she thought. "It may be open." And she marched round the building. But the back door was shut, and although she pounded angrily on it, splitting her black kid gloves, nobody came to open it. Her face burned with exertion and rising fury. She started off again and completed the circuit of the hall. The frosted windows were all above the level of her eyes. The last one she came to was open at the bottom. Miss Campanula returned to the lane and saw that her chauffeur had followed her in the car from the church.

"Gibson!" she shouted. "Gibson, come here!"

He got out of the car and came towards her. He was a wooden-faced man with a fine physique; very smart in his dark maroon livery and shiny gaiters. He followed his mistress round the front of the hall to the far side.

"I want you to look inside that window," said Miss Campanula. "There's somebody in there who's behaving suspiciously."

"Very good, miss," said Gibson.

He gripped the window sill. The muscles under his smart tunic swelled as he raised himself until his eyes were above the sill.

Miss Campanula sneezed violently, blew her nose on her enormous handkerchief drenched in eucalyptus, and said, "Cad you see annddythingk?"

"No, miss. There's nobody there."

"But there *bust* be," insisted Miss Campanula.

"I can't see any one, miss. The place is all tidied up, like, for tomorrow."

"Where's the piano?"

"Down on the floor, miss, in front of the stage."

Gibson lowered himself.

"They bust have gone into one of the back rooms," muttered Miss Campanula.

"Could whoever it was have come out at the front door, miss, while you were round at the back?"

"Did you see addybody?"

"Can't say I did, miss. Not round the hall. But I was turning the car. They might have gone round the bend in the lane before I would notice."

"I consider it bost peculiar and suspicious."

"Yes, miss. There's Miss Prentice just coming out of church, miss."

"Is she?" Miss Campanula peered short sightedly down the lane. She could see the south porch of St. Giles and a figure in the doorway.

"I mustn't be late," she thought. "Eleanor has got in first, as usual." And she ordered Gibson to wait for her outside the church. She crossed the lane and strode down to the lych-gate. Eleanor was still in the porch. One did not stop to gossip when going to confession, but she gave Eleanor her usual nod and was astonished to see that she looked ghastly.

"There's something wrong with her," thought Miss Campanula, and somewhere, in the shifting hinterland between her conscious and unconscious thoughts, lay the warm hope that the rector had been displeased with Eleanor at confession.

Miss Campanula entered the church with joy in her heart.

iii

At the precise moment when Miss Prentice and Miss Campanula passed each other in the south porch, Henry, up at Pen Cuckoo, decided that he could remain indoors no longer. He was restless and impatient. He and Dinah had kept their pact, and since their morning on Cloudyfold had not met alone. Henry had announced their intention to his father at breakfast while Eleanor Prentice was in the room.

"It's Dinah's idea," he had said "She calls it an armistice. As our affairs seem to be so much in the public eye, and as her father has been upset by the conversation you had with him last night, Cousin Eleanor, Dinah thinks it would be a good thing if we promised him we would postpone what you have described as our clandestine meetings for three weeks. After that I shall speak to the rector myself." He had looked directly at Miss Prentice and added: "I shall be very grateful if you would not discuss the matter with him in the meantime. After all, it is primarily our affair."

"I shall do what I believe to be my duty, Henry," Miss Prentice had said; and Henry had answered, "I'm afraid you will," and walked out of the room.

He and Dinah had written to each other. Henry had found Miss Prentice eyeing Dinah's first letter as it lay beside his plate at breakfast. He had put it in the breast pocket of his coat, rather shocked at the look he had surprised in her face. After that morning he had come down early to breakfast.

During the three weeks' truce, Jocelyn never spoke to his son of Dinah, but Henry knew very well that Miss Prentice nagged at the squire whenever a chance presented itself. Several times Henry had walked into the study to find Eleanor closeted with Jocelyn. The silence that invariably followed his entrance, his father's uncomfortable attempts to break it, and Miss Prentice's tight smile as she glided away, left Henry in no doubt as to the subject of their conversation.

This afternoon, Jocelyn was hunting. Miss Prentice would come back from church before three, and Henry could not face the prospect of tea alone with his cousin. She had refused a car, and would return tired and martyred. Although Jocelyn had taught her to drive, it was her infuriating custom to refuse a car. She would walk to church after dark, on pouring wet nights, and give herself maddening colds in the head. To-day, however, was fine with glints of watery sunlight. He took a stick and went out.

Henry walked through the trees into a lane that came out near the church. Perhaps there would be a job of work to be done at the hall. If Dinah was there she would be surrounded by helpers, so that would be all right.

But about half-way down he walked round a sharp bend in the lane and found himself face to face and alone with Dinah.

For a moment they stood and stared at each other. Then Henry said, "I thought I might be able to help in the hall."

"We finished for to-day at two o' clock."

"Where are you going?"

"Just for a walk. I didn't know you'd—I thought you'd be——"

"I didn't know, either. It was bound to happen sooner or later."

"Yes, I suppose so."

"Your face is white," said Henry, and his voice shook. "Are you all right?"

"Yes. It's only the shock. Yours is white, too."

"Dinah!"

"No, no. Not till to-morrow. We promised."

As if moved by some compulsion outside themselves, they moved like automatons into each other's arms.

When Miss Prentice, dry-eyed but still raging, came round the bend in the lane, Henry was kissing Dinah's throat.

iv

"I can't see," said Selia Ross, "that it matters what a couple of shocking, nasty old church-hens choose to say."

"But it does," answered Dr. Templett. He kicked a log on the fire. "Mine is one of the few jobs where your private life affects your practice. Why it should be so, the Lord alone knows. And I can't afford to lose my practice, Selia. My brother went through most of what was left when my father died. I don't want to sell Chippingwood, but it takes me all my time to keep it up. It's a beastly situation, I know. Other things being equal, I still couldn't ask Freda to divorce me. Lying there from one year's end to another! Spinal paralysis isn't much fun and—she's still fond of me."

"My poor darling," said Mrs. Ross softly. Templett's back was towards her. She looked at him speculatively. Perhaps she wondered if she should go to him. If so, she decided against it and remained, exquisitely neat and expensive, in a high-backed chair.

"Only just now," muttered Templett, "old Mrs. Cain said something about seeing my car outside. I've noticed things. They're beginning to talk, damn their eyes. And with the new fellow over at Penmoor I can't afford to take chances. It's all due to those two women. Nobody would have thought anything about it if they hadn't got their claws into me. The other day, when I fixed up old Prentice's finger, she asked after Freda, and in almost the same breath she began to talk about you. My God, I wish she'd get gangrene! And now this!"

"I'm sorry I told you."

"No, it was much better you should. I'd better see the damn' thing."

Mrs. Ross went to her writing-desk and unlocked a drawer. She took out a sheet of note-paper and gave it to him. He stared at six lines of black capitals.

"You are given notice to leave the district. If you disregard this warning, your lover shall suffer."

"When did it come?"

"This morning. The postmark was Chipping."

"What makes you think it's her?"

"Smell it."

"Eucalyptus, my God!"

"She's drenched in it."

"She probably carried it in her bag?"

"That's it. You'd better burn it, Billy."

Dr. Templett dropped the paper on the smouldering log and then snatched it up again.

"No," he said. "I've got a note from her at home. I'll compare the paper."

"Surely hers has a printed address."

"This might be a plain sheet for the following on. It's good paper."

"She'd never be such a fool."

"The woman's pathological, my dear. She might do anything. Anyway, I'll see."

He put the paper in his pocket.

"In my opinion," said Selia Ross, "she's green with jealousy because I've rather got off with the parson and the squire."

"So am I."

"Darling," said Mrs. Ross, "you can't think how pure I am with them."

Templett suddenly burst out laughing.

CHAPTER EIGHT

Catastrophe

i

AT TEN minutes to eight on the night of Saturday, November 27th, the parish hall at Winton St. Giles smelt of evergreens, wet mackintoshes, and humanity. Members of the Young People's Friendly Circle, harried and dragooned by Miss Campanula, had sold all the tickets in advance, so, in spite of the appalling weather, every seat was occupied. Even the Moorton Park people had come over with their house-party, and sat in the front row of less uncomfortable chairs at two shillings a head. Behind them were ranged the church workers including Mr. Prosser, chemist of Chipping, and Mr. Blandish, the police superintendent, both churchwardens. The Women's Institute was there with its husband and children. Farther back, in a giggling phalanx, were those girls of the Friendly Circle who were not acting as ushers, and behind them, on the back benches, the young men of the farms and villages, smelling of hair-grease and animal warmth. In the entrance, Miss Campanula had posted Sergeant Roper, of the Chipping Constabularly, and sidesman of St. Giles. His duties were to collect tickets and subdue the back-benchers, who were inclined to guffaw and throw paper pellets at their girls. At the end of the fourth row from the front, on the left of the centre aisle, sat Georgie Biggins with his parents. He seemed strangely untroubled by his dethronement from the position of call-boy. His hair was plastered down with water on his bullet-shaped head, his face shone rosily, and there was an unholy light in his black boot-button eyes, which were fixed on the piano.

The piano, soon to achieve a world-wide notoriety, stood beneath the stage and facing the centre aisle. One of the innumerable photographs that appeared in the newspapers on Monday, November 29th, shows a museum piece, a cottage pianoforte of the nineties, with a tucked silk panel, badly torn, in the front. It has a hard-bitten look. It would not be too fanciful to compare it to a spinster, dressed in dilapidated moth-eaten finery, still retaining an air of shabby gentility, but given over to some very dubious employment. This air is enhanced by the presence of five aspidistras, placed in a row on the top of the bunting, which has been stretched across the top, over the opening and the turned-back lid, tightly fixed to the edges with drawing pins, and allowed to fall in artistic festoons down the sides and in a sort of valance-like effect across the front. At ten to eight on the night of the concert, there on the fretwork rack under the valance of bunting was Miss Prentice's "Venetian Suite," rather the worse for wear, but ready for her attention.

There was a notice in the programmes about the object of the performance, a short history of the old piano, a word of thanks to Jocelyn Jernigham, Esq., of Pen Cuckoo, for his generous offer to make up the sum of money needed for a new instrument. The old piano came in for a lot of attention that evening.

At eight o'clock Dinah, sick with apprehension in the prompt corner, turned on the stage lights. Sergeant Roper, observing this signal, leant across the row of boys on the back bench and switched off the house lights. The audience made noises of pleasurable anticipation.

Improvised footlights shone upwards on the faded green curtain. After a moment's pause, during which many people in the audience said, "Ssh!" an invisible hand drew the curtain aside and the rector walked through. There was a great burst of applause in the second row, and the reporter from the *Chipping Courier* took out his pad and pencil.

Mr. Copeland's best cassock was green about the seams, the toes of his boots turned up because he always neglected to put trees in them. He was actually a good-looking, rather shabbily-dressed parish priest. But, lit dramatically from beneath, he looked magnificent. It was the head of a mediæval saint, austere and beautiful, sharp as a cameo against its own black shadow.

"He ought to be a bishop," said old Mrs. Cain to her daughter.

Behind the curtain, Dinah took a final look at the set. The squire, satisfactory in plus-fours and a good clean make-up, was in his right position up-stage, with a telegram in his hand. Henry stood off-stage at the prompt entrance, very nervous. Dinah moved into the wings with the bicycle bell in her hands.

"Don't answer the telephone till it's rung twice," she hissed at Jocelyn.

"All right, all right, all right."

"Clear, please," said Dinah severely. "Stand by."

She went into the prompt box, seized the curtain lines and listened to her father.

"—So you see," the rector was saying, "the present piano is almost a historical piece, and I'm sure you will be glad to hear that this old friend will be given an honourable place in the small recreation room at the back of the stage."

Sentimental applause.

"I have one other announcement. You will see on your programmes that Miss Prentice of Pen Cuckoo, in addition to taking a part, was to play the overture and entr'acte this evening. I am sorry to say that Miss Prentice has—ah—has—ah—an injured finger which has given—and I am sorry to say is still giving her—a great deal of pain. Miss Prentice, with her customary pluck and unselfishness"—Mr. Copeland paused hopefully and was awarded a tentative outbreak of clapping—"was anxious not to disappoint us and was prepared, up to a minute or two ago, to play the piano. However, as she has an important rôle to fill later on in the evening, and as her hand is really not fit, she—ah—Dr. Templett has—ah—has taken matters in hand and ordered her not to—to play."

The rector paused again while the audience wondered if it should applaud Dr. Templett's efficiency, but decided that, on the whole, it had better not.

"Now, although you will be disappointed and will sympathize, I am sure, with Miss Prentice, we all know we mustn't disobey doctor's orders. I am happy to say that we shall still have our music—and very good music, too. Miss Idris Campanula, at literally a moment's notice, has consented to play for us. Now, I think this is particularly generous and sporting of Miss Campanula, and I'll ask you all to show your appreciation in a really——"

Deafening applause.

"Miss Campanula," ended Mr. Copeland, "will play Rachmaninoff's 'Prelude in C Sharp Minor.' Miss Campanula."

He led her from the wings, handed her down the steps to the piano, and returned to the stage through the side curtains.

It was wonderful to see Idris Campanula acknowledge the applause with an austere bend, smile more intimately at the rector, descend the steps carefully and, with her back to the aisle, seat herself at the instrument. It was wonderful to see her remove the "Venetian Suite," and place her famous Prelude on the music rack, open it with a masterly flip, deal it a jocular slap, and then draw out her pince-nez from the tucked silk bosom that so closely resembled the tucked silk bosom of the instrument. Miss Campanula and the old piano seemed to face each other with an air of understanding and affinity. Miss Campanula's back hollowed as she drew up her bosom until it perched on the top of her stays. She leant forward until her nose was within three inches of the music, and she held her left hand poised over the bass. Down it came.

Pom. *Pom*. POM.

The three familiar pretentious chords.

Miss Campanula paused, lifted her big left foot and planked it down on the soft pedal.

ii

The air was blown into splinters of atrocious clamour. For a second nothing existed but noise—hard racketing noise. The hall, suddenly thick with dust, was also thick with a cloud of intolerable sound. And, as the dust fell, so the pandemonium abated and separated into recognisable sources. Women were screaming. Chair legs scraped the floor, branches of ever-greens fell from the walls, the piano hummed like a gigantic top.

Miss Campanula fell forward. Her face slid down the sheet of music, which stuck to it. Very slowly and stealthily she slipped sideways to the keys of the piano, striking a final discord in the bass. She remained there, quite still, in a posture that seemed to parody the antics of an affected virtuoso. She was dead.

iii

Lady Appleby in her chair by the piano turned to her husband as if to ask him a question and fainted.

Georgie Biggins screamed like a whistle.

The rector came through the curtain and ran down the steps to the piano. He looked at that figure leaning on the keys, wrung his hands and faced the audience. His lips moved, but he could not be heard.

Dinah came out of the prompt corner and stood transfixed. Her head was bent as if in profound meditation. Then she turned, stumbled past the curtain, calling, "Henry! Henry!" and disappeared.

Dr. Templett, in his appalling make-up, came through from the opposite side of the curtain. He went up to the rector, touched his arm and then descended to the piano. He bent down with his back to the audience, stayed so for a moment and then straightened up. He shook his head slightly at the rector.

Mr. Blandish, in the third row, pushed his way to the aisle and walked up to the stage.

He said, "What's all this?" in a loud, constabulary tone, and was heard. The hall went suddenly quiet. The voice of Mr. Prosser, the Chipping organist, said all by itself: "It was a gun. That's what it was. It was a gun."

Mr. Blandish was not in uniform, but he was dressed in authority. He examined the piano and spoke to Dr. Templett. There was a screen masking the corner on the prompt side between the stage and the wall. The two men fetched it and put it round the piano.

The rector mounted the steps to the stage and faced his parishioners.

"My dear people," he said in a trembling voice, "there has been a terrible accident. I beg of you all to go away quietly to your own homes. Roper, will you open the door?"

"Just a minute," said Mr. Blandish. "Just a minute, if *you* please, sir. This is an affair for the police. Charlie Roper, you stay by that door. Have you got your notebook on you?"

"Yes, sir," said Sergeant Roper.

"All right." Mr. Blandish raised his voice. "As you pass out," he roared, "I'll ask you to leave your names and addresses with the sergeant on duty at the door. Anybody, who has had anything to do with this entertainment," continued Mr. Blandish with no trace of irony in his voice, "either in the way of taking part or decorating the hall or so forth, will kindly remain behind. Now move along quietly, please, there's no need to rush. The back benches first. Keep your seats till your turn comes."

To the rector he said, "I'd be much obliged if you'd go to the back door, sir, and see nobody leaves that way. If it can be locked and you've got the key, lock it. We'll have this curtain up, if you please. I'm going to the telephone. It's in the back room, isn't it? Much obliged."

He went through the back of the stage, passing Dinah and Henry, who stood side by side in the wings.

"Good-evening, Mr. Jernigham," said the superintendent. "Do you mind raising the curtain?"

"Certainly," said Henry.

The curtain rose in a series of uneven jerks, revealing to the people still left in the hall a group of four persons: Jocelyn

Jernigham, Selia Ross, Eleanor Prentice and the rector, who had returned from the back door with the key in his hand.

"I can't believe it," said the rector. "I simply cannot believe that it has happened."

"Is it murder?" asked Mrs. Ross sharply. Her voice pitched a note too high, sounded shockingly loud.

"I—I can't believe——" repeated Mr. Copeland.

"But see here, Copeland," interrupted the squire, "I don't know what the devil everybody's driving at. Shot through the head! What d'you mean? Somebody must have seen something. You can't shoot people through the head in a crowded hall without being spotted."

"The shot seems to have come from—from——"

"From where, for heaven's sake?"

"From inside the piano," said the rector unhappily. "We mustn't touch anything; but it seems to come from inside the piano. You can see through the torn silk."

"Good God!" said Jocelyn. He looked irritably at Miss Prentice, who rocked to and fro like a middle-aged marionette and moaned repeatedly.

"Do be quiet, Eleanor," said the squire. "Here! Templett!"

Dr. Templett had again gone behind the screen, but he came out and said, "What?" in an irascible voice.

"Has she been shot through the head?"

"Yes."

"How?"

"From inside the piano."

"I never heard such a thing," said Jocelyn. "I'm coming to look."

"Yes. But, I say," objected Dr. Templett, "I don't think you ought to, you know. It's a matter for the police."

"Well, you've just been in there."

"I'm police surgeon for the district."

"Well, by God," said the squire, suddenly remembering it, "I'm Acting Chief Constable for the county."

"Sorry," said Dr. Templett. "I'd forgotten."

But the squire was prevented from looking behind the screen by the return of Mr. Blandish.

"That's all right," said the superintendent peaceably. He turned to the squire. "I've just rung up the station and asked for two chaps to come along, sir."

"Oh, yes. Yes. Very sensible," said Jocelyn.

"Just a minute, Blandish," said Dr. Templett. "Come down here, would you?"

They disappeared behind the screen. The others waited in silence. Miss Prentice buried her face in her hands. The squire walked to the edge of the stage, looked over the top of the piano, turned aside, and suddenly mopped his face with his handkerchief.

Blandish and Templett came out and joined the party on the stage.

"Lucky, in a way, your being here on the spot, sir," Blandish said to Jocelyn. "Your first case of this sort since your appointment, I believe."

"Yes."

"Very nasty affair."

"It is."

"Yes, sir. Well now, with your approval, Mr. Jernigham, I'd just like to get a few notes down. I fancy Mr. Henry Jernigham and Miss Copeland are with us."

He peered into the shadows beyond the stage.

"We're here," said Henry.

He and Dinah came on the stage.

"Ah, yes. Good-evening, Miss Copeland."

"Good-evening," said Dinah faintly.

"Now," said Blandish, looking round the stage, "this is the whole company of performers, I take it. *With* the exception of the deceased, of course."

"Yes," said Jocelyn.

"I'll just make a note of the names."

They sat round the stage while Blandish wrote in his note-book. A group of ushers and two youths were huddled on a bench at the far end of the hall under the eyes of Sergeant Roper. Dinah fixed her gaze on this group, on Blandish, on the floor, anywhere but on the top of the piano jutting above the footlights and topped with pots of aspidistra. For down through the aspidistras, heavily shadowed by the screen, and not quite covered by the green and yellow bunting they had thrown over it, was Miss Campanula's body, face down on the keys of the piano. Dinah found herself wondering who was responsible for the aspidistras. She had meant to have them removed. They must mask quite a lot of the stage from the front rows.

"*Don't look at them*," said her mind. She turned quickly to Henry. He took her hands and pulled her round with her back to the footlights.

"It's all right, Dinah," he whispered, "it's all right darling."

"I'm not panicked or anything," said Dinah.

"Yes," said Blandish, "that's all the names. Now, sir—— Well, what is it?"

A uniformed constable had come in from the front door and stood waiting in the hall.

"Excuse me," said Blandish, and went down to him. There was a short rumbling conversation. Blandish turned and called to the squire.

"Can you spare a moment, sir?"

"Certainly," said Jocelyn, and joined them.

"Can you beat this, sir?" said Blandish, in an infuriated whisper. "We've had nothing better than a few old drunks and speed merchants in this place for the last six months or more, and now, to-night, there's got to be a breaking and entering job at Moorton Park with five thousand pounds' worth of her ladyship's jewellery gone and Lord knows what else besides. Their butler rang up the station five minutes ago, and this chap's come along on his motor bike and he says the whole place is upside down. Sir George and her ladyship and the party haven't got back yet. It looks like the work of the gang that cleaned up a couple of jobs in Somerset a fortnight back. It'll be a big thing to tackle. Now what am I to do, sir?"

Jocelyn and Blandish stared at each other.

"Well," said Jocelyn at last, "you can't be in two places at once."

"That's right, sir," said Blandish. "It goes against the grain when we've scarcely got started, but it looks as if it'll have to be the Yard."

CHAPTER NINE

C. I. D.

i

Five hours after Miss Campanula struck the third chord of the Prelude, put her foot on the soft pedal, and died, a police car arrived at the parish hall of Winton St. Giles. It had come from Scotland Yard. It contained Chief Detective-Inspector Alleyn, Detective-Inspector Fox, Detective-Sergeant Bailey, and Detective-Sergeant Thompson.

Alleyn, looking up from his road map, saw a church spire against a frosty, moonlit hill, trees against stars, and nearer at hand the lighted windows of a stone building.

"This looks like the hidden treasure," he said to Thompson who was driving. "What's the time?"

"One o'clock, sir."

As if in confirmation a clock, outside in the night, chimed for the hour and tolled one.

"Out we get," said Alleyn.

The upland air was cold after the stuffiness of the car. It smelt of dead leaves and frost. They walked up a gravelled path to the front door of the building. Fox flashed a torch on a brass plate.

"Winton St. Giles Parish Hall. The Gift of Jocelyn Jernigham Esquire of Pen Cuckoo, 1805. To the Glory of God. In memory of his wife Prudence Jernigham who passed away on May 7th, 1801."

"This is the place, sir," said Fox.

"Sure enough," said Alleyn, and rapped smartly on the door.

It was opened by Sergeant Roper, bleary-eyed after a five hours' vigil.

"Yard," said Alleyn.

"Thank Gawd," said Sergeant Roper.

They walked in.

"The super asked me to say, sir," said Sergeant Roper, "that he was very sorry not to be here when you arrived, but seeing as how there's been a first-class breaking and entering up to Moorton Park——"

"That's all right," said Alleyn. "What's it all about?"

"Murder," said Roper. "Will I show you?"

"Do."

They walked up the centre aisle between rows of empty benches and chairs. The floor was littered with programmes.

"I'll just turn on the other lights, sir," said Roper. "Deceased's behind the screen."

He trudged up the steps to the stage. A switch clicked and Dinah's foot- and proscenium-lights flooded the stage. Bailey and Thompson pulled the screen to one side.

There was Miss Campanula with her face on the keyboard of the piano, waiting for the expert, the camera, and the pathologist.

"Good Lord!" said Alleyn.

Rachmaninoff's (and Miss Campanula's) Prelude was crushed between her face and the keys. A dark crimson patch had seeped out towards the margin of the music, but the title showed clearly. A hole had been blown through the centre. Without touching the music, Alleyn could see several pencilled reminders. After the last of the opening chords was an emphatic "S.P." The left hand had been pinned down by the face but the right had fallen, and hung inconsequently at the end of a long purple arm. The face itself was hidden. They stared down at the back of the head. Its pitiful knot of grey hair, broken and loosened, hung over a dark hole. Weepers of stained hair stuck to the thin neck.

"Through the back of the skull," said Fox.

"That's the wound of exit," said Alleyn. "We shall have to find the bullet."

Bailey turned away and began to search along the aisle.

Alleyn shone his torch on the tucked silk front of the piano. There was a rent exactly in the centre, extending above and below the central hole made by the bullet. Inside the hole, but quite close to the surface, the light picked up a shining circle. Alleyn leaned forward, peering, and uttered a soft exclamation.

"That's the gun that did the job, sir," said Roper. "Inside the piano."

"Has it been touched?"

"No, sir, no. The super was in the audience and he took over immediately, did super. Except for doctor, not a soul's been near."

"The doctor. Where is he?"

"He's gone home, sir. Dr. Templett it is, up to Chippingwood.

He's police surgeon. He was here when it happened. He said would I ring him up when you came and if you wanted him he'd be over. It's only a couple of miles off."

"I think he'd better come. Ring him up now, will you?"

When Roper had gone, Alleyn said, "This is a rum go, Fox."

"Very peculiar, Mr. Alleyn. How's it been worked?"

"We'll take a look-see when we've got some pictures. Take every angle, Thompson."

Thompson had already begun to set up his paraphernalia. Soon the flashlight threw Miss Campanula into startling relief. For the second and last time she was photographed, seated at the instrument.

Roper came back from the telephone and watched the experts with avid interest.

"Funniest go you ever did see," he said to Bailey, who had moved to the end of the aisle. "I was on the spot. The old lady sits down at the piano in her bold way and wades into it. Biff, biff, plonk, and before you know where you are the whole works go off like a packet of crackers and she's lying there a corpse."

"Cuh!" said Bailey and stooped swiftly to the floor. "Here we are, sir," he said. "Here's the bullet."

"Got it? I'll look at it in a minute."

Alleyn marked the position of the head and arm and squatted on the floor to run a chalk line round the feet.

"Size eight," he murmured. "The left foot looks as if it's slipped on the soft pedal. Now, I wonder. Well, we'll soon find out. Got gloves on, all of you? Good. Go carefully, I should, and keep away from the front. Will you, sergeant—what is your name, by the way?"

"Roper, sir."

"Right. Will you clear the stuff off the top?"

Roper shifted the aspidistras and began to unpin the bunting. Alleyn went up to the stage and squatted over the footlights like a sort of presiding deity.

"Gently does it, the thing's tottering. Look at that!"

He pointed at the inside of the top lid, which was turned back.

"Wood-rot. No wonder they wanted a new one. Good Lord!"

"What, sir?"

"Come and look at this, Fox."

Alleyn shone his torch in at the top. The light glinted on a steel barrel. He slipped in his gloved fingers. There was a sharp click.

"I've just snicked over the safety-catch on a perfectly good automatic. Now, then."

Roper pulled away the bunting.

"Well, I'll be damned!" said Fox.

ii

"Very fancy, isn't it?" said Alleyn.

"A bit too fancy for me, sir. How does it work?"

"It's a Colt. The butt's jammed between the pegs, where the wires are made fast, and the front of the piano. The nozzle fits into a hole in this fretwork horror in front of the silk bib. The bib's rotten with age and bulging. It could be tweaked in front of the nozzle. Anyway, the music would hide it. Of course the top was smothered in bunting and vegetables."

"But what pulled the trigger?"

"Half a second. There's a loop of string round the butt and over the trigger. The string goes on to an absurd little pulley in the back of the inner case. Then forward to another pulley on a front strut. Then it goes down." He moved his torch. "Yes, now you can see. The other end of the string is fixed to the batten that's part of the soft pedal action. When you use the pedal the batten goes backwards. Moves about two inches, I fancy. Quite enough to give a sharp jerk to the string. We'll have some shots of this, Thompson. It's a bit tricky. Can you manage?"

"I think so, Mr. Alleyn."

"It looks like a practical joke," said Fox.

Alleyn looked up quickly.

"Funny you should say that," he said. "You spoke my thoughts. A small boy's practical joke. The Heath Robinson touch with the string and pulleys is quite in character. I believe I even recognise those little pulleys, Fox. Notice how very firmly they've been anchored. My godson's got their doubles in one of those building sets, an infernal dithering affair that's supposed to improve the mind, and nearly sent me out of mine. 'Twiddletoy,' it's called. Yes, and by George, Brer Fox, that's the sort of cord they provide: thin green twine, very tough, like fishing line, and fits nicely into the groove of the pulley."

"D'you reckon some kid's gone wild and rigged this for the old girl?" asked Fox.

"A child with a Colt .32?"

"Hardly. Still, he might have got hold of one."

Alleyn swore softly.

"What's up, sir?" asked Fox.

"It's the whole damn lay-out of the thing! It's exactly like a contraption they give in the book of the words of these toys. 'Fig. I. Signal.' It's no more like a signal than your nose. Less, if anything. But you build it on this principle. I made the thing for my godson. The cord goes up in three steps to pulleys that are fixed to a couple of uprights. At the bottom it's tied to a little arm and at the top to a bigger one. When you push down the lower arm, the upper one waggles. I'll swear it inspired this job. You see how there's just room for the pulley in the waist of the Colt at the back? They're fiddling little brutes, those pulleys, as I know to my cost. Not much bigger than the end of a cigarette. Hole through the middle. Once you've threaded the twine it can't slip out. It's guarded by the curved lips of the groove. You see, the top one's anchored to the wires above that strip of steel. The bottom one's tied to a strut in the fretwork. All right, Thompson, your witness."

Thompson manœuvred his camera.

A car drew up outside the hall. A door slammed.

"That'll be the doctor, sir," said Roper.

"Ah, yes. Let him in, will you?"

Dr. Templett came in. He had removed his make-up and his beard and had changed the striped trousers and morning coat proper to a French Ambassador, for a tweed suit and sweater.

"Hullo," he said. "Sorry if I kept you waiting. Car wouldn't start."

"Dr. Templett?"

"Yes, and you're from Scotland Yard, aren't you? Didn't lose much time. This is a nasty business."

"Beastly," said Alleyn. "I think we might move her now."

They brought a long table from the back of the hall and on it they laid Miss Campanula. She had been shot between the eyes.

"Smell of eucalyptus," said Alleyn.

"She had a cold."

Dr. Templett examined the wounds while the others looked on. At last he straightened up, took a bottle of ether from his pocket, and used a little to clean his hands.

"There's a sheet in one of the dressing-rooms, Roper," he said. Roper went off to get it.

"What've you got there?" Templett asked Alleyn.

Alleyn had found Miss Prentice's Venetian Suite behind the piano. He turned it over in his hands. Like the Prelude, it was a very jaded affair. The red back of the cover had a discoloured circular patch in the centre. Alleyn touched it. It was damp. Roper returned with the sheet.

"Can't make her look very presentable, I'm afraid," said Dr. Templett. "Rigor's fairly well advanced in the jaw and neck. Rather quick after five hours. She fell at an odd angle. I didn't do more than look at her. The exit wound showed clearly enough what had happened. Of course, I assured myself she was dead."

"Did you realise at once that it was a wound of exit?"

"What? Yes. Well, after a second or two I did. Thought at first she'd been shot through the back of the head and then I noticed characteristics of an exit wound, direction of the matted hair and so on. I bent down and tried to see the face. I could just see the blood. Then I noticed the hole in the music. The frilling round the edge of the hole showed clearly enough which way the bullet had come."

"Very sound observation," said Alleyn. "You knew, then, what had happened?"

"I was damn' puzzled and still am. When we'd rigged up the screen I had another look and spotted the nozzle of the revolver or whatever it is, behind the silk trimmings. I told Blandish, the local superintendent, and he had a look too. How the devil was it done?"

"A mechanical device that she worked herself."

"Not suicide?"

"No, murder. You'll see when we open the piano."

"Extraordinary business."

"Very," agreed Alleyn. "Bailey, you might get along with your department now. When Thompson's finished, you can go over the whole thing for prints and then dismantle it. In the meantime, I'd better produce my note-book and get a few hard facts."

They carried the table into a corner and put the screen round it. Roper came down with a sheet and covered the body.

"Let's sit down somewhere," suggested Dr. Templett. "I want a pipe. It's given me a shock, this business."

They sat in the front row of stalls. Alleyn raised an eyebrow at Fox who came and joined them. Roper stood in the offing. Dr. Templett filled his pipe, Alleyn and Fox opened their note-books.

"To begin with," said Alleyn, "who was this lady?"

"Idris Campanula," said Templett. "Spinster of this parish."

"Address?"

"The Red House, Chipping. You passed it on your way up."

"Have the right people been told about this?"

"Yes. The rector did that. Only the three maids. I don't know about the next-of-kin. Somebody said it was a second cousin in

Kenya. We'll have to find that out. Look here, shall I tell you the story in my own words?"

"I wish you would."

"I thought I'd find myself in the double rôle of police surgeon and eye-witness, so I tried to sort it out while I waited for your telephone call. Here goes. Idris Campanula was about fifty years of age. She came to the Red House as a child of twelve to live with her uncle, General Campanula, who adopted her on the death of her parents. He was an old bachelor and the girl was brought up by his acidulated sister, whom my father used to call one of the nastiest women he'd ever met. When Idris was about thirty, the general died, and his sister only survived him a couple of years. The house and money, a lot of money by the way, were left to Idris, who by that time was shaping pretty much like her aunt. Nil nisi and all that, but it's a fact. She never had a chance. Starved and repressed and hung about with a mass of shibboleths and Victorian conversation. Well, here she's stayed for the last twenty years, living on rich food, good works and local scandal. Upon my word, it's incredible that she's gone. Look here, I'm being too diffuse, aren't I?"

"Not a bit. You're giving us a picture in the round which is what we like."

"Well, there she was until to-night. I don't know if you've heard from Roper about the play."

"We haven't had time," said Alleyn, "but I hope to get volumes from him before dawn."

Roper looked gratified and drew nearer.

"The play was got up by a group of local people."

"Of whom you were one," said Alleyn.

"Hullo!" Dr. Templett took his pipe out of his mouth and stared at Alleyn. "Now, did any one tell you that, or is this the real stuff?"

"I'm afraid it's not even up to Form I at Hendon. There's a trace of grease paint in your hair. I wish I could add that I have written a short monograph on grease paint."

Dr. Templett grinned.

"I'll lay you ten to one," he said, "that you can't deduce what sort of part I had."

Alleyn glanced sideways at him.

"We are not allowed to show off," he said, "but with Inspector Fox's austere eye on me, I venture to have a pot shot. A character part, possibly a Frenchman, wearing a rimless eyeglass. Any good?"

"Did we bet in shillings?"

"It was no bet," said Alleyn apologetically.

"Well, let's have the explanation," said Templett. "I enjoy feeling a fool."

"I'm afraid I'll feel rather a fool making it," said Alleyn. "It's very small beer indeed. In the words of all detective heroes, you only need to consider. You removed your make-up in a hurry. Spirit gum, on which I have not written a monograph, leaves its mark unless removed with care and alcohol. Your chin and upper lips show signs of having been plucked and there's a very remote trace of black crêpe hairiness. Only on the tip of your chin and not on your cheeks. Ha! A black imperial. The foreign ambassadorial touch. A sticky reddish dint by the left eye suggests a rimless glass, fixed with more spirit gum. The remains of a heated line across the brow suggests a top hat. And, when you mentioned your part, you moved your shoulders very slightly. You were thinking subconsciously of your performance. Broken English. " 'Ow you say?" with a shrug. That sort of thing. For heaven's sake say I'm right."

"By gum!" said Sergeant Roper, devoutly.

"Amen," said Dr. Templett. "In the words of Mr. Holmes——"

"—of whom nobody shall make mock in my presence. Pray continue your most interesting narrative," said Alleyn.

CHAPTER TEN

According to Templett

i

"——AND SO you see," concluded Templett, "there is absolutely nothing about any of us that is at all out of the ordinary. You might find the same group of people in almost any of the more isolated bits of English countryside. The parson, the squire, the parson's daughter, the squire's son, the two church hens and the local medico."

"And the lady from outside," added Alleyn, looking at his notes. "You have forgotten Mrs. Ross."

"So I have. Well, she's simply a rather charming new-comer. That's all. I'm blessed if I can see who, by the wildest flight of imagination, could have wanted to kill this very dull middle-aged frumpish spinster. I shouldn't have thought she had an enemy in the world."

"I wouldn't say that," said Sergeant Roper, unexpectedly. Alleyn looked up at him.

"No?"

"No, sir, I wouldn't say that. To speak frankly, she was a very sharp-tongued lady. Mischievous like. Well, over-bearing. Very curious, too. Proper nosey-parker. My missus always says you couldn't change your mind without it being overheard at the Red House. My missus is friendly with the cook up to Red House, but she never says anything she doesn't want everybody in the village to hear about. Miss Campanula used to order the meals and then wait for the news, as you might say. They call her the Receiving Set in Chipping."

"Do they indeed," murmured Alleyn.

"You don't murder people for being curious," said Templett.

"I can't imagine it with Miss Campanula."

"I don't reckon anybody *did* want to murder Miss Campanula," said Roper, stolidly.

"Hullo!" Alleyn ejaculated. "What's all this?"

"I reckon they wanted to murder Miss Prentice."

"Good God!" said Templett. "I never thought of that!"

"Never thought of what?" said Alleyn.

"I forgot to tell you. Good Lord, what a fool! Why didn't you remind me, Roper? Good Lord!"

"May we hear now?" asked Alleyn patiently.

"Yes, of course."

In considerable confusion, Templett explained about Miss Prentice's finger and the change of pianists.

"This is altogether another kettle of fish," said Alleyn. "Let's get a clear picture. You say that up to twenty minutes to eight Miss Prentice insisted that she was going to do the overture and entr'acte?"

"Yes. I told her three days ago she'd better give it up. There was this whitlow on her middle finger and she mucked about with it and got some sort of infection. It was very painful. D'you think she'd give in? Not a bit of it. Said she'd alter the fingering of her piece. Wouldn't hear of giving up. I asked her to-night if she'd let me look at it. Oh, no! It was 'much easier'! She'd got a surgical stall over it. At about twenty to eight I passed the ladies dressing-room. The door was half-open and I heard a sound like somebody crying. I could see her in there alone, rocking backwards and forwards holding this damned finger. I went in and insisted on looking at it. All puffed up and as fiery as hell! She was in floods of tears but she still said she'd manage. I put my foot down. Dinah Copeland came in, saw what was up, and fetched her father who's got more authority over these women than anybody else. He made her give in. Old Idris, poor old girl, had turned up by then and was all agog to play the famous Prelude. She's played it in and out of season for the last twenty years, if it's been written as long as that. Somebody was sent off to the Red House for the music and a dress; she was dressed up for her part, you see. The rector said he'd make an announcement about it. By that time Miss Prentice had settled down to being a martyr and—but, look here, I'm being most amazingly indiscreet. Now, don't go and write all this down in that note-book and quote me as having said it."

Dr. Templett looked anxiously at Fox whose note-book was flattened out on his enormous knee.

"That's all right, sir," said Fox blandly. "We only want the essentials."

"And I'm giving you all the inessentials. Sorry."

"I didn't say that, now, doctor."

"We can take it," Alleyn said, "that, in your opinion, up to twenty to eight everybody, including Miss Campanula and Miss Prentice, believed the music would be provided by Miss Prentice."

"Certainly."

"And this Venetian Suite was Miss Prentice's music?"

"Yes."

"Nobody could have rigged this apparatus inside the piano after seven-forty?"

"Lord, no! The audience began to arrive at about half-past seven, didn't it, Roper? You were on the door."

"The Cains turned up at seven-twenty," said Roper, "and Mr. and Mrs. Biggins and that young limit Georgie, were soon after them. I was on duty at seven. Must have been done before then, sir."

"Yes. What about the afternoon and morning? Anybody here?"

"We were all in and out during the morning," said Dr. Templett. "The Y.P.F.C. girls did the decorating and fixed up the supper arrangements and so on, and we got out stuff ready behind the scenes. Masses of people."

"You'd been rehearsing here, I suppose?"

"Latterly. We did most of the rehearsing up in the study in Pen Cuckoo. It was too cold here until they got extra heaters in. We had our dress rehearsal here on Thursday night. Yesterday afternoon at five, Friday I mean, we went up to Pen Cuckoo and had what Dinah calls a run-through for words."

"What about this afternoon before the performance?"

"It was shut up during the afternoon. I called in at about three o'clock to drop some of my gear. The place was closed then and the key hung up between the wall of the outside place and the main building. We'd arranged that with Dinah."

"Did you notice the piano?"

"Now, did I? Yes. Yes, I did. It was where it is now, with bunting all over the top and a row of pot plants. They'd fixed it up like that in the morning."

"Did anybody else look in at three o'clock while you were here?"

"Let me think. Yes, Mrs. Ross was there with some foodstuff. She left it in the supper-room at the back of the stage."

"How long were you both in the place?"

"Oh, not long. We—talked for a minute or two and then came away."

"Together?"

"No. I left Mrs. Ross arranging sandwiches on plates. By the way, if you want anything to eat, do help yourselves. And there's some beer under the table. I provided it, so don't hesitate."

"Very kind of you," said Alleyn.

"Not a bit. Be delighted. Where were we? Oh, yes. I had a case over near Moorton and I wanted to look in at the cottage hospital. I wasn't here long."

"Nobody else came in?"

"Not then."

"Who was the first to arrive in the evening?"

"I don't know. I was the last. Had an emergency case at six. When I got home I found my wife not so well again. We didn't get here till half-past seven. Dinah Copeland thought I wasn't going to turn up and had worked herself into a frightful stew. She'd be able to tell you all about times of arrival. I bet she got here long before the rest of the cast. Dinah Copeland. That's the parson's daughter. She produced the play."

"Yes. Thank you."

"Well, I suppose you don't want me any longer. Good Lord, it's nearly two o'clock!"

"Awful, isn't it? We shall be here all night, I expect. No, we won't bother you any more, Dr. Templett."

"What about moving the body? Shall I fix up for the mortuary van to come along as early as possible?"

"I wish you would."

"I'll have to do the P.M., I suppose?"

"Yes. Yes, of course."

"Pretty plain sailing, it'll be, poor old girl. Well, good-night or good-morning, er—I don't know your name, do I?"

"Alleyn."

"What, Roderick Alleyn?"

"Yes."

"By George, I've read your book of criminal investigation. Damned good. Fascinating subject, isn't it?"

"Enthralling."

"For the layman, what? Not such fun for the expert."

"Not quite such fun."

Dr. Templett shook hands, turned to go, and then paused.

"I tell you what," he said. "I'd like to see how this booby-trap worked."

"Yes, of course. Come and have a look."

Bailey was at the piano with an insufflator and a strong lamp.

Thompson stood by with his cameras.

"How's it going, Bailey?" asked Alleyn.

"Finished the case, sir. Not much doing. Somebody must have dusted the whole show. We may get some latent prints but I don't think there's a chance, myself. Same with the Colt. We're ready to take it down."

"All right. Go warily, we don't want to lose any prints if they're there. I'll move the front of the piano off and you hold the gun."

Bailey reached a gloved hand inside the top.

"I'll take off the pulley on the front panel, sir."

"Yes. That'll give us a better picture than if you dismantled the twine altogether."

Fox undid the side catches and Alleyn lifted away the front of the piano and put it on one side.

"Hullo," he said, "this silk panelling seems as though it's had water spilt on it. It's still dampish. Round the central hole."

"Blood?" suggested Dr. Templett.

"No. There's a little blood. This was water. A circular patch of it. Now, I wonder. Well, let's have a look at the works."

The Colt, supported at the end of the barrel by Bailey's thumb and forefinger, was revealed with its green twine attachments. The butt was still jammed against the pegs at the back. Alleyn picked up the detached pulley and held it in position.

"Good God!" said Dr. Templett.

"Ingenious, isn't it?" Alleyn said. "I think we'll have a shot of it like this, Thompson. It'll look nice and clear for the twelve good men and true."

"Is the safety catch on?" demanded Dr. Templett, suddenly stepping aside.

"It is. You've dealt with the soft pedal, haven't you, Bailey?" He stooped and pressed the left pedal down with his hand. The batten with its row of hammers moved towards the string. The green twine tightened in the minute pulleys.

"That's how it worked. You can see where the pressure comes on the trigger."

"A very neat-fingered person, wouldn't you say, Mr. Alleyn?" said Fox.

"Yes," said Alleyn. "Neat and sure fingers."

"Oh. I don't know," said Templett. "It's amazingly simple really. The only tricky bit would be passing the twine through the trigger guard, round the butt, and through the top pulley. That could be done before the gun was jammed in position. No, it's simpler than it looks."

"It's like one of these affairs in books," said Bailey disgustedly. "Someone trying to think up a new way to murder. Silly, I call it."

"What do you say, Roper?" said Alleyn.

"To my way of thinking, sir," said Sergeant Roper, "these thrillers are ruining our criminal classes."

Dr. Templett gave a shout of laughter. Roper turned scarlet and stared doggedly at the wall.

"What d'you mean by that, my lad?" asked Fox, who was on his knees, staring into the piano.

Thompson, grinning to himself, touched off his flashlight.

"What I mean to say, Mr. Fox," said Roper. "It puts ideas in their foolish heads. And the talkies, too. Especially the young chaps. They get round the place talking down their noses and making believe they're gangsters. Look at this affair! I bet the chap that did this got the idea of it out of print."

"That's right, Roper, stick to it," said Dr. Templett. Roper disregarded him. Templett repeated his goodnights and went away.

"Go on, Roper. It's an idea," said Alleyn when the door had slammed. "What sort of print do you imagine would inspire this thing?"

"One of those funny drawings with bits of string and cogs and umbrellas and so forth?" suggested Thompson.

"Heath Robinson? Yes."

"Or more likely, sir," said Roper, "one of they four-penny boys' yarns in paper covers like you buy at the store in Chipping. I used to buy them myself as a youngster. There's always a fat lad and a comic lad and the comical chap plays off the fat one. Puts lighted crackers in his pants and all that. I recollect trying the cracker dodge under the rector's seat at Bible class, and he gave me a proper tanning for it, too, did rector."

"The practical joke idea again, you see, Fox," said Alleyn.

"Well," said Fox, stolidly. "Do we start off reading the back numbers of a boys' paper, or what?"

"You never know, Brer Fox. Have you noticed the back of the piano where the bunting's pinned down? There are four holes in the centre drawing pin and three to each of the others. Will you take the Colt out now, and all the rest of the paraphernalia? I'm going to take a look round the premises. We'll have to start seeing these people in the morning. Who the devil's that?"

There was a loud knock at the front entrance.

"Will I see?" asked Sergeant Roper.

"Do."

Roper tramped off down the centre aisle and threw open the doors.

"Good-morning," said a man's voice outside. "I wonder if I can come in for a moment. It's raining like Noah's half-holiday and I'd like to have a word with——"

"Afraid not, sir," said Roper.

"But I assure you I want to see the representative from Scotland Yard. I've come all the way from London," continued the voice plaintively. "I have, indeed. I represent the *Evening Mirror*. He'll be delighted to see me. Is it by any chance——"

"Yes, it is," said Alleyn loudly and ungraciously. "You can let him in, Roper."

A figure in a dripping mackintosh and streaming hat made a quick rush past Roper, gave a loud exclamation expressive of delight, and hurried forward with outstretched hand.

"I am *not* pleased to see you," said Alleyn.

"Good-morning, Mr. Bathgate," said Fox. "Fancy it being you."

"Yes, just fancy!" agreed Nigel Bathgate. "Well, well, well! I never expected to find the old gang. Bailey, too, and Thompson. It's like the chiming of old bellses to see you all happily employed together."

"How the blue hell did you get wind of this?" inquired Alleyn.

"The gentleman who does market and social notes for the *Chipping Courier* was in the audience to-night and like a bright young pressman he rang up the Central News. I was in the office when it came through and you couldn't see my rudder for the foam. Down here in four hours with one puncture. God bless my soul, now, what's it all about?"

"Sergeant Roger will perhaps spare a moment to throw you a bone or two. I'm busy. How are you?"

"Grand. Angela would send her love if she knew I was here, and your godson wants you to put him down for Hendon. He's three on Monday. Is it too late?"

"I'll inquire. Roper, you will allow Mr. Bathgate to sit quietly in a corner somewhere. I'll be back in a few minutes. Coming, Fox?"

Alleyn and Fox went up on the stage, looked round the box-set, and explored the wings.

"We'll have to go over this with a tooth-comb," Alleyn said, "looking for Lord knows what, as usual. Miss Dinah Copeland seems to have gone to a lot of trouble. The scenery's been patched up. Improvised footlights, you see, and I should think the two big overheads are introduced."

He went into the prompt corner.

"Here's the play. *Shop Window*, by Hunt. Rather a good comedy. Very professional, with all the calls marked and so on. A bicycle bell. Probably an adjunct of the telephone of the stage. Let's have a look behind."

A short flight of steps on each side of the back wall led down into a narrow room that ran the length of the stage.

"Mrs. Ross's supper arrangements all laid out on the table. Lord, Fox, those sandwiches look good."

"There's a lot more in this basket," said Fox. "Dr. Templett did say——"

"And beer under the table," murmured Alleyn. "Brer Fox?"

"A keg of it," said Fox, who was exploring. "Dorset draught beer. Very good, Dorset draught."

"You're right," said Alleyn after an interval. "It's excellent. Hullo!"

He stooped and picked something out of a box on the floor.

"Half a Spanish onion. Any onion in your sandwiches?"

"No."

"Nor in mine. It's got flour or something on it." He put the onion on the table and began to examine the plates of sandwiches. "Two kinds only, Fox. Ham and lettuce on the one hand, cucumber on the other. Hullo, here's a tray all set out for a stage tea. Nobody eats anything. Wait a bit."

He lifted the lid of the empty silver teapot and sniffed at the inside.

"The onion appears to have lived in the teapot. Quaint conceit, isn't it? Very rum, indeed. Come on."

They explored the dressing-rooms. There were two on each side of the supper-room.

"Gents to the right, ladies to the left," said Alleyn. He led the way into the first room on the left. He and Fox began a methodical search through the suitcases and pockets.

"Not quite according to Cocker, perhaps," Alleyn remarked, peering at Miss Prentice's black marocain on the wall. "But I think we'll ask afterwards. Anyway, I'm provided with a blank search-warrant so we're all right. Damn this onion, my hand stinks of it. This must be the two spinsters' rooms, judging by the garments."

"Judging by the pictures," said Fox, "it's a Bible classroom in the ordinary way."

"Yes. The Infant Samuel. What about next door? Ah, rather more skittish dresses. This will be Dinah Copeland and Mrs. Ross. Dr. Templett seemed rather self-conscious about Mrs. Ross, I thought. Miss Copeland's grease paints are in a cardboard box with her name on it. They've been used a lot. Mrs. Ross's, in a brand new japanned tin affair and brand new themselves, from which, inspired by Dorset draught, I deduce that Miss Copeland may be a professional, but Mrs. Ross undoubtedly is not. Here's a card in the new tin box. 'Best luck for to-night, B.' A present, by gum! Who's B., I wonder. Now for the men's rooms."

They found nothing of interest in the men's rooms until Alleyn came to a Donegal tweed suit.

"This is the doctor's professional suit," he said. "It reeks of surgery. Evidently the black jacket is not done in a country practice. I suppose, in the hubbub, he didn't change but went home looking like a comic-opera Frenchman. He must have——"

Alleyn stopped short. Fox looked up to see him staring at a piece of paper.

"Found something, sir?"

"Look."

It was a piece of plain blue paper. Fox read the lines of capitals:

"YOU ARE GIVEN NOTICE TO LEAVE THIS DISTRICT. IF YOU DISREGARD THIS WARNING YOUR LOVER SHALL SUFFER."

"Where did you find this, Mr. Alleyn?"

"In a wallet. Inside breast pocket of the police surgeon's suit," said Alleyn. He dropped it on the dressing-table and then bent down and sniffed at it.

"It smells of eucalyptus," he said.

CHAPTER ELEVEN

According to Roper

i

"THAT'S AWKWARD," grunted Fox, after a pause.

"Couldn't be more awkward."

" 'Your *lover* shall suffer,' " quoted Fox. "That looks as if it was written to a woman, doesn't it?"

"It's not common usage nowadays the other way round, but it's English. Common enough in the mixed plural."

"He's a married man," Fox remembered.

"Yes, it sounded as if his wife's an invalid, didn't it? This may have been written to his mistress or possibly to him, or it may have been shown him by a third person who is threatened and wants advice."

"Or he may have done it himself."

"Yes, it's possible, of course. Or it may be the relic of a parlour game. Telegrams, for instance. You made a sentence from a string of letters. He'd hardly carry that about next to his heart, though, would he? Damn! I'm afraid we're in for a nasty run, Brer Fox."

"How did the doctor strike you, Mr. Alleyn?"

"What? Rather jumpy. Bit too anxious to please. Couldn't stop talking."

"That's right," agreed Fox.

"We'll have to flourish the search-warrant a bit if we work on this," said Alleyn. "It'll be interesting to see if he misses it before we tackle him about it."

"He's doing the P.M."

"I know. We shall be present. Anyway, the lady was shot through the head. We've got the weapon and we've got the projectile. The post-mortem is not likely to be very illuminating. Hullo, Bailey, what is it?"

Bailey had come down the steps from the stage.

"I thought you'd better know, sir. This chap Roper's recognised the automatic. Mr. Bathgate ran him down to the station and they've checked up the number."

"Where is he?"

"Out in the hall." A reluctant grin appeared on Bailey's face. "I reckon he still thinks it's great to be a policeman. He wants to tell you himself."

"Very touching. All right. Bailey, I want you to test this paper for prints. Do it at once, will you, and put it between glass when you've finished. And, Bailey, have a shot at the teapot out there. Inside and out."

"Teapot, sir?"

"Yes. Also the powdered onion on the table. I dare say it's quite immaterial, but it's queer, so we'd better tackle it."

They returned to the hall where they found Roper standing over the automatic with something of the air of a clever retriever.

"Well, Roper," said Alleyn, "I hear you've done a bit of investigation for us."

"Yes, sir, I have so. I've recognised the lethal weapon, sir."

"Well, whose is it?"

"I says to myself when I see it," said Roper, "I know you, my friend, I've had you in my hands, I said. And then I remembered. It was when we checked up on firearms licences six months ago. Now, I suppose a hundred weapons must have passed under my notice that time, this being a sporting part of the world, so I reckon it's not surprising I didn't pick this affair so soon as I clapped eyes on her. I reckon that's not surprising, and yet she looked familiar, you understand?"

"Yes, Roper, I quite understand. Who is the owner?"

"This weapon, sir, is a Colt .32 automatic, the property of Jocelyn Jernigham, Esquire, of Pen Cuckoo."

"Is it, indeed?" murmured Alleyn.

"This gentleman, Mr. Bathgate, ran me down to the station, sir, and it didn't take me over and above five minutes to lay my finger on the files. You can take a look at the files, sir, and——"

"I shall do so. Now, Roper, see if you can give me some model answers. Short, crisp, and to the point. When did you see the automatic? Can you give me the date?"

"In the files!" shouted Sergeant Roper, triumphantly. "May 31st of the current year."

"Where was it?"

"In the study at Pen Cuckoo, sir, that being the room at the extreme end of the west wing facing the Vale."

"Who showed it to you?"

"Squire, himself, showed it to me. We'd checked up all the weapons in the gun-room, of which there was a number, and squire takes me into his study and says, 'There's one more,' he says, and he lays his hand on a wooden box on the table and opens the lid. There was this lethal masterpiece laying on her side, with a notice written clear in block letters. 'Loaded.' 'It's all right,' says Mr. Jernigham, seeing me step aside as he takes her out. 'The safety catch is on,' he says. And he showed me. And he says, 'It went all through the war with me,' he says, 'and there's half a clip left in it. I'd fired two shots when I got my Blighty one,' he says, 'and I've kept it like this ever since. I let it be known there's a loaded automatic waiting at Pen Cuckoo for anybody that feels like coming in uninvited.' We'd had some thieving in the district at that time, same as we've got it now. He told me this weapon had lain loaded in that box for twenty years, did squire."

"Was the box locked?"

"No, sir. But he said all the maids was warned about it."

"Anybody else in the room?"

"Yes, sir. Mr. Henry was there, and Miss Prentice, sitting quietly by the fire and smiling, pussy-like, same as she always does."

"Don't you like Miss Prentice?"

"I think she's all right, but my missus says she's proper sly. My missus is a great one for the institute and Miss Prentice is president of same."

"I see. Any local gossip about Miss Prentice?"

Roper expanded. He placed his hands in his belt with the classic heaving movement of all policemen. He then appeared to remember he was in the presence of authority and rearranged himself in an attitude of attention.

"Aye," he said, "they talk all right, sir. You see, Miss Prentice, she came along, new to the Vale, on three years back when Mrs. Jernigham died. I reckon the late Mrs. Jernigham was nigh-on the best liked lady in this part of Dorset. A Grey of Stourminster-Weston she was, Dorset born and bred, and a proper lady. Now, this Miss Prentice, for all she's half a Jernigham, is a foreigner as you might say, and she doesn't know our ways here. Mrs. Jernigham was welcome everywhere, cottage and big houses alike, and wherever she went she was the same. Never asking questions or if she did, out of real niceness and not nosey-parkishness. Now, folk about here say Miss Prentice is the other way round. Sly. Makes trouble between cottages and rectory, or would if she could. Cor!" said

Roper, passing his ham of a hand over his face. "The way that old maiden got after rector! My missus says—well, my missus is an outspoken woman and come off a farm."

Alleyn did not press for a repetition of Mrs. Roper's agricultural similes.

"There was only one worse than her," continued Roper, "and that was the deceased. She was a dragon after rector. And before Miss Prentice came, Miss Campanula had it all her own way, but I reckon Miss Campanula kind of lost driving power when t'other lady got going with her insinuating antics."

"How did they get on together?"

"Fast as glue," said Roper. "Thick as thieves. My missus says they knew too much about each other to be anything else. Cook up to Red House, she says Miss Campanula was jealous fair-to-bust of Miss Prentice, but she was no match for her, however, being the type of woman that lets her anger be seen and rages out in the open, whereas Miss Prentice, with her foxy ways, goes quiet to work. Cook told my missus that deceased was losing ground daily and well-nigh desperate over it."

"How do you mean, losing ground?"

"With rector."

"Dear me," murmured Alleyn. "How alarming for the rector."

"Reckon he picks his way like that chap in Bible," said Roper. "He's a simple sort of chap is rector but he's a Vale man and he suits us. His father and grandfather were rectors here before him and he knows our ways."

"Quite so, Roper," said Alleyn, and lit a cigarette.

"No. But the rector met his match in those two ladies, sir, and it's a marvel one of them hasn't snapped him up by this time. Likely he holds them off with holy conversation, but I've seen the hunted look in the man's eyes more than once."

"I see," said Alleyn. "Do you think it generally known that Mr. Jernigham kept this loaded automatic in the study?"

"I should say it was, sir. If I make so bold, sir, I'd say it was never squire that did this job. He's peppery, is Mr. Jernigham, but I'd bet my last penny he's not a murderer. Flares up and forgets all about it the next minute. Very outspoken. Mr. Henry, now, he's deeper. A nice young fellow but quiet-like. You never know what he's thinking. Still, he's got no call to kill anybody, and wouldn't if he had."

"Who is Mrs. Ross of Duck Cottage, Cloudyfold?"

"Stranger to these parts. She only came here last April." Roper's blue eyes became hard and bright.

"Young?" asked Alleyn.

"Not what you'd say so very young. Thin. Pale hair, done very neat, and very neat in her dressing. Her clothes look different to most ladies. More like the females in the talkies only kind of simpler. Dainty. She's dressed very quiet, always, but you notice her." Roper paused, six-foot-two of dim masculine appreciation. "I reckon she's got It," he said at last. "It's not my place to say so, but I suppose a chap always knows her sort. By instinct."

There was an odd little silence during which the other five men stared at Sergeant Roper.

"Dr. Templett does, anyway," he said at last.

"Oh," said Alleyn. "More local gossip?"

"The women-folk. You know what they are, sir. Given it a proper thrashing, they have. Well, there's a good deal of feeling on account of Mrs. Templett being an invalid."

"Yes, I suppose so. Let me see, that's all the cast of the play, isn't it? Except Miss Copeland."

"Miss Dinah? She'll be in a taking-on, I make no doubt. After all the work she's given to this performance for it to go up, as you might say, in a cloud of dust. Still, she's courting, that'll be a kind of comfort to the maid. Mr. Henry was watching over her after the tragedy, holding her hand for all to see. They're well-matched and we're hoping to hear it's a settled matter any time now. My missus says it'll be one in the eye for Miss Prentice."

"Why on earth?"

"She won't be fancying another lady at Pen Cuckoo. I saw her looking blue murder at them even while deceased was lying, you might say, a corpse at their feet. She's lucky it wasn't her. Should be thanking her Creator she's still here to make trouble."

"Miss Prentice," said Nigel, "seems to be a very unpleasant cup of tea. Perhaps her sore finger was all a bluff and she rigged the tackle for the girl-friend."

"Dr. Templett said it was no bluff, Mr. Bathgate," said Fox. "He said she held out till the last moment that she was going to play."

"That's right enough, sir," said Roper. "I went round to the back to see Miss Dinah just after it had happened and there was Miss Prentice crying her eyes out, with her finger looking that unwholesome it'd turn your stomach, and Miss Dinah telling her she was ruining the paint on her face and the doctor saying, 'I absolutely forbid it. Your finger's in a very nasty state and if you weren't playing this part tonight,' he said, 'I'd open it up.' Yes, he threatened her with the knife, did doctor. Mr. Henry says, 'You'll make a mess of Mr. Nevin's ecstasies.' Her piece was composed by a chap of that name as you'll see in the programme. 'You'll never stay the course, Cousin Eleanor,' says Mr. Henry. 'I know it's hurting you like stink,' says Mr. Henry, 'because you're crying,' he says. But no, she wouldn't give in till Miss Dinah fetched her father. 'Come,' he says, 'we all know how you feel about it, but there are times when generosity is better than heroism.' She looked up at rector, then, and she said, 'If you say so, Father,' and with that Miss Campanula says, 'Now, who'll go and get my music? Where's Gibson?' Which is the name of her chauffeur. So she give in, but very reluctant."

"A vivid enough picture of the rival performances, isn't it?" said Alleyn. "Well, there's the history of the case. It's getting on for three o'clock. I think, on second thoughts, Fox, we won't wait for the light of day. We'll make a night of it. This place must be overhauled sometime and it looks as though we'll have a busy day tomorrow. You can turn in if you like, Roper. Some one can relieve us at seven."

"Are you going to search the premises, sir?"

"Yes."

"Reckon I'd like to give a hand if it's agreeable to you."

"Certainly. Fox, you and Thompson make sure we've missed nothing in the dressing-rooms and supper-room. Bailey, you can take Roper with you on the stage. Go over every inch of it. I'll tackle the hall and join you if I finish first."

"Are you looking for anything in particular?" asked Nigel.

"The usual unconsidered trifles. Spare bits of Twiddletoy, for instance. Even a water-pistol."

"Not forgetting any kid's annuals that happen to be lying round," added Fox.

"Poor things!" said Nigel. "Back to childhood's day, I see. Is there a telephone here?"

"In a dressing-room," said Alleyn. "But it's only an extension."

"I'll ring up the office from a pub, then. In the meantime, I may as well write up a pretty story."

He took out his pad and settled himself at a table on the stage.

Police investigation is for the most part a dull business. Nothing could be more tedious than searching for things. Half a detective's life is spent in turning over dreary objects, finding nothing, and replacing them. Alleyn started in the entrance porch of the parish hall and began a meticulous crawl over dusty surfaces. He moved like a snail, across and across, between the rows of benches. He felt cold and dirty and he smelt nothing but dust. He could not allow his thoughts to dwell pleasantly on his own affairs, his coming marriage, and the happiness that kept him company nowadays; because it is when his thoughts are abstracted from the business in hand that the detective misses the one small sign events have set in his path. Sometimes the men on the stage heard a thin whistling down in the hall. Sergeant Roper's voice droned interminably. At intervals the church clock sweetly recorded the journey of the hours. Miss Campanula lay stealthily stiffening behind a red baize screen, and Nigel Bathgate recorded her departure in efficient journalese.

Alleyn had passed the benches and chairs and was grovelling about in the corner with an electric torch. Presently he uttered a soft exclamation. Nigel looked up from his writing and Bailey, who had the loose seat of a chair in his hands, shaded his eyes and peered down into the corner.

Alleyn stood by the stage, on the audience's left. He held a small shining object between finger and thumb. His hand was gloved. One of his eyebrows was raised and his lips were pursed in a soundless whistle.

"Struck a patch, sir?" asked Bailey.

"Yes, I rather think so, Bailey."

He walked over to the piano.

"Look."

Bailey and Nigel came to the footlights.

The shining object Alleyn held in his hands was a boy's water-pistol.

iii

"As you said yourself, Bathgate, back to childhood days."

"What's the idea, sir?" asked Bailey.

"It seems to be a recurrent idea," said Alleyn. "I found this thing stuffed away in a sort of locker under the stage over there. It was poked in a dark corner, but there's little or no dust on it. The rest of the stuff in the locker's smothered in dirt. Look at the butt, Bailey. Do you see that shiny scratch? It's rather a super sort of water pistol, isn't it? None of your rubber bulbs that you squeeze—but a proper trigger action. Fox!"

Fox and Thompson appeared from the direction of the supper-room.

Alleyn went to the small table where Bailey had placed the rest of the exhibits, lifted the covering cloth and laid his find beside the Colt automatic.

"The length is the same to within a fraction of an inch," he said; "and there's a mark on the butt of the Colt very much like the mark on the butt of the water-pistol. That, I believe, is where it was rammed in the piano, between the steel pegs where the strings are fastened."

"But what the devil," asked Nigel, "is the explanation?"

Alleyn pulled off his gloves and fished in his pockets for his cigarette-case.

"Where's Roper?"

"Out at the back, sir," said Bailey. "He'll be back shortly with a new set of reminiscences. His super ought to issue a gag to that chap."

"This is a rum go," said Fox profoundly.

" 'Jones Minor' all over it," said Alleyn. "You were right, Bailey, I believe, when you suggested the death-trap in the piano was too elaborate to be true. It *is* only in books that murder is quite as fancy as all this. The whole thing carries the hall-mark of the booby-trap and the signature of the practical joker. It is somehow difficult to believe that a man or woman would, as Bailey has said, think up murder on these lines. But what if a man with murder in his heart came upon this booby-trap, this water-pistol aimed through a hole in the torn silk bib? What if this potential murderer thought of substituting a Colt for the water-pistol? It becomes less far-fetched, then, doesn't it? What's more, there are certain advantages. The murderer can separate himself from his victim and from the *corpus delicti*. The spade-work has been done. All the murderer has to do is remove the water-pistol, jam in the Colt and tie the loose end of twine round the butt. It's not his idea, it's Jones Minor's."

"He'd want to be sure the Colt was the same length," said Fox.

"He could measure the water-pistol."

"And then go home and check up his Colt?"

"Or somebody else's Colt," said Bailey.

"One of the first points we have to clear up," Alleyn said, "is the accessibility of Jernigham's war souvenir. Roper says he thinks everybody knew about it, and apparently it was there in the study for the picking up. They've all been rehearsing in the study. They were there last night—Friday night, I mean. It's Sunday now, heaven help us."

"If Dr. Templett recognised the Colt," observed Fox, "he didn't let on."

"No more he did."

The back door banged and boots resounded in the supper-room.

"Here's Roper," said Fox.

"Roper!" shouted Alleyn.

"Yes, sir?"

"Come here."

Sergeant Roper stumbled up the steps and appeared on the stage.

"Come and have a look at this."

"Certainly, sir."

Roper placed his palm on the edge of the stage and vaulted deafeningly to the floor. He approached, the table with an air of efficiency and contemplated the water-pistol.

"Know it?" asked Alleyn.

Roper reached out his hand.

"Don't touch it!" said Alleyn sharply.

"'T, 't, 't!" said Fox and Bailey.

"Beg pardon, sir," said Roper. "Seeing that trifling toy, and recognising it in a flash, I had a natural impulse, as you might say——"

"Your natural impulses must be mortified if you want to grow up into a detective," said Alleyn. "Whose water-pistol is this?"

"Mind," said Roper warningly, "there may be two of this class in the district, sir. Or more. I'm not taking my oath there aren't. But barring that eventuality I reckon I can put an owner on it. And seeing he had the boldness to take a shot at me outside the Jernigham Arms, me being in uniform——"

"Roper," said Alleyn, "it is only about three hours to the dawn. Don't let the sun rise on your parentheses. Whose water-pistol is this?"

"George Biggins's," said Roper.

CHAPTER TWELVE

Further Vignettes

i

AT SEVEN o'clock the Yard car dropped Alleyn and Fox at the Jernigham Arms.

The rain had stopped, but it was a dank, dreary morning, and so cloudy that only a mean thinning of the night, a grudging disclosure of vague, wet masses, gave evidence that somewhere beyond the Vale there was dawnlight.

Bailey and Thompson drove off for London. Alleyn stared after the tail-light of the car while Fox belaboured the front door of the Jernigham Arms.

"There's *somebody* moving about in there," he grumbled.

"Here they come."

It was the pot-boy, very tousled and peepy, and accompanied by a gust of stale beer. Alleyn thought that he looked like all pot-boys at dawn throughout time and space.

"Good-morning," Alleyn said. "Can you give us rooms for a day or two, and breakfast in an hour? There's a third man on his way here."

"I'll aask Missus," said the pot-boy. He gaped at them, blinked, and went off down a passage. They could hear him calling with the cracked uncertainty of adolescence:

"Missus! 'Be detec-er-tives from Lunnon, along of Miss Campanula's murder, likely. Mrs. Pe-e-each! Missus!"

"The whole place buzzing with it," said Alleyn.

ii

At seven o'clock Henry found himself suddenly awake. He lay still, wondering for a moment why this day would be different from any other day. Then he remembered. He saw with precision a purple heap, the top of a head, the nape of a neck laced with dark, shining streaks. He saw a sheet of music, crumpled, pinned to the keys of a piano by the head. The picture was framed in aspidistras like a nightmarish valentine and across the lower margin was the top of a piano.

"I have looked down at a murdered woman." And for a time his thoughts would not move beyond this sharp memory, so that he found himself anxiously retracing the pattern of the head, the neck, the white sheet of music, and the fatuous green leaves. Then the memory of Dinah's cold fingers crept into his hands. He closed his hands on the memory, clenching them as he lay in bed, and the whole idea of Dinah came into his mind.

"If it had been Eleanor, there would have been an end to our troubles."

He pushed this thought away from him, telling himself it was horrible, but it returned repeatedly, and at last he said, "It is stupid to pretend otherwise. I do wish it had been Eleanor." He began to think of all that happened after Idris Campanula died; of how his father went aside with Superintendent Blandish, and of the solemn, ridiculous look on his father's face. He remembered Dr. Templett's explanations and Miss Prentice's moans which had irritated them all very much. He remembered that when he looked at Mr. Copeland he saw that his lips were moving, and realised, with embarrassment, that the rector was at prayer. He remembered Mrs. Ross's almost complete silence and the way she and Templett had not spoken to each other. And again his thoughts returned to Dinah. He had walked to the rectory with Dinah and her father, and on the threshold he had kissed her openly, the rector seeming scarcely aware of it. On the way home to Pen Cuckoo, the squire had not forgotten that, in the absence of Sir George Dillington, he was Chief Constable, and had discoursed solemnly on the crime, saying again and again that Henry was to treat everything he heard as confidential, and relating how, with Blandish, he had come to a decision to call in Scotland Yard. When they were indoors at last, Eleanor Prentice had fainted, and the squire had forced brandy down her throat with such an uncertain hand that he had half-asphyxiated her. They helped her to her room and Jocelyn, nervously assiduous, had knocked the bandaged finger so that she screamed with pain. Henry and his father had a solemn drink together in the dining-room, Jocelyn still discoursing on his responsibilities.

Henry went cold all over, his heart dropped like a plummet, and he faced the worst memory of all, the one that he had been pushing away ever since he woke.

It was when Jocelyn told him how, strong in his position of Acting Chief Constable, he had peered through the hole in the tucked silk front, and had seen the glimmer of a firearm.

"A revolver," Jocelyn had said, "or else an automatic."

At that moment the picture of the box in the study had risen in Henry's imagination. He had hurried his father to bed, but when he was alone had been afraid to go into the study and lift the lid of the box. Now he knew that he must do it. Quickly, before the servants were up. He leapt out of bed, threw on his dressing-gown, and crept downstairs through the dark house. There was an electric torch in the hall. He found it and made his way to the study.

The box was empty. The notice "LOADED" in block capitals lay at the bottom.

Henry turned away with panic in his heart, and a minute later he was knocking at his father's door.

iii

Selia Ross had been awake for a very long time. She was wondering when she could telephone to Dr. Templett or whether it would be altogether too unsafe to get into touch with him. She knew the telephone rang at his bedside until eight o'clock in the morning, and that he slept far enough away from his wife's room for it not to disturb her. Mrs. Ross wanted to ask him what he had done with the anonymous letter. She knew that he had put it in his wallet, and that he kept the wallet in his breast pocket. She remembered that after the catastrophe he had not changed back into his ordinary suit, and she was hideously afraid that the letter might still be in his coat at the hall. He was very forgetful and careless about such things, and had once left one of her letters, open, on his dressing-table, only remembering it later on in the day.

She had no knowledge of what the police would do. She had a sort of an idea she had read in a criminal novel that they were not allowed to search through private houses without a permit of some kind. But did that apply to a public hall? And surely if the body of a murdered person was there, in the hall, they would hunt everywhere. What would they think if they found that letter? She wanted to warn Dr. Templett to be ready with an answer.

But he himself was an official.

But he had almost certainly remembered the letter.

Would it be better to say he knew the author to be someone else—his wife, even? Any one but one of those two women.

Her thoughts, needle-sharp, darted in and out of the fabric of her terror.

Perhaps if he went down early . . .

Perhaps she should have telephoned an hour ago.

She switched on her bedside lamp and looked at her clock. It was five minutes to eight.

Perhaps she was too late.

In a panic she reached for the telephone and dialled his number.

iv

Miss Prentice's finger had kept her awake, but it is doubtful if she would have slept even if it had not throbbed all night. Her thoughts were too hurried and busy, weaving backwards and forwards between the rector, herself and Idris Campanula, who was murdered. She thought of all sorts of things: of how when she first came to Pen Cuckoo she and Idris had been such friends, confiding the secrets of their bosoms to each other like schoolgirls. She remembered all the delicious talks they had had together, talks full of exciting conjectures about the behaviour of other people in the village and the county. There would be nobody now who would speak her language and discuss things and people in that way. They had been so intimate until Idris grew jealous. That was the form Miss Prentice gave to their differences: Idris grew jealous of her friend's rising influence in the village and in church affairs.

She would not think yet of Mr. Copeland. The memory of things he had said to her at confession must be thrust down into oblivion, and that other memory, that other frightful revelation of Idris's perfidy.

No. Better to remember the old friendly days and to think of Idris's will. It had been a very simple will. A lot for Mr. Copeland, a little for the distant nephew, and seven thousand for Eleanor herself. Idris had said she'd never had a real friend until Eleanor came, and that if she died first she would be happy in the thought that she had been able to do this. Eleanor even then rather resented her friend's air of patronage.

But it was true that if she had this money she would no longer be so dependent on Jocelyn.

Mr. Copeland would be very well off indeed, for Idris was an extremely rich woman.

Dinah would be an heiress.

She had not thought of that before. There would be no worldly reason now why Dinah and Henry should not marry.

If she were to withdraw her opposition quickly, before the will was known—would not that seem generous and kind? If she could only stifle the recollection of that scene on Friday afternoon. Dinah limp in Henry's arms, lost in rapture. It had nearly driven Eleanor mad. How could she unsay all that she had said before she turned away and stumbled up the lane, escaping from so much agony? But with Dinah married to Henry, then her father would be lonely. A rich lonely man, fifty years old, and too dignified to look for a young wife. Surely, then!

Then! Then!

The first bell, calling the people to eight o'clock service, roused her from her golden plans. She rose, dressed and went out into the dark morning.

v

The rector was astir at seven. It was Sunday, and he would be in church in an hour. He dressed hurriedly, unable to lie thinking any longer of the events of the night that was past. All sorts of recollections flocked into his thoughts, and in all of them the murdered woman was present, turning them into nightmares. He felt as if he was dyed in guilt, as if he would never rid himself of his dreadful memories. His thoughts were chaotic and quite uncontrollable.

Long before the warning bell sounded for early celebration, he stole out of the house and walked, as he had done every Sunday for twenty years, down the drive, through the nut walk and over the stile into the churchyard.

When he was alone inside the dark church he fell on his knees and tried to pray.

vi

Somewhere, a long way off, somebody was knocking at a door. Bang, bang, *bang*. Must be old Idris pounding away at that damned lugubrious tune. Blandish needn't have locked Eleanor up inside the piano. As Deputy Chief Constable, I object to that sort of thing; it isn't cricket. Let her out! If she knocks much louder she'll blow the place up, and then we'll have to get in the Yard. Bang, bang——

The squire woke with a sickening leap of his nerves.

"Wha-a-a?"

"Father, it's me! Henry! I want to speak to you."

vii

When Dinah heard her father go downstairs long before his usual hour, she knew that he hadn't slept, that he was miserable, and that he would go into church and pray. She hoped that he had remembered to wear a woollen cardigan under his cassock, because he seemed to catch cold more easily in church than anywhere else. She knew last night that she was in for a difficult time with him. For some extraordinary reason, he had already begun to blame himself for the tragedy, saying that he had been weak and vacillating, not zealous enough in his duties as a parish priest.

Dinah was unable to follow her father's reasoning, and with a sinking heart she had asked him if he suspected any one as the murderer of Idris Campanula. That was when they got home last night and she was fortified by Henry's kiss.

"Daddy, do you think you know?"

"No, darling, no. But I haven't helped them as I should. And when I did try, it was too late."

"But what do you mean?"

"You mustn't ask me, darling."

And then she had realised that he was thinking of the confessional. What on earth had Idris Campanula told him on Friday? What had Eleanor Prentice told him? Something that had upset him very much, Dinah was sure. Well, one of them was gone and wouldn't make mischief any more. It was no good trying to be sorry. She wasn't sorry, she was only frightened and filled with horror whenever she thought of the dead body. It was the first dead body Dinah had ever seen.

Of course it was obvious to everybody that the trap had been set for Eleanor Prentice. Her father must realise that. Who, then, had a motive to kill Eleanor Prentice?

Dinah sat up in bed, cold with terror. She remembered the meeting in the lane on Friday afternoon, the things Eleanor Prentice had said in a breathless whisper, and the answer Henry had made.

"If she tells them what he said," thought Dinah, "they'll say Henry had a motive."

And with her whole soul she tried to send out a warning message to Henry.

But Henry, at that moment, was pounding his father's bedroom door, and into his startled mind there came no warning message from Dinah. There was no need for one, for already he was afraid.

viii

Dr. Templett was dreamlessly and peacefully asleep when the telephone rang at his bedside. At once, and with the accuracy born of long practice, he reached out in the half-light for the receiver.

"Dr. Templett here," he said, as he always did when the telephone rang at an ungodly hour. He remembered that young Mrs. Cartwright might be now in labour.

But it was Selia Ross.

"Billy? Billy, have you got that letter?"

"What!"

He lay there quite still, holding the receiver to his ear and listening to his own thumping heart.

"Billy! Are you there?"

"Yes," he said, "yes. It's all right. There's nothing to worry about. I'll look in some time to-day."

"Do, for God's sake."

"All right. Good-bye."

He hung up the receiver and lay staring at the ceiling. What had he done with that letter?

CHAPTER THIRTEEN

Sunday Morning

i

ALLEYN AND Fox were at breakfast and Nigel was still asleep when Superintendent Blandish walked in. He was blue about the chin and his eyes and nose were watery.

"You must wonder if there is anybody except that jabbering chap Roper in the Great Chipping Constabulary," he said as he shook hands. "I'm sorry to have neglected you like this; but we're in for a picnic, and no mistake, with this case up at Moorton Park."

"Damn' bad luck, the two cases cropping up at the same time," said Alleyn. "Of course, you'd have liked to handle our business yourself. Have you had breakfast?"

"Haven't taken a look at food since six o'clock yesterday."

Alleyn went to the hatch and shouted:

"Mrs. Peach! Another lot of eggs and bacon, if you can manage it."

"Well, I won't say no," said Blandish, and sat down. "And I won't say I wouldn't have liked to try my hand at this business. But there you are: never rains but it pours, does it?"

"That's right," agreed Fox. "We get the same thing at the Yard. Though lately it's been quietish—hasn't it, Mr. Alleyn?"

Blandish chuckled. "Maybe that's why we've been honoured with the top-notchers," he said. "Well, Mr. Alleyn, it will be quite an experience for us to see you working. Needless to say, we'll give you all the help we can."

"Thank you," said Alleyn. "We'll need it. This is a remarkably rum business. You were in the audience, weren't you?"

"I was, and I can give you my word I got a fright. Thought the whole place had exploded. The old piano went on buzzing for Lord knows how long. By gum, it took all my self-control not to have a peep inside the lid before I went off to Moorton. But, 'No,' I thought. 'You're handing over, and you'd better not meddle.' "

"Extraordinarily considerate. We breathed our fervent thanks, didn't we, Fox? I suppose that conversation piece you've got for a sergeant has told you all about it?"

Blandish pulled an expressive grimace.

"I shut him up after the second recital," he said. "He wants sitting on, does Roper, but he's got his wits about him. I'd like to hear your account."

While he devoured his eggs and bacon, Alleyn gave him the history of the night. When he came to the discovery of the message in Dr. Templett's coat, Blandish laid down his knife and fork and stared at him.

"Glory!" he said.

"I know."

"This is hell," said Blandish. "I mean to say, it's awkward."

"Yes."

"Not to put too fine a point on it, Mr. Alleyn, it's bloody awkward."

"It is."

"By gum, I'm not so sure I do regret being out of it. It may not be anything, of course, but it can't be overlooked. And I've been associated with the doctor I don't know how many years."

"Like him?" asked Alleyn.

"Do I like him? Well, now, yes. I suppose I do. We've always got on very pleasantly, you know. Yes, I—well, I'm accustomed to him."

"You'll know the questions we're going to ask. In this sort of affair we have to batten on local gossip."

Alleyn went to the corner of the dining-room, got his case and took from it the anonymous letter. It was flattened between two sheets of glass joined, at the edges, with adhesive tape. The corner, back and sides of the paper bore darkened impressions of fingers.

"There it is. We brought up three sets of latent prints. One of them corresponds with a print taken from a powder box in the dressing-room used by the victim and Miss Prentice. It has been identified as the victim's. A second has its counterpart on a new japanned make-up box, thought to be the property of Mrs. Ross. The third is repeated on other papers in the wallet, and is obviously Dr. Templett's."

"Written by deceased, sent to Mrs. Ross and handed by her to the doctor?"

"It seems indicated. Especially as two of Mrs. Ross's prints, if they are hers, appear to be superimposed on the deceased prints, and one of Dr. Templett's lies across two of the others. We'll get more definite results when Bailey develops his photographs."

"This is an ugly business. You mentioned local gossip, Mr. Alleyn. There's been a certain amount in this direction, no denying it, and the two ladies in question were mainly responsible, I fancy."

"But is it a motive for murder?" asked Fox of nobody in particular.

"Well, Brer Fox, it might be. A doctor, in a country district especially, doesn't thrive on scandal. Is Templett a wealthy man, do you know. Blandish?"

"No, I wouldn't say he was," said Blandish. "They're an old Vale family, and the doctor's a younger son. His elder brother was a bit of a rip. Smart regiment before the war, and expensive tastes. It's always been understood the doctor came in for a white elephant when he got Chippingwood. I'd say he needs every penny he earns. He's a hunting man, too, and that costs money."

"What about Mrs. Ross?"

"Well, there you are! If you're to believe everything you hear, they are pretty thick. But gossip's not evidence, is it?"

"No, but it's occasionally based on some sort of foundation, more's the pity. Ah, well! It indicates a line and we'll follow the pointer. Now, about the automatic. It's Mr. Jernigham's all right."

"I've heard all about that, Mr. Alleyn, and that's not too nice either, though I wouldn't believe, if I saw the weapon smoking in his hand, that the squire would shoot a woman, let alone plan to murder his own flesh and blood. Unlikely enough people have turned out to be murderers, as we all know, and I suppose that it is not beyond the possibilities that Mr. Jernigham might kill his man in hot blood; but I've known him all my life, and I'd stake my reputation he's not the sort to do an underhand fantastic sort of job like this. The man's not got it in him. That's not evidence, either——"

"It's expert opinion, though," said Alleyn, "and to be respected as such."

"The squire's acting Chief Constable while Sir George Dillington's away."

"We seem to be on official preserves wherever we turn," said Alleyn. "I'll call at Pen Cuckoo later in the morning. The mortuary van came before it was light. Dr. Templett's doing the post-mortem this afternoon. Either Fox or I will be there. I think our first job now is to call on Mr. Georgie Biggins."

"Young limb of Satan! You'll find him in the last cottage on the left, going out of Chipping. The station's in Great Chipping, you know—only five miles from here. Roper and a P-c. enjoy their mid-day snooze at a substation in this village. Both are at your service."

"Is there a car of sorts I could hire for the time being? You'll need the official bus for your own work, of course."

"As a matter of fact, I'm afraid we shall. It's a tidy stretch over to Moorton Park, and we'll be going backwards and forwards. No doubt about our men being Posh Jimmy & Co. Typical job. Funny how they stick to their ways, isn't it? About a car. As a matter of fact, the Biggins have got an old Ford they hire."

"Splendid. An admirable method of approaching Mr. Georgie. How old is he?"

"In years," said Blandish, "he's about thirteen. In sin he's a hundred. A limb, if ever there was one. Nerve of a rhinoceros."

"We'll see if we can shake it," said Alleyn.

The superintendent departed, lamenting the amount of work that lay before him.

ii

Alleyn and Fox lit their pipes and walked through Chipping. By daylight it turned out to be a small hamlet with a row of stone cottages on each side of the road, a general store, a post office, and the Jernigham Arms. Even the slope of Cloudyfold, rising steeply above it from the top of Pen Cuckoo Vale, did not rob Chipping of its upland character. It felt high in the world, and the cold wind blew strongly down the Vale road.

The Biggins's cottage stood a little apart from the rest of the village, and had a truculent air. It was one of those bare-faced Dorset cottages, less picturesque than its neighbours, and more forbidding.

As Alleyn and Fox approached the front door, they heard a woman's voice:

"Whatever be the matter with you, then, mumbudgeting so close to my apron strings? Be off with you!"

Silence.

"To be sure," continued the voice, "if you wasn't so strong as a young foal, Georgie Biggins, I'd think something ailed you. Stick out your tongue."

Silence.

"As clean as a whistle. Stick it in again, then. Standing there like you was simple Dick with your tongue lolling! I never see! What ails you?"

"Nuthun," said a small voice.

"Nuthun killed nobody."

Alleyn tapped on the door.

Another silence was broken by a sharp whispering and an unmistakable scuffle.

"Do what I tell you!" ordered the voice. "Me in my working apron, and Sunday morning! Go *on* with you."

There was a sound of rapid retreat and then the door opened three inches to disclose a pair of boot-button eyes and part of a very white face.

"Hullo," said Alleyn. "I've come to see if I can hire a car. This is Mr. Biggins's house, isn't it?"

"Uh."

"Have you got a car for hire?"

"Uh."

"Well, how about opening the door a bit wider and we can talk about it?"

The door opened very slowly to another five inches. Georgie Biggins stood revealed in his Sunday suit. His moon-face was colourless and he had the look of a boy who may bolt without warning.

Alleyn said, "Now, what about this car? Is your father at home?"

"Along to pub corner," said Georgie in a stifled voice. "Mum's comeun."

The cinema has made all little boys familiar with the look of a detective. Alleyn kept a change of clothes in the Yard in readiness for sudden departures. His shepherd's plaid coat, flannel trousers and soft hat may have reassured George Biggins, but when the boot-button eyes ranged farther afield and lit on Inspector Fox, in his dark suit, mackintosh and bowler, their owner uttered a yelp of pure terror, turned tail and charged into his mother, who had at that moment walked out of the bedroom. She was a large woman, and she caught her son with a practised hand.

"Now!" she said. "That's enough and more, for sure. What's the meanings of these goings-on? You wait till your Dad comes home. I never see!"

She advanced to the door, bringing her son with her by the scruff of the neck.

"I'm sure I'm sorry to keep you waiting," she said.

Alleyn asked about the car and was told he could have it. Mrs. Biggins examined both of them with frank curiosity and led the way round the house to a dilapidated shed where they found a Ford car, six years old, but, as Alleyn cheerfully remarked, none the worse for that. He paid a week's rental in advance. Mrs. Biggins kept a firm but absent-minded grip on her son's shirt-collar.

"I'll get you a receipt," she said. "Likely you're here on account of this terrible affair."

"That's it," said Alleyn.

"Are you from Scotland Yard, then?"

"Yes, Mrs. Biggins, that's us." Alleyn looked good naturedly at Master Biggins. "Is this Georgie?" he asked.

The next second, Master Biggins had left the best part of his Sunday collar in his mother's hand and had bolted like a rabbit, only to find himself held as if in a vice by the terrible man in the mackintosh and bowler.

"Now, now, now," said Fox. "What's all this?"

The very words he had so often heard on the screen.

"Georgie!" screamed Mrs. Biggins in a maternal fury. Then she looked at her son's face and at the hands that held him.

"Here, you!" she stormed at Fox. "What are you at, laying your hands on my boy?"

"There's nothing to worry about, Mrs. Biggins," said Alleyn. "Georgie may be able to help us, that's all. Now, look here, wouldn't it be better if we went indoors out of sight and sound of your neighbours?"

The shot went home.

"Mighty me!" said Mrs. Biggins, still almost as white as her child, but rallying. "Mighty me, it's true enough they spend most of the Lord's Day minding other folks' business and clacking their tongues. Georgie Biggins, if you don't hold your noise I'll have the skin off you. Do us go in, then."

iii

In a cold but stuffy parlour, Alleyn did his best with mother and son. Georgie was now howling steadily. Mrs. Biggins's work-reddened hands pleated and repleated the folds of her dress. But she listened in silence.

"It's just this," said Alleyn. "Georgie is in no danger, but we believe he is in a position to give us extremely important information."

Georgie checked a lamentable roar and listened.

Alleyn took the water-pistol from his pocket and handed it to Mrs. Biggins.

"Do you recognise it?"

"For sure," she said slowly. "It's his'en."

George burst out again.

"Young Biggins," said Alleyn, "is this your idea of being a detective? Come here."

Georgie came.

"See here, now. How would you like to help the police bring a murderer to justice? How would you like to work with us? We're from Scotland Yard, you know. It's not often you'll get the chance to work with the Yard, is it?"

The black eyes fastened on Alleyn's and brightened.

"What are the other chaps going to think if you, if you"—Alleyn hunted for the right phrase—"if you solve the problem that has baffled the greatest sleuths of all time?" He glanced at his colleague. Fox, looking remarkably bland, closed one eye.

"If you come in with us," Alleyn continued, "you'll be doing a man's job. How about it?"

A faintly hard-boiled expression crept over Georgie Biggins's undistinguished face.

"Okay," he said in a treble voice still fuddled with tears.

"Good enough." Alleyn took the water-pistol from Mrs. Biggins. "This is your gun, isn't it?"

"Yaas," said Georgie; and, remembering James Cagney the week before last at Great Chipping Plaza, he added with a strong Dorset accent: "Sure it's my gat."

"You fixed that water-pistol in the piano in the hall, didn't you?"

"So what?" said Georgie.

This was a little too much for Alleyn. He contemplated the child for a moment and then said:

"Look here, Georgie, never you mind about the pictures. This is real. There's somebody about who ought to be locked up. You're an Englishman, a man of Dorset, and you want to see right done, don't you? You thought it would be rather fun if Miss Prentice got a squirt of water in the eye when she put her foot on the soft pedal. I'm afraid I agree. It would have been funny."

Georgie grinned.

"But how about the music? You'd forgotten about that, hadn't you?"

"Nah, I had not. My pistol's proper strong pistol. 'Twould have bowled over the music, for certain, sure."

"You may be right," said Alleyn. "Did you try it after you had fixed it up?"

"Nah."

"Why not?"

"'Cause something happened."

"What happened?"

"Nuthin! Somebody made a noise. I went away."

"Where did you get the idea?" said Alleyn after a pause. "Come on, now."

"I'll be bound I know, the bad boy," interrupted his mother. "If our Georgie's been up to such-like capers, it's out of one of the clap-trappy tales he's always at. Ay, only last week he tied an alarm clock under faather's chair and set 'un for seven o'clock when he takes his nap, and there was the picture in this rubbish to give him away."

"Was it out of a book, Georgie?"

"Yaas. Kind of."

"I see. And partly out of your Twiddletoy model, wasn't it?"

Georgie nodded.

"When did you do it?"

"Froiday."

"What time?"

"Aafternoon. Two o'clock, about."

"How did you get into the hall?"

"Was there with them girls and I stayed behind."

"Tell me about it. You must have been pretty smart for them not to see what you were up to."

Georgie, it seemed, had slipped into a dark corner as the Friendly Young People left at about a quarter-past two. His idea had been to shoot at them with his water-pistol as they passed; but at the last moment a more amusing notion occurred to him. He remembered the diverting tale of a piano booby-trap which he had read with the greatest enjoyment in the last number of *Bingo Bink's Weekly*. He had some odds and ends of Twiddletoy in his pockets, and as soon as the front door slammed he got to work. First he silently examined the piano and made himself familiar with the action of the pedals. At this juncture his mother told Alleyn that Georgie was of a markedly mechanical turn of mind and had made many astonishing models from Twiddletoy all of which could be made to revolve or even propel. Georgie had gone solidly to work. Stimulated by Alleyn's ardent attention, he described his handiwork. When it was finished he played a triumphant stanza or two of chop-sticks, taking care to use the loud pedal only.

"And nobody came?"

The devilish child turned white again.

"Nobody saw," he muttered. "They never saw nuthun. Only banged at door and shouted."

"And you didn't answer? I see. Know who it was?"

"I never seen 'em."

"All right. How did you leave?"

"By front door. I shut 'un behind me."

There was a brief silence. Georgie's face suddenly twisted into a painful grimace, his lip trembled again, and he looked piteously at Alleyn.

"I never meant no harm," he said. "I never meant it to kill her."

"That's all right," said Alleyn. He reached out a hand and took the child by the shoulder.

"It's nothing to do with you, young Biggins," said Alleyn.

But over the boy's head he saw the mother's stricken face and knew he could not help her so easily.

CHAPTER FOURTEEN

According to the Jernighams

i

ALLEYN WENT alone to Pen Cuckoo. He left Fox to visit Miss Campanula's servants, find out the name of her lawyers, and pick up any grain of information that might be the fruit of his well-known way with female domestics.

The Biggins's car chugged doggedly up the Vale Road in second gear. It was a stiff grade. The Vale rises steeply above Chipping, mounting past Winton to Pen Cuckoo Manor and turning into Cloudyfold Rise at the head of the valley. It is not an obviously picturesque valley, but it has a charm that transcends mere prettiness. The lower slopes of Cloudyfold make an agreeable pattern, the groups of trees are beautifully disposed about the flanks of the hills, and the scattered houses, being simple, seem to have grown out of the country, as indeed they have, since they are built of Dorset stone. It is not a tame landscape, either. The four winds meet on Cloudyfold, and in winter the small lake in Pen Cuckoo grounds holds its mask of ice for days together.

Alleyn noticed that several lanes came down into the Vale Road. He could see that at least one of them led crookedly up to the Manor, and one seemed to be a sort of bridle path from the Manor down to the church. He drove on through the double gates, up the climbing avenue and out on the wide sweep before Pen Cuckoo house.

A flood of thin sunshine had escaped the heavy clouds, and Pen Cuckoo looked its wintry best, an ancient and gracious house, not so very big, not at all forbidding, but tranquil. "A happy house," thought Alleyn, "with a certain dignity."

He gave his card to Taylor.

"I should like to see Mr. Jernigham, if I may."

"If you will come this way, sir."

As he followed Taylor through the west wing, he thought: "With any luck, it'll be the study."

It was, and the study was empty.

As soon as the door had shut behind Taylor, Alleyn looked for the box described by Sergeant Roper. He found it on a table underneath one of the windows. He lifted the lid and saw that the box was empty. He looked closely at the notice "LOADED," which was printed in block capitals. Alleyn gently let fall the lid and walked over to the french window. It was not locked. It looked across the end of the gravelled sweep and over the tops of the park trees right down Pen Cuckoo Vale to Chipping and beyond.

Alleyn was still tracing the course of the Vale Road as it wound through the valley when the squire walked in.

Jocelyn looked fresh and composed. Perhaps his eyes were a little more prominent than usual and his face a little less red, but he had the look of a man who has come to a decision and there was a certain dignity and resolution in his manner.

"I'm glad to see you," he said as he shook hands. "Sit down, won't you? This is a terrible affair."

"Yes," said Alleyn. "It's both terrible and bewildering."

"Good God, I should think it was bewildering! It's the most damned complicated, incomprehensible business I ever want to come up against. I suppose Blandish has told you that in Dillington's absence I've got his job?"

"As Chief Constable? Yes, sir, he told me. That's partly my reason for calling on you."

The squire stared solemnly into the fire and said, "Quite."

"Blandish says you were present when the thing happened."

"Good God, yes. I don't know why it happened, though, or exactly how. As soon as we decided to call you in, Blandish was all for leaving things severely alone. Be damn' glad if you'd explain."

Alleyn explained. Jocelyn listened with his eyes very wide open and his mouth not quite closed.

"Beastly, underhand, ingenious sort of thing," he said. "Sounds more like a woman's work to me. I don't mean to say I think women are particularly underhand, you know; but when they do turn nasty, in my opinion they are inclined to turn crooked-nasty."

He laughed unexpectedly and uncomfortably.

"Yes," agreed Alleyn.

"Sort of inverse ratio or something, what?" added the squire dimly.

"That's it, sir. Now, the first thing we've got to tackle is the ownership of the Colt. I don't know——"

"Wait a bit," said Jocelyn. He stood up, drove his hands into his breeches pockets and walked over to the french windows.

"It's mine," he said.

Alleyn did not answer. The squire turned and looked at him. Seeing nothing but polite attention in Alleyn's face, he made a slight inarticulate noise, strode to the table under the window and opened the box.

"See for yourself," he said. "It's been in that box for the last twenty years. It was there last week. Now it's gone."

Alleyn joined him.

"Hellish unpleasant," said Jocelyn, "isn't it? I only found out this morning. My son was thinking about the business, it seems, and suddenly remembered that the Colt is always lying there, loaded. He came downstairs and looked, and then he came to my room and told me. I'm wondering if I ought not to resign my position as C.C."

"I shouldn't do that, sir," said Alleyn. "With any luck, we ought to be able to clear up the disappearance of the automatic."

"I feel pretty shaken up about it, I don't mind telling you."

"Of course you do. As a matter of fact, I've brought the Colt up here to show you. May I just fetch it? I can slip out to the car this way."

He went straight through the french windows and returned with his case, from which he took the automatic wrapped in a silk handkerchief.

"There's really no need for all these precautions," said Alleyn as he unwrapped it. "We've been all over it for prints and found none. My fingerprint man travels with half a laboratory in his kit. This thing's been dusted, peered at and photographed. It was evidently very thoroughly cleaned after it was put in position."

He laid the automatic in the box. It exactly fitted the indentation in the green baize lining.

"Seems a true bill," said Alleyn.

"How many rounds gone?" asked Jocelyn.

"Three," answered Alleyn.

"I fired the first two in 1917," said Jocelyn; "but I swear before God I'd nothing to do with the third."

"I hope you'll at least have the satisfaction of knowing who had," said Alleyn. "Did you write this notice, 'Loaded,' sir?"

"Yes," said Jocelyn. "What of it?"

Alleyn paused for a fraction of a second before he said, "Only routine, sir. I was going to ask if it always lay on top of the Colt."

"Certainly."

"Do you mind, sir, if I take this box away with me? There may be prints; but I'm afraid your housemaids are too well trained."

"I hope to God you find something. Do take it. I tell you, I'm nearly worried to death by the whole thing. It's a damned outrage that this blasted murderer——"

The door opened and Henry came into the room.

"This is my son," said Jocelyn.

ii

From an upstairs window Henry had watched the arrival of Alleyn's car. Ever since his visit to the study at dawn and his subsequent interview with the abruptly awakened Jocelyn, Henry had been unable to think coherently, to stay still, or to do anything definite. It struck him that he was in very much the same condition as he had been last night while waiting in the wings for the curtain to go up. He had telephoned to Dinah and arranged to see her at the rectory. He had prowled miserably about the house. At intervals he had tried to reassure his father, who had taken the news well, but was obviously very shaken. He had wondered what they would do with Eleanor when she chose to appear. She had gone straight to her room on her return from church, and was reported to be suffering from a headache.

When Jocelyn went downstairs to meet Alleyn, Henry's condition became several degrees more uncomfortable. He imagined his father making a bad job of the automatic story, getting himself further and further involved, and finally losing his temper. The Yard man would probably be maddeningly professional and heavy handed. Henry pictured him seated on the edge of one of the study chairs, staring at his father with sharp, inhuman eyes set in a massive policeman's face. "He will carry his bowler in with him and his boots will be intolerable," thought Henry. "A mammoth of officialdom!"

At last his own idleness became insupportable, and he ran downstairs and made for the study.

He could hear his father's voice raised, as it seemed, in protest. He opened the door and walked in.

"This is my son," said Jocelyn.

Henry's first thought was that this was some stranger, or perhaps a friend of Jocelyn's arrived with hideous inconvenience to visit them. He saw an extremely tall man, thin, and wearing good clothes, with an air of vague distinction.

"This is Mr. Alleyn," said Jocelyn, "from Scotland Yard."

"Oh," said Henry.

He shook hands, felt suddenly rather young, and sat down. His next impression was that he had seen Mr. Alleyn before. He found himself looking at Alleyn in terms of a pencil drawing. A drawing that might have been done by Durer with a sharp, hard pencil and then washed delicately with blue-blacks and ochres. "A grandee turned monk," thought Henry, "but retaining some amusing memories." And he sought to find a reason for this impression which seemed more like a recollection. The accents of the brows, the winged corners to the mouth and eyes, the sharp insistence of the skull—he had seen them all before.

"Henry!" said his father sharply.

Henry realised that Alleyn had been speaking.

"I'm so sorry," he said. "I'm afraid I didn't—— I'm very sorry."

"I was only asking," said Alleyn, "if you could help us with this business of the Colt. Your father says it was in its box last week. Can you get any nearer to it than that?"

"It was there on Friday afternoon at five," said Henry.

"How d'you know?" demanded the squire.

"You'll scarcely credit it," said Henry slowly, "but I've only just remembered. It was before you came down. I was here with Cousin Eleanor waiting for the others to come in for Dinah's run-through for words. They all arrived together, or within two or three minutes of each other. Somebody, Dr. Templett, I think, said something about the burglaries in Somerset last week. Posh Jimmy and his Boys, and all that. We wondered if they'd come this way. Miss Campanula talked about burglar alarms and what she'd do if she heard stealthy footsteps in the small hours. I told them about your war relic, Father, and we all looked at it. Mrs. Ross said she didn't think it was safe to have a loaded firearm lying about. I showed her that the safety catch was on. Then we talked about something else. You came in and we started the rehearsal."

"That's a help," said Alleyn. "It narrows the time down to twenty-seven hours. That was Friday evening. Now, did either of you go to the hall on Friday afternoon?"

"I was hunting," said Jocelyn. "I didn't get back till five, in time for this run-through."

Alleyn looked at Henry.

"I went for a walk," said Henry. "I left at about half-past two. I remember now. It was half-past two."

"Did you go far?"

Henry looked straight before him.

"No. About half-way down to the church."

"How long were you away?"

"About two hours."

"You stopped somewhere, then?"

"Yes."

"Did you speak to anybody?"

"I met Dinah Copeland." Henry looked at his father. "*Not* by appointment. We talked. For some time. Then my cousin, Eleanor Prentice, came up. She had been to church. If it's of any interest, I remember hearing the church clock strike three when she came up. After that Dinah went back to the rectory and I struck up a path to Cloudyfold. I came home by the hill path."

"At what time did you get home?"

"Tea-time. About half-past four."

"Thank you. Now for Friday at five, when the company met here and you showed them the automatic. Did they all leave together?"

"Yes," said Henry.

"At what time?"

"Soon after six."

"Nobody was alone in here at any time before they left?"

"No. We rehearsed in here. They all went out by the french window. It saves trailing through the house."

"Yes. Is it always unlocked?"

"During the day it is."

"I lock it before we go to bed," said Jocelyn, "and fasten the shutters. Lock up the whole place."

"You did this on Friday night, sir?"

"Yes. I was in here reading, all Friday evening."

"Alone?"

"I was here part of the time," Henry said. "Something had gone wrong with one of Dinah's light plugs in the hall and I'd brought it up here to mend. I started in here, and then went to my own room where I had a screwdriver. I tried to ring Dinah up, but our telephone was out of order. A branch had fallen across it in Top Lane."

"I see. Now, how about yesterday? Any visitors?"

"Templett came up in the morning to borrow an old four-in-hand tie of mine," said Jocelyn. "He seemed to think he'd like to wear it in the play. He offered to look at my cousin's finger, but she wouldn't come down."

"She was afraid he'd tell her she couldn't play her filthy 'Venetian Suite,' " said Henry. "Do you admire the works of Ethelbert Nevin, Mr. Alleyn?"

"No," said Alleyn.

"They're gall and wormwood to me," said Henry gloomily. "And I suppose we'll have them here for the rest of our lives. Not that I like the bloody Prelude much better. Do you know what that Prelude is supposed to illustrate?"

"Yes, I think I do. Isn't it——"

"Burial," said Henry. "It's supposed to be a man buried alive. Bump, bump, bump on the coffin lid. Well, I suppose it's not so frightfully inappropriate."

"Not so frightfully," agreed Alleyn rather grimly. "Now, about yesterday's visitors."

But Henry and his father were rather vague about yesterday's visitors. The squire had driven into Great Chipping in the morning.

"And Miss Prentice?" asked Alleyn.

"Same thing. She went with us. She was in the hall all the morning. They were all there."

"All?"

"Well, not Templett," said Henry. "He called in here as we've described, at about ten o'clock, and my father gave him the tie. And a pretty ghastly affair it is, I may add."

"They were damn' smart at one time," said the squire hotly. "I remember I wore that tie——"

"Well, anyway," said Henry, "he got the tie. I didn't see him. I was hunting up my own clothes. We all went out soon after he'd gone. You saw him off, didn't you, Father?"

"Yes," said the squire. "Funny sort of fellow, Templett. First I knew about him was that Taylor told me he was in here and wanted the four-in-hand. I told Taylor to hunt it up and came down and found Templett. We talked for quite a long time and I'm blessed if, when I walked out with him to the car, poor little Mrs. Ross wasn't sitting there. Damn' funny thing to do," said Jocelyn, brushing up his moustache. " 'Pon my word, I think the fellow wanted to keep her to himself."

Alleyn looked thoughtfully at him.

"How was Dr. Templett dressed?" he asked.

"What? I don't know. Yes, I think I do. Donegal tweed."

"An overcoat?"

"No."

"Bulging pockets?" asked Henry, with a grin at Alleyn.

"I don't think so. Why? Good Lord, you don't suppose he took my Colt, do you?"

"We've got to explore the possibilities, sir," said Alleyn.

"My God," said Jocelyn, "I suppose they're all under suspicion! What?"

"Including us," said Henry. "You know," he added, "theoretically one wouldn't put it past Templett. Eleanor's been poisonous about his alleged—notice how I protect myself, Mr. Alleyn—his alleged affair with Selia Ross."

"Good God!" shouted Jocelyn angrily, "haven't you got more sense than to talk like that, Henry? This is a damn' serious business, let me tell you, and you go blackening Mr.—Mr. Alleyn's mind against a man who——"

"I spoke theoretically, remember," said Henry. "I don't really suppose Templett is a murderer, and as for Mr. Alleyn's mind——"

"It doesn't blacken very readily," said Alleyn.

"And after all," Henry continued, "you might make out just as bad a case against me. If I thought I could murder Cousin Eleanor in safety I dare say I should undertake it. And I should think Mr. Copeland would feel sorely tempted after the way she's——"

"Henry!"

"But, my dear Father, Mr. Alleyn is going to hear all the local gossip if he hasn't done so already. Of course, Mr. Alleyn will suspect each of us in turn. Even dear Cousin Eleanor herself is not above suspicion. She may have infected her finger in the approved manner with a not too deadly toxin. Or made it up to look septic. Why not? There were the grease paints. True, she overdid it a bit, but that may have been pure artistry."

"Damn' dangerous twaddle," shouted Jocelyn. "It was hurting her like hell. I've known Eleanor since we were children, and I've never seen her cry before. She's a Jernigham."

"A good deal of it was straight-out annoyance at not being able to perform the 'Venetian Suite,' if you ask me. Tears of anger, they were, and the only sort you'll ever wring from Eleanor's eyes. Did she cry when they yawked out her gall-bladder? No. She's a Jernigham."

"Be quiet, sir," stormed Jocelyn.

"As far as I can see, the only one of us who could *not* have set the trap is poor old Idris Campanula. Oh, God!"

Alleyn, watching Henry, saw him turn very white before he moved away to the window.

"All right," Henry said to the landscape. "One's got to do something about it. Can't go on all day thinking of an old maid with her brains blown out. Might as well be funny in our hard, decadent modern way."

"I remember getting the same reaction in the war," said Alleyn vaguely. "As they say in vaudeville, 'I had to laugh.' It's not an uncommon rebound from shock."

"I don't suppose I was being anything but excessively commonplace," said Henry tartly.

iv

"Then you don't know if anybody came while you were out yesterday morning?" asked Alleyn, after some considerable time spent in collecting the attention of the two Jernighams.

"I'll ask the servants," said Jocelyn importantly, and rang for Taylor.

As Alleyn expected, the evidence of the servants was completely inconclusive. Nobody had actually rung the door bells, but on the other hand anybody might have walked into the study and done anything. They corroborated Jocelyn and Henry's statements about their own movements and Taylor remembered seeing Miss Prentice come in at four on Friday afternoon. When the last maid had gone Alleyn asked if they had all been at Pen Cuckoo for some time.

"Lord, yes," said the squire. "Out of the question they should have anything to do with this affair. No motive, no opportunity."

"And not nearly enough sense," added Henry.

"In addition to which," said Alleyn, "they have provided each other with alibis for the whole day until they all went down in a solid body to the church hall at seven-thirty."

"I understand the entertainment provided," said Henry, "caused cook to vomit three times on the way home, and this morning, Father, I am told, the bootboy heaved everything he had into the tops of your hunting boots."

"Well, that's a nice thing!" began Jocelyn crossly.

Alleyn said, "You told me it is out of the question that the automatic could have been substituted for the water-pistol during yesterday morning."

"Unless it was done under the noses of a bevy of Friendly Young People and most of the company," said Henry.

"How about the afternoon?"

"It was locked up then and the key, instead of being at the rectory as usual, was hidden, fancifully enough, behind the outside lavatory," said Henry. "Dinah invented the place of concealment, and announced it at rehearsal. Cousin Eleanor was too put-out to object. Nobody but the members of the cast knew about it. As far as I know, only Templett and Mrs. Ross called in during the afternoon."

"What did you do?" asked Alleyn.

"I went for a walk on Cloudyfold. I met nobody," said Henry, "and I can't prove I was there."

"Thank you," said Alleyn mildly. "What about you, sir?"

"I went round the stables with Rumbold, my agent," said Jocelyn, "and then I came in and went to sleep in the library. I was waked by my cousin at five. We had a sort of high tea at half-past six and went down to the hall at a quarter to seven."

"All three of you?"

"Yes."

"And now, if you please," said Alleyn, "I should like to see Miss Prentice."

CHAPTER FIFTEEN

Alleyn Goes to Church

i

Miss Prentice came in looking, as Henry afterwards told Dinah, as much like an early Christian martyr as her clothes permitted. Alleyn, who had never been able to conquer his proclivity for first impressions, took an instant dislike to her.

The squire's manner became nervously proprietary.

"Well, Eleanor," he said, "here you are. We're sorry to bring you down. May I introduce Mr. Alleyn? He's looking into this business for us."

Miss Prentice gave Alleyn a forbearing smile and a hand like a fish. She sat on the only uncomfortable chair in the room.

"I shall try not to bother you too long," Alleyn began.

"It's only," said Miss Prentice, in a voice that suggested the presence of Miss Campanula's body in the room, "it's only that I hope to go to church at eleven."

"It's a few minutes after ten. I think you'll have plenty of time."

"I'll drive you down," said Henry.

"Thank you, dear, I think I should like to walk."

"I'm going, anyway," said Jocelyn.

Miss Prentice smiled at him. It was an approving, understanding sort of smile, and Alleyn thought it would have kept him away from church for the rest of his life.

"Well, Miss Prentice," he said, "we are trying to see daylight through a mass of strange circumstances. There is no reason why you shouldn't be told that Miss Campanula was shot by the automatic that is kept in a box in this room."

"Oh, Jocelyn!" said Miss Prentice, "how terrible! You know, dear, we *have* said it wasn't really quite advisable, haven't we?"

"You needn't go rubbing it in, Eleanor."

"Why wasn't it advisable," asked Henry. "Had you foreseen,

Cousin Eleanor, that somebody might pinch the Colt and rig it up in a piano as a lethal booby-trap?"

"Henry dear, please! We just said sometimes that perhaps it wasn't very wise."

"Are you employing the editorial or the real 'we'?"

Alleyn said, "One minute, please. Before we go any further I think, as a matter of pure police routine, I would like to see your finger, Miss Prentice."

"Oh, dear! It's very painful. I'm afraid——"

"If you would rather Dr. Templett unwrapped it——"

"Oh, no. No."

"If you will allow me, I think I can do a fairly presentable bandage."

Miss Prentice raised her eyes to Alleyn's and a very peculiar expression visited her face, a mixture of archness and submission. She advanced her swathed hand with an air of timidity. He undid the bandage very quickly and lightly and exposed the finger with a somewhat battered stall drawn over a closer bandage. He peeled off the stall and completely unwrapped the finger. It was inflamed, discoloured and swollen.

"A nasty casualty," said Alleyn. "You should have it dressed again. Dr. Templett——"

"I do not wish Dr. Templett to touch it."

"But he could give you fresh bandages and a stall that has not been torn."

"I have a first-aid box. Henry, would you mind, dear?"

Henry was despatched for the first-aid box. Alleyn redressed the finger very deftly. Miss Prentice watched him with a sort of eager concentration, never lowering her gaze from his face.

"How beautifully you manage," she said.

"I hope it will serve. You should have a sling, I fancy. Do you want the old stall?"

She shook her head. He dropped it in his pocket and was startled when she uttered a little coy murmur of protestation for all the world as if he had taken her finger-stall from some motive of gallantry.

"You deserve a greater reward," she said.

"Lummy!" thought Alleyn in considerable embarrassment. He said, "Miss Prentice, I am trying to get a sort of timetable of everybody's movements from Friday afternoon until the time of the tragedy. Do you mind telling me where you were on Friday afternoon?"

"I was in church."

"All the afternoon?"

"Oh, no," said Eleanor, softly.

"Between what hours were you there, please?"

"I arrived at two."

"Do you know when the service was over?"

"It was not a service," said Miss Prentice with pale forbearance.

"You were there alone?"

"It was confession," said Henry impatiently.

"Oh, I see." Alleyn paused. "Was anybody else there besides yourself and—and your confessor?"

"No. I passed poor Idris on my way out."

"When was that?"

"I think I remember the clock struck half-past two."

"Good. And then?"

"I went home."

"Directly?"

"I took the top lane."

"The lane that comes out by the church?"

"Yes."

"Did you pass the parish hall?"

"Yes."

"You didn't go in?"

"No."

"Was any one there, do you think?"

"The doors were shut," said Miss Prentice. "I think the girls only went in for an hour."

"Were the keys in their place of concealment on Friday?" asked Alleyn.

Miss Prentice instantly looked grieved and shocked. Henry grinned broadly and said, "There's only one key. I don't know if it was there on Friday. I think it was. Dinah would know about that. Some of the committee worked there on Friday, as Cousin Eleanor says, but none of us. They may have returned the key to the rectory. I only went halfway down."

"At what part of the top lane on Friday afternoon did you meet Mr. Henry Jernigham and Miss Copeland, Miss Prentice?"

Alleyn heard her draw in her breath and saw her turn white. She looked reproachfully at Henry and said:

"I'm afraid I do not remember."

"I do," said Henry. "It was at the sharp bend above the footbridge. You came round the corner from below."

She bent her head. Henry looked as if he dared her to speak.

"There's something damned unpleasant about this," thought Alleyn.

He said, "How long did you spend in conversation with the others before you went on to Pen Cuckoo?"

An unlovely red stained her cheeks.

"Not long."

"About five minutes, I should think," said Henry.

"And you arrived home, when?"

"I should think at about half-past three. I really don't know."

"Did you go out again on Friday, Miss Prentice?"

"No," said Miss Prentice.

"You were about the house? I'm sorry to worry you like this, but you see I really do want to know exactly what everybody did on Friday."

"I was in my room," she said. "There are two little offices that Father Copeland has given us for use after confession."

"Oh, I see," said Alleyn, in some embarrassment.

ii

Alleyn waded on. Miss Prentice's air of patient martyrdom increased with every question, but he managed to get a good deal of information from her. On Saturday, the day of the performance, she had spent the morning in the parish hall with all the other workers. She left when the others left, and, with Jocelyn and Henry, returned to Pen Cuckoo for lunch. She had not gone out again until the evening but had spent the afternoon in her sitting-room. She remembered waking the squire at tea-time. After tea she returned to her room.

"During yesterday morning you were all at the hall?" said Alleyn. "Who got there first?"

"Dinah Copeland, I should think," said Jocelyn promptly. "She was there when we arrived. She was always the first."

Alleyn made a note of it and went on, "Did any of you notice the position and appearance of the piano?"

They all looked very solemn at the mention of the piano.

"I think I did," said Miss Prentice in a low voice. "It was as it was for the performance. The girls had evidently arranged the drapery and pot-plants on Friday. I looked at it rather particularly as I was—I was to play it."

"Good Lord!" ejaculated the squire, "you were strumming on the damned thing. I remember now."

"Jocelyn, dear, please! I did just touch the keys. I believe, with my right hand. Not my left," said Miss Prentice with her most patient smile.

"This was yesterday morning, wasn't it?" said Alleyn. "Now, please. Miss Prentice, try to remember. Did you use the soft pedal at all when you tried the piano?"

"Oh, dear, now I wonder. Let me see. I did sit down for a moment. I expect I did use the soft pedal. I always think soft playing is so much nicer. Yes, I should think almost without doubt I used the soft pedal."

"Was anybody by the piano at the time?" asked Alleyn.

Miss Prentice turned a reproachful gaze on him.

"Idris," she whispered. "Miss Campanula."

"Here, wait a bit," shouted Jocelyn. "I've remembered the whole thing. Eleanor, you sat down and strummed about with your right hand and she came up and asked you why you didn't try with your left to see how it worked."

"So she did," said Henry, softly. "And so, of course, she would."

"And you got up and went away," said the squire. "Old Camp—well, Idris Campanula—gave a sort of laugh and dumped herself down and——"

"And away went the Prelude!" cried Henry. "You're quite right, Father. 'Pom. *Pom!* POM!! And then down with the soft pedal. That's it, sir," he added, turning to Alleyn. "I watched her. I'll swear it."

"Right," said Alleyn. "We're getting on. This was yesterday morning. At what time?"

"Just before we packed up," said Henry. "About midday."

"And—I know I've been over this before, but it's important—you all left together?"

"Yes," said Henry. "We three drove off in the car. I remember that I heard Dinah slam the back door just as we started. They were all out by then."

"And none of you returned until the evening? I see. When you arrived at a quarter to seven you found Miss Copeland there."

"Yes," said Jocelyn.

"Where was she?"

"On the stage with her father, putting flowers in vases."

"Was the curtain down?"

"Yes."

"What did you all do?"

"I went to my dressing-room," said the squire.

"I stayed in the supper-room and talked to Dinah," said Henry. "Her father was on the stage. After a minute or two I went to my dressing-room."

"Here!" ejaculated Jocelyn, and glared at Miss Prentice.

"What, dear?"

"Those girls were giggling about in front of the hall. I wonder if any of them got up to any hanky-panky with the piano."

"Oh, my dear Father!" said Henry.

"They were strictly forbidden to touch the instrument," said Miss Prentice. "Ever since Cissie Drury did such damage."

"How long was it before the others arrived? Dr. Templett and Mrs. Ross?" asked Alleyn.

"They didn't get down until half-past seven," said Henry. "Dinah was in a frightful stew and so were we all. She rang up Mrs. Ross's cottage in the end. It took ages to get through. The hall telephone's an extension from the rectory and we rang for a long time before anybody at the rectory answered and at last, when it was connected with Mrs. Ross's house, there was no reply, so we knew she'd left."

"She came with Dr. Templett?"

"Oh, yes," murmured Miss Prentice.

"The telephone is in your dressing-room, isn't it, Mr. Jernigham?"

"Mine and Henry's. We shared. We were all there round the telephone."

"Yes." said Alleyn. He looked from one face to another. Into the quiet room there dropped the Sunday morning sound of chiming bells. Miss Prentice rose.

"Thank you so much," said Alleyn. "I think I've got a general idea of the two days now. On Friday afternoon Miss Prentice went to church, Mr. Jernigham hunted, Mr. Henry Jernigham went for a walk. On her return from church, Miss Prentice met Mr. Henry Jernigham and Miss Copeland, who had themselves met by chance in the top lane. That was at about three. Mr. Henry Jernigham returned home by a circuitous route, Miss Prentice by the top lane. Miss Prentice went to her room. At five you had your rehearsal for words in this room, and everybody saw the automatic. You all three dined at home and remained at home. It was also on Friday afternoon that some helpers worked for about an hour at the hall, but apparently they had finished at two-thirty when Miss Prentice passed that way. On Saturday (yesterday) morning Dr. Templett and Mrs.

Ross called here for the tie. You all went down to the hall and you, sir, drove to Great Chipping. You all returned for lunch. By this time the piano was in position with the drapery and aspidistras on top. In the afternoon Mr. Henry Jernigham walked up Cloudyfold and back. As far as we know, only Dr. Templett and Mrs. Ross visited the hall yesterday afternoon. At a quarter to seven you all arrived there for the performance."

"Masterly, sir," said Henry.

"Oh, I've written it all down," said Alleyn. "My memory's hopeless."

"What about your music, Miss Prentice? When did you put it on the piano?"

"Oh, on Saturday morning, of course."

"I see. You had it here until then?"

"Oh, no," said Miss Prentice. "Not *here*, you know."

"Then, where?"

"In the hall, naturally."

"It lives in the hall?"

"Oh, no," she said, opening her eyes very wide, "why should it?"

"I'm sure I don't know. When did you take it to the hall?"

"On Thursday night for the dress-rehearsal. Of course."

"I see. You played for the dress-rehearsal?"

"Oh, no."

"For the love of heaven!" ejaculated Jocelyn. "Why the dickens can't you come to the point, Eleanor. She wanted to play on Thursday night but her finger was like a bad sausage," he explained to Alleyn.

Miss Prentice gave Alleyn her martyred smile, shook her head slightly at the bandaged finger, and looked restlessly at the clock.

"H'm," she said unhappily.

"Well," said Alleyn. "The music was in the hall from Thursday onwards and you put it in the rack yesterday morning. And none of you went into the hall before the show last night. Good."

Miss Prentice said, "Well—I think I shall just—Jocelyn, dear, that's the first bell, isn't it?"

"I'm sorry," said Alleyn, "but I should like, if I may, to have a word with you, Miss Prentice. Perhaps you will let me drive you down. Or if not——"

"Oh," said Miss Prentice, looking very flurried, "thank you. I think I should prefer—I'm afraid I really can't——"

"Cousin Eleanor," said Henry, "I will drive you down, father will drive you down, or Mr. Alleyn will drive you down. You might even drive yourself down. It is only twenty-five to eleven now and it doesn't take more than ten minutes to *walk* down, so you can easily spare Mr. Alleyn a quarter of an hour."

"I'm afraid I do fuss rather, don't I, but you see I like to have a few quiet moments before——"

"Now, look here, Eleanor," said the squire warmly, "this is an investigation into murder. Good Lord, it's your best friend that's been killed, my dear girl, and when we're right in the thick of it, damme, you want to go scuttling off to church."

"Jocelyn!"

"Come on, Father," said Henry. "We'll leave Mr. Alleyn a fair field."

iii

"——you see," said Alleyn, "I don't think you quite realise your own position. Hadn't it occurred to you that you were the intended victim?"

"It is such a dreadful thought," said Miss Prentice.

"I know it is, but you've got to face it. There's a murderer abroad in your land and as far as one can see his first coup hasn't come off. It's been a fantastic and horrible failure. For your own, if not for the public's good, you must realise this. Surely you want to help us."

"I believe," said Miss Prentice, "that our greatest succour lies in prayer."

"Yes," Alleyn said slowly, "I can appreciate that. But my job is to ask questions, and I do ask you, most earnestly, if you believe that you have a bitter enemy among this small group of people."

"I cannot believe it of any one."

Alleyn looked at her with something very like despair. She had refused to sit down after they were alone, but fidgeted about in the centre of the room, looked repeatedly down the Vale, and was thrown into a fever of impatience by the call of the church bells.

A towering determined figure, he stood between Eleanor and the window, and concentrated his will on her. He thought of his mind as a pin-pointed weapon and he drove it into hers.

"Miss Prentice. Please look at me."

Her glance wavered. Her pale eyes travelled reluctantly to his. Deliberately silent until he felt he had got her whole attention, he held her gaze with his own. Then he spoke. "I may not try to force information from you. You are a free agent. But think for a moment of the position. You have escaped death by an accident. If you had persisted in playing last night you would have been shot dead. I am going to repeat a list of names to you. If there is anything between any one of these persons and yourself which, if I knew of it, might help me to see light, ask yourself if you should not tell me of it. These are the names:

"Mr. Jocelyn Jernigham?

"His son, Henry Jernigham?

"The rector, Mr. Copeland?"

"No!" she cried, "no! Never! Never!"

"His daughter, Dinah Copeland?

"Mrs. Ross?"

He saw the pale eyes narrow a little.

"Dr. Templett?"

She stared at him like a mesmerised rabbit.

"Well, Miss Prentice, what of Mrs. Ross and Dr. Templett?"

"I can accuse nobody. Please let me go."

"Have you ever had a difference with Mrs. Ross?"

"I hardly speak to Mrs. Ross."

"Or with Dr. Templett?"

"I prefer not to discuss Dr. Templett," she said breathlessly.

"At least," said Alleyn, "he saved your life. He dissuaded you from playing."

"I believe God saw fit to use him as an unworthy instrument."

Alleyn opened his mouth to speak and thought better of it. At last he said, "In your own interest, tell me this. Has Mrs. Ross cause to regard you as her enemy?"

She wetted her lips and answered him with astounding vigour:

"I have thought only as every decent creature who sees her must think. Before she could silence the voice of reproach she would have to murder a dozen Christian souls."

"Of whom Miss Campanula was one?"

She stared at him vacantly and then he saw she had understood him.

"That's why he wouldn't let me play," she whispered.

On his way back, Alleyn turned off the Vale road and drove up past the church to the hall. Seven cars were drawn up outside St. Giles and he noticed a stream of villagers turning in at the lych-gate.

"Full house, this morning," thought Alleyn grimly. And suddenly he pulled up by the hall, got out, and walked back to the church.

"The devil takes a holiday," he thought, and joined in with the stream.

He managed to elude the solicitations of a sidesman and slip into a seat facing the aisle in the back row where he sat with his long hands clasped round his knee. His head looked remotely austere in the cold light from the open doors.

Winton St. Giles is a beautiful church and Alleyn, overcoming that first depression inseparable from the ecclesiastical smell, and the sight of so many people with decorous faces, found pleasure in the tranquil solidity of stone shaped into the expression of devotion. The single bell stopped. The organ rumbled vaguely for three minutes, the congregation stood, and Mr. Copeland followed his choir into church.

Like everybody else who saw him for the first time, Alleyn was startled by the rector's looks. The service was a choral Eucharist and he wore a cope, a magnificent vestment that shone like a blazon in the candle light. His silver hair, the incredible perfection of his features, his extreme pallor, and great height, made Alleyn think of an actor admirably suited for the performance of priestly parts. But when the time came for the short sermon, he found evidence of a simple and unaffected mind with no great originality. It was an unpretentious sermon touched with sincerity. The rector spoke of prayers for the dead and told his listeners that there was nothing in the teaching of their church that forbade such prayers. He invited them to petition God for the peace of all souls departed in haste or by violence, and he commended meditation and a searching of their own hearts lest they should harbour anger or resentment.

As the service went on, Alleyn, looking down the aisle, saw a dark girl with so strong a resemblance to the rector that he knew she must be Dinah Copeland. Her eyes were fixed on her father and in them Alleyn read anxiety and affection.

Miss Prentice was easily found, for she sat next the aisle in the front row. She rose and fell like a ping-pong ball on a water jet, sinking in solitary genuflexions and crossing herself like a sort of minor soloist. The squire sat beside her. The back of his neck wore an expression of indignation and discomfort, being both scarlet and rigid. Much nearer to Alleyn, and also next the aisle, sat a woman whom he recognised as probably the most fashionable figure in the congregation. Detectives are trained to know about clothes and Alleyn knew hers were impeccable. She wore them like a Frenchwoman. He could only see the thin curve of her cheek and an immaculate wing of straw-coloured hair, but presently, as if aware of his gaze, she turned her head and he saw her face. It was thinnish and alert, beautifully made-up, hard, but with a look of amused composure. The pale eyes looked into his and widened. She paused with unmistakable deliberation for a split second, and then turned away. Her luxuriously gloved hand went to her hair.

"That was once known as the glad eye," thought Alleyn.

Under cover of a hymn he slipped out of church.

V

He crossed the lane to the hall. Sergeant Roper was on duty at the gate and came smartly to attention.

"Well, Roper, how long have you been here?"

"I relieved Constable Fife an hour ago, sir. The super sent him along soon after you left. About seven-thirty, sir."

"Anybody been about?"

"Boys," said Roper, "hanging round like wasps and as bold as brass with that young Biggins talking that uppish you'd have thought he was as good as the murderer, letting on as he was as full of inside knowledge as the Lord Himself, not meaning it in the way of blasphemy. I subdued him, however, and his mother bore him off to church. Mr. Bathgate took a photograph of the building, and asked me to say, sir, that he'd look back in a minute or two in case you were here."

"I dare say," grunted Alleyn.

"And the doctor came along, too, in a proper taking on. Seems he left one of his knives for slashing open the body in the hall last night, and he wanted to fetch her out for to lay bare the youngest Cain's toe. I went in with the doctor but she was nowhere to be found, no not even in the pockets of his suit which seemed a strange casual spot for a naked blade, no doubt so deadly sharp as 'twould penetrate the very guts of a man in a flash. Doctor was proper put about by the loss and made off without another word."

"I see. Any one else?"

"Not a living soul," said Roper. "I reckon rector will have brought this matter up in his sermon, sir. The man couldn't well avoid it, seeing it's his job to put a holy construction on the face of disaster."

"He did just touch on it," Alleyn admitted.

"A ticklish affair and you may be sure one that he didn't greatly relish, being a timid sort of chap."

"I think I'll have a look round the outside of the hall, Roper."

"Very good, sir."

Alleyn wandered round the hall on the lane side, his eyes on the gravelled path. Roper looked after him wistfully until he disappeared at the back. He came to the rear door, saw nothing of interest, and turned to the outhouses. Here, in a narrow gap between two walls, he found a nail where he supposed the key had hung yesterday. He continued his search round the far side of the building and came at last to a window, where he stopped.

He remembered that they had shut this window last night before they left the hall. It was evidently the only one that was ever opened. The others were firmly sealed in accumulated grime. Alleyn looked at the wall underneath it. The surface of the weathered stone was grazed in many places, and on the ground he discovered freshly detached chips. Between the gravelled path and the side of the building was a narrow strip of grass. This bore a rectangular impress that the night's heavy rain had softened but not obliterated. Within the margin of the impress he found traces of several large footprints and two smaller ones. Alleyn returned to a sort of lumbershed at the back and fetched an old box. The edges at the open end bore traces of damp earth. He took it to the impression and found that it fitted exactly. It also covered the lower grazes on the wall. He examined the box minutely, peering into the joints and cracks in the rough wood. Presently he began to whistle. He took a pair of tweezers from his pocket, and along the edge, from a crack where the wood had split, he pulled out a minute red scrap of some spongy substance. He found two more shreds caught in the rough surface of the wood, and on a projecting nail. He put them in an envelope and sealed it. Then he replaced the box. He measured the height from the box to the window-sill.

"Good-morning," said a voice behind him. "You must be a detective."

Alleyn glanced up and saw Nigel Bathgate leaning over the stone fence that separated the parish hall grounds from a path on the far side.

"What a fascinating life yours must be," continued Nigel.

Alleyn did not reply. Inadvertently he released the catch on the steel tape. It flew back into the container.

"Pop goes the weasel," said Nigel.

"Hold your tongue," said Alleyn, mildly, "and come here."

Nigel vaulted over the wall.

"Take this tape for me. Don't touch the box if you can help it."

"It would be pleasant to know why."

"Five-foot-three from the box to the sill," said Alleyn. "Too far for Georgie, and in any case we know he didn't. That's funny."

"Screamingly."

"Go to the next window, Bathgate, and raise yourself by the sill. If you can."

"Only if you tell me why."

"I will in a minute. Please be quick. I want to get this over before the hosts of the godly are upon us. Can you do it?"

"Listen, Chief. This is your lucky day. Look at these biceps. Three months ago I was puny like you. By taking my self-raising course——"

Nigel reached up to the window sill, gave a prodigious heave, and cracked the crown of his head smartly on the sill.

"Great strength rings the bell," said Alleyn. "Now try and get a foothold."

"Blast and damn you!" said Nigel, scraping at the wall with his shoes.

"That will do. I'm going into the hall. When I call out, I want you to repeat this performance. You needn't crack your head again."

Alleyn went into the hall, forced open the second window two inches, and went over to the piano.

"Now!"

The shape of Nigel's head and shoulders rose up behind the clouded glass. His collar and tie appeared in the gap. Alleyn had a fleeting impression of his face.

"All right."

Nigel disappeared and Alleyn rejoined him.

"Are we playing Peep Bo or what?" asked Nigel sourly.

"Something of the sort. I saw you all right. Yes," continued Alleyn, examining the wall. "The lady used the box. We will preserve the box. Dear me."

"At least you might say I can come down."

"I'm so sorry. Of course. And your head?"

"Bloody."

"But unbowed, I feel sure. Now I'll explain."

CHAPTER SIXTEEN

The Top Lane Incident

i

ALLEYN GAVE Nigel his explanation as they walked up Top Lane by the route Dinah had taken on Friday afternoon. They walked briskly, their heads bent, and a look of solemn absorption on their faces. In a few minutes they crossed a rough bridge and reached a sharp turn in the lane.

"It was here," said Alleyn, "that Henry Jernigham met Dinah Copeland on Friday afternoon. It was here that Eleanor Prentice found them on her return from the confessional. I admit that I am curious about their encounters, Bathgate. Miss Prentice came upon them at three, yet she left the church at half-past two. Young Jernigham says he was away two hours. He left home at two-thirty. It can take little more than five minutes to come down here from Pen Cuckoo. They must have been together almost half an hour before Miss Prentice arrived."

"Perhaps they are in love."

"Perhaps they are. But there is something that neither Miss Prentice nor Master Henry cares to remember when one speaks of this meeting. They turn pale. Henry becomes sardonic and Miss Prentice sends out waves of sanctimonious disapproval in the manner of a polecat."

"What can you mean?"

"It doesn't matter. She left the church at three. She only spent five minutes here with the others and yet she did not reach Pen Cuckoo till after four. There seems to be a lot of time to spare. Henry struck up this path to the hill-top. Miss Copeland returned by the way we have come, Miss Prentice went on to Pen Cuckoo. I have a picture of three specks of humanity running together, exploding, and flying apart."

"There are a hundred explanations."

"For their manner of meeting and parting? Yes, I dare say there are, but not so many explanations for their agitation when the meeting is discussed. Say that she surprised them in an embrace, Master Henry might feel foolish at the recollection, but why should Miss Prentice go white and trembly?"

"She's an old maid, isn't she? Perhaps it shocked her."

"It may have given her a shock."

Alleyn was searching the wet lane.

"The rain last night was the devil. This great bough must have been blown down quite recently. Master Henry told me that their telephone was dumb on Friday night. He said it was broken by a falling bough in Top Lane. There are the wires and it almost follows as the night the day that this is the bough. It's protected the ground. Wait, I believe we've struck a little luck."

They moved the still unwithered bough.

"Yes. See here, Bathgate, here is where they stood. How much more dramatic footprints can be than the prints of hands. Look, here are Dinah Copeland's if indeed they are hers, coming round the bend into the protection of the bank. The ground was soft but not too wet. Coming downhill we pick *his* prints up, as they march out of the sodden lane into the lee of the bank and overlapping trees. Surface water has seeped into them but there they are. And here, where the bough afterwards fell, they met."

"And what a meeting!" ejaculated Nigel, looking at the heavy impressions of overlapping prints.

"A long meeting. Yes, and a lover's meeting. She looks a nice girl. I hope Master Henry——"

He broke off.

"Here we are, by George. Don't come too far. Eleanor Prentice must have rounded the corner, taken two steps or so, and stopped dead. There are her feet planted side by side. She stood for some time in this one place, facing the others and then—what happened? Ordinary conversation? No, I don't think so. I'll have to try and get it from the young ones. *She* won't tell me. Yes, there are her shoes, no doubt of it. Black-calf with pointed toes and low heels. Church hen's shoes. She was wearing them this morning."

Alleyn squatted by the two solitary prints, reached out a long finger and touched the damp earth. Then he looked up at Nigel.

"Well, it's proved one thing," he said.

"What?"

"If these are Eleanor Prentice's prints, and I think they are, it wasn't Eleanor Prentice who tried to see in at the window of the parish hall. Wait here, will you, Bathgate? I'm going down to the car for my stuff. We'll have a cast of these prints."

ii

At half-past twelve Alleyn and Nigel arrived at the Red House, Chipping. An elderly parlourmaid told them that Mr. Fox was still there, and showed them into a Victorian drawing-room which, in the language of brassware and modernish silk Japanese panels, spoke unhappily of the late General Campanula's service in the East. It was an ugly room, over-furnished and unfriendly. Fox was seated at a writing desk in the window and before him were many neat stacks of papers. He rose and looked placidly at them over the tops of his glasses.

"Hullo, Brer Fox," said Alleyn. "How the hell are you getting on?"

"Fairly comfortably, thank you, sir. Good-morning, Mr. Bathgate."

"Good-morning, inspector."

"What have you got there?" asked Alleyn.

"A number of letters, sir, none of them very helpful."

"What about that ominous wad of foolscap, you old devil? Come on, now; it's the will, isn't it?"

"Well, it is," said Fox.

He handed it to Alleyn and waited placidly while he read it.

"This was a wealthy woman," said Alleyn.

"How wealthy?" demanded Nigel, "and what has she done with it?"

"Nothing that's for publication."

"All right, all right."

"She's left fifty thousand. Thirty of them go to the Reverend Walter Copeland of Winton St. Giles in recognition of his work as a parish priest and in deep gratitude for his spiritual guidance and unfailing wisdom. Lummy! He is to use this money as he thinks best but she hopes that he will not give it all away to other people. Fifteen thousand to her dear friend, Eleanor Jernigham Prentice, four thousand to Eric Campanula, son of William Campanula, and second cousin to the testatrix. Last heard of in Nairobi, Kenya. A stipulation that the said four thousand be invested by Miss Campanula's lawyers, Messrs. Waterworth, Waterworth and Biggs, and the beneficiary to receive the interest at their hands. The testatrix adds the hope that the beneficiary will not spend the said interest on alcoholic beverages or women, and will think of her and mend his ways. One thousand to be divided among the servants. Dated May 21st, 1938."

"There was a note enclosed dated May 21st of this year," said Fox. "Here it is, sir."

Alleyn read aloud with one eyebrow raised:

"To all whom it may concern. This is my last Will and Testament so there's no need for anybody to go poking about among my papers for another. I should like to say that the views expressed in reference to the principal beneficiary are the views I hold at the moment. If I could add anything to this appreciation of his character to make it more emphatic, I would do so. There have been disappointments, and friends who have failed me, but I am a lonely woman and see no reason to alter my Will. Idris Campanula."

"She seems to have been a very outspoken lady, doesn't she?" asked Fox.

"She does. That's a nasty jab in the eye for her dear friend, Eleanor Prentice," said Alleyn.

"Well, now," said Nigel briskly, "do you think either of these two have murdered her? You always say, Alleyn, that money is the prime motive."

"I don't say so in this instance," Alleyn said. "It may be, but I don't think it is. Well, there we are, Fox. We must get hold of the Waterworths and Mr. Biggs, before they read about it in the papers."

"I've rung them up, Mr. Alleyn. The parlourmaid knew Mr. Waterworth senior's private address."

"Excellent, Fox. Anything else?"

"There's the chauffeur, Gibson. I think you might like to talk to him."

"All right. Produce Gibson."

Fox went out and returned with Miss Campanula's chauffeur. He wore his plum-coloured breeches and shining gaiters and had the air of having just crammed himself into his tunic.

"This is Gibson, sir," said Fox. "I think the chief inspector would like to hear about this little incident on Friday afternoon, Mr. Gibson."

"Good-morning," said Alleyn. "What's the incident?"

"It concerns deceased's visit to church at two-thirty, sir," Fox explained. "It seems that she called at the hall on her way down."

"Really?" said Alleyn.

"Not to say called, sir," said Gibson. "Not in a manner of speaking, seeing she didn't go in."

"Let's hear about it?"

"She used to go regular, you see, sir, to the confessing affair. About every three weeks. Well, Friday, she orders the car and we go down, getting there a bit early. She says, drive on to the hall, so I did and she got out and went to the front door. She'd been in a good mood all the morning. Pleased at going down to church and all, but soon as I saw her rattling the front door I knew one of her tantrums was coming on. As I was explaining to Mr. Fox, sir, she was a lady that was given to tantrums."

"Yes."

"I watched her. Rattle, rattle, rattle! And then I heard her shouting, 'Who's in there! Let me in!' I thought I could hear the piano, too. Off she goes round to the back. I turned the car. When I looked out again she had come round the other side, the one away from the lane. Her face was red, and, Gawd help us, I thought, here we go, and sure enough she starts yelling out for me to come. 'There's someone in there behaving very suspicious,' she says. 'Take a look through that open window.' I hauled myself up and there wasn't a blooming thing to be seen. 'Where's the piano?' Well, I told her. The piano was there right enough down on the floor by the stage. I knew she was going to tell me to go to the rectory for the key, when I see Miss Prentice coming out of the church. So I drew her attention to Miss Prentice and she was off like a scalded cat, across the lane and down to the church. I followed along slow, it's only a couple of chain or so, and pulled up outside the church."

"What about the box?"

"Pardon, sir?"

"Didn't you get a box out of the shed at the back of the hall for Miss Campanula to stand on in order to look through the window?"

"No, sir. No."

Nigel grinned and whistled softly.

"All right," said Alleyn. "It's no matter. Anything else?"

"No, sir. Miss Prentice come out looking very upset, passed me, and went up the lane. I reckon she was going home by Top Lane."

"Miss Prentice looked upset?"

"She did so, sir. It's my belief Mr. Copeland had sent her off with a flea in her ear, if you'll excuse the liberty."

"Did you watch her go? Look after her, I mean?"

"No, sir, I didn't like, seeing she was looking so queer."

"D'you mean she was crying?"

"She wasn't actually that way, sir. Not shedding tears or anything, but she looked queer. Upset, very down in the mouth."

"You don't know if she went to the hall?"

"No, sir, I can't say. I did have a look in the driving mirror and I saw her cross the road as soon as she'd gone a few steps, but she'd do that, anyway, sir, very likely."

"Gibson, can you remember exactly how the piano looked? Describe it for me as accurately as you possibly can."

Gibson scraped his jaw with his mechanic's hand.

"Down on the floor where it was in the evening, sir. Stool in front of it. No music on it. Er—let's see now. It wasn't quite the same. No, that's right. It *was* kind of different."

Alleyn waited.

"I got it," said Gibson loudly. "Yes, by gum, I got it."

"Yes?"

"Those pot plants was on the edge of the stage and the top of the piano was open."

"Ah," said Alleyn, "I hoped so."

iii

"What's the inner significance of all that?" demanded Nigel when Gibson had gone. "What about this box? Is it the one you had under the window?"

"It is." Alleyn spoke to Fox. "At some time since Gibson hauled himself up to look in at the window, somebody has put an open box there and stood on it. It's left a deep rectangular scar overlapping one of Gibson's prints. I found the box in the outhouse. It wasn't young Georgie. He used the door, and anyway the window would have been above his eye-level. The only footprints are Miss C's and some big ones, no doubt Gibson's. They trod on the turf. The box expert must have come later, perhaps on Saturday, and only stood on the gravel. We'll try the box for prints, but I don't think we'll do any good. When I heard Gibson's story I expected we would find that Miss Campanula had used it. Evidently not. It's a tedious business but we'll have to clear it up. Have you said much to the maids?"

"It looks as if deceased was a proper tartar," said Fox. "I've heard enough to come to the conclusion. Mary, the parlourmaid, you saw just now, sir, seems to have acted as a kind of lady's-maid as well.

Miss Campanula had a very open way with Mary when she was in the mood. Surprising some of the things she used to tell her."

"For instance, Brer Fox?"

"Well, Mr. Alleyn, to Mary's way of thinking, Miss C. was a bit queer on the subject of Mr. Copeland. Potty on him is the way Mary puts it. She says that about the time the rector walks through the village of a morning, deceased used to go and hang about under one pretext or another until she could meet him."

"Oh Lord!" said Alleyn distastefully.

"Yes, it's kind of pitiful, sir, isn't it? Mary says she'd dress herself up, very particularly, walk up to Chipping, and go into the little shop. She'd keep the woman there talking, while she bought some trifle or another, and all the time she'd be looking through the glass door. If the rector showed up, Miss Campanula would be off like lightning. She was a very uncertain tempered lady, and when things went wrong she used to scare the servants by the wild way she talked, saying she'd do something violent, and so on."

"This is getting positively Russian," said Alleyn, "and remarkably depressing. Go on."

"It wasn't so bad till Miss Prentice came. She had it her own way in the parish till then. But Miss Prentice seems to have put her in the shade, as you might say. Miss Prentice beat her to all the top places. She's president of this Y.P.F.C. affair and Miss C. was only secretary. Same sort of thing with the Girl Guides."

"She's never a Girl Guide!" Alleyn ejaculated.

"Seems like it, and she beat Miss C. hands down, teaching the kids knots and camp cookery. Got herself decorated with badges and so on. Started at the bottom and swotted it all up. The local girls didn't fancy it much, but she kind of got round them; and when Lady Appleby gave up the Commissioner's job Miss Prentice got it. Same sort of thing at the Women's Circle and all the other local affairs. Miss P. was too smart for Miss C. They were as thick as thieves; but Mary says sometimes Miss C. would come back from a Friendly meeting or something of the sort, and the things she'd say about Miss Prentice were surprising."

"Oh, Lord!"

"She'd threaten suicide and all the rest of it. Mary knew all about the will. Deceased often talked about it, and as short time back as last Thursday, when they had their dress rehearsal, she said it'd serve Miss Prentice right if she cut her out, but she was too charitable to do that, only she hoped if she did go first the money would be like scalding water on Miss Prentice's conscience. On Friday,

Mary says, she had one of her good days. Went off to confession and came back very pleased. Same thing after the five o'clock affair at Pen Cuckoo, and in the evening she went to some Reading Circle or other at the rectory. She was in high feather when she left, but she didn't get back until eleven—very much later than usual. Gibson says she didn't speak on the way back, and Mary says when she came in she had a scarf pulled round her face and her coat collar turned up and——"

"It wasn't her," said Nigel. "Miss Prentice had disguised herself in Miss C.'s clothes in order to have a look at the will."

"Will you be quiet, Bathgate. Go on, Fox."

"Mary followed her to her room; but she said she didn't want her, and Mary swears she was crying. She heard her go to bed. Mary took in her first tea first thing yesterday morning, and she says Miss Campanula looked shocking. Like an Aunt Sally that had been left out in the rain, was the way Mary put it."

"Graphic! Well?"

"Well, she spent yesterday morning at the hall with the others, but when she came back she wrote a note to the lawyers and gave it to Gibson to post; but she stayed in all yesterday afternoon."

"I knew you had something else up your sleeve," said Alleyn. "Where's the blotting paper?"

Fox smiled blandly.

"It's all right, as it turns out, sir. Here it is."

He took a sheet of blotting paper from the writing-table and handed it to Alleyn. It was a clean sheet with only four lines of writing. Alleyn held it up to an atrocious mirror and read:

"De S

K dly dn our presentative to ee me at our arliest on enience

ours faithfully

RIS C MP NULA."

"Going to alter her will," said Nigel over Alleyn's shoulder.

"Incubus!" said Alleyn. "Miserable parasite! I wouldn't be surprised if you were right. Anything else, Fox?"

"Nothing else, sir. She seemed much as usual when she went down to the performance. She left here at seven. Not being wanted till the second act, she didn't need to be so early."

"And they know of nobody, beyond the lawyers, whom she should inform?"

"Nobody, Mr. Alleyn."

"We'll have some lunch and then visit the rectory. Come on."

When they returned to the Jernigham Arms they found that the representative of the *Chipping Courier* had been all too zealous. A crowd of young men wearing flannel trousers and tweed coats greeted Nigel with a sort of wary and suspicious cordiality, and edged round Alleyn. He gave them a concise account of the piano and its internal arrangements, said nothing at all about the water-pistol, told them the murder appeared to be motiveless, and besought them not to follow him about wherever he went.

"It embarrasses me and it's no use to you. I'll see that you get photographs of the piano."

"Who's the owner of the Colt, chief inspector?" asked a pert young man wearing enormous glasses.

"It's a local weapon, thought to have been stolen," said Alleyn. "If there's anything more from the police, gentlemen, you shall hear of it. You've got enough in the setting of the thing to do your screaming worst. Off you go and do it. Be little Pooh Bahs. No corroborative details required. The narrative is adequately unconvincing, and I understand artistic verisimilitude is not your cup of tea."

"Try us," suggested the young man.

"*Pas si bête*," said Alleyn, "I want my lunch."

"When are you going to be married, Mr. Alleyn?"

"Whenever I get a chance. Good-morning to you."

He left them to badger Nigel.

Alleyn and Fox finished their lunch in ten minutes, left the inn by the back door, and were off in Biggins's car before Nigel had exhausted his flow of profanity. Alleyn left Fox in the village. He was to seek our Friendly Young People, garner more local gossip, and attend the post-mortem. Alleyn turned up the Vale Road, and in five minutes arrived at the rectory.

iv

Like most clerical households on Sunday, the rectory had a semi-public look about it. The front door was wide open. On a hall table Alleyn saw a neat stack of children's hymn-books. A beretta lay beside them. In a room some way down the hall they heard a female voice.

"Very well, Mr. Copeland. Now the day is over."

"I think so," said the rector's voice.

"Through the night of doubt and sorrow," added the lady brightly.

"Do they like that?"

"Aw, they love it, Mr. Copeland."

"Very well," said the rector wearily. "Thank you, Miss Wright."

A large village maiden came out into the hall. She gathered the hymn-books into a straw bag and bustled out, not neglecting to look pretty sharply at Alleyn.

Alleyn rang the bell again, and presently an elderly maid appeared.

"May I see Mr. Copeland?"

"I'll just see, sir. What name, please?"

"Alleyn. I'm from Scotland Yard."

"Oh! Oh, yes, sir. Will you come this way, please?"

He followed her through the hall. She opened a door and said:

"Please, sir, the police."

He walked in.

Mr. Copeland looked as if he had sprung to his feet. At his side was the girl whom Alleyn had recognised as his daughter. They were indeed very much alike, and at this moment their faces spoke of the same mood: they looked startled and alarmed.

Mr. Copeland, in his long cassock, moved forward and shook hands.

"I'm so sorry to worry you like this, sir," said Alleyn. "It's the worst possible day to badger the clergy, I know; but, unfortunately, we can't delay things."

"No, no," said the rector, "we are only too anxious. This is my daughter. I'm afraid I don't——"

"Alleyn, sir."

"Oh, yes. Yes. Do sit down. Dinah, dear?"

"Please don't go, Miss Copeland," said Alleyn. "I hope you may be able to help us."

Evidently they had been sitting with the village maiden in front of the open fireplace. The chairs, drawn up in a semi-circle, were comfortably shabby. The fire, freshly mended with enormous logs, crackled companionably and lent warmth to the faded apple-green walls, the worn beams, the rector's agreeable prints, and a pot of bronze chrysanthemums from the Pen Cuckoo glasshouses.

They sat down, Dinah primly in the centre chair, Alleyn and the rector on either side of her.

Something of Alleyn's appreciation of this room may have appeared in his face. His hand went to his jacket pocket and was hurriedly withdrawn.

"Do smoke your pipe," said Dinah quickly.

"That was very well observed," said Alleyn. "I'm sure you will be able to help us. May I, really?"

"Please."

"It's very irregular," said Alleyn; "but I think I might, you know."

And as he lit his pipe he was visited by a strange thought. It came into his mind that he stood on the threshold of a new friendship, that he would return to this old room and again sit before the fire. He thought of the woman he loved, and it seemed to him that she would be there, too, at this future time, and that she would be happy. "An odd notion!" he thought, and dismissed it.

The rector was speaking: "——Terribly distressed. It is appalling to think that among the people one knows so well there should have been one heart that nursed such dreadful anger against a fellow-creature."

"Yes," said Alleyn. "The impulse to kill, I suppose, is dormant in most people; but when it finds expression we are so shockingly astonished. I have noticed that very often. The reaction after murder is nearly always one of profound astonishment."

"To me," said Dinah, "the most horrible thing about this business is the grotesque side of it. It's like an appalling joke."

"You've heard the way of it, then?"

"I don't suppose there's a soul within twenty miles who hasn't," said Dinah.

"Ah," said Alleyn. "The industrious Roper."

He lit his pipe and, looking over his thin hands at them, said, "Before I forget, did either of you put a box outside one of the hall windows late on Friday or some time on Saturday?"

"No."

"No."

"I see. It's no matter."

The rector said, "Perhaps I shouldn't ask, but have you any idea at all of who——?"

"None," said Alleyn. "At the moment, none. There are so many things to be cleared up before the case can begin to make a pattern. One of them concerns the key of the hall. Where was it on Friday?"

"On a nail between an outhouse and the main building," said Dinah.

"I thought that was only on Saturday."

"No. I left it there on Friday for the Friendly Circle members who worked in the lunch hour. They moved the furniture and swept up, and things. When they left at two o'clock they hung the key on the nail."

"But Miss Campanula tried to get in at about half-past two and couldn't."

"I don't think Miss Campanula knew about the key. I told the girls, and I think I said something about it at the dress rehearsal in case the others wanted to get in, but I'm pretty sure Miss Campanula had gone by then.

"We've never hung it there before."

"Did you go to the hall on Friday?"

"Yes," said Dinah. "I went in the lunch hour to supervise the work. I came away before they had quite finished, and returned here."

"And then you walked up Top Lane towards Pen Cuckoo?"

"Yes," said Dinah in surprise, and into her eyes came that same guarded look he had seen in Henry's.

"Was Georgie Biggins in the hall when you left at about two o'clock?"

"Yes. Making life hideous with his masterly water-pistol. He *is* a naughty boy, Daddy," said Dinah. "I really think you ought to exorcise Georgie. I'm sure he's possessed of a devil."

"Then you haven't heard about Georgie?" murmured Alleyn. "Roper has his points."

"What about Georgie?"

Alleyn told them.

"I want," he said, "to make as little as possible of the obvious implication. There seems to be little doubt that Georgie, plus Twiddletoy, and his water-pistol made the bullets that the murderer subsequently fired. It's an unpleasant responsibility to lay on a small boy's shoulders, however bad he may be. I'm afraid it must come out in evidence, but as far as possible I think we ought to try and avoid village gossip."

"Certainly," said the rector. "At the same time, he knew he was doing something wrong. The terrible consequences——"

"Are disproportionately terrible, don't you think."

"I do. I agree with you," said Dinah.

Alleyn, seeing priest's logic in the rector's eye, hurried on.

"You will see," he said, "that the substitution of the Colt for the water-pistol must have taken place after two o'clock on Friday when Georgie was flourishing his pistol. I know he stayed behind on Friday and rigged it up. He had admitted this. Miss Campanula's chauffeur, at her request, looked through the open window at two-thirty and saw the piano with the top open. His story leads us to believe that at that time Georgie was hiding somewhere in the building. Georgie did not tell me that at all willingly, and I confess I am afraid the memory of Miss Campanula, banging at the doors and demanding admittance, is likely to become a childish nightmare. I don't pretend to understand child psychology."

"The law," said Dinah, "in the person of her officer, seems to be surprisingly merciful."

Alleyn disregarded this.

"So that gives us two-thirty on Friday as a starting-off point. You, Miss Copeland, walked up Top Lane and by chance encountered Mr. Henry Jernigham."

"What!" the rector ejaculated. "Dinah!"

"It's all right," said Dinah in a high voice. "It *was* by accident, Daddy. I did meet Henry and we did behave as you might have expected. Our promise was almost up. It's my fault. I couldn't help it."

"Miss Prentice arrived some time later, I believe," said Alleyn.

"Has she told you that?"

"Mr. Henry Jernigham told me and Miss Prentice agreed. Do you mind, Miss Copeland, describing what happened at this triple encounter?"

"If they haven't told you," said Dinah, "I won't."

CHAPTER SEVENTEEN

Confession From a Priest

i

"WON'T YOU?" said Alleyn mildly. "That's a pity. We shall have to do the Peer Gynt business."

"What's that?"

"Go roundabout. Ask servants about the relationship between Miss Prentice and her young cousin. Tap the fabulous springs of village gossip—all that."

"I thought," flashed Dinah, "that nowadays the C.I.D. was almost a gentleman's job."

"Oh, no!" said Alleyn. "You couldn't be more mistaken."

Her face was scarlet. "That was a pretty squalid remark of mine," said Dinah.

"It was inexcusable, my dear," said her father. "I am ashamed that you have been capable of it."

"I find no offence in it at all," Alleyn said cheerfully. "It was entirely apposite."

But Mr. Copeland's face was pink with embarrassment, and Dinah's still crimson with mortification. The rector addressed her as if she was a children's service. His voice became more markedly clerical, and in the movement of his head Alleyn recognised one of his pulpit mannerisms. He said, "You have broken a solemn promise, Dinah, and to this fault you add a deliberate evasion and an ill-bred and entirely unjustifiable impertinence. You force me to make Mr. Alleyn some sort of explanation." He turned to Alleyn. "My daughter and Henry Jernigham," he said, "have formed an attachment of which his father and I do not approve. Dinah suggested that they should give their word not to meet alone for three weeks. Friday was the final day of the three weeks. Miss Prentice was also of our mind in this matter. If she came upon them at a moment when, as Dinah has admitted, they had completely forgotten or ignored this promise, I am sure she was extremely disappointed and distressed."

"She wasn't!" exclaimed Dinah, rallying a little. "She wasn't a bit like that. She was absolutely livid with rage and beastliness."

"Dinah!"

"Oh, Daddy, *why* do you shut your eyes? You must know what she's like—you of all people!"

"Dinah, I must insist——"

"No!" cried Dinah. "No! First you say I've been underhand; and then, when I go all upperhand and open, you don't like it any better. I'm sorry in a way that Henry and I didn't stay the course; but we nearly did, and I *won't* think there was anything very awful about Friday afternoon. I won't have Henry and me made seem grubby. I'm sorry I was rude to Mr. Alleyn and I—well, I mean it's quite obvious it wasn't only rude, but silly. I mean, it's obvious from the way he's taken it—I mean—oh, hell! Oh, Daddy, I'm sorry."

Alleyn choked down a laugh.

The rector said, "Dinah! Dinah!"

"Yes, well, I *am* sorry. And now Mr. Alleyn will think heaven knows what about Friday afternoon. I may as well tell you, Mr. Alleyn, that in Henry's and my opinion Miss Prentice is practically ravers. It's a well-known phenomenon with old maids. She's tried to sublimate her natural appetites and—and—work them off in religion. I can't help it, Daddy, she *has*. And it's been a failure. She's only repressed and repressed, and when she sees two natural, healthy people making love to each other she goes off pop."

"It is I," said the rector, looking hopelessly at his child, "who have been a failure."

"*Don't*. You haven't. It's just that you don't understand these women. You're an angel, but you're not a modern angel."

"I should be interested to know," said Alleyn, "how an angel brings himself up to date. Stream-lined wings, I suppose."

Dinah grinned.

"Well, you know what I mean," she said. "And I'm right about these two. If you had heard Miss Prentice! It was simply too shaming and hideous. She actually shook all over and sort of gasped. And she said the most ghastly things to us. She threatened at once to tell you, Daddy, and the squire. She suggested—oh, she was beyond belief. What's more, she dribbles and spits."

"Dinah, my dear!"

"Well, Daddy, she *does*. I noticed the front of her beastly dress, and it was *disgusting*. She either dribbles and spits, or else she spills her tea. Honestly! And, anyway, she was perfectly *sceptic*, the things she said."

"Didn't either of you try to stop her?" asked Alleyn.

"Yes," said Dinah. She turned rather white and added quickly: "In the end she just blundered past us and went on up the lane."

"What did you do?"

"I went home."

"And Mr. Jernigham?"

"He went up to Cloudyfold, I think."

"By the steep path? He didn't walk down with you?"

"No," said Dinah. "He didn't. There's nothing in that."

ii

"I cannot see," said the rector, "that this unhappy story can have any bearing on the tragedy."

"I think I can promise," said Alleyn, "that any information found to be irrelevant will be completely blotted out. We are, quite literally, not interested in any facts that cannot be brought into the pattern."

"Well, that can't," Dinah declared. She threw up her chin and said loudly:

"If you think, because Miss Prentice made us feel uncomfortable and embarrassed, it's a motive for murder, you're quite wrong. We're not in the least afraid of Miss Prentice or anything she may say or do. It can't make any difference to Henry and me." Dinah's lower lip trembled and she added: "We simply look at her from a detached analytical angle and are vaguely sorry for her. That's all." She uttered a dry sob.

The rector said: "Oh, my darling child, what nonsense," and Dinah walked over to the window.

"Well," said Alleyn mildly, "let's go on being detached and analytical. What did you both do on Saturday afternoon? That's yesterday."

"We were both in here," said Dinah. "Daddy went to sleep. I went over my part."

"What time did you get to the hall last evening?"

"We left here at half-past six," answered Mr. Copeland, "and walked over by the path through our garden and wood."

"Was anybody there?"

"Yes. Yes, Gladys Wright was there, wasn't she, Dinah? She is one of our best workers and was in charge of the programmes. She was in the front of the hall. I think the other girls were either there, or came in soon after we did."

"Can you tell me exactly what you did up to the time of the catastrophe?"

"I can, certainly," rejoined the rector. "I saw that the copy of the play and the bicycle bell I had to ring were in their right places, and then I sat in an arm-chair on the stage to keep out of the way and see that nobody came in from the front of the hall. I was there until Dinah came for me to speak to Miss Prentice."

"Did you expect Miss Prentice would be unable to play?"

"No, indeed. On the contrary, she told me her finger was much better. That was soon after she arrived."

"Had you much difficulty in persuading Miss Prentice not to play?"

"Yes, indeed I had. She was most determined about it, but her finger was really very bad. It was quite impossible, and I told her I should be very displeased if she persisted."

"And apart from that time you never left the stage?"

"Oh! Oh, yes, I *did* go to the telephone before that, when they were trying to get Mrs. Ross's house. That was at half-past seven. The telephone is an extension of ours and our maid, Mary, is deaf and takes a long time to answer."

"We were all frantic," said Dinah, from the window. "The squire and Henry and father and I were all standing round the telephone, with Miss Campanula roaring instructions, poor old thing. The squire hadn't got any trousers on, only pink woollen underpants. Miss Prentice came along, and when she saw him she cackled like a hen and flew away, but no one else minded about the squire's pants, not even Miss C. We were all in a flat spin about the others being late, you see. Father was just coming over to ring from here, when we got through."

"I returned to the stage then," said the rector.

"I can't tell you exactly what I did," said Dinah. "I was all over the place." She peered through the window. "Here's Henry now."

"Why not go and meet him?" suggested Alleyn. "Tell him how I've bullied you."

"You haven't, but I will," said Dinah.

She opened the window and stepped over the low sill into the garden.

"I'm so sorry," said Alleyn, when the window had slammed.

"She's a good child, really," said the rector sadly.

"I'm sure she is. Mr. Copeland, you see what a strange position we are in, don't you? If Miss Prentice was the intended victim we must trace her movements, her conversation—yes, and if we could, even her thoughts during these last days. We are in the extraordinary position of having, apparently, a living victim in a case of homicide. There is even the possibility that the murderer may make a second attempt."

"No! No! That's too horrible."

"I am sure that, as your daughter says, you know a great deal about these two ladies—the actual and, as far as we know, the intended victim. Can you tell me anything, anything at all, that may throw a glint of light on this dark tangle of emotions?"

The rector clasped his hands and stared into the fire.

"I am very greatly troubled," he said. "I cannot see my way."

"Do you mean that you have got their confidence, and that under ordinary circumstances you would never speak of your knowledge?"

"Let me make myself clear. As no doubt you already know, I have heard the confessions of many of my parishioners. Under no condition will I break the seal of the confessional. That goes without saying. Moreover, it would serve no purpose if I did. I tell you this lest you should think I hold a key to the mystery."

"I recognise the position," said Alleyn, "and I shall respect it."

"I'm glad of that. There are many people, I know, who regard the sacrament of confession in the Anglo-Catholic Church as an amateurish substitute for the Roman use. It is no such thing. The Romans say, 'You must,' the Protestant Nonconformists say, 'You must not,' the Catholic Church of England says, 'You may!' "

But Alleyn was not there for doctrinal argument, and wouldn't have welcomed it under any circumstances.

He said, "I realise that a priest who hears confession, no matter what faith he professes, must regard the confessional as inviolate. That, I take, is not what troubles you. Do you perhaps wonder if you should tell me something that you have heard from one of your penitents outside the confessional?"

The rector gave him a startled glance. He clasped his hands more tightly and said:

"It is not that I believe it would be any help. It's only that I am burdened with the memory and with a terrible doubt. You say that this murderer may strike again. I don't believe that is possible. I am sure it is not possible."

"Why?" asked Alleyn in astonishment.

"Because I believe that the murderer is dead," said the rector.

iii

Alleyn turned in his chair and regarded Mr. Copeland for some seconds before he answered.

At last he said: "You think she did it herself?"

"I am sure of it."

"Will you tell me why?"

"I suppose I must. Mr. Alleyn, I am not, unfortunately, a man of strong character. All my life I have avoided unpleasantness. I know this very well and try to conquer my weakness. I have vacillated when I should have insisted; temporised when I should have taken definite action. Because of these veritable sins of omission I believe I am morally responsible, or at any rate in part responsible, for this terrible crime."

He paused, still looking at the fire. Alleyn waited.

"On Friday night," said Mr. Copeland, "the Reading Circle met in the rectory dining-room. It usually meets in St. Giles Hall; but because of the preparations for the play they all came here instead. It was Miss Campanula's turn to preside. I went in for a short time. Dinah read a scene from *Twelfth Night* for them, and after that they went on with their book. It is G. K. Chesterton's *The Ball and the Cross,* and Miss Campanula had borrowed my copy. When they had finished she came in here to return it. I was alone. It was about a quarter past ten."

"Yes?"

"Mr. Alleyn, it is very difficult and disagreeable for me to tell you of this incident. Really, I—I—don't know quite how to begin. You may not be familiar with parochial affairs, but I think many clergy find that there is an unfortunately rather common type of church worker who is always a problem to her parish priest. I don't know if you will understand me when I say that one finds this type among—dear me—among ladies who are not perhaps very young and who have no other interests."

The rector was now very pink.

"I think I understand," said Alleyn.

"Do you? Well, I am sorry to say poor Miss Campanula was really an advanced—er—specimen of this type. Poor soul, she was lonely and she had a difficult temperament which I am sure she did her best to discipline, but at times I could not help thinking that she needed a doctor as well as a priest to help her. I have even suggested as much."

"That was very wise advice, sir."

"She didn't take it," said the rector wistfully. "She stuck to me, you see, and I'm afraid I failed her."

"About Friday night?" Alleyn reminded him gently.

"Yes, I know. I'm coming to Friday night; but, really, it's *very* difficult. There was a terrible scene. She—I think she had got it into her head that if Dinah married or went away again—Dinah is on the stage, you know—I should be as lonely as she was. She said as much. I was very much startled and alarmed and I was at a loss how to reply. I think she misunderstood my silence. I really can't quite remember the order of events. It was rather like a bad dream, and still is. She was trembling dreadfully and looking at me with such a desperate expression in her eyes that I—I—I——"

He shut his eyes tight and added in a great hurry: "I patted her hand."

"That was quite a natural thing to do, wasn't it?"

"You wouldn't have said so if you'd seen the result."

"No?"

"No, indeed. The next moment she was, to be frank, in my arms. It was without any exception the most awful thing that has ever happened to me. She was sobbing and laughing at the same time. I was in agony. I couldn't release myself. We never draw our blinds in this room, and there was I in this appalling and even ludicrous situation. I was obliged actually to—to support her. And I was so sorry for her, too. It was so painfully evident that she had made a frightful mistake. I believe she was hysterically delighted. It makes me feel ashamed and, as we used to say when I was young, caddish to repeat all this."

"It's beastly for you," said Alleyn; "but I'm sure you should tell me."

"I would have preferred, before doing so, to take the advice of one of my brother clergy, but there is no one who—— However, that is beside the point. You are being very patient."

"How did it end?"

"Very badly," said the rector, opening his eyes wide. "It couldn't have ended worse. When she had quietened down a little—and it was a long time before she did—I hastened to release myself, and I am afraid the first thing I did was to draw the curtains. You see, some members of the Reading Circle might still have been about. Their young men come up to meet them. Worse than that, Miss

Prentice rang up in the morning and said she wanted to speak to me that evening. While Miss Campanula was still with me she telephoned to say she was not coming. That was about 10.15. Dinah took the message and afterwards said she sounded upset. I—I'm afraid I had been obliged to be rather severe with her—I mean as her priest—that afternoon. I had given her certain instructions which would keep her at home, and in any case I think perhaps her finger was too painful. But at the time I expected her, and if she had seen, it would have been—well, really——"

The rector gulped and added quickly: "But that is beside the point. I drew the curtains, and in my flurry I said something to Miss Campanula about expecting Miss Prentice. It turned out that I couldn't have said anything worse, because when I tried to tell this unfortunate soul that she was mistaken, she connected my explanation with Miss Prentice's visit."

"Help!" said Alleyn.

"What did you say? Yes. Yes, indeed. She became quite frantic and I really can *not* repeat what she said, but she uttered the most dreadful abuse of Miss Prentice and, in a word, she suggested that Miss Prentice had supplanted her, not only in the affairs of the parish, but in my personal regard. I became angry—just angry, as I thought at the time. As her priest I ordered her to stop. I rebuked her and reminded her of the deadly sin of envy. I told her that she must drive out this wickedness from her heart by prayer and fasting. She became much quieter, but as she left she said one sentence that I shall never forget. She turned in the doorway and said, 'If I killed myself she would suffer for it; but if, as I stand here in this room, I could strike Eleanor Prentice dead, I'd do it!' And before I could answer her she had gone out and shut the door."

iv

"Darling," said Henry, "I think I'd better tell him."

"But *why?*"

"Because I believe Eleanor will if I don't."

"How could she? It would be too shaming for her. She'd have to say how she behaved when she saw us."

"No, she wouldn't. She'd just twist it round somehow so that it looked as if she found us in a compromising position and that you were covered with scarlet shame and I was furious and threatened to scrag her."

"But, Henry, that would be a deliberate attempt to make him suspect you."

"I wouldn't put it past her."

"Well, I would. If you were tried for murder, it'd be a pretty good scandal, and she wouldn't care for that at all."

"No, that's true enough. Perhaps I may as well keep quiet."

"I should say you'd better."

"Dinah," said Henry, "who do you think——?"

"I *can't* think. It seems incredible that any of us should do it. It just isn't possible."

"Daddy thinks she did it herself. He won't say why."

"What, fixed it up for Eleanor and then at the last minute decided to take the count herself?"

"I suppose so. It must be something she said to him."

"What do you think of Alleyn?" asked Henry abruptly.

"I like him. Golly, I was rude to him," said Dinah, hurling another log of wood on the schoolroom fire.

"Were you, my sweet?"

"Yes. I implied he was no gent."

"Well, that was a lie," said Henry cheerfully.

"I know it was. He couldn't have been nicer about it. How I could! Daddy was livid."

"Naturally. Honestly, Dinah!"

"I know."

"I love you all the way to the Great Bear and round the Southern Cross and back again."

"Henry," said Dinah suddenly, "don't let's ever be jealous."

"All right. Why?"

"I keep thinking of those two. If they hadn't been jealous I don't believe this would have happened."

"Good heavens, Dinah, you don't think Eleanor——"

"No. But I sort of feel as if the whole thing was saturated in their jealousy. I mean, it was only jealousy that made them so beastly to each other and to us and to that shifty beast, Mrs. Ross."

"Why do you call her a shifty beast?"

"Because I know in my bones she is," said Dinah.

"I must say I wish my papa would restrain his middle-aged ardours when he encounters her. His antics are so damn' silly."

"Daddy's completely diddled by her conversion to his ways. She's put her name down for the retreat in Advent."

"That's not so bad as my parent's archness. I could wish she didn't respond in kind, I must say. Apart from that, I don't mind the lady."

"You're a man."

"Oh, nonsense," said Henry, answering the implication.

"I wouldn't trust her," said Dinah, "as far as I could toss a grand piano."

"Why bring pianos into it?"

"Well, I wouldn't. She's the sort that's always called a man's woman."

"It's rather a stupid sort of phrase," said Henry.

"It simply means," said Dinah, "that she's nice to men and would let a woman down as soon as look at her!"

"I should have thought it just meant that she was too attractive to be popular with her own sex."

"Darling, that's simply a masculine cliché," said Dinah. "I don't think so."

"There are tons of devastating women who are enormously popular with their own sex."

Henry smiled.

"Do you think she's attractive?" asked Dinah casually.

"Yes, very. I dare say she's rather a little bitch, but she is pleasing. For one thing, her clothes fit her."

"Yes, they do," said Dinah sombrely. "They must cost the earth."

Henry kissed her.

"I'm a low swine," he muttered. "I was being tiresome. You're my dear darling and I'm no more fit to love you than a sweep, but I do love you so much."

"We must never be jealous," whispered Dinah.

"Dinah!" called the rector in the hall below.

"Yes, Daddy?"

"Where are you?"

"In the schoolroom."

"May I go up, do you think?" asked a deep voice.

"That's Alleyn," said Henry.

"Come up here, Mr. Alleyn," called Dinah.

CHAPTER EIGHTEEN

Mysterious Lady

i

"SIT DOWN, Mr. Alleyn," said Dinah. "The chairs are all rather rickety in this room, I'm afraid. You know Henry, don't you?"

"Yes, rather," said Alleyn. "I'll have this, if I may."

He squatted on a stuffed footstool in front of the fire.

"I told Henry how rude I'd been," said Dinah.

"I was horrified," said Henry. "She's very young, poor girl."

"You couldn't by any chance just settle down and spin us some yarns about crime?" suggested Dinah.

"I'm afraid not. It would be delightful to settle down, but you see we're not allowed to get familiar when we're on duty. It looks impertinent. I've got a monstrous lot of things to do before to-night."

"Do you just collect stray bits of evidence," asked Henry, "and hope they'll make sense?"

"More or less. You scavenge and then you arrange everything and try and see the pattern."

"Suppose there's no pattern?"

"There must be. It's a question of clearing away the rubbish."

"Any sign of it so far?" asked Dinah.

"Not a great many signs."

"Do you suspect either of us?"

"Not particularly."

"Well, we didn't do it," said Dinah.

"Good."

"Cases of homicide," said Henry, "must be different from any other kind. Especially cases that occur in these sorts of surroundings. You're not dealing with the ordinary criminal classes."

"True enough," said Alleyn. "I'm dealing with people like yourselves who will be devastatingly frank up to a certain point—far franker than the practical criminal, who lies to the police from sheer force of habit—but who will probably bring a good deal more *savoir faire* to the business of withholding essentials. For instance, I know jolly well there's something more to that meeting you both had with Miss Prentice on Friday afternoon; but it's no good saying to you, as I would to Posh Jimmy: 'Come on, now. It's not you I'm after. Tell me what I want to know and perhaps we'll forget all about that little job over at Moorton.' Unfortunately, I've nothing against you."

"That's exactly what I mean," said Henry. "Still, you can always go for my Cousin Eleanor."

"Yes. That's what I'll have to do," agreed Alleyn.

"Well, I hope you don't believe everything she tells you," said Dinah, "or you *will* get in a muddle. Where we're concerned she's as sour as a quince."

"And, anyway, she's practically certifiable," added Henry. "It's a question which was dottiest: Eleanor or Miss C."

"Lamentable," said Alleyn vaguely. "Mr. Jernigham, did you put a box outside one of the hall windows after 2.30 on Friday?"

"No."

"What *is* this about a box?" asked Dinah.

"Nothing much. About the piano. When did those aspidistras make their appearance?"

"They were there on Saturday morning, anyway," said Dinah. "I meant to have them taken away. They must have masked the stage from the audience. I think the girls put them there after I left on Friday."

"In which case Georgie moved them off to rig his pistol."

"And the murderer," Henry pointed out, "must have moved them again."

"Yes."

"I wonder when," said Henry.

"So do we. Miss Copeland, did you see Miss Campanula on Friday night?"

"Friday night? Oh, I saw her at the Reading Circle meeting in the dining-room."

"Not afterwards?"

"No. As soon as I got out of the dining-room I came up here. She went into the study to see Daddy. I could just hear her voice scolding away as usual, I should think, poor thing."

"The study is beneath this room, isn't it?"

"Yes. I wanted to have a word with Daddy, but I waited until I heard her and the other person go."

Alleyn only paused for a second before he said:

"The other person?"

"There was somebody else in the study with Miss C. I can't help calling her 'Miss C.' We all did."

"How do you know there was someone else there?"

"Well, because they left after Miss C.," said Dinah impatiently. "It wasn't Miss Prentice, because she rang up from Pen Cuckoo just about that time. Mary called me to the telephone, so I suppose it must have been Gladys Wright. She's leader of the Reading Circle. She lives up the lane. She must have gone out by the window in the study, because I heard the lane gate give a squeak. That's how I knew she'd been here."

Alleyn walked over to the window. It looked down on a gravelled path, a lawn, and a smaller earthen path that led to a rickety gate and evidently ran on beyond it through a small plantation to the lane.

"I suppose you always go that way to the hall?" asked Alleyn.

"Oh, yes. It's much shorter than going round the house from the front door."

"Yes," said Alleyn, "it would be."

He looked thoughtfully at Dinah and said, "Did you hear this other person's voice?"

"Hi!" said Dinah. "What *is* all this? No, I didn't. Ask Daddy. He'll tell you who it was."

"Stupid of me," said Alleyn. "Of course he will."

ii

He didn't ask the rector, but before he left he crunched boldly round the gravel path and walked across the lawn to the gate. It certainly creaked very loudly. It was one of those old-fashioned gates that has a post stile beside it. The path was evidently used very often. There was no hope of finding anything useful on its hard but greasy surface. There had been too much rain since Friday night. "Much too much rain," sighed Alleyn. But just inside the gate he found two softened but unmistakable depressions. Horseshoe-shaped holes about two inches in diameter that had held water. "Heels," he thought, "but not a hope of saying whose. Female. Stood there a long time facing the house." He could see the rector crouched over the study fire. "Oh, well," he said, and plunged into the little wood. "Nothing at all that's to the purpose. Nothing."

He saw that the hall was only a little way up on the other side from where this path came out on the lane. He returned, circled the rectory, perfectly aware that Dinah and Henry had watched him from the schoolroom window. As he got into the car Henry opened the window and leaned out.

"I say," he shouted.

"Shut up," said Dinah's voice behind him. "*Don't*, Henry."

"What is it?" called Alleyn, squinting up through his driving-window.

"It's nothing," said Dinah. "He's gone ravers, that's all. Good-bye."

Henry's head shot out of sight and the window slammed.

"Now I wonder," thought Alleyn, "if Master Henry has got the same idea as I have."

He drove away.

At the Jernigham Arms he found Nigel, but no Fox.

"Where are you going?" Nigel demanded when Alleyn returned to the car.

"To call on a lady."

"Let me come."

"Why the devil?"

"I won't go in with you if you'd rather not."

"Naturally. All right. I can do with some comic relief."

"Oh, God, your only jig-maker," said Nigel and got in. "Now, who's the lady?" he said. "Speak up, dearie."

"Mrs. Ross."

"The mysterious stranger."

"Why do you call her that?"

"It's the part she played in their show. I've got a programme."

"So it is," said Alleyn.

He turned the car up the Vale Road and presently he began to talk. He went over the history of the case from midday on Friday. As far as he could, he traced the movements of the murdered woman and each of her seven companions. He correlated their movements and gave Nigel a time-table he had jotted down in his note-book.

"I hate these damn' things," Nigel grumbled. "They shatter my interest; they remind me of a Bradshaw, and they are therefore completely unintelligible."

"It's a pity about you," said Alleyn dryly. "Look at the list at the bottom."

Nigel looked and read:

"Piano. Drawing-pin holes. Automatic. Branch. Onion. Chopsticks. Key. Letter. Creaky gate. Window. Telephone."

"Thank you," said Nigel. "Now, of course, I see the whole thing in a blinding flash. It's as clear as the mud in your eye. The onion is particularly obvious, and as for the drawing-pins—— It's ludicrous that I didn't spot the exquisite reason of the drawing-pins."

He returned the paper to Alleyn.

"Go on," he continued acidly. "Say it. 'You have the facts, Bathgate. You know my methods, Bathgate. What of the little grey cells, Bathgate?' Sling in a quotation; add: 'Oh, my dear chap,' and vanish in a fog of composite fiction."

"This is Cloudyfold," said Alleyn. "Cold, isn't it? They had twelve degrees of frost on the pub thermometer last night."

"Oh, Mr. Mercury, how you did startle me!"

"That must be Mrs. Ross's cottage down there."

"Can't I come in as your stenographer?"

"Very well. I may send you out on an errand into the village."

Duck Cottage stands in a bend of the road before it actually reaches Cloudyfold Village. It is a typical Dorset cottage, plain fronted, well proportioned, cold-grey and weather-worn. Mrs. Ross had smartened it up. The window sashes and sills and the front door were painted vermilion, and a vermilion tub with a Noah's Ark tree stood on each side of the entrance which led straight off the road.

Alleyn gave a double rap on the shiny brass knocker.

The door was opened by a maid, all cherry-red and muslin. Mrs. Ross was at home. The maid took Alleyn's card away with her and returned to usher them in.

Alleyn had to stoop his head under the low doorway, and the ceilings were not much higher. They walked through a tiny ante-room, down some uneven steps and into Mrs. Ross's parlour. She was not there. It was a charming parlour looking out on a small formal garden. There were old prints on the walls, one or two respectable pieces of furniture, a deep carpet, some very comfortable chairs, and a general air of chintz, sparkle and femininity. It was a delicate little room. Alleyn looked at a bookcase filled with modern novels. He noticed one or two works by authors whose sole distinction had been conferred by the censor, and at three popular collections of famous criminal cases. They all had startling wrappers and photographic illustrations. Within their covers one would find the cases of Brown and Kennedy, Bywaters, Seddon, and Stinie Morrison. Their style would be characterized by a certain arch taciturnity. Alleyn grinned to himself and took one of them from the shelf. He let it fall open in his hands and a discourse on dactylography faced him. The groove between the pages was filled with cigarette ash. A photograph of prints developed and enlarged from a letter illustrated the written matter. A woman's voice sounded. Alleyn returned the book to its place. The door opened and Mrs. Ross came in.

She was the lady Alleyn had noticed in church. This did not surprise him much, but it made him feel wary. She greeted him with a sensible good-humoured air, shook hands and them gave him a slanting smile.

"This is Mr. Bathgate," said Alleyn. He noticed that Nigel's fingers had flown to his tie.

She settled them by the fire with the prettiest air in the world, and he saw her glance at the little cupid clock on the mantlepiece.

"I do think all this is too ghastly," she said. "That poor wretched old creature! How anybody could!"

"It's a bad business," said Alleyn.

She offered them cigarettes. Alleyn refused and Nigel, rather unwillingly, followed suit. Mrs. Ross took one and leaned towards Alleyn for a light.

"*Chanel, Numero Cinq*," thought Alleyn.

"I've never been 'investigated' before," said Mrs. Ross. "Dear me, that sounds rather peculiar, doesn't it? I don't mean what you mean."

She chuckled. Nigel uttered rather a flirtatious laugh, caught Alleyn's eye and was silent.

Alleyn said, "I shan't bother you for long, I hope. We've got to try and find out where everybody was from about midday on Friday up to the moment of the disaster."

"Heavens!" said Mrs. Ross. "I'll never be able to remember that; and if I do, it's sure to sound too incriminating for words."

"I hope not," said Alleyn sedately. "We've got a certain amount of it already. On Friday you went to a short five o'clock rehearsal at Pen Cuckoo, didn't you?"

"Yes. Apart from that, I was at home all day."

"And Friday evening?"

"Still at home. We aren't very gay in Cloudyfold, Mr. Alleyn. I think I've dined out twice since I came here. The county is simply rushing me, as you see."

"On Saturday evening I suppose you joined the others at the hall?"

"Yes. I carted down one or two things they wanted for the stage. We towed them in a trailer behind Dr. Templett's Morris."

"Did you go straight to the hall?"

"No. We called at Pen Cuckoo. I'd quite forgotten that. I didn't get out of the car."

"Dr. Templett went into the study?"

"He went into the house," she said lightly. "I don't know which room."

"He didn't return by the french window?"

"I don't remember." She paused and then added: "The squire, Mr. Jernigham, came and talked to me. I didn't notice Dr. Templett until he was actually at the car window."

"Ah, yes. You came back here for lunch?"

"Yes."

"And in the afternoon?"

"Saturday afternoon. That's only yesterday, isn't it? Heavens, it seems a lifetime! Oh, I took the supper down to the hall."

"At what time?"

"I think it was about half-past three when I got there."

"Was the hall empty?"

"Yes. No, it wasn't. Dr. Templett was there. He arrived just after I did. He'd brought down his clothes."

"How long did you stay there, Mrs. Ross?"

"I don't know. Not long. It might have been half an hour."

"And Dr. Templett?"

"He left before I did. I was putting out sandwiches."

"And cutting up onions?"

"*Onions!* Good Lord, why should I do that? No, thank you. I'm sick at the sight of one, and I have got some respect for my hands."

They were luxurious little hands. She held them to the fire.

"I'm sorry," said Alleyn. "There was an onion in the supper-room."

"I don't know how it got there. The supper-room was all scrubbed out on Friday."

"It's no matter. Did you look at the piano on Saturday afternoon?"

"No, I don't think so. The curtain was down, so I suppose if anything had been out of order I shouldn't have noticed. I didn't go to the front of the hall. The one key opens both doors."

"And only Dr. Templett came in?"

"Yes."

"Could any one have come unnoticed into the front of the hall while you were in the supper-room?"

"I suppose they might have. No. No, of course they couldn't. We had the key and the front door was locked."

"Did Dr. Templett go into the auditorium at all?"

"Only to shut the window."

"Which window was open?"

"It's rather odd," she said quickly. "I'm sure I shut it in the morning."

iii

"It's the window on the side away from the lane, nearest the front," continued Mrs. Ross after a pause. "I remember that, just as we were leaving, I pulled it down in case the rain blew in. That was at midday."

"Were you the last to leave at noon?"

"No. Well, we all left together; but I think Dr. Templett and I actually walked out first. The Copelands always leave by the back door."

"So presumably someone reopened the window?"

"Presumably."

"Were you on the stage when Dr. Templett shut the window?"

"Yes."

"What were you doing there?"

"We—I tidied it up and arranged one or two ornaments I'd brought."

"Dr. Templett helped you?"

"He—well, he looked on."

"And all this time the window was open?"

"Yes, I suppose so. Yes, of course it was."

"Did you tell him you thought you had shut it?"

"Yes."

"You don't think somebody pushed it open from outside?"

"No," she said positively. "We were certain they didn't. The curtain was up. We'd have seen."

"I thought you said the curtain was down."

"Oh, how stupid of me. It was up when we got there, but we let it down. It was supposed to be down. I wanted to try the effect of a lamp I'd taken."

"Did you lower the curtain before or after you noticed the window?"

"I don't remember. Oh. Yes, please, I think it was afterwards."

She leaned forward and looked at Nigel, who had been making notes.

"It's simply petrifying to see all this going down," she said to him. "Do I read it over and sign it?"

"It would have to go into long-hand first," said Nigel.

"Do let me see."

He gave her his notes.

"They look exactly like journalists' copy," said Mrs. Ross.

"That's our cunning," said Nigel boldly, but rather red in the face.

She laughed and gave them back to him.

"Mr. Alleyn thinks we're terribly flippant, I can see," she said. "Don't you, inspector?"

"No," said Alleyn. "I regard Bathgate as a zealous and serious-minded young officer."

Nigel tried to look zealous and serious-minded. He was a little shaken.

"You mustn't forget that telegram, Bathgate," added Alleyn. "I think you'd better go into Cloudyfold and send it. You can pick me up on the way back. Mrs. Ross will excuse you."

"Very good, sir," said Nigel and left.

"What a very charming young man," said Mrs. Ross, with her air of casual intimacy. "Are all your officers as Eton and Oxford as that?"

"Not quite all," rejoined Alleyn.

What a curious trick she had of widening her eyes! The pupils actually seemed to dilate. It was as if she was aware of something, recognised it, and gave just that one brief sign. Alleyn read into it a kind of polite wantonness. "She proclaims herself," he thought, "by that trick. She is a woman with a strong, determined appetite." He knew very well that, for all her impersonal manner, she had made small practised signals to him, and he wondered if he should let her see he had recognized these signals.

He leaned forward in his chair and looked deliberately into her eyes.

"There are two more questions," he said.

"Two more? Well?"

"Do you know whose automatic it was that shot Miss Campanula between the eyes and through the brain?"

She sat quite still. The corners of her thin mouth drooped a little. Her short blackened lashes veiled her light eyes.

"It was Jocelyn Jernigham's, wasn't it?" she said.

"Yes. The same Colt that Mr. Henry Jernigham showed you on Friday evening."

"That's awful," she said and looked squarely at him. "Does it mean that you suspect one of us?"

"By itself, it doesn't amount to so much. But it was his automatic that killed her."

"*He'd* never do it," she said contemptuously.

"Did you put a box outside one of the hall windows at any time after 2.30 on Friday?" asked Alleyn.

"No. Why?"

"It's of no importance."

Alleyn put his hand in the breast pocket of his coat and took out his note-book.

"Heavens!" said Selia Ross. "What next?"

His long fingers drew out a folded paper. That trick with her eyes must after all be unconscious. She looked slantways at the paper and the lines of block capitals, painstakingly executed by Inspector Fox. She took it from Alleyn, raising her eyebrows, and handed it back.

"Can you tell me anything about this?" asked Alleyn.

"No."

"I think perhaps I should tell you we regard it as an important piece of evidence."

"I've never seen it before. Where did you find it?"

"It just cropped up," said Alleyn.

Somebody had come into the adjoining room. There came the sound of stumbling feet on the uneven steps. The door burst open. Alleyn thought, "Blast Bathgate!" and glanced up furiously.

It was Dr. Templett.

CHAPTER NINETEEN

Statement From Templett

i

"SELIA?" said Dr. Templett, and stopped short.

The paper dangled from Alleyn's fingers.

"Hullo, chief inspector," said Templett breathlessly. "I thought I might find you here. I've just done the P.M."

"Yes?" said Alleyn. "Anything unexpected?"

"Nothing."

Alleyn held out the paper.

"Isn't this your letter?"

Templett stood absolutely still. He then shook his head, but the gesture seemed to repudiate the implication rather than the statement.

"Were you not looking for it this morning in the breast pocket of your coat?"

"Is it yours, Billy?" she said. "Who's been writing comic letters to you?"

The skin of his face seemed to tighten. Two sharp little chords sprang up from his nostrils to the corners of his mouth. He turned to the fire and stooped as if to warm his hands. They trembled violently and he thrust them into his pockets. His face was quite without colour, but the firelight dyed it crimson.

Alleyn waited.

Mrs. Ross lit a cigarette.

"I think I'd like to speak to Mr. Alleyn alone," said Templett.

"Can you come back to Chipping with me?" asked Alleyn.

"What? Yes. Yes, I'll do that."

Alleyn turned to Mrs. Ross and bowed.

"Good-evening, Mrs. Ross."

"Is it so late? Good-bye. Billy, is anything wrong?"

Alleyn saw him look at her with a sort of wonder. He shook his head and walked out. Alleyn followed him.

Nigel was sitting in the Biggins's car. Alleyn signalled quickly to him and followed Templett to his Morris.

"I'll come with you, if I may," said Alleyn.

Templett nodded. They got in. Templett turned the car and accelerated violently. Cloudyfold Rise leapt at them. They crossed the hill-top in two minutes. It was already dusk and the houses down in the Vale were lit. A cold mist hung about the hills.

"God damn it," said Dr. Templett, "you needn't watch me like that! I'm not going to take cyanide."

"Of course not."

As they skidded round Pen Cuckoo corner, Templett said, "I didn't do it."

"All right."

At the church lane turning the car skated twenty yards on the greasy road, and fetched up sideways. Alleyn held his peace and trod on imaginary brakes. They started off again more reasonably, but entered Chipping at forty miles an hour.

"Will you stop outside the Jernigham Arms for a minute?" asked Alleyn.

Templett did not slow down until they were within two hundred yards of the inn. They shot across the road and stopped with screaming brakes. The pot-boy came running out.

"Is Mr. Fox there? Ask him to come out, will you?" called Alleyn cheerfully. "And when Mr. Bathgate arrives, send him on to the police station at Great Chipping. Ask him to bring my case with him."

Fox came out, bare-headed.

"Pop in at the back, Brer Fox," said Alleyn. "We're going into Great Chipping. Dr. Templett will take us."

"Good-evening, doctor," said Fox, and got in.

Dr. Templett put in his clutch and was off before the door shut. Alleyn's arm hung over the back of the seat. He twiddled his long fingers eloquently.

They reached the outskirts of Great Chipping in ten minutes, and here Templett seemed to come to his senses. He drove reasonably enough through the narrow provincial streets and pulled up at the police station.

Blandish was there. A constable showed them into his office and stood inside the door.

"Good-evening, gentlemen," said the superintendent, who seemed to be in superb form. "Some good news for me, I hope? Glad to say we're getting on quite nicely with our little job, Mr. Alleyn. I wouldn't be surprised if we won't be able to give the City a bit of very sound information by to-morrow. The bird's flown to Bermondsey, and we ought to be able to pull him in. Very gratifying. Well, now, sit down, all of you. Smith! The chair by the door."

He bustled hospitably, caught sight of Templett's face and was abruptly silent.

"I'll make a statement," said Templett.

"I think perhaps I should warn you——" said Alleyn.

"I know all that. I'll make a statement."

Fox moved up to the table. Superintendent Blandish, very startled and solemn, shoved across a pad of paper.

ii

"On Friday afternoon," said Dr. Templett, "on my return from hunting, an anonymous letter came into my possession. I believe the police now have this letter. Inspector Alleyn has shown it to me. I attached very little importance to it. I do not know who wrote it. I put it in my pocket-book in the inside breast pocket of my coat. I intended to destroy it. At five o'clock on Friday I attended a rehearsal at Pen Cuckoo. On my return home I was immediately called out on a difficult case. I did not get back until late night. I forgot all about the letter. Yesterday, Saturday, wearing the same suit, I left my house at about 8.30, having only just got up. I collected some furniture from Duck Cottage, called at Pen Cuckoo, went on to the hall, where I left the furniture. She was with me. The rest of Saturday was spent on my rounds. I was unusually busy. They gave me some lunch at the cottage hospital. In the afternoon I called at the hall. I was there for about half an hour. I did not go near the piano and I didn't remember the letter. I was not alone at the hall at any time. I arrived there for the evening performance at half-past seven, or possibly later. I went straight to my dressing-room and changed, hanging up my coat on the wall. Henry Jernigham came in and helped me. After the tragedy I did not change until I got home. At no time did I remember the letter. The next time I saw it, was this afternoon when Inspector Alleyn showed it to me. That's all."

Fox looked up.

Blandish said, "Make a full transcript of Inspector Fox's notes, Smith."

Smith went out with the notes.

Alleyn said, "Before we go any further, Dr. Templett, I think I should tell you that the letter I showed you was a copy of the original and made on identical paper. The original is in our possession and it is in my bag. Fox, do you mind seeing if Bathgate has arrived?"

Fox went out and in a minute returned with Alleyn's case.

"Have you," Alleyn asked Templett, "as far as your memory serves, given us the whole truth in the statement you have just made?"

"I've given you everything that's relevant."

"I am going to put several questions to you. Would you like to wait until your lawyer is present?"

"I don't want a lawyer. I'm innocent."

"Your answers will be taken down and——"

"And may be used in evidence. I know."

"—And may be used in evidence," Alleyn repeated.

"Well?" asked Templett.

"Have you shown the letter to any one else?"

"No."

"Did you receive it by post?"

"Yes."

Alleyn nodded to Fox, who opened the case and took out the original letter between its two glass cover-sheets.

"Here it is," said Alleyn. "You see, we have developed the prints. There are three sets—yours, the deceased's, and another's. I must tell you that the unknown prints will be compared with any that we find on the copy which Mrs. Ross has held in her hands. You can see, if you look at the original, that one set of prints is superimposed on the other two. Those are your own. The deceased's prints are the undermost."

Templett did not speak.

"Dr. Templett, I am going to tell you what I believe to have happened. I believe that this letter was sent in the first instance to Mrs. Ross. The wording suggests that it was addressed to a woman rather than a man. I believe that Mrs. Ross showed it to you on Saturday, which was yesterday morning, and that you put it in your pocket-book. If this is so, you know as well as I do that you will be ill-advised to deny it. You have told us the letter came by post. Do you now feel it would be better to alter this statement?"

"It makes no difference."

"It makes all the difference between giving the police facts instead of fiction. If we find what we expect to find from the fingerprints, you will not help matters by adding your misstatement to the one that was made at Duck Cottage."

Alleyn paused and looked at the undistinguished, dogged face.

"You have had a great shock," he said, and added in a voice so low that Blandish put his hand to his ear like a deaf rustic: "It's no good trying to protect people who are ready at any sacrifice of loyalty to protect themselves."

Templett laughed.

"So it seems," he said. "All right. That's how it was. It's no good denying it."

"Mrs. Ross gave you the letter on Saturday?"

"I suppose so. Yes."

"Did you guess at the authorship?"

"I *guessed*."

"Did you notice the smell of eucalyptus?"

"Yes. But I'm innocent. My God, I tell you I had no opportunity. I can give you an account of every moment of the day."

"When you were at the hall with Mrs. Ross, did you not leave her to go down to the auditorium?"

"Why should I?"

"Mrs. Ross told me you shut one of the windows."

"Yes. I'd forgotten. Yes, I did."

"But if Mrs. Ross says she had shut the window herself in the morning?"

"I know. We couldn't make it out."

"You noticed the open window, shut it, returned to the stage, and lowered the curtain?"

"Did she tell you that!"

Templett suddenly collapsed into the chair behind him and buried his face in his hands. "My God," he said. "I've been a fool. *What* a fool!"

"They say it happens once to most of us," said Alleyn unexpectedly and not unkindly. "Did Mrs. Ross not mention at the time that she thought she had already shut the window."

"Yes, yes, yes. She said so. But the window was *open*. It was opened about three inches. How can I expect you to believe it? You think I lowered the curtain, went to the piano, and fixed this bloody trap. I tell you I didn't."

"Why did you lower the curtain?"

Templett looked at his hands.

"Oh, God," he said. "Have we got to go into all that?"

"I see," said Alleyn. "No, I don't think we need. There was a scene that would have compromised you both if anybody had witnessed it?"

"Yes."

"Did you at any time speak about the letter?"

"She asked me if I'd found out—I may as well tell you I've got a note somewhere from Miss Campanula. I thought I'd compare the paper. I'd been so rushed during the day I hadn't had time. That's why I didn't destroy the thing."

"When you opened the window did you look out?"

"What? Yes. Yes. I think I did." There was a curious note of uncertainty in his voice.

"Have you remembered something?"

"What's the good! It sounds like something I've made up at the last moment."

"Let us have it anyway."

"Well, she caught sight of the window. She noticed it first; saw it over my shoulder, and got an impression that there was something that dodged down behind the sill. It was only a flash, she said. I thought it was probably one of those damned scouts. When I got to the window I looked out. There was nobody there."

"Were you upset by the discovery of an eavesdropper?"

Templett shrugged his shoulders.

"Oh, what's the good!" he said. "Yes, I suppose we were."

"Who was this individual?"

"I can't tell you."

"But didn't Mrs. Ross say who it was? She must have had some impression."

"Ask her if you must," he said violently. "I can't tell you."

"When you looked out they had gone," murmured Alleyn. "But you looked out."

He watched Dr. Templett, and Blandish and Fox watched him. Fox realised that they had reached a climax. He knew what Alleyn's next question would be, he saw Alleyn raise one eyebrow and screw his mouth sideways before he asked his question.

"Did you look down?" asked Alleyn.

"Yes."

"And you saw?"

"There was a box under the window."

"Ah!" It was the smallest sigh. Alleyn seemed to relax all over. He smiled to himself and pulled out his cigarette case.

"That seemed to suggest," said Templett, "that somebody had

stood there, using the box. It wasn't there when I got to the hall because I went round that way to get the key."

Alleyn turned to Fox.

"Have you asked them about the box?"

"Yes, sir. Mr. Jernigham, Miss Prentice, every kid in the village, *and* all the helpers. Nobody knows anything about it."

"Good," said Alleyn, heartily.

For the first time since they got there, Dr. Templett showed some kind of interest.

"Is it important?" he asked.

"Yes," said Alleyn. "I think it's of the first importance."

iii

"You knew about this box?" asked Templett after a pause.

"Yes, why don't you smoke, Dr. Templett?" Alleyn held out his case.

"Are you going to charge me?"

"No. Not on present information."

Templett took a cigarette and Alleyn lit it for him.

"I'm in a hell of a mess," said Templett. "I see that."

"Yes," agreed Alleyn. "One way and another you've landed yourself in rather a box." But there was something in his manner that drove the terror out of Templett's eyes.

Smith came in with the transcript.

"Sergeant Roper's outside, sir," he said. "He came down with Mr. Bathgate and wants to see you particular."

"He can wait," said Blandish. "He's wanted to see me particular about ten times a day ever since we got busy."

"Yes, sir. Will I leave this transcript?"

"Leave it here," said Blandish, "and wait outside."

When Smith had gone Blandish spoke to Dr. Templett for the first time that evening.

"I'm very sorry about this, doctor."

"That's all right," said Templett.

"I think Mr. Alleyn will agree with me that if it's got no bearing on the case we'll do our best to bury it."

"Certainly," said Alleyn.

"I don't care much what happens," said Templett.

"Oh, come now, doctor," said Blandish uncomfortably, "you mustn't say that."

But Alleyn saw a gay little drawing-room with a delicate straw-coloured lady, whose good nature did not stretch beyond a very definite point, and he thought he understood Dr. Templett.

"I think," he said, "you had better give us a complete time-table of your movements from two-thirty on Friday up to eight o'clock last night. We shall check it, but we'll make the process an impersonal sort of business."

"But for those ten minutes in the hall, I'm all right," said Templett. "God, I was with her all the time, until I shut the window! Ask her how long it took! I wasn't away two minutes over the business. Surely to God she'll at least bear me out in that. She's nothing to lose by it."

"She shall be asked," said Alleyn.

Templett began to give the names of all the houses he had visited on his rounds. Fox took them down.

Alleyn suddenly asked Blandish to find out how long the Pen Cuckoo telephone had been disconnected by the falling branch. Blandish rang up the exchange.

"From eight-twenty until the next morning."

"Yes," said Alleyn. "Yes."

Dr. Templett's voice droned on with its flat recital of time and place.

"Yes, I hunted all day Friday. I got home in time to change and go to the five o'clock rehearsal. The servants can check that. When I got home again I found this urgent message. . . . I was out till after midnight. Mrs. Bains at Mill Farm. She was in labour twenty-four hours . . . yes. . . ."

"May I interrupt?" asked Alleyn. "Yesterday morning, at Pen Cuckoo, Mrs. Ross did not leave the car?"

"No."

"Were you shown into the study?"

"Yes."

"You were there alone?"

"Yes," said Templett, showing the whites of his eyes.

"Dr. Templett, did you touch the box with the automatic?"

"Before God, I didn't."

"One more question. Last night did you use all your powers of authority and persuasion to induce Miss Prentice to allow Miss Campanula to take her place?"

"Yes, but—she wouldn't listen to me."

"Will you describe again how you found her?"

"I told you last night. I came in late. I thought Dinah would be worried and after I'd changed, I went along to the women's dressing-room to show her I was there. I heard some one snivelling and moaning, and through the open door I saw Miss Prentice in floods of tears, rocking backwards and forwards and holding her hand. I went in and looked at it. No doctor in his senses would have let her thump the piano. She *couldn't* have done it. I told her so, but she kept on saying, 'I will do it. I will do it.' I got angry and spoke my mind. I couldn't get any further with her. It was damned near time we started and I wasn't even made-up."

"So you fetched Miss Copeland and her father, knowing the rector would possibly succeed where you had failed."

"Yes. But I tell you it was physically impossible for her to use her finger. I could have told her that——"

He stopped short.

"Yes? You could have told her that, how long ago?" said Alleyn.

"Three days ago."

iv

Smith returned.

"It's Sergeant Roper, sir. He says it's very particular indeed and he knows Mr. Alleyn would want to hear it."

"Blast!" said Blandish. "All right, all right."

Smith left the door open. Alleyn saw Nigel crouched over an anthracite stove and Roper, sweating and expectant, in the middle of the room.

"Right oh, Roper," said Smith audibly. Roper hurriedly removed his helmet, cleared his throat, and marched heavily into the room.

"Well, Roper?" said Blandish.

"Sir," said Roper, "I have a report." He took his official notebook from a pocket in his tunic and opened it, bringing it into line with his nose. He began to read very rapidly in a high voice.

"This afternoon, November 28th, at 4 p.m. being on duty at the time outside the parish hall of Winton St. Giles I was approached and accosted by a young female. She was well-known to me being by name Gladys Wright (Miss) of Top Lane, Winton. The following conversation eventuated. Miss Wright enquired of me if I was waiting for my girl or my promotion. Myself (P.S. Roper): I am on duty, Miss Wright, and would take it kindly if you would pass along the lane. Miss Wright: Look what our cat's brought in. P.S. Roper: And I don't want no lip or saucy boldness. Miss Wright: I could tell you something and I've come along to do it, but seeing you're on duty maybe I'll keep it for your betters. P.S. Roper: If you know anything, Gladys, you'd better speak up for the law comes down with majesty on them that aids and abets and withholds. Miss Wright: What will you give me? The succeeding remarks are not evidence and bear no connection with the matter in hand. They are therefore omitted."

"What the hell did she tell you?" asked Blandish. "Shut that damned book and come to the point."

"Sir, the girl told me in her silly way that she came down to the hall at six-thirty on yesterday evening being one of them selected to usher. She let herself in and finding herself the first to arrive, living nearby and not wishing to return home, the night being heavy rain with squalls and her hair being artificially twisted up with curls which to my mind——"

"What did she tell you?"

"She told me that at six-thirty she sat down as bold as brass and played 'Nearer my Gawd to Thee' with the soft pedal on," said Roper.

CHAPTER TWENTY

According to Miss Wright

i

SERGEANT ROPER, sweating lightly, allowed an expression of extreme gratification to suffuse his enormous face. The effect of his statement on his superiors left nothing to be desired. Superintendent Blandish stared at his sergeant like a startled codfish, Detective-Inspector Fox pushed his glasses up his forehead and brought his hands down smartly on his knees. Dr. Templett uttered in a whisper a string of amazing blasphemies. Chief Inspector Alleyn pulled his own nose, made a peculiar grimace, and said:

"Roper, you shall be hung with garlands, led through the village, and offered up at the Harvest Festival."

"Thank you, sir," said Roper.

"Where," asked Alleyn, "is Gladys Wright?"

Roper flexed his knees and pointed with his thumb over his shoulder.

"Stuck to her like glue, I have. I telephoned Fife from the hall to relieve me, keeping the silly maiden under observation the while. I brought her here, sir, on the bar of my bike, all ten stones of her, and seven mile if it's an inch."

"Magnificent. Bring her in, Roper."

Roper went out.

"I didn't get there till half-past seven," whispered Dr. Templett, shaking his finger at Alleyn. "Not till half-past seven. You see! You see! The hall was full of people. Ask Dinah Copeland. She'll tell you I never went on the stage. Ask Copeland. He was sitting on the stage. I saw him through the door when I called him down. Ask any of them. My God!"

Alleyn reached out a long arm and gripped his wrist.

"Steady, now," he said. "Fox, there's the emergency flask in that case."

He got Templett to take the brandy before Roper returned.

"Miss Gladys Wright, sir," said Roper, flinging back the door and expanding his chest.

He shepherded his quarry into the room with watchful pride, handed her over, and retired behind the door to wipe his face down excitedly with the palm of his hand.

Miss Wright was the large young lady whom Alleyn had encountered in the rectory hall. Under a mackintosh she wore a plushy sort of dress with a hint of fur about it. Her head was indeed a mass of curls. Her face was crimson and her eyes black.

"Good-evening, Miss Wright," said Alleyn. "I'm afraid we've put you to a lot of trouble. Will you sit down?"

He gave her his own chair and sat on the edge of the desk.

Miss Wright backed up to the chair rather in the manner of a draught-horse, got half-way towards sitting on it, but thought better of this, and giggled.

"Sergeant Roper tells us you've got some information for us," continued Alleyn.

"Aw him!" said Miss Wright. She laughed and covered her mouth with her hand.

"Now I understand that you arrived at the parish hall at half-past six last night. Is that right?"

"That's right."

"Sure of the time?"

"Yass," said Miss Wright. "I heard the clock strike, see?"

"Good. How did you get in?"

"I got the key from outside and came in by the back door," said Miss Wright, and looked at the floor. "Miss Dinah was soon after me."

"Nobody else was in the hall. You switched on the light, I suppose?"

"Yas, that's right."

"What did you do next?"

"Well, I looked round, like."

"Yes. Have a good look round?"

"Aaw, yaas, I suppose so."

"Back and front of the stage, what? Yes. And then?"

"I took off my mac. And put out my programmes, like, and counted up my change, see, for selling."

"Yes?"

"Aw deer," said Miss Wright, "it does give me such a turn when I think about it."

"I'm sure it does."

"You know! When you think! What I was saying to Charley Roper, you never know. And look, I never thought of it till this afternoon at the Children's Service. I was collecting up hymn-books and it come all over me, so when I see Charley Roper hanging about outside the hall, I says, 'Pardon me, Mr. Roper,' I says, 'but I have a piece of information I feel it my duty to pass on.' "

"Very proper," said Alleyn, with a glance at Roper.

"Yass, and I told him. I told him I might be laying where she is, seeing what I did!"

"What did you do?"

"I sat down and played a hymn on that rickety old affair. Aw, *well!*"

"Did you play loudly or softly?"

"Well, well, both, ackshully. I was seeing which pedal worked best on that shocking old affair, see?"

"Yes," said Alleyn. "I see. Did you put the pedal on suddenly and hard?"

"Aw no. Because one time the soft pedal went all queer because Cissie Dewry put her foot on it, so we always use it gentle-like. I didn't try it but the bare once. The loud one worked better," said Miss Wright.

"Yes," agreed Alleyn. "I expect it would."

"Well, it did," confessed Miss Wright, and giggled again.

"But you did actually press the soft pedal down?" insisted Alleyn.

"Yass. Firm like. Not sharp."

"Exactly. Was there a piece of music on the rack?"

"Oo yass, Miss Prentice's piece. I never touched it. Truly!"

"I'm sure you didn't. Miss Wright, suppose you were in a court of law, and someone put a Bible in your hand, and you were asked to swear solemnly in God's name that at about twenty to seven last night you put your foot firmly on the left pedal, would you swear it?"

Miss Wright giggled.

"It's very important," said Alleyn. "You see, there would be a prisoner in the court on trial for murder. Please think very carefully indeed. Would you make this statement on oath?"

"Oh *yass*," said Miss Wright.

"Thank you," said Alleyn. He looked at Templett. "I don't think we need keep you, Dr. Templett, if you are anxious to get home."

"I—I'll drive you back," said Templett.

"That's very nice of you—I shan't be long." He turned back to Gladys Wright. "Did any one come in while you were playing?"

"I stopped when I heard them coming. Cissie Dewry come first and then all the other girls."

"Did you notice any of the performers?"

"No. We was all talking round the door, like." She rolled her eyes at Roper. "That was when you come, Mr. Roper."

"Well, Roper?"

"They were in the entrance, sir, giggling and cackling in their female manner, sure enough."

"Oo you *are*," said Miss Wright.

"And had any of the company arrived at that time?"

"Yes, sir," said Roper. "Miss Copeland was there ahead of me, but she went to the back door same as all the performers, I don't doubt. And the Pen Cuckoo party was there, sir, but I didn't know that till I went round to back of stage when I found them bedizening their faces in the Sunday-school rooms."

"So that there was a moment when the ladies were at the front door, talking, and the Pen Cuckoo party and Miss Copeland were behind the scenes?"

"That's right, sir."

"They were ringing and ringing at the telephone," interjected Miss Wright, "all the time us girls was there."

"And you say, Miss Wright, that none of the performers came into the front of the hall."

"Not one. Truly."

"Sure?"

"Yass. Certain sure. We would have seen them. Soon after that the doors were open and people started to come in."

"Where did you stand?"

"Up top by the stage, ushering the two shillingses."

"So if anybody had come down to the piano from the stage you would have seen them?"

"Nobody came down. Not ever. I'd take another Bible oath on that," said Miss Wright, with considerable emphasis.

"Thank you," said Alleyn. "That's splendid. One other question. You were at the Reading Circle meeting at the rectory on Friday night. Did you go home by the gate into the wood. The gate that squeaks?"

"Oo *no!* None of us girls goes that way at night." Miss Wright giggled, extensively. "It's too spooky. Oo, I wouldn't go that way for anything. The others, they all went together, and my young gentleman, he took me home by lane."

"So you're sure nobody used the gate?"

"Yass, for sure. They'd all gone," said Miss Wright, turning scarlet, "before us. And we used lane."

"You passed the hall, then. Were there any lights in the hall?"

"Not in front."

"You couldn't see the back windows, of course. Thank you so much, Miss Wright. We'll get you to sign a transcript of everything you have told us. Read it through carefully, first. If you wouldn't mind waiting in the outer office I think I can arrange for you to be driven home."

"Oo well, thanks ever so," said Miss Wright, and went out.

ii

Alleyn looked at Templett.

"I ought to apologise," he said, "I've given you a damned bad hour."

"I don't know why you didn't arrest me," said Templett with a shaky laugh. "Ever since I realised I'd left that bloody note in the dressing-room I've been trying to think how I could prove I hadn't rigged the automatic. There seemed to be no possible proof. Even now I don't see—— Oh, well, it doesn't matter. Nothing much matters. If you don't mind, I'll wait outside in the car. I'd like a breath of fresh air."

"Certainly."

Dr. Templett nodded to Blandish and went out.

"Will I shadow the man?" asked Roper, earnestly.

Blandish's reply was unprintable.

"You might ask Mr. Bathgate to drive your witness home, Roper," said Alleyn. "Let her sign her statement first. Tell Mr. Bathgate I'm returning with Dr. Templett. And Roper, as tactfully as you can, just see how Dr. Templett's getting on. He's had a shock."

"Yes, sir."

Roper went out.

"He's got about as much tact as a cow," said Blandish.

"I know, but at least he'll keep an eye on Templett."

"The lady let him down, did she?"

"With a thump that shook the crockery."

"S-s-s-s!" said Blandish appreciatively. "Is that a fact?"

"He's had two narrow escapes," said Fox, "and *that's* a fact. The lady's let him down with a jerk and he's lucky the hangman won't follow suit."

"Fox," said Alleyn, "you have the wit of a Tyburn broadsheet, but there's matter in it."

"I don't know where I am," said Blandish. "Are we any nearer to an arrest?"

"A good step," said Alleyn. "The pattern emerges."

"What does that mean, Mr. Alleyn?"

"Well," said Alleyn, apologetically, "I mean all these mad little things like the box, and the broken telephone, and the creaking gate—I'm not so sure of the onion——"

"The onion!" cried Fox, triumphantly. "I know all about the onion, Mr. Alleyn. Georgie Biggins is responsible for that, the young limb. I saw him this afternoon and asked him, as well as every other youngster in the village, about the box. He's going round as pleased as punch, letting on he's working at the case with the Yard. Answers me as cool as you please, and when I'm going he says, 'Did you find an onion in the teapot, mister?' Well, it seems that they had a tea-party on the stage, with Miss Prentice and Miss Campanula quarrelling about which should pour out. If the young devil didn't go and put an onion in the pot. It seems they each had to take the lid off and look in the pot and this was another of George's bright ideas. I suppose someone found it in time and threw it into the box on the floor, where you picked it up."

"Dear little Georgie," said Alleyn. "Dear little boy! We've had red herrings before now, Fox, but never a Spanish onion. Well, as I was saying, all these mad little things begin to bear some sort of relationship."

"That's nice, Mr. Alleyn," said Fox, woodenly. "You're going to tell us you know who did it, I suppose?"

"Oh, yes," said Alleyn looking at him in genuine surprise. "I do *now*, Brer Fox. Don't you?"

iii

When a man learns that his mistress, faced with putting herself in a compromising position, will quite literally see him hanged first, he is not inclined for conversation. Templett drove slowly back towards Chipping and was completely silent until the first cottage came into view. Then he said, "I don't see how any one could have done it. The piano was safe at six-thirty. The girl used the soft pedal. It was safe."

"Yes," agreed Alleyn.

"I suppose, putting the pedal down softly, the pressure wasn't enough to pull the trigger?"

"It's a remarkably light pull," said Alleyn. "I've tried."

Templett brushed his hand across his eyes. "I suppose my brain won't work."

"Give the thing a rest."

"But how could anybody fix that contraption inside the piano after half-past six when those girls were sky-larking about in the front of the house? It's impossible."

"If you come down to the hall to-morrow night, I'll show you."

"All right. Here's your pub. What time's the inquest? I've forgotten. I'm all to pieces." He pulled up the car.

"Eleven o'clock to-morrow."

Alleyn and Fox got out. It was a cold windy evening. The fine weather had broken again and it had begun to rain. Alleyn stood with the door open and looked at Templett. He leaned heavily on the wheel and stared with blank eyes at the windscreen.

"The process of convalescence," said Alleyn, "should follow thc initial shock. Take heart of grace, you will recover."

"I'll go home," said Templett. "Good-night."

"Good-night."

He drove away.

They went upstairs to their rooms.

"Let's swap stories, Brer Fox," said Alleyn. "I'll lay my case, for what it's worth, on the dressing-table. I want a shave. You can open your little heart while I'm having it. I don't think we'll unburden ourselves to Bathgate just yet."

They brought each other up-to-date before they went downstairs again in search of a drink.

They found Nigel alone in the bar parlour.

"I'm not going to pay for so much as half a drink and I intend to drink a very great deal. I've had the dullest afternoon of my life and all for your benefit. Miss Wright smells. When I took her to her blasted cottage she made me go in to tea with her brother who turns out to be the village idiot. Yes, and on the way back from Duck Cottage, your lovely car sprang a puncture. Furthermore——"

"Joe!" shouted Alleyn. "Three whiskies-and-sodas."

"I should damn well think so. What are you ordering for yourselves?"

Nigel calmed down presently and listened to Alleyn's account of the afternoon. Mrs. Peach, a large flowing woman, told them she had proper juicy steak for their dinner and there was a fine fire in the back parlour. They moved in, taking their drinks with them. It was pleasant, when the curtains were drawn and the red-shaded oil lamp was lit, to hear the rain driving against the leaded windows and to listen to the sound of grilling steak beyond the kitchen slide.

"Not so many places left like this," said Fox. "Cosy, isn't it? I haven't seen one of those paraffin lamps for many a long day. Mrs. Peach says old Mr. Peach, her father-in-law, you know, won't have electricity in the house. He's given in as far as the tap-room's concerned but nowhere else. Listen to the rain! It'll be a wild night again."

"Yes," said Alleyn. "It's strange, isn't it, to think of the actors in this silly far-fetched crime, all sitting over their fires, as we are now, six of them wondering what the answer is, and the seventh nursing it secretly in what used to be known as a guilty heart."

"Oo-er," said Nigel.

Mrs. Peach's daughter brought in the steak.

"Are you going out again?" asked Nigel after an interval.

"I've got a report to write," answered Alleyn. "When that's done I think I might go up to the hall."

"Whatever for?"

"Practical demonstration of the booby-trap."

"I might come," said Nigel. "I can ring up the office from there."

"You'll have to square up with the Copelands if you do. The hall telephone is on an extension from the rectory. Great hopping fleas!" shouted Alleyn, "why the devil didn't I think of that before!"

"What!"

"The telephone."

"Excuse him," said Nigel to Fox.

iv

"We'll take half an hour's respite," said Alleyn, when the cloth had been drawn and a bottle of port, recommended by old Mr. Peach, had been set before them. "Let's go over the salient features."

"Why not?" agreed Nigel, comfortably.

Alleyn tried the port, raised an eyebrow, and lit a cigarette.

"It's respectable," he said. "An honest wine and all that. Well, as I see it, the salient features are these. Georgie Biggins rigged his booby-trap between two and three on Friday afternoon. Miss Campanula rattled on the door just before two-thirty. Georgie was in the hall, but must have hidden, because when Gibson looked through the window, the top of the piano was open and Georgie nowhere to be seen. Miss Campanula didn't know that the key was hung up behind the outhouse. The rest of the company were told but they are vague about it. Now Georgie didn't test his booby-trap because, as he says, 'somebody came.' I think this refers to Miss Campanula's onslaught on the door. I'm afraid Miss Campanula is a nightmare to Georgie. He won't discuss her. I'll have to try again. Anyway, he didn't test his booby-trap. But *somebody* did, because the silk round the hole made by the bullet was still damp last night. That means something was on the rack, possibly Miss Prentice's 'Venetian Suite' which seems to have been down in the hall for the last week. It has a stain on the back which suggests that the jet of water hit it and splayed out, wetting the silk. Now, Georgie left the hall soon after the interruption, because he finished up by playing chopsticks with the loud pedal on, and Miss Campanula overheard this final performance. The next eighteen hours or so are still wrapped in mystery but, as far as we know, any of the company may have gone into the hall. Miss Prentice passed it on her way home from confession, the Copelands live within two minutes of the place. Master Henry says that after his meeting with Dinah Copeland he roamed the hills most of that unpleasantly damp afternoon. He may have come down to the hall. Jernigham senior seems to have hunted all day and so does Templett, but either of them may have come down in the evening. Miss Prentice says that she spent the evening praying in her room, Master Henry says he tinkered with a light plug in his room, the squire says he was alone in the study. It takes about eight minutes to walk down Top Lane to the hall and perhaps fifteen to return. On Friday night the rector had an agonising encounter in his own study. I'll tell you about it."

Alleyn told them about it.

"Now the remarkable thing about this is that I believe he spoke the truth, but his story is made so much nonsense if Dinah Copeland was right in thinking there was a third person present. Miss C. would hardly make passionate advances and hang herself round the rector's neck, with a Friendly Helper to watch the fun. Dinah Copeland bases her theory on the fact that she heard the gate opposite the study window squeak, as if somebody had gone out that way. She tells us it couldn't have been Miss Prentice because Miss Prentice rang up a few minutes later to say she wasn't coming down. We know Miss Prentice was upset when she left confession that afternoon. The rector had ticked her off and given her a penance or something and he thinks that's why she didn't come. It wasn't any of the readers. Who the devil was it?"

"The rector himself," said Nigel promptly, "taking a short cut to the hall."

"He says that after Miss C. left him he remained a wreck by his fireside."

"That may not be true."

"It may be as false as hell," agreed Alleyn. "There are one or two points about this business. I'll describe the lay-out again and repeat the rector's story."

When he had done this he looked at Fox.

"Yes," said Fox. "Yes, I think I get you there, Mr. Alleyn."

"Obviously, I'm right," said Nigel, flippantly. "It's the reverend."

"Mr. Copeland's refusing the money, Mr. Bathgate," said Fox. "I was telling the chief, just now. I got that bit of information this afternoon. Mr. Henry told the squire in front of the servants and it's all round the village."

"Well, to finish Friday," said Alleyn. "Dr. Templett spent the best part of the night on a case. That can be checked. Mrs. Ross says she was at home. To-morrow, Foxkin, I'll get you to use your glamour on Mrs. Ross's maid."

"Very good, sir."

"Now then. Some time before noon yesterday, the water-pistol disappeared, because at noon Miss P. strummed with her right hand and used the soft pedal. Nothing happened."

"Perhaps George's plan didn't work," suggested Nigel.

"We are going to see presently if Georgie's plan works. Whether it works or not, the fact remains that somebody found the water-pistol, removed and hid it, and substituted the Colt."

"That must have been later still," said Nigel.

"I agree with you, but not, I imagine, for the same reason. Dr. Templett's story seems to prove that the box was placed outside the window while he and Mrs. Ross were in the hall. He got the impression that someone dodged down behind the sill. Now this eavesdropper was not Miss Campanula because the servants agree that she didn't go out yesterday afternoon. Miss Prentice, the squire, Dinah Copeland and her father were all in their respective houses, but any of them could have slipped out for an hour. Master Henry was again roving the countryside. None of them owns to the box outside the window. Fox has asked every soul in the place and not a soul professes to know anything about the box."

"That's right," said Fox. "I reckon the murderer was hanging about with the Colt and had a look in to see who was there. He'd see the cars in the lane but he'd want to find out if the occupants were in the hall or had gone that way into the vicarage. On the far side of the hall he'd have been out of sight, and he'd have plenty of time to dodge if they sounded as if they were coming round that way. But they never would, of course, seeing it's the far side. He'd be safe enough. Or she," added Fox with a bland glance at Nigel.

"That's how I read it," agreed Alleyn. "Now, look here."

He took an envelope from his pocket, opened it, and, using tweezers, took out four minute reddish-brown scraps, which he laid on a sheet of paper.

"Salvage from the box," he said.

Nigel prodded at them with the tweezers.

"Rubber," said Nigel.

"Convey anything?"

"Somebody wearing goloshes. Miss Prentice, by gosh. I bet she wears goloshes. Or Miss C. herself. Good Lord," said Nigel, "perhaps the rector's right. Perhaps it is a case of suicide."

"These bits of rubber were caught on a projecting nail and some rough bits of wood inside the box."

"Well, she might have trodden inside the box before she picked it up."

"You have your moments," said Alleyn. "I suppose she might."

"Goloshes!" said Fox and chuckled deeply.

"Here!" said Nigel, angrily. "Have you got a case?"

"The makings of one," said Alleyn. "We're not going to tell you just yet, because we don't want to lower our prestige."

"We like to watch your struggles, Mr. Bathgate," said Fox.

"We are, as it might be," said Alleyn, "two experts on a watchtower in the middle of a maze. 'Look at the poor wretch,' we say as we nudge each other, 'there he goes into the same old blind alley. Jolly comical,' we say, and then we laugh like anything. Don't we, Fox?"

"So we do," agreed Fox. "But never you mind, Mr. Bathgate, you're doing very nicely."

"Well, to hell with you anyway," said Nigel. "And moreover what about Gladys Wright putting her splay foot on the soft pedal an hour and a half before the tragedy?"

"Perhaps she wore goloshes," said Fox, and for the first time in these records he broke into a loud laugh.

CHAPTER TWENTY-ONE

According to Mr. Saul Tranter

i

ALLEYN FINISHED his report by nine o'clock. At a quarter-past nine they were back in the Biggins's Ford, driving through pelting rain to the hall.

"I'll have to go up to the Yard before this case is many hours older," said Alleyn. "I telephoned the A.C. this morning but I think I ought to see him and there are a lot of odd things to be cleared up. Perhaps tomorrow night. I'd like to get to the bottom of that meeting between Master Henry, Dinah Copeland and Miss Prentice. I rather think Master Henry wishes to unburden himself and Miss Dinah won't let him. Here we are."

Once more they crunched up the gravel path to the front door. The shutters had been closed and they and the windows were all locked. P.C. Fife was on duty. He let them in and being an incurious fellow retired thankfully when Alleyn said he would not be wanted for two hours.

"I'll ring up the Chipping station when we're leaving," said Alleyn.

The hall smelt of dying evergreens and varnish. It was extremely cold. The piano still stood in its old position against the stage. The hole in the faded silk gaped mournfully. The aspidistras drooped a little in their pots. A fine dust had settled over everything. The rain drove down steadily on the old building and the wind shook the shutters and howled desperately under the eaves.

"I'm going to light these heaters," said Nigel. "There's a can of paraffin in one of the back rooms. This place smells of mortality."

Alleyn opened his case and took out Georgie Biggins's water-pistol. Fox wedged the butt between steel pegs in the iron casing. The nozzle fitted a hole in the fretwork front. They had left the cord and pulleys in position.

"On Friday," said Alleyn, "there was only the long rent in the tucked silk. You see there are several of them. The material has rotted in the creases. No doubt Georgie arranged the silk tastefully behind the fret-work, so that the nozzle didn't catch the light. We'll have a practical demonstration from Mr. Bathgate, Fox. Now, if you fix the front pulley, I'll tie the cord round the butt of the pistol. Hurry up. I hear him clanking in the background."

They had just dropped a sheet of newspaper on the rack when Nigel reappeared with a large can.

"There's some fairly good beer in that room," said Nigel. He began to fill the tank of the heater from his can.

Alleyn sat down at the piano, struck two or three chords, and began to vamp *"Il était une Bergère."*

"That's odd, Fox," he said.

"What's wrong, Mr. Alleyn?"

"I can't get the soft pedal to budge. You try. Don't force it."

Fox seated himself at the piano and picked out "Three Blind Mice," with a stubby forefinger.

"That's right," he said. "It makes no difference."

"What's all this?" demanded Nigel, and bustled forward.

"The soft pedal doesn't work."

"Good Lord!"

"It makes no difference to the sound," said Fox.

"You're not using it."

"Yes, I am, Mr. Bathgate," lied Fox.

"Here," said Nigel, "let me try."

Fox got up. Nigel took his place with an air of importance.

"Rachmaninoff's Prelude in C—Minor," he said. He squared his elbows, raised his left hand and leant forward. The voice of the wind mounted in a thin wail and seemed to encircle the building. Down came Nigel's left hand like a sledge-hammer.

"Pom. *Pom*. POM!"

Nigel paused. A violent gust shook the shutters so impatiently that, for a second, he raised his head and listened. Then he trod on the soft pedal.

The newspaper fell forward on his hands. The thin jet of water caught him between the eyes like a cold bullet. He jerked backwards, uttered a scandalous oath, and nearly lost his balance.

"It does work," said Alleyn.

But Nigel did not retaliate. Above all the uneasy clamour of the storm, and like an echo of the three pretentious chords, sounded a loud triple knock on the front door.

"Who the devil's that?" said Alleyn.

He started forward, but before he could reach the door it crashed open, and on the threshold stood Henry Jernigham with streaks of rain lacing his chalk-white face.

ii

"What the hell's happening in here?" demanded Henry.

"Suppose you shut the door," said Alleyn.

But Henry stared at him as if he had not heard. Alleyn walked past him, slammed the door, and secured the catch. Then he returned to Henry, took him by the elbow, and marched him up the hall.

Fox waited stolidly. Nigel wiped his face with his handkerchief and stared at Henry.

"Now what is it?" demanded Alleyn.

"My God!" said Henry, "who played those three infernal chords?"

"Mr. Bathgate. This is Mr. Bathgate, Mr. Jernigham, and this is Detective-Inspector Fox." Henry looked dimly at the other two and sat down suddenly.

"Oh, Lord," he said.

"I say," said Nigel. "I'm most extraordinarily sorry if I gave you a shock, but I assure you I never thought——"

"I'd come into the lane," said Henry, breathlessly, "the rectory trees were making such a noise in the wind that you couldn't hear anything else."

"Yes?" said Alleyn.

"Don't you see? I'd come up the path and just as I reached the door a great gust of wind and rain came screeching round the building like the souls of the damned. And then, when it dropped, those three chords on a cracked piano! My God, I tell you I nearly bolted."

Henry put his hand to his face and then looked at his fingers.

"I don't know whether it's sweat or rain," he said, "and that's a fact. Sorry! Not the behaviour of a pukka sahib. No, by Gad, sir. Blimp wouldn't think anything of it."

"I can imagine it was rather trying," said Alleyn. "What were you doing there, anyway?"

"Going home. I stayed on to supper at the rectory. Only just left. Mr. Copeland's in such a hoo that he's forgotten all about choking me off. When I occurred at cold supper he noticed me no more than the High Church blanc-mange. I say, sir, I am sorry I made such an ass of myself. Honestly! How I could!"

"That's all right," said Alleyn. "But why did you turn in here?"

"I thought if that splendid fellow Roper held the dog-watch, I might say, 'Stand ho! What hath this thing appeared?' and get a bit of gossip out of him."

"I see."

"Have a cigarette?" said Nigel.

"Oh, thank you. I'd better take myself off."

"Would you like to wait and see a slight experiment?" asked Alleyn.

"Very much indeed, sir, if I may."

"Before we begin, there's just one thing I'd like to say to you, as you are here. I shall call on Miss Prentice to-morrow and I shall use every means within the law to get her to tell me what took place on that encounter in Top Lane on Friday. I don't know whether you'd rather give me your version first."

"I've told you already, she's dotty," said Henry with nervous impatience. "It's my belief she is actually and literally out of her senses. She looks like death and she won't leave her room except for meals, and then she doesn't eat anything. She said at dinner to-night that she's in danger, and that in the end she'll be murdered. It's simply ghastly. God knows whom she suspects, but she suspects somebody, and she's half dead with fright. What sort of sense will you get out of a woman like that?"

"Why not give us a sane version first?"

"But it's nothing to do with the case," said Henry, "and if you feel like saying 'tra-la,' I'd be grateful if you'd restrain yourselves."

"If it turns out to be irrelevant," said Alleyn, "it shall be treated as such. We don't use irrelevant statements."

"Then why ask for them?"

"We like to do the winnowing ourselves."

"Nothing happened in Top Lane."

"You mean Miss Prentice stood two feet away from you both, stared into your face until her heels sank an inch into the ground, and then walked away without uttering a word?"

"It was private business. It was altogether our affair."

"You know," said Alleyn, "that won't do. This morning at Pen Cuckoo, and this afternoon at the rectory, frankness was the keynote of your conversation. You have said that you wouldn't put it past Miss Prentice to do murder, and yet you boggle at repeating a single word that she uttered in Top Lane. It looks as though it's not Miss Prentice whom you wish to protect."

"What do you mean?"

"Hasn't Miss Copeland insisted on your taking this stand because she's nervous on your account? What were you going to call out to me this afternoon when she stopped you?"

"Well," said Henry unexpectedly, "you're quite right."

"See here," said Alleyn, "if you are innocent of murder, I promise you that you are not going the right way to make us think so. Remember that in a little place like this we are bound to hear of all the rifts and ructions and this thing only happened twenty-six hours ago. We've scarcely touched the fringe of local gossip, and already I know that Miss Prentice is opposed to your friendship with Miss Dinah Copeland. I know very well that to you police methods must seem odious and——"

"No, they don't," said Henry. "Of course, you've got to do it."

"Very well, then."

"I'll tell you this much, and I dare say it's no more than you've guessed: My Cousin Eleanor was thrown into a dither by finding us there together, and our conversation consisted of a series of hysterical threats and embarrassing accusations on her part."

"And did you make no threats?"

"She'll probably tell you I did," said Henry; "but, as I have said six or eight times already, she's mad. And I'm sorry, sir, but that's all I can tell you."

"All right," said Alleyn with a sigh. "Let's get to work, Fox."

iii

They removed the water-pistol and set up the Colt in its place. Alleyn produced the "Prelude" from his case and put it on the rack. Henry saw the hole blown through the centre and the surrounding ugly stains. He turned away and then, as if he despised this involuntary revulsion, moved closer to the piano and watched Alleyn's hands as they moved inside the top.

"You see," said Alleyn, "all the murderer had to do was exactly what I'm doing now. The Colt fits into the same place, and the loose end of cord which was tied round the butt of the water-pistol is tied round the butt of the Colt. It passes across the trigger. It is remarkably strong cord, rather like fishing line. I've left the safety catch on. Now look."

He sat on the piano stool and pressed the soft pedal. The two pulleys stood out rigidly from their moorings, the cord tautened as the dampers moved towards the strings and checked.

"It's stood firm," said Alleyn. "Georgie made sure of his pulleys. Now."

"By gum!" ejaculated Nigel, "I never thought of——"

"I know you didn't."

Alleyn reached inside and released the safety catch. Again he trod lightly on the soft pedal. This time the soft pedal worked. The cord tightened in the pulleys and the trigger moved back. They all heard the sharp click of the striker.

"Well, there you are for what it's worth," said Alleyn lightly.

"Yes, but last night the top of the piano was smothered in bunting and six he-men aspidistras," objected Henry.

"So you think it was done last night," said Alleyn.

"I don't know when it was done, and I don't think it could have been done last night, unless it was before we all got to the hall."

Alleyn scowled at Nigel, who was obviously pregnant with a new theory.

"It's perfectly true," said Nigel defiantly. "Nobody could have moved those pots after 6.30."

"I so entirely agree with you," said Alleyn. A bell pealed distantly. Henry jumped.

"That's the telephone," he said and started forward.

"I'll answer it, I think," said Alleyn. "It's sure to be for me."

He crossed the stage, found a light switch and made his way to the first dressing-room on the left. The old-fashioned manual telephone pealed irregularly until he lifted the receiver.

"Hullo?"

"Mr. Alleyn? It's Dinah Copeland. Somebody wants to speak to you from Chipping."

"Thank you."

"Here you are," said Dinah. The telephone clicked and the voice of Sergeant Roper said, "Sir?"

"Hullo?"

"Roper, sir. I thought I should find you, seeing as how Fife is still asleep here. I have a small matter in the form of a recent arrest to bring before your notice, sir."

"In *what* form?"

"By name Saul Tranter, and by employment as sly a poacher as ever you see; but we've cotched him very pretty, sir, and the man's sitting here at my elbow with guilt written all over him in the form of two fine cock-pheasants."

"What the devil——?" began Alleyn, and checked himself. "Well, Roper, what about it?"

"This chap says he's got a piece of information that'll make the court think twice about giving him the month's hard he's been asking for these last two years. He won't tell me, sir, but in his bold way he asks to be faced with you. Now, we've got to get him down to the lock-up some time and——"

"I'll send Mr. Bathgate down, Roper. Thank you." Alleyn hung up the receiver and stared thoughtfully at the telephone.

"I'll have to see about you," he told it and returned to the front of the hall.

"Hullo," he said, "where's Master Henry?"

"Gone home," said Fox. "He's a funny sort of young gentleman, isn't he?"

"Rather a bumptious infant, I thought," said Nigel.

"He's about the same age as you were when I first met you," Alleyn pointed out, "and not half as bumptious. Bathgate, I'm afraid you'll have to go into Chipping and get a poacher."

"A poacher!"

"Yes. Treasure-trove of Roper's. Apparently the gentleman wishes to make a blunderbuss about his impending sentence. He says he's got a story to unfold. Bring Fife with him. Stop at the pub on the way back and get your own car, and let Fife drive the Ford here and he can use it afterwards to deliver this gentleman to the lock-up. We'll clear up this place to-night."

"Am I representative of a leading London daily or your odd-boy?"

"You know the answer to that better than I do. Away you go."

Nigel went, not without further bitter complaint. Alleyn and Fox moved to the supper-room.

"All this food can be thrown away to-morrow," said Alleyn. "There's something else I want to see down here, though. Look, there's the tea-tray ready to be carried on in the play. Mrs. Ross's silver, I dare say. It looks like her. Modern, expensive and streamlined."

He lifted the lid of the teapot.

"It reeks of onion. Dear little Georgie."

"I suppose someone spotted it and threw it out. You found it lying on the floor here, didn't you, Mr. Alleyn?"

"In that box over there. Yes. Bailey has found Georgie's and Miss P's prints in the pot, so presumably Miss P. hawked out the onion.

He stooped down and looked under the table.

"You went all over here last night, didn't you, Fox? Last night! This morning! 'Little Fox, we've had a busy day.' "

"All over it, sir. You'll find the onion peel down there. Young Biggins must have skinned it and then put it in the teapot."

"Did you find any powder in here?"

"Powder? No. No, I didn't. Why?"

"Or flour?"

"No. Oh, you're thinking of the flour on the onion."

"I'll just get the onion."

Alleyn fetched the onion. He had put it in one of his wide-necked specimen bottles.

"We haven't had time to deal with this as yet," he said. "Look at it, Fox, it's pinkish. That's powder, not flour."

"Perhaps young Biggins fooled round with it in one of the dressing-rooms."

"Let's look at the dressing-rooms."

They found that on each dressing-table there was a large box of theatrical powder. They were all new, and it looked as if Dinah had provided them. The men's boxes contained a yellowish powder, the women's a pinkish cream. Mrs. Ross, alone, had brought her own in an expensive-looking French box. In the dressing-room used by Miss Prentice and Miss Campanula, some of their powder had been spilled across the table. Alleyn stooped and sniffed at it.

"That's it," he said. "Reeks of onion." He opened the box. "But this doesn't. Fox, ring up Miss Copeland and ask when the powder was brought into these rooms. It's an extension telephone. You just turn the handle."

Fox plodded away. Alleyn, in a sort of trance, stared at the top of the dressing-table, shook his head thoughtfully and returned to the stage. He heard a motor-horn, and in a minute the door opened. Roper and Fife came in shepherding between them a pigmy of a man who looked as if he had been plunged in a water-butt.

Mr. Saul Tranter was an old man with a very bad face. His eyes were no bigger than a pig's and they squinted, wickedly close together, on either side of his mean little nose. His mouth was loose and leered uncertainly, and his few teeth were objects of horror. He smelt very strongly indeed of dirty old man, dead birds and whisky. Roper thrust him forward as if he was some fabulous orchid, culled at great risk.

"Here he be, sir," said Roper. "This is Saul Tranter, sure enough, with all his wickedness hot in his body, having been taken in the act with two of squire's cock-pheasants and his gun smoking in his hands. Two years you've dodged us, haven't you, Tranter, you old fox? I thought I'd come along with Fife, sir, seeing I've got the hang of this case, having brought my mind to bear on it."

"Very good of you, Roper."

"Now then, Tranter," said Roper, "speak up to the chief inspector and let him have the truth—if so be it lies in you to tell it."

"Heh, my sonnies!" said the poacher in a piping voice. "Be that the instrument that done the murder?"

And he pointed an unspeakably dirty hand at the piano.

"Never you mind that," ordered Roper. "That's not for your low attention."

"What have you got to tell us, Tranter?" asked Alleyn. "Good Lord, man, you're as wet as a water-rat!"

"Wuz up to Cloudyfold when they cotched me," admitted Mr. Tranter. He drew a little closer to the heater and began stealthily to steam.

"Ay, they cotched me," he said. "Reckon it do have to happen so soon or so late. Squire'll sit on me at court and show what a mighty man he be, no doubt, seeing it's his woods I done trapped and shot these twenty year. 'Od rabbit the man, he'd change his silly, puffed-up ways if he knew what I had up my sleeve for 'un."

"That's no way to talk," said Roper severely, "you, with a month's hard hanging round your neck."

"Maybe. Maybe not, Charley Roper." He squinted up at Alleyn. "Being I has my story to tell which will fix the guilt of this spring-gun on him as set it, I reckon the hand of the law did ought to be light on my ancient shoulders."

"If your information is any use," said Alleyn, "we might put in a word for you. I can't promise. You never know. I'll have to hear it first."

" 'Tain't good enough, mister. Promise first, story afterwards, is my motter."

"Then it's not ours," said Alleyn coolly. "It looks as though you've nothing to tell, Tranter."

"Is threats nothing? Is blasting words nothing? Is a young chap caught red-handed same as me, with as pretty a bird as ever flewed into a trap, nothing?"

"Well?"

Fox came down into the hall, joined the group round the heater and stared with a practised eye at Tranter. Nigel arrived and took off his streaming mackintosh. Tranter turned his head restlessly and looked sideways from one face to another. A trickle of brown saliva appeared at the corner of his mouth.

"Well?" Alleyn repeated.

"Sour, tight-fisted men be the Jernighams," said Tranter. "What's a bird or two to them! I'm up against all damned misers, and so be all my side. Tyrants they be, and narrow as the grave, father and son."

"You'd better take him back, Roper."

"Nay, then, I'll tell you. I'll tell you. And if you don't give me my dues, dang it, if I don't fling it in the faces of the J.P.s. Where be your pencils and papers, souls? This did oughter go down in writing."

CHAPTER TWENTY-TWO

Letter to Troy

i

"ON FRIDAY afternoon," said Mr. Tranter, "I were up to Cloudyfold. Never mind way. I come down by my own ways, and proper foxy ways they be, so quiet as moonshine. I makes downhill to Top Lane. Never mind why."

"I don't in the least mind," said Alleyn. "Do go on."

Mr. Tranter shot a doubtful glance at him and sucked in his breath.

"A'most down to Top Lane, I wuz, when I heard voices. A feymell voice and a man's voice, and raised in anger. 'Ah,' thinks I. 'There's somebody down there kicking up Bob's-a-dying in the lane and, that being the case, the lane's no place for me, with never-mind-what under my arm and never-mind-what in my pockets, neither.' So I worms my way closer, till at last I'm nigh on bank above lane. There's a great ancient beech tree a-growing theer, and I lays down and creeps forward, so cunning as a serpent, till I looks down atwixt the green stuff into the lane. Yass. And what do I see?"

"What *do* you see?"

"Ah! I sees young Henry Jernigham, as proud as death and with the devil himself in his face, and rector's wench in his arms."

"That's no way to talk," admonished Roper. "Choose your words."

"So I will, and mind your own business, Charley Roper. And who do I see standing down in lane a-facing of they two with her face so sickly as cheese and her eyes like raging fires and her limbs trimbling like a trapped rabbit. Who do I see?"

"Miss Eleanor Prentice," said Alleyn.

Mr. Tranter, who was now steaming like a geyser and smelling like a polecat, choked and blinked his eyes.

"She's never told 'ee?"

"No. Go on."

"Trimbling as if to take a fit, she was, and screeching feeble, but uncommon venomous. Threating 'em with rector, she was, and threating 'em with squire. She says she caught 'em red-handed in vice and she'd see every decent critter in parish heard of their goings-on. And more besides. You'd never believe that old maiden had the knowledge of sinful youth in her, like she do seem to have. Nobbut what she don't tipple."

"Really?" Alleyn ejaculated.

"Aye. One of them hasty secret drinkers, she is. She'd sloshed her tipple down her bosom, as I clearly saw. No doubt that's what'd inflamed the old wench and caused her to rage and storm at 'em. She give it 'em proper hot and sizzling, did Miss Prentice. And when she was at the full blast of her fury, what does t' young spark do but round on 'er. Aye, t' young toad! Grabs her by shoulders and hisses in 'er face. If she don't let 'em be, 'e says, and if she tries to blacken young maid's name in eyes of the world, he says, he'll stop her wicked tongue for good an' all. He were in a proper rage, more furious than her. Terrible. And rector's maid, she says, 'Doan't, Henry, doan't!' But young Jernigham 'e take no heed of the wench, but hammer-and-tongs he goes to it, so white as a sheet and blazing like a furnace. Aye, they've all got murderous, wrathy, passionate tempers, they Jernighams, as is well known hereabouts; I've heard the manner of this bloody killing, and I reckon there's little doubt he set his spring-gun for t'one old hen and catched t'other. Now!"

ii

"Damn!" said Alleyn, when Mr. Tranter had been removed. "What a *bloody* business this is."

"Is it what you expected?" asked Nigel.

"Oh, I half expected it, yes. It was obvious that something pretty dramatic had happened on Friday afternoon. Miss Prentice and Henry Jernigham showed the whites of their eyes whenever it was mentioned, and the rector told me that he and the squire and Miss Prentice had all been opposed to this match. Why, the Lord alone knows. She seems a perfectly agreeable girl, rather a nice girl, blast it. And look at the way Master Henry responded to inquiry! Fox, did you ever know such a case? One cranky spinster is enough, heaven knows; and here we have two, each a sort of Freudian prize packet, and one a corpse on our hands."

"The whole thing seems very unlikely sort of stuff to me, Mr. Alleyn, and yet there it is. She *was* murdered. If that kid had never read his comic paper, and if he hadn't had his Twiddletoy outfit, it wouldn't have happened."

"I believe you're right there, Brer Fox."

"I suppose, sir, that was what Miss Prentice wanted to see the rector about on Friday evening. The meeting in Top Lane, I mean."

"Yes, I dare say it was. Oh, hell, we'll have to tackle Miss Prentice in the morning. What did Dinah Copeland say about the face-powder?"

"She brought it down with her last night. Georgie Biggins wasn't behind the scenes at all last night. He made such a nuisance of himself that they gave him the sack. He was call-boy at the dress rehearsal, but the tables and dressing-rooms have all been scrubbed out since then. That powder must have been spilt after half-past six last evening. And another thing: Miss Dinah Copeland never heard about the onion—or says she didn't."

"That makes sense, anyway!"

"*Does it?*" said Nigel bitterly. "I don't mind owning that I fail to see the faintest significance in anything you've been saying. Why this chat about an onion?"

"Why, indeed," sighed Alleyn. "Come on. We'll pack up and go home. Even a policeman must sleep."

iii

But before Alleyn went to sleep that night he wrote to his love:

The Jernigham Arms,
November 29th.

MY DARLING TROY,

What a chancey sort of lover you've got. A fly-by-night who speaks to you at nine o'clock on Saturday evening, and soon after midnight is down in Dorset looking at lethal pianos. Shall you mind this sort of thing when we are married? You say not, and I suppose and hope not. You'll turn that dark head of yours and find your husband gone from your side. "Off again, I see," you'll say, and fall to thinking of the picture you are to paint next day. My dear and my darling Troy, you shall disappear, too, when you choose, into the austerity of your work, and never, never, never shall I look sideways, or disagreeably, or in the manner of the martyred spouse. Not as easy a promise as you might think, but I make it.

This is a disagreeable and unlikely affair. You will see the papers before my letter reaches you, but in case you'd like to know the official version, I enclose a very short account written in Yard language, and kept as colourless as possible. Fox and I have come to a conclusion, but are hanging off and on, hoping for a bit more evidence to turn up before we make an arrest. You told me once that your only method in detection would be based on character: and a very sound method, too, as long as you've got a flair for it. Now, here are our seven characters for you. What do you make of them?

First, the squire, Jocelyn Jernigham of Pen Cuckoo, and Acting Chief Constable to make it more difficult. He's a reddish, baldish man, with a look of perpetual surprise in his rather prominent light eyes. A bit pomposo. You would always know from the tone of his voice whether he spoke to a man or a woman. I think he would bore you and I think you would frighten him. The ladies, you see, should be gay and flirtatious and winsome. You are not at all winsome, darling, are you? They should make a man feel he's a bit of a dog. He's not altogether a fool, though, and, I should think, has a temper of his own. I think his cousin, Eleanor Prentice, frightens him, but he's full of family pride, and probably considers that even half a Jernigham can't be altogether wrong.

Miss Eleanor Prentice is half a Jernigham. She's about forty-nine or fifty, and I think rather a horrid woman. She's quite colourless and she's got buck teeth. She disseminates an odour of sanctity. She smiles a great deal, but with an air of forbearance as if hardly anything was really quite nice. I think she's a religious fanatic, heavily focused on the rector. This morning when I interviewed her she was thrown into a perfect fever by the sound of the church bells. She could scarcely listen to the simplest question, much less return a reasonable answer, so ardent and impatient was her longing to go to church. Now, in your true religious that's understandable enough. If you believe in the God Christ preached, you must be overwhelmed by your faith, and in time of trouble turn, with a heart of grace, to prayer. But I don't think Eleanor Prentice is that sort of religious. God knows I'm no psycho-analyst, but I imagine she'd be meat and drink to any one who was. Does one talk about a sex-fixation? Probably not. Anyway, she's gone the way modern psychology seems to consider axiomatic with women of her age and condition. This opinion is based partly on the statements of Henry Jernigham and Dinah Copeland and partly on my own impression of the woman.

Henry Jernigham is a good-looking young man. He's dark, with a jaw, grey eyes and an impressive head. He adopts the conversational manner of the moment, ironic and amusing, and gives the impression that he says whatever comes . . . into his head. But I don't believe any one has ever done that. How deep are our layers of thought, Troy. So deep that the thought of thought is terrifying to most of us. After many years, or perhaps only a few years, you and I may sometimes guess at each other's thoughts before they are spoken; and how strange that will seem to us. 'A proof of our love!' we shall cry.

This young Jernigham is in love with Dinah Copeland. Why didn't we meet when I was his age and you were a solemn child? Should I have loved you when you were fourteen and I was twenty-three? In those days I seem to remember I had a passion for full-blown blondes. But, without doubt, I would have loved and you would have never noticed it. Well, Henry loves Dinah, who is a nice, intelligent child and vaguely on the stage, as almost all of them seem to be nowadays. I long to drivel on about the damage that magnificent chap Irving did to his profession when he made it respectable. No art should be fashionable, Troy, should it? But Dinah is evidently a serious young actress and probably quite a good one. She adores Master Henry.

Dr. Templett, as you will see, looks very dubious. He could have taken the automatic, he could have fixed it in position, he has a motive, and he used all his authority to bring about the change of pianists. But he didn't get down to the hall until the audience had arrived, and he was never alone from the time he arrived until the time of the murder. To meet, he's a common-place enough fellow. Under ordinary circumstances, I think he'd be tiresomely facetious. There is no doubt that he was infected with a passion for Mrs. Selia Ross, and woe betide the man who loves a thin straw-coloured woman with an eye to the main chance. If she doesn't love him she'll let him down, and if she does love him she'll suck away his character like a leech. He'll develop anæmia of the personality. Mrs. Ross, as you will have gathered, *is* a thin, straw-coloured woman, with the sort of sex appeal that changes men's faces when they speak of her. Their eyes turn bright and at the same time guarded, and the muscle from the nostril to the corner of the mouth becomes accentuated. Do you think that a very humourless observation? It's very true, my girl, and if you ever want to draw a sensualist, draw him like that. Trust a policeman: old Darwin found it out in spite of those whiskers. Mrs. Ross could have nipped out of the car and dodged through the french window into the squire's study while Templett was handing his hat and coat to the butler. Had you thought of that? But she came down to the hall with Templett for the evening performance.

The rector, Walter Copeland, B.A. Oxon.: The first thing you think of is his head. He's an amazingly fine-looking fellow. Everything the photographer or the producer ordered for a magnificent cleric. Silver hair, dark eyebrows, saintly profile. It's like a nead on a coin or a statue, and much too much like any magazine illustration of "A Handsome Man." He seems to be less startling than his looks, and appears, in fact, to be a conscientious priest, rather disinclined for difficult jobs, but capable, suddenly, of digging in his toes. He is High Church, and I am sure very sincerely so. I should say that, if his belief came into question, he could be obstinate and even ruthless, but the general impression is of gentle vagueness.

The murdered woman seems to have been an arrogant, lonely, hysterical spinster. She and Miss Prentice might be taken as the positive and negative poles of parochial fanaticism with the rector as the needle. Not a true analogy. The general opinion is that she was a tartar.

It's midnight. I didn't get to bed last night, so I must leave you now. Troy, shall we have a holiday cottage in Dorset? A small house with a stern grey front, not too picturesque, but high up in the world so that you could paint the curves of the hills and the solemn changing cloud shadows that hurry over Dorset? Shall we have one? I'm going to marry you next April, and I love you with all my heart.

Good-night,
R.

iv

Alleyn laid down his pen and stretched his cramped fingers.

He was, he supposed, the only waking being in the inn, and the silence of a country dwelling at night flowed in upon his mind. The wind had dropped again, and he realised that for some time there had been no sound of rain. The fire had fallen into a glow. The timbers of the inn cracked abruptly and startled him. He was suddenly weary. His body was a stranger to his mind and he looked at it in wonder. He stood as if in a trance, alarmed at meeting himself as a stranger, yet aware of this experience which was not new to him. As always, some part of his mind tried to step across the threshold of the unknown, but was unable to give purpose to his whole thought. He returned to himself and, rousing, lit his candle, turned out the lamp, and climbed the stairs to his room.

His window looked up the Vale. High above him he could see a light. "They are late at bed at Pen Cuckoo," he thought, and opened the window. The sound of water dripping from the eaves came into the room and the smell of wet grass and earth. "Perhaps it will be fine to-morrow," he thought, and went happily to bed.

CHAPTER TWENTY-THREE

Frightened Lady

i

"—LET ME remind you, gentlemen," said the coroner, looking severely at Mr. Prosser, "that you are not concerned with theories. It is your duty to decide how this unfortunate lady met with her death. If you find you are able to do so, you must then make up your minds whether you are to return a verdict of accident, suicide or murder. If you are unable to arrive at this second decision, you must say so. Now, there is no difficulty in describing the manner of death. On Friday afternoon a small boy, after the manner of small boys, set an ingenious booby-trap. At some time before Saturday night, someone interfered with this comparatively harmless piece of mechanism. A Colt automatic was substituted for a water-pistol. You have heard that this automatic, the property of Mr. Jocelyn Jernigham, was in a room which is accessible from outside all day and every day. You have heard that it was common knowledge that the weapon was kept loaded in this room. You realise, I am sure, that on Saturday it would have been possible for anybody to enter the room through the french window and take the automatic. You have listened to a lucid description of the mechanism of this death-trap. You have examined the Colt automatic. You have been told that at 6.30 Miss Gladys Wright used the left-hand pedal of the piano, and that nothing untoward occurred. You have heard her say that from 6.30 until the moment of the catastrophe the front of the hall was occupied by herself, her fellow-helpers and, as they arrived, the audience. You have been shown photographs of the piano as it was at 6.30. The open top was covered in bunting which was secured to the sides by drawing-pins. On top of the piano and standing on the bunting, which stretched over the turned-back lid, were six pot plants. You realise that up to within fifteen minutes of the tragedy, every member of the company of performers, and every person in the audience, believed that it was Miss Prentice who was to play the overture. You may therefore have formed the opinion that Miss Prentice, and not Miss Campanula, was the intended victim. This need not affect your decision and, as a coroner's jury, does not actually concern you. If you agree that at eight o'clock Miss Campanula pressed the left-hand or soft pedal and was killed by a charge from the automatic and that somebody had put the automatic in the piano with felonious intent, in short with intent to murder, and if you consider there is no evidence to show who this person was—why, then, gentlemen, you may return a verdict to this effect."

"O upright beak!" said Alleyn as Mr. Prosser and the jury retired. "O admirable and economic coroner! Slap, bang, and away they go. Slap, bang, and here they are again."

They had indeed only gone into a huddle in the doorway, and returned looking rather as if they had all washed their faces in rectitude.

"Yes, Mr. Prosser?"

"We are all agreed, sir."

"Yes?"

"We return a verdict of murder," said Mr. Prosser, looking as if he feared he hadn't got it quite as it ought to be, "against person or persons unknown."

"Thank you. The only possible conclusion, gentlemen."

"I should like to add," said the smallest juryman, suddenly, "that I think them water-pistols ought to be put down by law."

ii

Immediately after the inquest, Fox and Ford left for Duck Cottage. Alleyn's hand was on the door of Nigel's car, when he heard his name called. He turned and found himself face to face with Mrs. Ross.

"Mr. Alleyn—I'm so sorry to bother you, but may I come and see you? I've remembered something that I think you ought to know."

"Certainly," said Alleyn. "Now, if it suits you."

"You're staying at the Jernigham Arms, aren't you? May I come there in ten minutes?"

"Yes, of course. I shall drive straight there."

"Thank you so much."

Alleyn replaced his hat and climbed into the car.

"*Now*, what the devil?" he wondered. "It's fallen out rather well, as it happens. Fox will have a longer session with the pretty housemaid."

Nigel came out and drove him to the inn. Alleyn asked Mrs. Peach if he could use the back parlour as an office for an hour. Mrs. Peach was volubly agreeable.

Nigel was told to take himself off.

"Why should I? Who are you going to see?"

"Mrs. Ross."

"Why can't I be there?"

"Because I think she'll speak more freely if she sees me alone."

"Well, let me sit in the next room with the slide a crack open."

Alleyn looked thoughtfully at him.

"Very well," he said, "you may do that. Take notes. It can't be used in evidence, but it may be handy. Wait a second. You've got your camera?"

"Yes."

"See if you can get a shot of her as she comes in. Careful about it. Get there quickly. She'll arrive in a second."

Nigel was only just in time. In five minutes the pot-boy announced Mrs. Ross, who came in looking much more like the Ritz than the Jernigham Arms.

"It *is* nice of you to see me," she said. "Ever since I remembered it, I've been so worried about this thing. I felt very bold, accosting you outside the hall of justice or whatever it was. You must be rushed off your feet."

"It's my job to listen," said Alleyn.

"May I sit down?"

"Please. I think this is the most comfortable chair."

She sat down with a pretty air of intimacy. She drew off her gloves, rummaged in her bag for her cigarettes, and then accepted one of his. Alleyn remained standing.

"You know," said Mrs. Ross, "you're not a bit my idea of a detective."

"No?"

"Not a *bit*. That enormous man who drives about with you looks much more the thing done at the Yard."

"Perhaps you would rather see Inspector Fox?"

"No, I'd much rather see you. Don't snub me."

"I'm sorry if I seemed to do that. What is it you would like to tell me?"

She leant forward. Her manner lost its flippancy and took on an air of practical concern, but it also managed to suggest that she knew he would understand and sympathize with her motive in coming to him.

"You'll think I was such a fool not to remember it before," she said; "but the whole thing's been rather a shock. I suppose I simply had a blank moment or something. Not that I had any affection for the poor old thing; but, for all that, it was rather a shock."

"I'm sure it was."

"When you came to see me yesterday I had a ghastly headache and could hardly think. Did you ask me if I went out on Friday night?"

"Yes. You told me you were at home."

"I *thought* I did. Honestly, I don't know what I could have been thinking about. I *was* at home practically all the evening, but I went out for about half an hour. I drove from here to post a letter. I quite forgot."

"That's not very serious."

"I'm extremely relieved to hear you say so," she said, and laughed. "I was afraid you'd be *angry* with me."

She had a comical trick of over-emphasis, as if she parodied her own conversation. She drew out the word *angry*, making a grimace over it and opening her eyes very wide.

"Is that the whole story?" asked Alleyn.

"No, it's not," she said flatly. "The thing is, on my way down I came by Church Lane, past the hall. Church Lane goes on over the hills, you know, and comes out close to my cottage."

"Yes."

"Well, there was a light in one of the dressing-rooms."

"What time was this?"

"It was eleven when I got back. Say about twenty to eleven. No, a little earlier."

"Which dressing-room was it, do you know?"

"Yes. I've worked it out. It was too far away to be either of the women's rooms, and anyway they've got blinds. Miss Prentice, who is a very pure woman, thought it wasn't quite nice for us not to have blinds. The one Billy Templett uses has its window on the far side. It must have been the squire's. Mr. Jernigham's. But the funny thing about it was that it only flashed on for a few seconds and then went out again."

"Are you quite sure it wasn't the reflection of your headlights?"

"Absolutely positive. It was much too far to my right, and anyway it wasn't a bit like that. The glass is that thick stuff. No, a yellow square just popped up and popped out again."

"I see."

"It may not be anything at all, but it was on my conscience, so I thought I'd own up, and *come clean* and all that. I didn't think anything of it at the time. It might have been Dinah Copeland messing about over there, or any old thing; but as every moment after Friday seems important——"

"It's much better to let the police know of anything you remember that may have even the smallest significance," said Alleyn.

"I hoped you'd say that. Mr. Alleyn, I'm so terribly worried, and you're so human and unofficial, I wonder if I dare ask you something rather awkward."

Alleyn's manner could scarcely have been more formal as he replied: "I am here as a policeman, you know."

"Yes, I know. Well, when in doubt, ask a policeman." She grinned charmingly. "No, but honestly I'm in a horrid—awful muddle. It's about Billy Templett. I'm sure you've already heard all the local gossip, and you'll have found out for yourself that the charming people in this aristocratic part of the world have got minds like sinks and worse. No doubt they've told you all the local lies about Billy Templett and me. Well, we *are* great friends. He's the only soul in the entire district with an idea beyond hunting and other people's business, and we've got a lot in common. Of course, as a doctor, he's not supposed to look on women as anything but sets of insides and collections of complaints. I never dreamt it might actually do his practice no good if he saw rather more of me than old Mrs. Cain and the oldest inhabitant. Oh, dear, this *is* difficult. May I have another cigarette, please?"

Alleyn gave her another cigarette.

"I may as well choke it out before I lose my nerve altogether. Do you suspect Billy of this beastly crime?"

"As the case stands," said Alleyn, "it appears to be quite impossible that Dr. Templett should have had any hand in it."

"Is that true?" she asked, and her voice was as sharp as a knife.

"It is a very serious offence for a policeman to set traps or deliberately mislead his witnesses."

"I'm sorry. I know that. It was just the relief. You remember that letter you showed me yesterday? The anonymous letter?"

"Yes."

"It was written to me."

"Yes."

"I knew I hadn't taken you in. You are a clever beast, aren't you?" She laughed again. Alleyn wondered how many people had told her she laughed like a gamine and whether she ever forgot it.

"Do you want to amend your statement about the letter?" he asked.

"Yes, please. I want to explain. I showed the letter to Billy and we discussed it and decided to take no notice. When you showed it to me I supposed you'd picked it up somewhere in the hall, and as I knew it had nothing to do with this murder, and I wanted to protect poor old Billy, I said I didn't know anything about it. And then he came in and I thought he'd take his cue from me and—well, it went wrong."

"Yes," said Alleyn, "it went very wrong."

"Mr. Alleyn, what did he tell you last evening when he went away with you? Was he—was he angry with me? He didn't realise I'd tried to help him, did he?"

"I don't think so."

"He might have known! It's one of those hideous things that turn into a muddle."

"I'm afraid your explanation has gone equally astray."

"What do you mean?"

"I mean that you knew where Dr. Templett put the letter and that it is very unlikely we picked it up in the hall. I mean that yesterday you spoke instinctively and with the object of getting out of an awkward position. You have since remembered that there is a fingerprint system, so you come to me with a story of altruistic motives. When I told you Dr. Templett is not, on the evidence we have, a likely suspect you regretted that you had shown your hand. I think I know a frightened woman when I see one, and yesterday you were very frightened, Mrs. Ross."

She had let her cigarette burn down to her fingers. Her hand jerked and she dropped the butt on the floor. He picked it up and threw it in the fire.

"You're wrong," she said. "I did it for *him*."

Alleyn made no answer.

She said, "I thought she'd written it. The murdered woman. And I thought old Prentice was going to play."

"Dr. Templett didn't tell you on Saturday morning that it would be a physical impossibility for Miss Prentice to play?"

"We didn't discuss it. Billy didn't do it and neither did I. We didn't get to the place till nearly eight o'clock."

"You arrived soon after 7.30," Alleyn corrected her.

"Well, anyway, it was too late to do anything to the piano. The hall was packed. We were never alone."

"Mrs. Ross, when I asked you yesterday about the episode of the window, why did you not tell me you saw someone dodge down behind the sill?"

She seemed startled but not particularly alarmed at this. She looked at him, as he thought, speculatingly, as though she deliberately weighed his question and pondered the answer. At last she said:

"I suppose Billy told you that. It was only an impression, through the thick glass. The window was only open about two inches."

"I suggest that you were alarmed at the idea of an eavesdropper. I suggest that you noticed this shadow at the window only after you had been for some little time on the stage with Dr. Templett, and that enough had taken place in that time for you to be seriously compromised. I suggest that you told Dr. Templett to shut the window and that you lowered the curtain to ensure privacy."

She tilted her head to one side and looked at him under her lashes.

"You really ought to join the Women's Circle. They'd adore that story at a tea-party."

"I shall work," said Alleyn, "on the theory that you said nothing more to Dr. Templett of this shadowy impression, as you did not wish to alarm him, but that it was not too shadowy or too fleeting for you to recognise the watcher at the window."

That shot did go home. Her whole face seemed to sharpen and she made a quick involuntary movement of her hands. She waited for a moment, and he knew that she was mustering her nerves. Then in one swift movement she was on her feet, close to him, her hands on his coat.

"You don't believe I'd do anything like that, do you? You're not such a fool. I don't even understand how it worked, and I've never been able to tie a knot in my life. Mr. Alleyn? Please?"

"If you are innocent you're in no danger."

"Do you promise that?"

"Certainly."

Before he could move she dropped her head against him and clung to his coat. She murmured broken phrases. Her hair was scented. He felt her uneven breathing.

"No, no," he said, "this won't do."

"I'm sorry—you've frightened me. Don't be nervous, I'm not trying to seduce you. I'm only rather shaken. I'll be all right in a moment."

"You're all right now," said Alleyn. He took her wrists and held her away from him. "That's better."

She stood before him with her head bent down. She achieved a look of helpless captivity. Her whole posture seemed to proclaim her subjection. When she raised her face it wore a gamine grin.

"You're either made of dough," she said, "or else you're afraid I'll compromise you. Poor Mr. Alleyn."

"You would have been wiser to call on Mr. Jernigham," said Alleyn. "He's Acting Chief Constable, you know."

iii

When she had been gone some minutes, Nigel looked cautiously into the back parlour.

"Hell knows no fury," he said.

"An intensely embarrassing lady," said Alleyn. "Did you get a shot of her?"

"Yes. Ought to be all right. I got her as she came in."

"Let me have the film or plate, or whatever it is."

"Do explain all this, Alleyn."

"It's as plain as daylight. She's got a genius for self-preservation. When I showed her the anonymous letter she was hell-bent on keeping out of suspicion, and on the spur of the moment denied all knowledge of it. She'd do her best for Templett up to a point, but a charge of homicide is definitely beyond that point. Yesterday she let him down with a thud. Now she's regretting it. I think she's probably as much in love with him as she could be with anybody. She's read a popular book on criminal investigation. She remembered that she'd handled the letter and realised we'd find her prints. So she hatched up this story. Now she knows we're not after Templett she'll try to get him back. But she's a sensible woman, and she wouldn't hang for him."

"I wonder if he'll believe her," said Nigel.

"Probably," said Alleyn. "If she gets a chance to see him alone."

Fox came in.

"I've seen Mrs. Ross's maid, sir. There's nothing much, except that Mrs. Ross did go out on Friday night. It was the maid's night off, but her boy had a cold and it was raining, so she stayed in. She only mentioned this to Mrs. Ross this morning."

"And Mrs. Ross mentioned it to me in case the maid got in first."

"Is that a fact, sir?"

"It is, Brer Fox. You shall hear of our interview."

Fox listened solemnly to the account of the interview.

"Well," he said, "she's come off worst in that bout, sir. What'll she do now?"

"I think she'd like to have a shot at old Jernigham. She's frightened and rattled. A shrewd woman, but not really clever."

"Does she think you suspect her, Mr. Alleyn?"

"She's afraid I might."

"*Do* you suspect her?" asked Nigel.

"Of all sorts of things," said Alleyn lightly. He sniffed at his coat. "Blast the woman. I stink of Chanel No. 5."

Nigel burst out laughing.

"Don't you think she's attractive?" he said. "I do."

"Fortunately I don't. I can see she might be; but she gives me housemaid's creeps. What do you think, Fox?"

"Well, sir, under more favourable conditions I dare say she'd be quite an experience in a way. There's something about her."

"You licentious old article."

"She's not very comfortable, if you know what I mean. More on the frisky side. I'd say she's one of these society ladies who, if they were born in a lower walk of life, would set up for themselves in a rather exclusive way, but well within the meaning of the act."

"Yes, Fox."

"What do we do now, Mr. Alleyn?"

"We lunch. After lunch we have a word together. And to-night I think we play a forcing hand, Fox. We've got about as much information as we'll ever screw out of them by separate interviews. Let's see how we get on with a mixed bunch. There's a fast train from Great Chipping in an hour. I think I'll catch it. Will you see the telephone people? Have one more stab at the villagers for Saturday afternoon. The person who stood at the box and peeped through the window. Ask if anyone saw anybody about the place. You won't get anything, but we've got to try. Arrange the meeting with Jernigham senior. I'd better see him myself beforehand. There are one or two things—— Go carefully with him, Fox. And telephone to me at the Yard before half-past five."

"I'll come up with you, if I may," said Nigel.

"Do. There's a good train that gets to Great Chipping at 8.15. I'll return by that, and send a car ahead with two people and clanking chains, in case we feel like arresting somebody. All right?"

"Very good, sir," said Fox.

"Then we'd better lunch."

CHAPTER TWENTY-FOUR

The Peculiarity of Miss P.

i

"It's no good taking it like this, Eleanor," said the squire, laying down his napkin and glaring at his cousin. "How do you suppose we feel? You won't help matters by starving yourself."

"I'm sorry, Jocelyn, but I cannot eat."

"You can't go on like this, my dear girl. You'll get ill."

"Would that matter very much?"

"Don't be an ass, Eleanor. Henry, give her some apple tart."

"No, thank you, Henry."

"What you want, Cousin Eleanor," said Henry from the side table, "is a good swinging whisky."

"Please, dear. I'm sorry if I'm irritating you both. It would be better if I didn't come down to lunch."

"Good Gad, woman," shouted the squire. "Don't talk such piffling drivel. We simply don't want you to kill yourself."

"It's a pity," said Miss Prentice stonily, "that I wasn't killed. I realise that. It would have been a blessed release. They say poor Idris didn't feel anything. It's the living who suffer."

"Cousin Eleanor," said Henry, returning with a loaded plate, "have you ever read *Our Mutual Friend*?"

"No, Henry."

"Because you're giving a perfectly brilliant impersonation of Mrs. R. W."

"Was she very irritating?"

"Very."

"That'll do, Henry," said the squire. He darted an uncomfortable glance at Miss Prentice, who sat upright in her chair with her head bowed. At intervals she drew in her breath sharply and closed her eyes.

"Is your finger hurting you?" demanded Jocelyn after a particularly noticeable hiss from the sufferer. She opened her eyes and smiled palely.

"A little."

"You'd better let Templett see it again."

"I'm not very likely to do that, Jocelyn."

"Why not?" asked Henry. "Do you think he's the murderer?"

"Oh, Henry, Henry," said Miss Prentice. "Some day you'll be sorry you have grieved me so much."

"Upon my word," said Henry, "I can't for the life of me see why that should grieve you. One of us is a murderer. I only asked if you thought it might be Templett."

"You are fortunate to be able to speak so lightly of this terrible, terrible tragedy."

"We're as much worried as you are," protested Jocelyn with an appealing glance at his son. "Aren't we, boy?"

"Of course we are," said Henry cheerfully.

"As a matter of fact, I've asked Copeland to come up here and talk the whole thing over."

Miss Prentice clasped her hands and gave a little cry. A dull flush stained her cheeks and her eyes brightened.

"Is he coming? How wise of you, Jocelyn! He is so wonderful. He will help us all. It will all come out right. It will come out quite, quite all right."

She laughed hysterically and clapped her hands.

"When is he coming?"

Jocelyn looked at her with positive terror.

"This evening," he said. "Eleanor, you're not well."

"And is dear Dinah coming, too?" asked Miss Prentice shrilly.

"Hullo!" said Henry. "Here's a change." And he stared fixedly at his cousin.

"Henry," said Miss Prentice very rapidly. "Shall we forget our little differences? I have your happiness so much at heart, dear. If you had been more candid and straightforward with me——"

"Why should I?" asked Henry.

"—I think you would have found me quite understanding. Shall we let bygones be bygones? You see, dear, you have no mother to——"

"Will you excuse me, sir?" said Henry. "I feel slightly sick." And he walked out of the room.

"I thought," said Miss Prentice, "that I had been deeply enough injured already. So deeply, deeply injured. I am sorry I am rather excited, Jocelyn dear, but, you see, when someone is waiting down at St. Giles to shoot you—— *Jocelyn, is that somebody coming?*"

"What the devil's the matter, Eleanor?"

"It's that woman! It was her car! I saw it through the window. Jocelyn, I won't meet that woman. She'll do me an injury. She's wicked, wicked, wicked. A woman of Babylon. They're all the same. All bad, horrible creatures."

"Eleanor, be quiet."

"You're a man. You don't understand. *I will not meet her*."

Taylor came in.

"Mrs. Ross to see you, sir."

"Damnation!" said the squire. "All right. Take her to the study."

ii

The squire was worried about Eleanor. She was really very odd indeed, far odder than even these uncomfortable circumstances warranted. There was no knowing what she'd say next. If he didn't look out, she'd land him in a pretty tight corner with one of these extraordinary statements of hers. She'd got such a damned knowing look in her eye. When she thought he wasn't noticing her, she'd sit in a corner watching him, with an expression which could only be described as a leer. If she was going mad! Well, there was one thing: mad people couldn't give evidence. Perhaps the best thing would be to ask an alienist down for the weekend. He hoped to heaven she wouldn't take it into her head to come raging into the study and go for poor little Mrs. Ross. His thoughts raced through his head as he crossed the hall, passed through the library and entered his study. Anyway, it'd be a relief to talk to an attractive woman.

She did look very attractive. Pale-ish, but that was understandable. She wore her clothes like a French-woman. He'd always liked black. Damn' good figure and legs. He took the little hand in its delicate glove and held it tightly.

"Well," he said, "this *is* nice of you."

"I simply had to see you. You'll think me a most frightful bore, coming at this time."

"Now you knew that wasn't true before you said it."

The little hand started in his.

"Have I hurt you?" asked the squire. "I am a clumsy brute."

"No. Not really. Only you are rather strong, aren't you? It's just my ring."

"I insist on investigating."

He peeled back the soft glove and drew it down.

"Look at that! A red mark on the inside of your finger. Now, what can be done about that?"

A subdued laugh. He separated the white fingers and kissed them.

"Ha-ha, my boy!" thought the squire, and led her to a chair.

"You've done me good already," he said. "Do you realise that, madam?"

"Have I?"

"Don't you think you're rather an attractive little thing?"

"What am I supposed to say to that?"

"You know it damned well, so you needn't say anything. Ha, ha, ha!"

"Well, I *have* heard something like it before."

"How often?" purred the squire.

"Never you mind."

"Why are you so attractive?"

"Just made that way."

"Little devil," he said and kissed the hand again. He felt quite excited. Everything was going like clockwork.

"Oh, dear," whispered Mrs. Ross. "You're going to be simply livid with me."

"Simply furious?" he asked tenderly.

"Yes. Honestly. I don't want to tell you; but I must!"

"Don't look at me like that or I shall have to kiss you."

"No, please. You must listen. Please."

"If I listen I expect to be rewarded."

"We'll see about that," she said.

"Promise?"

"Promise."

"I'm listening," said the squire, rather feverishly.

"It's about this awful business. I want to tell you first of all, very, very sincerely that you've nothing to fear from me."

"Nothing——?"

He still held her hand, but his fingers relaxed.

"No," she said, "nothing. If you will just trust me——"

Her voice went on and on. Jocelyn heard her to the end, but when it was over he did not remind her of her promise.

iii

When Alleyn left the assistant commissioner and returned to his own office, he found Bailey there.

"Well, Bailey?"

"Well, sir, Thompson's developed Mr. Bathgate's film. He's got a couple of shots of the lady."

He laid the still wet prints on the desk.

There was Mrs. Ross in profile on the front step of the Jernigham Arms, and there she was again full face as she came up the path. Nigel must have taken his snapshots through the open window. Evidently she had not seen him. The pointed chin was set a little to one side, the under lip projected very slightly, and the thin mouth was drawn down at the corners. They were not flattering photographs.

"Any luck?" asked Alleyn.

With his normal air of mulish disapproval Bailey laid a card beside the prints. On it was mounted a double photograph. Sharp profile, thin mouth, pointed chin; and the front view showed the colourless hair, drawn back in two immaculate shining wings, from the rather high forehead.

Alleyn muttered: "Sarah Rosen. Age 33. Height 5 ft. 5¼ ins. Eyes, light blue. Hair, pale blonde. Very well dressed, cultured speech, usually poses as widow. Detained with Claude Smith on blackmailing charge, 1931. Subsequently released—insufficient evidence. Claude got ten years, didn't he?"

"That's right, sir. They stayed at the Ritz as brother and sister."

"I remember. What about the prints?"

"They're good enough."

"Blackmail," said Alleyn thoughtfully.

"I've looked up the case. She was in the game all right, but they hadn't a thing on her. She seems to have talked her way out."

"She would. Thank you, Bailey. I wish I'd known this a little earlier. Oh, well, no matter, it fits in very prettily."

"Anything else, Mr. Alleyn?"

"I'm going to my flat for half an hour. If Fox rings up before I'm back tell him I'm there. The car ought to leave now. I'll fix that up. We'd better take a wardress, I suppose. All right, Bailey. Thank you."

iv

Henry wondered what the devil Mrs. Ross had to say to his father. He had watched, with extreme distaste, their growing intimacy. "How sharper than a serpent's tooth it is," he thought, "to have a prancing parent." When Jocelyn spoke to Mrs. Ross his habit of loud inexplicable laughter, his manner of leaning backwards, of making a series of mysterious little bows, the curious gesture he employed, the inclination his eyes exhibited towards protuberance, and the naked imbecility of his conversation, all vexed and embarrassed his son to an almost insupportable degree. If Jocelyn should marry her! Henry had no particular objection to Mrs. Ross, but the thought of her as a stepmother struck dismay to his heart. His affection for his father was not weakened by Jocelyn's absurdities. He loved him deeply, he realised, and now the thought that his father might be making a fool of himself in there with that woman was more than he could endure. Miss Prentice had, no doubt, gone to her room; Dinah was out; there was nothing to do.

He wandered restlessly into the library, half-hoping that the door into the study would be open. It was closed. He could hear the murmur of a woman's voice. On and on. What the hell could she have to say? Then a baritone interjection in which he read urgency and vehemence. Then a long pause.

"My God!" thought Henry. "If he has proposed to her!"

He whistled raucously, took an encyclopædia from the shelves, banged the glass door and slammed the book down on the table.

He heard his father exclaim. A chair castor squeaked and the voices grew more distant. They had moved to the far end of the room.

Henry flung himself into an arm-chair, and once again the conundrum of the murder beset him. Who *did* the police believe had tried to murder Eleanor Prentice? Which would they say had the greatest reason for wishing Eleanor dead? With the thud of fear that came upon him whenever he thought of this, he supposed that he himself had most reason for wishing Eleanor out of the way. Was it possible that Alleyn suspected him? Whom *did* Alleyn suspect? Not Dinah, surely, not the rector, not his own father. Templett, then? Or—yes—Mrs. Ross? But, Alleyn would surely reason, if Templett was the murderer, it was a successful murder, since it was Templett who insisted that Eleanor shouldn't play the piano. Alleyn would wonder if Templett had told Mrs. Ross he would not allow Eleanor to play. Did Dinah's tirade against Mrs. Ross mean that Dinah suspected her? Had the police any idea who could have gone to the piano after there were people in the hall, and yet not been seen? Already the story of Gladys Wright had reached Pen Cuckoo. And as final conjecture, perhaps they would ask themselves if Eleanor Prentice in some way had faked her finger and set the trap for her bosom enemy. Or might they agree with the rector and call it a case of attempted murder and suicide?

He leapt to his feet. There was no longer a sound of voices in the study. They must have gone out by the french window.

Henry opened the door and walked in. No, they were still there. Mrs. Ross sat in the window with her back to the light. Jocelyn Jernigham faced the door. When Henry saw Jocelyn he cried out: "Father, what's the matter?"

Jocelyn said, "Nothing's the matter."

Mrs. Ross said, "Hullo! Good-afternoon."

"Good-afternoon," said Henry. "Father, are you ill?"

"No. Don't come bursting into the room asking people if they're ill. It's ridiculous."

"But your face! It's absolutely ashen."

"I've got indigestion."

"I don't believe it."

"I thought he looked pale," said Mrs. Ross solicitously.

"He's absolutely green."

"I'm nothing of the sort," said Jocelyn angrily. "Mrs. Ross and I are talking privately, Henry."

"I'm sorry," said Henry stubbornly, "but I know there's something wrong here. What is it?"

"There's nothing wrong, my dear boy," she said lightly.

He stared at her.

"I'm afraid I still think there is."

"Well, I very much hope you won't still think there is when we tell you all about it. At the moment I'm afraid it's a secret." She looked at Jocelyn. "Isn't it?"

"Yes. Of course. Go away, boy, you're making a fool of yourself."

"Are you sure," Henry asked slowly, "that nobody is making a fool of you?"

Taylor came in. He looked slightly disgruntled.

"Inspector Fox to see you, sir. I told him——"

"Good-afternoon, sir," said a rumbling voice, and the bulk of Inspector Fox filled the doorway.

V

Henry saw the squire look quickly from the open window to Mrs. Ross. Taylor stood aside and Fox walked in.

"I hope you'll excuse me coming straight in like this, sir," said

Fox. "Chief Inspector Alleyn asked me to call. I took the liberty of following your butler. Perhaps I ought to have waited."

"No, no," said Jocelyn. "Sit down, er——"

"Fox, sir. Thank you very much, sir."

Fox placed his bowler on a near-by table. He turned to Henry.

"Good-afternoon, sir. We met last night, didn't we?"

"This is Inspector Fox, Mrs. Ross," said Henry.

"Good-afternoon, madam," said Fox tranquilly. Then he sat down. As Alleyn once remarked to Nigel, there was a certain dignity about Fox.

Mrs. Ross smiled charmingly.

"I must take myself off," she said, "and not interrupt Mr. Fox. Don't move, anybody, please."

"If it's not troubling you too much, Mrs. Ross," said Fox, "I'd be obliged if you'd wait for a moment. There are one or two little routine questions for general inquiry, and it will save me taking up your time later on."

"But I'm longing to stay, Mr. Fox."

"Thank you, madam."

Fox took out his spectacles and placed them on his nose. He then drew his note-book from an inside pocket, opened it and stared at it.

"Yes," he said. "Now, the first item's a small matter, really. Did anybody present find the onion in the teapot?"

"*What!*" Henry ejaculated.

Fox fixed his eyes on him.

"The onion in the teapot, sir."

"Which onion in what teapot?" demanded Jocelyn.

Fox turned to him.

"Young Biggins, sir, has admitted that he put a Spanish onion in the teapot used on the stage. We'd like to know who removed it."

Mrs. Ross burst out laughing.

"I'm so sorry," she said, "but it *is* rather funny."

"It sounds rather a ridiculous sort of thing, doesn't it, madam?" agreed Fox gravely. "Do you know anything about it?"

"I'm afraid not. I think Mr. Alleyn has already accused me of an onion."

"Did you happen to hear anything of it, sir?"

"Good Lord, no," said Jocelyn.

"And you, Mr. Henry?"

"Not I," said Henry.

"The next matter," said Fox, making a note, "is the window. I understand you found it open on Saturday afternoon, Mrs. Ross."

"Yes. We shut it."

"Yes. You'd already shut it once, hadn't you? At midday?"

"Yes, I had."

"Who opened it?" inquired Fox, and he looked first at Jocelyn and then at Henry. They both shook their heads.

"I should think it was probably Miss Prentice. My cousin," said Henry. "She has a deep-rooted mania——" He checked himself. "She's a fresh-air fiend of the worst variety and continually complained that the hall was stuffy."

"I wonder if I might ask Miss Prentice?" said Fox. "Is she at home, sir?"

The squire looked extremely uncomfortable.

"I think she's—ah—she's—ah—in. Yes."

"Do you want me any longer, Mr. Fox?" asked Mrs. Ross.

"I think that will be all for the present, thank you, madam. The chief inspector would be much obliged if you could come down to the hall at about 9.15 this evening."

"Oh? Yes, very well."

"Thank you very much, madam."

"I'll see you out," said the squire hurriedly.

They went out by the french window.

Henry offered Fox a cigarette.

"No. Thank you very much, all the same, sir."

"Mr. Fox," said Henry. "What do you think of the rector's theory? I mean, the idea that Miss Campanula set the trap for my cousin, and that something happened to make her so miserable that when she was asked to play she thought: 'Oh, well, this settles it. Here goes!' "

"Would you have said the deceased lady seemed very unhappy, sir?"

"Well, you know, I didn't notice her very much. But I've been thinking it over, and—yes—she was rather odd. She was damned odd. For one thing, she'd evidently had a colossal row with my cousin. Or rather my cousin seemed friendly enough, but Miss C. wouldn't say a word to her. She was a cranky old cup of tea, you know, and we none of us took much notice. Know what I mean?"

"I understand, sir," said Fox, looking hard at Henry. "Perhaps if I could just have a word with Miss Prentice."

"Oh, Lord!" said Henry ruefully. "Look here, Mr. Fox, you'll find her pretty rum. You'll think we specialize in eccentric spinsters in this part of the world, but I promise you I think the shock of this business has pushed her off at the deep-end. She seems to think the murderer's made a mess of the first attempt, and sooner or later will have another go at her."

"That's not unnatural, is it, sir? Perhaps the lady would feel more comfortable with police protection."

"I pity the protector," said Henry. "Well, I suppose I'd better see if she'll come down."

"If you wouldn't mind, sir," said Fox comfortably.

In some trepidation, Henry mounted the stairs and tapped on Miss Prentice's door. There was no answer. He tapped again. The door opened suddenly and Miss Prentice was revealed with her fingers to her lips, like some mysterious bucktoothed sybil.

"What's happened!" she whispered.

"Nothing's happened, Cousin Eleanor. It's simply one of the men from Scotland Yard with a rather childish question to ask you."

"Is that woman there? I won't meet that woman."

"Mrs. Ross has gone."

"Henry, is that true?"

"Of course it's true."

"Now I've made you angry again. You're very unkind to me, Henry."

"My dear Cousin Eleanor!"

Her hand moved restlessly across the bosom of her dress.

"Yes, you are. So unkind. And I'm so fond of you. It's only for your own good. You're young and strong and handsome. All the Jernighams are very strong and beautiful. Don't listen to women like that, Henry. Don't listen to any woman. They'll do you harm. Except dear Dinah."

"Will you come down and speak to Inspector Fox?"

"It's not a trap to make me meet that woman? Why is it a different man? Fox? Where's the other man? He was a gentleman. So tall! Taller than Father Copeland."

He saw with astonishment that the movement of her hand traced a definite pattern on her bosom. She was crossing herself.

"This man is perfectly harmless," said Henry. "Do come."

"Very well. My head's splitting. I suppose I must come."

"That's better," said Henry. He added awkwardly: "Cousin Eleanor, your dress is undone."

"Oh!" She blushed crimson and, to his horror, laughed shrilly and turned aside her head. Her fingers fumbled with the fastening of her dress. Then she shrank past him and, with a kind of coquettishness in her gait, hurried downstairs.

Henry followed with a sinking heart and escorted her to the study. His father had returned and stood before the fire. Jocelyn glared uncomfortably at Miss Prentice.

"Hullo, Eleanor, here you are. This is Inspector Fox."

Miss Prentice offered her hand and, as soon as Fox touched it, snatched it away. Her eyes were downcast, her hands pleated a fold in her dress. Fox looked calmly at her.

"I'm sorry to trouble you, Miss Prentice. I only wanted to ask if you opened one of the hall windows as you left at noon on Saturday."

"Oh, yes," she whispered. "Was that the unpardonable sin?"

"I beg your pardon, miss?"

"Did I let it in?"

"Let what in, Miss Prentice?"

"You know. But I only opened it the least little bit. A tiny crack. Of course it can make itself very small, can't it?"

Fox adjusted his spectacles and made a note.

"You did open the window?" he said.

"You shouldn't keep on asking. You know I did."

"Miss Prentice, did you find anything in the teapot you were to use on the stage?"

"Is that where it hid?"

"Where what hid?"

"The unpardonable sin. You know. The thing she did!"

"You're talking nonsense, Eleanor," said Jocelyn. He got behind her and made violent grimaces at Fox.

"I'm sorry if I irritate you, Jocelyn."

"You don't know anything about an onion that a small boy put in the teapot, Miss Prentice?"

She opened her eyes very wide and shaped her mouth like an O. Then she slowly shook her head. Once started, she seemed unable to leave off shaking her head, but went on and on until the movement lost all meaning.

"Well," said Fox, "I think that's all I need trouble you about, thank you, Miss Prentice."

"Henry," said Jocelyn. "See your cousin upstairs."

She went without another word. Henry hurried after her. Jocelyn turned to Fox.

"See how it is!" he said. "The shock sent her out of her mind.

There are no two ways about it. See for yourself. Have to get a specialist. Better not believe a word she says."

"She's never been like this before, sir?"

"Good God, no."

"That's very distressing, sir, isn't it? The chief inspector asked me to speak to you, sir, about this evening. He thinks it would be a good idea to see, at the same time, all the people who were in the play, and he wonders if you would be good enough to send your party down to the hall."

"I must say I don't quite see—— As a matter of fact, I've asked the Copelands for dinner to talk things over."

"That will fit in very nicely, then, won't it, sir? You can come on to the hall."

"Yes, but I don't see what good it'll do."

"The chief inspector will explain when he comes, sir. He asked me to say he'd be very much obliged if you would give the lead in this little matter. In view of your position in the county, sir, he thought you would prefer to come before the others. You've two cars, haven't you, sir?"

"I suppose I'd better." Jocelyn stared very hard at a portrait of his actress-ancestress and said, "Have you got any idea who it is?"

"I couldn't say what the chief intends just at the moment, sir," answered Fox so blandly that the evasion sounded exactly like a direct answer. "No doubt he will report to you himself, sir. Would nine o'clock suit you at the hall, Mr. Jernigham?"

"What? Oh, yes. Yes, certainly."

"I'm much obliged, sir. I'll say good-afternoon."

"Good-afternoon," said Jocelyn restlessly.

vi

"This is Miss Bruce," said the supervisor. "She was on duty on Friday night, but I doubt if she'll be able to help you."

Fox looked placidly at Miss Bruce and noted that she seemed a bright young person.

He said, "Well, Miss Bruce, we'll be very pleased if you can put us right in this little matter. I understand you were on duty as an operator at ten o'clock on Friday evening."

"Yes, that's right."

"Yes. Now the call we're interested in came through somewhere round about 10.30. It was to the rectory, Winton St. Giles. It's a party line with the old manual telephones and a long extension. Not many of those left, are there?"

"They'll be gone by this time next year," said the supervisor.

"Is that a fact?" said Fox comfortably. "Well, well. Now, Miss Bruce, can you help us?"

"I don't remember any calls on the rectory phone on Friday night," said Miss Bruce. "Chipping 10, the number is. I'm in the Y.P.F.C., so I know. We always have to ring a long time there, because the old housemaid Mary's a bit deaf, and Miss Dinah's room's away upstairs, and the rector never answers until he's fetched. It's a line that's used a lot, of course."

"It would be."

"Yes. Friday was Reading Circle night, and they're usually over at the hall, so everybody knows not to ring up on Friday, see, because they won't be in. Actually, last Friday it was at the rectory because of the play; but people wouldn't know that, see. They'd think: 'Well, Friday. It's no use ringing on Friday.' "

"So you're sure nobody rang?"

"Yes. Yes, I'm sure of it. I'd swear to it if that's what's wanted."

"If the extension was used you wouldn't know, I suppose?"

"I wouldn't know anything about that."

"No," agreed Fox. "Well, thank you very much, miss. I'm greatly obliged. Good-afternoon."

"Pleasure, I'm sure," said Miss Bruce. "Ta-ta."

CHAPTER TWENTY-FIVE

Final Vignettes

i

THE EXPRESS from London roared into Great Chipping station. Alleyn, who had been reading the future in the murky window pane, rose hurriedly and put on his overcoat.

Fox was on the platform.

"Well, Brer Fox?" said Alleyn when they reached the Biggins's Ford.

"Well, sir, the Yard car's arrived. They're to drive up quietly after we've all assembled. Alison can come into the supper-room with his two men and I'll wait inside the front door."

"That'll be all right. I'd better give you all a cue to stand by, as Miss Copeland would say. Let's see. I'll ask Miss Prentice if she's feeling the draught. We'll sit on the stage round that table so there'll probably be a hell of a draught. How did you get on at Pen Cuckoo?"

"She was there."

"Not?"

"Ross or Rosen. You had a lucky strike there, Mr. Alleyn. Fancy her being Claude Smith's girl. We were on the Quantock case at that time, weren't we?"

"We weren't at the Yard, anyway. I've never seen her before this."

"More've I. Well, she was there. Something up—between him and her—I should say."

"Between who and her, Mr. Fox?" asked Nigel. "You're very dark and cryptic this evening."

"Between Jernigham senior and Mrs. Ross, Mr. Bathgate. When I arrived he was looking peculiar, and Mr. Henry seemed as if he thought something was up. She was cool enough, but I'd say the other lady was a case for expert opinion."

"Miss Prentice?" murmured Alleyn.

"That's right, sir. Young Jernigham went and fetched her. She owned up to opening the window as sweet as you please, and then began to talk a lot of nonsense about letting in the unpardonable sin. I took it all down, but you'd be surprised how silly it was."

"The unpardonable sin? Which one's that, I wonder?"

"Nobody owned to the onion," said Fox gloomily.

"I think onions, in any form, the unpardonable sin," said Nigel.

"I reckon you're right about the onion, Mr. Alleyn."

"I think so, Fox. After all, on finding onions in teapots, why not exclaim on the circumstance? Why not say, 'Georgie Biggins for a certainty,' and raise hell?"

"That's right, sir. Well, from the way they shaped up to the question, you'd say none of them had ever smelt one. Mr. Jernigham's talking about getting a doctor in. Do you know what? I think he's sweet on her. On Rosen, I mean."

Fox changed into second gear for Chipping Rise and said, "The telephone's right. I told you that when I rang up, didn't I?"

"Yes."

"And I've seen the four girls who helped Gladys Wright. Three of them are ready to swear on oath that nobody came down into the hall from the stage, and the fourth is certain nobody did, but wouldn't swear, as she went into the porch for a minute. I've rechecked the movements of all the people behind the scenes. Mr. Copeland sat facing the footlights from the time he got there until he went in to Mr. Jernigham's room, when they tried to telephone to Mrs. Ross. He went back to the stage and didn't leave it again until they all crowded round Miss Prentice."

"I think it's good enough, Fox."

"I think so, too. This Chief Constable business is awkward, isn't it, Mr. Alleyn?"

"It is, indeed. I know of no precedent. Oh, well, we'll see what the preliminary interview does. You arranged that?"

"Yes, sir, that's all right. Did you dine on the train?"

"Yes, Fox. The usual dead fish and so on. Mr. Bathgate wants to know who did the murder."

"I do know," said Nigel in the back seat; "but I won't let on."

"D'you want to stop at the pub, Mr. Alleyn?"

"No. Let's get it over, Brer Fox, let's get it over."

ii

At Henry's suggestion, they had invited Dinah and the rector to dinner.

"You may as well take Dinah and me for granted, father. We're not going to give each other up, you know."

"I still think—however!"

And Henry, watching his father, knew that the afternoon visit of Miss Campanula's lawyers to the rectory, was Vale property. Jocelyn boggled and uttered inarticulate noises; but already, Henry thought, his father was putting a new roof on Winton. It would be better not to speak, thought Henry, of his telephone conversation with Dinah after Fox had gone. For Dinah had told Henry that her father felt he could not accept the fortune left him by Idris Campanula.

Henry said, "I don't suppose you suspect either the rector or Dinah, do you, even though they do get the money? They don't suspect us. Cousin Eleanor, who suspects God knows who, is in her room and won't appear until dinner."

"She ought not to be alone."

"One of the maids is with her. She's quietened down again and is quite normally long-suffering and martyred."

Jocelyn looked nervously at Henry.

"What do you think's the matter with her?"

"Gone ravers," said Henry cheerfully.

The Copelands accepted the invitation to dinner. Sherry was served in the library, but Henry managed to get Dinah into the study, where he had made up a large fire and had secretly placed an enormous bowl of yellow chrysanthemums.

"Darling Dinah," said Henry, "there are at least fifty things of the most terrific importance to say to you, and when I look at you I can't think of one of them. May I kiss you? We're almost publicly betrothed, aren't we?"

"Are we? You've never really asked for my hand."

"Miss Copeland—may I call you Dinah?—be mine. Be mine."

"I may not deny, Mr. Jernigham, that my sensibilities; nay, since I will not dissemble, my affections are touched by this declaration. I cannot hear you unmoved."

Henry kissed her and muttered in her ear that he loved her very much.

"All the same," said Dinah, "I do wonder why Mr. Alleyn wants us to go down to the hall to-night. I don't want to go. The place gives me the absolute horrors."

"Me, too. Dinah, I made such a fool of myself last night."

He told her how he had heard the three chords of the "Prelude" as he came through the storm.

"I would have died of it," said Dinah. "Henry, *why* do they want us to-night? Are they—are they going to arrest someone?"

"Who?" asked Henry.

They stared solemnly at each other.

"Who indeed," said Dinah.

iii

"I tell you, Copeland, I'm pretty hard hit," said the squire, giving himself a whisky-and-soda. "It's so beastly uncomfortable. Have some more sherry? Nonsense, it'll do you good. You're not looking particularly happy yourself."

"It's the most dreadful thing that has ever happened to any of us," said the rector. "How's Miss Prentice?"

"That's partly what I want to talk about. I ought to warn you——"

The rector listened with a steadily blanching face to Jocelyn's account of Miss Prentice.

"Poor soul," he said, "poor soul."

"Yes, I know, but it's damned inconvenient. I'm sorry, rector, but it—well, it's—it's—— Oh, God!"

"Would you like to tell me?" asked the rector, and if he spoke at all wearily Jocelyn did not notice it.

"No," said Jocelyn, "no. There's nothing to tell. I'm simply rather worried. What d'you suppose is the meaning of this meeting to-night?"

The rector looked curiously at him.

"I thought you probably knew. Your position, I mean——"

"As the weapon happens to be my property, I felt it better to keep right out of the picture. Technically, I'm a suspect."

"Yes. Dear me, yes." The rector sipped his sherry. "So are we all, of course."

"I wonder," said the squire, "what Alleyn is up to."

"You don't think he's going to—to arrest anybody?"

They stared at each other.

"Dinner is served, sir," said Taylor.

iv

"Good-night, dear," said Dr. Templett to his wife. "I expect you'll be asleep when I get home. I'm glad it's been a good day."

"It's been a splendid day," said the steadfastly gallant voice. "Good-night, my dear."

Templett shut the door softly. The telephone pealed in his dressing-room at the end of the landing. The hospital was to ring before eight. He went to his dressing-room and lifted the receiver.

"Hullo?"

"Is that you, Billy?"

He sat frozen, the receiver still at his ear.

"Billy? Hullo? Hullo?"

"Well?" said Dr. Templett.

"Then you are alive," said the voice.

"I haven't been arrested, after all."

"Nor, strangely enough, have I, in spite of the fact that I've been to Alleyn and taken the whole responsibility of the letter——"

"Selia! Not on the telephone!"

"I don't much care what happens to me now. You've let me down. Nothing else matters."

"What do you mean? No, don't tell me! It's not true."

"Very well. Good-bye, Billy."

"Wait! Have you been told to parade at the hall this evening?"

"Yes. Have you?"

"Yes." Dr. Templett brushed his hand across his eyes. He muttered hurriedly: "I'll call for you."

"What?"

"If you like I'll drive you there."

"I've got my own car. You needn't bother."

"I'll pick you up at nine."

"And drop me a few minutes later, I suppose?"

"That's not quite fair. What do you suppose I thought when——?"

"You obviously don't trust me. That's all."

"My God——!" began Dr. Templett. The voice cut in coolly:

"All right. At nine. Why do you suppose he wants us in the hall? Is he going to arrest someone?"

"I don't know. What do you think?"

"I don't know."

V

The church clock struck nine as the police car drew up outside the hall. Alleyn and Fox got cut, followed by Detective-Sergeant Alison and two plain-clothes men. At the same moment, Nigel drove up in his own car with Sergeant Roper. They all went in through the back door. Alleyn switched on the stage lights and the supper-room light.

"You see the lie of the land, don't you," he said. "Two flights of steps from the supper-room to the stage. We'll have the curtain down, I think, Fox. You can stay on the stage. So can you, Bathgate, in the wings, and with not a word out of you. You know when to go down and what to do?"

"Yes," said Nigel nervously.

"Good. Alison, you'd better move to the front door, and you others can go into the dressing-rooms. They'll come straight through the supper-room and won't see you. Roper, you're to go outside and direct them to the back door. Then come in. But quietly, if you don't want me to tear your buttons off and half-kill you. The rest of you can stay in the dressing-rooms until the company's complete. When it is complete, I'll slam both doors at the top of the steps. You can then come into the supper-room and sit on the steps. The piano's in position, isn't it, Fox? And the screens? Yes. All right, down with the curtain."

The curtain came down in three noisy rushes, releasing a cloud of dust.

With the front of the hall shut out, the stage presented a more authentic appearance. Dinah's box set, patched and contrived though it was, resembled any touring company's stock scenery, while Mrs. Ross's chairs and ornaments raised the interior to still greater distinction. The improvised lights shone bravely enough on chintz and china. The stage had taken on a sort of eerie half-life and an air of expectancy. On the round table Alleyn laid the anonymous letter, the "Prelude in C Minor," the "Venetian Suite," the pieces of rubber in their box, the onion, the soap-box and the teapot. He then covered this curious collection with a cloth.

Fox and Alison brought extra chairs from the dressing-rooms and put one of the paraffin lamps on the stage.

"Eight chairs," counted Alleyn. "That's right. Are we ready? I think so."

"Nothing else, sir?"

"Nothing. Remember your cue. Leave on the supper-room lights. Here he comes, I think. Away you go."

Fox walked over to the prompt corner. Nigel went through the opposite door and sat out of sight in the shadow of the proscenium. Alison went down to the auditorium, the two plain-clothes men disappeared into the dressing-rooms, and Roper, breathing stertorously, made for the back door.

"Shock tactics," muttered Alleyn. "Damn, I hate 'em. So infernally unfair, and they look like pure exhibitionism on the part of the police. Oh, well, can't be helped."

"I don't hear a car," whispered Nigel.

"It's coming."

They all listened. The wind howled and the rain drummed on the shutters.

"I'll never think of this place," said Nigel, "without hearing that noise."

"It's worse than ever," said Fox.

"Here he is," said Alleyn.

And now they all heard the car draw up in the lane. A door slammed. Boots crunched up the gravel path. Roper's voice could be heard. The back door opened. Roper, suddenly transformed into a sort of major-domo, said loudly:

"Mr. Jernigham senior, sir."

And the squire walked in.

CHAPTER TWENTY-SIX

Miss Prentice Feels the Draught

i

"—So you see," said Alleyn, "I was led to wonder if, to speak frankly, the object of her visit was blackmail."

The squire's face was drained of all its normal colour, but now it flushed a painful crimson.

"I cannot believe it."

"In view of the record——"

The squire made a violent, clumsy gesture with his right hand. Standing in the centre of the stage under those uncompromising lights, he looked at once frightened and defiant. Alleyn watched him for a moment and then he said:

"You see, I think I know what she had to say to you."

Jernigham's jaw dropped.

"I don't believe you," he said hoarsely.

"Then let me tell what I believe to be her hold on you."

Alleyn's voice went on and on, quietly, dispassionately. Jernigham listened with his gaze on the floor. Once he looked up as though he would interrupt, but he seemed to think better of this impulse and fell to biting his nails.

"I give you this opportunity," said Alleyn. "If you care to tell me now——"

"There is nothing to tell you. It's not true."

"Mrs. Ross did not come this afternoon with this story. She did not make these very definite terms with you?"

"I cannot discuss the matter."

"Even," said Alleyn, "in view of this record?"

"I admit nothing."

"Very well. I was afraid you would take this line."

"In my position——"

"It was because of your position I gave you this opportunity. I can do no more."

"I can't see why you want this general interview."

"Shock tactics, sir," said Alleyn.

"I—I don't approve."

"If you wish, sir, I can hand my report in and you may make a formal complaint at the Yard."

"No."

"It would make no difference," said Alleyn. "I think the others have arrived. This is your last word?"

"I have nothing to say."

"Very well, sir."

Roper tapped at one of the supper-room doors.

"Hullo!" shouted Alleyn.

"Here they be, sir, every living soul, and all come together."

"All right, Roper. Show them in."

ii

Miss Prentice came in first, followed by Dinah, the rector and Henry. Alleyn asked Miss Prentice to sit in the most comfortable chair, which he had placed on the prompt side of the table. When she dithered, he was so crisply polite that she was there before she realised it. She looked quickly towards the rector, who took the chair on her right. Dinah sat on her father's right with Henry beside her. The squire looked furtively at Alleyn.

"Will you sit down, sir?" invited Alleyn.

"What! Yes, yes," said the squire convulsively, and sat beside Henry.

Mrs. Ross came in. She was dressed in black and silver, a strangely exotic figure in those surroundings. She said: "Good-evening," with her customary side-long smile, bowed rather more pointedly to Alleyn, and sat beside the squire. Templett, seeming ill at ease and shame-faced, followed her.

Miss Prentice drew in her breath and began to whisper:

"No, no, no! Never at the same table. I can't——!"

Alleyn sat on her left in the one chair remaining vacant and said, "Miss Prentice—please!"

His voice had sufficient edge to silence Miss Prentice and call the others to a sort of guarded alertness.

His long hands lay clasped before him on the table. He leant forward and looked with deliberation round the circle of attentive faces.

He said, "Ladies and gentlemen, I shall not apologise for calling you together to-night. I am sure that most—not all, but most—of you are only too anxious that this affair should be settled, and I may tell you that we have now collected enough evidence to make an arrest. Each of you in turn has provided evidence; each of you has withheld evidence. From the information you have given, and from the significance of your several reticences, has emerged a pattern which, as we read it, has at its centre a single person: the murderer of Miss Idris Campanula."

They sat as still as figures in a tableau, and the only sound, when Alleyn paused, was the sound of rain and the uneasy stirring of the wind outside.

"From the beginning, this strange affair has presented one particularly unusual problem: the problem of the murderer's intention. Was it Miss Idris Campanula for whom this trap was set, or was it Miss Eleanor Prentice? If it was indeed Idris Campanula, then the number of possible suspects was very small. If it was Miss Prentice, the field was a great deal wider. During most of yesterday and part of to-day my colleague, Inspector Fox, interviewed the people who have known and come into contact with both ladies. He could find no motive for the murder of either of them, outside the circle of people we have found motive. Money, jealousy, love and fear are the themes most usually found behind homicide. All four appeared in this case if Miss Campanula was the intended victim: the last three, if the intended victim was Miss Prentice. The fact that on Friday evening at five o'clock Mr. Henry Jernigham showed the automatic to all of you, except his father, who is the owner, was another circumstance that suggested one of you as the guilty person."

Henry rested his head on his hand, driving his fingers through his hair. Templett cleared his throat.

"At the inquest this morning you all heard the story of the water-pistol. The booby-trap was ready at 2.30 on Friday. The water-pistol was no longer in position at noon on Saturday when Miss Prentice used the soft pedal. Yet some time between Friday at 2.30 and noon on Saturday, somebody sat at the piano and used the soft pedal and the booby-trap worked."

Alleyn lifted the cloth from the table. Miss Prentice gave a nervous yelp. He took up the "Venetian Suite" and pointed to the circular blister and discoloured splashes on the back.

"Five hours after the catastrophe, this was still damp. So was the torn silk round the hole in the front of the piano. Miss Prentice has told us that her music was left on the piano earlier in the week. All

Saturday morning the hall was occupied. It seems, therefore, that the water-pistol was removed before Saturday morning, and presumably by the guilty person, since an innocent person would not have kept silent about the booby-trap. On Friday afternoon and evening the hall was deserted. At this stage I may say that Mr. Jernigham and Dr. Templett both have alibis for Friday afternoon, when they hunted up till a short time before the rehearsal-for-words at Pen Cuckoo. Dr. Templett has an alibi for Friday and well into Saturday morning, during which time he was occupied with professional duties. It is hardly conceivable that he would enter the hall in the small hours of Saturday morning to play the piano. The helpers arrived soon after nine o'clock on Saturday, and by that time the pistol had been removed.

"Now for the automatic. If, as we suppose, the water-pistol was discovered on Friday, it is of course possible that the automatic was substituted before Saturday. This possibility we consider unlikely. It was known that the helpers would be in the hall all Saturday morning, and the murderer would have run the risk of discovery. It was only necessary for someone to disarrange the rotten silk in the front of the piano to reveal the nozzle of the Colt. True, this piece of music was on the rack; but it might have been removed. Somebody might have dusted the piano. It is also true that nobody was likely to look in the top, as the person who removed the water-pistol had taken pains to re-fasten the bunting with drawing-pins and to cover the top with heavy pot plants. Still, there would have been considerable risk. It seems more probable that the murderer would leave the setting of the automatic until as late as possible. Say about four o'clock on Saturday afternoon."

Templett made a sudden movement, but said nothing.

"For four o'clock on Saturday afternoon," said Alleyn, "none of you has an alibi that would stand up to five minutes' cross-examination."

"But——"

"I've told you——"

"I explained yesterday——"

"Do you want me to go into this? Wait a little and listen. At about half-past three, Mrs. Ross arrived at the hall. Dr. Templett got there a few minutes later. She had come to complete the supper arrangements, he to put his acting clothes in his dressing-room. They had both called at Pen Cuckoo in the morning. Mrs. Ross tells us that while Dr. Templett went into the house she remained in the car. I imagine there is no need to remind you all of the french window into the study at Pen Cuckoo."

"I knew," whispered Miss Prentice. "I knew, I knew!"

"You're going beyond your duty, Mr. Alleyn," said Mrs. Ross.

"No," said Alleyn. "I merely pause here to point out how easy it would have been for any of you to come up Top Lane and slip into the study. To return to the 3.30 visit to the hall. Dr. Templett has given what I believe to be a true account of this visit. He has told us that he arrived to find Mrs. Ross already there and occupied with the supper arrangements. After a time they came here on to this stage. They noticed that the last window on the right, near the front door, was a few inches open. Mrs. Ross, who first noticed this, told Dr. Templett that she saw someone dodge down behind the sill. To reach the window this onlooker used a box."

He turned the cloth farther back and the dilapidated soap-box was revealed. Miss Prentice giggled and covered her mouth with her hand.

"This is the box. It fits into the marks under the window. Do you recognise it, Dr. Templett?"

"Yes," said Templett dully, "I remember that splash of white on the top. I saw it as I looked down."

"Exactly. I should explain that when Dr. Templett reached the window he looked out to see if he could discover anybody. He saw nobody, but he noticed the box. He tells me it was not there when he arrived. Now Mrs. Ross said that she did not recognise this person. But I have experimented, and have found that if one sees anybody at all under the conditions she has described, one stands a very good chance of recognising them. One would undoubtedly know, for instance, whether it was a man or a woman whose image showed for a moment and disappeared behind the sill. It will be urged by the police that Mrs. Ross did, in fact recognise this person." Alleyn turned to Templett.

"Mrs. Ross did not tell you who it was?"

"I didn't know who it was," said Mrs. Ross.

"Dr. Templett?"

"I believe Mrs. Ross's statement."

Alleyn looked at the squire.

"When you saw Mrs. Ross alone this afternoon, sir, did she refer to this incident?"

"I can't answer that question, Alleyn," muttered the squire. Henry raised his head and looked at his father with a sort of wonder.

"Very well, sir," said Alleyn. "I must remind you all that you are free to refuse answers to any questions you may be asked. The police may not set traps, and it is my duty to tell you that we have established the identity of the eavesdropper." He took the lid from a small box.

"One of those fragments of rubber," he said, "was found on the point of a nail on the inside of the box. The others were caught behind projecting splinters also on the inside of the box."

He opened an envelope and from it he shook a torn surgical finger-stall.

"The fragments of rubber," he said, "correspond with the holes in this stall."

Miss Prentice electrified the company by clapping her hands with great violence.

"Oh, inspector," she cried shrilly, "how perfectly, perfectly wonderful you are!"

iii

Alleyn turned slowly and met her enraptured gaze. Her prominent eyes bulged, her mouth was open, and she nodded her head several times with an air of ecstasy.

"Then you acknowledge," he said, "that you put this box outside the window on Saturday afternoon?"

"Of course!"

"And that you stood on it in order to look through the window?"

"Alas, yes!"

"Miss Prentice, why did you do this?"

"I was guided."

"Why did you not admit you recognised the box when Inspector Fox asked you about it?"

With that unlovely air of girlishness she covered her face with her fingers.

"I was afraid he would ask me what I saw."

"This is absolute nonsense!" said Templett angrily.

"And why," continued Alleyn, "did you tell me you were indoors all Saturday afternoon?"

"I was afraid to say what I'd done."

"Afraid? Of whom?"

She seemed to draw herself inwards to a point of venomous concentration. She stretched out her arm across the table. The finger pointed at Mrs. Ross.

"Of *her*. She tried to murder me. She's a murderess. I can prove it. I can prove it."

"No!" cried the squire. "No! Good God, Alleyn——"

"Is there any doubt in your mind, Mr. Alleyn," said Mrs. Ross, "that this woman is mad?"

"I can prove it," repeated Miss Prentice.

"How?" asked Alleyn. "Please let this finish, Mr. Jernigham. We shall see daylight soon."

"She knew I saw her. She tried to kill me because she was afraid."

"You hear that, Mrs. Ross? It is a serious accusation. Do you feel inclined to answer it? I must warn you, first, that Dr. Templett has made a statement about this incident."

She looked quickly at Templett.

He said, "I thought you hadn't considered me over the other business. I told the truth."

"You fool," said Mrs. Ross. For the first time she looked really frightened. She raised her hands to her thin neck and touched it surreptitiously. Then she hid her hands in her lap.

"I do not particularly want to repeat the gist of Dr. Templett's statement," said Alleyn.

"Very well." Her voice cracked, she took a breath and then said evenly, "Very well. I recognised Miss Prentice. I've nothing whatever to fear. One doesn't kill old maids for eavesdropping."

"Mr. Jernigham," said Alleyn, "did Mrs. Ross tell you of this incident this afternoon?"

The squire was staring at Mrs. Ross as if she was a sort of Medusa. Without turning his eyes, he nodded.

"She suggested that Miss Prentice had come down to the hall with the intention of putting the automatic in the piano?"

"So she had. I'll swear," said Mrs. Ross.

"Mr. Jernigham?"

"Yes. Yes, she suggested that."

"She told you perhaps, that you could trust her?"

"Oh, my God!" said the squire.

"I arrived too late at this place," said Mrs. Ross, "to be able to do anything to the piano." She looked at Dinah. "You know that."

"Yes," said Dinah.

"It was soon after that," said Miss Prentice abruptly, "that she began to set traps for me, you know. Then I saw it all in a flash. She must have seen me through a glass darkly, and because I witnessed the unpardonable sin she will destroy me. You understand, don't you, because it is very important. She is in league with The Others, and it won't be long before one of them catches me."

Templett said, "Alleyn, you must see. This has gone on long enough. It's perfectly obvious what's wrong here."

"We will go on, if you please," said Alleyn. "Mr. Copeland, you told me that on Friday night you expected Miss Prentice at the rectory."

The rector, very pale, said, "Yes."

"She didn't arrive?"

"No. I told you. She telephoned."

"At what time?"

"Not long after ten."

"From Pen Cuckoo?"

"It was my hand, you know," said Miss Prentice rapidly. "I wanted to rest my hand. It was so *very* naughty. The blood tramped up and down my arm. Thump, thump, thump. So I said I would stay at home."

"You rang up from Pen Cuckoo?"

"I took the message, Mr. Alleyn," said Dinah. "I told you."

"And what do you say, Miss Copeland, if I tell you that on Friday night the Pen Cuckoo telephone was out of order from 8.20 until the following morning?"

"But—it couldn't have been."

"I'm afraid it was." He turned to Henry Jernigham. "You agree?"

"Yes," said Henry without raising his head.

"You can thank The Others for that," said Miss Prentice in a trembling voice.

"The Others?"

"*The Others*, yes. They are always doing those sort of tricks; and she's the worst of the lot, that woman over there."

"Well, Miss Copeland?"

"I took the message," repeated Dinah. "Miss Prentice said she was at home and would remain at home."

"This contradiction," said Alleyn, "takes us a step further. Mrs. Ross, on Friday night you drove down to Chipping by way of Church Lane?"

"Yes."

"You have told me that you saw a light in this hall."

"Yes."

"You think it was in Mr. Jernigham's dressing-room?"

"Yes."

"The telephone is in that room, Miss Dinah, isn't it?"

"Yes," whispered Dinah. "Oh, yes."

Alleyn took a card from his pocket and scribbled on it. He handed it over to Henry.

"Will you take Miss Dinah to the rectory?" he said. "In half an hour I want you to ring through to here on the extension. Show this card to the man at the door and he will let you out."

Henry looked fixedly at Alleyn.

"Very well, sir," he said. "Thank you."

Henry and Dinah went out.

iv

"Now," said Alleyn, "we come to the final scene. I must tell you—though I dare say you have heard it all by now—that at 6.30 Miss Gladys Wright used the piano and pressed down the soft pedal. Nothing untoward happened. Since it is inconceivable that anybody could remove the pot plants and rig the automatic after 6.30, we know that the automatic must have been already in position. The safety-catch, which Mr. Henry Jernigham showed to all of you, and particularly to Mrs. Ross, accounts for Gladys Wright's immunity. How, then, did the guilty person manage to release the safety-catch after Gladys Wright and her fellow-helpers were down in the front of the hall? I will show you how it could have been done."

He went down to the footlights.

"You notice that the curtain falls on the far side of the improvised footlights and just catches on the top of the piano. Now, if you'll look."

He stooped and pushed his hand under the curtain. The top of the piano, with its covering of green and yellow bunting, could just be seen.

"This bunting is pinned down as it was on Saturday. It is stretched tight over the entire top of the piano. The lid is turned back, but of course that doesn't show. The pot plants stand on the inside of the lid. I take out the centre drawing-pin at the back and slide, my hand under the bunting. I am hidden by the curtain, and the pot plants also serve as a mask for any slight movement that might appear from the front of the hall. My fingers have reached the space beyond the open lid. Inside the opening they encounter the cold, smooth surface of the Colt. Listen."

Above the sound of rain and wind they all heard a small click.

"I have pushed over the safety-catch," said Alleyn. "The automatic is now ready to shoot Miss Campanula between the eyes."

"Horrible," said the rector violently.

"There is one sequence of events about which we can be certain," said Alleyn. "We know that the first person to arrive was Gladys Wright. We know that she entered the hall at 6.30, and was in front of the curtain down there with her companions until and after the audience came in. We know that it would have been impossible for anybody to come down from the stage into the front of the hall unnoticed. Miss Wright is ready to swear that nobody did this. We know that Miss Dinah Copeland arrived with her father soon after Gladys Wright, and was here behind the scenes. We know Mr. Copeland sat on the stage until he made his announcement to the audience, only leaving it for a moment to join the others at the telephone, and once again when he persuaded Miss Prentice not to play. Mr. Copeland, did you at any time see anybody stoop down to the curtains as I did just then?"

"No. No! I am quite certain that I didn't. You see, my chair faced the exact spot."

"Yes, therefore we know that unless Mr. Copeland is the guilty person, the safety-catch must have been released during one of his two absences. But Mr. Copeland believed, up to the last moment, that Miss Prentice was to be the pianist. We are satisfied that Mr. Copeland is not the guilty person."

The rector raised one of his large hands in a gesture that seemed to repudiate his immunity. The squire, Miss Prentice, Mrs. Ross and Templett kept their eyes fixed on Alleyn.

"Knowing the only means by which the safety-catch might be released, it seems evident that Miss Prentice was not the intended victim. Miss Prentice, you are cold. Do you feel a draught?"

Miss Prentice shook her head, but she trembled like a wet dog and looked not unlike one. There was a faint sound of movement behind the scenes. Alleyn went on:

"When you were all crowded round her and she gave in and consented to allow Miss Campanula to play, it would have been easy enough to come up here and put the safety-catch on again. Why run the risk of being arrested for the murder of the wrong person?"

Alleyn's level voice halted for a moment. He leant forward, and when he spoke again it was with extreme deliberation:

"No! The trap was set for Miss Campanula. It was set before Miss Prentice yielded her right to play, and it was set by someone who knew she would not play. The safety-catch was released at the only moment when the stage was empty. The moment when you were all crowded round the telephone. Then the murderer sat back and waited for the catastrophe to happen. Beyond the curtain at this moment someone is sitting at the piano. In a minute you will hear the opening chords of the "Prelude" as you heard them on Saturday night. If you listen closely you will hear the click of the trigger when the soft pedal goes down. That will represent the report of the automatic. Imagine this guilty person. Imagine someone whose hand stole under the curtain while the hall was crowded and set that trap. Imagine someone who sat, as we sit now, and waited for those three fatal chords."

Alleyn paused.

As heavy as lead and as loud as ever the dead hand had struck them out, in the empty hall beyond the curtain, thumped the three chords of Miss Campanula's "Prelude."

"Pom. *Pom*. POM!"

And very slowly, in uneven jerks, the curtain began to rise.

As it rose, so did Miss Prentice. She might have been pulled up by an invisible hand in her hair. Her mouth was wide open, but the only sound she made was a sort of retching groan. She did not take her eyes from the rising curtain, but she pointed her hand at the rector and waved it up and down.

"It was for you," screamed Miss Prentice. *"I did it for you!"*

And Nigel, seated at the piano, saw Alleyn take her by the arm.

"Eleanor Prentice, I arrest you——"

CHAPTER TWENTY-SEVEN

Case Ends

i

HENRY AND Dinah sat by the fire in the rectory study and watched the clock.

"*Why* does he want us to ring up?" said Dinah for perhaps the sixth time. "I don't understand."

"I think I do. I think the telephoning's only an excuse. He wanted us out of the way."

"But why?"

Henry put his arm round her shoulders and pressed his cheek against her hair.

"Oh, Dinah," he said.

"What, darling?"

Dinah looked up. He sat on the arm of her chair and she had to move a little in his embrace before she could see his eyes.

"Henry! What is it?"

"I think we're in for a bad spin."

"But—isn't it Mrs. Ross?"

"I don't think so."

Without removing her gaze from his face she took his hand.

"I think it's Eleanor," said Henry.

"Eleanor!"

"It's the only answer. Don't you see that's what Alleyn was driving at all the time?"

"But she *wanted* to play. She made the most frightful scene over not playing."

"I know. But Templett said two days before that she'd never be able to do it. Don't you see, she worked it so that we should find her crying and moaning, and insist on her giving up?"

"Suppose we hadn't insisted."

"She'd have left the safety-catch on or not used the soft pedal, or perhaps she'd have 'discovered' the automatic and accused Miss C. of putting it there. That would have made a glorious scene."

"I can't believe it."

"Can you believe it of any one else?"

"Mrs. Ross," said Dinah promptly.

"No, darling. I rather think Mrs. Ross has merely tried to blackmail my papa. It is my cousin who is a murderess. Shall you enjoy a husband of whom every one will say: 'Oh, yes, Henry Jernigham! Wasn't he the Pen Cuckoo murderess's nephew or son or something?' "

"I shall love my husband and I shan't hear what they say. Besides, you don't know. You're only guessing."

"I'm certain of it. There are all sorts of things that begin to fit in. Things that don't fit any other way. Dinah, I know she's the one."

"Anyway, my dear darling, she's mad."

"I hope so," said Henry. "God, it's awful, isn't it?"

He sprang up and began to walk nervously up and down.

"I can't stand this much longer," said Henry.

"It's time we rang up."

"I'll do it."

But as he reached the door they heard voices in the hall.

The rector came in, followed by Alleyn and the squire.

"Dinah! Where's Dinah?" cried the rector.

"Here she is," said Henry. "Father!"

The squire turned a chalk-white face to his son.

"Come here, old boy," he said. "I want you."

"That chair," said Alleyn quickly.

Henry and Alleyn put the squire in the chair.

"Brandy, Dinah," said the rector. "He's fainted."

"No, I haven't," said Jocelyn. "Henry, old boy, I'd better tell you——"

"I know," said Henry. "It's Eleanor."

Alleyn moved back to the door and watched them. He was now a detached figure. The arrest came like a wall of glass between himself and the little group that hovered round Jocelyn. He knew that most of his colleagues accepted these moments of isolation. Perhaps they were scarcely aware of them. But, for himself, he always felt a little like a sort of Mephistopheles, who looked on at his own handiwork. He didn't enjoy the sensation. It was the one moment when his sense of detachment deserted him. Now, as they remembered him, he saw in the faces turned towards him the familiar guarded antagonism of herded animals.

He said, "If Mr. Jernigham would like to see Miss Prentice, it shall be arranged. Superintendent Blandish will be in charge."

He bowed, and was going when Jocelyn said loudly:

"Wait a minute."

"Yes, sir?" Alleyn moved quickly to the chair. The squire looked up at him.

"I know you tried to prepare me for this," he said. "You guessed that woman had told me. I couldn't admit that until—until it was all up—I wouldn't admit it. You understand that?"

"Yes."

"I'm all to blazes. Think what to do in the morning. Just wanted to say I appreciate the way you've handled things. Considerate."

"I would have avoided the final scene, sir, if I had seen any other way."

"I know that. Mustn't ask questions, of course. There are some things I don't understand—— Alleyn, you see she's out of her mind?"

"Dr. Templett, I'm sure, will advise you about an alienist, sir."

"Yes. Thank you."

The squire blinked up at him and then suddenly held out his hand.

"Good-night."

"Good-night, sir."

Henry said, "I'll come out with you."

As they walked to the door, Alleyn thought there were points about being a Jernigham of Pen Cuckoo.

"It's queer," said Henry. "I suppose this must be a great shock to us; but at the moment I feel nothing at all. Nothing. I don't realise that she's—— Where is she?"

"The Yard car is on the way to Great Chipping. She'll need things from Pen Cuckoo. We'll let you know what they are."

Henry stopped dead at the rectory door. His voice turned to ice. "Is she frightened?"

Alleyn remembered that face with the lips drawn back from the projecting teeth, the tearless bulging eyes, the hands that opened and closed as if they had let something fall.

"I don't think she is conscious of fear," he said. "She was quite composed. She didn't weep."

"She can't. Father's often said she never cried as a child."

"I remembered your father told me that."

"I hated her," said Henry. "But that's nothing now; she's insane. It's strange, because there's no insanity in the family. What happens? I mean, when will they begin to try her. We—what ought we to do?"

Alleyn told him what they should do. It was the first time he had ever advised the relatives of a person accused of murder, and he said, "But you must ask your lawyer's advice first of all. That is really all I may tell you."

"Yes. Yes, of course. Thank you, sir." Henry peered at Alleyn. He saw him against rods of rain that glinted in the light from the open door.

"It's funny," said Henry jerkily. "Do you know, I was going to ask you about Scotland Yard—how one began."

"Did you think seriously of this?"

"Yes. I want a job. Hardly suitable for the cousin of the accused."

"There's no reason why you shouldn't try for the police."

"I've read your book. Good Lord, it's pretty queer to stand here and talk like this."

"You're more shocked than you realise. If I were you I should take your father home."

"Ever since yesterday, sir, I've had the impression I'd seen you before. I've just remembered. Agatha Troy did a portrait of you, didn't she?"

"Yes."

"It was very good, wasn't it? Rather a compliment to be painted by Troy. Is she pleasant or peculiar?"

"I think her very pleasant indeed," said Alleyn. "I have persuaded her to say she will marry me. Good-night."

He smiled, waved his hand and went out into the rain.

ii

Nigel had driven his own car over to the rectory, and he took Alleyn to Great Chipping.

"The others have only just got away," said Nigel. "She fainted after you left, and Fox had to get Templett to deal with her. They're picking the wardress up at the sub-station."

"Fainted, did she?"

"Yes. She's completely dotty, isn't she?"

"I shouldn't say so. Not completely."

"Not?"

"The dottiness has only appeared since Saturday night. She's probably extremely neurotic. Unbalanced, hysterical, all that. In law, insanity is very closely defined. Her counsel will probably go for moral depravity, delusion, or hallucination. If he can prove a history of disturbance of the higher levels of thought, he may get away with it. I'm afraid poor old Copeland will have to relate his experiences. They'll give me fits for your performance on the piano, but I've covered myself by warning the listeners. I don't mind betting that even if lunacy is not proved, there'll be a recommendation for mercy. Of course, they may go all out for 'not guilty' and get it."

"You might give me an outline, Alleyn."

"All right. Where are we? It's as dark as hell."

"Just coming into Chipping. There's the police car ahead."

"Ah, yes. Well, here's the order of events as we see it. On Friday, by 2.40, Georgie had set the booby-trap. Miss Campanula tried to get into the hall before he left it. He hid while the chauffeur looked through the window. When the chauffeur had gone, Georgie repinned the bunting over the open top of the piano, replaced the aspidistras and decamped. At a minute or two after half-past two, Miss C. passed Miss P. in the church porch. Miss P. was seen by Gibson. She crossed Church Lane and would pass the hall on her way to Top Lane. In Top Lane she met Dinah Copeland and Henry Jernigham at three o'clock.

"Apparently she had taken half an hour to walk a quarter of a mile. We did it yesterday in five minutes. Our case is that she'd gone into the hall in a great state of upset because the rector had ticked her off at confession. She must have sat at the piano, worked the booby-trap and got the jet of water full in the face. She removed the pistol, and probably the first vague idea of her crime came into her head, because she kept quiet about the booby-trap. Perhaps she remembered the Colt and wondered if it would fit. We don't know. We only know that at three o'clock she had the scene in Top Lane with Henry and Dinah, the scene that was watched and overheard by that old stinker, Tranter. Tranter and Dinah noticed that the bosom of her dress was wet. That, with the lapse in time, are the only scraps of evidence we've got so far to give colour to this bit of our theory, but I'd like to know how else the front of her bodice got wet, if not from the pistol. It wasn't raining, and anyhow rain wouldn't behave like that. And I'd like to know how else you can account for her arrival, as late as three, at a spot five minutes away."

"Yes, it'll certainly take a bit of explaining."

"The butler remembered she got back at four. At five Henry explained the mechanism of the Colt to the assembled company, stressing and illustrating the action of the safety-catch. Miss P. had told the rector she wanted to see him that evening. Of course, she wanted to give him a distorted and poisonous version of the meeting between Henry and his Dinah. She was to come to the rectory after Reading Circle activities. About ten o'clock, that would be. Now, soon after ten, Miss C. flung herself into the rector's arms in the rectory study."

"Christopher!"

"Yes. I hope for his sake we won't have to bring this out; but it's a faint hope. The curtains were not drawn, and anybody on the path to the hall could have seen. Round about 10.15, Miss Dinah heard the gate into the wood give its customary piercing shriek. She thought somebody had gone out that way and believed it was Miss C. We contend it was Miss P. coming in for her appointment. We contend she stood inside the gate transfixed by the tableau beyond the window, that she put the obvious interpretation on what she saw, and fell a prey to whatever furies visit a woman whose ageing heart is set on one man and whose nerves, desires and thoughts have been concentrated on the achievement of her hope. We think she turned, passed through the post-stile and returned to Church Lane. To help this theory we've got two blurred heel-prints, the statements that nobody else used the gate that night, and the fact that Miss P. rang up shortly afterwards from the hall."

"How the devil d'you get that?"

"The telephone operator is prepared to swear nobody rang up the rectory. But Miss P. rang up and the old housemaid called Dinah Copeland, who went to the telephone. She evidently didn't notice it was an extension call. Miss P. said she was speaking from Pen Cuckoo. Miss P. has admitted she rang up. The hall telephone is an extension and doesn't register at the exchange. Mrs. Ross saw a light in the hall telephone room, at the right moment. It's the only explanation. Miss P. didn't know the Pen Cuckoo telephone was out of order and thought she was safe enough to establish a false alibi. She probably got the water-pistol that night and took it away with her to see if the Colt was the same length. It was an eleventh of an inch shorter which meant that the nozzle would fit in the hole without projecting. Now we come to Saturday afternoon. She told me she was in her room. Mrs. Ross recognised her through the hall window, and we've got the scraps of rubber to prove that she handled the box. She looked through the hall window to see if the coast was clear. I imagine Templett was embracing his dubious love, who saw the onlooker over his shoulder. Miss P. took to cover, leaving the box. When they'd gone, she crept into the hall and put the Colt in position. She'd had four emotional shocks in twenty-six hours. The rector had given her fits. She'd seen Henry making ardent love to Dinah. She'd seen Idris Campanula, apparently victoriously happy, in the rector's arms, and she'd watched Templett and Mrs. Ross in what I imagine must have been an even more passionate encounter. And though I do *not* consider her insane in law, I do consider that these experiences drove her into an ecstasy of fury. Since it is the rector with whom she herself is madly and overwhelmingly in love, Idris Campanula was the object of her hatred. It was Idris who had robbed her of her hopes. Incidentally, it is Idris who left her a fortune. Georgie Biggins had shown her the way. It's worth noting here that she won a badge for tying knots, and taught the local Guides in this art. At half-past four she was back at Pen Cuckoo and waked the squire in time for tea. This account, too, sounds like conjecture, but the finger-stall proves she lied once, the telephone proves she lied twice, and the fingerprints in the teapot prove she lied three times."

"In the teapot?"

"I'll explain them in a minute."

They reached the top of Great Chipping Rise, and the lights of the town swam brokenly beyond the rain.

"There's not much more," said Alleyn. "The prosecution will make the most of this last point. The only time the stage was deserted, after they arrived in the evening, was when all the others stood round the telephone trying to get through to Mrs. Ross and Dr. Templett. Only Miss Prentice was absent. She appeared for a moment, saw the squire in his under-pants, scuttled off to the stage and did her stunt with the safety-catch. Our case really rests on this. We can check and double-check the movements of every one of them from half-past six onwards. The rector sat on the stage, and will swear nobody touched the piano from that side. Gladys Wright and her helpers were in the hall and will swear nobody touched it from that side. The only time the catch could have been moved was when they were all round the telephone, and Miss P. was absent. She is literally the only person who could have moved the catch."

"By George," said Nigel, "she must be a coldblooded creature! What a nerve!"

"It's given way a little since the event," said Alleyn grimly. "I think she found she wasn't as steady as she expected to be, so she allowed her hysteria to mount into the semblance of insanity. Her nerve had gone at the shock of her dear friend's death, you see. Now she's going to work the demented stunt for all it's worth. I wonder when she first began to be afraid of me. I wonder if it was when I put the finger-stall in my pocket. Or was it at the first tender mention of the onion?"

"The onion!" shouted Nigel. "Where the devil does the onion come in?"

"Georgie Biggins put the onion in the teapot. We found it in a cardboard box in the corner of the supper-room. It had pinkish powder on it. There was pinkish powder on the table in Miss P.'s dressing-room. It smelt of onion. The dressing-rooms were locked while Georgie was in the hall, so he didn't drop the onion in Miss P.'s powder. My theory is that Miss P. found the onion in the teapot, which she had to use, took it to her dressing-room and put it down on the table amongst the spilt powder. The teapot has her prints on the inside, and hers and Georgie's on the outside."

"But what the suffering cats did she want with an onion? She wasn't going to make Irish stew."

"Haven't you heard that she has never been known to shed tears until Saturday night, when floods were induced by sheer pain and disappointment because she couldn't play the piano? She took a good sniff at the onion, opened her dressing-room door, swayed to and fro, moaned and wept and wept and wept until Dr. Templett heard her and behaved exactly as she knew he would behave. Later on she chucked the onion into the débris in the supper-room. She ought to have returned it to the teapot."

"I boggle at the onion."

"Boggle away, my boy. If it was an innocent onion, why didn't she own to it? There are her powder and her prints. Nobody else extracted it from the teapot. But it doesn't matter. It's only another corroborative detail."

"The whole thing sounds a bit like Pooh Bah."

"It's a beastly business. I detest it. She's a horrible woman, not a generous thought in her make-up; but that doesn't make much odds. If Georgie Biggins hadn't set his trap she'd have gone on to the end of her days, most likely, hating Miss C., scheming, scratching, adoring. Everybody will talk psychiatry and nonsense. Her *ideé fixe* will be pitchforked about the studios of the intelligentsia. That old fool Jernigham, who's a nice old fool, and his son, who's no fool at all, will go through hell. The rector, who supplied the *ideé fixe, will* blame himself; and God knows he's not to blame. Templett will hover on the brink of professional odium, but he'll be cured of Mrs. Ross."

"What of Mrs. Ross?"

"At least she's scored a miss in the Vale of Pen Cuckoo. No hope now of blackmailing old Jernigham into matrimony, or out of hard cash. We'll catch the Rosen sooner or later, please heaven, for she's a nasty bit of work, and that's a fact. She would have seen Templett in the dock before she'd have risked an eye-lash to clear him, and yet I imagine she's very much attracted by Templett. As soon as she knew we thought him innocent, she was all for him. Here we are."

Nigel pulled up outside the police station.

"May I come in with you?" he asked.

"If you like, certainly."

Fox met Alleyn in the door.

"She's locked up," said Fox. "Making a great old rumpus. The doctor's gone for a strait-jacket. Here's a letter for you, Mr. Alleyn. It came this afternoon."

Alleyn looked at the letter and took it quickly. The firm small writing of the woman he loved brought the idea of her into his mind.

"It's from Troy," he said.

And before he went into the lighted building he looked at Nigel.

"If one could send every grand passion to the laboratory, do you suppose, in each resulting formula, we should find something of Dinah and Henry's young idyll, something of Templett's infatuation, something of Miss P.'s madness, and even something of old Jernigham's foolishness?"

"Who knows?" said Nigel.

"Not I," said Alleyn.

THE END

Ngaio MARSH

Death at the Bar

For my friends in the Dunedin Repertory Society

CAST OF CHARACTERS

LUKE WATCHMAN, K.C.
SEBASTIAN PARISH, his cousin.
NORMAN CUBITT, R.A.
ABEL POMEROY, proprietor, Plume of Feathers, Devon.
WILL POMEROY, his son.
MRS. IVES, housekeeper at the Plume of Feathers.
THE HONOURABLE VIOLET DARRAGH, of County Clare, Ireland.
ROBERT LEGGE, Secretary and Treasurer to the Coombe Left Movement.
DECIMA MOORE, of Cary Edge Farm and of Oxford.
GEORGE NARK, farmer, of Ottercombe.
RICHARD OATES, P.C. of the Illington and Ottercombe Constabulary.
DR. SHAW, Police Surgeon, Illington.
NICHOLAS HARPER, Superintendent of Police, Illington.
DR. MORDANT, Coroner for Illington.
RODERICK ALLEYN, Chief Detective-Inspector, Criminal Investigation Department.
T.R. FOX, Inspector, Criminal Investigation Department.
COLONEL, THE HONOURABLE MAXWELL BRAMMINGTON, Chief Constable.

CONTENTS

CHAPTER ONE

The Plume of Feathers

i

As Luke Watchman drove across Otterbrook Bridge the setting sun shone full in his eyes. A molten flood of sunlight poured towards him through the channel of the lane and broke into sequins across Otterbrook waters. He arched his hand over his eyes and peered through the spattered dazzle of the windscreen. Somewhere about here was the turning for Ottercombe. He lowered the window and leant out.

The warmth of evening touched his face. The air smelt of briar, of fern, and, more astringently of the distant sea. There, fifty yards ahead, was the fingerpost with its letters almost rubbed out by rain. "Ottercombe, *7 miles*."

Watchman experienced the fulfillment of a nostalgic longing and was content. Only now, when he was within reach of his journey's end, did he realize how greatly he had desired this return. The car moved forward and turned from the wide lane into the narrow. The curves of hills marched down behind hedgerows. There was no more sunlight. Thorns brushed the windows on each side, so narrow was the lane. The car bumped over pot-holes. The scent of spring-watered earth rose coldly from the banks.

"Downhill all the way now," Watchman murmured. His thoughts travelled ahead to Ottercombe. One should always time arrivals for this hour when labourers turned homewards, when lamps were lit, when the traveller had secret glimpses into rooms whose thresholds he would never cross. At the Plume of Feathers, Abel Pomeroy would stand out in the roadway and look for incoming guests. Watchman wondered if his two companions had got there before him. Perhaps his cousin, Sebastian Parish, had set out on his evening prowl round the village. Perhaps Norman Cubitt had already found a subject and was down on the jetty dabbing nervously at a canvas. This was the second holiday they had spent together in

Ottercombe. A curious trio when you came to think of it. Like the beginning of a funny story . . . "A lawyer, an actor, and a painter once went to a fishing village in Devon." Well, he'd rather have Cubitt and Parish than any of his own learned brethren. The law set too deep a seal on character. The very soul of a barrister took silk. And he wondered if he had failed to escape the mannerisms of his profession, if he exuded learned counsel, even at Ottercombe in South Devon.

The lane dived abruptly downhill. Watchman remembered Decima Moore. Would she still be there? Did the Coombe Left Movement still hold its meetings on Saturday night and would Decima allow her arguments with himself to end as they had ended that warm night nearly a year ago? He set his thoughts on the memory of the smell of seaweed and briar, and of Decima, trapped halfway between resentment and fright, walking as if by compulsion into his arms.

The hamlet of Diddlestock, a brief interlude of whitewash and thatch, marked the last stage. Already as he slid out of the shadow of Ottercombe Woods, he fancied that he heard the thunder of the sea.

Watchman checked his car, skidded, and changed into low gear. Somewhere about here, Diddlestock Lane crossed Ottercombe Lane and the intersection was completely masked by banks and hedgerows. A dangerous turning. Yes, there it was. He sounded his horn and the next second crammed on his brakes. The car skidded, lurched sideways, and fetched up against the bank, with its right-hand front bumpers locked in the left-hand rear bumpers of a baby two-seater.

Watchman leant out of the driving window.

"What the hell do you think you're doing?" he yelled. The two-seater leapt nervously and was jerked back by the bumpers.

"Stop that!" roared Watchman.

He got out and stumbled along the lane to the other car.

It was so dark down there between the hedgerows that the driver's features, shadowed both by the roof of his car and the brim of his hat, were scarcely discernible. He seemed about to open the door when Watchman, bareheaded, came up to him. Evidently he changed his mind. He leant farther back in his seat. His fingers pulled at the brim of his hat.

"Look here," Watchman began, "you're a hell of a fellow, aren't you, bucketing about the countryside like a blasted tank! Why the devil can't you sound your horn? You came out of that lane about twenty times as fast as—*What?*"

The man had mumbled something.

"What?" Watchman repeated.

"I'm extremely sorry. Didn't hear you until . . ." The voice faded away.

"All right. Well, we'd better do something about it. I don't imagine much damage has been done." The man made no move and Watchman's irritation revived. "Give me a hand, will you."

"Yes, certainly. Of course." The voice was unexpectedly courteous. "I'm very sorry. Really, very sorry. It was all my fault."

This display of contrition mollified Watchman.

"Oh well," he said, "no harm done, I dare say. Come on."

The man got out on the far side and walked round to the back of the car. When Watchman joined him he was stooping over the locked buffers.

"I can heave mine up if you don't mind backing an inch or two," said the man. With large callused hands he gripped the buffers of his own car.

"All right," agreed Watchman.

They released the buffers without much trouble. Watchman called through his driving-window: "All clear!" The man lowered his car and then groped uncertainly in his pockets.

"Cigarette?" suggested Watchman and held out his case.

"Very kind," said the man. "Coals of fire!" He hesitated and then took a cigarette.

"Light?"

"I've got one, thanks."

He turned aside and cupped his hands round the match, dipping his head with extravagant care as if a wind threatened the flame.

"I suppose you're going to Ottercombe?" said Watchman.

He saw a flash of teeth.

"Looks like it, doesn't it? I'm sorry I can't let you through till then."

"I shan't be on your heels at the pace you travel," grinned Watchman.

"No," agreed the man, and his voice sounded remote as he moved away. "I'll keep out of your way. Good night."

"Good night."

The ridiculous little car was as good as its driver's word. It shot away down the lane and vanished over the brow of a steep drop. Watchman followed more cautiously and by the time he rounded the hill the other car had turned a further corner. He caught the distant toot of a horn. It sounded derisive.

ii

The lane ran out towards the coast and straight for Coombe Rock, a headland that rose sharply from the downs to thrust its nose into the Channel. A patch on the hillside seemed to mark an inconsequent end to the route. It was only when he drew close to this patch that a stranger might recognize it as an entrance to a tunnel, the only gate into Ottercombe. Watchman saw it grow magically until it filled his range of vision. He passed a road-sign—"OTTERCOMBE. Dangerous Corner. Change down,"—and entered the mouth of the tunnel. He slowed down and switched on his lights. Dank walls closed about him, the sound of his progress echoed loudly and he smelt wet stones and seaweed. Before him, coldly and inkily blue, framed in black, was the sea. From within, the tunnel seemed to end in a shelf; actually it turned sharply to the left. Watchman had to stop and back his car before he could get round. There, down on his left and facing the sea, was Ottercombe.

Probably the alarming entrance into this village has saved it from becoming another Clovelly or Polperro. Ladies with Ye Olde Shoppe ambitions would hesitate to drive through Coombe Tunnel, and very large cars are unable to do so. Moreover, the village is not too picturesque. It is merely a group of houses whose whitewash is tarnished by the sea. There are no secret stairs in any of them, no ghosts walk Ottercombe Steps, no smuggler's cave looks out from Coombe Rock. For all that, the place has its history of grog-running and wrecking. There is a story of a fight in the tunnel between excisemen and the men of Coombe, and there are traces of the gate that once closed the tunnel every night at sunset. The whole of Ottercombe is the property of an irascible eccentric who keeps the houses in good repair, won't let one of them to a strange shopkeeper, and breathes venom on the word "publicity." If a stranger cares to stay in Ottercombe he must put up at the Plume of Feathers, where Abel Pomeroy has four guest rooms, and Mrs. Ives does the housekeeping and cooking. If the Coombe men like him, they will take him out in their boats and play darts with him in the evening. He may walk round the cliffs, fish off the rocks, or drive seven miles to Illington where there is a golf course and a three-star hotel. These are the amenities of Ottercombe.

The Plume of Feathers faces the cobbled road of entrance. It is a square building, scrupulously whitewashed. It has no great height but its position gives it an air of dominance over the cottages that surround it. On the corner of the Feathers, the road of approach splits and becomes a sort of inn-yard off which Ottercombe Steps lead through the village and down to the wharf. Thus the windows of the inn, on two sides, watch for the arrival of strangers. By the corner entrance is a bench occupied on warm evenings by Abel Pomeroy and his cronies. At intervals Abel walks into the middle of the road and looks up towards Coombe Tunnel as his father and grandfather did before him.

As Watchman drove down, he could see old Pomeroy standing there in his shirt sleeves. Watchman flicked his headlights and Pomeroy raised his hand. Watchman sounded his horn and a taller figure, dressed in the slacks and sweater of some superb advertisement, came through the lighted doorway.

It was Watchman's cousin, Sebastian Parish. Then the others *had* arrived.

He drew up and opened the door.

"Well, Pomeroy."

"Well, Mr. Watchman, we'm right-down glad to see you again. Welcome to you."

"I'm glad to get here," said Watchman, shaking hands. "Hullo, Seb. When did you arrive?"

"This morning, old boy. We stopped last night at Exeter with Norman's sister."

"I was at Yeovil," said Watchman. "Where is Norman?"

"Painting down by the jetty. The light's gone. He'll be in soon. He's started a portrait of me on Coombe Rock. It's going to be rather wonderful. I'm wearing a red sweater and the sea's behind me. Very virile!"

"Good Lord!" said Watchman cheerfully.

"We'll get your things out for you, sir," said old Pomeroy. "Will!"

A tall, fox-coloured man came through the doorway. He screwed up his eyes, peered at Watchman, and acknowledged his greeting without much show of enthusiasm.

"Well, Will."

"Evening, Mr. Watchman."

"Bear a hand, my sonny," said old Pomeroy.

His son opened the luggage carrier and began to haul out Watchman's suit-cases.

"How's the Movement, Will?" asked Watchman. "Still well on the Left?"

"Yes," said Will shortly. "It's going ahead. Will these be all?"

"Yes, thanks. I'll take the car around, Seb, and join you in the bar. Is there a sandwich or so anywhere about, Abel?"

"We can do a bit better than that, sir. There's a fine lobster Mrs. Ives has put aside, special."

"By George, you're a host in a million. God bless Mrs. Ives."

Watchman drove round to the garage. It was a converted stable, a dark building that housed the memory of sweating horses rubbed down by stable lads with wisps of straw. When he stopped his engine Watchman heard a rat plop across the rafters. In addition to his own, the garage held four cars. There was Norman Cubitt's Austin, a smaller Austin, a Morris, and there, demure in the corner, a battered two-seater.

"You again!" said Watchman, staring at it. "Well, I'll be damned!"

He returned to the pub, delighted to hear the familiar ring of his own steps, to smell the tang of the sea and of burning driftwood. As he ran upstairs he heard voices and the unmistakable tuck of a dart in a cork board.

"Double-twenty," said Will Pomeroy, and above the general outcry came a woman's voice.

"Splendid, my dear. We win!"

"So, she *is* here," thought Watchman as he washed his hands. "And why 'my dear'? And who wins?"

iii

Watchman, with his cousin for company, ate his lobster in the private tap-room. There is a parlour at the Feathers but nobody ever uses it. The public and the private tap-rooms fit into each other like two Ls, the first standing sideways on the tip of its short base, the second facing backwards to the left. The bar-proper is common to both. It occupies the short leg of the Public, has a counter for each room, and faces the short leg of the Private. The top of the long leg forms a magnificent inglenook flanked with settles and scented with three hundred years of driftwood smoke. Opposite the inglenook at the bottom angle of the L hangs a dart board made by Abel Pomeroy himself. There, winter and summer alike, the Pomeroys' chosen friends play for drinks. There is a board in the Public for the rank and file. If strangers to the Feathers choose to play in the Private the initiates wait until they have finished. If the initiates invite a stranger to play, he is no longer a stranger.

The midsummer evening was chilly and a fire smouldered in the inglenook. Watchman finished his supper, swung his legs up on to the settle, and felt for his pipe. He squinted up at Sebastian Parish, who leant against the mantelpiece in an attitude familiar to every West End playgoer in London.

"I like this place," Watchman said. "Extraordinarily pleasant, isn't it, returning to a place one likes?"

Parish made an actor's expressive gesture.

"Marvellous!" he said richly. "To get away from everything! The noise! The endless racket! The artificiality! God, how I loathe my profession!"

"Come off it, Seb," said Watchman. "You glory in it. You were born acting. The gamp probably burst into an involuntary round of applause on your first entrance and I bet you played your mother right off the stage."

"All the same, old boy, this good clean air means a hell of a lot to me."

"Exactly," agreed Watchman drily. His cousin had a trick of saying things that sounded a little like quotations from an interview with himself. Watchman was amused rather than irritated by this mannerism. It was part and parcel, he thought, of Seb's harmless staginess; like his clothes which were too exactly what a gentleman roughing it in South Devon ought to wear. He liked to watch Seb standing out on Coombe Rock, bareheaded to the breeze, in effect waiting for the camera man to say "O.K. for sound." No doubt that was the pose Norman had chosen for his portrait of Sebastian. It occurred to him now that Sebastian was up to something. That speech about the artificiality of the stage was the introduction to a confidence, or Watchman didn't know his Parish. Whatever it was, Sebastian missed his moment. The door opened and a thin man with untidy fair hair looked in.

"Hullo!" said Watchman. "Our distinguished artist." Norman Cubitt grinned, lowered his painter's pack, and came into the inglenook.

"Well, Luke? Good trip?"

"Splendid! You're painting already?"

Cubitt stretched a hand to the fire. The fingers were grimed with paint.

"I'm doing a thing of Seb," he said. "I suppose he's told you about it. Laying it on with a trowel, I am. That's in the morning. To-night I started a thing down by the jetty. They're patching up one of the posts. Very pleasant subject, but my treatment of it, so far, is bloody."

"Are you painting in the dark?" asked Watchman with a smile.

"I was talking to one of the fishing blokes after the light went. They've gone all politically-minded in the Coombe."

"That," said Parish, lowering his voice, "is Will Pomeroy and his Left Group."

"Will and Decima together," said Cubitt. "I've suggested they call themselves the Decimbrists."

"Where are the lads of the village?" demanded Watchman. "I thought I heard the dart game in progress as I went upstairs."

"Abel's rat-poisoning in the garage," said Parish. "They've all gone out to see he doesn't give himself a lethal dose of prussic acid."

"Good Lord!" Watchman ejaculated. "Is the old fool playing round with cyanide?"

"Apparently. . . . Why wouldn't we have a drink?"

"Why not, indeed," agreed Cubitt. "Hi, Will!"

He went to the bar and leant over it, looking into the Public.

"The whole damn place is deserted. I'll get our drinks and chalk them up. Beer?"

"Beer it is," said Parish.

"What form of cyanide had Abel got hold of?" Watchman asked.

"Eh?" said Parish savagely. "Oh, let's see now. I fetched it for him from Illington. The chemist hadn't got any of the stock rat-banes but he poked round and found this stuff. I think he called it Scheele's acid."

"Good God!"

"What? Yes, that was it—Scheele's acid. And then he said he thought the fumes of Scheele's acid mightn't be strong enough so he gingered it up a bit."

"With what, in the name of all the Borgias?"

"Well—with prussic acid, I imagine."

"You imagine! You imagine!"

"He said that was what it was. He said it was acid or something. I wouldn't know. He warned me in sixteen different positions to be careful. Suggested Abel wear a half-crown gas mask, so I bought it in case Abel hadn't got one. Abel's using gloves and everything."

"It's absolutely monstrous!"

"I had to sign for it, old boy," said Parish. "Very solemn we were. God, he was a stupid man! Bone from the eyes up, but so, so kind."

Watchman said angrily: "I should damn' well think he was stupid. Do you know that twenty-five drops of Scheele's acid will kill a man in a few minutes? Why, good Lord, in *Rex v. Bull*, if I'm not mistaken, it was alleged that accused gave only seven drops. I myself defended a medical student who gave twenty minims in error. Charge of manslaughter. I got him off but—how's Abel using it?"

"What's all this?" inquired Cubitt. "There's your beer."

"Abel said he was going to put it in a pot and shove it in a rathole," explained Parish. "I think he's filled with due respect for its deadliness, Luke, really. He's going to block the hole up and everything."

"The chemist had no business to give you Scheele's, much less this infernal brew. He ought to be struck off the books. The pharmacopoeial preparation would have been quite strong enough. He could have diluted even that to advantage."

"Well, God bless us," said Cubitt hastily, and took a pull at his beer.

"What happens, actually, when someone's poisoned by prussic acid?" asked Parish.

"Convulsion, clammy sweat, and death."

"Shut up!" said Cubitt. "What a filthy conversation!"

"Well—cheers, dears," said Parish raising his tankard.

"You do get hold of the most repellent idioms, Seb," said his cousin. *"Te saluto!"*

"But not *moriturus*, I trust," added Parish. "With all this chat about prussic acid! What's it look like?"

"You bought it."

"I didn't notice. It's a blue bottle."

"Hydrocyanic acid," said Watchman with his barrister's precision, "is, in appearance, exactly like water. It is a liquid miscible with water, and this stuff is a dilution of hydrocyanic acid."

"The chemist," said Parish, "put a terrific notice on it. I remember I once had to play a man who's taken cyanide. 'Fool's Errand,' the piece was; a revival with whiskers on it but not a bad old drama. I died in a few seconds."

"For once the dramatist was right," said Watchman. "It's one of the sudden poisons. Horrible stuff! I've got cause to know it. I was once briefed in a case where a woman took—"

"For God's sake," interrupted Norman Cubitt violently, "shut up, both of you. I've got a poison phobia."

"Have you really, Norman?" asked Parish. "That's very interesting. Can you trace it?"

"I think so." Cubitt rubbed his hair and then looked absent-mindedly at his paint-grimed hand. "As a matter of fact, my dear Seb," he said, with his air of secretly mocking at himself, "you have named the root and cause of my affection. You have perpetrated a coincidence. Sebastian. The very play you mentioned just now started me off on my Freudian road to the jim-jams. 'Fool's Errand' and well-named. It is, as you say, a remarkably naïve play. At the age of seven, however, I did not think so. I found it terrifying."

"At the age of seven?"

"Yes. My eldest brother, poor fool, fancied himself as an amateur and essayed the principal part. I was bullied into enacting the small boy who, as I remember, perpetually bleated 'Papa, why is Mama so pale?' and later on: 'Papa, why is Mama so quiet? Where has she gone, Papa?' "

"We cut all that in the revival," said Parish. "It was terrible stuff."

"I agree with you. As you remember, Papa had poisoned Mama. For years afterwards I had the horrors at the very word. I remember that I used to wipe all the schoolroom china for fear our Miss Tobin was a Borgian governess. I invented all sorts of curious devices in order that Miss Tobin should drink my morning cocoa and I hers. Odd, wasn't it? I grew out of it, but I still dislike the sound of the word and I detest taking medicine labelled in accordance with the Pure Food Act."

"Labelled *what?*" asked Parish with a wink at Watchman.

"Labelled 'poison,' damn you," said Cubitt.

Watchman looked curiously at him.

"I suppose there's something in this psycho stuff," he said, "but I always rather boggle at it."

"I don't see why you should," said Parish. "You yourself get a fit of the staggers if you scratch your finger. You told me once you fainted when you had a blood test. That's a phobia, same as Norman's."

"Not quite," said Watchman. "Lots of people can't stand the sight of their own blood. The poison-scare's much more unusual. But you don't mean to tell me, do you, Norman, that because at an early age you helped your brother in a play about cyanide you'd feel definitely uncomfortable if I finished my story?"

Cubitt drained his tankard and set it down on the table.

"If you're hell-bent on your beastly story—" he said.

"It was only that I was present at the autopsy on this woman who died of cyanide poisoning. When they opened her up, I fainted. Not from emotion but from the fumes. The pathologist said I had a pronounced idiosyncrasy for the stuff. I was damned ill after it. It nearly did for me."

Cubitt wandered over to the door and lifted his pack.

"I'll clean up," he said, "and join you for the dart game."

"Splendid, old boy," said Parish. "We'll beat them tonight."

"Do our damned'st, anyway," said Cubitt. At the doorway he turned and looked mournfully at Parish.

"She's asking about perspective," he said.

"Give her rat-poison," said Parish.

"Shut up," said Cubitt, and went out.

"What was he talking about?" demanded Watchman.

Parish smiled. "He's got a girl-friend. Wait till you see. Funny chap! He went quite green over your story. Sensitive old beggar, isn't he?"

"Oh yes," agreed Watchman lightly. "I must say I'm sensitive in a rather different key where cyanide's concerned, having been nearly killed by it."

"I didn't know you could have a—what did you call it?"

"An idiosyncrasy."

"It means you'd go under to a very small amount?"

"It does." Watchman yawned and stretched himself full-length on the settle.

"I'm sleepy," he said. "It's the sea air. A very pleasant state of being. Just tired enough, with the impressions of a long drive still floating about behind one's consciousness. Flying hedges, stretches of road that stream out before one's eyes. The relaxation of arrival setting in. Very pleasant!"

He closed his eyes for a moment and then turned his head to look at his cousin.

"So Decima Moore is still here," he said.

Parish smiled. "Very much so. But you'll have to watch your step, Luke."

"Why?"

"There's an engagement in the offing."

"What d'you mean?"

"Decima and Will Pomeroy."

Watchman sat up.

"I don't believe you," he said sharply.

"Well—why not?"

"Good Lord! A politically minded pot-boy."

"Actually they're the same class," Parish murmured.

"Perhaps; but she's not of it."

"All the same—"

Watchman grimaced.

"She's a little fool," he said, "but you may be right," and lay back again. "Oh well!" he added comfortably.

There was a moment's silence.

"There's another female here," said Parish, and grinned.

"Another? Who?"

"Norman's girl-friend, of course. My oath!"

"Why? What's she like? Why are you grinning away like a Cheshire cat, Seb?"

"My dear soul," said Parish, "if I could get that woman to walk on the boards every morning and do her stuff exactly as she does it here—well, of course! I'd go into management and die a millionaire."

"Who is she?"

"She's the Honourable Violet Darragh. She waters."

"She *what?*"

"She does water-colours. Wait till you hear Norman on Violet."

"Is she a nuisance?" asked Watchman apprehensively.

"Not exactly. Well, in a way. Pure joy to me. Wait till you meet her."

Parish would say no more about Miss Darragh, and Watchman, only mildly interested, relapsed into a pleasant doze.

"By the way," he said presently, "some driving expert nearly dashed himself to extinction against my bonnet."

"Really?"

"Yes. At Diddlestock Corner. Came bucketing out of the blind turning on my right, beat me by a split second, and hung his silly little stern on my front buffers. Ass!"

"Any damage?"

"No, no. He heaved his pygmy up by the bottom and I backed away. Funny sort of fellow, he is."

"You knew him?" asked Parish in surprise.

"No." Watchman took the tip of his nose between thumb and forefinger. It was a gesture he used in cross-examination. "No, I don't know him, and yet—there was something—I got the impression that *he* didn't want to know *me*. Quite an educated voice. Labourer's hands. False teeth, I rather fancy."

"You're very observant," said Parish, lightly.

"No more than the next man, but there was something about the fellow—I was going to ask if you knew him. His car's in the garage."

"Surely it's not—Hullo, here are the others."

Boots and voices sounded in the public bar. Will Pomeroy came through and leant over the counter. He looked, not towards Watchman or Parish, but into a settle on the far side of the Private, a settle whose high back was towards them.

" 'Evening, Bob," said Will cordially. "Kept you waiting?"

"That's all right, Will," said a voice from beyond the settle. "I'll have a pint of bitter when you're ready."

Luke Watchman uttered a stifled exclamation.

"What's up?" asked his cousin.

"Come here."

Parish strolled nearer to him and in obedience to a movement of Watchman's head, stooped towards him.

"What's up?" he repeated.

"That's the same fellow," muttered Watchman. "He must have been here all the time. That's his voice."

"Hell!" said Parish delightedly.

"D'you think he heard?"

"Of course he heard."

"Blast the creature! Serves him right."

"Shut up."

The door into the private bar opened. Old Abel came in followed by Norman Cubitt. Cubitt took three darts from a collection in a pewter pot on the bar and moved in front of the dart board.

"I'll be there in a moment," said a woman's voice from the passage. "Don't start without me."

Abel walked into the inglenook and put a bottle on the mantelpiece.

"Well, souls," he said, "reckon we'm settled the hash of they vermin. If thurr's not a corpse on the premises afore long, I'll be greatly astonished."

CHAPTER TWO

Advance by Watchman

i

THE BOTTLE was a small one and, as Sebastian Parish had remarked, it was conspicuously labelled. The word POISON in scarlet on a white ground, ran diagonally across an attached label. It struck a note of interjection and alarm, and focussed the attention of the five men. Few who read that warning escape a sudden jolt of the imagination.

Parish said: "Mr. Watchman thinks you are a public danger, Abel. He's afraid we'll all be poisoned."

"I'm afraid he'll poison himself," said Watchman.

"Who, sir? Me?" asked Abel. "Not a bit of it. I be a mortal cautious sort of chap when it comes to this manner of murderous tipple, Mr. Watchman."

"I hope you are," said Cubitt from the dart board.

"You're not going to leave it on the mantelshelf, Father?" asked Will.

"No fear of that, sonny. I'll stow it away careful."

"You'd much better get rid of it altogether," said Watchman. "Don't put it away somewhere. You'll forget about it and some day someone will take a sniff at it to find out what it is. Let me take it back to the chemist at Illington. I'd very much like to have a word with that gentleman."

"Lord love you," said Abel opening his eyes very wide, "us've not finished with they bowldacious varmints yet, my sonnies. If so be they've got a squeak left in 'em us'll give 'em another powerful whiff and finish 'em off."

"At least," said Cubitt throwing a dart into double-twenty, "at least you might put it out of reach."

"Mr. Cubitt has a poison-phobia," said Watchman.

"A what, sir?"

"Never mind about that," said Cubitt. "I should have thought anybody might boggle at prussic acid."

"Don't fret yourselves, gentlemen," said Abel. "Thurr'll be none of this brew served out at the Feathers tap."

He mounted the settle and taking the bottle from the mantelpiece pushed it into the top shelf of a double-cupboard in the corner of the inglenook. He then pulled off the old gloves he wore, threw them on the fire, and turned the key.

"Nobody can call me a careless man," he said. "I'm all for looking after myself. Thurr's my first-aid box in thurr, ready to hand, and if any of the chaps cuts themselves with a mucky fish-knife or any other infectious trifle of that sort, they gets a swill of iodine in scratch. Make 'em squirm a bit and none the worse for that. I learnt that in the war, my sonnies. I was a surgeon's orderly and I know the mighty powers thurr be in drugs."

He stared at the glass door. The label POISON still showed, slightly distorted, in the darkness of the little cupboard.

"Safe enough thurr," said Abel, and went over to the bar.

With the arrival of the Pomeroys the private bar took on its customary aspect for a summer's evening. They both went behind the counters. Abel sat facing the Private and on Cubitt's order drew pints of draught beer for the company. A game of darts was started in the Public.

The man in the settle had not moved, but now Watchman saw his hand reach out for his pint. He saw the calluses, the chipped nails, the coarsened joints of the fingers. Watchman got up, stretched himself, grimaced at Parish, and crossed the room to the settle.

The light shone full in the face of the stranger. The skin of his face was brown but Watchman thought it had only recently acquired this colour. His hair stood up in white bristles, his forehead was garnished with bumps that shone in the lamplight. The eyes under the bleached lashes seemed almost without colour. From the nostrils to the corners of the mouth ran grooves that lent emphasis to the fall of the lips. Without raising his head the man looked up at Watchman and the shadow of a smile seemed to visit his face. He got up and made as if to go to the door, but Watchman stopped him.

"May I introduce myself?" asked Watchman.

The man smiled broadly. "They *are* teeth," thought Watchman and he added: "We have met already this evening but we didn't exchange names. Mine is Luke Watchman."

"I gathered as much from your conversation," said the man. He paused a moment and then said: "Mine is Legge."

"I'm afraid I sounded uncivil," said Watchman. "I hope you'll allow me a little motorists' license. One always abuses the other man, doesn't one?"

"You'd every excuse," mumbled Legge, "every excuse." He scarcely moved his lips. His teeth seemed too large for his mouth. He looked sideways at Watchman, picked up a magazine from the settle, and flipped it open, holding it before his face.

Watchman felt vaguely irritated. He had struck no sort of response from the man and he was not accustomed to falling flat. Obviously, Legge merely wished to be rid of him and this state of affairs piqued Watchman's vanity. He sat on the edge of the table, and, for the second time that evening, offered his cigarette case to Legge.

"No, thanks—pipe."

"I'd no idea I should find you here," said Watchman and noticed uncomfortably that his own voice sounded disproportionately cordial, "although you did tell me you were bound for Ottercombe. It's a good pub, isn't it?"

"Yes, yes," said Legge hurriedly. "Very good."

"Are you making a long visit?"

He pulled out his pipe and began to fill it. His fingers moved clumsily and he had an air of rather ridiculous concentration. Watchman felt marooned on the edge of the table. He saw that Parish was listening with a maddening grin, and he fancied that Cubitt's ears were cocked. "Damn it," he thought, "I will not be put out of countenance by the brute. He *shall* like me." But he could think of nothing to say and Mr. Legge had begun to read his magazine.

From beyond the bar came the sound of raucous applause. Someone yelled: "Double serventeen and we'm beat the Bakery."

Norman Cubitt pulled out his darts and paused for a moment. He looked from Watchman to Parish. It struck him that there was a strong family resemblance between these cousins, a resemblance of character rather than physique. Each in his way, thought Cubitt, was a vain man. In Parish one recognized the ingenuous vanity of the actor. Off the stage he wooed applause with only less assiduity than he commanded it when he faced an audience. Watchman was more subtle. Watchman must have the attention and respect of every new acquaintance, but he played for it without seeming to do so. He would take endless trouble with a complete stranger when he seemed to take none. "But he's getting no change out of Legge," thought Cubitt maliciously. And with a faint smile he turned back to the dart board.

Watchman saw the smile. He took a pull at his tankard and tried again.

"Are you one of the dart experts?" he asked. Legge looked up vaguely and Watchman had to repeat the question.

"I play a little," said Legge.

Cubitt hurled his last dart at the board and joined the others.

"He plays like the Devil himself," he said. "Last night I took him on, 101 down. I never even started. He threw fifty, one, and the fifty again."

"I was fortunate that time," said Mr. Legge with rather more animation.

"Not a bit of it," said Cubitt. "You're merely odiously accurate."

"Well," said Watchman, "I'll lay you ten bob you can't do it again, Mr. Legge."

"You've lost," said Cubitt.

"Aye, he's a proper masterpiece, is Mr. Legge," said old Abel.

Sebastian Parish came across from the inglenook. He looked down good-humouredly at Legge. "Nobody," thought Cubitt, "has any right to be as good-looking as Seb."

"What's all this?" asked Parish.

"I've offered to bet Mr. Legge ten bob he can't throw fifty, one and fifty."

"You've lost," said Parish.

"This is monstrous," cried Watchman. "Do you take me, Mr. Legge?"

Legge shot a glance at him. The voices of the players beyond the partition had quieted for the moment. Will Pomeroy had joined his father at the private bar. Cubitt and Parish and the two Pomeroys waited in silence for Legge's reply. He made a curious grimace, pursing his lips and screwing up his eyes. As if in reply Watchman used the K.C.'s trick of his and took the tip of his nose between thumb and forefinger. Cubitt, who watched them curiously, was visited by the fantastic notion that some sort of signal had passed between them.

Legge rose slowly to his feet.

"Oh yes," he said. "Certainly, Mr. Watchman, I take you on."

ii

Legge moved, with a slovenly dragging of his boots, into a position in front of the board. He pulled out the three darts and looked at them.

"Getting a bit worn, Mr. Pomeroy," said Legge. "The rings are loose."

"I've sent for a new set," said Abel. "They'll be here tomorrow. Old lot go into Public."

Will Pomeroy left the public bar and joined his father. "Showing 'em how to do it, Bob?" he asked.

"There's a bet on, sonny," said old Pomeroy.

"Don't make me nervous, Will," said Legge with a grin.

He looked at the board, poised his first dart and, with a crisp movement of his hand, flung it into the Bull's-eye.

"Fifty," said Will. "There you are, gentlemen! Fifty!"

"Three-and-fourpence in pawn," said Watchman.

"We'll put it into the C.L.M. if it comes off, Will," said Legge.

"What's the C.L.M.?" demanded Watchman.

Will stared straight in front of him and said: "The Coombe Left Movement, Mr. Watchman. We've a branch of the South Devon Left, now."

"Oh Lord!" said Watchman.

Legge threw his second dart. It seemed almost to drop from his hand but he must have used a certain amount of force since it sent home solidly into the top right-hand division.

"And the one. Six-and-eightpence looking a bit off-colour, Mr. Watchman," said Abel Pomeroy.

"He's stymied himself for the other double twenty-five, though," said Watchman. "The first dart's lying right across it."

Legge raised his hand and this time took more deliberate aim. He threw from a greater height. For a fraction of a second the dart seemed to hang in his fingers before it sped downwards athwart the first, into the narrow strip round the centre.

"And fifty it is!" said Will. "There you are. Fifty. Good for you, comrade."

A little chorus went up from Parish, Cubitt and old Abel.

"The man's a wizard."

"Shouldn't be allowed!"

"You'm a proper masterpiece."

"Well done, Bob," added Will, as if determined to give the last word of praise.

Watchman laid a ten-shilling note on the table.

"I congratulate you," he said.

Legge looked at the note.

"Thank you, Mr. Watchman," he said. "Another ten bob for the fighting fund, Will."

"Good enough, but it's straight-out generous to give it."

Watchman sat down again on the table-edge.

"All very nice," he said. "Does you credit, Mr. Legge. I rather think another drink's indicated. With me, if you please. Loser's privilege."

Will Pomeroy glanced uncomfortably at Legge. By Feather's etiquette, the winner of a bet at darts pays for the next round. There was a short silence broken by old Pomeroy who insisted that the next round should be on the house, and served the company with a potent dark ale, known to the Coombe as Treble Extra.

"We'll all play like Mr. Legge with this inside us," said Parish.

"Yes," agreed Watchman, looking into his tankard, "it's a fighting fund in itself. A very pretty tipple indeed." He looked up at Legge. "Do you know any other tricks like that one, Mr. Legge?"

"I know a prettier one than that," said Legge quietly, "if you'll assist me."

"I assist you?"

"Yes. If you'll stretch your hand out flat on the board I'll outline it with darts."

"Really? You ought to be in the sawdust ring. No. I don't think I trust you enough for that, you know. One would need a little more of Mr. Pomeroy's Treble Extra."

He stretched out his hand and looked at it.

"And yet, I don't know," he said. "I'd like to see you do it. Some other time. You know, Mr. Legge, as a good Conservative, I feel I should deplore your gesture. Against whom is your fighting fund directed?"

But before Legge could speak, Will answered quickly: "Against the capitalist, Mr. Watchman, and all his side."

"Really? So Mr. Legge is also an ardent proletarian fan?"

"Certainly," said Legge. "I have the honour to be Secretary and Treasurer for the Coombe Left Movement."

"Secretary *and* Treasurer," repeated Watchman. "Responsible jobs, aren't they?"

"Aye," said Will, "and it's a responsible chap that's taken 'em on for us."

Legge turned away and moved into the inglenook. Watchman looked after him. Cubitt noticed that Watchman's good humour seemed to be restored. Anyone would have thought that he had won the bet and that it had been for a much larger sum. And for no reason in the world Cubitt felt that there had been a passage of arms between Legge and Watchman, and that Watchman had scored a bit.

"What about you, Abel?" Watchman asked abruptly. "Are you going to paint the feathers red?"

"Me, sir? No, I don't hold with Will's revolutionary ideas and he knows it, but us've agreed to differ. Does no harm, I reckon, for these young chaps to meet every Friday and make believe they're hashing up the laws and serving 'em out topsy-turvy: game in servants' hall and prunes and rice for gentry. Our Will was always a great hand for make-believe from the time he learned to talk. Used to strut about tap-room giving orders to the furniture. 'I be as good as Squire, now,' he'd say in his little lad's voice and I reckon he's saying it yet."

"You're blind to reason, Father," said Will. "Blind-stupid and hidebound. Either you can't see or you won't. Us chaps are working for the good of all; not for ourselves."

"Right enough, sonny. A fine noble ideal, I don't doubt, and when you've got us all toeing the line with no handicaps and nothing to run for—"

"The good of the State to run for. Each man equal—"

"And all coming in first. Damn queer sort of race."

"The old argument," said Legge from the fireplace, "and based as usual on a false analogy."

"Is it a false analogy?" asked Watchman. "You propose to kill private enterprise—"

"A chap," said Will Pomeroy, "will be as ambitious for the public good as he will for his own selfish aims. Give him the chance, that's all. Teach him to think. The people—"

"The people!" interrupted Watchman, looking at Legge's back. "What do you mean by the people? I suppose you mean that vast collection of individuals whose wages are below a certain sum and who are capable of being led by the nose when the right sort of humbug comes along."

"That's no argument," began Will angrily. "That's no more than a string of silly opinions."

"That'll do, sonny," said Abel.

"It's all right, Abel," said Watchman, still looking at Legge. "I invited the discussion. No offence. I should like to hear what Mr. Legge has to say about private enterprise. As Treasurer—"

"Wait a bit, Bob," said Will as Legge turned from the fireplace. "I don't like the way you said that, Mr. Watchman. Bob Legge here is well-respected in the Coombe. He's not been long in these parts—ten months, isn't it, Bob?—but we've learned to like him.

Reckon we've showed we trust him, too, seeing the position we've given him."

"My dear Will," said Watchman delicately, "I don't dispute for a moment. I think Mr. Legge has done remarkably well for himself, in ten months."

Will's face was scarlet under his thatch of fox-coloured hair. He moved forward and confronted Watchman, his tankard clenched in a great ham of a fist, his feet planted apart.

"Shut up, now, Luke," said Sebastian Parish softly and Cubitt murmured, "Don't heckle, Luke, you're on holiday."

"See here, Mr. Watchman," said Will. "You can afford to sneer, can't you, but I'd like to know—"

"Will!" Old Abel slapped the bar with an open hand. "That's enough. You'm a grown chap, not a lad, and what's more, the son of this house. Seems like I ought to give 'ee light draught and lemonade till you learn to take a man's pint like a man. If you can't talk politics and hold your temper then you'll not talk politics at all. 'Be a job for you in Public here. 'Tend it."

"I'm sorry, Will," said Watchman. "Mr. Legge is fortunate in his friend."

Will Pomeroy stood and looked under his brows from Watchman to Legge. Legge shrugged his shoulders, muttered something about moving into the public bar, and went out. Will turned to Watchman.

"There's something behind all this," he said. "I want to know what the game is, Mr. Watchman, and damme I'm going to find out."

"Did I hear something about a game?" said a woman's voice. They all turned to look at the doorway. There they saw a short fat figure clad in a purple tweed skirt and a green jersey.

"May I come in?" asked the Honourable Violet Darragh.

iii

Miss Darragh's entrance broke up the scene. Will Pomeroy turned, ducked under the flap of the private bar, and leant over the counter into the Public. Watchman stood up. The others turned to Miss Darragh with an air of relief, and Abel Pomeroy, with his innkeeper's heartiness, intensified perhaps by a feeling of genuine relief, said loudly, "Come in then, miss, company's waiting for you and you'm in time for a drink, with the house."

"Not Treble Extra, Mr. Pomeroy, if you don't mind. Sherry for me, if you please."

She waddled over to the bar, placed her hands on the counter and with agility that astonished Watchman, made a neat little vault on to one of the tall stools. There she sat beaming upon the company.

She was a woman of perhaps fifty, but it would have been difficult to guess her age since time had added to her countenance and figure merely layer after layer of firm wholesome fat. She was roundabout and compact. Her face was babyish and this impression was heightened by the tight grey curls that covered her head. In repose she seemed to pout and it was not until she spoke that her good humour appeared in her eyes, and was magnified by her spectacles. All fat people wear a look of inscrutability and Violet Darragh was not unlike a jolly sort of sphinx.

Abel served her and she took the glass delicately in her small white paws.

"Well now," she said, "is everybody having fun?" and then caught sight of Watchman. "Is this your cousin, Mr. Parish?"

"I'm sorry," said Parish hurriedly. "Mr. Watchman, Miss Darragh."

"How d'ye do," said Miss Darragh.

Like many Irishwomen of her class she spoke with such a marked brogue that one wondered whether it was inspired by a kind of jocularity that had turned into a habit.

"I've heard about you, of course, and read about you in the papers, for I dearly love a good murder and if I can't have me murder I'm all for arson. That was a fine murder case you defended last year, now, Mr. Watchman. Before you took silk, 'twas. You did your best for the poor scoundrel."

Watchman expanded.

"I didn't get him off, Miss Darragh."

"Ah well, and a good job you didn't, for we'd none of us been safe in our beds. And there's Mr. Cubitt come from his painting down by the jetty, in mortal terror, poor man, lest I plague him with me perspective."

"Not at all," said Cubitt, turning rather pink.

"I'll leave you alone, now. I know very well I'm a trouble to you but it's good for your character, and you may look upon me as a kind of holiday penance."

"You're a painter, too, Miss Darragh?" said Watchman.

"I'm a raw amateur, Mr. Watchman, but I've a kind of itch for ut. When I see a little peep I can't rest till I'm at it with me paints.

There's Mr. Cubitt wincing as if he had a nagging tooth, when I talk of a pretty peep. You've a distinguished company in your house, Mr. Pomeroy," continued Miss Darragh. "I thought I was coming to a quiet little village and what do I find but a galaxy of the talents. Mr. Parish who's turned me heart over many a time with his acting; Mr. Cubitt, down there painting within stone's-throw of meself; and now haven't we the great counsel to add to your intellectual feast. I wonder now, Mr. Watchman, if you remember me poor cousin Bryonie's case?"

"I—Yes," said Watchman, greatly disconcerted. "I—I defended Lord Bryonie. Yes."

"And didn't he only get the mere eighteen months due entirely to your eloquence? Ah, he's dead now, poor fellow. Only a shadow of himself, he was, when he came out. It was a terrible shock to um."

"Undoubtedly."

" 'Twas indeed. He never had any brains, poor fellow, and it was an unlucky day for the family when he took it into his head to dabble in business. Where's Miss Moore? I thought I heard you speak of a game of darts."

"She's coming," said Cubitt.

"And I hope you'll all play again for I found it a great entertainment. Are you a dart player, too, Mr. Watchman?"

"I try," said Watchman.

Footsteps sounded on the stairs.

"Here is Decima," said Cubitt.

iv

A tall young woman came into the room and stood, very much at her ease, screwing her eyes up a little in the glare of the lights.

"I'm so sorry if I've kept you waiting," said Decima Moore. "Good evening, everyone."

They all greeted her. There was a second's pause and then Watchman moved into the centre of the room.

"Good evening," said Watchman.

She faced him and met his gaze.

"So you have arrived," she said. "Good evening."

She touched his outstretched hand, walked over to the bar, and settled herself on one of the tall stools. She wore a fisherman's jersey and dark blue slacks. Her hair was cut like a poet's of the romantic period and was moulded in short locks about her head and face. She was good-looking with a classic regularity of beauty that was given an individual quirk by the blackness of her brows and the singular intensity of her eyes. She moved with the kind of grace that only just escapes angularity. She was twenty-four years of age.

If an observant stranger had been at the Feathers that evening he might have noticed that on Decima's entrance the demeanour of most of the men changed. For Decima owned the quality which Hollywood had loudly defined for the world. She owned a measure of attraction over which she herself had little governance. Though she must have been aware of this she seemed unaware; and neither in her manner nor in her speech did she appear to exercise conscious charm. Yet from the moment of her entrance the men, when they spoke to each other, looked at her, and in each of them was the disturbance of Decima's attraction reflected. Watchman's eyes brightened, he became more alert, and he spoke a little louder. Parish expanded as if in a spotlight and he exuded gallantry. Cubitt's air of vague amiability contracted to a sharp awareness. Abel Pomeroy beamed upon Decima. Will, still flushed from his passage with Watchman, turned a deeper red. He answered her greeting awkwardly and was very much the solemn and self-conscious rustic.

Decima took a cigarette from Parish and looked round the tap-room.

"Has the dart game begun?" she asked.

"We're waiting for you, my angel," said Parish. "What have you been doing with yourself all this time?"

"Washing. I've attended a poison-party. I hope you didn't spill prussic acid about the garage, you two Pomeroys."

"You're not 'feared, too, are you. Miss Dessy?" asked Abel. "A fine, bold, learned female like you."

Decima laughed.

"A revolting picture," she said. "What do you think, Will?"

She leant across the bar and looked beyond Abel into the Public. Will's back was towards her. He turned and faced Decima. His eyes devoured her, but he said nothing. Decima raised her tankard and drank to him. He returned the gesture clumsily, and Cubitt saw Watchman's eyebrows go up.

"Will," said Decima suddenly, "what have you all been talking about? You're very silent now, I must say."

Before any of the others could reply Watchman said, "We've been arguing, my dear."

"Arguing?" She still looked at Will. Watchman drained his tankard, moved up to the bar, and sat on the stool next to hers.

"Yes," he said. "Until Miss Darragh came in, we did nothing else."

"And why should I stop you?" asked Miss Darragh. She slipped neatly off her high stool and toddled into the inglenook. "I've a passion for argument. What was it about, now? Art? Politics? Love?"

"It was about politics," said Watchman, still looking at Decima. "The State, the People, and—private enterprise."

"You," Decima said. "But you're hopeless. When our way of things comes round, you'll be one of our major problems."

"Really? Won't you need any barristers?"

"I wish I could say 'no,' " said Decima.

Watchman laughed.

"At least," he said, "I may hold a watching brief for you." She didn't answer and he insisted: "Mayn't I?"

"You're talking nonsense," said Decima.

"Well," said Parish suddenly, "how about a Round-the-Clock contest to enliven the proceedings?"

"Why not, indeed?" murmured Cubitt.

"Will you play?" Watchman asked Decima.

"Of course. Let's all play. Coming, Will?"

But Will Pomeroy jerked his head towards the public tap-room where two or three newcomers noisily demanded drinks.

"Will you play, Miss Darragh?" asked Decima.

"I will not, thank you, my dear. I've no eye at all for sport. When I was a child didn't I half-blind me brother Terence with an apple intended to strike me brother Brian? I'd do some mischief were I to try. Moreover, I'm too fat. I'll sit and watch the fun."

Cubitt, Parish, and Decima Moore stood in front of the dart board. Watchman walked into the inglenook. From the moment when Will Pomeroy had taken up cudgels for him against Watchman, Legge had faded out. He had taken his drink, his pipe, and his thoughts, whatever they might be, into the public bar.

Presently a burst of applause broke out and Will Pomeroy shouted that Legge was a wizard and invited Decima and Cubitt to look at what he had done. The others followed, peering into the public bar. A colossal red-faced man stood with his hand against the public dart board. His fingers were spread out, and in the gaps between, darts were embedded, with others outside the thumb and the little finger.

"Look at that!" cried Will. "Look at it!"

"Ah," said Watchman. "So Mr. Legge has found another victim. A great many people seem to have faith in Mr. Legge."

There was a sudden silence. Watchman leant over the private bar and raised his voice.

"We are going to have a match," he said. "Three-a-side. Mr. Legge, will you join us?"

Legge took his pipe out of his mouth and said: "What's the game?"

"Darts. Round-the-clock."

"Darts. Round-the-clock?"

"Yes. Haven't you played that version?"

"A long time ago. I've forgotten—"

"You have to get one dart in each segment in numerical sequence, ending on a double," explained Cubitt.

"In fact," said Watchman, very pleasantly, "you might call it, 'Doing Time.' Haven't you ever done time, Mr. Legge?"

"No," said Legge, "but I'll take you on. I'll be there in a minute."

"Right. And if you beat me at this I'm damned if tomorrow night I don't let you take a pot at my hand."

"Thank you," said Legge. "I'll remember."

CHAPTER THREE

Further Advance by Watchman

i

"THE CHIEF fault in Luke," said Sebastian Parish, "is that he is quite incapable of letting well alone."

Norman Cubitt tilted his hat over his eyes, peered from Parish to his canvas and began to scuffle among his tubes of paint. He uttered a short grunt.

"More than that," added Parish, "he glories in making bad a good deal worse. Do you mind my talking, old boy?"

"No. Turn the head a little to the right. Too much. That's right. I won't keep you much longer. Just while the sun's on the left side of the face. The shoulders are coming too far round again."

"You talk like a doctor about my members—*the* head, *the* face, *the* shoulders."

"You're a vain fellow, Seb. Now, hold it like that, do. Yes, there's something persistently impish in Luke. He jabs at people. What was he up to last night with Will Pomeroy and Legge?"

"Damned if I know. Funny business, wasn't it? Do you think he's jealous of Will?"

"Jealous?" repeated Cubitt. With his palette knife he laid an unctuous stroke of blue beside the margin of the painted head. "Why jealous?"

"Well, because of Decima."

"Oh, nonsense! And yet I don't know. He's not your cousin for nothing, Seb. Luke's got his share of the family vanity."

"I don't know why you say I'm vain, damn you. I don't think I'm vain at all. Do you know, I get an average of twelve drivelling letters a day from females in front? And do they mean a thing to me?"

"You'd be bitterly disappointed if there was a falling off. Don't move your shoulders. But you may be right about Luke."

"I'd like to know," said Parish, "just how much last year's little flirtation with Decima added up to."

"Would you? I don't think it's relevant."

"Well," said Parish, "she's an attractive wench. More 'It' to the square inch than most of them. It's hard to say why. She's got looks, of course, but not the looks that usually get over that way. Not the voluptuous type. Her—"

"Shut up," said Cubitt violently, and added: "I'm going to paint your mouth."

His own was set in an unusually tight line. He worked for a time in silence, stood back, and said abruptly:

"I don't really think Will Pomeroy was his objective. He was getting at Legge, and why the devil he should pick on a man he'd never seen in his life until last night is more than I can tell."

"I thought he seemed to be sort of probing. Trying to corner Legge in some way."

Cubitt paused with his knife over the canvas.

"Yes," he said slowly. "That's perfectly true. I thought so, too. Trick of the trade, perhaps, Counsel's curiosity. Almost, one expected him to put his foot on the seat of a chair and rest his elbow on his knee. Now I come to think of it, I believe he did hitch his coat up by the lapels."

"Characteristic," pronounced Parish seriously. He himself had used these touches several times in trial scenes.

Cubitt smiled. "But he sounded definitely malicious," he added.

"He's not malicious," said Parish uncomfortably.

"Oh yes, he is," said Cubitt coolly. "It's one of his more interesting qualities. He can be very malicious."

"He can be very generous, too."

"I'm sure he can. I like Luke, you know. He interests me enormously."

"Apparently he likes you," said Parish. "Apparently."

"Hullo!" Cubitt walked back from his canvas and stood squinting at it. "You said that with a wealth of meaning, Seb. What's in the air? You can rest a minute, if you like."

Parish moved off the boulder where he had been sitting, stretched himself elaborately, and joined Cubitt. He gazed solemnly at his own portrait. It was a large canvas. The figure in the dull red sweater was three-quarter life-size. It was presented as a dark form against the lighter background which was the sea and the sky. The sky appeared as a series of paling arches, the sea as a simple plane, broken by formalized waves. A glint of sunlight had found the cheek and jaw-bone on the right side of the face.

"Marvellous, old boy," said Parish. "Marvellous!"

Cubitt, who disliked being called "old boy," grunted.

"Did you say you'd show it in this year's Academy?" asked Parish.

"I didn't, Seb, but I will. I'll stifle my aesthetic conscience, prostitute my undoubted genius, and send your portrait to join the annual assembly of cadavers. Do you prefer 'Portrait of an Actor,' 'Sebastian Parish, Esq.,' or simply 'Sebastian Parish'?"

"I think I would like my name," said Parish seriously. "Not, I mean, that everybody wouldn't know—"

"Thank you. But I see your point. Your press agent would agree. What were you going to say about Luke? His generosity, you know, and his apparently liking me so much?"

"I don't think I ought to tell you, really."

"But of course you are going to tell me."

"He didn't actually say it was in confidence," said Parish. Cubitt waited with a slight smile.

"You'd be amazed if you knew," continued Parish.

"Yes."

"Yes. Oh, rather. At least I imagine you would be. I was. I never expected anything of the sort, and after all I *am* his nearest relation. His next of kin."

Cubitt turned and looked at him in real astonishment.

"Are you by any chance," he asked, "talking about Luke's will?"

"How did you guess?"

"My dear, good Seb—"

"All right, all right. I suppose I did give it away. You may as well hear the whole thing. Luke told me the other day that he was leaving his money between us."

"Good Lord!"

"I know. I happened to look him up after the show one evening, and I found him browsing over an official-looking document. I said something, chaffingly, you know, about it, and he said: 'Well, Seb, you'll find it out some day, so you may as well know now.' And then he told me."

"Extraordinarily nice of him," said Cubitt uncomfortably, and he added: "Damn! I wish you hadn't told me."

"Why, on earth?"

"I don't know. I enjoy discussing Luke and now I'll feel he's sort of sacrosanct. Oh well, he'll probably out-live both of us."

"He's a good bit older than I am," said Parish. "Not, I mean, that I don't hope with all my heart he will. I mean—as far as I'm concerned—"

"Don't labour it, Seb," said Cubitt kindly. "I should think Luke will certainly survive me. He's strong as a horse and I'm not. You'll probably come in for the packet."

"I hate talking about it like that."

Parish knocked his pipe out on a stone. Cubitt noticed that he was rather red in the face.

"As a matter of fact," he muttered, "it's rather awkward."

"Why?"

"Well, I'm plaguily hard up at the moment and I'd been wondering—"

"If Luke would come to the rescue?"

Parish was silent.

"And in the light of this revelation," Cubitt added, "you don't quite like to ask. Poor Seb! But what the devil do you do with your money? You ought to be rolling. You're always in work. This play you're in now is a record run, isn't it, and your salary must be superb."

"That's all jolly fine, old man, but you don't know what it's like in the business. My expenses are simply ghastly."

"Why?"

"Why, because you've got to keep up a standard. Look at my house. It's ruinous, but I've got to be able to ask the people that count to a place they'll accept, and, if possible, remember. You've got to look prosperous in this game, and you've got to entertain. My agent's fees are hellish. My clubs cost the earth. And like a blasted fool I backed a show that flopped for thousands last May."

"What did you do that for?"

"The management are friends of mine. It looked all right."

"You give money away, Seb, don't you? I mean literally. To out-of-luck actors? Old-timers and so on?"

"I may. Always think 'There but for the grace of God . . . !' It's such a damn chancy business."

"Yes. No more chancy than painting, my lad."

"You don't have to show so well if you're an artist. People expect you to live in a peculiar way."

Cubitt looked at him, but said nothing.

Parish went on defensively: "I'm sorry, but you know what I mean. People expect painters to be Bohemians and all that."

"There was a time," said Cubitt, "when actors were content to be 'Bohemians,' whatever that may mean. I never know. As far as I am concerned, it means going without things you want."

"But your pictures sell."

"On an average I sell six pictures a year. Their prices range from twenty pounds to two hundred. It usually works out at about four hundred. You earn that in as many weeks, don't you?"

"Yes, but—"

"Oh, I'm not grumbling. I've got a bit of my own and I could make more, I daresay, if I took pupils or had a shot at commercial art. I've suited myself and it's worked out well enough until—"

"Until what?" asked Parish.

"Nothing. Let's get on with the work, shall we? The light's no good after about eleven."

Parish walked back to the rock, and took up his pose. The light wind whipped his black hair away from his forehead. He raised his chin and stared out over the sea. He assumed an expression of brooding dominance.

"That right?" he asked.

"Pretty well. You only want a pair of tarnished epaulettes and we could call it 'Elba.' "

"I've always thought I'd like to play Napoleon."

"A fat lot you know about Napoleon."

Parish grinned tranquilly.

"Anyway," he said, "I'd read him up a bit if I had to. As a matter of fact, Luke looks rather like him."

"The shoulders should come round," said Cubitt. "That's more like it. Yes, Luke is rather the type."

He painted for a minute or two in silence and then Parish suddenly laughed.

"What's up?" asked Cubitt.

"Here comes your girl."

"What the devil do you mean?" demanded Cubitt angrily and looked over his shoulder. "Oh—I see."

"Violet," said Parish. "Who did you think it was?"

"I thought you'd gone dotty. Damn the woman!"

"Will *she* paint me, too?"

"Not if I know it."

"Unkind to your little Violet?" asked Parish.

"Don't call her that."

"Why not?"

"Well, damn it, she's not very young and she's—well, she may be a pest but she's by way of being a lady."

"Snob!"

"Don't be so dense, Seb. Can't you see—oh Lord, she's got all her gear. She *is* going to paint. Well, I've just about done for to-day."

"She's waving."

Cubitt looked across the headland to where Miss Darragh, a droll figure against the sky, fluttered a large handkerchief.

"She's put her stuff down," said Parish. "She's going to sketch. What is there to paint over there?"

"A peep," said Cubitt. "Now, hold hard and don't talk. There's a shadow under the lower lip—"

He worked with concentration for five minutes and then put down his palette.

"That'll do for to-day. We'll pack up."

But when he'd hitched his pack on his shoulders and stared out to sea for some seconds, he said suddenly:—

"All the same, Seb, I wish you hadn't told me."

ii

It was understood among the three friends that each should go his own way during the weeks they spent at Ottercombe. Watchman had played with the notion of going out in the dawn with the fishing boats. He woke before it was light and heard the tramp of heavy boots on cobblestones and the sound of voices down on Ottercombe Steps. He told himself comfortably that here was a link with the past. For hundreds of years the Coombe men had gone down to their boats before dawn. The children of Coombe had heard them stirring, their wives had fed them and seen them go, and for centuries their voices and the sound of their footsteps had roused the village for a moment in the coldest hour of the night. Watchman let the sounds die away, snuggled luxuriously down in his bed, and fell asleep.

He woke again at half-past nine and found that Parish had already breakfasted and set out for Coombe Rock.

"A mortal great mammoth of a picture Mr. Cubitt be at," said Abel Pomeroy, as Watchman finished his breakfast. "Paint enough to cover a wall, sir, and laid on so thick as dough. At close quarters it looks like one of they rocks covered in shellfish, but 'od rabbit it, my sonnies, when you fall away twenty feet or more, it's Mr. Parish so clear as glass. Looking out over the Rock he be, looking out to sea, and so natural you'd say the man was smelling the wind and thinking of his next meal. You might fancy a stroll out to the Rock, sir, and take a look at Mr. Cubitt flinging his paint left and right."

"I feel lazy, Abel. Where's Will?"

"Went out-along, with the boats, sir." Abel rasped his chin, scratched his head, and rearranged the objects on the bar.

"He's restless, is Will," he said suddenly. "My own boy, Mr. Watchman, and so foreign to me as a changeling."

"Will is?" asked Watchman, filling his pipe.

"Ah, Will. What with his politics and his notions he's a right-down stranger to me, is Will. A very witty lad, too, proper learned, and so full of arguments as a politician. He won't argufy with me, naturally, seeing I'm not his equal in the way of brains, nor anything like it."

"You're too modest, Abel," said Watchman lightly.

"No, sir, no. I can't stand up to that boy of mine when it comes to politics and he knows it and lets me down light. I'm for the old ways, a right-down Tory, and for why? For no better reason than it suits me, same as it suited my forebears."

"A sound enough reason."

"No, sir, not according to my boy. According to Will it be a damn-fool reason and a selfish one into the bargain."

"I shouldn't let it worry you."

" 'More I do, Mr. Watchman. It's not our differences that worry me. It's just my lad's restless, mum-budgeting ways. You saw how he was last night. Speaking to you that fashion. Proper 'shamed of him, I was."

"It was entirely my fault, Abel, I baited him."

"Right-down generous of you to put it like that but all the same he's not himself these days. I'd like him to settle down. Tell you the truth, sir, it's what's to become of the Feathers that troubles me and it troubles me sore. I'm nigh on seventy, Mr. Watchman. Will's my youngest. T'other two boys wurr took in war, and one girl's married and in Canada, and t'other in Australia. Will'll get the Feathers."

"I expect," said Watchman, "that Will'll grow out of his red ideas and run the pub like any other Pomeroy."

Old Abel didn't answer and Watchman added: "When he marries and settles down."

"And when will that be, sir? Likely you noticed how 'tis between Will and Miss Dessy? Well now, that's a funny state of affairs, and one I can't get used to. Miss Dessy's father's Jim Moore up yurr to Cary Edge Farm, and an old friend of mine. Good enough. But what happens when Dessy's a li'l maid no higher than my hand?

’Od rabbit it, if old Jim don’t come in for a windfall. Now his wife being a ghastly proud sort of a female and never tired of letting on she came down in society when she married, what do they do but send young Dessy to a ladies’ school where she gets some kind of free pass into a female establishment at Oxford.”

“Yes. I know.”

“ ’Ess, and comes home at the end of it a dinky li’l chit, sure enough, and husband-high; but speaking finicky-like and the equal of all the gentlefolks in the West Country.”

“Well?” said Watchman.

“Well, sir, that’s fair enough. If she fancies our Will above the young sparks she meets in her new walk of life, good enough. I’m proper fond of the maiden, always have been. Good as a daughter to me, and just the same always, no matter how ladylike she’m grown.”

Watchman stood up and stretched himself.

“It sounds idyllic, Abel. A charming romance.”

“Wait a bit, sir, wait a bit. ’Bain’t so simple as all that. These yurr two young folks no sooner meets again than my Will sets his heart, burning strong and powerful, on Decima Moore. Eaten up with love from time he sets eyes on her, was Will, and hell-bent to win her. She come back with radical notions same as his own, and that’s a bond atween ’em from the jump. Her folks don’t fancy my Will, however, leastways not her mother, and they don’t fancy her views neither, and worst of all they lays blame on Will. Old Jim Moore comes down yurr and has a tell with me, saying life’s not worth living up to Farm with Missus at him all day and half night to put his foot down and stop it. That’s how it was after you left last year, sir, and that’s how ’tis still. Will burning to get tokened and wed, and Dessy—”

“Yes?” asked Watchman as Abel paused and looked fixedly at the ceiling. “What about Decima?”

“That’s the queerest touch of the lot, sir,” said Abel.

Watchman, lighting his pipe, kept his eye on his host and saw that he now looked profoundly uncomfortable.

“Well?” Watchman repeated.

“It be what she says about wedlock,” Abel muttered.

“What does she say?” asked Watchman sharply.

“ ’Be shot if she haven’t got some new-fangled notion about wedlock being no better than a name for savagery. Talks wild trash about freedom. To my way of thinking the silly maiden don’t know what she says.”

"What," asked Watchman, "does Will say to all this?"

"Don't like it. The chap wants to be tokened and hear banns read like any other poor toad, for all his notions. He wants no free love for his wife or himself. He won't talk to me, not a word; but Miss Dessy does, so open and natural as a daisy. Terrible nonsense it be, I tells her, and right-down dangerous into bargain. Hearing her chatter, you might suppose she've got some fancy-chap up her sleeve. Us knows better, of course, but it's an uncomfortable state of affairs and seemingly no way out. Tell you what, sir, I do blame this Legge for the way things are shaping. Will'd have settled down. He *was* settling down, afore Bob Legge came yurr. But now he've stirred up all their revolutionary notions again, Miss Dessy's along with the rest. I don't fancy Legge. Never have. Not for all he'm a masterpiece with darts. My way of thinking, he'm a cold calculating chap and powerful bent on having his way. Well, thurr 'tis, and talking won't mend it."

Watchman walked to the door and Abel followed him. They stood looking up the road to Coombe Tunnel.

"Dallybuttons!" exclaimed Abel. "Talk of an angel and there she be. That's Miss Dessy, the dinky little dear, coming in to do her marketing."

"So it is," said Watchman. "Well, Abel, on second thoughts I believe I'll go and have a look at that picture."

iii

But Watchman did not go directly to Coombe Rock. He lingered for a moment until he had seen Decima Moore go in at the post office door, and then he made for the tunnel. Soon the darkness swallowed him, his footsteps rang hollow on the wet stone floor, and above him, a luminous disc, shone the top entry. Watchman emerged, blinking, into the dust and glare of the high road. To his left the country rolled gently away to Illington, to his right a path led round the cliffs to Coombe Rock, and then wound inland to Cary Edge Farm where the Moores lived.

He arched his hand over his eyes, and on Coombe Head could make out the shape of canvas and easel with Cubitt's figure moving to and fro, and beyond, a tiny dot which must be Sebastian Parish's head. Watchman left the road, climbed the clay bank, circled a clump of furze, and beneath a hillock from where he could see the entrance to the tunnel, he lay full length on the short turf. With the cessation of his own movement the quiet of the countryside engulfed him. At first the silence seemed complete but after a moment or two the small noises of earth and sky welled up into his consciousness. A lark sang above his head with a note so high that it impinged upon the outer borders of hearing and at times soared into nothingness. When he turned and laid his ear to the earth it throbbed with the faraway thud of surf against Coombe Rock and when his fingers moved in the grass it was with a crisp stirring sound. He began to listen intently, lying so still that no movement of his body could come between his sense and more distant sound. He closed his eyes and to an observer he would have seemed to sleep. Indeed, his face bore that look of inscrutability which links sleep in our minds with death. But he was not asleep. He was listening; and presently his ears caught a new rhythm, a faint hollow beat. Someone was coming up through the tunnel.

Watchman looked through his eyelashes and saw Decima Moore step into the sunlight. He remained still while she mounted the bank to the cliff path. She rounded the furzebush and was almost upon him before she saw him. She stood motionless.

"Well, Decima," said Watchman and opened his eyes.

"You startled me," she said.

"I should leap to my feet, shouldn't I? And apologize?"

"You needn't trouble. I'm sorry I disturbed you. Goodbye." She moved forward.

Watchman said: "Wait a moment, Decima."

She hesitated. Watchman reached out a hand and seized her ankle.

"Don't do that," said Decima. "It makes us both look silly. I'm in no mood for dalliance."

"Please say you'll wait a moment and I'll behave like a perfect little gent. I've something serious to say to you."

"I don't believe it."

"I promise you. Of the first importance. Please."

"Very well," said Decima.

He released her and scrambled to his feet.

"Well, what is it?" asked Decima.

"It'll take a moment or two. Do sit down and smoke a cigarette. Or shall I walk some of the way with you?"

She shot a glance at the distant figures on Coombe Head and then looked at him. She seemed ill at ease, half-defiant, half-curious.

"We may as well get it over," she said.

"Splendid. Sit down now, do. If we stand here, we're in full view of anybody entering or leaving Ottercombe, and I don't want to be interrupted. No, I've no discreditable motive. Come now."

He sat down on the hillock under the furze-bush and after a moment's hesitation she joined him.

"Will you smoke? Here you are."

He lit her cigarette, dug the match into the turf and then turned to her.

"The matter I wanted to discuss with you," he said, "concerns this Left Movement of yours."

Decima's eyes opened wide.

"That surprises you?" observed Watchman.

"It does rather," she said. "I can't imagine why you should suddenly be interested in the C.L.M."

"I've no business to be interested," said Watchman, "and in the ordinary sense, my dear Decima, I am not interested. It's solely on your account—no, do let me make myself clear. It's on your account that I want to put two questions to you. Of course if you choose you may refuse to answer them."

Watchman cleared his throat, and pointed a finger at Decima.

"Now in reference to this society—"

"Dear me," interrupted Decima with a faint smile. "This green plot shall be our court, this furze-bush our witness-box; and we will do in action as we will do it before the judge."

"A vile paraphrase. And if we are to talk of midsummer-night's dreams, Decima—"

"We certainly won't do that," she said, turning very pink. "Pray continue your cross-examination, Mr. Watchman."

"Thank you, my lord. First question: is this body—society, club, movement or whatever it is—an incorporated company?"

"What does that mean?"

"It means among other things, that the books would have to be audited by a chartered accountant."

"Good Heavens, no. It's simply grown up, largely owing to the efforts of Will Pomeroy and myself."

"So I supposed. You've a list of subscribing members?"

"Three hundred and forty-five," said Decima proudly.

"And the subscription?"

"Ten bob. Are you thinking of joining us?"

"Who collects the ten bobs?"

"The Treasurer."

"And Secretary . . . , Mr. Legge?"

"Yes. What are you driving at? What were you at, last night, baiting Bob Legge?"

"Wait a moment. Do any other sums of money pass through his hands?"

"I don't see why I should tell you these things," said Decima.

"There's no reason, but you have my assurance that I mean well."

"I don't know what you mean."

"And you may be sure I shall regard this conversation as strictly confidential."

"All right," she said uneasily. "We've raised sums for different objects. We want to start a Left Book Club in Illington and there are one or two funds: Spanish, Czech, and Austrian refugees, and the fighting fund, and so on."

"Yes. At the rate of how much a year? Three hundred, for instance?"

"About that. Quite that I should think. We've some very generous supporters."

"Now look here, Decima. Did you inquire very carefully into this man Legge's credentials?"

"I—no. I mean, he's perfectly sound. He's secretary for several other things: some philatelic society and a correspondence course, and he's agent for one or two things."

"He's been there ten months, hasn't he?"

"Yes. He's not strong; touch of T.B., I think, and some trouble with his ears. His doctor told him to come down here. He's been very generous and subscribed to the movement himself."

"May I give you a word of advice? Have your books audited."

"Do you know Bob Legge? You can't make veiled accusations—"

"I have made no accusations."

"You've suggested that—"

"That you should be businesslike," said Watchman. "That's all."

"Do you know this man? You must tell me."

There was a very long silence and then Watchman said:

"I've never known anybody of that name."

"Then I don't understand," said Decima.

"Let us say I've taken an unreasonable dislike to him."

"I've already come to that conclusion. It was obvious last night."

"Well, think it over." He looked fixedly at her and then said suddenly: "Why won't you marry Will Pomeroy?"

Decima turned white and said: "That, at least, is entirely my own business."

"Will you meet me here to-night?"

"No."

"Do I no longer attract you, Decima?"

"I'm afraid you don't."

"Little liar, aren't you?"

"The impertinent lady-killer stuff," said Decima, "doesn't wear very well. It has a way of looking merely cheap."

"You can't insult me," said Watchman. "Tell me this. Am I your only experiment?"

"I don't want to start any discussion of this sort. The thing's at an end. It's been dead a year."

"No. Not on my part. It could be revived, and very pleasantly. Why are you angry? Because I didn't write?"

"Good Lord, no!" ejaculated Decima.

"Then why—?"

He laid his hand over hers. As if unaware of his touch, her fingers plucked the blades of grass beneath them.

"Meet me here to-night," he repeated.

"I'm meeting Will to-night at the Feathers."

"I'll take you home."

Decima turned on him.

"Look here," she said, "we'd better get this straightened out. You're not in the least in love with me, are you?"

"I adore you."

"I daresay, but you don't love me. Nor do I love you. A year ago I fell for you rather heavily and we know what happened. I can admit now that I was—well, infatuated. I can even admit that what I said just then wasn't true. For about two months I *did* mind your not writing. I minded damnably. Then I recovered in one bounce. I don't want any recrudescence."

"How solemn," murmured Watchman, "how learned, and how young."

"It may seem solemn and young to you. Don't flatter yourself I'm the victim of remorse. I'm not. One has to go through with these things, I've decided. But don't let's blow on the ashes."

"We wouldn't have to blow very hard."

"Perhaps not."

"You admit that, do you?"

"Yes. But I don't want to do it."

"Why? Because of Pomeroy?"

"Yes."

"Are you going to marry him, after all?"

"I don't know. He's ridiculously class-conscious about sex. He's completely uneducated in some ways but—I don't know. If he knew about last year he'd take it very badly and I can't marry him without telling him."

"Well," said Watchman suddenly, "don't expect me to be chivalrous and decent. I imagine chivalry and decency don't go with sex-education and freedom, anyway. Don't be a fool, Decima. You know you think it would be rather fun."

He pulled her towards him. Decima muttered, "No, you don't," and suddenly they were struggling fiercely. Watchman thrust her back till her shoulders were against the bank. As he stooped his head to kiss her, she wrenched one hand free and she struck him, clumsily but with violence, across the mouth.

"You—" said Watchman.

She scrambled to her feet and stood looking down at him.

"I wish to God," she said savagely, "that you'd never come back."

There was a moment's silence.

Watchman, too, had got to his feet. They looked into each other's eyes; and then, with a gesture that, for all its violence and swiftness, suggested the movement of an automaton, he took her by the shoulders and kissed her. When he had released her they moved apart stiffly, with no eloquence in either of their faces or figures.

Decima said: "You'd better get out of there. If you stay here it'll be the worse for you. I could kill you. Get out."

They heard the thud of footsteps on turf and Cubitt and Sebastian Parish came over the brow of the hillock.

CHAPTER FOUR

The Evening in Question

i

WATCHMAN, CUBITT and Parish lunched together in the tap-room. Miss Darragh did not appear. Cubitt and Parish had last seen her sucking her brush and gazing with complacency at an abominable sketch. She was still at work when they came up with Watchman and Decima. At lunch, Watchman was at some pains to tell the others how he and Decima Moore met by accident, and how they had fallen to quarrelling about the Coombe Left Movement.

They accepted his recital with, on Parish's part, rather too eager alacrity. Lunch, on the whole, was an uncomfortable affair. Something had gone wrong with the relationship of the three men. Norman Cubitt, who was acutely perceptive in such matters, felt that the party had divided into two, with Parish and himself on one side of an intangible barrier, and Watchman on the other. Cubitt had no wish to side, however vaguely, with Parish against Watchman. He began to make overtures, but they sounded unlikely and only served to emphasize his own discomfort. Watchman answered with the courtesy of an acquaintance. By the time they had reached the cheese, complete silence had overcome them.

They did not linger for their usual postprandial smoke. Cubitt said he wanted to get down to the jetty for his afternoon sketch, Parish said he was going to sleep. Watchman, murmuring something about writing a letter, disappeared upstairs.

They did not see each other again until the evening when they met in the private tap-room for their usual cocktail. The fishing boats had come in, and at first the bar was fairly full. The three friends joined in local conversation and were not thrown upon their own resources until the evening meal which they took together in the inglenook. The last drinker went out saying that there was a storm hanging about, and that the air was unnaturally heavy. On his departure complete silence fell upon the three men. Parish made one or two half-hearted attempts to break it but it was no good, they had nothing to say to each other. They finished their meal and Watchman began to fill his pipe.

"What's that?" said Parish suddenly. "Listen!"

"High tide," said Watchman, "it's the surf breaking on Coombe Rock."

"No, it's not. Listen."

And into the silence came a vague gigantic rumour.

"Isn't it thunder?" asked Parish.

The others listened for a moment but made no answer.

"What a climate!" added Parish.

The village outside the inn seemed very quiet. The evening air was sultry. No breath of wind stirred the curtains at the open windows. When, in a minute or two, somebody walked round the building, the footsteps sounded unnaturally loud. Another and more imperative muttering broke the quiet.

Cubitt said nervously: "It's as if a giant, miles away on Dartmoor, was shaking an iron tray."

"That's exactly how they work thunder in the business," volunteered Parish.

"*The business*," Watchman said with violent irritation. "What business? Is there only one business?"

"What the hell's gone wrong with you?" asked Parish.

"Nothing. The atmosphere," said Watchman.

"I hate thunder-storms," said Cubitt quickly. "They make me feel as if all my nerves were on the surface. A loathsome feeling."

"I rather like them," said Watchman.

"And that's the end of *that* conversation," said Parish with a glance at Cubitt.

Watchman got up and moved into the window. Mrs. Ives came in with a tray.

"Storm coming up?" Parish suggested.

" 'Ess, sir. Very black outside," said Mrs. Ives.

The next roll of thunder lasted twice as long as the others and ended in a violent tympanic rattle. Mrs. Ives cleared the table and went away. Cubitt moved into the inglenook and leant his elbows on the mantelpiece. The room had grown darker. A flight of gulls, making for the sea, passed clamorously over the village. Watchman pulled back the curtains and leant over the window-sill. Heavy drops of rain had begun to fall. They hit the cobblestones of the inn yard with loud slaps.

"Here comes the rain," said Parish unnecessarily.

Old Abel Pomeroy came into the Public from the far door. He began to shut the windows and called through into the Private:

"We'm in for a black storm, souls."

A glint of lightning flickered in the yard outside. Parish stood up, scraping his chair-legs on the floor.

"They say," said Parish, "that if you count the seconds between the flash and the thunder it gives you the distance—"

A peal of thunder rolled up a steep crescendo.

"—the distance away in fifths of a mile," ended Parish.

"Do shut up, Seb," implored Watchman, not too unkindly.

"Damn it all," said Parish, "I don't know what the hell's the matter with you. Do you, Norman?"

Abel Pomeroy came through the bar into the tap-room.

"Be colder soon I reckon," he said. "If you'd like a fire, gentlemen—"

"We'll light it, Abel, if we want it," said Cubitt.

"Good enough, sir." Abel looked from Cubitt and Parish to Watchman who still leant over the window-sill.

"She'll come bouncing and teeming through that window, Mr. Watchman, once she do break out. Proper deluge she'll be."

"All right, Abel. I'll look after the window."

A livid whiteness flickered outside. Cubitt and Parish had a momentary picture of Watchman in silhouette against a background of inn yard and houses. A second later the thunder broke in two outrageous claps. Then, in a mounting roar, the rain came down.

"Yurr she comes," said Abel.

He switched on the light and crossed to the door into the passage.

"Reckon Mr. Legge'll bide to-night, after all," said Abel.

Watchman spun round.

"Is Mr. Legge going away?" he asked.

"He'm called away on business, sir, to Illington. But that lil' car of his leaks like a lobster-pot. Reckon the man'd better wait till tomorrow. I must look to the gutters or us'll have the rain coming in through upstairs ceilings."

He went out.

The evening was now filled with the sound of rain and thunder. Watchman shut the window and came into the room. His head was wet.

He said: "It's much colder. We might have that fire."

Cubitt lit the fire and they watched the first flames rise uncertainly among the driftwood.

"The rain's coming down the chimney," said Parish. "Hullo! Who's this?"

The tap-room door opened slowly. There, on the threshold, stood the Honourable Violet Darragh, dripping like a soused hen. Her cotton dress was gummed to her person with such precision that it might as well have melted. Her curls were flattened into streaks, and from the brim of her hat poured little rivers that rushed together at the base of her neck, and, taking the way of least resistance, streamed centrally to her waist where they deployed and ran divergently to the floor. With one hand she held a canvas hold-all, with the other a piece of paper that still bore streaks of cobalt-blue and veridian across its pulpy surface. She might have been an illustration from one of the more Rabelaisian pages of *La Vie Parisienne*.

"My dear Miss Darragh!" ejaculated Watchman.

"Ah, look at me!" said Miss Darragh. "What a pickle I'm in, and me picture ruined. I was determined to finish it and I stayed on till the thunder and lightning drove me away in terror of me life, and when I emerged from the tunnel didn't it break over me like the entire contents of the ocean? Well, I'll go up now, and change, for I must look a terrible old sight."

She glanced down at herself, gasped, cast a comical glance at the three men, and bolted.

Will Pomeroy and two companions entered the Public from the street door. They wore oil-skin hats and coats, and their boots squelched on the floorboards. Will went into the bar and served out drinks. Parish leant over the private bar and gave them good-evening.

"You seem to have caught it in the neck," he observed.

"That's right, Mr. Parish," said Will. "She's a proper masterpiece. The surface water'll be pouring through the tunnel if she keeps going at this gait. Here you are, chaps, I'm going to change."

He went through the Private into the house, leaving a wet trail behind him. They heard him at the telephone in the passage. He had left the door open and his voice carried above the sound of the storm.

"That you, Dessy? Dessy, this storm's a terror. You'd better not drive that old car over to-night. Tunnel'll be a running stream. It's not safe."

Watchman began to whistle under his breath. Abel returned and took Will's place in the bar.

"I'd walk over, myself," Will was saying, "only I can't leave Father single-handed. We'll have a crowd in, likely, with this weather."

"I'm going to have a drink," said Watchman suddenly.

"Walk?" said Will. "You're not scared of lightning, then? Good enough, and nobody better pleased than I am. I'll lend you a sweater and—Dessy, you'd better warn them you'll likely stay the night. Why not? So I do, then, and you'll find it out, my dear. I'll come a fetch along the way to meet you."

The receiver clicked. Will stuck his head round the door.

"Dessy's walking over, Dad. I'll go through the tunnel to meet her. Have you seen Bob Legge?"

"He said he'd be up to Illington to-night, sonny."

"He'll never make it. Has he left?"

"In his room, yet, I fancy."

"I'll see," said Will. "I've told Dessy she'd better stay the night."

"Very welcome, I'm sure. Ask Mrs. Ives to make a room ready."

"So I will, then," said Will and disappeared.

"Walking over!" said Abel. "A matter of two miles it is, from yurr to Cary Edge. Wonderful what love'll do, gentlemen, 'bain't it?"

"Amazing," said Watchman. "Is nobody else going to drink?"

ii

By eight o'clock the public tap was full and the private nearly so. Decima Moore and Will had looked in, but at the moment were closeted upstairs with Mr. Legge who had apparently decided not to go to Illington. Miss Darragh came down in dry clothes with her curls rubbed up, and sat writing letters by the fire.

Two of Abel's regular cronies had come in: Dick Oates, the Ottercombe policeman, and Arthur Gill, the grocer. A little later they were joined by Mr. George Nark, an elderly bachelor-farmer whose political views chimed with those of the Left Movement and who was therefore a favourite of Will Pomeroy's. Mr. Nark had been a great reader of the liberal literature in his youth, and had never got over the surprise and excitement that he had experienced, thirty years ago, on reading Winwood Reade, H. G. Wells, and the *Evolution of Man*. The information that he had derived from these and other serious works had, with the passage of time, become transmuted into simplified forms which, though they would have astonished the authors, completely satisfied Mr. Nark.

The rain still came down in torrents and Mr. Nark reported that Coombe tunnel was a running stream.

"It's a crying shame," he said, gathering the attention of the Private. "Bin going on for hundreds of years and no need for it. We can be flooded out three times a year and capitalistic government only laughs at us. Science would have druv a Class-A high road into the Coombe if somebody had axed it. But does a capitalistic government ax the advice of Science? Not it. It's afraid to. And why? Because Science knows too much for it."

"Ah," said Mr. Gill.

"That's capitalism for you," continued Mr. Nark. "Blind-stupid, and arrogant. Patching up where it should pitch-in and start afresh. What can you expect, my sonnies, from a parcel of wage-slavers and pampered aristocrats that don't know the smell of a day's work? So long as they've got their luxuries for themselves—"

He stopped and looked at Miss Darragh.

"Axing your pardon, Miss," said Mr. Nark. "In the heat of my discourse I got carried off my feet with the powerful rush of ideas and forgot your presence. This'll be all gall and wormwood to you, doubtless."

"Not at all, Mr. Nark," said Miss Darragh cheerfully. "I'm myself a poor woman and I've moods when I'm consumed with jealousy for anybody who's got a lot of money."

This was not precisely the answer Mr. Nark, who was a prosperous farmer, desired.

"It's the Government," he said, "that does every manjack of us out of our scientific rights."

"As far as that goes," said P. C. Oates, "I reckon one government's as scientific as the other. Look at sewage, for instance."

"Why?" demanded Mr. Nark, "should we look at sewage? What's sewage got to do with it? We're all animals."

"Ah," said Mr. Gill, "so we are, then."

"Do you know, Dick Oates," continued Mr. Nark, "that you've got a rudimentary tail?"

"And if I have, *which* I don't admit—"

"Ask Mr. Cubitt, then. He's an artist and no doubt has studied the skeleton of man in its present stage of evolution. The name escapes me for the moment but we've all got it. Isn't that correct, sir?"

"Yes, yes," said Norman Cubitt hurriedly. "Quite right, Mr. Nark."

"There you are," said Mr. Nark. "Apes, every manjack of us, and our arms have only grown shorter through us knocking off the habit of hanging from limbs of trees."

"What about our tongues?" asked Mr. Oates.

"Never mind about that," answered Mr. Nark warmly. "Do you know that an unborn child's got gills like a fish?"

"That doesn't make it a monkey, however."

"It goes to show, though."

"What?"

"You want to educate yourself. In a proper government the State 'ud educate the police so's they understood these deep matters for themselves. They know all about that in Russia. Scientific necessity, that's what it is."

"I don't see how knowing I've got a bit of a tail and once had a pair of gills is going to get me any nearer to a sergeant's stripe," reasoned Mr. Oates. "What I'd like is a case. You know how it happens in these crime stories, chap," he continued, looking round the company. "I read a good many of them and it's always the same thing. The keen young P. C. happens to be on the spot when there's a homicide. His Super has to call in the Yard and before you know where you are the P. C.'s working with one of the Big Four and getting praised for his witty deductions. All I can say is, I wished it happened like that in the Illington and Ottercombe Riding. Well, I'd best go round the beat, I reckon. Down the Steps and up again is about all this drowned hole'll see of me to-night. I'll look in again, chaps."

Mr. Oates adjusted his helmet, fastened his mackintosh, looked to his lamp, and went out into the storm.

"Ah, the poor fellow!" murmured Miss Darragh comfortably from inside the inglenook settle.

"In a properly conducted state—" began Mr. Nark.

His remark was drowned in a clap of thunder. The lights wavered and grew so dim that the filaments in the bulbs were reduced to luminous threads.

"Drat they electrics," said old Abel. "That's the storm playing Bobs-a-Dying with the wires somewhere. Us'll be in darkness afore closing time, I daresay." And he raised his voice to a bellow.

"Will! Oi, Will!"

Will's voice answered from above. The lights brightened. After a minute or two, Decima and Will came downstairs and into the Private. Each carried an oil lamp.

"Guessed what you were hollowing for," said Will, with a grin. "Here's the lamps. We'll put 'em on the two bars, Dessy, and matches handy. Bob Legge's fetching the other, Dad. Ceiling in his room's sprung a leak and the rain's coming in pretty heavy. The man was sitting there, so lost in thought he might have drowned. I've fixed up a bucket to catch it, and told him to come down."

Will stared for a second at Watchman, and added rather truculently: "We told Bob we missed his company in the Private, didn't we, Dess?"

"Yes," said Decima.

Watchman looked at her. She turned her back to him and said something to Will.

"Let us by all means have Mr. Legge among us," Watchman said. "I hope to beat him; all round the clock."

And in a minute or two Mr. Legge came in with the third unlit lamp.

iii

On the day following the thunder storm, the patrons of the Plume of Feathers tried very hard to remember in some sort of order, the events of the previous evening; the events that followed Mr. Legge's entrance into the private tap-room. For one reason and another their stories varied, but no doubt the principal reason for their variation might be found in the bottle of Courvoisier '87 that Abel Pomeroy had brought up from the cellar. That was after Mr. Gill had gone home, and before Mr. Oates returned from a somewhat curtailed beat round the village.

It was Watchman who started the discussion on brandy. Watchman apparently had got over whatever unfriendly mood had possessed him earlier in the evening, and was now as communicative as he had been silent. He began to tell legal stories and this he did very well indeed, so that in a minute or two he had the attention of both bars; the patrons of the public tap-room leaning on the bar counter and trying to see into the other room. He told stories of famous murder trials, of odd witnesses, and finally of his biggest case before he took silk. He did not give the names of the defendants, only describing them as the embezzling experts of the century. He had led for the defence of one of them and had succeeded in shifting most of the blame to the other who got, he said, a swinging big sentence. He became quite exalted over it all.

Sebastian always said that his cousin would have made an actor. He was certainly an excellent mimic. He gave a character sketch of the judge and made a living creature of the man. He described how, after the verdict, when the defendant's house was sold up, he had bought three dozen of brandy from the cellar.

"Courvoisier '87," said Watchman. "A superb year."

"Me cousin Bryonie," said Miss Darragh, looking round the corner of her settle, "had the finest cellar in County Clare, I believe. Before the disaster, of course."

Watchman started, and stared at Miss Darragh in confusion.

"Dear me, Mr. Watchman," she said composedly, "what is the matter with you? Had you forgotten I was here?"

"I—it sounds very ungallant but I believe I had."

"What brandy did you say, sir?" asked Abel, and when Watchman repeated mechanically, "Courvoisier '87," Abel said placidly that he believed he had three bottles in his own cellar.

"I picked 'em up when old Lawyer Payne over to Diddlestock died and was sold up," said Abel. "Half-dozen thurr was, and squire split 'em with me. I think that's the name. It's twelve month or more since I looked at 'em."

Watchman had already taken three glasses of Treble Extra and, although sober, was willing to be less so. Parish, suddenly flamboyant, offered to bet Abel a guinea that the brandy was not Courvoisier '87, and on Abel shaking his head, said that if it was Courvoisier '87, damn it, they'd kill a bottle of it there and then. Abel took a candle and went off to the cellar. The three men in the public tap-room went away. Will Pomeroy left the public bar and came to the private one. He had shown little interest in Watchman's stories. Legge had gone into the inglenook where he remained reading a book on the Red Army in Northern China. Watchman embarked on a discussion with Cubitt on the subject of capital punishment. Soon it became a general argument with Decima, Cubitt, and Parish on one side; and Watchman, dubiously supported by Mr. Nark, on the other.

"It's a scientific necessity," said Mr. Nark. "The country has to be purged. Cast out your waste material is what I say, and so does Stalin."

"So does Hitler if it comes to that," said Cubitt. "You're talking of massed slaughter, aren't you?"

"You can slaughter in a righteous manner," said Mr. Nark, "and you can slaughter in an unrighteous manner. It's all a matter of evvylution. Survival of the fittest."

"What on earth's that to say to it?" asked Cubitt.

"We're talking about capital punishment in this country, aren't we?" Decima asked.

Throughout the discussion, though she had launched several remarks at Watchman, she had not spoken directly to him. In each instance Watchman had answered exactly as if the conversation was between those two alone. He now cut in quickly.

"I thought so," said Watchman. "My learned friend is a little confused."

"I regard it," Decima continued, always to Cubitt, "as a confession of weakness."

"I think it's merely barbarous and horrible," said Parish.

"Terrible," murmured Miss Darragh drowsily. "Barbarous indeed! If we can't stop men from killing each other by any better means than killing in return, then they'll persist in it till their dying day."

Cubitt, with some difficulty, stifled a laugh.

"Quite right, Miss Darragh," he said. "It's a concession to the savage in all of us."

"Nonsense," said Watchman. "It's an economic necessity."

"Ah," said Mr. Nark with the air of one clutching at a straw. "Ah, now you're talking."

Abel came back with a bottle in his hands.

"There you are, gentlemen," he said. "It's Mr. Watchman's brand and no doubt about it. See for yourself, sir."

Watchman looked at the bottle.

"By God, you're right, Abel."

"This is magnificent," cried Parish. "Come on. We'll open it. Have you any brandy glasses? Never mind, tumblers'll do. It's a bit cold, but we'll humour it."

Abel opened the bottle.

"This," said Watchman, "is my affair. Shut up, Seb; I insist, Abel, you and Will must join us."

"Well, thank you very much, sir, I'm sure," said Abel.

"I'm afraid," said Decima, "that I really dislike brandy. It'd be wasted on me."

"What will you have, then?"

"I'm sorry to be so tiresome but I'd really rather not have a drink."

"My poor girl," said Watchman.

"Dessy'll have a stone-ginger with me," said Will Pomeroy suddenly.

"With me," said Watchman. "Eight brandies, two stone-gingers, Abel, and kill the bottle."

"Good Lord, Luke," expostulated Cubitt, "you'll have us rolling."

"None for me, thank you, Mr. Watchman," said Miss Darragh. "I'm afraid that I, too, am a Philistine."

"You'll have a drink, though?"

"I shall join you," said Miss Darragh, "in the non-alcoholic spirit."

"Seven brandies, Abel," amended Watchman. "The first half now, and the second hereafter."

Abel poured out the brandy. They watched him in silence.

The rain still poured down, but the thunder sounded more distantly.

Watchman took the first tot to Legge and put it on a table at his elbow.

"I hope you'll join us, Mr. Legge," he said.

Legge looked at the brandy and then directly at Watchman.

"It's very kind of you," he said. "As a matter of fact I've some work to do, and—"

" 'Let other hours be set apart for business,' " quoted Watchman. "To-day is our pleasure to be drunk. Do you like good brandy, Mr. Legge?"

"This," said Legge, "is the vintage of my choice."

He took the glass and nursed it between those callused hands.

"An exquisite bouquet," said Mr. Legge.

"I knew you'd appreciate it."

"Your health," said Legge, and took a delicate sip.

The others, with the exception of Mr. Nark, murmured self-consciously and sipped. Mr. Nark raised his glass.

"Your very good health, sir. Long life and happiness," said Mr. Nark loudly, and emptied his glass, at one gulp. He drew in his breath with a formidable whistle, his eyes started from his head and he grabbed at the air.

"You'm dashed at it too ferocious, George," said Abel.

Mr. Nark shuddered violently and fetched his breath.

"It's a murderous strong tipple," he whispered. "If you'll pardon me, Mr. Watchman, I'll break it down inwardly with a drop of water."

But presently Mr. Nark began to smile and then to giggle and as he giggled so did Cubitt, Parish, and Watchman. By the time the first tot of Courvoisier '87 had been consumed there was much laughter in the private bar, and a good deal of rather loud aimless conversation. Watchman proposed that they have a Round-the-Clock competition on the dart board.

Parish reminded him of Legge's trick with the darts.

"Come on, Luke," cried Parish. "If you let him try it on you, damme if I won't let him try it on me."

Mr. Legge was understood to say he was willing.

Watchman pulled the darts out of the board.

"Come on now," he said. "I'm equal to the lot of you. Even Mr. Legge. Round-the-Clock it is, and if he beats me this time, we'll have the other half and he can do his circus trick with my hand. Is it a bargain, Mr. Legge?"

"If you're not afraid," said Legge indistinctly, "I'm not. But I'd like a new set of darts."

"Afraid? With a brandy like this on board, I'd face the Devil himself."

"Good old Luke," cried Parish.

Abel fished under the shelves and brought up a small package which he clapped down on the bar counter.

"Brand new set o' darts, my sonnies," said Abel. "Best to be bought, and come this evening from London. I'll fix the flights in 'em while you play Round-the-Clock with the old 'uns. Bob Legge can christen 'em with this masterpiece of an exhibition."

He broke the string and opened the package.

"Come now, Mr. Legge," said Watchman. "Is it a bargain?"

"Certainly," said Legge. "A bargain it is."

CHAPTER FIVE

Failure of Mr. Legge

i

P. C. OATES had gone as far as the tunnel, had returned, and had descended the flight of stone steps that leads to the wharf from the right-hand side of the Feathers. He had walked along the passage called Fish Lane, flashing his lamp from time to time on steaming windows and doorways. Rain drummed on Oates's mackintosh cape, on his helmet, on cobblestones, and on the sea, that only a few feet away in the darkness, lapped at the steaming waterfront. The sound of the rain was almost as loud as the sound of thunder and behind both of these was the roar of surf on Coombe Rock. A ray of lamplight from a chink in the window-blind shone obliquely on rods of rain and, by its suggestion of remote comfort, made the night more desolate.

Far above him, dim and forlorn, the post office clock told a quarter past nine.

Oates turned at the end of Fish Lane and shone his light on the second flight of Ottercombe Steps. Water was pouring down them in a series of miniature falls. He began to climb, holding tight to the handrail. If anyone could have seen abroad in the night, lonesome and dutiful, his plodding figure might have suggested a progression into the past, when the night-watchman walked through Ottercombe to call the hours to sleeping fishermen. Such a flight of fancy did not visit the thoughts of Mr. Oates. He merely told himself that he was damned if he'd go any farther, and when the red curtains of the Plume of Feathers shone through the rain, he mended his pace and made for them.

But before he had gone more than six steps he paused. Some noise that had not reached him before threaded the sound of the storm. Someone was calling out—shouting—yelling. He stopped and listened.

"O-O-Oates! Hullo! Dick! D-i-i-ick! O-O-Oates!"

"Hullo!" yelled Oates, and his voice sounded very desolate.

"Hullo! Come—back—here."

Oates broke into a lope. The voice had come from the front of the pub. He crossed the yard, passed the side of the house and the door into the Public, and came in sight of the front door. A tall figure, shading its eyes, was silhouetted against the lighted entry. It was Will Pomeroy. Oates strode out of the night into the entry.

"Here!" he said, "what's up?" And when he saw Will Pomeroy's face: "What's happened here?"

Without speaking Will jerked his thumb in the direction of the private tap. His face was the colour of clay and the corner of his mouth twitched.

"Well, what *is* it?" demanded Oates impatiently.

"In there. Been an accident."

"*Accident*. What sort of a accident?"

But before Will could answer, Decima Moore came out of the tap-room, closing the door behind her.

"Here's Dick," said Will.

"Will," said Decima, "there's no doubt about it. He's dead."

"My Gawd, who's dead?" shouted Oates.

"Watchman."

ii

Oates looked down at the figure on the settle. He had remembered to remove his helmet but the water dripped off his cape in little streams. When he bent forward three drops fell on the blind face. Oates dabbed at them with his finger and glanced round apologetically.

He said, "What happened?"

Nobody answered. Old Pomeroy stood by the bar, his hands clasped in front of him. His face spoke only of complete bewilderment. He looked from one to another of the men as if somewhere there was some sort of explanation which had been withheld from him. Sebastian Parish and Norman Cubitt stood together in the inglenook. Parish's face was stained with tears. He kept smoothing back his hair with a nervous and meaningless gesture of the right hand. Cubitt's head was bent down. He seemed to be thinking deeply. Every now and then he glanced up sharply from under his brows. Mr. Nark sat on one of the bar stools clenching and unclenching his hands and struggling miserably with intermittent but profound hiccoughs. Legge, as white as paper, bit at his fingers and stared at Oates. Decima and Will stood together in the doorway. Miss Darragh sat just outside the inglenook on a low chair. Her moonlike face was colourless but she seemed composed.

Watchman lay on a settle near the dart board and opposite the bar. His eyes were wide open. They seemed to stare with glistening astonishment at the ceiling. The pupils were wide and black. His hands were clenched; the right arm lay across his body, the left dangled, and where the knuckles touched the floor they, like the back of the hand, were stained red.

"Well," repeated Oates violently, "can't any of you speak? What happened? Where's your senses? Have you sent for a doctor?"

"The telephone's dead," said Will Pomeroy. "And he's past doctoring, Dick."

Oates picked up the left wrist.

"What's this? Blood?"

"He got a prick from a dart."

Oates looked at the clenched hand and felt the wrist. In the third finger there was a neat puncture on the outside, below the nail. It was stained brown. The nails were bluish.

"I did that," said Legge suddenly. "It was my dart."

Oates laid the hand down and bent over the figure. A drop of water fell from his coat on one of the staring eyes. He fumbled inside the shirt, looking over his shoulder at Will Pomeroy.

"We'll have to fetch a doctor, however," he said.

"I'll go," said Cubitt. "Is it Illington?"

"Dr. Shaw, sir. Main road in and the last corner. It's on the left after you pass the police-station. He's police surgeon. I'd be obliged if you'd stop at the station and report."

"Right." Cubitt went out.

Oates straightened up and unbuttoned his cape.

"I'll have to get some notes down," he said and felt in the pocket of his tunic. He stepped back and his boots crunched excruciatingly.

"There's glass all over the floor," said Will.

Decima Moore said: "Can't we—cover him up?"

"It would be better, don't you think?" said Miss Darragh, speaking for the first time. "Can I—?"

Will said: "I'll get something," and went out. Oates looked round the group and at last addressed himself to Sebastian Parish.

"How long ago was this, sir?" he asked.

"Only a few minutes. It happened just before you came in."

Oates glanced at his watch.

"Half-past nine," he said, and noted it down.

"Let's hear what happened," he said.

"But it's not a case for the police," said Parish. "I mean because he died suddenly—"

"You called me in, sir," said Oates. "It's no doubt a case for the doctor. Leave it, if you wish, sir, till he comes."

"No, no," said Parish. "I don't mean that I object. It's only that your notebook and everything—it's so awful, somehow." He turned to Abel Pomeroy. "You tell him."

"It was like this, Dick," said old Abel. "Mr. Legge, here, had told us how he could throw the darts like a circus chap between the fingers of a man's hand stretched out on board. You heard him, Mr. Watchman, in his bold way, said he'd hold his hand out and Mr. Legge was welcome to have a shot at it. 'Twouldn't do no great damage, Mr. Watchman said, if he did stick him. Us all said it was a silly rash kind of trick. But Mr. Watchman was hellbent on it."

"He insisted," said Will.

"So he did, then. And up goes his hand. Mr. Legge throws the first three as pretty as you please, outside little finger, atween little and third, atween third and middle. Then he throws the fourth, and 'stead of going atween middle and first finger it catches little finger. 'Got me', says Mr. Watchman, and then—then what?" asked Abel.

"It was curious," said Miss Darragh slowly. "He didn't move his hand once. He kept it there against the board. The blood trickled down his finger and spread like veins in a leaf over the back of his hand. One had time to wonder if the dart had gone right through and he was in a way, crucified."

"He turned mortal ghastly white," said Abel.

"And then pulled the dart out," said Parish, "and threw it down on the floor. He shuddered, didn't he?"

"Yes," said Abel. "He shuddered violent."

"He always turned queer at the sight of his own blood, you know," said Parish.

"Well, what next?" asked Oates.

"I think he took a step towards the settle," said Parish.

"He sat on the settle," said Decima. "Miss Darragh said, 'He's feeling faint, give him a sip of brandy.' Mr. Legge said he looked ill and could he have lockjaw? Someone else, Mr. Pomeroy I think, said he ought to have iodine on his finger. Anyway, Mr. Pomeroy got the first-aid box out of the bottom cupboard. I looked for a glass with brandy in it but they were all empty. I got the bottle. While I was doing that—pouring out the brandy, I mean—Mr. Pomeroy dabbed iodine on the finger. Mr. Watchman clenched his teeth and cried out. He jerked up his arms."

She stopped and closed her eyes.

Will Pomeroy had come back with a sheet. He spread it over Watchman and then turned to Decima.

"I'll take you out of this," he said. "Come upstairs to Mrs. Ives, Dessy."

"No, I'll finish."

"No need."

Will put his arm across Decima's shoulder and turned to Oates.

"I'll tell you, Mr. Parish, here, said Mr. Watchman couldn't stand the sight of blood. Father said something about iodine like Dessy told you and he got the first-aid box out of the cupboard. He took out the bottle and it was nearly empty. Father tipped it up and poured some on Mr. Watchman's finger and then got out a bandage. Then Dessy gave him his brandy. He knocked the glass out of her hand."

"Miss Darragh was just going to tie his finger up," said Abel, "when the lights went out."

"Went out?"

" 'Ess. They'd been upping and downing ever since thunder set in and this time they went out proper for about a minute."

"It was frightful," said Parish rapidly. "We could hear him breathing. We were all knocking against each other with broken glasses everywhere and—those awful noises. Nobody thought of the oil lamps, but Legge said he'd throw some wood on the fire to make a blaze. He did, and just then the lights went up."

"Hold hard, if you please, sir," said Oates. "I'll get this down in writing."

"But, look here—"

Parish broke off and Will began again:—

"When the lights went on again we all looked at Mr. Watchman. He was in a kind of fit, seemingly. He thrashed about with his arms and legs and then fell backwards on settle where he is now. His breathing came queer for a bit and then—didn't come at all. I tried to get the doctor but the wires must be down. Then I came out and called you."

Will turned Decima towards the door.

"If you want me, Father," he said, "I'll be up-along. Coming, Dessy?"

"I'm all right," said Decima.

"You'll be better out of here."

She looked at him confusedly, seemed to hesitate, and then turned to Miss Darragh.

"Will you come, too?" asked Decima.

Miss Darragh looked fixedly at her and then seemed to make up her mind.

"Yes, my dear, certainly. We're better out of the way now, you know."

Miss Darragh gathered up her writing block and plodded to the door. Decima drew nearer to Will and, obeying the pressure of his hand, went out with him.

Legge walked across and looked down at the shrouded figure.

"My God," he said, "do you think it was the dart that did it? My God, I've never missed before. He moved his finger. I swear he moved his finger. My God, I shouldn't have taken that brandy!"

"Where is the dart?" asked Oates, still writing.

Legge began hunting about the floor. The broken glass crackled under his boots.

"If it's all the same to you, Abel," said Oates suddenly, "I reckon we'd better leave this end of the room till doctor's come. If it's all the same to you I reckon we'll shift into the Public."

"Let's do that, for God's sake," said Parish.

Mr. Nark was suddenly and violently ill.

"That settles it," said old Abel. "Us'll move."

iii

"Steady," said the doctor. "There's no particular hurry, you know. It's no joke negotiating Coombe Tunnel on a night like this. We must be nearly there."

"Sorry," said Cubitt. "I can't get it out of my head you might—might be able to do something."

"I'm afraid not, from your account. Here's the tunnel now. I should change down to first, really I should."

Cubitt changed down.

"I expect you wish you'd driven yourself," he said grimly.

"If it hadn't been for that slow puncture—there's the turning. Can you do it in one in this car? Splendid. I must confess I don't enjoy driving into the Coombe, even on clear nights. Now the road down. Pretty steep, really, and it's streaming with surface water. Shameful state of repair. Here we are."

Cubitt put on his brakes and drew up with a side long skid at the front door of the Feathers. The doctor got out, reached inside for his bag, and ducked through the rain into the entry. Cubitt followed him.

"In the private bar, you said?" asked Dr. Shaw.

He pushed open the door and they walked in.

The private bar was deserted but the lights were up in the Public beyond and they heard a murmur of voices.

"Hullo!" called Dr. Shaw.

There was a scuffling of feet and Will Pomeroy appeared on the far side of the bar.

"Here's doctor," said Will over his shoulder.

"Just a minute, Will," said the voice of Mr. Oates. "I'll trouble you stay where you are, if you please, gentlemen."

He loomed up, massively, put Will aside, and reached Dr. Shaw by way of the tap-proper, ducking under both counters.

"Well, Oates," said Dr. Shaw, "what's the trouble?"

Cubitt, stranded inside the door, stayed where he was. Oates pointed to the settle. Dr. Shaw took off his hat and coat, laid them with his bag on a table, and then moved to the shrouded figure. He drew back the sheet and after a moment's pause, stooped over Watchman.

Cubitt turned away. There was a long silence.

At last Dr. Shaw straightened up and replaced the sheet.

"Well," he said, "let's have the whole story again. I've had it once from Mr. Cubitt but he says he was a bit confused. Where are the others?"

"In here, Doctor," said Abel Pomeroy. "Will you come through?"

Oates and Will held up the counter-flap and Dr. Shaw went into the public bar. Parish, Mr. Nark and Abel had got to their feet.

Dr. Shaw was not the tallest man there but he dominated the scene. He was pale and baldish and wore glasses. His intelligence appeared in his eyes, which were extremely bright and a vivid blue. His lower lip protruded. He had an unexpectedly deep voice, a look of serio-comic solemnity, and a certain air of distinction. He looked directly and with an air of thoughtfulness at each of the men before him.

"His relations must be told," he said.

Parish moved forward. "I'm his cousin," he said, "and his nearest relation."

"Oh yes," said Dr. Shaw. "You're Mr. Parish?"

"Yes."

"Yes. Sad business, this."

"What was it?" asked Parish. "What happened? He was perfectly well. Why did he—I don't understand."

"Tell me this," said Dr. Shaw. "Did your cousin become unwell as soon as he received this injury from the dart?"

"Yes. At least he seemed to turn rather faint. I didn't think much of it because he's always gone like that at the sight of his own blood."

"Like what? Can you describe his appearance?"

"Well, he—Oh God, what did he do, Norman?"

Cubitt said: "He just said 'Got me' when the dart struck and then afterwards pulled it out and threw it down. He turned terribly pale. I think he sort of collapsed on that seat."

"I've seen a man with tetanus," said Legge suddenly. "He looked just the same. For God's sake, Doctor, d'you think he could have taken tetanus from that dart?"

"I can't tell you that off-hand, I'm afraid. What happened next?" Dr. Shaw looked at Cubitt.

"Well, Abel here—Mr. Pomeroy—got a bandage and a bottle of iodine, and put some iodine on the finger. Then Miss Darragh, a lady who's staying here, said she'd bandage the finger and while she was getting out the bandage Miss Moore gave him brandy."

"Did he actually take the brandy?"

"I think he took a little but after she'd tipped the glass up he clenched his teeth and knocked it out of her hand."

"Complain of pain?"

"No. He looked frightened."

"And then? After that?"

"After that? Well, just at that moment, really, the lights went out, and when they went up again he seemed much worse. He was in a terrible state."

"A fit," said Mr. Nark, speaking for the first time. "The man had a fit. Ghastly!" He belched uproariously.

"There's a very strong smell of brandy," said Dr. Shaw.

"It spilt," explained Mr. Nark hurriedly. "It's all over the floor in there."

"Where's the dart, Oates?" asked Dr. Shaw.

"In there, sir. I've put it in a clean bottle and corked it up."

"Good. I'd better have it. You'll have to leave the room in there as it is, Mr. Pomeroy, until I've had a word with the Superintendent. The body may be removed in the morning."

"Very good, sir."

"And I'm afraid, Mr. Parish, that under the circumstances I must report this case to the coroner."

"Do you mean there'll have to be an inquest?"

"If he thinks it necessary."

"And—and a post-mortem?"

"If he orders it."

"Oh God!" said Parish.

"May I have your cousin's full name and his address?"

Parish gave them. Dr. Shaw looked solemn and said it would be a great loss to the legal profession. He then returned to the private bar. Oates produced his notebook and took the floor.

"I'll have all your names and addresses, if you please, gentlemen," he said.

"What's the use of saying that?" demanded Mr. Nark, rallying a little. "You know 'em already. You took our statements. We've signed 'em, and whether we should in law, is a point I'm not sure of."

"Never mind if I know 'em or don't, George Nark," rejoined Oates, "I know my business and that's quite sufficient. What's your name?"

He took all their names and addresses and suggested that they go to bed. They filed out through a door into the passage. Oates then joined Dr. Shaw in the private bar.

"Hullo, Oates," said the doctor. "Where's that dart?"

"Legge picked the dart off the floor," Oates said.

He showed it to Dr. Shaw. He had put it into an empty bottle and sealed it.

"Good," said Dr. Shaw, and put the bottle in his bag. "Now the remains of the brandy glass. They seem to have tramped it to smithereens. We'll see if we can gather up some of the mess. There's a forceps and an empty jar in my bag. Where did the iodine come from?"

"Abel keeps his first-aid outfit in that corner cupboard, sir. He's a great one for iodine. Sloushed it all over Bob Legge's face to-day when he cut himself with his razor."

Dr. Shaw stooped and picked up a small bottle that had rolled under the settle.

"Here it is, I suppose." He sniffed at it. "Yes, that's it. Where's the cork?"

He hunted about until he found it.

"Better take this, too. And the brandy bottle. Good Heavens, they seem to have done themselves remarkably proud. It's nearly empty. Now where's the first-aid kit?"

Dr. Shaw went to the cupboard and stared up at the glass door.

"What's that bottle in there?" he said sharply.

Oates joined him.

"That sir? Oh yes, I know what that is. It's some stuff Abel got to kill the rats in the old stables. He mentioned it earlier this evening."

Oates rubbed his nose vigorously.

"Seems more like a week ago. There was the deceased gentleman standing drinks and chaffing Abel not much more than a couple of hours ago. And now look at him. Ripe for coroner as you might say."

"Did Abel say what this rat-poison was?"

"Something in the nature of prussic acid, I fancy, sir."

"Indeed?" said Dr. Shaw. "Get my gloves out of my overcoat pocket, will you, Oates?"

"Your gloves, sir?"

"Yes, I want to open the cupboard."

But when Oates brought the gloves Dr. Shaw still stared at the cupboard door.

"Your gloves, sir."

"I don't think I'll use 'em. I don't think I'll open the door, Oates. There may be fingerprints all over the shop. We'll leave the cupboard doors, Oates, for the expert."

CHAPTER SIX

Inquest

i

The Illington Coroner was James Mordant, Esq., M.D. He was sixty-seven years old and these years sat heavily upon him, for he suffered from dyspepsia. He seemed to regard his fellow men with brooding suspicion, he sighed a great deal, and had a trick of staring despondently at the merest acquaintances. He had at one time specialized in bacteriology and it was said of him that he saw human beings as mere playgrounds for brawling micrococci. It was also said that when Dr. Mordant presided over an inquest, the absence in court of the corpse was not felt. He sat huddled up behind his table and rested his head on his hand with such a lack-lustre air that one might have thought he scarcely listened to the evidence. This was not the case, however. He was a capable man.

On the morning of the inquest on Luke Watchman, the third day after his death, Dr. Mordant, with every appearance of the deepest distrust, heard his jury sworn and contemplated the witnesses. The inquest was held in the Town Hall, and because of the publicity given to Watchman's death in the London paper, was heavily attended by the public. Watchman's solicitor, who in the past had frequently briefed him, had come down from London. So had Watchman's secretary and junior, and a London doctor who had attended him recently. There was a fair sprinkling of London pressmen. Dr. Mordant, staring hopelessly at an old man in the front row, charged the jury to determine how, when, where, and by what means, deceased came by his death; and whether he died from criminal, avoidable, or natural causes. He then raised his head and stared at the jury.

"Is it your wish to view the body?" he sighed.

The jury whispered and huddled, and its foreman, an auctioneer, said they thought perhaps under the circumstances they *should* view the body.

The coroner sighed again and gave an order to his officer. The jury filed out and returned in a few minutes looking unwholesome. The witnesses were then examined on oath by the coroner.

P. C. Oates gave formal evidence of the finding of the body. Then Sebastian Parish was called and identified the body. Everybody who had seen his performance of a bereaved brother, in the trial scene of a famous picture, was now vividly reminded of it. But Parish's emotion, thought Cubitt, could not be purely histrionic unless, as he had once declared, he actually changed colour under the stress of a painful scene. Sebastian was now very pale indeed, and Cubitt wondered uneasily what he thought of this affair, and how deeply he regretted the loss of his cousin. He gave his evidence in a low voice but it carried to the end of the building, and when he faltered at the description of Watchman's death, at least two of the elderly ladies in the public seats were moved to tears. Parish wore a grey suit, a soft white shirt, and a black tie. He looked amazingly handsome, and on his arrival had been photographed several times.

Cubitt was called next and confirmed Parish's evidence.

Then Miss Darragh appeared. The other witnesses exuded discomfort and formality but Miss Darragh was completely at her ease. She took the oath with an air of intelligent interest. The coroner asked her if she had remembered anything that she hadn't mentioned in her first statement, or if there was any point that had been missed by the previous witness.

"There is not," said Miss Darragh. "I told the doctor, Dr. Shaw 'twas all I had seen; and when the policeman, Constable Oates 'twas, came up on the morning after the accident, I told 'um all I knew all over again. If I may be allowed to say so, it is my opinion that the small wound Mr. Watchman had from the dart had nothing whatever to do with his death."

"What makes you think that, Miss Darragh?" asked the coroner with an air of allowing Miss Darragh a certain amount of latitude.

"Wasn't it a small paltry prick from a brand-new dart that couldn't hurt a child. As Mr. Parish said at the time, he was but frightened at the sight of his own blood. That was my own impression. 'Twas later that he became so ill."

"When did you notice the change in his condition?"

"Later."

"Was it after he had taken the brandy?"

"It was. Then, or about then, or after."

"He took the brandy after Mr. Pomeroy put iodine on his finger?"

"He did."

"You agree for the rest with the previous statement?"

"I do."

"Thank you, Miss Darragh."

Decima Moore came next. Decima looked badly shaken but she gave her evidence very clearly and firmly. The coroner stopped her when she came to the incident of the brandy. He had a curious trick of prefacing many of his questions with a slight moan, rather in the manner of a stage parson.

"N-n-n you say, Miss Moore, that the deceased swallowed some of the brandy."

"Yes," said Decima.

"N-n-now you are positive on that point?"

"Yes."

"Yes. Thank you. What happened to the glass?"

"He knocked it out of my hand on to the floor."

"Did you get the impression that he did this deliberately?"

"No. It seemed to be involuntary."

"And was the glass broken?"

"Yes." Decima paused. "At least—"

"N-n-n-yes?"

"It was broken, but I don't remember whether that happened when it fell, or afterwards when the light went out. Everybody seemed to be treading on broken glass after the lights went out."

The coroner consulted his notes.

"And for the rest, Miss Moore, do you agree with the account given by Mr. Parish, Mr. Cubitt and Miss Darragh?"

"Yes."

"In every particular?"

Decima was now very white indeed. She said: "Everything they said is quite true, but there is one thing they didn't notice."

The coroner sighed.

"What is that, Miss Moore?" he asked.

"It was after I gave him the brandy. He gasped and I thought he spoke. I thought he said one word."

"What was it?"

" 'Poisoned,' " said Decima.

A sort of rustling in the room seemed to turn the word into an echo.

The coroner added to his notes.

"You are sure of this?" he asked.

"Yes."

"Yes. And then?"

"He clenched his teeth very hard. I don't think he spoke again."

"Are you positive that it was Mr. Watchman's own glass that you gave him?"

"Yes. He put it on the table when he went to the dart board. It was the only glass there. I poured a little into it from the bottle. The bottle was on the bar."

"Had anyone but Mr. Watchman touched the glass before you gave him the brandy?"

Decima said: "I didn't notice anyone touch it."

"Quite so. Have you anything further to tell us? Anything that escaped the notice of the previous witnesses?"

"Nothing," said Decima.

Her deposition was read to her, and, like Parish and Cubitt, she signed it.

Will Pomeroy took the oath with an air of truculence and suspicion, but his statement differed in no way from the others, and he added nothing material to the evidence. Mr. Robert Legge was the next to give evidence on the immediate circumstances surrounding Watchman's death.

On his appearance there was a tightening of attention among the listeners. The light from a high window shone full on Legge. Cubitt looked at his white hair, the grooves and folds of his face, and the calluses on his hands. He wondered how old Legge was and why Watchman had baited him, and exactly what sort of background he had. It was impossible to place the fellow. His clothes were good; a bit antiquated as to cut perhaps, but good. He spoke like an educated man and moved like a labourer. As he faced the coroner he straightened up and held his arms at his side almost in the manner of a private soldier. His face was rather white and his fingers twitched, but he spoke with composure. He agreed that the account given by the previous witnesses was correct. The coroner clasped his hands on the table and gazed at them with an air of distaste.

"About this n-n-n-experiment with the darts, Mr. Legge," he said. "When was it first suggested?"

"I believe on the night of Mr. Watchman's arrival. I mentioned, I think, that I had done the trick and he said something to the effect that he wouldn't care to try. I think he added that he might, after all, like to see me do it." Legge moistened his lips. "Later on that evening, I did the trick in the public tap-room and he said that if I beat him at Round-the-Clock he'd let me try it on him."

"What," asked the coroner, drearily, "is Round-the-Clock?"

"You play into each segment of the dart board, beginning at Number One. As soon as you miss a shot the next player has his turn. You have three darts, that is three chances to get a correct opening shot, but after that you carry on until you do miss. You have to finish with fifty."

"You all played this game?"

Legge hesitated: "We were all in it except Miss Darragh. Miss Moore began. When she missed, Mr. Cubitt took the next turn; then I came."

"Yes?"

"I didn't miss."

"You mean you n-n-ran out in one turn?"

"Yes."

"And then?"

"Mr. Watchman said he believed he would trust me to do the hand trick."

"And did you do it?"

"No. I was not anxious to do it and turned the conversation. Later, as I have said, I did it in the public room."

"But the following night, last Friday, you attempted it on the deceased?"

"Yes."

"Will you tell us how this came about?"

Legge clenched his fingers and stared at an enlargement of a past mayor of Illington.

"In much the same circumstances. I mean, we were all in the private bar. Mr. Watchman proposed another game of Round-the-Clock and said definitely that, if I beat him, I should try the trick with the hand. I did win and he at once insisted on the experiment."

"Were you reluctant?"

"I—No. I have done the trick at least fifty times and I have only failed once before. On that occasion no harm was done. The dart grazed the third finger, but it was really nothing. I told Mr. Watchman of this incident, but he said he'd stick to his bargain, and I consented."

"Go on, please, Mr. Legge."

"He put his hand against the dart board with the fingers spread out as I suggested. There were two segments of the board showing between the fingers in each instance." Legge paused and then said: "So you see it's really easier than Round-the-Clock. Twice as easy."

Legge stopped and the coroner waited.

"Yes?" he said to his blotting paper.

"I tried the darts, which were new ones, and then began. I put the first dart on the outside of the little finger and the next between the little and third fingers and the next between the third and middle."

"It was the fourth dart, then, that miscarried?"

"Yes."

"How do you account for that?"

"At first I thought he had moved his finger. I am still inclined to think so."

The coroner stirred uneasily.

"Would you not be positive on this point if it was so? You must have looked fixedly at the fingers."

"At the space between," corrected Legge.

"I see." Dr. Mordant looked at his notes.

"The previous statements," he said, "mention that you had all taken a certain amount of a vintage brandy. Exactly how much brandy, Mr. Legge, did you take?"

"Two nips."

"How large a quantity? Mr. William Pomeroy states that a bottle of Courvoisier '87 was opened at Mr. Watchman's request, and that the contents were served out to everyone but himself, Miss Daragh, and Miss Moore. That would mean a sixth of a bottle to each of the persons who took it?"

"Er—yes. Yes."

"Had you finished your brandy when you threw the dart?"

"Yes."

"Had you taken anything else previously?"

"A pint of beer," said Legge unhappily.

"N-n-n-yes. Thank you. Now, where did you put the darts you used for this experiment?"

"They were new darts. Mr. Pomeroy opened the package and suggested—" Legge broke off and wetted his lips. "He suggested that I should christen the new darts," he said.

"Did you take them from Mr. Pomeroy?"

"Yes. He fitted the flights while we played Round-the-Clock and then gave them to me for the experiment."

"No one else handled them?"

"Mr. Will Pomeroy and Mr. Parish picked them up and looked at them."

"I see. Now, for the sequel, Mr. Legge."

But again Legge's story followed the others. His deposition was read to him and he signed it, making rather a slow business of writing his name. The coroner called Abel Pomeroy.

ii

Abel seemed bewildered and nervous. His habitual cheerfulness had gone and he gazed at the coroner as at a recording angel of peculiar strictness. When they reached the incident of the brandy, Dr. Mordant asked Abel if he had opened the bottle. Abel said he had.

"And you served it, Mr. Pomeroy?"

" 'Ess, sir."

"Will you tell us from where you got the glasses and how much went into each glass?"

" 'Ess, sir. I got glasses from cupboard under bar. They was the best glasses. Mr. Watchman said we would kill the bottle in two halves, sir. So I served half-bottle round. 'Twas about two fingers each. Us polished that off and then they played Round-the-Clock, sir, and then us polished off t'other half. 'Least, sir, I didn't take my second tot. Tell the truth, sir, I hadn't taken no more than a drop of my first round and that was enough for me. I'm not a great drinker," said old Abel innocently, "and I mostly bides by beer. But I just took a drain to pleasure Mr. Watchman. I served out for the rest of the company 'cepting my Will and Miss Darragh and Miss Dessy—Miss Moore, sir. But I left fair drain in bottle."

"Why did you do that?"

Abel rubbed his chin and glanced uncomfortably at the other witnesses.

"Seemed like they'd had enough, sir."

"This was before the experiment with the deceased's hand, of course," said the coroner to the jury. "Yes, Mr. Pomeroy? How much was in the glasses on the second round?"

" 'Bout a finger and half, sir, I reckon."

"Did you hand the drinks round yourself?"

Abel said: "I don't rightly remember. Wait a bit, though. I reckon Mr. Watchman handed first round to everyone." Abel looked anxiously at Will, who nodded. " 'Ess, sir. That's how 'twas."

"You must not communicate with other persons, Mr. Pomeroy, before giving your answers," said Dr. Mordant darkly. "And the second round?"

"Ah. I poured it out and left glasses on bar," said Abel thoughtfully. "Company was fairly lively by then. There was a lot of talk.

I reckon each man took his own, second round. Mr. Watchman carried his over to table by dart board."

"Would you say that at this juncture the men who had taken brandy were sober?"

"Not to say sober, sir, and not to say proper drunk. Bosky-eyed, you might say, 'cepting old George Nark and he was proper soaked. 'Ess, he was drunk as a fish was George Nark."

Two of the jury men laughed at this and several of the public. The coroner looked about him with an air of extreme distaste and silence set in immediately.

"Is it true," said the coroner, "that you have been poisoning rats in your garage, Mr. Pomeroy?"

Old Abel turned very white and said, "Yes."

"What did you use?"

" 'Twas some stuff from chemist."

"Yes. Did you purchase it personally?"

"No, sir. It was got for me."

"By whom?"

"By Mr. Parish, sir. I axed him and he kindly fetched it. I would like to say, sir, that when he give it to me 'twas all sealed up, chemist-fashion."

"N-n-n-yes. Do you know the nature of this poison?"

"I do believe, sir, it was in the nature of prussic acid. It's not marked anything but poison."

"Please tell the jury how you used this substance and when."

Abel wetted his lips and repeated his story. He had used the rat-poison on Thursday evening, the evening of Watchman's arrival. He had taken great care and used every precaution. A small vessel had been placed well inside the mouth of the rat-hole and some of the fluid poured into it. The hole was plugged up with rags and the bottle carefully corked. No waste drops of the fluid had escaped. Abel had worn old gloves which he afterwards threw on the fire. He had placed the bottle in a corner cupboard in the inglenook. It had stood alone on the shelf and the label *POISON* could be seen through the glass door. Everyone in the house was aware of the bottle and its contents.

"We have heard that the iodine was taken from a cupboard in the inglenook. Was this the same cupboard?"

" 'Ess fay," said Abel quickly, "but 'twasn't same shelf, sir. 'Twas in a tin box in another shelf and with a different door, but same piece of furniture."

"You fetched the iodine?"

"So I did, then, and it was snug and tight in first-aid tin, same as it always is. And, axing your pardon, sir, I used to dab of that same iodine on Bob Legge's chin only that evening, and there the man is as fit as a flea to bear witness."

"Quite. Thank you, Mr. Pomeroy. Call Bernard Noggins, chemist, of Illington."

Mr. Bernard Noggins could have been called nothing else. His eyes watered, his face was pink, his mouth hung open, and he suffered from hay fever. He was elderly and vague, and he obviously went in great terror of the coroner. He was asked if he remembered Mr. Parish's visit to his shop. He said he did.

"Mr. Parish asked you for a rat-poison?"

"Yes. Yes, he did."

"What did you supply?"

"I—er—I had no proprietary rat-bane in stock," began Mr. Noggins miserably, "and no arsenic. So I suggested that the fumes of a cyanide preparation might prove beneficial."

"Might prove *what?*"

"Efficacious. I suggested Scheele's acid."

"You sold Mr. Parish Scheele's acid?"

"Yes. No—I—actually—I diluted—I mean I added—I mean I produced a more concentrated solution by adding H.CN. I—er—I supplied a fifty per cent solution. Yes."

The coroner dropped his pen and gazed at Mr. Noggins, who went on in a great hurry:

"I warned Mr. Parish. He will agree I warned him most carefully and he signed the register—every formality and precaution—most particular. Full instructions. Label."

The coroner said: "Why did you make this already lethal fluid so much more deadly?"

"Rats," said Mr. Noggins. "I mean, Mr. Parish said it was for rats, and that Mr. Pomeroy had tried a commercial rat-bane without success. Mr. Parish suggested—suggested—I should—"

"Should what, Mr. Noggins?"

"That I should ginger it up a bit, as he put it." Mr. Noggins, in the excess of his discomfort, uttered a mad little laugh. The coroner turned upon him a face sickly with disapprobation and told him he might stand down. Dr. Mordant than addressed the jury.

"I think, gentlemen, we have heard enough evidence as to fact and circumstance surrounding this affair and may now listen to the medical evidence. Dr. Shaw, if you please."

Dr. Shaw swore himself in very briskly and, at the coroner's invitation, described the body as it was when he first saw it. The coroner's attitude of morbid introspection increased but he and Dr. Shaw seemed to understand each other pretty well.

"The eyes were wide open and the pupils widely dilated, the jaws tightly clenched . . ." Dr. Shaw droned on and on. Parish and Cubitt, who had remained in court, both looked rather sick. Legge eyed Dr. Shaw with a sort of mesmerized glare. Will Pomeroy held Decima's hand, and old Abel stared at his boots. Mr. Nark, who had expected to be called, looked alternately huffy and sheepish. A large, bald man, who looked as if he ought to be in uniform, seemed to prick up his ears. He was Superintendent Harper of the Illington Police Force.

"You have performed an autopsy?" asked the coroner.

"Yes."

"What did you find?"

"I found the blood much engorged and brilliant in colour. I found nothing unusual in the condition of the stomach. I sent the contents to be analyzed, however, and the report has reached me. Nothing unexpected has been found. I also sent a certain quantity of the blood to be analyzed."

Dr. Shaw paused.

"N-n-yes?"

"In the case of the sample of blood, the analyst has found definite traces of hydrocyanic acid. These traces point to the presence of at least a grain and a half of the acid in the blood stream."

"And the fatal dose?"

"One may safely say less than a grain."

"Did you send the brandy bottle and the iodine bottle, which was found under the bench, to the analyst?"

"Yes."

"What was the result, Dr. Shaw?"

"The test was negative. The analyst can find no trace of hydrocyanic acid in either bottle."

"And the dart?"

"The dart was also tested for traces of hydrocyanic acid." Dr. Shaw looked directly at the coroner and said crisply, "Two tests were used. The first was negative. The second positive. Indications of a very slight trace of hydrocyanic acid were found upon the dart."

iii

There was only one other witness, a representative of the firm that made the darts. He stated with considerable emphasis that at no stage of their manufacture did they come in contact with any form of cyanide, and that no cyanic preparation was to be found in the entire factory.

The coroner summed up at considerable length and with commendable simplicity. His manner suggested that the jury as a whole was certifiable as mentally unsound, but that he knew his duty and would perform it in the teeth of stupidity. He surveyed the circumstances surrounding Watchman's death. He pointed out that the only word spoken by the deceased, the word "poisoned," overheard by one witness alone, should not weigh too heavily in the minds of the jury. In the first place the evidence might be regarded as hearsay, and therefore inadmissible at any other court. In the second, there was nothing to show why the deceased had uttered this word or whether his impression had been based on any actual knowledge. They might attach considerable importance to the point that the post-mortem analysis gave positive signs of the presence of some kind of cyanide in the blood. They might, while remembering the presence of a strong solution of hydrocyanic acid in the room, also note the assurance given by several of the witnesses that all reasonable precaution had been taken in the use and disposal of the bottle. They would very possibly consider that the use, for domestic purposes, of so dangerous a poison, was extremely ill-advised. He reminded them of Watchman's idiosyncrasy for the acid. He delivered a short address on the forms in which this, the most deadly of the cerebral depressants, was usually found. He said that, since hydrogen cyanide is excessively volatile, the fact that none was found in the stomach did not preclude the possibility that the deceased had taken it by the mouth. He reminded them again of the expert evidence. No cyanide had been found in the brandy bottle or the iodine bottle. The fragments of the broken brandy glass had also given a negative result in the test for cyanide, but they might remember that as these fragments were extremely minute, the test, in this instance, could not be considered conclusive. They would of course note that the point of the dart had yielded a positive result in the second test made by the analyst. This dart was new, but had been handled by three persons before Mr. Legge used it. He wound up by saying that if the jury came to the conclusion that the deceased died of cyanide poisoning but that there was not enough evidence to say, positively, how he took the poison, they might return a verdict to this effect.

Upon this hint the jury retired for ten minutes and came back to deliver themselves, as well as they could remember them, in Dr. Mordant's own words. They added a shocked and indignant remark on the subject of prussic acid in the home.

The inquest on Luke Watchman was ended and his cousin was free to bury his body.

CHAPTER SEVEN

Complaint from a Publican

i

"SUMMER," SAID Chief Detective-Inspector Alleyn moodily, "is acoming in and my temper is agoing out. Lhude sing cuccu. I find that the length of my patience, Fox, fluctuates in an inverse ratio with the length of the days."

"Don't you like the warm weather?" asked Detective-Inspector Fox.

"Yes, Fox, but not in London. Not in the Yard. Not in the streets, where one feels dirty half an hour after one has bathed. Not when one is obliged to breathe the fumes of petrol and the body-odour of those who come to make statements and remain to smell. That creature who has just left us stank abominably. However, the case is closed, which is a slight alleviation. But I don't like summer in London."

"Ah well," said Fox, shifting his thirteen stone from one leg to the other, *"chacun à son goût."*

"Your French improves."

"It ought to, Mr. Alleyn. I've been sweating at it for two years now, but I can't say I feel what you might call at home with it. Give me time and I can see my way with the stuff but that's not good enough. Not nearly good enough."

"Courage, Fox. Dogged as does it. What brought you up here?"

"There's a chap came into the waiting-room an hour ago with rather a rum story, sir. They sent him along to me. I don't know that there's much in it but I thought you might be interested."

"Why?" asked Alleyn apprehensively.

"I nearly sent him off," continued Fox, who had his own way of imparting information. "I did tell him it was nothing to do with us and that he'd better go to the local Super which is, of course, what he'll have to do anyway if there's anything in it."

"Fox," said Alleyn, "am I a Tantalus that you should hold this beaker, however unpalatable, beyond my reach? What was this fellow's story? What prevented you from following the admirable course you have outlined? And why have you come in here?"

"It's about the Watchman business."

"Oh?" Alleyn swung round in his chair. "What about it?"

"I remembered you'd taken an interest in it, Mr. Alleyn, and that deceased was a personal friend of yours."

"Well—an acquaintance."

"Yes. You mentioned that there were one or two points that were not brought out at the inquest."

"Well?"

"Well, this chap's talking about one of them. The handling of the darts."

Alleyn hesitated. At last he said: "He must go to the local people."

"I thought you might like to see him before we got rid of him."

"Who is he?"

"The pub-keeper."

"Has he come up from Devon to see us?"

"Yes, he has. He says the Super at Illington wouldn't listen to him."

"None of our game."

"I thought you might like to see him," Fox repeated.

"All right, blast you. Bring him up."

"Very good, sir," said Fox, and went out.

Alleyn put his papers together and shoved them into a drawer of his desk. He noticed with distaste that the papers felt gritty and that the handle of the drawer was sticky. He wished suddenly that something important might crop up somewhere in the country, somewhere, for preference, in the South of England; and his thoughts switched back to the death of Luke Watchman in Devon. He called to mind the report on the inquest. He had read it attentively.

Fox returned and stood with his hand on the door.

"In here, if you please, Mr. Pomeroy," said Fox.

Alleyn thought his visitor would have made a very good model for the portrait of an innkeeper. Abel's face was broad, ruddy and amiable. His mouth looked as if it had only just left off smiling and was ready to break into a smile again; for all that, at the moment, he was rather childishly solemn. He wore his best suit and it sat uneasily upon him. He walked halfway across the floor and made a little bow.

"Good afternoon, sir," said Abel.

"Good afternoon, Mr. Pomeroy. I hear you've come all the way up from the West Country to see us."

"I have so, sir. First time since Coronation and not such a pleasant errand. I bide home-along mostly."

"Lucky man. Sit down, Mr. Pomeroy."

"Much obliged, sir."

Abel sat down and spread his hands on his knees.

"This gentleman," he said, looking at Fox, "says it do be none of your business here, sir. That's a bit of a facer. I got no satisfaction along to Illington, and I says to myself: 'I'll go up top. I'll cut through all their pettifogging, small-minded ways, and lay my case boldly before the witty brains of those masterpieces at Scotland Yard.' Seems like I've wasted time and money."

"That's bad luck," said Alleyn. "I'm sorry, but Inspector Fox is right. The Yard only takes up an outside case at the request of the local Superintendent, you see. But if you'd care to tell me, unofficially, what the trouble is, I think I may invite you to do so."

"Better than nothing, sir, and thank you very kindly." Abel moistened his lips and rubbed his knees. "I'm sore troubled," he said. "It's got me under the weather. First time anything of a criminal nature has ever come my way. The Feathers has got a clean sheet, sir. Never any trouble about after-hours in my house. Us bides by the law and now it seems as how the law don't bide by we."

"A *criminal* nature?" said Alleyn.

"What else am I to think of it, sir? 'Twasn't accident! 'Twasn't neglect on my part, for all they're trying to put on me."

"Suppose," said Alleyn, "we begin at the beginning, Mr. Pomeroy. You've come to see us because you've information—"

Abel opened his mouth but Alleyn went on: "Information or an opinion about the death of Mr. Luke Watchman."

"Opinion!" said Abel. "That's the word."

"The finding at the inquest was death by cyanide-poisoning, with nothing to show exactly how it was taken."

"And a proper fidgeting, suspicioning verdict it was," said Abel warmly. "What's the result? Result is George Nark, so full of silly blusteracious nonsense as an old turkey-cock, going round 't Coombe with a story as how I killed Mr. Watchman along of criminal negligence with prussic acid. George Nark axing me of an evening if I've washed out glasses in my tap, because he'd prefer not to die in agony same as Mr. Watchman. George Nark talking his ignorant blusteracious twaddle to anyone as is stupid enough to listen to him."

"Very irritating," said Alleyn. "Who is Mr. Nark?"

"Old fool of a farmer, sir, with more long words than wits in his yed. I wouldn't pay no attention, knowing his tongue's apt to make a laughing-stock of the man, but other people listen and it's bad for trade. I know," said Abel steadily, "I know as certain-sure as I know anything in the life, that it was no fault of mine Mr. Watchman died of poison in my private tap. Because why? Because so soon as us had done with that stuff in my old stables, it was corked up proper. For all there wasn't a drop of wetness on the bottle, I wiped it thorough and burned the rag. I carried it in with my own hands, sir, and put it in the cupboard. Wearing gas mask and gloves, I was, and I chucked the gloves on the fire and washed my hands afterwards. And thurr that bottle stood, sir, for twenty-four hours; and if any drop of stuff came out of it, 'twas by malice and not by accident. I've axed my housekeeper and li'l maid who works for us, and neither on 'em's been near cupboard. Too mortal scared they wurr. Nor has my boy, Will. And what's more, sir, the glasses Mr. Watchman and company drank from that ghastly night was our best glasses, and I took 'em special, out of cupboard under bar. Now, sir, could this poison, however deadly, get itself out of stoppered bottle, through glass door, and into tumbler under my bar? Could it? I ax you!"

"It sounds rather like a conjuring trick," agreed Alleyn with a smile.

"So it do."

"What about the dart, Mr. Pomeroy?"

"Ah!" said Abel. "Thicky dart! When George Nark don't be saying I did for the man in his cups, he be swearing his soul away I mussed up thicky dart with prussic acid. Mind this, sir, the darts wurrn't arrived when us brought in poison on Thursday night, and they wurr only unpacked five minutes before the hijjus moment itself. Now!"

"Yes, they were new darts, weren't they? I seem to remember—"

" 'Ess fay, and never used till then. I opened 'em up myself, while company was having their last go Round-the-Clock. I opened 'em up on bar counter. Fresh in their London wrappings, they wurr. Mr. Parish and my boy, Will, they picked 'em up and looked at 'em, casual-like, and then Bob Legge, he scooped 'em up and took a trial throw with the lot. He said they carried beautiful. Then he had his shot at Mr. Watchman's hand. They wurr clean new, they darts."

"And yet," said Alleyn, "the analyst found a trace of cyanide on the dart that pierced Mr. Watchman's finger."

Abel brought his palms down with a smack on his knees.

" 'Od rabbit it," he shouted, "don't George Nark stuff that-thurr chunk of science down my gullet every time he opens his silly face? Lookee yurr, sir! 'Twas twenty-four hours, and more, since I put a bottle 'o poison in cupboard. I'd washed my hands half a dozen times since then. Bar had been swabbed down. Ax yourself, how could I infectorate they darts?"

Alleyn looked at the sweaty, earnest countenance before him, and whistled soundlessly.

"Yes," he said at last, "it seems unlikely."

"Unlikely! It's slap-down impossible."

"But—"

"If pison got on thicky dart," said Abel, " 'twasn't by accident nor yet by carelessness. 'Twas by malice. 'Twas with murderacious intent. Thurr!"

"But how do you account . . . ?"

"Account? Me?" asked old Abel, agitatedly. "I don't. I leaves they intellectual capers to Superintendent Nicholas Harper, and a pretty poor fist he do be making of it. That's why—"

"Yes, yes," said Alleyn hurriedly. "But remember that Mr. Harper may be doing more than you think. Policemen have to keep their own counsel, you see. Don't make up your mind that because he doesn't say very much—"

"It's not what he don't say, it's the silly standoffishness of what he do say. Nick Harper! Damme, I was to school with the man, and now he sits behind his desk and looks at me as if I be a fool. 'Where's your facts,' he says. 'Don't worry yourself,' he says, 'if there's anything fishy, us'll fish for it.' Truth of the matter is, the man's too small and ignorant for a murderous matter. Can't raise himself above the level of motor licenses and after-hour trade, and more often than not he makes a muck of them. What'll come to the Feathers if this talk goes on? Happen us'll have to give up the trade, after a couple of centuries."

"Don't you believe it," said Alleyn. "We can't afford to lose our old pubs, Mr. Pomeroy, and it's going to take more than a week's village gossip to shake the trade at the Plume of Feathers. It is just a week since the inquest, isn't it? It's fresh in Mr. George Nark's memory. Give it time to die down."

"If this affair dies down, sir, there'll be a murder unhung in the Coombe."

Alleyn raised his brows.

"You feel like that about it?"

" 'Ess, I do. What's more, sir, I'll put a name to the man."

Alleyn lifted a hand but old Abel went on doggedly:

"I don't care who hears me, I'll put a name to him, and that-there name's Robert Legge. Now!"

"A very positive old article," said Alleyn, when Fox returned from seeing Abel Pomeroy down the corridor.

"I don't see why he's made up his mind this chap Legge is a murderer," said Fox. "He'd only known deceased twenty-four hours. It sounds silly."

"He says Watchman gibed at Legge," said Alleyn. "I wonder if he did. And why."

"I've heard him in court, often enough," said Fox. "He was a prime heckler. Perhaps it was a habit."

"I don't think so. He was a bit malicious, though. He was a striking sort of fellow. Plenty of charm and a good deal of vanity. He always seemed to me to take unnecessary trouble to be liked. But I didn't know him well. The cousin's a damn' good actor. Rather like Watchman, in a way. Oh well, it's not our pidgin, thank the Lord. I'm afraid the old boy's faith in us wonderful police has been shaken."

"D'you know the Super at Illington, Mr. Alleyn?"

"Harper. Yes, I do. He was in on that arson case in South Devon in '37. Served his apprenticeship in L. Division. You must remember him."

"Nick Harper?"

"That's the fellow. Devon, born and bred. I think perhaps I'd better write and warn him about Mr. Pomeroy's pilgrimage."

"I wonder if old Pomeroy's statement's correct. I wonder if he did make a bloomer with the rat-poison and is simply trying to save his face."

"His indignation seemed to me to be supremely righteous. I fancy he thinks he's innocent."

"Somebody else may have mucked about with the bottle and won't own up," Fox speculated.

"Possible. But who'd muck about with hydrocyanic acid for the sheer fun of the thing?"

"The alternative," said Fox, "is murder."

"Is it? Well, you bumble off and brood on it. You must be one of those zealous officers who rise to the top of the profession."

"Well, sir," said Fox, "it's funny. On the face of it, it's funny."

"Run away and laugh at it, then. I'm going home, Br'er Fox."

But when Fox had gone, Alleyn sat and stared at the top of his desk. At last he drew a sheet of paper towards him and began to write.

Dear Nick,

It's some time since we met, and you'll wonder why the devil I'm writing. A friend of yours had just called on us: Abel Pomeroy of the Plume of Feathers, Ottercombe. He's in a state of injury and fury, and is determined to get to the bottom of the Luke Watchman business. I tried to fob him off with fair words, but it wasn't a howling success and he's gone away with every intention of making things hum, until you lug a murderer home to justice. I thought I'd just warn you but you'll probably hear from him before this reaches you. Don't, for the love of Mike, think we want to butt in. How are you? I envy you your job, infuriated innkeepers and all. In this weather we suffocate at C.I.

Yours ever,
RODERICK ALLEYN.

Alleyn sealed and stamped this letter. He took his hat and stick from the wall, put on one glove, pulled it off again, cursed, and went to consult the newspaper files for the reports on the death of Luke Watchman.

An hour passed. It is significant that when he finally left the Yard and walked rapidly down the Embankment, his lips were pursed in a soundless whistle.

CHAPTER EIGHT

Alleyn at Illington

i

Superintendent Nicholas Harper to Chief Detective-Inspector Alleyn:—

Illington Police Station
South Devon
August 8th

Dear Mr. Alleyn,

Yours of the 6th inst. to hand for which I thank you. As regards Mr. Abel Pomeroy I am very grateful for information received as per your letter as it enabled me to deal with Pomeroy more effectively, knowing the action he had taken as regards visiting C.I. For your private information we are working on the case which presents one or two features which seem to preclude possibility of accident. Well, Mr. Alleyn—Rory, if you will pardon the liberty—it was nice to hear from you. I have not forgotten that arson case in '37 nor the old days in L. Division. A country Super gets a bit out of things.

With kind regards and many thanks.

Yours faithfully,
N. W. Harper
(Superintendent)

Part of a letter from Colonel the Honourable Maxwell Brammington, Chief Constable of South Devon, to the Superintendent of the Central Branch of New Scotland Yard:—

. . . And on the score of the deceased's interests and activities being centred in London, I have suggested to Superintendent Harper that he consult you. In my opinion the case is somewhat beyond the resources and experience of our local force. Without wishing for a moment to exceed my prerogative in this matter, I venture to suggest that as we are already acquainted with Chief Detective-Inspector Alleyn of C.I., we should be delighted if he was appointed to this case. That, however, is of course entirely for you to decide.

I am,
Yours faithfully,
MAXWELL BRAMMINGTON, C.C.

"Well, Mr. Alleyn," said the Superintendent of C.I., staring at the horseshoe and crossed swords that garnished the walls of his room, "you seem to be popular in South Devon."

"It must be a case, sir," said Alleyn, "of sticking to the ills they know."

"Think so? Well, I'll have a word with the A.C. You'd better pack your bag and tell your wife."

"Certainly, sir."

"You knew Watchman, didn't you?"

"Slightly, sir. I've had all the fun of being turned inside out by him in the witness-box."

"In the Davidson case?"

"And several others."

"I seem to remember you were equal to him. But didn't you know him personally?"

"Slightly."

"He was a brilliant counsel."

"He was, indeed."

"Well, watch your step and do us proud."

"Yes, sir."

"Taking Fox?"

"If I may."

"That's all right. We'll hear from you."

Alleyn returned to his room, collected his emergency suitcase and kit, and sent for Fox.

"Br'er Fox," he said, "this is a wish-fulfillment. Get your fancy pyjamas and your tooth-brush. We catch the midday train for South Devon."

ii

The branch-line from Exeter to Illington meanders amiably towards the coast. From the train windows, Alleyn and Fox looked down on sunken lanes, on thatched roofs, and on glossy hedgerows that presented millions of tiny mirrors to the afternoon sun. Alleyn let down the window, and the scent of hot grass and leaves drifted into the stuffy carriage.

"Nearly there, Br'er Fox. That's Illington church-spire over the hill, and there's the glint of sea beyond."

"Very pleasant," said Fox, dabbing at his enormous face with his handkerchief. "Warm, though."

"High summer, out there."

"You never seem to show the heat, Mr. Alleyn. Now I'm a warm man. I perspire very freely. Always have. It's not an agreeable habit, though they tell me it's healthy."

"Yes, Fox."

"I'll get the things down, sir."

The train changed its pace from slow to extremely slow. Beyond the window, a main road turned into a short-lived main street, with a brief network of surrounding shops. The word "Illington" appeared in white stones on a grassy bank, and they drew into the station.

"There's the Super," said Fox. "Very civil."

Superintendent Harper shook hands at some length. Alleyn, once as touchy as a cat, had long ago accustomed himself to official hand-clasps. And he liked Harper who was bald, scarlet-faced, blue-eyed, and sardonic.

"Glad to see you, Mr. Alleyn," said Harper. "Good afternoon. Good afternoon, Mr. Fox. I've got a car outside."

He drove them in a police Ford down the main street. They passed a Woolworth store, a departmental store, a large hotel, and a row of small shops amongst which Alleyn noticed one labelled "Bernard Noggins, Chemist."

"Is that where Parish bought the cyanide?"

"You haven't lost any time, Mr. Alleyn," said Harper, who seemed to hover on the edge of Alleyn's Christian name and to funk it at the last second. "Yes, that's it. He's a very stupid sort of man, is Bernie Noggins. There's the station. The colonel will be along presently. He's in a shocking mood over this affair, but you may be able to cope with him. I thought that before we moved on to Ottercombe, you might like to see the files and have a tell," said Harper, whose speech still held a tang of West Country.

"Splendid. Where are we to stay?"

"That's as you like, of course, Mr. Alleyn, but I've told that old blatherskite Pomeroy to hold himself in readiness. I thought you might prefer to be on the spot. I've warned him to say nothing about it and I think he'll have the sense to hold his tongue. No need to put anybody on the alert, is there? This car's at your service."

"Yes, but look here—"

"It's quite all right, Mr. Alleyn. I've a small two-seater we can use here."

"That sounds perfectly splendid," said Alleyn, and followed Harper into the police station.

They sat down in Harper's office, while he got out his files. Alleyn looked at the photographs of past Superintendents, at the worn linoleum and varnished woodwork, and he wondered how many times he had sat in country police stations waiting for the opening gambit of a case that, for one reason or another, had been a little too much for the local staff. Alleyn was the youngest chief-inspector at the Central Branch of New Scotland Yard, but he was forty-three. "I'm getting on," he thought without regret. "Old Fox must be fifty, he's getting quite grey. We've done all this so many times together." And he heard his own voice as if it was the voice of another man, uttering the familiar phrases.

"I hope we won't be a nuisance to you, Nick. A case of this sort's always a bit tiresome, isn't it? Local feeling and so on."

Harper clapped a file down on his desk, threw his head back and looked at Alleyn from under his spectacles.

"Local feeling?" he said. "Local stupidity! I don't care. They work it out for themselves and get a new version every day. Old Pomeroy's not the worst, not by a long chalk. The man's got something to complain about, or thinks he has. It's these other experts, George Nark & Co., that make all the trouble. Nark's written three letters to the *Illington Courier*. The first was about fingerprinting. He called it 'the Bertillion system,' of course, ignorant old ass, and wanted to know if we'd printed everyone who was there, when Watchman died. So I got him round here and printed him. So he wrote another letter to the paper about the liberty of the subject and said the South Devon Constabulary were a lot of Hitlers. Then Oates, the Coombe P. C., found him crawling about outside Pomeroy's garage with a magnifying glass, and kicked him out. So he wrote another letter, saying the police were corrupt. Then the editor, who ought to know better, wrote a damn-fool leader and then three more letters about me appeared. They were signed 'Vigilant,' 'Drowsy,' and 'Moribund.' Then all the pressmen who'd gone away, came back again. I don't care. What of it? But the C.C. began ringing me up three times a day and I got fed up and suggested he ask you, and he jumped at it. There's the file."

Alleyn and Fox hastened to make sympathetic noises.

"Before we see the file," Alleyn said, "we'd very much like to hear your own views. We've looked up the report on the inquest so we've got the main outline or ought to have it."

"My views?" repeated Mr. Harper moodily. "I haven't got any. I don't think it was an accident."

"Don't you, now?"

"I don't see how it could have been. I suppose old Pomeroy bleated about his injuries when he went screeching up to the Yard. I think he's right. 'Far as I can see, the old man did take reasonable precautions. Well, perhaps not that, the stuff ought never to have been left on the premises. But I don't see how, twenty-four hours after he'd stowed the bottle away in the cupboard, he could have infected that dart accidentally. We've printed the cupboard. It's got his prints on it and nobody's else's."

"Oh," said Alleyn, "then it isn't a case of somebody else having tampered with the bottle and been too scared to own up."

"No."

"How many sets of Pomeroy's prints are on the cupboard door?"

"Several. Four good ones on the knob. And he turned the key in the top cupboard when he put the cyanide away. His print's on the key all right and you can't do the pencil trick, for I've tried. It's a fair teaser."

"Any prints on the bottle?"

"None. But he explained he wore gloves and wiped the bottle."

"The cupboard door's interesting."

"Is it? Well, when he opened the parcel of darts he broke the seals. I got hold of the wrapping and string. The string had only been tied once and the seals have got the shop's mark on them."

"Damn good, Nick," said Alleyn. Mr. Harper looked a little less jaundiced.

"Well, it goes to show," he admitted, "the dart was O.K. when old Pomeroy unpacked it. Then young Will and Parish handled the darts, and then Legge tried them out. Next thing—one of 'em sticks into deceased's finger and in five minutes he's a corpse."

"The inference being . . . ?"

"God knows! They found cyanide on the dart, but how the hell it got there's a masterpiece. I suppose old Pomeroy's talked Legge to you."

"Yes."

"Yes. Well, Legge had his coat off and his sleeves rolled up. Cubitt and young Pomeroy swear he took the darts with his left hand and held them point outward in a bunch while he tried them. They say he didn't wait any time at all. Just threw them into the board, said they were all right and then waded in with his trick. You see, they were all watching Legge."

"Yes."

"What about the other five, Super?" asked Fox. "He used six for the trick, didn't he?"

"Meaning one of them might have contrived to smear cyanide on one dart, while they looked at the lot?"

"It doesn't make any sort of sense," said Alleyn. "How was Cubitt or young Pomeroy to know Legge was going to pink Watchman?"

"That's right," agreed Harper, relapsing. "So it must be Legge but it couldn't be Legge; so it must be accident but it couldn't be accident. Funny, isn't it?"

"Screamingly."

"The iodine bottle's all right and so's the brandy bottle."

"The brandy glass was broken?"

"Smashed to powder, except the bottom, and that was in about thirty pieces. They couldn't find any cyanide."

"Whereabouts on the dart was the trace of cyanide?"

"On the top and halfway up the steel point. We've printed the dart, of course. It's got Legge's prints all over it. They've covered Abel's or anybody else's who touched it, except Oates, and he kept his head and only handled it by the flight. The analyst's report is here. And all the exhibits."

"Yes. Have you fished up a motive?"

"The money goes to Parish and Cubitt. Two thirds to Parish and one third to Cubitt. That's excepting one or two small legacies. Parish is the next-of-kin. It's a big estate. The lawyer was so close as an oyster, but I've found out it ought to wash up at something like fifty thousand. We don't know much beyond what everybody knows. Reckon most folks have seen Sebastian Parish on the screen, and Mr. Cubitt seems to be a well-known artist. The C.C. expects the Yard to tackle that end of the stick."

"Thoughtful of him! Anyone else?"

"They've found a bit already. They've found Parish's affairs are in a muddle and he's been to the Jews. Cubitt had money in that Chain Stores Unlimited thing, that bust the other day. There's motive there, all right."

"Anyone else? Pomeroy's fancy? The mysterious Legge?"

"Him? Motive? You've heard Pomeroy, Mr. Alleyn. Says deceased behaved peculiar to Legge. Chaffed him, like. Well, what is there in that? It seems there was a bit of a collision between them, the day Mr. Watchman drove into the Coombe. Day before the fatality that was. Legge's a bad driver, anyway. Likely enough, Mr. Watchman felt kind of irritated, and let Legge know all about it when they met again. Likely, Legge's views irritated Mr. Watchman."

"His views?"

"He's an out-and-out communist is Legge. Secretary and Treasurer of the Coombe Left Movement and in with young Will and Miss Moore. Mr. Watchman seems to have made a bit of a laughing-stock of the man, but you don't do murder because you've been made to look silly."

"Not very often, I should think. Do you know anything about Legge? He's a newcomer, isn't he?"

Harper unhooked his spectacles and laid them on his desk.

"Yes," he said, "he's foreign to these parts. We've followed up the usual routine, Mr. Alleyn, but we haven't found much. He says he came here for his health. He's opened a small banking account at Illington, three hundred and fifty pounds. He came to the Feathers ten months ago. He gets a big lot of letters, and writes a lot to all parts of the West Country, and sends away a number of small packages. Seems he's agent for some stamp collecting affair. I got the name, 'Phillips Philatelic Society,' and got one of our chaps to look up the headquarters in London. Sure enough, this chap Legge's the forwarding agent for the west of England. Well, he chummed up with young Will, and about three months ago they gave him this job with the Coombe Left business. I don't mind saying I don't like the looks of the man. He's a funny chap. Unhealthy, I'd say. Something the matter with his ears. We've searched all their rooms and I found a chemist's bottle and a bit of a squirt in his. Had it tested, you bet, but it's only some muck he squirts into his beastly lug. So I returned it. Cubitt's room was full of painting gear. We found oil, and turpentine and varnish. Went through the lot. Of course we didn't expect to find anything. Parish," said Harper in disgust, "uses scent.

Well, not to say scent, but some sort of toilet water. No, I don't mind saying I don't like the looks of Legge, but there again, Miss Moore says Mr. Watchman told her he'd never set eyes on the man before."

"Well," said Alleyn, "let's go through the list while we're at it. What about young Pomeroy?"

"Will? Yes. Yes, there's young Will." Harper opened the file and stared at the first page, but it seemed to Alleyn that he was not reading it. "Will Pomeroy," said Harper, "says he didn't like Mr. Watchman. He makes no bones about it. Mr. Parish says they quarrelled on account of this chap, Legge. Will didn't like the way Mr. Watchman got at Legge, you see, and being a hotheaded loyalish kind of fellow, he tackled Mr. Watchman. It wasn't much of an argument, but it was obvious Will Pomeroy had taken a scunner on Mr. Watchman."

"And—what is the lady's name?—Miss Decima Moore? What about her?"

"Nothing. Keeps company with Will. She's a farmer's daughter. Old Jim Moore, up to Cary Edge. Her mother's a bit on the classy side. Foreigner to these parts and can't forget she came down in society when she married Farmer Moore. Miss Decima was educated at Oxford and came home a red Leftist. She and deceased used to argufy a bit about politics, but that's all."

Alleyn counted on his long, thin fingers.

"That's five," he said, "six, counting old Pomeroy. We're left with the Honourable Violet Darragh and Mr. George Nark."

"You can forget 'em," rejoined Harper. "The Honourable Violet's a rum old girl from Ireland, who takes views in paints. She was there writing letters when it happened. I've checked up on her and she's the genuine article. She'll talk the hind leg off a donkey. So'll George Nark. He's no murderer. He's too damned silly to kill a wood-louse except he treads on it accidental."

"How many of these people are still in Ottercombe?"

"All of 'em."

"Good Lord!" Alleyn exclaimed. "Didn't they want to get away when it was all over? I'd have thought—"

"So would anybody," agreed Harper. "But it seems Mr. Cubitt had started off on several pictures down there, and wants to finish them. One's a likeness of Mr. Parish, so he's stayed down-along too. They waited for the funeral, which was here. Deceased had no relatives nearer than Mr. Parish, and Mr. Parish said he thought his cousin would have liked to be put away in the country. Several legal gentlemen came down from London, and the flowers were a masterpiece. Well, they just stopped on, Mr. Cubitt painting as quiet as you please. He's a cool customer, is Mr. Cubitt."

"How much longer will they be here?"

"Reckon another week. They came for three. Did the same thing last year. It's a fortnight to-night since this case cropped up. We've kept the private bar shut up. Everything was photographed and printed. There was nothing of interest in the deceased's pockets. He smoked some outlandish kind of cigarettes. Daha—something, but that's no use. We've got his movements taped out. Arrived on Thursday night and didn't go out. Friday morning, went for a walk but don't know exactly where, except it was through the tunnel. Friday afternoon, went upstairs after lunch and was in his room writing letters. Seen in his room by Mrs. Ives, the housekeeper, who went up at 3.30 to shut windows and found him asleep on his bed. Also seen at 4 o'clock by Mr. Cubitt, who looked in on his way back from painting down on the wharf. Came downstairs at 5.15, or thereabouts, and was in the private bar from then onwards till he died. I don't think I missed anything."

"I'm sure you didn't."

"You know," said Harper, warming a little, "it's a proper mystery, this case. Know-what-I-mean, most cases depend on routine. Boil 'em down and it's routine that does the trick as a general rule. May do it here, but all the same this is a teaser. I'm satisfied it wasn't accident but I can't prove it. When I'm told on good authority that there was cyanide on that dart, and that Mr. Watchman died of cyanide in his blood, I say: 'Well, there's your weapon,' but alongside of this there's six people, let alone my own investigation, that prove to my satisfaction nobody could have tampered with the dart. But the dart was poisoned. Now, the stuff in the rat-hole was in a little china jar. I've left it there for you to see. I got another jar of the same brand. They sell some sort of zinc ointment in them, and Abel had several; he's mad on that sort of thing. Now, the amount that's gone from the bottle, which Noggins says was full, is a quarter of an ounce more than the amount the jar holds and Abel swears he filled the jar. The jar was full when we saw it."

"Full?" said Alleyn sharply. "When did you see it?"

"The next morning."

"Was the stuff in the jar analyzed?"

Harper turned brick-red.

"No," he said, "Abel swore he'd filled it and the jar's only got his prints on it. And, I tell you, it *was* full."

"Have you got the stuff?"

"Yes. I poured it off and kept it. Seeing there's a shortage, the stuff on the dart must have come from the bottle."

"For how long was the bottle uncorked?"

"What? Oh, he said that when he used it he uncorked the bottle and put it on the shelf above the hole, with the cork beside it. He was very anxious we should know he'd been careful, and he said he didn't want to handle the cork more than was necessary. He said he was just going to pour the stuff in the jar, when he thought he'd put the jar in position first. He did that and then filled it, holding the torch in his other hand. He swears he didn't spill any, and he swears nobody touched the bottle. The others were standing in the doorway."

"So the bottle may have been uncorked for a minute or two?"

"I suppose so. He plugged up the hole with rag, before he did anything else. He had the bottle on the floor beside him."

"And then?"

"Well, then he took up the bottle and corked it. I suppose," said Harper, "I should have had the stuff analyzed, but we've no call to suspect Abel Pomeroy. There was none missing from the jar and there are only his prints on it, and there's the extra quarter-ounce missing from the bottle. No, it's gone from the bottle. Must have. And, see here, Mr. Alleyn, the stuff was found on the dart and nowhere else. What's more, if it was the dart that did the trick, and it's murder, then Legge's our bird, because only Legge controlled the flight of the dart."

"Silly sort of way to kill a man," said Fox, suddenly. "It'd be asking for a conviction. Super, now wouldn't it?"

"Maybe he reckoned he'd get a chance to wipe the dart," said Harper.

"He had his chance," said Alleyn, quickly. "Wasn't it brought out that Legge helped the constable—Oates, isn't it?—to find the dart? He had his chance, then, to wipe it."

"And if he was guilty, why didn't he?" ended Fox.

"You're asking *me*," said Superintendent Harper. "Here's the Colonel."

iii

The Chief Constable was an old acquaintance of Alleyn's. Alleyn liked Colonel Brammington. He was a character, an oddity, full of mannerisms that amused rather than irritated Alleyn. He was so unlike the usual country-minded chief constable, that it was a matter for conjecture how he ever got the appointment for he spent half his life in giving offence and was amazingly indiscreet. He arrived at Illington Police Station in a powerful racing-car that was as scarred as a veteran. It could be heard from the moment it entered the street and Harper exclaimed agitatedly:

"Here he comes! He knows that engine's an offence with the meaning of the Act and he doesn't care. He'll get us all into trouble one of these days. There are complaints on all sides. On all sides!"

The screech of heavy tyres and violent braking announced Colonel Brammington's arrival and in a moment he came in. He was a vast red man with untidy hair, prominent eyes, and a loud voice. The state of his clothes suggested that he'd been dragged by the heels through some major disaster.

He shouted an apology at Harper, touched Alleyn's hand as if it was a bomb, stared at Fox, and then hurled himself into a seagrass chair with such abandon that he was like to break it.

"I should have been here half an hour ago," shouted Colonel Brammington, "but for my car, my detestable, my abominable car."

"What was the matter, sir?" asked Harper.

"My good Harper, I have no notion. Fortunately I was becalmed near a garage. The fellow thrust his head among her smoking entrails, uttered some mumbojumbo, performed suitable rites with oil and water, and I was enabled to continue."

He twisted his bulk in the creaking chair and stared at Alleyn.

"Perfectly splendid that you have responded with such magnificent celerity to our *cri du coeur*, Alleyn. We shall now resume, thankfully, the upholstered leisure of the not-too-front front stall."

"Don't be too sure of that, sir," said Alleyn. "It looks as if there's a weary grind ahead of us."

"Oh God, how insupportably dreary! What, hasn't the solution been borne in upon you in a single penetrating flash? Pray expect no help from me. Have you got a cigarette, Harper?"

Alleyn offered his case.

"Thank you. I haven't even a match, I'm afraid. Ah, thank you." Colonel Brammington lit his cigarette and goggled at Alleyn. "I suppose Harper's given you the whole tedious rigmarole," he said.

"He's given me the file. I suggest that Fox and I take it with us to Ottercombe and digest it."

"Oh Lord! Yes, do. Yes, of course. But you've discussed the case?"

"Yes, sir. Mr. Harper has given me an excellent survey of the country."

"It's damned difficult country. Now, on the face of it, what's your opinion; accident or not?"

"On the face of it," said Alleyn, "not."

"Oh Lord!" repeated Colonel Brammington. He got up, with surprising agility, from his tortured chair and moved restlessly about the room. "Yes," he said, "I agree with you. The fellow was murdered. And of all the damned unconscionable methods of despatching a man! An envenom'd stick, by God! How will you hunt it home to this fellow?"

"Which fellow, sir?"

"The murderer, my dear man. Legge! A prating, soap-box-orator of a fellow, I understand—some squalid little trouble-hatcher. Good God, my little Alleyn, of course he's your man! I've said so from the beginning. There was cyanide on the dart. He threw the dart. He deliberately pinked his victim."

"Harper," said Alleyn, with a glance at the superintendent's shocked countenance, "tells me that several of the others agree that Legge had no opportunity to anoint the dart, with cyanide or anything else."

"Drunk!" cried Colonel Brammington. "Soaked in a damn' good brandy, the lot of 'em. My opinion."

"It's possible, of course."

"It's the only answer. My advice, for what it's worth, is, haul him in for manslaughter. Ought to have been done at first, only that drooling old pedagogue Mordant didn't put it to the jury. However, you must do as you think best."

"Thank you, sir," said Alleyn gravely. Brammington grinned.

"The very pineapple of politeness," he quoted. "Come and dine with me to-morrow. Both of you."

"May I ring up?"

"Yes, yes," said Colonel Brammington impatiently. "Certainly."

He hurried to the door as if overcome by an intolerable urge to move on somewhere. In the doorway he turned.

"You'll come round to my view," he said, "I'll be bound you will."

"At the moment, sir," said Alleyn, "I have no view of my own."

"Run him in on the minor charge," added Colonel Brammington, raising his voice to a penetrating shout as he disappeared into the street, "and the major charge will follow as the night the day."

A door slammed and in a moment the violence of his engines was reawakened.

"Well, now," said Alleyn. "I wonder."

CHAPTER NINE

Alleyn at the Feathers

i

THE SUN had nearly set when Alleyn and Fox drove down Ottercombe Road towards the tunnel. As the car mounted a last rise they could see Coombe Road, a quarter of a mile away across open hills. So clear was the evening that they caught a glint of gold where the surf broke into jets of foam against the sunny rocks. Alleyn slowed down and they saw the road sign at the tunnel entrance.

"Ottercombe. Dangerous corner. Change down."

"So I should think," muttered Alleyn, as the sheer drop appeared on the far side. He negotiated the corner and there, at the bottom of the steep descent, was the Plume of Feathers and Ottercombe.

"By George," said Alleyn, "I don't wonder Cubitt comes here to paint. It's really charming, Fox, isn't it? A concentric design, with the pub as its axis. And there, I fancy, is our friend Pomeroy."

"On the look-out, seemingly," said Fox.

"Yes. Look at the colour of the sea, you old devil. Smell that jetty-tar-and-iodine smell, blast your eyes. Fox, murder or no murder, I'm glad we came."

"So long as you're pleased, sir," said Fox, drily.

"Don't snub my ecstasies, Br'er Fox. Good evening, Mr. Pomeroy."

Abel hurried forward and opened the door.

"Good evening, Mr. Alleyn, sir. We'm glad to see you. Welcome to the Feathers, sir."

He used the same gestures, almost the same words, as those with which he had greeted Watchman, fourteen days ago. And Alleyn, if he had realized it, answered as Watchman had answered.

"We're glad to get here," he said.

"Will!" shouted old Abel. "Will!"

And Will, tall, fox-coloured, his eyes screwed up in the sunlight, came out and opened the back of the car. He was followed by a man whom Alleyn recognized instantly. He was nearly as striking off the stage as on it. The walk was unmistakable; the left shoulder raised very slightly, the long graceful stride, imitated with more ardour than discretion by half the young actors in London.

The newcomer glanced at Alleyn and Fox, and walked past the car.

"Another marvellous evening, Mr. Pomeroy," he said airily.

"So 'tis, then, Mr. Parish," said Abel.

Alleyn and Fox followed Will Pomeroy into the Feathers. Abel brought up the rear.

"Show the rooms, sonny. These are the gentlemen we're expecting. They're from London. From Scotland Yard," said Abel.

Will Pomeroy gave them a startled glance.

"Move along, sonny," said Abel. "This way, sir. Us'll keep parlour for your private use, Mr. Alleyn, in case so be you fancy a bit of an office like."

"That sounds an excellent arrangement," said Alleyn.

"Have you had supper, sir?"

"Yes, thank you, Mr. Pomeroy. We had it with Mr. Harper."

"I wonder," said Abel, unexpectedly, "that it didn't turn your stomachs back on you, then."

"This way, please," said Will.

They followed Will up the steep staircase. Abel stood in the hall, looking after them.

The Feathers, like all old buildings, had its own smell. It smelt of wallpaper, driftwood smoke, and very slightly of beer. Through the door came the tang of the water-front to mix with the house-smell. The general impression was of coolness and seclusion. Will showed them two small bedrooms whose windows looked over Ottercombe Steps and the chimney-tops of Fish Lane, to the sea. Alleyn took the first of these rooms and Fox, the second.

"The bathroom's at the end of the passage," said Will, from Alleyn's doorway. "Will that be all?"

"We shall be very comfortable," said Alleyn, and as Will moved away, he added: "You're Mr. Pomeroy's son?"

"Yes," said Will, stolidly.

"I expect Mr. Harper has explained why we are here."

Will nodded and said nothing.

"I'd be very glad," added Alleyn, "if you could spare me a minute or two, later on."

Will said: "I'll be serving in the bar all the evening."

"I'll see you there, then. Thank you."

But Will didn't move. He stared at the window and said: "This affair's upset my father. He takes it to heart, like; the talk that goes on."

"I know."

"I reckon he's right about it being no accident."

"Do you?"

"Yes. Nobody touched the bottle by mistake—'tisn't likely."

"Look here," said Alleyn, "can you spare a moment, now, to show me the rat-hole in the garage?"

Will's eyelashes flickered.

"Yes," he said, "reckon I can do that." He shifted his weight from one foot to the other, and added with a kind of truculence: "Reckon when the police come in, there's not much use in refusing. Not unless you've got a pull somewhere."

"Oh, come," Alleyn said mildly, "we're not as corrupt as all that, you know."

Will's face turned scarlet but he said doggedly: "It's not the men, it's the system. It's the way everything is in this country."

"One law," suggested Alleyn, amiably, "for the rich, and so on?"

"It's true enough."

"Well, yes. In many ways, I suppose it is. However, I'm not open to any bribery at the moment. We always try to be honest for the first few days, it engenders confidence. Shall we go down to the garage?"

"It's easy enough," Will said, "to make the truth look silly. A man never seems more foolish-like than he does when he's speaking his whole mind and heart. I know that."

"Yes," agreed Alleyn, "that's quite true. I dare say the apostles were as embarrassing in their day, as the street-orator, with no audience, is in ours."

"I don't know anything about that. They were only setting up a superstition. I'm dealing with the sober truth."

"That's what I hope to do myself," said Alleyn. "Shall we join the rats?"

Will led Alleyn across the yard to the old stables. A small evening breeze came in from the sea, lifting Alleyn's hair and striking chill through his tweed coat. Gulls circled overhead. The sound of men's voices drifted up from the waterfront.

"It'll be dark in-along," said Will.

"I've got a torch."

"The rat-hole's not in the proper garage, like. It's in one of the loose-boxes. It's locked and we haven't got the key. Harper's men did that."

"Mr. Harper gave me the key," said Alleyn.

The old loose-box had been padlocked, and sealed with police tape. Alleyn broke the tape and unlocked it.

"I wonder," he said, "if you'd mind asking Mr. Fox to join me. He's got a second torch. Ask him to bring my case."

"Yes," said Will, and after a fractional pause, "sir."

Alleyn went into the stable. It had been used as an extra garage but there was no car in it now. Above the faint reek of petrol oozed another more disagreeable smell, sweetish and nauseating. The cyanide, thought Alleyn, had evidently despatched at least one rat. The place was separated from the garage-proper, an old coach-house, by a semi-partition; but the space between the top of the partition and the roof had recently been boarded up, and Alleyn awarded Harper a good mark for attention to detail. Harper, he knew, had also taken photographs of the rat-hole and tested the surrounding walls and floor for prints. He had found dozens of these.

Alleyn flashed his torch round the bottom of the walls and discovered the rat-hole. He stooped down. Harper had removed the rag and jar, tested them for prints, and found Abel's. He had then drained off the contents of the jar and replaced it. There was the original rag, stuffed tight in the hole. Alleyn pulled it and the smell of dead rat became very strong indeed. The ray of light glinted on a small jar. It was less than an inch in diameter and about half an inch deep.

Fox loomed up in the doorway. He said:

"Thank you, Mr. Pomeroy, I'll find my way in."

Will Pomeroy's boots retreated across the cobblestones.

"Look here, Br'er Fox," said Alleyn.

A second circle of light flickered on the little vessel. Fox peered over Alleyn's shoulder.

"And it was full," said Fox.

"Yes," said Alleyn. "That settles it, I fancy."

"How d'you mean, sir?"

"It's a case of murder."

ii

The parlour of the Feathers is the only room in the house that is generally uninhabited. For the usual patrons, the private tap is the common room. The parlour is across the side passage and opposite the public tap-room. It overlooks Ottercombe Steps, and beneath its windows are the roofs of the Fish Lane houses. It has a secret and deserted life of its own. Victoria's Jubilee and Edward the Seventh's Wedding face each other across a small desert of linoleum and plush. Above the mantelpiece hangs a picture of two cylindrical and slug-like kittens. Upon the mantelpiece are three large shells. A rag-rug, lying in front of the fireplace, suggests that in a more romantic age Harlequin visited the Feathers and slouched his skin before taking a leap up the chimney.

For Alleyn's arrival, the parlour came to life. Someone had opened the window and placed a bowl of flowers on the plush-covered table. Abel Pomeroy hurriedly added a writing pad, a pencil, a terrible old pen and a bottle of ink. He surveyed these arrangements with an anxious smile, disappeared for a minute, and returned to ask Alleyn if there was anything else he needed.

"Two pints of beer, Mr. Pomeroy," said Alleyn, "will set us up for the rest of the evening."

Abel performed a sort of slow-motion trick with his right hand, drawing away his apron to reveal a thickly cobwebbed bottle.

"I wondered, sir," he said, "if you'd pleasure me by trying a drop of this yurr tipple. 'Twurr laid down by my old Dad, many a year back. Sherry 'tis. 'Montillady. I did used to call 'er Amadillo, afore I knew better."

"But, my dear Mr. Pomeroy," said Alleyn, "this is something very extra indeed. It's wine for the gods."

"Just what the old Colonel said, sir, when I told him us had it. It would pleasure the Feathers, sir, if you would honour us."

"It's extraordinarily nice of you."

"You wurr 'straordinary nice to me, sir, when I come up to London. If you'll axcuse me, I'll get the glasses."

"It should be decanted, Mr. Pomeroy."

"So it should, then. I'll look out a decanter tomorrow, sir, and in the meanwhile, us'll open the bottle."

They opened the bottle and took a glass each.

"To the shade of Edgar Allan Poe," murmured Alleyn, and raised his glass.

"The rest is yours, gentlemen," said Abel. " 'Twill be set aside special. Thurr's a decanter in the Private. If so be you bain't afeared, same as George Nark, that all my bottles is full of pison, to-morrow I'll decant this yurr tipple in your honour."

Alleyn and Fox murmured politely.

"Be thurr anything else I can do, gentlemen?" asked Abel.

"We'll have a look at the private bar, Mr. Pomeroy, if we may."

"Certainly, sir, certainly, and terrible pleased us'll be to have her opened up again. 'Tis like having the corpse itself on the premises, with Private shuttered up and us chaps all hugger-mugger of an evening in Public. Has His Royal Highness the Duke of Muck condescended to hand over the keys, sir?"

"What? Oh—yes, I have the keys."

"Nick Harper!" said Abel, "with his fanciful blown-up fidgeting ways. Reckon the man laces his boots with red tape. This way, if you please, gentlemen, and watch yourselves for the step. 'Dallybuttons, Nick,' I said to him, 'you've aimed your camera, and blowed a thicky childish li'l squirter over every inch of my private tap, you've lain on your belly and scraped the muck off the floor. What do 'ee want?' I said. 'Do 'ee fancy the corpse will hant the place and write murderer's name in the dust?' I axed him. This is the door, sir."

Alleyn produced his bunch of keys and opened the door.

The private tap had been locked up, by Oates, a fort-night ago, and reopened by Harper and his assistants only for purposes of investigation. The shutter over the bar-counter had been drawn down and locked. The window shutters also were fastened. The place was in complete darkness.

Abel switched on the light.

It was a travesty of the private tap that Alleyn saw. The comfort and orderliness of its habitual aspect were quite gone. It had suffered such a change as might overtake a wholesome wench, turned drab in a fortnight. Dust covered the tables, settles, and stools. The butt ends of cigarettes strewed the floor, tobacco ash lay everywhere in small patches and trails. The open hearth was littered with ashes of the fire that had warmed Watchman on the night he died. Five empty tumblers were stained with the dregs of Courvoisier '87, two with the dregs of the ginger-beer. Of the eighth glass, such powdered fragments as had escaped Harper's brush crunched jarringly underfoot. The room smelt indescribably stale and second-rate.

"It do gall me uncommon," said Abel, "for my private tap-room to display itself in thicky shocking state."

"Never mind, Mr. Pomeroy," said Alleyn, "we're used to it, you know."

He stood just inside the door, with Fox at his shoulder. Abel watched them anxiously, but it is doubtful if he remarked the difference in their attitudes. Fox's eyes, light grey in colour, brightened and sharpened as he looked about the room. But Alleyn might have been a guest in the house, and with no more interest than politeness might allow his gaze shifted casually from one dust-covered surface to another.

After a few minutes, however, he could have given a neat drawing, and nice attention to detail, of the private tap-room. He noticed the relative positions of the dart board, the bar, and the settle. He paid attention to the position of the lights, and remarked that the spot, chalked on the floor by Oates, where Legge had stood when he threw the darts, was immediately under a strong lamp. He saw that there was a light switch inside the door and another by the mantelpiece. He walked over to the corner cupboard.

"Nick Harper," said Abel, "took away that-theer cursed pison bottle. He took away bits of broken glass and brandy bottle and iodine bottle. He took away the new darts, all six on 'em. All Nick Harper left behind is dirt and smell. Help yourself to either of 'em."

"Don't go just yet," said Alleyn. "We want your help, Mr. Pomeroy, if you'll give it to us."

"Ready and willing," Abel said, with emphasis. "I'm ready and willing to do all I can. By my way of thinking you two gentlemen are here to clear my name, and I be mortal set on that scheme."

"Right. Now will you tell me, as well as you can remember, where everybody stood at the moment when you poured out the second round of brandies. Can you remember? Try to call up the picture of this room as it was a fortnight ago to-night."

"I can call all it to mind right enough," said Abel, slowly. "I been calling to mind every night and a mighty number of times every night, since that ghastly moment. I was behind bar—"

"Let's have those shutters away," said Alleyn.

Fox unlocked the shutters and rolled them up. The private tap, proper, was discovered. A glass door, connecting the two bars, was locked, and through it Alleyn could see into the Public. Will Pomeroy was serving three fishermen. His shoulder was pressed against the glass door. He must have turned his head when he heard the sound of the shutters. He looked at Alleyn through his eyelashes, and then turned away.

Alleyn examined the counter in the private tap. It was stained with dregs, fourteen days old. Abel pointed to a lighter ring.

"Thurr's where brandy bottle stood," he said. " 'Ess fay, thurr's where she was, sure enough."

"Yes. Now, where were the people? You say you stood behind the bar?"

" 'Ess, and young Will was in corner 'twixt bar and dart board. Rest of 'em had just finished Round-the-Clock. Bob Legge had won. They used the old darts, and when he ran home, he put 'em back in that thurr wooden rack by board. Yurr they be. Nick Harper come over generous," said Abel, with irony, "and left us they old darts. He collared the new 'uns."

"Ah, yes," said Alleyn hurriedly. "What about the rest of the party?"

"I'm telling you, sir. Chap Legge'd won the bout. Mr. Watchman says, 'By God it's criminal, Legge. Men have been jailed for less,' he says, in his joking way. 'Come on,' he says, 'us'll have t'other half,' he says, 'and then, be George, if I don't let 'ee have a go at my hand.' He says it joking, sir; but to my mind, Mr. Watchman knew summat about Legge, and to my mind, Legge didn't like it."

Abel glanced through the glass door at Will, but Will's back was turned. The three customers gaped shamelessly at Alleyn and Fox.

"Well, now," Abel went on, lowering his voice, "Legge paid no 'tention to Mr. Watchman, 'cept to say casual-like: 'I'll do it all right, but don't try it if you feel nervous,' which wurr very wittiest manner of speech the man could think of to egg on Mr. Watchman, to set his fancy, hellbent, on doing it. 'Ess, Legge egged the man on, did Legge. That's while he was putting away old darts. Then he moved off, tantalizing, to t'other end of room. T'other ladies and gentlemen was round bar, 'cepting Miss Darragh, who was setting with her writing in inglenook. Thurr's her glass on t'old settle, sir. Stone ginger, she had, Miss Dessy, that's Miss Moore, sir, she was setting on the bar, in the corner yurr, swinging her legs. That'll be her glass on the ledge thurr. Stone ginger. The three gentlemen, they wurr alongside bar. Mr. Cubitt next Miss Dessy, then Mr. Watchman and then Mr. Parish. I 'member that, clear as daylight, along of Miss Darragh making a joke about 'em. 'Three graces,' she called 'em, being a fanciful kind of middle-aged lady."

"That leaves Mr. George Nark."

"So it does then, the silly old parrot. 'Ess. George Nark wurr setting down by table inside of door, laying down the law, as is the foolish habit of the man. Well now, I poured out the second tot beginning with Mr. Cubitt. Then Mr. Watchman and then Mr. Parish. Then George Nark brings his glass over, with his tongue hanging out, and insults t'murdered gentleman by axing for soda in this masterpiece of a tipple, having nigh-on suffercated hisself with first tot, golloping it down ferocious. No sooner does he swallow second tot that he's proper blind tipsy. 'Ess, so soused as a herring, wurr old George Nark. Lastly, sir, Mr. Watchman gets Legge's glass from mantelshelf and axes me to pour out the second tot."

"Leaving his own glass on the bar between Mr. Parish and Mr. Cubitt?"

" 'Ess. Legge wurr going to wait till after he'd done his trick. Us knows what wurr in the evil thoughts of the man. He wanted to keep his eye in so's he could stick Mr. Watchman with thicky murderous dart."

"Mr. Pomeroy," said Alleyn, "I must warn you against making statements of that sort. You might land yourself in a very pretty patch of trouble, you know. What happened next? Did you pour out Mr. Legge's brandy for him?"

" 'Ess, I did. And Mr. Watchman tuk it to him saying he'd have no refusal. Then Mr. Watchman tuk his own dram over to table by dart board. He drank 'er down slow, and then says he: 'Now for it.' "

"And had Mr. Legge been anywhere near Mr. Watchman's glass?"

Abel looked mulish. "No, sir, no. Not azacly. Not at all. He drank his over in inglenook, opposite Miss Darragh. 'Twasn't then the mischief wurr done, Mr. Alleyn."

"Well," said Alleyn, "we shall see. Now for the accident itself."

The story of those few minutes, a story that Alleyn was to hear many times before he reached the end of this case, was repeated by Abel and tallied precisely with all the other accounts in Harper's file, and with the report of the inquest.

"Very well," said Alleyn. He paused for a moment and caught sight of Will's three customers, staring with passionate interest through the glass door. He moved out of their range of vision.

"Now we come to the events that followed the injury. You fetched the iodine from that cupboard?"

"Sure enough, sir, I did."

"Will you show me what you did?"

"Certainly. Somebody—Legge 'twas, out of the depths of his hypocrisy, says, 'Put a drop of iodine on it,' he says. Right. I goes to thicky cupboard which Nick Harper has played the fool with, mucking round with his cameras and squirts of powder. I opens bottom door this way, and thurr on shelf is my first-aid box."

Alleyn and Fox looked at the cupboard. It was a double corner cabinet, with two glass doors one above the other. Abel had opened the bottom door. At the back of the shelf was a lidless tin, containing the usual first-aid equipment, and a very nice ship's decanter. Abel removed the decanter.

"I'll scald and scour 'er out," he said. "Us'll have your sherry in this yurr, gentlemen, and I'll join you to-morrow in fust drink to show there's no hanky-panky."

"We'll be delighted if you'll join us, Mr. Pomeroy, but I don't think we need feel any qualms."

"Ax George Nark," said Abel bitterly. "Have a tell with George Nark, and get your minds pisened. I'll look after your stomachs."

Alleyn said hurriedly: "And that's the first-aid equipment?"

"That's it, sir. Bottle of iodine was laying in empty slot, yurr," Abel explained. "I tuk it out and I tuk out bandage at same time."

"You should keep your first-aid box shut up, Mr. Pomeroy," said Alleyn, absently.

"Door's air-tight, sir."

Alleyn shone his torch into the cupboard. The triangular shelf, forming the roof of the lower cupboard and the floor of the top one, was made of a single piece of wood, and fitted closely.

"And the bottle of prussic acid solution was in the upper cupboard?" asked Alleyn.

" 'Ess, tight-corked. Nick Harper's taken—"

"Yes, I know. Was the upper door locked?"

"Key turned in lock, same as it be now."

"You said at the inquest that you had used the iodine earlier in the evening."

"So I had, then. Bob Legge had cut hisself with his razor. He said he wurr shaving hisself along of going to Illington. When storm came up—it wurr a terror that thurr storm—us told Legge he'd better bide home-along. I reckon that's the only thing I've got to blame myself for. Howsumdever the man came in for his pint at five o'clock, and I give him a lick of iodine and some sticking plaster."

"Are you certain, Mr. Pomeroy? It's important."

"Bible oath," said Abel. "Thurr y'are, sir. Bible oath. Ax the man hisself. I fetched out my first-aid box and give him the bottle. Ax him."

"Yes, yes. And you're certain it was at five o'clock?"

"Bob Legge," said Abel, "has been into tap for his pint *at* five o'clock every day, 'cepting Sunday, fur last ten months. Us opens at five in these parts, and when I give him the iodine I glanced at clock and opened up."

"When you put the bottle in the top cupboard on the Thursday night you wore gloves. Did you take them off before you turned the key?"

" 'Ess fay, and pitched 'em on fire. Nick Harper come down off of his high horse furr enough to let on my finger marks is on key. Don't that prove it?"

"It does, indeed," said Alleyn.

Fox, who had been completely silent, now uttered a low growl.

"Yes, Fox?" asked Alleyn.

"Nothing, Mr. Alleyn."

"Well," said Alleyn, "we've almost done. We now come to the brandy Miss Moore poured out of the Courvoisier bottle into Watchman's empty glass. Who suggested he should have brandy?"

"I'm not certain-sure, sir. I b'lieve Mr. Parish first, and then Miss Darragh, but I wouldn't swear to her."

"Would you swear that nobody had been near Mr. Watchman's glass between the time he took his second nip and the time Miss Moore gave him the brandy?"

"Not Legge," said Abel, thoughtfully. And then with that shade of reluctance with which he coloured any suggestion of Legge's innocence: "Legge wurr out in middle o'floor afore dart board. Mr. Watchman stood atween him and table wurr t'glass stood. Mr. Parish walked over to look at Mr. Watchman spreading out his fingers. All t'others stood hereabouts, behind Legge. No one else went anigh t'glass."

"And after the accident? Where was everybody then?"

"Crowded round Mr. Watchman. Will stepped out of corner. I come through under counter. Miss Darragh stood anigh us, and Dessy by Will. Legge stood staring where he wurr. Reckon Mr. Parish did be closest still to glass, but he stepped forward when Mr. Watchman flopped down on settle. I be a bit mazed-like wurr they all stood. I disremember."

"Naturally enough. Would you say anybody could have touched that glass between the moment when the dart struck and the time Miss Moore poured out the brandy?"

"I don't reckon anybody could," said Abel, but his voice slipped a half-tone and he looked profoundly uncomfortable.

"Not even Mr. Parish?"

Abel stared over Alleyn's head and out of the window. His lower lip protruded and he looked as mulish as a sulky child.

"Maybe he could," said Abel, "but he didn't."

CHAPTER TEN

The Tumbler and the Dart

i

"We may as well let him have this room," said Alleyn, when Abel had gone. "Harper's done everything possible in the way of routine."

"He's a very thorough chap, is Nick Harper."

"Yes," agreed Alleyn. "Except in the matter of the rat-hole jar. However, Fox, we'll see if we can catch him out before we let the public in. Let's prowl a bit."

They prowled for an hour. They kept the door locked and closed the bar shutters. Dim sounds of topping penetrated from the public tap-room. Alleyn had brought Harper's photographs and they compared these with the many chalk marks Harper had left behind him. A chalk mark under the settle showed where the iodine bottle had rolled. The plot of the bottle of Scheele's acid was marked in the top cupboard. The shelves of the corner cupboard were very dusty, and the trace left by the bottle showed clearly. Alleyn turned to the fireplace.

"He hasn't shifted the ashes, Br'er Fox. We may as well do that, I think."

Fox fetched a small sieve from Alleyn's case. The ashes at first yielded nothing of interest but in the last handful they found a small misshapen object which Alleyn dusted and took to the light.

"Glass," he said. "They must have had a good fire. It's melted and gone all bobbly. There's some more. Broken glass, half-melted by the fire."

"They probably make the fire up on the old ashes," said Fox. "It may have lain there through two or three fires."

"Yes, Fox. And then again, it may not. I wonder if those fragments of the brandy glass were complete. This has been a thickish piece, I should say."

"A bit of the bottom?"

"We'll have to find out. You never know. Where was the broken glass?"

The place where most of the broken glass had been found was marked on the floor.

"Oh careful, Mr. Harper!" Alleyn sighed. "But it doesn't get us much farther. I'm afraid, Fox, I'm like to get in a muddle over this. You must keep me straight. You know what an ass I can make of myself. No," as Fox looked amiably sceptical. "No, I mean it. There are at least three likely pitfalls. I wish to heaven they hadn't knocked over that glass and tramped it to smithereens."

"D'you think there was cyanide in the glass, Mr. Alleyn?"

"God bless us, Fox, I don't know. I don't know, my dear old article. How can I? But it would help a lot if we *could* know one way or the other. Finding none on those tiny pieces isn't good enough."

"At least," said Fox, "we know there was cyanide on the dart. And knowing that, sir, and ruling out accident, I must say I agree with old Pomeroy. It looks like Legge."

"But how the devil could Legge put prussic acid on the dart with eight people all watching him? He was standing under the light, too."

"He felt the points," said Fox, without conviction.

"Get along with you, Foxkins. Prussic acid is extremely volatile. Could Legge dip his fingers in the acid and then wait a couple of hours or so—with every hope of giving himself a poisoned hand? He'd have needed a bottle of the stuff about him."

"He may have had one. He may be a bit of a conjurer. Legerdemain," added Fox.

"Well—he may. We'll have to find out."

Alleyn lit a cigarette and sat down.

"Let's worry it out," he said. "May I talk? And when I go wrong, Fox, you stop me."

"It's likely then," said Fox, drily, "to be a monologue. But go ahead, sir, if you please."

Alleyn went ahead. His pleasant voice ran on and on and a kind of orderliness began to appear. The impossible, the possible, and the probable were sorted into groups, and from the kaleidoscopic jumble of evidence was formed a pattern.

"Imperfect," said Alleyn, "but at least suggestive."

"Suggestive, all right," Fox said. "And if it's correct, the case, in a funny sort of way, still hinges on the dart."

"Yes," agreed Alleyn. "The bare bodkin. The feathered quarrel and all that. Well, Fox, we've wallowed in speculation and now we'd better get on with the job. I think I hear Pomeroy senior in the public bar, so presumably Pomeroy junior is at liberty. Let's remove to the parlour."

"Shall I get hold of young Pomeroy?"

"In a minute. Ask him to bring us a couple of pints. You'd better not suggest that he join us in a drink. He doesn't like us much, and I imagine he'd refuse, which would not be the best possible beginning."

Alleyn wandered into the inglenook, knocked out his pipe on the hearthstone, and then stooped down.

"Look here, Fox."

"What's that, sir?"

"Look at this log-box."

Fox bent himself at the waist and stared into a heavy wooden box in which Abel kept his pieces of driftwood and the newspaper used for kindling. Alleyn pulled out a piece of paper and took it to the light.

"It's been wet," observed Fox.

"Very wet. Soaked. It was thrust down among the bits of wood. A little pool had lain in the pocket. Smell it."

Fox sniffed, vigorously.

"Brandy?" he asked.

"Don't know. Handle it carefully, Br'er Fox. Put it away in your room and then get Pomeroy junior."

Alleyn returned to the parlour, turned on the red-shaded lamp and settled himself behind the table.

Fox came in, followed by Will Pomeroy. Will carried two pint pots of beer. He set them down on the table.

"Thank you," said Alleyn. "Can you spare us a moment?"

"Yes."

"Sit down, won't you?"

Will hesitated awkwardly, and then chose the least comfortable chair and sat on the extreme edge. Fox took out his note-book and Will's eyes flickered. Alleyn laid three keys on the table.

"We may return these now, I think," he said. "I'm sure you'll be glad to see the Plume of Feathers set right again."

"Thanks," said Will. He stretched out his hand and took the keys.

"The point we'd like to talk about," said Alleyn, "is the possibility of the dart that injured Mr. Watchman being tainted with the stuff used for rat-poison—the acid was kept in the corner cupboard of the private tap. Now, your father—"

"I know what my father's been telling you," interrupted Will, "and I don't hold with it. My father's got a damn' crazy notion in his head."

"What notion is that?" asked Alleyn.

Will looked sharply at him, using that trick of lowering his eyelashes. He did not answer.

"Do you mean that your father's ideas about Mr. Robert Legge are crazy?"

"That's right. Father's got his knife into Bob Legge because of his views. There's no justice nor sense in what he says. I'll swear, Bible oath, Bob Legge never interfered with the dart. I'll swear it before any judge or jury in the country."

"How can you be so positive?"

"I was watching the man. I was in the corner between the dart board and the bar. I was watching him."

"All the time? From the moment the darts were unpacked until he threw them?"

"Yes," said Will, doggedly. "All the time."

"Why?"

"Eh?"

"Why did you watch him so closely?"

"Because of what the man was going to do. We all watched him."

"Suppose," said Alleyn, "that for the sake of argument I told you we knew positively that Mr. Legge, while he held the darts in his left hand, put his right hand in his pocket for a moment—"

"I'd say it was a lie. He didn't. He never put his hand in his pocket."

"What makes you so positive, Mr. Pomeroy?"

"For one thing he was in his shirt-sleeves."

"What about his waistcoat and trousers' pockets?"

"He hadn't a waistcoat. His sleeves was rolled up and I was watching his hands. They never went near his trousers' pockets. He held the darts in his left hand, and I was watching the way he felt the points, delicate-like, with the first finger of his other hand. He was saying they was right-down good darts, well made and well balanced." Will leant forward and scowled earnestly at Alleyn.

"Look 'ee here, sir," he said. "If Bob Legge meant any harm to they darts would he have talked about them so's we all looked at the damn' things? Would he, now?"

"That's a very sound argument," agreed Alleyn. "He would not."

"Well, then!"

"Right. Now the next thing he did, was to throw all six darts, one after the other, into the board. He had six, hadn't he?"

"Yes. There were six new 'uns in the packet. Usual game's only three, but he took all six for this trick."

"Exactly. Now, what did he do after he'd thrown them?"

"Said they carried beautiful. He'd thrown the lot round the centre, very pretty. Mr. Watchman pulled 'em out and looked at 'em. Then Mr. Watchman spread out his left hand on the board and held out the darts with his right. 'Fire ahead,' he says, or something like that."

Alleyn uttered a short exclamation and Will looked quickly at him.

"That wasn't brought out at the inquest," said Alleyn.

"Beg pardon? What wasn't?"

"That Mr. Watchman pulled out the darts and gave them to Mr. Legge."

"I know that, sir. I only thought of it to-day. I'd have told Mr. Harper next time I saw him."

"It's a little odd that you should not remember this until a fortnight after the event."

"Is it, then?" demanded Will. "I don't reckon it is. Us didn't think anything at the time. Ask any of the others. Ask my father. They'll remember, all right, when they think of it."

"All right," said Alleyn. "I suppose it's natural enough you should forget."

"I know what it means," said Will quickly. "I know that, right enough. Mr. Watchman handled those darts, moving them round in his hands, like. How could Bob Legge know which was which, after that?"

"Not very easily one would suppose. What next?"

"Bob took the darts and stepped back. Then he began to blaze away with 'em. He never so much as glanced at 'em, I know that. He played 'em out quick."

"Until the fourth one stuck into the finger?"

"Yes," said Will doggedly, "till then."

Alleyn was silent. Fox, note-book in hand, moved over to the window and stood looking over the roofs of Ottercombe at the sea.

"I'll tell you what it is," said Will suddenly.

"Yes?" asked Alleyn.

"I reckon the poison on those dart's a blind."

He made this announcement with an air of defiance, and seemed to expect it would bring some sort of protest from the other two. But Alleyn took it very blandly.

"Yes," he said, "that's possible, of course."

"See what I mean?" said Will eagerly. "The murderer had worked it out he'd poison Mr. Watchman. He'd worked it out he'd put the stuff in his drink, first time he got a chance. Then, when Bob Legge pricks him by accident, the murderer says to himself: 'There's a rare chance.' He's got the stuff on him. He puts it in the brandy glass and afterwards, while we're all fussing round Mr. Watchman, he smears it on the dart. The brandy glass gets smashed to pieces but they find poison on the dart. That's how I work it out. I reckon whoever did this job tried, deliberate, to fix it on Bob Legge."

Alleyn looked steadily at him.

"Can you give us anything to support this theory?"

Will hesitated. He looked from Alleyn to Fox, made as if to speak, and then seemed to change his mind.

"You understand, don't you," said Alleyn, "that I am not trying to force information. On the other hand, if you do know of anything that would give colour to the theory you have yourself advanced, it would be advisable to tell us about it."

"I know Bob Legge didn't interfere with the dart."

"After it was all over, and the constable looked for the dart, wasn't it Legge who found it?"

"Sure-ly! And that goes to show. Wouldn't he have taken his chance to wipe the dart if he'd put poison in it?"

"That's well reasoned," said Alleyn. "I think he would. But your theory involves the glass. Who had an opportunity to put prussic acid in the glass?"

Will's fair skin reddened up to the roots of his fox-coloured hair.

"I've no wish to accuse anybody," he said. "I know who's innocent and I speak up for him. There won't be many who'll do that. His politics are not the colour to make powerful friends for him when he's in trouble. I know Bob Legge's innocent, but I say nothing about the guilty."

"Now, look here," said Alleyn, amiably, "you've thought this thing out for yourself and you seem to have thought it out pretty thoroughly. You must see that we can't put a full-stop after your pronouncement on the innocence of Mr. Legge. The best way of establishing Legge's innocence is to find where the guilt lies."

"I don't know anything about that."

"Really?"

"Yes, sir," said Will. "Really."

"I see. Well, can you tell us if Mr. Legge stood anywhere near the brandy glass, before he threw the darts?"

"He was nowhere near it. Not ever. It was on the table by the board. He never went near it."

"Do you remember who stood near the table?"

Will was silent. He compressed his lips into a hard line.

"For instance," Alleyn pursued, "was Mr. Sebastian Parish anywhere near the table?"

"He might have been," said Will.

ii

"And now, Fox," said Alleyn, "we'll have a word with Mr. Sebastian Parish, if he's on the premises. I don't somehow think he'll have strayed very far. See if you can find him."

Fox went away. Alleyn took a long pull at his beer and read through the notes Fox had made during the interview with Will Pomeroy. The light outside had faded and the village had settled down for the evening. Alleyn could hear the hollow sounds made by men working with boats; the tramp of heavy boots on stone, a tranquil murmur of voices, and, more distantly, the thud of breakers. Within the house, he heard sounds of sweeping and of quick footsteps. The Pomeroys had lost no time cleaning up the private bar. In the public bar, across the passage, a single voice seemed to drone on and on as if somebody made a speech to the assembled topers. Whoever it was came to an end. A burst of conversation followed and then a sudden silence. Alleyn recognized Fox's voice. Someone answered, clearly and resonantly: "Yes, certainly."

"That's Parish," thought Alleyn.

The door from the public tap-room into the passage was opened and shut. Sebastian Parish and Fox came into the parlour.

The evening was warm and Parish was clad in shorts and a thin blue shirt. He wore these garments with such an air that the makers might well have implored him to wear their shorts and shirts, free of cost, in and out of season, for the rest of his life. His legs were olive-brown and slightly glossy, the hair on his olive-brown chest was golden brown. He looked burnished and groomed to the last inch. The hair on his head, a darker golden brown, was ruffled, for all the world as if his dresser had darted after him into the wings, and run a practised hand through his locks. There was something almost embarrassing in so generous a display of masculine beauty.

He combined in his appearance all the most admired aspects of a pukka sahib, a Greek god, and a wholesome young Englishman. Fox came after him like an anticlimax in good serviceable worsted.

"Oh, good evening, Inspector," said Parish.

"Good evening," said Alleyn. "I'm sorry to worry you."

Parish's glance said, a little too plainly: "Hullo, so you're a gentleman." He came forward, and, with an air of manly frankness, extended his hand.

"I'm very glad to do anything I can," he said.

He sat on the arm of a chair and looked earnestly from Alleyn to Fox.

"We hoped for this," he said. "I wish to God they'd called you in at once."

"The local men," Alleyn murmured, "have done very well."

"Oh, they've done what they could, poor old souls," said Parish. "No doubt they're very sound at bottom, but it's rather a long way before one strikes bottom. Considering my cousin's position I think it was obvious that the Yard should be consulted."

He looked directly at Alleyn, and said: "But I know you!"

"Do you?" said Alleyn politely. "I don't think—"

"I know you!" Parish repeated dramatically. "Wait a moment. By George, yes, of course. You're the—I've seen your picture in a book on famous trials." He turned to Fox with the air of a Prince Regent.

"What *is* his name?" demanded Parish.

"This is Mr. Alleyn, sir," said Fox, with a trace of a grin at his superior.

"Alleyn! By God, yes, of course! Alleyn!"

"Fox," said Alleyn, austerely, "be good enough to shut the door." He waited until this was done and then addressed himself to the task of removing the frills from the situation.

"Mr. Parish," Alleyn said, "we have been sent down here to make enquiries about the death of your cousin. The local superintendent has given us a very full and explicit account of the circumstances surrounding his death, but we are obliged to go over the details for ourselves."

Parish made an expressive gesture, showing them the palms of his hands. "But of course," he said.

"Yes. Well, we thought that before we went any further, we should ask to see you."

"Just a moment," interrupted Parish. "There's one thing I must know. Mr. Alleyn, was my cousin murdered?"

Alleyn looked at his hands, which were joined together on the table. After a moment's thought, he raised his eyes.

"It is impossible to give you a direct answer," he said, "but as far as we have gone, we can find no signs of accident."

"That's terrible," said Parish, and for the first time his voice sounded sincere.

"Of course something that will point to accident may yet come out."

"Good God, I hope so."

"Yes. You will understand that we want to get a very clear picture of the events leading up to the moment of the accident."

"Have you spoken to old Pomeroy?"

"Yes."

"I suppose he's talked about this fellow Legge?"

Alleyn disregarded the implication and said: "About the position of everybody when Mr. Legge threw the darts. Can you remember—"

"I've thrashed the thing out a hundred times a day. I don't remember, particularly clearly."

"Well," said Alleyn, "let's see how we get on."

Parish's account followed the Pomeroys' pretty closely, but he had obviously compared notes with all the others.

"To tell the truth," he said, "I'd had a pint of beer and two pretty stiff brandies. I don't say I've got any very clear recollection of the scene. I haven't. It seems more like a sort of nightmare than anything else."

"Can you remember where you stood immediately before Mr. Legge threw the darts?"

Alleyn saw the quick involuntary movement of those fine hands, and he thought there was rather too long a pause before Parish answered.

"I'm not very certain, I'm afraid."

"Were you, for instance, near the table that stands between the dart board and the settle?"

"I may have been. I was watching Legge."

"Try to remember. Haven't you a clear picture of Legge as he stood there ready to throw the darts?"

Parish had a very expressive face. Alleyn read in it the reflection of a memory. He went on quickly:

"Of course you have. As you say, you were watching him. Only, in the medley of confused recollections, that picture was, for a time, lost. But, as you say, you were watching him. Did he face you?"

"He—yes."

Alleyn slid a paper across the table.

"Here, you see, is a sketch plan of the private bar." Parish looked at it over his shoulder. "Now, there's the dart board, fairly close to the bar counter. Legge must have stood there. There isn't room for more than one person to stand in the corner by the bar counter, and Will Pomeroy was there. So, to face Legge, you must have been by the table."

"All right," said Parish restively. "I don't say I wasn't, you know, I only say I'm a bit hazy."

"Yes, of course, we understand that perfectly. But what I'm getting at is this. Did you see Legge take the darts after the trial throw?"

"Yes. My cousin pulled them out of the board and gave them to Legge. I remember that."

"Splendid," said Alleyn. "It's an important point and we're anxious to clear it up. Thank you. Now, standing like that, as we've agreed you were standing, you would see the whole room. Can you remember the positions of the other onlookers?"

"I remember that they were grouped behind Legge. Except Abel, who was behind the bar counter. Oh, and Will. Will was in the corner, as you've said. Yes."

"So that it would have been impossible, if any of the others came to the table, for their movement to escape your notice?"

"I suppose so. Yes, of course it would. But I can't see why it matters."

"Don't you remember," said Alleyn gently, "that Mr. Watchman's glass was on that table? The glass that was used afterwards when Miss Moore gave him the brandy?"

iii

Parish was not a rubicund man but the swift ebbing of what colour he had was sufficiently startling. Alleyn saw the pupils of his eyes dilate; his face was suddenly rather pinched.

"It was the dart that was poisoned," said Parish. "They found that out. It was the dart."

"Yes. I take it nobody went to the table?"

"I—don't think anybody—Yes, I suppose that's right."

"And after the accident?"

"How d'you mean?"

"What were your positions?"

"Luke—my cousin—collapsed on the settle. I moved up to him. I mean I stooped down to look at him. I remember I said—oh, it doesn't matter."

"We should like to hear, if we may."

"I told him to pull himself together. You see, I didn't think anything of it. He's always gone peculiar at the sight of his own blood. When we were kids, he used to faint if he scratched himself."

"Did anybody but yourself know of this peculiarity?"

"I don't know. I should think Norman knew. Norman Cubitt. He may not have known, but I rather think we've talked about it recently. I seem to remember we did."

"Mr. Parish," said Alleyn, "will you focus your memory on those few minutes after your cousin collapsed on the settle? Will you tell us everything you can remember?"

Parish got to his feet and moved restlessly about the room. Alleyn had dealt with people of the theatre before. He had learnt that their movements were habitually a little larger than life, and he knew that in many cases this staginess was the result of training and instinct, and that it was a mistake to put it down to deliberate artifice. He knew that, in forming an opinion of the emotional integrity of actors, it was almost impossible to decide whether their outward-seeming was conscious or instinctive; whether it expressed their sensibility or merely their sense of theatre. Parish moved restlessly, as though some dramatist had instructed him to do so. But he may not, thought Alleyn, know at this moment how beautifully he moves.

"I begin to see it," said Parish, suddenly. "Really it's rather as if I tried to recall a dream, and a very bad dream at that. You see, the lights kept fading and wobbling, and then one had drunk rather a lot, and then, afterwards, all that happened makes it even more confused. I am trying to think about it as a scene on the stage; a scene, I mean, of which I've had to memorize the positions."

"That's a very good idea," said Alleyn.

The door opened and a tall man with an untidy head looked in.

"I beg your pardon. Sorry!" murmured this man.

"Mr. Cubitt?" asked Alleyn. Parish had turned quickly. "Do come in, please."

Cubitt came in and put down a small canvas with its face to the wall. Parish introduced him.

"I'd be glad if you'd stay," said Alleyn. "Mr. Parish is going to try and recall for us the scene that followed the injury to Mr. Watchman's hand."

"Oh," said Cubitt, and gave a lop-sided grin. "All right. Go ahead, Seb. Sorry I cut in."

He sat on a low chair near the fireplace and wound one thin leg mysteriously round the other. "Go ahead," he repeated.

Parish, at first, seemed a little disconcerted, but he soon became fortified by his own words.

"Luke," he said, "is lying on the settle. The settle against the left-hand wall."

"Actors' left or audience's left?" asked Cubitt.

"Audience's left. I'm deliberately seeing it as a stage setting, Norman."

"So I understand."

"And Inspector Alleyn knows the room. At first nobody touches Luke. His face is very white and he looks as if he'll faint. I'm standing near his head. Legge's still out in front of the dart board. He's saying something about being sorry. I've got it now. It's strange, but thinking of it like this brings it back to me. You, Norman, and Decima, are by the bar. She's sitting on the bar in the far corner. Will has taken a step out into the room and Abel's leaning over the bar. Wait a moment. Miss Darragh is further away near the inglenook, and is sitting down. Old George Nark, blind tight, is teetering about near Miss Darragh. That's the picture."

"Go on, please," said Alleyn.

"Well, the lights waver. Sometimes it's almost dark, then the figures all show up again. Or—" Parish looked at Cubitt.

"No," said Cubitt, "that wasn't the brandy, Seb. You're quite right."

"Well, I can't go any further," said Parish petulantly. "The rest's still a filthy nightmare. Can you sort it out?"

"Please do, if you can, Mr. Cubitt," said Alleyn.

Cubitt was filling his pipe. His fingers, blunt-ended, were stained, as usual, with oil paint.

"It's as everybody described it at the inquest," he said. "I think Seb and I both had the same idea, that Watchman was simply upset at the sight of his own blood. It's true about the lights. The room seemed to—to sort of pulse with shadows. I remember Luke's right hand. It groped about his chest as if he felt for a handkerchief or something. Legge said something like: 'My God! I'm sorry, is it bad?' Something like that. And then Legge said something more. 'Look at his face! My God, it's not lockjaw, is it?' And you, Seb, said 'Not it,' and trotted out the old story about Luke's sensibilities."

"How was I to know? You make it sound—"

"Of course you weren't to know. I agreed with you, but Legge was very upset and, at the mention of lockjaw, Abel went to the cupboard and got out the iodine and a bandage. Miss Darragh came to life, and took the bandage from Abel. Abel dabbed iodine on the finger, and Luke sort of shuddered, like you do with the sting of the stuff. Miss Darragh said something about brandy. Decima Moore took the bottle off the bar and poured some into Luke's glass. His glass was on the table."

"The table by the dart board close to Mr. Parish?"

Cubitt looked up from his pipe.

"That's it," he said. "Decima gave Luke the brandy. He seemed to get worse, just about then. He had a sort of convulsion." Cubitt paused. "It was beastly," he said and his voice changed. "The glass went flying. Miss Darragh pressed forward with the bandage and then—then the lights went out."

"That's very clear," said Alleyn. "I take it that, from the time Abel Pomeroy got the iodine and bandage until Mr. Watchman died, you were all gathered round the settle?"

"Yes. We didn't really change positions, much; not Legge, or Will, or Seb here, or me. Abel and the two women came forward."

"And when the lights went up again," said Alleyn, "were the positions the same?"

"Pretty much. But—"

"Yes?"

Cubitt looked steadily at Alleyn. His pipe was gripped between his teeth. He felt in his pockets.

"There was a devil of a lot of movement while the lights were out."

CHAPTER ELEVEN

Routine

i

"WHAT SORT of movement?" asked Alleyn.

"I know what you mean," said Parish, before Cubitt could answer. "It was Luke. He must have had a sort of attack after the lights went out. It was appalling."

"I don't mean that," said Cubitt. "I know Luke made a noise. His feet beat a sort of tattoo on the settle. He flung his arms about and—he made other noises."

"For God's sake," Parish broke out, "don't talk about it like that! I don't know how you can sit there and discuss it."

"It looks as if we've got to," said Cubitt.

"I'm afraid it does," agreed Alleyn. "What other movements did you notice, beyond those made by Mr. Watchman?"

"Somebody was crawling about the floor," Cubitt said.

Parish made a gesture of impatience. "My dear old Norman," he said, " 'Crawling about the floor!' You're giving Mr. Alleyn a wrong impression. Completely wrong! I've no doubt one of us may have stooped down in the dark, knelt down, perhaps, to try and get hold of Luke."

"I don't mean that at all," said Cubitt calmly. "Someone was literally crawling about the floor. Whoever it was banged his head against my knees."

"Where were you standing?" asked Alleyn.

"By the foot of the settle. I had my back to the settle. The backs of my knees touched it."

"How d'you know it was a head?" demanded Parish. "It might have been a foot."

"I can distinguish between a foot and a head," said Cubitt, "even in the dark."

"Somebody feeling round for the brandy glass," said Parish.

"It was after the brandy glass was broken." Cubitt looked at

Alleyn. "Somebody trod on the glass soon after the lights went out. There's probably nothing in it, anyway. I've no idea at all whose head it was."

"Was it Legge's head?" demanded Parish, suddenly.

"I tell you, Seb," said Cubitt, quite mildly, "I don't know whose head it was. I merely know it was there. It simply butted against my knees and drew away quickly."

"Well, of course!" said Parish. "It was Abel."

"Why Abel?"

Parish turned to Alleyn.

"Abel dropped the bottle of iodine just before the lights went out. I remember that. He must have stooped down to try and find it."

"If it was Abel, he didn't succeed," said Alleyn. "The bottle was found under the settle, you know."

"Well, it was dark."

"So it was," agreed Alleyn. "Why did you think it might be Mr. Legge's head?"

Parish at once became very solemn. He moved to the hearthrug. He thrust his hands into the pockets of his shorts, pulled in his belly, and stuck out his jaw.

"God knows," he began, "I don't want to condemn any man, but Norman and I have talked this thing over."

"Come off it, Seb," said Cubitt. "We haven't a blessed thing against the fellow, you know. Nothing that would be of any interest to Mr. Alleyn. I'm very well aware that my own ideas are largely self-protective. I suppose you know, Mr. Alleyn, that Watchman left me some of his money."

"Yes," said Alleyn.

"Yes. It's as good a motive as any other. Better than most. I don't fancy I'm in a position to make suggestions about other people."

He said this with a sort of defiance, looking out of the window and half-smiling.

"This sort of thing," added Cubitt, "finds out the thin patches in one's honesty."

"If you can admit as much," said Alleyn, quickly, "perhaps they are not so very thin."

"Thanks," said Cubitt, drily.

"Well," began Parish, with the air of running after the conversation, "I don't altogether agree with you, Norman. I make no secret about dear old Luke leaving the rest of his money to me. In a way, it was the natural thing for him to do. I'm his next-of-kin."

"But I," said Cubitt, "am no relation at all."

"Oh, my dear old boy!" cried Parish in a hurry. "You were his best friend. Luke said so when he—" Parish stopped short.

"To revert," said Alleyn, "to Mr. Legge. You were going to talk about Mr. Legge, weren't you?"

"I was," said Parish. "I can't help what you think, Norman old boy. It seems to me that Legge's hand in this ghastly business is pretty obvious. Nobody but Legge could have known the poisoned dart would take effect. I must say I don't see that there's much mystery about it."

"And the motive?" asked Cubitt.

Alleyn said: "I understand your cousin told you that he and Mr. Legge were strangers to each other."

"I know he did," said Parish, "but I don't believe it was true. I believe Luke recognized Legge. Not at first, perhaps, but later. During that first evening in the bar. I suppose you know that Legge smashed into my cousin's car before ever he got here? That's a bit funny, too, when you come to think of it."

"What," asked Cubitt, "is the dark inference, Seb? Why was it funny? Do you suppose that Legge lurked round Diddlestock Corner in a two-seater, and that every time he heard a powerful car coming down Ottercombe Road, he hurled his baby out of cover in the hopes of ramming Luke?"

"Oh, don't be an ass. I simply mean it was a coincidence."

"About the first evening in the bar?" suggested Alleyn, who had decided that there was a certain amount to be said for allowing Parish and Cubitt plenty of rein.

"Yes. Well, I was going to tell you," said Parish. "I talked to Luke while he had his supper in the bar. He told me about this business with the cars and rather let off steam on the subject of the other driver. Well, it turned out that Legge was sitting in the settle—the—actually it was the settle where Luke—where it happened. When Luke realized Legge must have heard he went across and sort of made the *amende-honorable*, if you know what I mean. He didn't make much headway. Legge was rather stuffy and up-stage."

"Was all this while the poison-party was going on in the stable?"

"What? Yes. Yes, it was."

"So that Mr. Legge did not attend the party in the stables?"

"I suppose not. But he knew all about it. When Abel came in he warned everybody in the place about what he'd done."

Parish hesitated. "It's hard to describe," he said. "But if you'd known my cousin you'd understand. He seemed to be getting at Legge. Even you'll agree to that, Norman."

"Yes," said Cubitt. "I put it down to Luke's vanity."

"His vanity?" asked Alleyn.

"Parish doesn't agree with me," said Cubitt with a faint smile, "on the subject of Watchman's vanity. I've always considered he attached importance to being on good terms with people. It seemed to me that when Legge snubbed his advances Watchman was at first disconcerted and put out of countenance, and then definitely annoyed. They had a bet on that first night about Legge's dart-throwing and Legge won. That didn't help. Then Watchman chipped Legge about his politics and his job. Not very prettily, I thought. It was then, or about then, that the trick with the darts was first mentioned."

"By Legge," Parish pointed out.

"I know, but Luke insisted on the experiment."

"Mr. Cubitt," said Alleyn, "did you not get the impression that these two men had met before?"

Norman Cubitt rumpled his hair and scowled.

"I don't say that," he said. "I wondered. But I don't think one should attach too much importance to what Watchman said." And like Parish, he added: "If you'd ever met him you'd understand."

Alleyn did not think it necessary to say that he had met Watchman. He said: "Can you remember anything definite that seemed to point to recognition?"

"It was more the way Luke spoke than what he actually said," explained Parish. "He kept talking about Legge's job and sort of suggesting he'd done pretty well for himself. Didn't he, Norman?"

"I seem to remember a phrase about leading the people by the nose," said Cubitt, "which sounded rather offensive. And the way Luke invited Legge to play Round-the-Clock was not exactly the glass of fashion *or* the mould of form. He asked Legge if he'd ever done time."

"Oh," said Alleyn.

"But it all sounds far too solemn and significant when you haul it out and display it like this."

"Anyone would think," said Parish, "that you were trying to protect Legge. I thought it was all damned odd."

"I'm not trying to protect Legge, but I've no particular wish to make him sound like a man of mystery. 'Who is Mr. X?' As far as we know, Mr. X is a rather dreary little Soviet-fan who combines philately with communism, and is pretty nippy with the darts. And what's more, I don't see how he could have infected the dart. In fact, I'm prepared to swear he didn't. I was watching his hands. They're ugly hands and he's a clumsy mover. Have you noticed he always fumbles and drops his money when he pays for his drinks? He's certainly quite incapable of doing any sleight-of-hand stuff with prussic acid."

Alleyn looked at Fox. "That answers your question," he said.

"What question?" asked Cubitt. "Or aren't we supposed to know?"

"Fox wondered if Mr. Legge could be an expert at legerdemain," said Alleyn.

"Well, you never know. That's not impossible," said Parish. "He's might be."

"I'll stake my oath he's not," said Cubitt. "He's no more likely to have done it than you are—"

Cubitt caught his breath and, for the first time, looked profoundly uncomfortable.

"Which is absurd," he added.

Parish turned on Cubitt. His poise had gone and for a moment he looked as though he both hated Cubitt and was afraid of him.

"You seem very sure of yourself, Norman," he said. "Apparently my opinion is of no value. I won't waste any more of Mr. Alleyn's time."

"My dear old Seb—" Cubitt began.

Alleyn said: "Please, Mr. Parish! I'm sure all this business of questions that seem to have neither rhyme nor reason is tedious and exasperating to a degree. But you may be sure that we shall go as carefully as we go slowly. If there is any link between this man and your cousin I think I may promise you that we shall discover it."

"I suppose so," said Parish, not very readily. "I'm sorry if I'm unreasonable, but this thing has hit me pretty hard."

"Oh dear," thought Alleyn; "he *will* speak by the book!" And aloud he said: "Of course it has. I've nearly done for the moment. There are one or two more points. I think you looked at the new darts before they were handed to Mr. Legge."

Parish froze at that. He stood there on the dappled hearthrug and stared at Alleyn. He looked like a frightened schoolboy.

"I only picked them up and looked at them," he said. "Anyone will tell you that." And then with a sudden spurt of temper: "Damnation, you'll be saying I killed my cousin, next!"

"I wasn't going to say that," said Alleyn peacefully. "I was going to ask you to tell me who handled the darts before and after you did."

Parish opened his mouth and shut it again. When he did speak it was with a kind of impotent fury.

"If you'd said at first—you've got me all flustered."

Cubitt said: "I think I can tell you that, Alleyn. Abel unpacked the darts and laid them on the counter. Parish simply picked two or perhaps three of them up and poised them. That's right, isn't it, Seb?"

"I don't know," said Parish sullenly. "Have it your own way. *I* don't know. Why should I remember?"

"No reason in the world," said Alleyn cheerfully.

"Well," said Cubitt, "Sebastian put them down and Will Pomeroy took them up. I remember that Will turned away and held them nearer the light. He said something about the way they were made, with the weight in the brass point and not in a lead band. He said that the card flights were better than feathers. Abel fitted the darts with card flights." Cubitt hesitated and then added: "I don't suppose it's relevant but I'm prepared to say, definitely, that Parish did nothing more than pick them up and put them down."

"Thank you, Norman," said Parish. "Is that all, Mr. Alleyn?"

"My last question for the moment—did you see Miss Moore pour out the brandy for Mr. Watchman?"

Dead silence. And then Parish, wrinkling his forehead, looking half-peevish, half-frightened, said: "I didn't watch her, but you needn't go on probing into all that. Decima Moore had nothing to do with—"

"Seb," interrupted Cubitt quietly, "you would do better to answer these questions as they are put to you. Mr. Alleyn will meet Decima. He will find out for himself that, as far as this affair is concerned, she is a figure of no importance. You must see that he's got to ask about these things." He turned to Alleyn with his pleasant lop-sided grin. "I believe the word is 'routine,' " said Cubitt. "You see, I know my detective fiction."

"Routine it is," said Alleyn. "And you're perfectly correct. Routine is the very fibre of police investigation. Your novelist too has now passed the halcyon days when he could ignore routine. He reads books about Scotland Yard, he swots up police manuals. He knows that routine is deadly dull and hopelessly poor material for a thriller; so, like a wise potboiler, he compromises. He heads one chapter 'Routine,' dismisses six weeks of drudgery in as many phrases, cuts the cackle and gets to the 'osses. I wish to the Lord we could follow his lead."

"I'll be bound you do," said Cubitt. "Well, if it's any help, I didn't notice much when Decima poured out the brandy, except that she was very quick about it. She stood with the rest of us round the settle; someone suggested brandy, she said something about his glass being empty, and went to the bar for the bottle. I got the impression that she simply slopped some brandy in the glass and brought it straight to Watchman. If I may, I should like to add that she was on the best of terms with Watchman and, as far as I know, had no occasion in the world to wish him dead."

"Good God!" said Parish in a hurry, "of course not. Of course not."

"Yes," said Alleyn, "I see. Thank you so much. Now then: Mr. Parish, until the accident, stood by the table where Mr. Watchman had left his empty glass. I take it that Mr. Parish would have noticed, would have been bound to notice, if anyone came near enough to interfere with the glass. He tells me that the rest of the party were grouped behind Legge. Do you agree to that, Mr. Cubitt?"

"Yes. Except Will. Will was in the corner beyond the dart board. He couldn't have got at the glass. Nobody—" Again Cubitt caught his breath.

"Yes?"

"In my opinion," said Cubitt, "nobody touched the glass, could have touched it; either before or after Decima fetched the brandy bottle. Nobody."

"Thank you very much," said Alleyn. "That's all for the moment."

ii

"What's the time, Fox?" asked Alleyn, looking up from his notes.

"Half-past nine, sir."

"Has Legge come in yet?"

"Not yet, Mr. Alleyn," said Fox. He stooped slightly and closed the parlour door. Fox always closed doors like that, inspecting the handle gravely as if the turning of it were a delicate operation. He then straightened up and contemplated his superior.

"Legge," said Fox, advancing slowly, "is only here on sufferance as you might put it. I've just had one in the public tap. They're not opening the Private till tomorrow. So I had one in the Public."

"Did you, you old devil!"

"Yes. This chap Nark's in there and I must say he suits his name."

"In the Australian sense? A fair nark?"

"That's right, sir. I don't wonder old Pomeroy hates the man. He wipes out his pint-pot with a red cotton handkerchief before they draw his beer. To be on the safe side, so he says. And talk!"

"What's he talk about?"

"The law," said Fox, with an air of the deepest disgust. "As soon as he knew who I was, he started on it, and a lot of very foolish remarks he made. You ought to have a chat with him, Mr. Alleyn, he'd give you the pip."

"Thanks," said Alleyn. "About Legge. Why's he here on sufferance?"

Fox sat down.

"Because of old Pomeroy," he said. "Old Pomeroy thinks Legge's a murderer and wanted him to look for other lodgings, but young Pomeroy stuck to it and they let him stay on, and Will got his way. However, Legge's given notice and has found rooms in Illington. He's moving over on Monday. He seems to be very well liked among the chaps in the bar, but they're a simple lot, taking them by and large. Young Oates the Ottercombe P. C.'s in there. Very keen to see you."

"Oh. Well, I'll have to see him sooner or later. While we're waiting for Legge, why not? Bring him in."

Fox went out and returned in half a minute.

"P. C. Oates, sir," said Fox.

P. C. Oates was brick-red with excitement and as stiff as a poker from a sense of discipline. He stood inside the door with his helmet under his arm and saluted.

"Good evening, Oates," said Alleyn.

"Good evening, sir."

"Mr. Harper tells me you were on duty the night Mr. Watchman died. Are you responsible for the chalk marks in the private taproom?"

P. C. Oates looked apprehensive.

"Furr some of 'em, sir," he said. "Furr the place where we found the dart, like, and the marks on the settle, like. I used the chalk off the scoring board, sir."

"Is it your first case of this sort?"

" 'Ess, sir."

"You seem to have kept your head."

Wild visions cavorted through the brain of P. C. Oates. He saw in a flash all the keen young P. C.'s of his favourite novels and each of them, with becoming modesty, pointed out a tiny detail that had escaped the notice of his superiors. To each of them did the Man from Higher Up exclaim: "By thunder, my lad, you've got it," and upon each of them was rapid promotion visited, while Chief Constables, the Big Four, yes, the Man at the Top, himself, all told each other that young Oates was a man to be watched . . . for each of these P. C.'s was the dead spit and image of P. C. Oates himself.

"Thank you, sir," said Oates.

"I'd like to hear about your appearance on the scene," said Alleyn.

"In my own words, sir?"

"If you please, Oates," said Alleyn.

Dick Oates took a deep breath, mustered his wits, and began.

"On the night of Friday, August 2nd," he began, and paused in horror. His voice had gone into the top of his head and had turned soprano on the way. It was the voice of a squeaking stranger. He uttered a singular noise in his throat and began again.

"On the night of Friday, August 2nd, at approximately 9:16 p.m.," said Oates, in a voice of thunder, "being on duty at the time, I was proceeding up South Ottercombe Steps with the intention of completing my beat. My attention was aroused by my hearing the sound of my own name, viz. Oates, being called repeatedly from a spot on my left, namely the front door of the Plume of Feathers, public house, Abel Pomeroy, proprietor. On proceeding to the said front door, I encountered William Pomeroy. He informed me that there had been an accident. Miss Decima Moore came into the entrance from inside the building. She said 'There is no doubt about it, he is dead.' I said, to the best of my knowledge and belief, 'My Gawd, who is dead?' Miss Moore then said 'Watchman.' I then proceeded into the private tap-room."

Oates paused. Alleyn said: "Yes, Oates, that's all right, but when I said your own words I meant your own words. This is not going to be taken down and used in evidence against you. I want to hear what sort of an impression you got of it all. You see, we have already seen your formal report in the file."

" 'Ess, sir," said Oates, breathing rather hard through his nostrils.

"Very well, then. Did you get the idea that these men were tight, moderately tight, or stone-cold sober?"

"I received the impression, sir, that they had been intoxicated but were now sobered."

"All of them?"

"Well, sir, when I left the tap at nine o'clock, sir, to proceed—

to go round the beat, they was not to say drunk but bosky-eyed, like. Merry, like."

"Including Mr. Legge?"

"By all means," said Oates firmly. "Bob Legge, sir, was sozzled. Quiet-like, but muddled. Well, the man couldn't find his way to his mouth with his pipe, not with any dash, as you might say."

"He was still pretty handy with the darts, though," observed Fox.

"So he was, then, sir. But I reckon, sir, that's second nature to the man, drunk or sober. He smelt something wonderful of tipple. And after I left, sir, he had two brandies. He must have been drunk."

"But sobered by shock?" suggested Alleyn.

"That's what I reckoned, sir."

"Did you notice anything in Legge's manner or in the manner of any of the others that led you to think the thing wasn't an accident?"

Oates fixed his knees, in the classic tradition, and eased his collar.

"Legge," he said, "was rather put about. Well, sir, that's natural, he having seemingly just killed a man and got over a booze, in one throw of a dart if you want to put it fanciful. Yes, he was proper put out, was Bob Legge. White as a bogey and trimbling. Kept saying the deceased gentleman had taken tetanus. Now that," said Oates, "might of been a blind, but it looked genu-ine to me. That's Legge. There wasn't anything unusual in Abel Pomeroy. Worried, but there again, who isn't with a fresh corpse on the premises? Young Will had his eye on Miss Dessy Moore. Natural again. She's so pretty as a daisy and good as promised to Will. Staring at him, with eyes like saucers, and ready to swoon away. Kind of frightened. Bore up all right, till she'd told me how she give the deceased brandy, and then seemed, in a manner of speaking, to cave in to it, and went off with Will, scared-like and looking at him kind of bewildered. Will give me the clearest answers of the lot, sir. Kept his head, did Will."

"And the two friends?"

"Two gentlemen, sir? Mr. Parish looked scared and squeamish. Very put out, he was, and crying too, something surprising. Answered by fits and starts. Not himself at all. Mr. Cubitt, the straight-out opposite. Very white and didn't go near the body while I was there. Wouldn't look at it, I noticed. But cool and collected, and answered very sensible. It was Mr. Cubitt fetched the doctor. I got the idea he wanted to get out into the open air, like. Seemed to me, sir, that Mr. Parish kind of let hisself go and Mr. Cubitt held hisself in. Seemed to me that, likely, Mr. Cubitt was the more upset."

"Yes," said Alleyn. "I see. Go on."

"The rest, sir? I didn't see the Honourable Darragh till the morning. The Honourable Darragh, sir, behaved very sensible. Not but what she wasn't in a bit of a quiver, but being a stout lady, you noticed it more. Her cheeks jiggled something chronic when she talked about it, but she was very sensible. She's a great one for talking, sir, and it's my belief that when she got over the surprise she fair revelled in it."

"Really? And now we're left as usual with Mr. George Nark."

"Nothing but vomit and hiccough, sir. Drunk as an owl."

"I see. Well, Oates, you've given us a clear enough picture of the actors. Now for the dart. Where was the dart when you found it?"

"Legge found it, sir. I asked for it almost immediate, sir, but they was all that flustered they paid no heed to me. 'Cepting Legge who had been going on about 'Was it the dart that did it?' and 'Had he killed the man?' and 'Wasn't it lockjaw?' and 'He must have shifted his finger,' and so forth; and so soon as I asked for the dart he stooped down and peered about and then he says 'There it is!' and I saw it and he picked it up from where it had fallen. It was stained and still looked damp, sir. Blood. And I suppose, sir, the poison."

Oates paused and then said: "If I may take the liberty, sir."

"Yes, Oates?"

"They all says, sir, that Mr. Watchman threw that there dart down, sir. They say he threw it down t'other side of the table."

"Yes."

"Well now sir, *it was laying on the floor*."

"What?" exclaimed Fox.

"It was," repeated Oates, "*alaying* on the floor. I saw it. Ax Legge, he'll bear me out."

"Whereabouts?" asked Alleyn sharply.

"Behind the table, sir, like they said, and well away from where they had been standing. The table was betwixt the settle and the board."

"I see," said Alleyn. And then the wildest hopes of Dick Oates were realized. The words with which he had soothed himself to sleep, the words that he heard most often in his dearest dreams, were spoken unmistakably by the Man from Higher Up.

"By George," said Chief Detective-Inspector Alleyn, "I believe you've got it!"

CHAPTER TWELVE

Curious Behavior of Mr. Legge

i

ON THAT first night in Ottercombe, from the time Oates left them until half-past eleven, Alleyn and Fox thrashed out the case and debated a plan of action. Alleyn was now quite certain Watchman had been murdered.

"Unless there's a catch, Br'er Fox, and I can't spot it if there is. The rat-hole, the dart, the newspaper, and the general evidence ought to give us 'Who,' but we're still in the dark about 'How.' There are those bits of melted glass, now."

"I asked old Pomeroy. He says the fireplace was cleared out the day before."

"Well, we'll have to see if the experts can tell us if it's the same kind as the brandy glass. Rather, let us hope they can say definitely that it's not the same. Oh, Lord!"

He got up, stretched himself, and leant over the window-sill. The moon was out and the sleeping roofs of Ottercombe made such patterns of white and inky black as woodcut-draughtsmen love. It was a gull's eye view Alleyn had from the parlour window, a setting for a child's tale of midnight wonders. A cat was sitting on one of the crooked eaves. It stared at the moon and might have been waiting for an appointment with some small night-gowned figure that would presently lean, dreaming, from the attic window. Alleyn had a liking for old fairy tales and found himself thinking of George Macdonald and *At the Back of the North Wind*. The Coombe was very silent in the moonlight.

"All asleep," said Alleyn, "except us, and Mr. Robert Legge. I wish he'd come home to bed."

"There's a car, now," said Fox, "up by the tunnel."

It was evidently a small car and an old one. With a ramshackle clatter it drew nearer the pub and then the driver must have turned his engine off and coasted down to the garage. There followed the squeak of brakes. A door slammed tinnily. Someone dragged open the garage door.

"That's him," said Fox.

"Good," said Alleyn. "Pop into the passage, Fox, and hale him in."

Fox went out, leaving the door open. Alleyn heard slow steps plod across the yard to the side entrance. Fox said, "Good evening, sir. Is it Mr. Legge?"

A low mumble.

"Could you spare us a moment, sir? We're police officers. Chief Inspector Alleyn would be glad to have a word with you."

A pause, another mumble, and then approaching steps.

"This way, sir," said Fox, and ushered in Mr. Robert Legge.

Alleyn saw a medium-sized man who stooped a little. He saw a large head, white hair, a heavily-lined face and a pair of callused hands. Legge, blinking in the lamplight, looked a defenceless, rather pathetic figure.

"Mr. Legge?" said Alleyn. "I'm sorry to bother you so late in the evening. Won't you sit down?"

Fox moved forward a chair and, without uttering a word, Legge sat in it. He was under the lamp. Alleyn saw that his clothes, which had once been good, were darned and faded. Everything about the man seemed bleached and characterless. He looked nervously from Alleyn to Fox. His lips were not quite closed and showed his palpably false teeth.

"I expect," said Alleyn, "that you have guessed why we are here."

Legge said nothing.

"We're making enquiries about the death of Mr. Luke Watchman."

"Oh yes?" said Legge breathlessly.

"There are one or two points we would like to clear up and we hope you will be able to help us."

The extraordinarily pale eyes flickered.

"Only too pleased," murmured Legge and looked only too wretched.

"Tell me," said Alleyn, "have you formed any theory about this affair?"

"Accident."

"You think that's possible?"

Legge looked at Alleyn as if he had said something profoundly shocking.

"Possible? But of course it's possible. Dreadfully possible. Such a way to do things. They should have bought traps. The chemist should be struck off the rolls. It's a disgrace."

He lowered his voice and became conspiratorial.

"It was a terrible, virulent poison," he whispered mysteriously. "A shocking thing that they should have it here. The coroner said so."

He spoke with a very slight lisp, a mere thickening of sibilants caused, perhaps, by his false teeth.

"How do you think it got on the dart you threw into Mr. Watchman's finger?"

Legge made a gesture that disconcerted and astonished Alleyn. He raised his hand and shook a finger at Alleyn as if he gently admonished him. If his face had not spoken of terror, he would have looked faintly waggish.

"You suspect me," he said. "You shouldn't."

Alleyn was so taken aback by this old-maidish performance that for a moment he could think of nothing to say.

"You shouldn't," repeated Legge. "Because I didn't."

"The case is as wide open as the grave."

"He's dead," whispered Legge, "and buried. *I* didn't do it. I was the instrument. It's not a very pleasant thing to be the instrument of death."

"No. You should welcome any attempt to get to the bottom of the affair."

"So I would," muttered Legge eagerly, "if I thought they would get to the truth. But I'm not popular here. Not in some quarters. And that makes me nervous, Chief Inspector."

"It needn't," said Alleyn. "But we're being very unorthodox, Mr. Legge. May we have your full name and address?"

Fox opened his note-book. Legge suddenly stood up and, in an uncertain sort of fashion, came to attention.

"Robert Legge," he said rapidly, "care of the Plume of Feathers, Ottercombe, South Devon. Business address: Secretary and Treasurer the Coombe Left Movement, G.P.O., Box 119, Illington."

He sat down again.

"Thank you, sir," said Fox.

"How long have you been here, Mr. Legge?" asked Alleyn.

"Ten months. My chest is not very good. Nothing serious, you know. I needn't be nervous on *that* account. But I was in very low health altogether. Boils. Even in my ears. Very unpleasant and painful. My doctor said it would be as well to move."

"Ah, yes. From where?"

"From Liverpool. I was in Liverpool. In Flattery Street, South, Number 17. Not a very healthy part."

"That was your permanent address?"

"Yes. I had been there for some little time. I had one or two secretaryships. For a time I was in vacuums."

"What?"

"In vacuum cleaners. But that did not altogether agree with my chest. I got very tired, and you wouldn't believe how rude some women can be. Positively odious! So I gave it up for stamps."

His voice, muffled and insecure though it was, seemed the voice of an educated man. Alleyn wondered if he had been born to vacuum cleaners and philately.

"How long were you in Liverpool, Mr. Legge?"

"Nearly two years."

"And before that?"

"I was in London. In the City. I was born in London. Why do you ask?"

"Routine, Mr. Legge," said Alleyn, and thought of Cubitt. "What I was going to ask you was this. Had you ever met Mr. Watchman before he arrived at Ottercombe?"

"Yes, indeed."

Alleyn looked up.

"Do you mind telling us where you met him? You need not answer any of these questions, of course, if you don't want to."

"I don't in the least object, Chief Inspector. I met him in a slight collision at Diddlestock Corner. He was very nice about it."

Alleyn stared at him and he blinked nervously. Fox, Alleyn noticed, was stifling a grin.

"Was that the first time you saw him?"

"Oh, no. I'd *seen* him before. In court."

"What?"

"I used to go a great deal to the courts when I was in London. I always found it very absorbing. Of course Mr. Watchman didn't know *me*."

"I see."

Alleyn moved Abel's best ink-pot from one side of the table to the other and stared thoughtfully at it.

"Mr. Legge," he said at last, "how much did you have to drink on that Friday night?"

"Too much," said Legge quickly. "I realize it now. Not so much as the others, but too much. I have a good head as a rule, a very good head. But unless he moved his finger, which I still think possible, I must have taken too much."

He gave Alleyn a sidelong glance.

"I usually play my best," said Mr. Legge, "when I am a little intoxicated. I must have overdone it. I shall never forgive myself, never."

"How long was it," Alleyn asked, "before you realized what had happened?"

"Oh, a very long time. I thought it must be tetanus. I've seen a man with tetanus. You see, I had forgotten about that dreadful stuff. I had forgotten that Mr. Pomeroy opened the cupboard that afternoon."

"That was for—"

"I know what you're going to say," Legge interrupted, again with that gesture of admonishment. "You're going to remind me that he opened it to get the iodine for my face. Do you suppose that I can ever forget that? I was doubly the instrument. That's what upsets me so dreadfully. He must have done something then, and accidentally got it on his fingers. I don't know. I don't pretend it's not a mystery." His face twitched dolorously. "I'm wretchedly unhappy," he whispered. "Miserable!"

People with no personal charm possess one weapon, an occasional appeal to our sense of pathos. There was something intolerably pitiable in Legge; in his furtiveness, his threadbare respectability, his obvious terror, and his little spurts of confidence. Alleyn had a violent desire to get rid of him, to thrust him away as something indecent and painful. But he said: "Mr. Legge, have you any objections to our taking your fingerprints?"

The chair fell over as Legge got to his feet. He backed towards the door, turning his head from side to side and wringing his hands. Fox moved to the door, but Legge seemed unaware of him. He gazed like a trapped animal at Alleyn.

"Oh God!" he said. "Oh dear! Oh dear me! Oh God, I *knew* you'd say that!" and broke into tears.

ii

"Come now, Mr. Legge," said Alleyn at last, "you mustn't let the affair get on your nerves like this. If, as you think, Mr. Watchman's death was purely accidental, you have nothing to fear. There's nothing very terrible in having your fingerprints taken."

"Yes, there is," contradicted Legge in a sort of fury. "It's a perfectly horrible suggestion. I resent it. I deeply resent it. I most strongly object."

"Very well, then," said Alleyn placidly, "we won't take them."

Mr. Legge blew his nose violently and looked over the top of his handkerchief at Alleyn.

"Yes," he said, "that's all very well, but I know what tricks you'll get up to. You'll get them by stealth, I know. I've heard of the practices that go on in the police. I've studied the matter. It's like everything else in a state governed by capitalism. Trickery and intimidation. . . . You'll give me photographs to identify and take my fingerprints from them."

"Not now you've warned us," said Alleyn.

"You'll get them against my will and then you'll draw false conclusions from them. That's what you'll do."

"What sort of false conclusions?"

"About me," cried Legge passionately, "about me."

"You know that's all nonsense," said Alleyn quietly. "You will do yourself no good by talking like this."

"I won't talk at all. I will not be trapped into making incriminating statements. I will not be kept in here against my will!"

"You may go whenever you wish," said Alleyn. "Fox, will you open the door?"

Fox opened the door. Legge backed towards it, but on the threshold he paused.

"If only," he said with extraordinary intensity, "if only you'd have the sense to see that I couldn't have done any thing, even if I'd wanted to. If only you'd realize that and leave me in peace. You don't know *what* damage you may do, indeed you don't. If only you would leave me in peace!"

He swallowed noisily, made a movement with his hands that was eloquent of misery and defeat, and went away.

Fox stood with his hand on the doorknob.

"He's gone back to the garage," said Fox. "Surely he won't bolt."

"I don't think he'll bolt. Fox. Not in that car."

Fox stood and listened, looking speculatively at Alleyn.

"Well," he said, "that was a rum go, Mr. Alleyn, wasn't it?"

"Very rum indeed. I suppose you're thinking what I'm thinking?"

"He's been inside," said Fox. "I'll take my oath that man's done his stretch."

"I think so, too, and what's more he had that suit before he went in. It was made by a decent tailor about six years ago, or more, and it was made for Mr. Legge. It fits him well enough and he's too odd a shape for reach-me-downs."

"Notice his hands?"

"I did. And the hair, and the walk, and the eyes. I thought he was going to sob it all out on my bosom. Ugh!" said Alleyn. "It's beastly, that furtive, wary look they get. Fox, ring up Illington and ask Harper to send the dart up to Dabs. It's got his prints. Not very nice ones, but they'll do to go on with."

Fox went off to the telephone, issued cryptic instructions, and returned.

"I wonder," said Fox, "who he is, and what they pulled him in for."

"We'll have to find out."

"He behaved very foolish," said Fox austerely. "All that refusing to have his prints taken. We're bound to find out. We'll have to get his dabs, sir."

"Yes," agreed Alleyn, "on the sly, as he foretold."

"I wonder what he's *doing* out there," said Fox.

"Wait a moment," said Alleyn. "I'll have a look."

He stole into the passage. Legge had left the side door ajar and Alleyn could see the yard outside, flooded with moonshine. He slipped out and moved like a cat across the yard into the shadow of the garage door. Here he stopped and listened. From inside the garage came a rhythmic whisper, interrupted at intervals by low thuds, and accompanied by the sound of breathing. A metal door opened and closed stealthily, a boot scraped across stone. The rhythmic whisper began again. Alleyn stole away and recrossed the yard, his long shadow going fantastically before him.

When he rejoined Fox in the parlour he was grinning broadly.

"What's he up to?" asked Fox.

"Being one too many for the infamous police," said Alleyn. "He's polishing his car."

"Well, I'll be blooming well blowed," said Fox.

"He must have nearly finished. Switch off the light, Fox. It'd be a pity to keep him waiting."

Fox switched off the light. He and Alleyn sat like shadows in the parlour. The Ottercombe town clock struck twelve and a moment later, the same dragging footsteps sounded in the yard. The side door was shut and the steps went past the parlour. The staircase light clicked and a faint glow showed underneath the door.

"Up he goes," whispered Alleyn.

Legge went slowly upstairs, turned the light off, and moved along the passage above their heads. A door closed.

"Now then," said Alleyn.

They went upstairs in the dark and slipped into Alleyn's room, the first on the top landing. The upstairs passage was bright with moonlight.

"His is the end one," murmured Alleyn. "He's got his light on. Do you suppose he'll set to work and wipe all the utensils in his room?"

"The thing's silly," whispered Fox. "I've never known anything like it. What's the good of it? We'll *get* his blasted dabs."

"What do you bet me he won't come down to breakfast in gloves?"

"He's capable of anything," snorted Fox.

"*Sssh*! He's coming out."

"Lavatory?"

"Possibly."

Alleyn groped for the door and unlatched it.

"What are you doing, sir?" asked Fox rather peevishly.

"Squinting through the crack," Alleyn whispered. "Now he's come out of the lavatory."

"I can hear that."

"He's in his pyjamas. He doesn't look very delicious. Good Lord."

"What?"

"He's crossed the passage," breathed Alleyn, "and he's stooping down at another door."

"What's he up to?"

"Can't see—shadow. Now he's off again. Back to his own room. Shuts the door. Light out. Mr. Legge, finished for the night."

"And not before it was time," grumbled Fox. "They've got a nice sort of chap as Secretary and Treasurer for their society. How long'll we give him, Mr. Alleyn? I'd like to have a look what he's been up to."

"I'll give him ten minutes and then go along the passage."

"Openly?"

"Yes. Quickly, but not stealthily, Fox. It's the room on the right at the end. It looked almost as if he was shoving a note under the door. Very odd."

"What age," asked Fox, "is the Honourable Violet Darragh?"

"What a mind you have! It was probably young Pomeroy's door."

"I hadn't thought of that, sir. Probably."

Alleyn switched on the light and began to unpack his suit-case. Whistling soundlessly, he set his room in order, undressed, and put on his pyjamas and dressing-gown.

"Now then," he said. He picked up his towel and spongebag and went out.

Fox waited, his hands on his knees. He heard a tap turned on. Water-pipes gurgled. In a distant room, someone began to snore in two keys. Presently Fox heard the pad of feet in the passage and Alleyn returned.

His towel was round his neck. His hair was rumpled and damp and hung comically over his eyes. He looked like a rather distinguished faun who had chosen to disguise himself in pyjamas and a dressing-gown. Between thumb and forefinger he held a piece of folded paper.

"Crikey, Fox!" said Alleyn.

"What have you got there, sir?"

"Lord knows! A threat? A billet-doux? Find my case, please, Fox, and get out a couple of tweezers. We'll open it carefully. At least it may have his prints. Thank the Lord I brought that camera."

Fox produced the tweezers. Alleyn dropped his paper on the glass top of the wash-stand. Using the tweezers, he opened it delicately. Fox looked over his shoulder and read ten words written in pencil.

Implore you usual place immediately. Most important. *Destroy at once.*

"Crikey again!" said Alleyn. "An assignation."

"Where did you get it, Mr. Alleyn?"

"Under the door. I fished for it with a hairpin I found in the bathroom. Luckily there was a good gap."

"Will Pomeroy's door?"

"Does Will Pomeroy wear high-heeled shoes, size four-and-a-half, made by Rafferty, Belfast?"

"Lor'!" said Fox. "The Honourable Violet."

CHAPTER THIRTEEN

Miss Darragh Stands Firm

i

THE SUMMER sun shines early on the Coombe, and when Alleyn looked out of his window at half-past five, it was at a crinkled and sparkling sea. The roofs of Fish Lane were cleanly pale. A column of wood-smoke rose delicately from a chimney-pot. Someone walked, whistling, down Ottercombe Steps.

Alleyn had been dressed for an hour. He was waiting for Mr. Robert Legge. He supposed that the word "immediately" in the note for Miss Darragh might be interpreted as "the moment you read this," which no doubt would be soon after Miss Darragh awoke.

Fox and Alleyn had been very industrious before they went to bed. They had poured iodine into a flat dish and they had put Mr. Legge's letter into the dish but not into the iodine. They had covered the dish and left it for five minutes, and then set up an extremely expensive camera, by whose aid they could photograph the note by lamplight. They might have spared themselves the trouble. There were no fingerprints on Mr. Legge's note. Fox had gone to bed in high dudgeon. Alleyn had refolded the note and pushed it under Miss Darragh's door. Four minutes later he had slipped peacefully into sleep.

The morning smelt freshly. Alleyn leant over the window-sill and glanced to his left. At the same moment, three feet away, Fox leant over his window-sill and glanced to his right. He was fully dressed and looked solidly prepared to take up his bowler hat and go anywhere.

"Good morning, sir," said Fox in a whisper, "pleasant morning. He's just stirring, I fancy."

"Good morning to you, Br'er Fox," rejoined Alleyn. "A very pleasant morning. I'll meet you on the stairs."

He stole to the door of his room and listened. Presently the now familiar footsteps sounded in the passage. Alleyn waited for a few seconds and then slipped through the door. Fox performed a similar movement at the same time.

"Simultaneous comedians," whispered Alleyn. "Come on."

Keeping observation is one of the most tedious of a detective officer's duties. Laymen talk of "shadowing." It is a poetic term for a specialized drudgery. In his early days at Scotland Yard, Alleyn had hated keeping observation and had excelled at it, a circumstance which casts some light on his progress as a detective. There are two kinds of observation, in the police sense. You may tail a man in such a manner that you are within his range of vision but unrecognized or unremarked by him. You may also be obliged to tail a man in circumstances that forbid his seeing you at all. In a deserted hamlet, at half-past five on a summer's morning, Mr. Legge could scarcely fail to recognize his tormentors of the previous evening. Alleyn and Fox wished to follow him without being seen.

They reached the entrance lobby of the pub as Mr. Legge stepped into the street. Alleyn moved into the private tap and Fox into a sort of office on the other side of the front entrance. Alleyn watched Mr. Legge go past the window of the private tap and signalled to Fox. They hurried down the side passage in time to see Mr. Legge pass the garage and make for the South Steps. Alleyn nodded to Fox who strolled across the yard, and placed himself in a position where he could see the South Steps, reflected handily in a cottage window. When the figure of Mr. Legge had descended the steps and turned to the left, Fox made decent haste to follow his example. Alleyn opened the garage and backed the police Ford into the yard. He then removed his coat and hat, let a good deal of air out of his spare tyre and began, in a leisurely manner, to pump it up again. He had inflated and replaced the spare tyre, and was peering into the engine, when Miss Darragh came out of the pub.

Alleyn had not questioned the superintendent at all closely about Miss Darragh, nor was her appearance dwelt upon in the files of the case. He was therefore rather surprised to see how fat she was. She was like a pouter-pigeon in lavender print. She wore an enormous straw hat, and carried a haversack and easel. Her round face was quite inscrutable but Alleyn thought she looked pretty hard at him. He dived further inside the bonnet of the car, and Miss Darragh passed down the South Steps.

Alleyn gave her a good start and then put on his coat and hat.

When he reached the foot of the steps he looked cautiously round the corner of the wall to the left. Miss Darragh had reached the south end of Fish Lane and now plodded along a stone causeway to the last of the jetties. Alleyn crossed Fish Lane and followed under lee of the houses. At the end of Fish Lane he behaved with extreme caution, manoeuvring for a vantage point. There was nobody about. The fishing fleet had gone out at dawn and the housewives of Ottercombe were either in bed or cooking breakfast. Alleyn paused at Mary Yeo's shop on the corner of Fish Lane and the causeway. By peering diagonally through both windows at once, he had a distorted view of the jetty and of Miss Darragh. She had set up a camp stool and had her back to Ottercombe. Alleyn saw her mount her easel. A sketching block appeared. Presently Miss Darragh began to sketch.

Alleyn walked down an alley toward the jetty, and took cover in an angle of one of the ramshackle cottages that sprawl about the waterfront. This is the rough quarter of Ottercombe. Petronella Broome has a house of ill-repute, four rooms, on the south waterfront; and William Glass's tavern was next door until Superintendent Harper made a fuss and had the license cancelled. This stretch of less than two hundred yards is called the South Front. At night it takes on a sort of glamour. Its lamps are reflected redly in the water. Petronella's gramophone advertises her hospitality, bursts of laughter echo over the harbour, and figures move dimly to and fro across the lights. But at ten to six in the morning it smells of fish and squalor.

Alleyn waited for five minutes before Legge appeared from behind a bollard at the far end of the jetty. Legge crossed the end of the jetty and stood behind Miss Darragh, who continued to sketch.

"Damn," said Alleyn.

The tide was out and three dinghies were beached near the jetty. A fourth was made fast to the far end and seemed to lie, bobbing complacently, directly under Miss Darragh. Alleyn thought the water looked fairly shallow for at least halfway down the jetty. He groaned and, with caution, moved towards the front. Miss Darragh did not turn, but from time to time Legge glanced over his shoulder. Alleyn advanced to the foreshore under cover of boats, fishing gear, and the sea wall. To an observer from one of the windows, he would have seemed to be hunting for lost property. He reached the jetty.

For halfway along the jetty, the water was about two feet deep. Alleyn, cursing inwardly, rolled up his trousers and took to it, keeping under the jetty. The water was cold and the jetty smelt. Abruptly the bottom shelved down. Alleyn could now hear the faintest murmur of voices and knew that he was not so very far from his objective. The dinghy was hidden by posts but he could hear the *glug-glug* of its movement and the hollow thud it made when it knocked against the post to which it was made fast. Just beyond it was a flight of steps leading up to the jetty. Alleyn mounted a cross-beam. It was slimy and barnacled but he found handholds at the end. If he could reach the dinghy! His progress was hazardous, painful, and maddeningly slow, but at last he grasped the post. He embraced it with both arms, straddled the cross-beams and wriggled round until he reached the far side.

Underneath him was the dinghy and lying full length in the dinghy was Inspector Fox. His note-book lay open on his chest.

Fox winked at his superior and obligingly moved over. Alleyn pulled the dinghy closer, and, not without difficulty, lowered himself into the bows.

"Two minds with but a single thought," he whispered. "Simultaneous comedy again."

He took out his note-book and cocked his ears.

From the jetty above, the voices of Miss Darragh and Mr. Legge sounded disembodied and remote. For a second or two Alleyn could hear nothing distinctly but, as his concentration sharpened, words and phrases began to take form. Miss Darragh was speaking. She spoke in little bursts of eloquence broken by pauses that fell oddly until he realized that while she talked, she painted.

". . . And haven't I gone sufficiently far, coming down here, to meet you? I go no farther at all. I'm sorry for the nasty pickle you're in . . . terribly cruel the way . . . haunts you . . . compromised myself . . . can't expect . . ." Her voice died into a mysterious murmur. Alleyn raised his eyebrows and Fox shook his head. Miss Darragh droned on. Suddenly she said very distinctly: "It's no good at all asking, for I'll not do ut."

Legge began to mumble, quite inaudibly. She interrupted him with a staccato: "Yes, yes, I realize all that." And a moment later: "Don't think I'm not sorry. I am." And then, incisively: "Of course, I know you're innocent of ut, but I can't—"

For the first time Mr. Legge became intelligible.

"My blood be on your head," said Mr. Legge loudly.

"Ah, don't say that. Will you be quiet, now? You've nothing to fear."

Legge's voice dropped again but Alleyn's hearing was now attuned to it. He heard isolated phrases. "Hounded to death . . . just when I was . . . expiated my fault . . . God knows . . . never free from it."

Footsteps plodded across the beams overhead and when Miss Darragh spoke, it was from a different place. She had moved, perhaps to look at the sketch, and now stood near the edge of the jetty. Her voice, seeming very close, was startlingly clear.

"I promise you," she said, "that I'll do my best, but I'll not commit perjury—"

"Perjury!" said Legge irritably. He had followed her.

"Well, whatever it is. I'll do my best. I've no fear at all of their suspecting you, for they'll have their wits about them and will soon see it's impossible."

"But don't you see . . . They'll think . . . they'll tell everyone . . ."

"I can see it's going to be hard on you and I've got my . . . You know well enough why I feel bound to help you. That'll do now. Rest easy, and we'll hope for the best."

"Don't forget how I came to my trouble."

"I do not and I will not. Be off, now, for it's getting late. I've finished me little peep and it's nothing better than a catastrophe; me mind was not on ut. We'd best not be seen walking back together."

"I'm at your mercy," said Legge. And they heard him walk away.

ii

Alleyn and Fox breakfasted in the dining-room. Cubitt and Parish were nowhere to be seen but Miss Darragh sat at a corner table and gave them good morning as they came in. Alleyn knew that from behind the paper she watched them pretty closely. He caught her at it twice, but she did not seem to be at all embarrassed and, the second time, twinkled and smiled at him.

"I see you've no paper," said Miss Darragh. "Would you like to have a look at the *Illington Courier*?"

"Thank you so much," said Alleyn, and crossed over to the table.

"You're Mr. Roderick Alleyn, are ye not?"

Alleyn bowed.

"Ah, I knew you from your likeness to your brother George," said Miss Darragh.

"I am delighted that you knew me," said Alleyn, "but I've never thought that my brother George and I were much alike."

"Ah, there's a kind of a family resemblance. And then, of course

I knew you were here, for the landlord told me. You're a good deal better-looking than your brother George. He used to stay with me cousins, the Sean O'Darraghs, for Punches-town. I met 'um there. I'm Violet Darragh, so now you know who 'tis that's so bold with you."

"Miss Darragh," said Alleyn, "would you spare us a moment when you have finished your breakfast?"

"I would. Is it about this terrible affair?"

"Yes."

"I'll be delighted. I'm a great lover of mysteries, myself, or I was before this happened. They're not such grand fun when you're in the middle of 'um. I'll be in the private tap-room when you want me. Don't hurry, now."

"Thank you," said Alleyn. Miss Darragh rose and squeezed past the table. Alleyn opened the door. She nodded cheerfully and went out.

"Cool," said Fox, when Alleyn joined him. "You'd never think she had anything up her sleeve, sir, now would you?"

"No, Fox, you wouldn't. I wonder what line I'd better take with her. She's as sharp as a needle."

"I'd say so," agreed Fox.

"I think, Fox, you had better ask her, in your best company manners, to walk into our parlour. It looks more official. I must avoid that friend-of-the-family touch—" Alleyn stopped short and rubbed his nose. "Unless, indeed, I make use of it," he said. "Dear me, now, I wonder."

"What's the friend-of-the-family touch, sir?"

"Didn't you hear? She has met my brother George who is physically as unlike me as may be. Mentally, too, I can't help hoping. But perhaps that's vanity. What do you think?"

"I haven't had the pleasure of meeting Sir George, Mr. Alleyn."

"He's rather an old ass, I'm afraid. Have you finished?"

"Yes, thank you, sir."

"Then I shall remove to the parlour. My compliments to Miss Darragh, Foxkin, and I shall be grateful if she will walk into my parlour. Lord, Lord, I hope I don't make a botch of this."

Alleyn went to the parlour. In a minute or two, Fox came in with Miss Darragh.

Ever since he entered the detective service, Alleyn has had to set a guard against a habit of instinctive reactions to new acquaintances. Many times has he repeated to himself the elementary warning that roguery is not incompatible with charm. But he has never quite overcome certain impulses towards friendliness, and his austerity of manner is really a safeguard against this weakness; a kind of protective colouring, a uniform for behaviour.

When he met Violet Darragh he knew that she would amuse and interest him, that it would be easy to listen to her and pleasant to strike up a sort of friendship. He knew that he would find it difficult to believe her capable of double-dealing. He summoned the discipline of a system that trains its servants to a high pitch of objective watchfulness. He became extremely polite.

"I hope you will forgive me," he said, "for suggesting that you should come in here. Mr. Pomeroy has given us this room as a sort of office, and as all our papers—"

"Ah, don't worry yourself," said Miss Darragh. She took the armchair that Fox wheeled forward, wriggled into the deep seat, and tucked her feet up.

"It's more comfortable here," she said, "and I'm a bit tired. I was out at the crack of dawn at me sketching. Down on the front, 'twas, and those steps are enough to break your heart."

"There must be some very pleasant subjects down there," murmured Alleyn. "At the end of the jetty, for instance."

"You've a good eye for a picture," said Miss Darragh. "That's where I was. Or perhaps you saw me there?"

"I think," said Alleyn, "that you passed me on your way out. I was in the garage yard."

"You were. But the garage yard does not overlook the jetty."

"Oh, no," said Alleyn vaguely. "Now, Miss Darragh, may we get down to what I'm afraid will be, for you, a very boring business. It's about the night of this affair. I've seen your statement to the police, and I've read the report of the inquest."

"Then," said Miss Darragh, "I'm afraid you'll know all I have to tell you and that's not much."

"There are one or two points we'd like to go over with you if we may. You told the coroner that you thought the wound from the dart had nothing to do with Mr. Watchman's death."

"I did. And I'm positive it hadn't. A little bit of a puncture no bigger than you'd take from a darning needle."

"A little bigger than that surely?"

"Not to make any matter."

"But the analyst found cyanide on the dart."

"I've very little faith in 'um," said Miss Darragh.

"In the analyst? It went up to London, you know. It was the very best analyst," said Alleyn with a smile.

"I know 'twas, but the cleverest of 'um can make mistakes. Haven't I read for myself how delicut these experiments are, with their fractions of a grain of this and that, and their acid tests, and their heat tests, and all the rest of it? I've always thought it's blown up with their theories and speculations these fine chemists must be. When they're told to look for prussic acid, they'll be determined to find it. Ah, well, maybe they did find poison on the dart, but that makes no difference at all to me theory, Mr. Alleyn. If there was prussic acid or cyanide, or Somebody's acid on the dart (and why for pity's sake can't they find one name for ut and be done with ut?), then 'twas put on in the factory or the shop, or got on afterwards, for 'twas never there at the time."

"I beg your pardon?" asked Alleyn apologetically. "I don't quite—"

"What I mean is this, Mr. Alleyn. Not a soul there had a chance to play the fool with the darts, and why should they when nobody could foretell the future?"

"The future? You mean nobody could tell that the dart would puncture the finger?"

"I do."

"Mr. Legge," said Alleyn, "might have known, mightn't he?"

"He might," said Miss Darragh coolly, "but he didn't. Mr. Alleyn, I never took my eyes off that 'un, from the time he took the darts till the time he wounded the poor fellow, and that was no time at all, for it passed in a flash. If it's any help I'm ready to make a sworn statement—an affidavit isn't it?—that Legge put nothing on the dart."

"I see," said Alleyn.

"Even Mr. Pomeroy, who is set against Mr. Legge, and Mr. Parish, too, will tell you he had no chance to infect the dart."

Miss Darragh made a quick nervous movement with her hands, clasping them together and raising them to her chin.

"I know very well," she said, "that there are people here will make things look black for Mr. Legge. You'll do well to let 'um alone. He's a delicut man and this affair's racking his nerves to pieces. Let 'um alone, Mr. Alleyn, and look elsewhere for your murderer, if there's murder in ut."

"What's your opinion of Legge?" asked Alleyn abruptly.

"Ah, he's a common well-meaning little man with a hard life behind 'um."

"You know something of him? That's perfectly splendid. I've been trying to fit a background to him and I can't."

For the first time Miss Darragh hesitated, but only for a second. She said: "I've been here nearly three weeks and I've had time to draw my own conclusions about the man."

"No more than that?"

"Ah, I know he's had a hard time and that in the end he's come into harbour. Let 'em rest there, Mr. Alleyn, for he's no murderer."

"If he's no murderer he has nothing to fear."

'You don't know that. You don't understand."

"I think perhaps we are beginning to understand. Miss Darragh, last night I asked Mr. Legge if, as a matter of routine, he would let us take his fingerprints. He refused. Why do you suppose he did that?"

"He's distressed and frightened. He thinks you suspect 'um."

"Then he should welcome any procedure that is likely to prove our suspicions groundless. He should rather urge us to take his prints than burst into a fit of hysterics when we ask for them."

A faint line appeared between Miss Darragh's eyes. Her brows were raised and the corners of her mouth turned down. She looked like a disgruntled baby.

"I don't say he's not foolish," she said. "I only say he's innocent of murder."

"There's one explanation that sticks out a mile," Alleyn said. "Do you know the usual reason for withholding fingerprints?"

"I do not."

"The knowledge that the police already have them."

Miss Darragh said nothing.

"Now if that should be the reason in this case," Alleyn continued, "it is only a matter of time before we arrive at the truth. If, to put it plainly, Legge has been in prison, we shall very soon trace his record. But we may have to arrest him for manslaughter, to do it."

"All this," exclaimed Miss Darragh with spirit, "all this to prove he didn't kill Watchman! All this disgrace and trouble! And who's to pay the cost of ut? 'Twould ruin him entirely."

"Then he would be well advised to make a clean breast and tell us of his record, before we find it out for ourselves."

"How do you know he has a record?"

"I think," said Alleyn, "I must tell you that I was underneath the south jetty at six o'clock this morning."

She opened her eyes very wide indeed, stared at him, clapped her fat little hands together, and broke into a shrill cackle of laughter.

"Ah, what an old fule you've made of me," said Miss Darragh.

iii

But although she took Alleyn's disclosure in good part, she still made no admissions. She was amused and interested in his exploit of the morning, didn't in the least resent it, and exclaimed repeatedly that it was no use trying to keep out of his clutches. But she did elude him, nevertheless, and he began to see her as a particularly slippery pippin, bobbing out of reach whenever he made a bite at it.

Alleyn was on difficult ground and knew it. The notes that he and Fox had made of the conversation on the jetty were full of gaps and, though they pointed in one direction, contained nothing conclusive.

Detective officers are circumscribed by rules which, in more than one case, are open to several interpretations. It is impossible to define exactly the degrees of pressure in questions put by the detective. Every time an important case crops up he is likely enough to take risks. If he is lucky, his departure from rule of thumb comes off, but at the end of every case, like a warning bogey, stands the figure of defending counsel, ready to pounce on any irregularity and shake it angrily before the jury.

Miss Darragh had not denied the suggestion that Legge had a police record and Allcyn decided to take it as a matter of course that such a record existed and that she knew about it.

He said: "It's charming of you to let me down so lightly."

"For what, me dear man?"

"Why, for lying on my back in a wet dinghy and listening to your conversation."

"Isn't it your job? Why should I be annoyed? I'm only afraid you've misinterpreted whatever you heard."

"Then," said Alleyn, "I shall tell you how I have interpreted it, and you will correct me if I am wrong."

"So you say," said Miss Darragh good-humoredly.

"So I hope. I think that Legge has been to gaol, that you know it, that you're sorry for him, and that as long as you can avoid making a false statement you will give me as little information as possible. Is that right?"

"It's right in so far as I'll continue to hold me tongue."

"Ugh!" said Alleyn with a rueful grin. "You *are* being firm with me, aren't you? Well, here we go again. I think that if Mr. Legge had not been to gaol, you would laugh like mad and tell me what a fool I was."

"You do, do you?"

"Yes. And what's more I do seriously advise you to tell me what you know about Legge. If you won't do that, urge Legge to come out of the thicket, and tell me himself. Tell him that we've always got the manslaughter charge up our sleeves. Tell him that his present line of behaviour is making us extremely suspicious." Alleyn paused and looked earnestly at Miss Darragh.

"You said something to this effect this morning, I know," he added. "Perhaps it's no good. I don't see why I should finesse. I asked Legge to let me take impressions of his fingerprints. Good prints would have been helpful but they're not essential. He picked up the dart, it had been tested and we've got results. I asked him for impressions because I already suspected he had done time and I wanted to see how he'd respond. His response convinced me that I was right. We've asked the superintendent at Illington to send the dart to the Fingerprint Bureau. Tomorrow they will telephone the result."

"Let 'um," said Miss Darragh cheerfully.

"You know, you're withholding information. I ought to be very stiff with you."

"It's not meself, I mind," she said. "I'm just wishing you'd leave the poor fellow alone. You're wasting your time and you're going to do 'um great harm in the end. Let 'um alone."

"We can't," said Alleyn. "We can't let any of you alone."

She began to look very distressed and beat the palms of her hands together.

"You're barking up the wrong tree," she said. "I'll accuse no one; but look further and look nearer home."

And when he asked her what she meant she only repeated very earnestly: "Look further and look nearer home. I'll say no more."

CHAPTER FOURTEEN

Crime and Mr. Legge

i

"Fox," SAID Alleyn. "Get your hat. We'll walk to Cary Edge Farm and call on Miss Moore. Miss Darragh says it's a mile and a quarter over the downs from the mouth of the tunnel. She says we shall pass Cubitt painting Parish on our way. An eventful trip. Let us take it."

Fox produced the particularly rigid felt hat that appcars when his duties take him into the country. Will Pomeroy was in the front passage and Alleyn asked him if he might borrow one of a collection of old walking sticks behind the door.

"Welcome," said Will, shortly.

"Thank you so much. To get to Cary Edge Farm we turn off to the right from the main road, don't wc?"

"Cary Edge?" repeated Will and glared at them.

"Yes," said Alleyn. "That's where Miss Moore lives isn't it?"

"She won't be up-along this morning."

"What's that, sonny?" called old Abel, from the private tap-room. "Be the gentlemen looking for Miss Dessy? She's on her way over by this time for Saturday marketing."

Will moved his shoulders impatiently.

"You know everyone's business, Father," he muttered.

"Thank you, Mr. Pomeroy," called Alleyn. "We'll meet her on the way, perhaps."

"Less she do drive over in old car," said Abel, coming to the door. "But most times her walks."

He looked apprehensively at Will and turned back into the bar.

"We'll risk it," said Alleyn. "Back to lunch, Mr. Pomeroy."

"Thank 'ee, sir."

Alleyn and Fox walked up to the tunnel mouth. When they reached it Alleyn glanced back at the Plume of Feathers. Will stood in the doorway looking after them. As Alleyn turned, Will moved back into the pub.

"He will now telephone Cary Edge in case Miss Moore has not left yet," observed Alleyn. "No matter. She'll have been expecting us to arrive sooner or later. Come on." They entered the tunnel.

"Curious, Fox, isn't it," said Alleyn, and his voice rang hollow against the rock walls. "Ottercombe must have been able to shut itself up completely on the landward side. I bet some brisk smuggling went forward in the old days. Look out, it's slippery. Miss Moore must be an intrepid driver if she motors through here in all weathers."

They came out into the sunshine. The highway, a dusty streak, ran from the tunnel. On each side the downs rolled along the coast in a haze of warmth, dappled by racing cloud shadows. Farther inland were the hills and sunken lanes, the prettiness of Devon; here was a sweep of country where Englishmen for centuries had looked coastwards, while ships sailed across their dreams, and their thoughts were enlarged beyond the seaward horizon.

"Turn to the right," said Alleyn.

They climbed the bank and rounded a furze-bush, in a sunken hollow.

"Good spot for a bit of courting," said Fox, looking at the flattened grass.

"Yes, you old devil. You may invite that remarkably buxom lady who brought our breakfast, to stroll up here after hours."

"Mrs. Ives?"

"Yes. You'll have to get in early, it's a popular spot. Look at those cigarette butts, squalid little beasts. Hullo!"

He stooped and picked up two of them.

"The cigarette butt," he said, "has been derided by our detective novelists. It has lost caste and now ranks with the Chinese and datura. No self-respecting demi-highbrow will use it. That's because old Conan Doyle knew his job and got in first. But you and I, Br'er Fox, sweating hacks that we are, are not so superior. This cigarette was a Dahabieh, an expensive Egyptian. Harper said they found some Egyptian cigarettes in Watchman's pockets. Not many Dahabieh-smokers in Ottercombe, I imagine. Parish and Cubitt smoke Virginians. This one has lip stick on it. Orange-brown."

"Not Miss Darragh," said Fox.

"No, Fox. Nor yet Mrs. Ives. Let's have a peer. There's been rain since the Dahabiehs were smoked. Look at those heel marks. Woman's heels. Driven into the bank."

"She must have been sitting down," said Fox. "Or lying. Bit of a struggle seemingly. What had the gentleman been up to?"

"What indeed. What did Miss Darragh mean by her 'Look further and look nearer home'? We've no case for a jury yet, Fox. We mustn't close down on a theory. Can you find any masculine prints? Yes. Here's one. Not a very good one."

"Watchman's?"

"We may have to find out. May be nothing in it. Wait a bit though. I'm going back to the pub."

Alleyn disappeared over the ridge and was away for some minutes. He returned with two stones, a bit of an old box, and a case.

"Better," he said, "in your favourite phrase, Br'er Fox, to be sure than sorry."

He opened the case. It contained a rubber cup, a large flask of water, some plaster-of-Paris, and a spray-pump. Alleyn sprayed the footprints with shellac, and collected twigs from under the furze-bushes, while Fox mixed plaster. They took casts of the four clearest prints, reinforcing the plaster with the twigs and adding salt to the mixture. Alleyn removed the casts when they had set, covered the footprints with the box, weighted it with stones, and dragged branches of the furze-bush down over the whole. The casts, he wrapped up and hid.

"You never know," he said, "let's move on."

They mounted the rise and, away on the headland, saw Cubitt, a manikin, moving to and fro before his easel.

"We'll have to join the infamous company of gapers," said Alleyn. "Look, he's seen us. How eloquent of distaste that movement was! There's Parish beyond. He's doing a big thing. I believe I've heard Troy[1] speak of Norman Cubitt's work. Let's walk along the cliffs, shall we?"

They struck out to the right and hadn't gone many yards before they came to a downward slope where the turf was trampled. Alleyn stooped and examined it.

"Camp-stool," he muttered. "And here's an empty tube. Water-colour. The Darragh spoor, I imagine. An eventful stretch of country, this. I wonder if she was here on that Friday. You can't see the other place from here, Fox. You might hear voices though."

"If they were raised a bit."

[1]Mrs. Roderick Alleyn, R. A.

"Yes. Angry voices. Well, on we go."

As they drew nearer Cubitt continued to paint, but Parish kept turning his head to look at them. When they came within earshot. Cubitt shouted at them over his shoulder.

"I hope to God you haven't come here to ask questions. I'm busy."

"All right," said Alleyn. "We'll wait."

He walked beyond them, out of sight of the picture. Fox followed him. Alleyn lay on the lip of the headland. Beneath them, the sea boomed and thudded against a rosy cliff. Wreaths of seaweed endlessly wove suave patterns about Coombe Rock. A flight of gulls mewed and circled, in and out of the sunlight.

"What a hullabaloo and a pother," said Alleyn. "How many thousands of times, before they come adrift, do these strands of seaweed slither out and swirl and loop and return? Their gestures are so beautiful that it is difficult to realize they are meaningless. They only show us the significance of the water's movements but for themselves they are helpless. And the sea is helpless too, and the winds which it obeys, and the wider laws that rule the winds, themselves are ruled by passive rulers. Dear me, Fox, what a collection of ordered inanities! Rather like police investigations. I can't look over any more, I've no head for heights."

"Here comes Mr. Cubitt, sir," said Fox.

Alleyn rolled over and saw Cubitt, a vast figure against the sky.

"We're resting now," said Cubitt. "Sorry to choke you off but I was on a tricky bit."

"We are extremely sorry to bother you," said Alleyn. "I know it is beyond a painter's endurance to be interrupted at a critical moment."

Cubitt dropped down on the grass beside him.

"I'm trying to keep a wet skin of paint all over the canvas," he said. "You have to work at concert pitch for that."

"Good Lord!" Alleyn exclaimed. "You don't mean you paint right through that surface in three hours?"

"It keeps wet for two days. I've got a new brand of slow-drying colours. Even so, it's a bit of an effort."

"I should think so, on a thing that size."

Parish appeared on the brow of the hill.

"Aren't you coming to see my portrait?" he cried.

Cubitt glanced at Alleyn and said: "Do, if you'd like to."

"I should, enormously."

They walked back to the easel.

The figure had come up darkly against the formalized sky. Though the treatment was one of extreme simplification, there was no feeling of emptiness. The portrait was at once rich and austere. There was no bravura in Cubitt's painting. It seemed that he had pondered each brushmark, gravely and deeply, and had then laid it down on a single impulse and left it so.

"Lord, it's good," said Alleyn. "It's grand, isn't it?"

Parish stood with his head on one side and said, "Do you like it?" but Cubitt said: "Do you paint, Alleyn?"

"No, not I. My wife does."

"Does she exhibit at all?"

"Yes," said Alleyn. "Her name is Troy."

"Oh God!" said Cubitt. "I'm sorry."

"She's good, isn't she?" said Alleyn humbly.

"To my mind," answered Cubitt, "the best we've got."

"Do you think it's like me?" asked Parish. "I tell Norman he hasn't quite got my eyes. Judging by my photographs, you know. Not that I don't like it. I think it's marvellous, old boy, you know that."

"Seb," said Cubitt, "your price is above rubies. So long as you consider it a pretty mockery of nature, I am content."

"Oh," said Parish, "I'm delighted with it, Norman, really. It's only a suggestion about the eyes."

"How long have you been at it?" asked Alleyn.

"This is the sixth day. I had two mornings before the catastrophe. We shelved it for a bit after that."

"Naturally," added Parish solemnly. "We didn't feel like it."

"Naturally," agreed Cubitt drily.

"Tell me," said Alleyn, "did you ever pass Mr. Watchman on your way to or from this place?"

Cubitt had laid a streak of blue across his palette with the knife. His fingers opened and the knife fell into the paint. Parish's jaw dropped. He looked quickly at Cubitt as if asking him a question.

"How do you mean?" asked Cubitt. "He was only here one day. He died the night after he got here."

"That was the Friday," said Alleyn. "Did you work here on the Friday morning?"

"Yes."

"Well, was Mr. Watchman with you?"

"Oh no," said Cubitt quickly, "he was still in bed when we left."

"Did you see him on the way home?"

"I don't think we did," said Parish.

"In a little hollow this side of a furze-bush and just above the main road."

"I don't think so," said Parish.

"No," said Cubitt, a little too loudly. "We didn't. Why?"

"He was there some time," said Alleyn vaguely.

Cubitt said: "Look here, do you mind if I get going again? The sun doesn't stand still in the heavens."

"Of course," said Alleyn quickly.

Parish took up the pose. Cubitt looked at him and filled a brush with the colour he had mixed. He raised the brush and held it poised. Alleyn saw that his hand trembled.

"It's no good," said Cubitt abruptly, "we've missed it. The sun's too far round."

"But it's not ten yet," objected Parish.

"Can't help it," said Cubitt and put down his palette.

"For pity's sake," said Alleyn, "don't go wrong with it now."

"I'll knock off, I think."

"We've been a hell of a nuisance. I'm sorry."

"My dear chap," said Parish, "you're nothing to the modest Violet. It's a wonder she hasn't appeared. She puts up her easel about five yards behind Norman's and brazenly copies every stroke he makes."

"It's not as bad as that, Seb."

"Well, personally," said Parish, "I've had quite as much as I want of me brother Terence and me brother Brian and me unfortunate cousin poor Bryonie."

"What!" exclaimed Alleyn.

"She has a cousin who is a noble lord and got jugged for something."

"Bryonie," said Alleyn. "He was her cousin, was he?"

"So it seems. Do you remember the case?"

"Vaguely," said Alleyn. "Vaguely. Was Miss Darragh anywhere about on that same morning?"

"She was over there," said Parish. "Back in the direction you've come from. She must have stayed there for hours. She came in, drenched to the skin and looking like the wrath of Heaven, late in the afternoon."

"An enthusiast," murmured Alleyn. "Ah well, we mustn't hang round you any longer. We're bound for Cary Edge Farm."

Something in the look Cubitt gave him reminded Alleyn of Will Pomeroy.

Parish said: "To call on the fair Decima? You'll be getting into trouble with Will Pomeroy."

"Seb," said Cubitt, "pray don't be kittenish. Miss Moore is out on Saturday mornings, Alleyn."

"So Will Pomeroy told us, but we hoped to meet her on her way to Ottercombe. Good luck to the work. Come along, Fox."

ii

A few yards beyond the headland they struck a rough track that led inland and over the downs.

"This will take us there, I expect," said Alleyn. "Fox, those gentlemen lied about Watchman and the furze-bush."

"I thought so, sir. Mr. Cubitt made a poor fist of it."

"Yes. He's not a good liar. He's a damn good painter. I must ask Troy about him."

Alleyn stopped and thumped the point of his stick on the ground.

"What the devil," he asked, "is this about Lord Bryonie?"

"He's the man that was mixed up in the Montague Thringle case."

"Yes, I know. He got six months. He was Thringle's cat's-paw. By George, Fox, d'you know what?"

"What, sir?"

"Luke Watchman defended Bryonie. I'll swear he did."

"I wouldn't remember."

"Yes, you would. You must. By gum, Fox, we'll look up that case. Watchman defended Bryonie, and Bryonie was Miss Darragh's cousin. Rum. Monstrous rum."

"Sort of fetches her into the picture by another route."

"It does. Well, come on. We've lots of little worries. I wonder if Miss Moore uses orange-brown lipstick. I tell you what, Fox, I think Cubitt is catched with Miss Moore."

"In love with her?"

"Deeply, I should say. Did you notice, last night, how his manner changed when he talked about her? The same thing happened just now. He doesn't like our going to Cary Edge. Nor did Will Pomeroy. I wonder what she's like."

He saw what Decima was like in thirty seconds. She came swinging over the hilltop. She wore a rust-coloured jumper and a blue skirt. Her hair was ruffled, her eyes were bright, and her lips were orange-brown. When she saw the two men she halted for a second and then came on towards them.

Alleyn took off his hat and waited for her.

"Miss Moore?"

"Yes."

She stopped, but her pose suggested that it would be only for a moment.

"We hoped that we might meet you if we were too late to find you at home," said Alleyn. "I wonder if you can give up a minute or two. We're police officers."

"Yes."

"I'm sorry to bother you, but would you mind . . . ?"

"You'd better come back to the farm," said Decima. "It's over the next hill."

"That will be a great bore for you, I'm afraid."

"It doesn't matter. I can go into the Coombe later in the morning."

"We shan't keep you long. There's no need to turn back."

Decima seemed to hesitate.

"All right," she said at last. She walked over to a rock at the edge of the track and sat on it. Alleyn and Fox followed her.

She looked at them with the kind of assurance that is given to women who are unusually lovely and sometimes to women who are emphatically plain. She was without self-consciousness. Nobody had told Alleyn that Decima was beautiful and he was a little surprised. "It's impossible," he thought, "that she can be in love with young Pomeroy."

"I suppose it's about Luke Watchman," said Decima.

"Yes, it is. We've been sent down to see if we can tidy up a bit."

"Does that mean they think it was murder?" asked Decima steadily. "Or don't you answer that sort of question."

"We don't," rejoined Alleyn smiling, "answer that sort of question."

"I suppose not," said Decima.

"We are trying," continued Alleyn, "to trace Mr. Watchman's movements from the time he got here until the time of the accident."

"Why?"

"Part of the tidying-up process."

"I see."

"It's all pretty plain sailing except for Friday morning."

Alleyn saw her head turn so that for a second she looked towards

Ottercombe Tunnel. It was only for a second, and she faced him again.

"He went out," said Alleyn, "soon after breakfast. Mr. Pomeroy saw him enter the tunnel. That was about ten minutes before you left Ottercombe. Did you see Mr. Watchman on your way home?"

"Yes," she said, "I saw him."

"Where, please?"

"Just outside the top of the tunnel by some furze-bushes. I think he was asleep."

"Did he wake as you passed him?"

She clasped her thin hands round her knees.

"Oh, yes," she said.

"Did you stop, Miss Moore?"

"For a minute or two, yes."

"Do you mind telling us what you talked about?"

"Nothing that could help you. We—we argued about theories."

"Theories?"

"Oh, politics. We disagreed violently over politics. I'm a red rebel, as I suppose you've heard. It rather annoyed him. We only spoke for a moment."

"I suppose it was apropos of the Coombe Left Movement?" murmured Alleyn.

"Do you?" asked Decima.

Alleyn looked apologetic. "I thought it might be," he said, "because of your interest in the Movement. I mean it would have been a sort of natural ingredient of a political argument, wouldn't it?"

"Would it?" asked Decima.

"You're quite right to snub me," said Alleyn ruefully. "I'm jumping to conclusions and that's a very bad fault in our job. Isn't it, Fox?"

"Shocking, sir," said Fox.

Alleyn pulled out his note-book.

"I'll just get this right if I may. You met Mr. Watchman at about what time?"

"Ten o'clock."

"At ten o'clock or thereabouts. You met him by accident. You think he was asleep. You had a political argument in which the Coombe Left Movement was not mentioned."

"I didn't say so, you know."

"Would you mind saying so or saying not so? Just for my notes?" asked Alleyn, with such a quaint air of diffidence that Decima suddenly smiled at him.

"All right," she said, "we did argue about the society, though it's nothing to do with the case."

"If you knew the numbers of these books that I've filled with notes that have nothing whatever to do with the case you'd feel sorry for me," said Alleyn.

"We'll manage things better when we run the police," said Decima.

"I hope so," said Alleyn gravely. "Was your argument amicable?"

"Fairly," said Decima.

"Did you mention Mr. Legge?"

Decima said: "Before we go any further there's something I'd like to tell you."

Alleyn looked up quickly. She was frowning. She stared out over the downs, her thin fingers were clasped together.

"You'd better leave Robert Legge alone," said Decima. "If Watchman was murdered it wasn't by Legge."

"How do you know that, Miss Moore?"

"I watched him. He hadn't a chance. The others will have told you that. Will, Norman Cubitt, Miss Darragh. We've compared notes. We're all positive."

"You don't include Mr Parish?"

"He's a fool," said Decima.

"And Mr. Abel Pomeroy?"

She blushed, unexpectedly and beautifully.

"Mr. Pomeroy's not a fool but he's violently prejudiced against Bob Legge. He's a ferocious Tory. He thinks we—he thinks Will and I are too much under Bob's influence. He hasn't got a single reasonable argument against Bob, he simply would rather it was Bob than anyone else and has hypnotized himself into believing he's right. It's childishly obvious. Surely you must see that. He's an example in elementary psychology."

Alleyn raised an eyebrow. She glared at him.

"I'm not disputing it," said Alleyn mildly.

"Well then—"

"The camp seems to be divided into pro-Leggites and anti-Leggites. The funny thing about the pro-Leggites is this: They protest his innocence and, I am sure, believe in it. You'd think they'd welcome our investigation. You'd think they'd say, 'Come on then, look into his record, find out all you like about him. He's a decent citizen and an innocent man. He'll stand up to any amount of investigation.' They don't. They take the line of resenting the mildest form of question about Legge. Why's that, do you suppose? Why do you warn us off Mr. Legge?"

"I don't—"

"But you do," insisted Alleyn gently.

Decima turned her head and stared searchingly at him.

"You don't look a brute," she said doubtfully.

"I'm glad of that."

"I mean you don't look a complete robot. I suppose, having once committed yourself to a machine, you have to tick-over in the appointed manner."

"Always providing someone doesn't throw a spanner in the works."

"Look here," said Decima. "Bob Legge had an appointment in Illington that evening. He was just going, he would have gone if Will hadn't persuaded him not to. Will told him he'd be a fool to drive through the tunnel with the surface water pouring through it."

She was watching Alleyn and she said quickly, "Ah! You didn't know that?"

Alleyn said nothing.

"Ask Will. Ask the man he was to meet in Illington."

"The local police have done that," said Alleyn. "We won't question the appointment. We only know Mr. Legge didn't keep it."

"He couldn't. You can't drive through that tunnel when there's a stream of surface-water pouring down it."

"I should hate to try," Alleyn agreed. "We're not making much of an outcry over Mr. Legge's failure to appear. It was you, wasn't it, who raised the question?"

"I was only going to point out that Bob didn't know there would be a thunderstorm, did he?"

"Unless the pricking of his thumbs or something—"

"If this was murder I suppose it was premeditated. You won't deny that?"

"No. I don't deny that."

"Well then! Suppose he was the murderer. He didn't know it would rain. It would have looked pretty fishy for him to put off his appointment for no reason at all."

"It would. I wonder why he didn't tell me this himself."

"Because he's so worried that he's at the end of his tether. Because you got hold of him last night and deliberately played on his nerves until he couldn't think. Because—"

"Hullo!" said Alleyn. "You've seen him this morning, have you?"

If Decima was disconcerted she didn't show it. She blazed at Alleyn.

"Yes, I've seen him and I scarcely recognized him. He's a mass of overwrought nerves. His condition's pathological. The next thing will be a confession of a crime he didn't commit."

"How about the crime he did commit?" asked Alleyn. "It would be more sensible."

And that did shake her. She caught her breath in a little gasping sigh. Her fingers went to her lips. She looked very young and very guilty.

"So you knew all the time," said Decima.

CHAPTER FIFTEEN

Love Interest

i

ALLEYN HAD expected that Decima would hedge, rage, or possibly pretend to misunderstand him. Her sudden capitulation took him by surprise and he was obliged to make an embarrassingly quick decision. He plumped for comparative frankness.

"We expect," he said, "a report on his fingerprints. When that comes through, we shall have official confirmation of a record that we suspected from the first and of which we are now certain."

"And you immediately put two and two together and make an absurdity."

"What sort of absurdity?"

"You will say that because he didn't come forward and announce 'I'm a man with a police record,' he's a murderer. Can't you see how he felt? Have you the faintest notion what it's like for a man who's been in prison to try to get back, to try to earn a miserable pittance? Have you ever thought about it at all or wondered for two seconds what becomes of the people you send to jail? To their minds? I know you look after their bodies with the most intolerable solicitude. You are there always. Every employer is warned. There is no escape. It would be better, upon my honour, I believe it would be better, to hang them outright than—than to tear their wings off and let them go crawling out into the sun."

"That's a horrible analogy," said Alleyn, "and a false one."

"It's a true analogy. Can't you see why Legge was so frightened? He's only just stopped having to report. Only now has he got his thin freedom. He thought, poor wretch, that we wouldn't keep him on if we knew he'd been to jail. Leave him alone! Leave him alone!"

"How long have you known this about him?" asked Alleyn.

She stood up abruptly, her palm against her forehead as though her head ached.

"Oh, for some time."

"He confided in you? When?"

"When he got the job," said Decima flatly. Alleyn did not believe her, but he said politely:—

"That was very straightforward, wasn't it?" And as she did not answer he added: "Do you know why he went to prison?"

"No. I don't want to know. Don't tell me. He's wiped it out, God knows, poor thing. Don't tell me."

Alleyn reflected, with a certain amount of amusement, that it was as well she didn't want to know what Legge's offence had been. Some image of this thought may have appeared in his face. He saw Decima look sharply at him and he said hurriedly: "All this is by the way. What I really want to ask you is whether, on the morning you encountered Mr. Watchman by the furze-bush, you were alone with him all the time."

He saw that now she was frightened for herself. Her eyes widened, and she turned extremely pale.

"Yes. At least—I—no. Not at the end. I rather think Norman Cubitt and Sebastian Parish came up."

"You rather think?"

"They did come up. I remember now. They did."

"And yet," said Alleyn, "when I asked them if they saw Watchman that morning, they said definitely that they did not."

"They must have forgotten."

"Please! You can't think I'll believe that. They must have been over every word that was spoken by Watchman during the last hours of his life. They have told me as much. Why, they must have walked back to the inn with him. How could they forget?"

Decima said: "They didn't forget."

"No?"

"It was for me. They are being little gents."

Alleyn waited.

"Well," she said, "I won't have it. I won't have their chivalry. If you must know, they surprised their friend in a spirited attempt upon my modesty. I wasn't pleased and I was telling him precisely what I thought of him. I suppose they were afraid you would transfer your attentions from Bob Legge to me."

"Possibly," agreed Alleyn. "They seem to think I am a sort of investigating chameleon."

"I imagine," said Decima in a high voice, "that because I didn't relish Mr. Watchman's embraces and told him so it doesn't follow that I set to work and murdered him."

"It's not a strikingly good working hypothesis. I'm sorry to labour this point but we've no sense of decency in the force. Had he shown signs of these tricks before?"

The clear pallor of Decima's face was again flooded with red. Alleyn thought: "Good Lord, she's an attractive creature, I wonder what the devil she's like." He saw, with discomfort, that she could not look at him. Fox made an uneasy noise in his throat and stared over the downs. Alleyn waited. At last Decima raised her eyes.

"He was like that," she murmured.

Alleyn now saw a sort of furtiveness in Decima. She was no longer tense, her pose had changed and she offered him no challenge.

"I suppose he couldn't help it," she said, and then with a strange look from Alleyn to Fox, she added: "It's nothing. It doesn't mean anything. You needn't think ill of him. I was all right."

In half a minute she had changed. The educational amenities, provided by that superior mother, had fallen away from her. She had turned into a rustic beauty, conscious of her power of provocation. The rumoured engagement to Will Pomeroy no longer seemed ridiculous. And as if she had followed Alleyn's thought, she said: "I'd be very glad if you wouldn't say anything of this to Will Pomeroy. He knows nothing about it. He wouldn't understand."

"I'll sheer off it if it can be done. It was not the first time you'd had difficulty with Watchman?"

She paused and then said: "We hadn't actually—come to blows before."

"Blows? Literally?"

"I'm afraid so."

She stood up. Alleyn thought she mustered her self-assurance. When she spoke again it was in a different key, ironically and with composure.

"Luke," she said, "was amorous by habit. No doubt it was not the first time he'd miscalculated. He wasn't in the least disconcerted. He—wasn't in the least in love with me."

"No?"

"It's merely a squalid little incident which I had rather hoped to forget. It was, I suppose, very magnificent of Seb and Norman to lie about it, but the gesture was too big for the theme."

"Now she's being grand at me," thought Alleyn. "We are back in St. Margaret's Hall."

He said: "And Watchman had never made himself objectionable before that morning?"

"I did not usually find him particularly objectionable."

"I intended," said Alleyn, "to ask you if he had ever made love to you before?"

"I have told you he wasn't in the least in love with me."

"I'm unlucky in my choice of words, I see. Had he ever kissed you, Miss Moore?"

"This is very tedious," said Decima. "I have tried to explain that my acquaintance with Luke Watchman was of no interest or significance to either of us, or, if you will believe me, to you."

"Then why," asked Alleyn mildly, "don't you give me an answer and have done with it?"

"Very well," said Decima breathlessly. "You can have your answer. I meant nothing to him and he meant less to me. Until last Friday he'd never been anything but the vaguest acquaintance." She turned on Fox. "Write it down. You'll get no other answer. Write it down."

"Thank you, Miss," said Fox civilly, "I don't think I've missed anything. I've got it down."

ii

"Well, have you finished?" demanded Decima, who had succeeded in working herself up into a satisfactory temper. "Is there anything else you want to know? Do you want a list in alphabetical order of my encounters with any other little Luke Watchmans who have come my way?"

"No," said Alleyn. "No. We limit our impertinences to the police code. Our other questions are, I hope, less offensive. They concern the brandy you gave Mr. Watchman, the glass into which you poured it, and the bottle from which it came."

"All right. What about them?"

"May we have your account of that particular phase of the business?"

"I told Oates and I told the coroner. Someone suggested brandy. I looked round and saw Luke's glass on the table, between the settle where he lay and the dart board. There wasn't any brandy left in it. I saw the bottle on the bar. I was very quick about it. I got it and poured some into the glass. I didn't put anything but brandy in the glass. I can't prove I didn't, but I didn't."

"But perhaps we can prove it. Was anyone near the table? Did anyone watch you pour the brandy?"

"Oh God!" said Decima wearily. "How should I know? Sebastian Parish was nearest to the table. He may have noticed. I don't know. I took the glass to Luke. I waited for a moment, while Abel Pomeroy put iodine on Luke's finger, and then I managed to pour a little brandy between his lips. It wasn't much. I don't think he even swallowed it, but I suppose you won't believe that."

"Miss Moore," said Alleyn suddenly, "I can't tell you how pathetically anxious we are to accept the things people tell us." He hesitated and then said: "You see, we spend most of our working life asking questions. Can you, for your part, believe that we get a kind of sixth sense and sometimes feel very certain indeed that a witness is speaking the truth, or, as the case may be, is lying? We're not allowed to recognize our sixth sense, and when it points a crow's flight towards the truth we may not follow it. We must cut it dead and follow the dreary back streets of collected evidence. But if they lead us anywhere at all it is almost always to the same spot."

"Eminently satisfactory," said Decima. "Everything for the best in the best of all possible police forces."

"That wasn't quite what I meant. Was it after you had given him the brandy that Mr. Watchman uttered the single word 'poisoned'?"

"Yes."

"Did you get the impression that he spoke of the brandy?"

"No. I don't know if your sixth sense will tell you I'm lying, but it seemed to me he *tried* to take the brandy, and perhaps did swallow a little, and that it was when he found he couldn't drink that he said—that one word. He said it between his clenched teeth. I had never seen such a look of terror and despair. Then he jerked his hand. Miss Darragh was going to bandage it. Just at that moment the lights went out."

"For how long were they out?"

"Nobody knows. It's impossible to tell. I can't. It seemed an age. Somebody clicked the switch. I remember that. To see if it had been turned off accidentally, I suppose. It was a nightmare. The rain sounded like drums. There was broken glass everywhere—crunch, crunch, squeak. And his voice. Not like a human voice. Like a cat, mewing. And his heels, drumming on the settle. And everybody shouting in the dark."

Decima spoke rapidly and twisted her fingers together.

"It's funny," she said, "I either can't talk about it at all, or I can't stop talking about it. Once you start, you go on and on. It's rather queer. I suppose he was in great pain. I suppose it was torture. As bad as the rack, or disembowelling. I've got a terror of physical pain. I'd recant anything first."

"Not," said Alleyn, "your political views?"

"No," agreed Decima, "not those. I'd contrive to commit suicide or something. Perhaps it was not pain that made him cry like that, and drum with his heels. Perhaps it was only reflex-something. Nerves."

"I think," said Alleyn, "that your own nerves have had a pretty shrewd jolt."

"What do you know about nerves?" demanded Decima with surprising venom. "Nerves! These things are a commonplace to you. Luke Watchman's death-throes are so much data. You expect me to give you a neat statement about them. Describe, in my own words, the way he clenched his teeth and drew back his lips."

"No," said Alleyn. "I haven't asked you about those things. I have asked you two questions of major importance. One was about your former relationship with Watchman and the other about the brandy you gave him before he died."

"I've answered you. If that's all you want to know you've got it. I can't stand any more of this. Let me—"

The voice stopped as if someone had switched it off. She looked beyond Alleyn and Fox to the brow of the hillock. Her eyes were dilated.

Alleyn turned. Norman Cubitt stood against the sky.

"Norman!" cried Decima.

He said: "Wait a bit, Decima," and strode down towards her. He stood and looked at her and then lightly picked up her hands.

"What's up?" asked Cubitt.

"I can't stand it, Norman."

Without looking at Alleyn or Fox, he said: "You don't have to talk to these two precious experts if it bothers you. Tell 'em to go to hell." And then he turned her round and over her shoulder grinned, not very pleasantly, at Alleyn.

"I've made a fool of myself," whispered Decima.

She was looking at Cubitt as though she saw him for the first time. He said: "What the devil are you badgering her for?"

"Just," said Alleyn, "out of sheer wanton brutality."

"It's all right," said Decima. "He didn't badger, really. He's only doing his loathsome job."

Her eyes were brilliant with tears, her lips not quite closed, and still she looked with a sort of amazement into Cubitt's face.

"Oh, Norman!" she said, "I've been so inconsistent and fluttery and feminine. Me!"

"You," said Cubitt.

"In a moment," thought Alleyn, "he'll kiss her." And he said: "Thank you so much, Miss Moore. I'm extremely sorry to have distressed you. I hope we shan't have to bother you again."

"Look here, Alleyn," said Cubitt, "if you do want to see Miss Moore again I insist on being present, and that's flat."

Before Alleyn could answer this remarkable stipulation Decima said: "But my dear man, I'm afraid you can't insist on that. You're not my husband, you know."

"That can be attended to," said Cubitt. "Will you marry me?"

"Fox," said Alleyn, "what are you staring at? Come back to Ottercombe."

iii

"Well, Mr. Alleyn," said Fox when they were out of earshot, "we see some funny things in our line of business, don't we? What a peculiar moment, now, for him to pick on for a proposal. Do you suppose he's been courting her for a fair while, or did he spring it on her sudden?"

"Suddenish, I fancy, Fox. Her eyes were wet and that, I suppose, went to his head. I must say she's a very lovely creature. Didn't you think so?"

"A very striking young lady," agreed Fox. "But I thought the Super said she was keeping company with young Pomeroy?"

"He did."

"She's a bit on the classy side for him, you'd think."

"You would, Fox."

"Well, now, I wonder what she'll do. Throw him over and take Mr. Cubitt? She looked to me to be rather inclined that way."

"I wish she'd told the truth about Watchman," said Alleyn.

"Think there'd been something between them, sir? Relations? Intimacy?"

"Oh Lord, I rather think so. It's not a very pleasant thought."

"Bit of a *femme fatale*," said Fox carefully. "But there you are. They laugh at what we used to call respectability, don't they? Modern women—"

Alleyn interrupted him.

"I know, Fox, I know. She is very sane and intellectual and

modern, but I don't mind betting there's a strong dram of rustic propriety that pops up when she least expects it. I think she's ashamed of the Watchman episode, whatever it was, and furious with herself for being ashamed. What's more, I don't believe she knew, until today, that Legge was an old lag. All guesswork. Let's forget it. We'll have an early lunch and call on Dr. Shaw. I want to ask him about the wound in the finger. Come on."

They returned by way of the furze-bush, collecting the casts and Alleyn's case. As they disliked making entrances with mysterious bundles, they locked their gear in the car and went round to the front of the Feathers. But here they walked into a trap. Sitting beside Abel Pomeroy on the bench outside the front door was an extremely thin and tall man with a long face, a drooping moustache, and foolish eyes. He stared very fixedly at Fox, who recognized him as Mr. George Nark and looked the other way.

"Find your road all right, gentlemen?" asked Abel.

"Yes, thank you, Mr. Pomeroy," said Alleyn.

"It's a tidy stretch, sir. You'll be proper warmed up."

"We're not only warm but dry," said Alleyn.

"Ripe for a pint, I dessay, sir?"

"A glorious thought," said Alleyn.

Mr. Nark cleared his throat. Abel threw a glance of the most intense dislike at him and led the way into the private bar.

" 'Morning," said Mr. Nark, before Fox could get through the door.

"Morning, Mr. Nark," said Fox.

"Don't know but what I wouldn't fancy a pint myself," said Mr. Nark firmly, and followed them into the Private.

Abel drew Alleyn's and Fox's drinks.

" 'Alf-'n-'alf, Abel," said Mr. Nark, grandly.

Somewhat ostentatiously Abel wiped out a shining pint-pot with a spotless cloth. He then drew the mild and bitter.

"Thank 'ee," said Mr. Nark. "Glad to see you're acting careful. Not but what, scientifically speaking, you ought to bile them pots. I don't know what the law has to say on the point," continued Mr. Nark, staring very hard at Alleyn: "I'd have to look it up. The law may touch on it and it may not."

"Don't tell us you'm hazy on the subject," said Abel bitterly. "Us can't believe it."

Mr. Nark smiled in an exasperating manner and took a pull at his beer. He made a rabbit-like noise with his lips, snapping them together several times with a speculative air. He then looked dubiously into his pint-pot.

"Well," said Abel tartly, "what's wrong with it? You'm not p'isoned this time, I suppose?"

"I dessay it's all right," said Mr. Nark. "New barrel, b'ain't it?"

Abel disregarded this enquiry. The ship's decanter, that they had seen in the cupboard, now stood on the bar counter. It was spotlessly clean. Abel took the bottle of Amontillado from a shelf above the bar. He put a strainer in the neck of the decanter and began, carefully, to pour the sherry through it.

"What jiggery-pokery are you up to now, Abel?" enquired Mr. Nark. "Why, Gor'dang it, that thurr decanter was in the pi'son cupboard."

Abel addressed himself exclusively to Alleyn and Fox. He explained the various methods used by Mrs. Ives to clean the decanter. He poured himself out a glass of the sherry and invited them to join him. Under the circumstances they could scarcely refuse. Mr. Nark watched them with extraordinary solicitude and remarked that they were braver men than himself.

"Axcuse me for a bit if you please, gentlemen," said Abel elaborately, to Alleyn and Fox. "I do mind me of summat I've got to tell Mrs. Ives. If you'd be so good as to ring if I'm wanted."

"Certainly, Mr. Pomeroy," said Alleyn.

Abel left them with Mr. Nark.

"Fine morning, sir," said Mr. Nark.

Alleyn agreed.

"Though I suppose," continued Mr. Nark wooingly, "all weathers and climates are one to a man of your calling? Science," continued Mr. Nark, drawing closer and closer to Alleyn, "is a powerful high-handed mistress. Now, just as a matter of curiosity, sir, would you call yourself a man of science?"

"Not I," said Alleyn, good-naturedly. "I'm a policeman, Mr. Nark."

"Ah! That's my point. See? That's my point. Now sir, with all respect, you did ought to make a power more use of the great wonders of science. I'll give in your fingerprints. There's an astonishing thing, now! To think us walks about unconscious-like, leaving our pores and loops all over the shop for science to pick up and have the laugh on us."

It was a peculiarity of Mr. Nark's conversational style that as he drew nearer to his victim he raised his voice. His face was now about twenty inches away from Alleyn's and he roared like an infuriated auctioneer.

"I'm a reader," shouted Mr. Nark. "I'm a reader and you might say a student. How many printed words would you say I'd absorbed in my life? At a guess, now?"

"Really," said Alleyn. "I don't think I could possibly—"

"Fifty-eight million!" bawled Mr. Nark. "Nigh on it. Not reckoning twice-overs. I've soaked up four hundred words, some of 'em as much as five syllables, mind you, every night for the last forty years. Started in at the age of fifteen. 'Sink or swim,' I said, 'I'll improve my brain to the tune of four hundred words per day till I passes out or goes blind!' And I done it. I don't suppose you know a piece of work called *The Evvylootion of the Spices?*"

"Yes."

"There's a tough masterpiece of a job. Took me a year and more, that did. Yes, I've tackled most branches of science. Now the last two years I've turned my eyes in the direction of crime. Trials of famous criminals, lives of murderers, feats of detection, all the whole biling of 'em. Can't get enough of 'em. I'm like that. Whole hog or nothing. Reckon I've sucked it dry."

Mr. Nark emptied his pint-pot and, perhaps as an illustrative gesture, sucked his moustache. He looked at Alleyn out of the corners of his eyes.

"This is a very pretty little case now," he said. "I don't say there's much in it, but it's quite a pretty bit of an affair in its way. You'll be counting on knocking it off in a day or two, I suppose?"

"I don't know about that, Mr. Nark."

"I was a witness."

"At the inquest? I thought—"

"Not at the inquest," interrupted Mr. Nark in a great hurry. "No. Superintendent Nicholas Gawd-Almighty Harper had the running of the inquest. I was a witness to the event. More than that I've made a study of the affair and I've drew my own deductions. I don't suppose they'd interest you. But I've drew 'em."

Alleyn reflected that it was extremely unlikely that Mr. Nark's deductions would be either intelligible or interesting, but he made an agreeable noise and invited him to have another drink. Mr. Nark accepted and drew it for himself.

"Ah," he said. "I reckon I know as much as anybody about this affair. There's criminal carelessness done on purpose, and there's criminal carelessness done by accident. There's motives here and there's motives there, each of 'em making t'other look like a fool, and all of 'em making the biggest fool of Nicholas Harper. Yes. Us chaps takes our lives in our hands when we calls in at Feathers for a pint. Abel knows it. Abel be too mortal deathly proud to own up."

"Carelessness, you said? How did it come about?"

If Mr. Nark's theory of how cyanide got on the dart was ever understood by him, he had no gift for imparting it to others. He became incoherent, and defensively mysterious. He dropped hints and when pressed to explain them, took fright and dived into obscurities. He uttered generalizations of bewildering stupidity, assumed an air of huffiness, floundered into deep water, and remained there, blowing like a grampus. Alleyn was about to leave him in this plight when, perhaps as a last desperate bid for official approval, Mr. Nark made a singular statement.

"The Garden of Eden," he said, "as any eddicated chap knows, is bunk. You can't tell me there's any harm in apples. I grow 'em. Us started off as a drop of jelly. We've come on gradual ever since, working our way up through slime and scales and tails to what we are. We had to *have* a female to do the job. Us knows that. Biological necessity. But she's been a poisonous snare and a curse to us, as even the ignorant author of Genesis had spotted and noted down, in his foolish fashion, under cover of a lot of clap-trap. She's wuzz than a serpent on her own, and she's mostly always at the back of our troubles. *Searchy la fem* as the French detectives say, and you ought to bear in mind. This ghastly affair started a year ago and there's three alive now that knows it. There *was* four."

Alleyn realized, with a sinking heart, that he would have to pay attention to Mr. Nark. He saw in Mr. Nark a desire for fame struggling with an excessive natural timidity. Mr. Nark hungered for the admiring attention of the experts. He also dreaded the law, to which he seemed to accord the veneration and alarm of a neophyte before the altar of some trick and fickle deity. Alleyn decided that he must attempt to speak to him in his own language.

He said: "That's very interesting, Mr. Nark. Strange, isn't it, Fox? Mr. Nark has evidently,"—He fumbled for the magic word,—"evidently made the same deductions as we have, from the evidence in hand."

Fox gave his superior a bewildered and disgusted glance. Alleyn said rather loudly: "See what I mean, Fox?"

Fox saw. "Very striking, sir," he said. "We'll have to get you into the force, Mr. Nark."

Mr. Nark buttoned his coat.

"What'll you take, gentlemen?" he asked.

But it was heavy going. To get any sense out of him Alleyn had to flatter, hint, and cajole. A direct suggestion threw him into a fever of incoherence, at a hint of doubt he became huffy and mysterious. As she seemed to be the only woman in the case, Alleyn attempted to crystallize on Decima.

"Miss Moore," he said at last, "is naturally very much upset by Mr. Watchman's death."

"Ah," said Mr. Nark. "Is she? She may be. P'raps! I don't know anything about women. She may be. Huh!"

Alleyn achieved a knowing laugh in which Fox joined.

"You look below the surface, I see," said Alleyn.

"I base my deductions on fact. Take an example," said Mr. Nark. His third drink, a Treble Extra, had begun to have a mellowing effect. His native burr returned to his usually careful utterance and he smiled knowingly. "Take an example. I don't say it's true to natur'. It's an illustration. A parrible. Ef I takes a stroll up-along Apple Lane of a warm night and hears a courting couple t'other side of hedge in old Jim Moore's orchard, I draws my own conclusions, doan't I?"

"No doubt."

"Ess. And *ef*," said Mr. Nark, "*ef* I do bide thurr, not with idea of eavesdropping but only to reflect and ponder in my deep bitter manner, on the wiles of females in gineral, and *ef* I yurrs a female voice I axpects to yurr, and a maskeline voice I doan't axpects to yurr, and *ef*" continued Mr. Nark fighting his way to the end of his sentence, "I says 'Hullo!' to myself and passes on a step, and *ef* I meet the owner of the maskeline voice I *did* axpect to yurr, standing sly and silent in hedge . . . what do I say? Wait a bit. Doan't tell me. I'll tell you. I says, 'Durn it!' I says, 'Thurr'll be bloodshed along of this-yurr if us doan't looks out!' And *ef* I bides a twelvemonth or more and nothing happens, and then something does happen, bloody and murderous, what do I say then?"

Mr. Nark raised his hand as a signal that this question also was rhetorical, and paused for so long that Fox clenched both his fists and Alleyn had time to light a cigarette.

"I sez," said Mr. Nark loudly, "not a damn thing."

"What!" ejaculated Alleyn.

"Not a damn thing. But I thinks like a furnace."

"What do you think, Mr. Nark?" asked Alleyn with difficulty.

"I thinks 'tis better to yold my tongue ef I want to keep breath in my body. And I yolds it. 'Ess fay, I be mum and I stays mum."

Mr. Nark brought off a mysterious gesture with his right forefinger, leered knowingly at Alleyn, and tacked rapidly towards the door. Once there, he turned to deliver his last word.

"Doan't you go calling my words 'statements,' " he said. "They're a n'allegory, and a n'allegory's got nothing to do with the law. You doan't trip me up thicky-fashion. I know natur of an oath. *Searchy la fem*."

CHAPTER SIXTEEN

Alleyn Exceeds His Duty

i

AFTER THEY had lunched Alleyn brought his report up-to-date, and Fox, sitting solemnly at the parlour table, typed it in duplicate. Alleyn had a brief interview with Abel Pomeroy and returned with three tumblers. One of these he smashed to splinters with the poker, keeping the pieces together, and emptying them into a tin. The other two he wrapped up and placed, with a copy of his report, in his case. He also spent some time throwing down darts and finding that they stuck in the floor. These employments at an end, they drove to Illington. The day had turned gloomy, heavy rain was falling, and the road was slimy.

Alleyn dropped Fox at Woolworth's and went on to Dr. Shaw's house at the end of the principal street. He was shown into a surgery that smelt of leather, iodine, and ether. Here he found Dr. Shaw, who was expecting him. Alleyn liked the look of Dr. Shaw. He had an air of authority and a pleasing directness of manner.

"I hope I'm not an infernal nuisance, coming at this hour," said Alleyn. "Your patients—"

"That's all right. Surgery doesn't start till two. Old trot sitting out there in the waiting room . . . *Malade imaginaire* . . . Do her good to wait a bit, she plagues my life out. Sit down. What do you want to talk about?"

"Principally about the wound and the dart. I've read the police report of the inquest."

"Thought it rather full of gaps? So it is. Mordant, the coroner you know, is a dry old stick, but he's got his wits about him. Respectable bacteriologist in his day. He and Harper got their heads together, I imagine, and decided just how much would be good for the jury. What about the wound?"

"Were there any traces of cyanide, prussic acid, or whatever the blasted stuff is?"

"No. We got a man from London, you know. One of your tame experts. Good man. Mordant and I were both there when he made his tests. We didn't expect a positive result from the wound."

"Why not?"

"Two reasons. He'd bled pretty freely and, if the stuff was introduced on the dart, what wasn't absorbed would be washed away by blood. Also, the stuff's very volatile."

"They found the trace on the dart."

"Yes. Oates kept his head and put the dart into a clean soda-water bottle and corked it up. Couldn't do that with the finger."

"Even so, wouldn't you expect the stuff to evaporate on the dart?"

Dr. Shaw uttered a deep growl and scratched his cheek.

"Perfectly correct," he said, "you would. Puzzling."

"Doesn't it look as if the Scheele's acid, or rather the fifty-percent prussic acid solution, must have been put on the dart a very short time before Oates bottled it up?"

"It does. Thought so all along."

"How long was it, after the event, that you got there?"

"Within half an hour after his death."

"Yes. Now, look here. For private consumption only, would you expect a cyanide solution, however concentrated, to kill a man after that fashion?"

Dr. Shaw thrust his hands in his pockets and stuck out his lower lip.

"I'm not a toxicologist," he said. "Mordant is, and we've taken the king-pin's opinion. Watchman, on his own statement, had a strong idiosyncrasy for cyanide. He told Parish and Cubitt about this the night before the tragedy."

"Yes. I saw that in the files. It's good enough, you think?"

"We've got no precedent for the affair. The experts seem to think it good enough. That dart was thrown with considerable force. It penetrated to the bone, or rather, it actually entered the finger at such an angle that it must have lain along the bone. It's good enough."

"There was no trace of cyanide in the mouth?"

"None. But that doesn't preclude the possibility of his having taken it by the mouth."

"Oh Lord!" sighed Alleyn, "nor it does. Did the room stink of it?"

"No, it stank of brandy. So did the body. Brandy, by the way, is one of the antidotes given for cyanide poisoning. Along with artificial respiration, potassium permanganate, glucose, and half a dozen other remedies, none of which is much use if the cyanide has got into the blood stream."

"Have you a pair of scales?" asked Alleyn abruptly. "Chemical scales or larger, but accurate scales?"

"What? Yes. Yes, I have. Why?"

"Fox, my opposite number, will be here in a minute. He's calling at the police station for the fragments of broken tumbler. I've got a rather fantastic notion. Nothing in it I dare say. We've a pair of scales at the pub but I thought you might be amused if we did a bit of our stuff here."

"Of course I would. Wait a moment while I get rid of that hypochondriacal crone. Shan't be long. Don't move. She only wants a flea in her ear."

Dr. Shaw went into the waiting room. Alleyn could hear his voice raised in crisp admonishment.

". . . Pull yourself together, you know—sound as a bell . . . Take up a hobby . . . Your own physician . . . Be a sensible woman . . ."

A doorbell rang and in a moment Fox and Superintendent Harper were shown into the surgery.

"Hullo, hullo!" said Harper. "What's all this I hear? Thought I'd come along. Got an interesting bit of news for you." He dropped his voice. "I sent a chap up to London by the milk train. He's taken the dart to Dabs and they've just rung through. The prints are good enough. What do you think they've found?"

"I can see they've found something, Nick," said Alleyn, smiling.

"You bet they have. Those prints belong to Mr. Montague Thringle, who did four years for embezzlement and came out of Broadmoor twenty-six months ago."

"Loud cheers," said Alleyn, "and *much* laughter."

"Eh? Yes, and that's not the best of it. Who do you think defended one of the accused and shifted all the blame on to Thringle?"

"None other than Luke Watchman, the murdered K.C.?"

"You're right. Legge's a gaol-bird who owes, or thinks he owes, his sentence to Watchman. He's just dug himself in pretty, with a nice job and lots of mugs eating out of his hand, and along comes the very man who can give him away."

"Now I'll tell you something *you* don't know," said Alleyn. "Who do you think was implicated with Montague Thringle and got off with six months?"

"Lord Bryonie. Big scandal it was."

"Yes. Miss Darragh's unfortunate cousin, the Lord Bryonie."

"You don't tell me that! Miss Darragh! I'd put her right out of the picture."

"She holds a watching-brief for Thringle-alias-Legge, I fancy," said Alleyn, and related the morning's adventure.

"By gum!" cried Harper, "I think it's good enough. I reckon we're just about right for a warrant. With the fact that only Legge could have known the dart would hit—what d'you think? Shall we pull him in?"

"I don't think we'll make an arrest just yet, Nick."

"Why not?"

"Well, I think the result would be what the highbrows call a miscarriage of justice. I'll tell you why."

ii

But before he had finished telling them why, an unmistakable rumpus in the street announced the arrival of Colonel Brammington's car. And presently Colonel Brammington himself came charging into the room with Dr. Shaw on his heels.

"I saw your car outside," he shouted. "A galaxy of all the talents with Aesculapius to hold the balance. Aesculapius usurps that seat of justice, poetic justice with her lifted scale."

Dr. Shaw put a small pair of scales on the table and grinned. Colonel Brammington took one of Alleyn's cigarettes and hurled himself into a chair.

"Curiosity," he said, "was praised by the great Doctor, as one of the permanent and certain characteristics of a vigorous intellect. His namesake, the rare Ben, remarked that he did love to note and to observe. With these noble precedents before me, I shall offer no excuse, but following the example of Beatrice, shall like a lapwing run, close to the ground to hear your confidence. An uncomfortable feat and one for which my great belly renders me unfit. Have you any matches? Ah, thank you."

Harper, with his back to the Chief Constable, turned his eyes up for the edification of Fox. He laid a tin box on the table.

"Here you are, Mr. Alleyn."

"Good." Alleyn weighed the box speculatively in his hands and then emptied its contents into the scale.

"What is that?" demanded Colonel Brammington. "Glass? Ah, the orts and fragments of the brandy glass, perhaps."

"That's it, sir," said Alleyn.

"And pray why do you put them on the scales?"

"Sir," murmured Alleyn politely, "to find out their weight."

Colonel Brammington said mildly: "You mock me, by Heaven. And what do they weigh?"

"Two ounces, forty-eight grains. That right, Dr. Shaw?"

"That's it."

Alleyn returned the fragments to their box and took a second box from his pocket.

"In this," he said, "are the pieces of an identically similar glass for which I gave Mr. Pomeroy one and six-pence. They are his best glasses. Now then."

He tipped the second shining heap into the scales.

"Yes, by George," said Alleyn softly. "Look. Two ounces, twenty-four grains."

"Here!" exclaimed Harper. "That's less. It must be a lighter glass."

"No," said Alleyn. "It's the same brand of glass. Abel took the glasses for the brandy from a special shelf. I've borrowed two more, unbroken. Let's have them, Fox."

Fox produced two tumblers. Each of them weighed two ounces, twenty-four grains.

"But look here," objected Harper. "We didn't get every scrap of that glass up. Some of it had been ground into the boards. Watchman's glass should, if anything, weigh less than the others."

"I know," said Alleyn.

"Well then—"

"Some other glass must have fallen," said Colonel Brammington. "They were full of distempering draughts, red-hot with drinking. One of them may have let fall some other glass. A pair of spectacles. Didn't Watchman wear an eyeglass?"

"It was round his neck," said Dr. Shaw, "unbroken."

"There seems to have been no other glass broken, sir," said Alleyn. "I've asked. Did you find all the pieces in one place, Harper?"

"Like you'd expect, a bit scattered and trampled about. I daresay there were pieces in the soles of their boots. Damn it all," cried Harper in exasperation, "*it must* weigh lighter."

He weighed the glass again, peering suspiciously at the scales. The result was exactly the same. The fragments of Watchman's glass weighed twenty-four grains heavier than the unbroken tumbler.

"This is rather amusing," said Colonel Brammington.

Alleyn sat at the table and spread the broken glass over a sheet of paper. Fox gave him a pair of tweezers and he began to sort the pieces into a graduated row. The other men drew closer.

"It's the same tumbler," said Colonel Brammington. "There, you see, are the points of one of those loathsome stars."

Alleyn took a jeweller's lens from his pocket.

"Ah!" muttered Colonel Brammington, staring at him with a bulging and raffish eye. "He peers. He screws a glass into his orb and with enlarged vision feeds his brain."

"We always feel rather self-conscious about these things," said Alleyn, "but they have their uses. Here, I think, are three, no four small pieces of glass that *might* be different from—well, let's weigh them."

He put them in the scales.

"Thirty-one grains. That, Harper, leaves a margin of eleven grains for the bits you missed. Any good?"

"Do you think these bits are a different class of stuff, Mr. Alleyn?" asked Harper.

"I think so. There's a difference in colour and if you look closely you can see they're a bit thicker."

"He has written a monograph on broken tumblers," cried Colonel Brammington delightedly. "Let me look through your lens."

He crouched over the table.

"They are different," he said. "You are quite right, my dear Alleyn. What can it mean? The iodine bottle? No, it was found unbroken beneath the settle."

"What did you discover at Woolworth's, Fox?" asked Alleyn.

"Nothing much, Mr. Alleyn. I tried all the other places as well. They haven't sold any and they say there's very little shop-lifting in Illington."

"Veil upon veil will lift," remarked Colonel Brammington, "but there will be veil upon veil behind. What is this talk of shoplifting?"

"I'll explain, sir," began Alleyn.

"On second thoughts, pray don't. I prefer, Alleyn, to be your Watson. You dine with me to-night? Very good. Give me the evidence, and let me brood."

"But don't you wish to hear Mr. Alleyn's case, sir?" asked Harper in a scandalized voice. "Your position—"

"I do not. I prefer to listen to voices in the upper air nor lose my simple faith in mysteries. I prefer to take the advice of the admirable Tupper and will let not the conceit of intellect hinder me from worshipping mystery. But nevertheless, give me your plain plump facts. I will sing, with Ovid, of facts."

"You will not have Ovid's privilege of inventing them," rejoined Alleyn. "I have brought a copy of my report on the case. It's up-to-date."

Colonel Brammington took the file and seemed to become the victim of an intolerable restlessness. He rose, hitched up his shapeless trousers and said rapidly in a high voice: "Well, good-bye, Shaw. Come to dinner to-night."

"Oh, thank you very much, sir," said Dr. Shaw. "I'd like to. Black tie?"

"As the fancy takes you. I shall make some gesture. Broadcloth and boiled line. You come, Harper?"

"Thank you, sir, I'm afraid I can't. I've got to—"

"All right. I see. Three then. You, Alleyn; Shaw, and—ah—"

"Fox," said Alleyn.

"Ah yes. Splendid. Well, *au revoir*."

"I was going to ask you, sir—" began Harper.

"Oh God! What?"

"It doesn't matter, sir, if you're in a hurry." Harper opened the door with emphasized politeness. "Good afternoon, sir."

"Oh, good-bye to you, Harper, good-bye," said Colonel Brammington, impatiently, and plunged out.

"If that," said Harper sourly, "is the modern idea of a Chief Constable it's not mine. You wouldn't credit it, would you, that when the gentleman's brother dies, he'll be a Lord. A lord, mind you! Bawling hurricane. Where's he get the things he says, Doctor? Out of his head or out of books?"

"Not having his brains, his memory, or his library I can't tell you," said Dr. Shaw.

iii

Alleyn, Fox, and Harper went to the police station. Here they had a long reiterative conversation. They compared Alleyn's casts with the shoes Watchman wore on the day of his death, and found that they tallied exactly. They went over the case step by step. Alleyn expounded, the others listened. They laid their collection of oddments on Harper's table; the brandy-bottle, the broken glass, the iodine bottle, the stained newspaper, the small china vessel from the rat-hole, and the bottle of Scheele's acid. Harper gave Alleyn a stoppered bottle.

"Ah," said Alleyn, "that's the stuff out of the rat-hole jar? I want you to get it analyzed. Perhaps Dr. Mordant would do it. No, I suppose that would be too unofficial. It had better go to London."

"You think our murderer got the stuff from the garage?" asked Harper.

"I do."

"But the thing was full."

"Because it was full," said Alleyn.

"You reckon that was water," asked Harper slowly.

"Yes, Nick."

"I see," said Harper.

"The poison-party," said Alleyn, "was attended by Abel, who put the prussic acid in the china pot and stopped the hole; by Will, by Miss Moore, by Legge, who only looked in for a moment, and by a couple of fishermen who were on their way to the public bar and who don't come into the picture. Subsequently Abel warned everybody in the place about what he had done, so that the actual attendance at the poison-party may not give us our answer. On the other hand it is possible that one of them lagged behind and pinched the poison. They all profess to have forgotten in what order they left. Now prussic acid in Mr. Noggins' fifty-per-cent solution is a highly volatile liquid. Judging by the stench, its fumes have accounted for at least one rat, so probably it was not removed immediately. On the other hand, it seems it would evaporate considerably in something under an hour. I'm not sure on this point. We'll experiment. The experts say, in their report, under an hour. Very good. My contention is that the murderer must have nipped into the garage, within an hour after Abel left it, and taken the poison, which would be kept in a tightly corked bottle until it was needed."

"But how the hell would he get it? The jar had Abel's prints. It hadn't been touched."

"Do you remember—"

"By God!" shouted Harper. "Don't tell me! I've got it."

He broke into a stream of oaths through which his enlightenment struggled for expression.

"That's it," said Alleyn. "Looks like it, doesn't it?"

"Looks like it!" ejaculated Harper. "It blasted well shrieks of it. I'm a hell of a detective I am! Look at me! I missed the point about that evaporation business! Took Abel in to look at the pot and he said it was just the amount he'd poured in. Well, the damn thing was full. I never thought it might be water. I took photographs and sealed the place up just as it was. I *did* pour off this stuff and keep it. I'll say that for myself. I made sure the poison had come out of the bottle in the cupboard. Blast it!"

"Abel's prints," Alleyn said, "were still on the key of the cupboard and on the knob. You can't open the door without turning the key and the knob. Dr. Shaw saw that, when he looked at the cupboard and waited until it had been tested for prints. If anyone else had been to the cupboard they would either have left their own prints, used gloves and smeared Abel's prints, or else wiped them off entirely. Nobody could have been to the cupboard."

"I knew that, but all the same . . . Well, I suppose I thought they might have got at the bottle while—oh hell!"

"Anybody might have missed it, Mr. Harper," said Fox. "I didn't pick it till Mr. Alleyn pointed it out."

"And I was lucky," said Alleyn. "I'd read Taylor on the cyanides, during our trip down."

"Well," said Harper, "the coroner and Dr. Shaw missed the point. Oates gave evidence of discovery of the stuff in the rat-hole. Old Pomeroy deposed it was the same amount he'd poured in. Nobody said anything about evaporation."

"Oates," Alleyn pointed out, "saw the first night with Dr. Shaw—before they knew the exact nature of the poison. Not much more than twenty-six hours after it was put there."

"He might have just dipped the dart in the stuff," said Harper. "I did think of that. But now—"

"Now we know the dart must have been doctored a very short time before Oates sealed it up. You see where we're heading?"

"Yes," said Harper unwillingly. "I see, all right. But suppose Legge had the stuff on him and put it on the dart just before he threw it—"

"He didn't," said Alleyn. "Believe me, he didn't. He's a clumsy man. He fumbles. His hands are coarse and his fingers are thick. To get cyanide on that dart with seven pairs of eyes watching him, he'd need the skill and the hands of a conjurer. Even Abel Pomeroy who thinks, or wants to think, Legge did the job, can't offer an idea of how he did it. Parish, who has thrown Legge in my teeth every time I've seen him, hasn't an argument to offer. And on the other side we've got Will, Miss Moore, Miss Darragh and Cubitt all ready to swear, with, I believe, perfect truth, that Legge, as he stood there under the light, had no chance of anointing the fourth, or any other dart."

"But we can't explain the poison in any other way."

"Oh yes," said Alleyn, "I think we can. This is our case."

iv

Five o'clock had struck and they were still at the police station. Alleyn had gone over every word of his report with Harper. He had described each interview and had sorted the scraps of evidence into two groups, the relevant and the irrelevant. He had poured prussic acid solution into Abel's little jar and, to reproduce rat-hole conditions, had placed it in a closed drawer. At the end of forty-six minutes half had evaporated.

"So you see," said Alleyn, "if the liquid you found in the tin is water, as I believe it is, it looks as if the murderer must have visited the garage within forty-five minutes. Now on that night—the night on which Watchman chipped Legge and Will Pomeroy lost his temper—Legge gave an exhibition of dart-throwing which lasted only a few seconds. This took place a few minutes after Abel had set the poison in the garage. The argument followed. Legge went into the public bar, where he brought off the trick with the darts. He then returned and joined the others in a game of Round-the-Clock—"

"There you are," interrupted Harper, "he could—sorry! Go on."

"I know he could, Nick, but wait a bit. According to your report they all, with the exception of Miss Darragh, who had gone to bed, stayed in the private tap-room until closing time. Our forty-five minutes have gone."

"I suppose," said Harper, "one of them might have gone out for a few minutes without being noticed."

"Yes, and that is a point that will be urged by counsel. All we can prove here is opportunity—possibility. We can't bring anything home. May we have the stuff you took from the rat-hole, Nick? Fox, would you get my bag? Mr. Noggins was generous with his prussic acid and there are at least three ounces of the water, if it is water. The analyst can lend us half. Let's poach on his preserves and find out for ourselves."

Fox opened Alleyn's bag. From it he took two open-mouthed vessels about two inches high, two watch glasses, and a small bottle. Alleyn squinted at the bottle.

"Silver nitrate. That's the stuff. Can you produce some warm water, Nick? Well, well I *am* exceeding my duty to be sure."

Harper went out and returned with a jug of water and a photographic dish. Alleyn poured a little water into the dish, half-filled one of his tiny vessels with the fluid found in the rat-hole, and the other with acid from Abel's bottle. He wetted the underside of the watch-glasses with nitrate solution and placed them over the vessels. He then stood the vessels, closed by the watch-glasses, in the warm water.

"Fox now says the Lord's Prayer backwards," he explained. "I emit a few oddments of ectoplasm and Hi Cockalorum the spell is wound up! Take a look at that, Nick."

They stared at the dish. On the surface of the prussic acid a little spiral had risen. It became denser, it flocculated, and the watch-glass was no longer transparent but covered with an opaque whiteness.

"That's cyanide, that was," said Alleyn. "Now, look at the other. A blank, my lord. It's water, Br'er Fox, it's water. Now let's pour them back into their respective bottles and don't give me away to the analyst."

"I suppose," said Harper, as Alleyn tidied up, "I suppose this means we needn't worry ourselves about the cupboard. The cupboard doesn't come into the blasted affair."

Alleyn held on the palm of his hand the three pieces of glass he had separated from the fragments of the broken brandy tumbler, and the small misshapen lumps he had found in the ashes of the fire.

"Oh yes," he said. "Yes. We're not home yet, not by a long march, but the cupboard still comes into the picture. Think."

Harper looked from the pieces of glass to Alleyn's face and back again.

"Yes," he said slowly, "yes. But you'll have the devil of a job to prove it."

"I agree," said Alleyn. "Nevertheless, Nick, I hope to prove it."

CHAPTER SEVENTEEN

Mr. Fox Takes Sherry

i

Parish came downstairs singing "*La Donna é Mobile*." He had a pleasant baritone voice which had been half-trained in the days when he had contemplated musical comedy. He sang stylishly and one could not believe that he sang unconsciously. He swung open the door of the private tap and entered on the last flourish of that impertinent, that complacently debonair refrain.

"Good evening sir," said Abel from behind the bar.

" 'Tis pleasant to hear you'm back to your churruping ways again."

Parish smiled wistfully.

"Ah, Abel," he said with a slight sigh, "it's not as easy as it sounds; but my cousin would have been the last man to want long faces, poor dear old fellow."

"So he would, then," rejoined Abel heartily, "the very last."

"Ah," said Mr. Nark, shaking his head. Norman Cubitt looked over the top of his tankard and raised his eyebrows. Legge moved into the inglenook where Miss Darragh sat knitting.

"What'll you take, Mr. Parish?" asked Abel.

"A Treble Extra. I need it. Hullo, Norman old man," said Parish with a sort of brave gaiety. "How's the work going?"

"Nicely, thank you, Seb." Cubitt glanced at the clock. It was a quarter past seven. "I'm thinking of starting a big canvas," he said.

"Are you? What subject?"

"Decima," said Cubitt. He put his tankard down on the bar. "She has very kindly said she'll sit to me."

"How'll you paint her?" asked Parish.

"I thought on the downs by Cary Edge. She's got a red sweater thing. It'll be life-size. Full length."

"Ah, now," exclaimed Miss Darragh from the inglenook, "you've taken my advice in the latter end. Haven't I been at you, now, ever since I got here, to take Miss Moore for your subject? I've never seen a better. Sure, the picture'll be your masterpiece, for she's a lovely young creature."

"But my dear chap," objected Parish, "we're off in a day or two. You'll never finish it."

"I was going to break it gently to you, Seb. If you don't object I think I'll stay on for a bit."

Parish looked slightly hurt.

"That's just as you like, of course," he said. "Don't ask me to stay. The place is too full of memories."

"Besides," said Cubitt drily, "you start rehearsals to-day week, don't you?"

"As a matter of fact I do." Parish raised his arms and then let them fall limply to his sides. "Work!" he said. "Back to the old grind. Ah well!" And he added with an air of martyrdom, "I can go back by train."

"I'll drive you into Illington, of course."

"Thank you, old boy. Yes, I'd better get back to the treadmill."

"Keep a stiff upper lip, Seb," said Cubitt with a grin.

The door opened and Alleyn came in. He wore a dinner jacket and stiff shirt. Someone once said of him that he looked like a cross between a grandee and a monk. In evening clothes the grandee predominated. Parish gave him a quick appraising glance, Mr. Nark goggled, and Miss Darragh looked up with a smile. Cubitt rumpled his hair and said: "Hullo! Here comes the county!"

Mr. Legge shrank back into the inglenook. Upon all of them a kind of wariness descended. They seemed to melt away from him and towards each other. Alleyn asked for two glasses of the special sherry and told Abel that he and Fox would be out till latish.

"May we have a key, Mr. Pomeroy?"

"Us'll leave side-door open," said Abel. "No need fur key, sir. Be no criminals in this neighbourhood. Leastways—" He stopped short and looked pointedly at Legge.

"That's splendid," said Alleyn. "How far is it to Colonel Bramminton's?"

" 'Bout eight mile, sir. Shankley Court. A great masterpiece of a place, sir, with iron gates and a deer park. Carry on for mile beyond Illington and turn left at The Man of Devon."

"Right," said Alleyn. "We needn't leave for half an hour."

Cubitt went out.

Alleyn fidgeted with a piece of rag round his left hand. It was clumsily tied and fell away, disclosing a trail of red.

He twitched the handkerchief out of his breast pocket, glanced at it and swore. There was a bright red spot on the handkerchief.

"Blast that cut," said Alleyn. "Now I'll have to get a clean one."

"Hurt hurrself, sir?" asked Abel.

"Tore my hand on a rusty nail in the garage."

"In the garage!" ejaculated Mr. Nark. "That's a powerful dangerous place to get a cut finger. Germs galore, I dessay, and as like as not some of the poison fumes still floating about."

"Aye," said Abel angrily, "that's right, George Nark. All my premises is still with poison. Wonder 'tis you come anigh 'em. Here, Mr. Alleyn, sir, I'll get 'ee a dressing fur that-thurr cut."

"If I could have a bit of rag and a dab of peroxide or something."

"Doan't you have anything out of that fatal cupboard," said Mr. Nark. "Not if you value the purity of your blood stream."

"You know as well as I do," said Abel, "that thurr cupboard's been scrubbed and fumigated. Not that thurr's anything in it. Thurr b'ain't. Nicholas Harper made off with my first-aid set, innocent though it wurr."

"And the iodine bottle," pointed out Mr. Nark, "so you can't give the inspector iodine, lethal or otherwise."

"Thurr's another first-aid box upstairs," said Abel. "In bathroom cupboard. Will!" He looked into the public bar. "Will! Get t'other out of bathroom cupboard, my sonny. Look lively."

"It doesn't matter, Mr. Pomeroy," said Alleyn. "Don't bother. I'll use this handkerchief."

"No trouble, sir, and you'll need a bit of antiseptic in that cut if you took it off a rusty nail. I'm a terror fur iodine, sir. I wurr a surgeon's orderly in France, Mr. Alleyn, and learned hospital ways. Scientific ideas b'ain't George Nark's private property though you might think they wurr."

Will Pomeroy came downstairs and into the private bar. He put a small first-aid box on the counter and returned to the public bar. Abel opened the box.

" 'Tis spandy-new," he said, "I bought it from a traveller only couple of days afore accident. Hullo! Yurr, Will!"

"What's up?" called Will.

"Iodine bottle's gone."

"Eh?"

"Where's iodine?"

"I dunno. It's not there!" shouted Will.

"Who's had it?"

"I dunno. I haven't."

"It really doesn't matter, Mr. Pomeroy," said Alleyn. "It's bled itself clean. Perhaps there wasn't any iodine."

"Course there wurr," said Abel. "Yurr's lil' bed whurr it lay. Damme, who's been at it? *Mrs. Ives!*"

He stumped out and could be heard roaring angrily about the back premises.

Alleyn put a bit of lint over his finger and Miss Darragh stuck it down with strapping. He went upstairs, carrying his own glass of sherry and Fox's. Fox was standing before the looking-glass in his room, knotting a sober tie. He caught sight of Alleyn in the glass.

"Lucky I brought my blue suit," said Fox, "and lucky you brought your dress clothes, Mr. Alleyn."

"Why didn't you let me tell Colonel Brammington that we'd neither of us change, Foxkin?"

"No, no, sir. It's the right thing for you to dress, just as much as it'd be silly for me to do so. Well, it'd be an affected kind of way for me to act, Mr. Alleyn. I never get a black coat and boiled shirt on my back except at the Lodge meetings and when I'm on a night-club job. The Colonel would only think I was trying to put myself in a place where I don't belong. Did you find what you wanted, Mr. Alleyn?"

"Abel bought another first-aid set, two days before Watchman died. The iodine has been taken. He can't find it."

"Is that so?"

Fox brushed the sleeves of his coat and cast a final searching glance at himself in the glass. "I washed that razor blade," he said.

"Thank you, Fox. I was a little too free with it. Bled all over Abel's bar. Most convincing. What's the time? Half-past seven. A bit early yet. Let's think this out."

"Right-o, sir," said Fox. He lifted his glass of sherry. "Good luck, Mr. Alleyn," he said.

ii

Decima had promised to come to Coombe Head at eight o'clock. Cubitt lay on the lip of the cliff and stared at the sea beneath him, trying, as Alleyn had tried, to read order and sequence into the hieroglyphics traced by the restless seaweed. The sequence was long and subtle, unpausing, unhurried. Each pattern seemed significant but all melted into fluidity and he decided, as Alleyn had decided, that the forces that governed these beautiful but inane gestures ranged beyond the confines of his imagination. He fell to appraising the colour and the shifting tones of the water, translating these things into terms of paint, and he began to think of how, in the morning, he would make a rapid study from the lip of the cliff.

"But I must fix one pattern only in my memory and watch for it to appear in the sequence, like a measure in some intricate saraband."

He was so intent on this project that he did not hear Decima come and was startled when she spoke to him.

"Norman?"

Her figure was dark and tall against the sky. He rose and faced her.

"Have you risen from the sea?" he asked. "You are lovely enough."

She did not answer and he took her hand and led her a little way over the headland to a place where their figures no longer showed against the sky. Here they faced each other again.

"I am so bewildered," said Decima. "I have tried since this morning to feel all sorts of things. Shame. Compassion for Will. Anxiety. I can feel none of them. I can only wonder why we should so suddenly have fallen in love."

"It was only sudden for you," said Cubitt. "Not for me."

"But—Is that true? How long . . . ?"

"Since last year. Since the first week of last year."

Decima drew away from him.

"But, didn't you know? I thought last year that you had guessed."

"About Luke? Yes, I guessed."

"Everything?"

"Yes, my dear."

"I wish very much that it hadn't happened," said Decima. "Of that I am ashamed. Not for the orthodox reason but because it made such a fool of me; because I pretended to myself that I was sanely satisfying a need, whereas in reality I merely lost my head and behaved like a dairymaid."

"Hullo," said Cubitt. "You're being very county. What's wrong with dairymaids in the proletariat?"

"Brute," muttered Decima and, between laughter and tears, stumbled into his arms.

"I love you very much," whispered Cubitt.

"You'd a funny way of showing it. Nobody ever would have dreamed you thought anything about me."

"Oh yes, they would. They did."

"Who?" cried Decima in terror. "Not Will?"

"No. Miss Darragh. She as good as told me so. I've seen her eyeing me whenever you were in the offing. God knows I had a hard job to keep my eyes off you. I've wanted like hell to do this."

But after a few moments Decima freed herself.

"This is going the wrong way," she said. "There mustn't be any of this."

Cubitt said, "All right. We'll come back to earth. I promised myself I'd keep my head. Here, my darling, have a cigarette, for God's sake, and don't look at me. Sit down. That's right. Now listen. You remember the morning of that day?"

"When you and Sebastian came over the hill?"

"Yes. Just as you were telling Luke you could kill him. Did you?"

"No."

"Of course you didn't. Nor did I. But we made a botch of things this morning. Seb and I denied that we saw Luke as we came back from Coombe Head and I think Alleyn knew we were lying. I got a nasty jolt when he announced that he was going to see you. I didn't know what to do. I dithered round and finally followed him, leaving Seb to come home by himself. I was too late. You'd told him?"

"I told him that Luke and I quarrelled that morning because Luke had tried—had tried to make love to me. I didn't tell him . . . Norman: I lied about the rest. I said it hadn't happened before. I was afraid. I was cold with panic. I didn't know what you and Sebastian had told him. I thought if he found out that I had been Luke's mistress and that we'd quarrelled, he might think . . . They say poison's a woman's weapon don't they? It was like one of those awful dreams. I don't know what I said. I lost my head. And that other man, Fox, kept writing in a book. And then you came and it was as if—oh, as if instead of being alone in the dark, and terrified, I had someone beside me."

"Why wouldn't you stay with me when they'd gone?"

"I don't know. I wanted to think. I was muddled."

"I was terrified you wouldn't come here to-night, Decima."

"I shouldn't have come. What are we to do about Will?"

"Tell him."

"He'll be so bewildered," said Decima, "and so miserable."

"Would you have married him if this hadn't happened?"

"I haven't said I would marry you."

"I have," said Cubitt.

"I don't know that I believe in the institution of marriage."

"You'll find that out when you've tried it, my darling."

"I'm a farmer's daughter. A peasant."

"The worst of you communists," said Cubitt, "is that you're such snobs. Always worrying about class distinctions. Come here."

"Norman," said Decima presently, "who do you think it was?"

"I don't know. I don't know."

Cubitt pressed her hands against him and, after a moment, spoke evenly. "Did Will ever guess about you and Luke?"

She moved away from him at arm's-length. "You can't think Will would do it?"

"Did he guess?"

"I don't think—I—"

"I rather thought he had guessed," said Cubitt.

iii

When Alleyn had gone out, the atmosphere of the tap-room changed. Parish began to talk to Abel, Miss Darragh asked Legge when he was moving into Illington, Mr. Nark cleared his throat and, by the simple expedient of shouting down everyone else, won the attention of the company.

"Ah," he said. "Axing the road to Shankley Court, was he? Ah. I expected it."

Abel gave a disgruntled snort.

"I expected it," repeated Mr. Nark firmly. "I had a chat with the Chief Inspector this morning."

"After which, in course," said Abel, "he knew his business. All he's got to do is to clap handcuffs on somebody."

"Abel," said Mr. Nark, "you're a bitter man. I'm not blaming you. A chap with a turrible load on his conscience, same as what you've got, is scarcely responsible for his words."

"On his conscience!" said Abel angrily. "What the devil do you mean? Why doan't 'ee say straight out I'm a murderer?"

"Because you're not, Abel. Murder's one thing and negligence is another. Manslaughter's the term for your crime. If proper care had been took, as I told the Chief Inspector; though, mind you, I'm not a chap to teach a man his own business—"

"What sort of a chap did you say you wasn't?"

Miss Darragh intervened.

"I'm sure," she said, "we all must hope for the end of this terrible affair. Whether 'twas accident, or whether 'twas something else, it's been a dreadful strain and an anxiety for us all."

"So it has then, Miss," agreed Abel. He looked at Legge who had turned his back and was engaged, with the assistance of a twisted handkerchief, on an unattractive exploration of his left ear. "Sooner they catch the murderer the happier all of us'll be."

Parish caught Abel's eyes and he too looked at Legge.

"I can't believe," said Parish, "that a crime like this can go unpunished. I shall not rest content until I know my cousin is avenged."

"Ah now, Mr. Parish," said Miss Darragh, "you must not let this tragedy make the bitter man of you. Sure, you're talking like the Count of Monte Cristo if 'twas he was the character I call to mind."

"Do I sound bitter?" asked Parish in his beautiful voice. "Perhaps I do. Perhaps I am."

A shadow of something that might have been a twinkle flitted across Miss Darragh's face.

"A little too bitter," she said, and it was impossible to tell whether or not she spoke ironically.

On the floor above them there was a sudden commotion. A man's voice spoke urgently. They heard a scuffle of feet and then someone ran along the upstairs passage.

"What's wrong with the sleuths?" asked Parish.

No one answered. Miss Darragh took up her knitting. Mr. Nark picked his teeth. Parish finished his beer.

"We all want to see the man caught," said Legge suddenly. He spoke in his usual querulous, muffled voice. He looked ill and he seemed extremely nervous. Miss Darragh glanced at him and said soothingly:

"Of course."

"Their behaviour," said Legge, "is abominable. Abominable! I intend writing a letter to the Commissioner of Scotland Yard. It is disgraceful."

Parish planted his feet apart, put his head on one side, and looked at Legge with the expression he used in films of the Bulldog Drummond type. His voice drawled slightly.

"Feelin' nervous, Legge?" he asked. "Now isn't that a pity."

"Nervous! I am not nervous, Mr. Parish. What do you mean by—"

"Gentlemen," said old Abel.

There was a brief silence broken by an urgent clatter of footsteps on the stairs.

The door into the private tap swung open. Alleyn stood on the threshold. When Miss Darragh saw his face she uttered a sharp cry that was echoed, oddly, by Parish.

Alleyn said:—

"Nobody is to move from this room. Understand? What's Dr. Shaw's telephone number?"

Abel said: "Illington 579, sir."

Alleyn kicked the door wide open and moved to the wall telephone just outside. He dialled a number and came into the doorway with the receiver at his ear.

"You understand," he said, "none of you is to move. Where's Cubitt?"

"He's gone out," said Parish. "What's the matter, Mr. Alleyn, for God's sake?"

Alleyn was speaking into the receiver:

"Dr. Shaw? At once, please, it's the police." He eyed them all as he waited.

"There has been an accident," he said. "Where's that decanter of sherry?"

"Here, sir," said Abel.

"Take it by the end of the neck, lock it in the cupboard behind you, and bring the key to me. That you, Shaw? Alleyn. Come at once. Same trouble as last time. I've given an emetic. It's worked, but he's half-collapsed. I'll do artificial respiration. For God's sake be quick."

He clicked the receiver and took the key Abel brought him. He dialled another number and spoke to Abel as he dialled it.

"Lock the shutters and all the doors. Both bars. Bring the keys here. Illington Police Station? Oates? Inspector Alleyn. I want Mr. Harper and yourself at once at the Plume of Feathers. Jump to it."

He hung up the receiver. Abel was clattering round the public bar. Alleyn slammed the shutters in the private bar.

"If anyone opens these shutters or tries to leave this room," he said, "there will be an arrest on a charge of attempted murder. Bring those others through here."

"But, look here—" said Parish.

"Quiet!" said Alleyn and was obeyed. Abel shepherded a couple of astonished fishermen into the private bar. Will Pomeroy followed. Abel slammed down the bar shutter and locked it. He came to Alleyn and gave him the keys. Alleyn pushed him outside, slammed the door and locked it.

"Now," he said, "come up here."

He ran up the stairs, taking three at a stride. Abel followed, panting. The door of Alleyn's room was open. Fox sat on the bed with the wash-hand basin at his feet. His face was curiously strained and anxious. When he saw Alleyn he tried to speak, but something had gone wrong with his mouth. He kept shutting his jaw with a sharp involuntary movement and his voice was thick. He jerked his hand at the bowl.

"Thank God," said Alleyn. "Can you do another heave, old thing?"

Fox jerked his head sideways and suddenly pitched forward. Alleyn caught him.

"Move that basin," he ordered. "I want to get him on the floor."

Abel moved the basin and together he and Alleyn moved Fox. Alleyn had wrenched open Fox's collar and tie. He now loosened his clothes. Somewhere in the background of his conscious thoughts was an impression that it was strange to be doing these things to Fox whom he knew so well. He began the movements of resuscitation, working hard and rhythmically. Abel quietly cleared an area round Fox.

"When you'm tiring, sir," said Abel, "I'll take a turn."

But Alleyn scarcely knew he had a body of his own. His body and breath, precariously and dubiously, belonged to Fox. His thoughts were visited by hurrying pictures. He saw a figure that shoved and sweated and set the wheels of a great vehicle in motion. A figure turned and turned again at a crank handle. He was aware, at moments most vividly, of his own glass of untouched sherry on the dressing-table. Fox's arms were heavy and stiff. Presently his eyes opened. The pupils had widened almost to the rim of the iris, the eyes had no expression. Alleyn's own eyes were half-blinded with sweat. Suddenly the body on the floor heaved.

"That's better," said Abel, stooping to the basin, "he'm going to vomit again."

Alleyn turned Fox on his side. Fox neatly and prolifically made use of the basin.

"Brandy," said Alleyn. "In a bag in the wardrobe."

He watched Abel fetch the flask. Alleyn unscrewed the top, smelt at the contents, and took a mouthful. He squatted on his haunches with the brandy in his mouth. The brandy was all right. He swallowed it, poured some into the cap of the flask, and gave it to Fox.

Downstairs the telephone was pealing.

"Go and answer it," said Alleyn.

Abel went out.

"Fox," said Alleyn. "Fox, my dear old thing."

Fox's lips moved. Alleyn took his handkerchief and wiped that large face carefully.

"Very inconvenient," said a voice inside Fox. "Sorry."

"You b——old b——," said Alleyn softly.

CHAPTER EIGHTEEN

Mr. Legge Commits a Misdemeanour

i

"I'M BETTER," said Fox presently. "I'd like to sit up."

Alleyn propped him against the bed.

A car pulled up outside and in a moment Alleyn heard a clatter of steps and the sound of voices. Abel came in.

"Your be doctor," Abel said, "and Nick Harper with police. And Colonel's on telephone roaring like proper grampus."

"Oh Lord!" Alleyn ejaculated. "Abel, tell him what's happened. He'll probably want to come over here. Apologize for me. Where's the doctor?"

"Here," said Dr. Shaw, and walked in. "What's the trouble? Hullo!"

He went to Fox.

"I'm better, Doctor," said Fox. "I've vomited."

Dr. Shaw took his pulse, looked at his eyes and nodded.

"You'll do," he said, "but we'll make a job of it. Come into the bathroom. You'd better keep that matter in the basin, Alleyn."

He opened his bag, took out a tube, and jerked his head at Fox.

"Here!" said Fox resentfully, eyeing the tube.

"How did it happen?" asked Dr. Shaw.

Harper came in.

"I've left Oates and another man downstairs," said Harper. "What's up?"

"Fox drank a glass of sherry," said Alleyn. "There's the glass. We'll detain all the crowd downstairs. You too, Mr. Pomeroy. Go down and join them."

"Move along, Abel," said Harper.

"I yurrd, I yurrd," grunted Abel irritably, and went out.

"You'd better go down with them, Nick," said Alleyn. "Tell Oates to watch our man like a lynx. Abel will show you a decanter. Bring it up here. Here's the key! Use my gloves. You'd better search them. You won't find anything but you'd better do it. Leave Miss Darragh for the moment."

Harper went out.

"Did you take any sherry, Alleyn?" asked Dr. Shaw sharply.

"I? No."

"Sure?"

"Perfectly. Why?"

"You look a bit dicky."

"I'm all right."

"Mr. Alleyn has just saved my life for me," whispered Fox.

"You come along," said Dr. Shaw, and led him out.

Alleyn took an envelope from his pocket and put it over the glass from which Fox had drunk. He weighted the envelope with a saucer from his wash-hand stand. He got his bag and took out an empty bottle and a funnel. He smelt the sherry in his own glass and then poured it into the bottle, stoppered it, and wrote on the label. He was annoyed to find that his hands shook. His heart thumped intolerably. He grimaced and took another mouthful of brandy.

Harper came back.

"Oates and my other chap are searching them," said Harper. "They made no objections."

"They wouldn't. Sit down, Nick," said Alleyn, "and listen. Put Fox's sick out of the way first, for the Lord's sake. Give it to Shaw. I've got palsy or something."

Harper performed this office and sat down.

"Yesterday evening," said Alleyn, "Abel Pomeroy opened a bottle of a very sound sherry. Fox and I had a glass each. At a quarter to one to-day Abel decanted the sherry. He, Fox and I had a glass each after it was decanted. George Nark was in the bar. Later on, Miss Darragh, Legge, Parish, Cubitt, and Will Pomeroy came in and we talked about the sherry. They all knew it was for our private use. Some forty minutes ago, Abel poured out two glasses. Fox drank his and within half a minute he was taken very ill. The symptoms were those of cyanide poisoning. I'll swear Abel didn't put anything in the glasses. There's Fox's glass. We'll do our stuff with what's left. I've covered it but we'd better get the dregs into an airtight bottle. You'll find one in my bag there. There's a funnel on the dressing-table. D'you mind doing it? Clean the funnel out first. I used it for the stuff in my glass."

Harper did this.

"It's a bad blunder," he said. "What good would it do him? Suppose you'd both been killed? I mean, it's foolish. Is it panic or spite or both?"

"Neither, I imagine. I see it as a last attempt to bolster up the accident theory. The idea is that in the same mysterious way as cyanide got on the dart so it got into the decanter. The decanter, you see, was brought out from the corner cupboard. Mrs. Ives had washed it in about two dozen changes of boiling water. I don't think anybody but Nark and Abel were aware of this. We were no doubt supposed to think the decanter was tainted by being in the cupboard."

Superintendent Harper uttered a vulgar and incredulous word.

"I know," agreed Alleyn. "Of course it is. But if Fox and—or—I had popped off, you'd have had a devil of a job proving it was murder. Oh, it's a blunder, all right. It shows us two things. The murderer must have kept a bit of cyanide up his sleeve and he must have visited the private bar after Abel decanted the sherry at a quarter to one this afternoon. We will now search their rooms. We won't find anything, but we'd better do it. I'll just see how Fox is getting on."

Fox, white and shaken, was sitting on the edge of the bath. Dr. Shaw was washing his hands.

"He'll do all right now," said Dr. Shaw. "Better go to bed and take it easy."

"I'm damned if I do," said Fox. "Excuse me, sir, but I'm damned if I do."

Alleyn took him by the elbow.

"Blast your eyes," he said, "you'll do as you're told. Come on."

Fox consented, with a bad grace, to lying on his bed. Alleyn and Harper searched the rooms.

ii

At first Harper said that the rooms, in all essentials, were as he had found them on the day after Watchman's death. In Cubitt's they found an overwhelming smell of studio and the painting gear that had engendered it. There were bottles of turpentine and oil, half-finished works, Cubitt's paint-box, and boxes of unopened tubes. Alleyn smelt the bottles and shook his head.

"We needn't take them," he said, "their stink is a lawful stink. You can't put turpentine or oil into vintage sherry and get away with it."

"What about prussic acid? It smells strong enough."

"Of almonds. A nutty flavour. Do you remember the account of the murder of Rasputin?"

"Can't say I do," said Harper.

"Youssoupoff put cyanide in the wine. Rasputin drank several glasses, apparently with impunity."

"But—"

"The theory is that the sugar in the wine took the punch out of the poison. That may account for Fox's escape. No doubt the sherry had a fine old nutty aroma. By God, I'll get this expert!"

"What are we looking for?"

"For anything that could have held the stuff he put in the decanter. Oh, he'll have got rid of it somehow, of course. But you never know."

They went into the bathroom. In a cupboard above the hand basin they found Abel's second first-aid outfit. Alleyn asked Harper if there had been a bottle of iodine there on the day after the murder. Harper said no. He had checked the contents of the cupboard. They separated and took the rest of the rooms between them, Alleyn going to Legge's and Parish's, Harper to the others. Alleyn took a small empty bottle from Parish's room. It had held pills and smelt of nothing at all. In Legge's dressing-table he found a phial half-full of a thick pinkish fluid that smelt of antiseptic. Mr. Legge's ear lotion . . . He kept it and searched all the drawers and pockets but found nothing else of interest. Abel's room was neat and spotless, Will's untidy and full of books. The wearisome and exciting business went on. Down below, in the private bar, Oates and his mate kept company with the patrons of the Plume of Feathers. They were very quiet. Occasionally Alleyn heard the voices of Parish and of Mr. Nark. Ottercombe clock struck ten, sweetly and slowly. There was a moment of complete quiet broken by a violent eruption of noise down in the bar. Alleyn and Harper met in the passage.

"Somebody cutting up rough," said Harper.

A falsetto voice screamed out an oath. A table was overturned and there followed a great clatter of boots. Harper ran downstairs and Alleyn followed. Inside the private bar they found Legge, mouthing and gibbering, between Oates and a second uniformed constable.

"What's all this?" asked Harper.

"Misdemeanour, sir," said Tates, whose nose was bleeding freely. "Assault *and* battery."

"I don't care what it is," screamed Legge. "I can't stand any more of this—"

"Shut up, you silly chap," admonished Oates. "He tried to make a breakaway, sir. Sitting there as quiet as you please, and all of a sudden makes a blind rush for the door and when we intercepts him he wades in and assaults and batters the pair of us. Won't give over, sir. You're under arrest, Robert Legge, and it is my duty to warn you that you needn't say anything, but what you do say may be used in evidence. Stop that."

"Persecuted," whispered Legge. "Persecuted, spied upon, driven and badgered and maddened. I know what it means. Let me go. Damn you, let me go!"

He kicked Oates on the shin. Oates swore and twisted Legge's arm behind his back. Legge screamed and went limp.

"You'll have to be locked up," said Harper sadly. "Now, are you going to behave or have we got to put the bracelets on you? Be a sensible chap."

"I'll resist," said Legge, " 'till you kill me."

"Oh, take him away," said Harper. "Put him in a room upstairs, both of you."

Legge, struggling and gasping horribly, was taken out.

"Ah, it's at his wits' end he is, poor wretch," said Miss Darragh.

Cubitt said: "Look here, this is ghastly. If he's not guilty why the hell—?"

Parish said: "Not guilty? I must say that for an innocent man, his behaviour is pretty fantastic."

Will Pomeroy crossed the room and confronted Alleyn and Harper.

"Why's he arrested?" demanded Will.

"Assaulting a constable and interfering with the police in the execution of their duty," said Harper.

"My God, he was drove to it! If this is justice the sooner there's a revolution in the country the better. It's enough to send the man mad, the way you've been pestering him. Haven't you the sense to see the state he's got into? Damme if I'm not nigh-ready to take on the lot of you myself. Let that man go."

"That'll do, Will," said Harper.

" 'That'll do!' The official answer for every blasted blunder in the force. Bob Legge's my comrade—"

"In which case," said Alleyn, "you'll do well to think a little before you speak. You can hardly expect Mr. Harper to set up constables in rows for your comrade Legge to bloody their noses. While his mood lasts he's better in custody. You pipe down like a sensible fellow." He turned to Harper. "Stay down here a moment, will you? I'll take a look at Fox and rejoin you."

He ran upstairs and met Oates in the landing.

"My mate's put Legge in his own room, sir," said Oates.

"Good. He'd better stay with him and you'd better dip your nose in cold water before you resume duty. Then come and relieve Mr. Harper."

Oates went into the bathroom. Alleyn opened Fox's door and listened. Fox was snoring deeply and rhythmically. Alleyn closed the door softly and returned to the tap-room.

iii

It was the last time that he was to see that assembly gathered together in the private tap-room of the Plume of Feathers. He had been little over twenty-four hours in Ottercombe but, it seemed more like a week. The suspects in a case of murder become quickly and strangely familiar to the investigating officer. He has an aptitude for noticing mannerisms, tricks of voice, and of movement. Faces and figures make their impression quickly and sharply. Alleyn now expected, before he saw them, Cubitt's trick of smiling lopsidedly, Parish's habit of sticking out his jaw, Miss Darragh's look of inscrutability, Will Pomeroy's mulish blushes, and his father's way of opening his eyes very widely. The movement of Nark's head, slanted conceitedly, and his look of burning self-importance, seemed to be memories of a year rather than of days. Alleyn felt a little as if they were marionettes obeying a few simple jerks of their strings and otherwise inert and stupid. He felt wholeheartedly bored with the lot of them; the thought of another bout of interrogation was almost intolerable. Fox might have been killed. Reaction had set in, and Alleyn was sick at heart.

"Well," he said crisply, "you may as well know what has happened. Between a quarter to one and five-past seven, somebody put poison in the decanter of sherry that was kept for our use. You will readily understand that we shall require a full account from each one of you of your movements after a quarter to one. Mr. Harper and I will see you in turn in the parlour. If you discuss the matter among yourselves it will be within hearing of Constable Oates, who will be on duty in this room. We'll see you first if you please, Mr. Cubitt."

But it was the usual exasperating job that faced him. None of them had a complete alibi. Each of them could have slipped unseen into the tap-room and come out again unnoticed. Abel had locked the bar-shutter during closing-hours but everyone knew where he kept his keys and several times when the bar was open it had been deserted. Cubitt said he was painting from two o'clock until six, when he returned for his evening meal. He had been one of the company in the tap-room when Alleyn came in for the sherry, but had left immediately to meet Decima Moore on Coombe Head. The others followed with similar stories—except old Pomeroy, who frankly admitted he had sat in the tap-room for some time, reading his paper. Each of them denied being alone there at any time after Abel had decanted the sherry. An hour's exhaustive enquiry failed to prove or disprove any of their statements. Last of all, Mr. Legge was brought down in a state of the profoundest dejection and made a series of protestations to the effect that he was being persecuted. He was a pitiful object and Alleyn's feeling of nausea increased as he watched him. At last Alleyn said:

"Mr. Legge, we only arrived here last evening but, as you must realize, we have already made many enquiries. Of all the people we have interviewed, you alone have objected to the way we set about our job. Why?"

Legge looked at Alleyn without speaking. His lower lip hung loosely, his eyes, half-veiled, in that now familiar way, by his white lashes, looked like the eyes of a blind man. Only his hands moved restlessly. After a moment's silence he mumbled something inaudible.

"What do you say?"

"It doesn't matter. Everything I say is used against me."

Alleyn looked at him in silence.

"I think," he said at last, "that it is my duty to tell you that a dart bearing your fingerprints was sent to the Bureau early this morning. They have been identified and the result has been telephoned to us."

Legge's hands moved convulsively.

"They have been identified," Alleyn repeated, "as those of Montague Thringle. Montague Thringle was sentenced to six years' imprisonment for embezzlement, a sentence that was afterwards reduced to four years and was completed twenty-six months ago." He paused. Legge's face was clay-coloured. "You must have known we'd find out," said Alleyn. "Why didn't you tell me last night who you were?"

"Why? Why?" demanded Legge. "You know why. You know well enough. The very sight and sound of the police! Anathema! Questions, questions, questions! At me all the time. Man with a record! Hound him out! Tell everybody! Slam every door in his face. And you have the impertinence to ask me why I was silent. My God!"

"All right," said Alleyn, "we'll leave it at that. How did you spend your afternoon?"

"There you go!" cried Legge, half-crying, but still with that curious air of admonishment. "There you go, you see! Straight off. Asking me things like that. It's atrocious."

"Nonsense," said Alleyn.

"Nonsense!" echoed Legge, in a sort of fury. He shook his finger in Alleyn's face. "Don't you talk like that to me, sir. Do you know who I am? Do you know that before my misfortune I was the greatest power in English finance? Let me tell you that there are only three men living who fully comprehended the events that brought about the holocaust of '29 and '30, and I am one of them. If I had not put my trust in titled imbeciles, if I had not been betrayed by a sulking moron, I should be in a position to send for you when I wished to command your dubious services, or dismiss them with a contemptuous *fiddle-de-dee*."

This astonishing and ridiculous word was delivered with such venom that Alleyn was quite taken aback. Into his thoughts, with the appropriate logic of topsy-turvy, popped the memory of a jigging line:—

To shirk the task were fiddle-de-dee.
To shirk the task were fiddle-de—, fiddle-de— . . .

He pulled himself together, cautioned and tackled Mr. Legge, and at last got a statement from him. He had spent the afternoon packing his books, papers, and effects, and putting them in his car. He had intended to take the first load into his new room that evening. He had also written some letters. He offered, frantically, to show Alleyn the letters. Alleyn had already seen them and they amounted to nothing. He turned Legge over to Oates, whose nose was now plugged with cotton-wool.

"You'd better take him to the station," said Alleyn.

"I demand bail," cried Legge in a trembling voice.

"Mr. Harper will see about that," said Alleyn. "You're under arrest for a misdemeanour."

"I didn't kill him. I know what you're up to. It's the beginning of the end. I swear—"

"You are under arrest for assaulting police officers," said Alleyn, wearily. "I will repeat the caution you have already heard."

He repeated it and was devoutly thankful when Legge, in a condition of hysterical prostration, was led away. Harper, with Oates and his mate, was to drive him to Illington and lodge him in the police station.

"The Colonel's at the station," said Harper acidly. "That was him on the telephone while you were upstairs. His car's broken down again. Why, in his position and with all his money, he doesn't—oh well! He wants me to bring him back here, or you to come in. Which'll it be? The man'll talk us all dotty, wherever he is."

"I'll have another look at Fox," said Alleyn. "If he's awake, I'll get him into bed and then follow you into Illington. I'd like the doctor to see him again."

"There'll be no need for that, sir, thank you."

Alleyn spun round on his heel to see Fox, fully dressed and wearing his bowler hat, standing in the doorway.

CHAPTER NINETEEN

The Chief Constable as Watson

i

"I've reported for duty, if you please, Mr. Alleyn," said Fox.

"You unspeakable old ninny," said Alleyn, "go back to bed."

"With all respect, sir, I'd rather not. I've had a very pleasant nap and am quite myself again. So if you'll allow me—"

"Br'er Fox," said Alleyn, "are we to have a row?"

"I hope not, sir, I'm sure," said Fox tranquilly. "Six years, I think it is now, and never a moment's unpleasantness, thanks to your tact and consideration."

"Damn you, go to bed."

"If it's all the same to you, sir, I'd rather—"

"Mr. Fox," Alleyn began very loudly and stopped short. They stared at each other. Harper coughed and moved to the door. Alleyn swore violently, seized Fox by the arm, and shoved him into an armchair. He then knelt on the harlequin rug and lit the fire.

"I'd be obliged, Nick," said Alleyn over his shoulder, "if you'd bring Colonel Brammington here. Would you explain that circumstances over which I appear to have no control oblige me to remain at the Plume of Feathers."

"I'm quite able to drive—" Fox began.

"You shut up," said Alleyn warmly.

Harper went out.

"Offences against discipline," said Alleyn, "are set forth in the Police Regulations under seventeen headings, including neglect of duty and disobedience to orders, together with a general heading covering discreditable conduct." He looked up from the fire. "Discreditable conduct," he repeated.

Fox was shaken up with soundless subterranean chuckles.

"I'm going into the tap-room," said Alleyn. "If you move out of that chair I'll damn well serve you with a Misconduct Form. See Regulation 13."

"I'll get the Super in as my witness, sir," said Fox. "See Regulation 17." And at this pointless witticism he went off into an ecstasy of apoplectic mirth.

Alleyn returned to the tap-room, where Oates still kept guard. Miss Darragh was knitting in the inglenook, Parish stood near the shuttered windows, Cubitt was drawing in the battered sketch-book he always carried in his pocket. Abel glowered in a corner. Mr. Nark wore the expression of one who had been made to feel unpopular.

Alleyn said: "You may open up again if you wish, Mr. Pomeroy. I'm sorry to have kept you all so long. Until you and your rooms had been searched, we had no alternative. To-morrow, you will be asked to sign the statements you have made to Mr. Harper. In the meantime, if you wish, you may go to your rooms. You will not be allowed to leave the premises until further orders. Mr. Nark may go home."

From the stairs came the sound of heavy steps. Harper and the second constable came down with Legge between them. Alleyn had left the tap-room door open. Six pairs of eyes turned to watch Legge go out.

Miss Darragh suddenly called out: "Cheer up, now. It's nothing at all, man. I'll go bail for you."

Will started forward.

"I want to speak to him."

"Certainly," said Alleyn.

"I'm sorry it has turned out this way, mate," said Will, "damned injustice and nothing less. It won't make any difference with the Party. You know that. We'll stick by you. Wish I'd bloodied t'other nose and gone to clink along with you."

"They've got a down on me," said Legge desolately.

"I know that. Good luck!"

"Come along, now," said Harper. "Get a move on. Ready, Oates?"

Oates went out to them and Alleyn shut the door.

"Well," said Parish. "I call that a step in the right direction, Mr. Alleyn."

"For God's sake, Seb, hold your tongue," said Cubitt.

"What d'you mean by that, Mr. Parish?" demanded Will. "You'd better be careful what you're saying, hadn't you?"

"That's no way to speak, sonny," said Abel.

"While I've a tongue in my head—" began Will.

"You'll set a guard on it, I hope," said Alleyn. "Good night, gentlemen."

They filed out one by one. Parish was the only one who spoke. With his actor's instinct for an efficient exit, he turned in the doorway.

"I imagine," he said, looking steadily at Alleyn, "that I shan't be run in for contempt, if I venture to suggest that this gentleman's departure marks the beginning of the end."

"Oh, no," said Alleyn politely. "We shan't run you in for that, Mr. Parish."

Parish gave a light laugh and followed the others upstairs.

Only Miss Darragh remained. She put her knitting into a large chintz bag, took off her spectacles and looked steadily at Alleyn.

"I suppose you had to take that poor fellow in charge," she said. "He behaved very foolishly. But he's a mass of nerves, you know. It's a doctor he's needing, not a policeman."

"Who? Mr. Montague Thringle?" asked Alleyn vaguely.

"So the cat's out of the bag, is ut?" said Miss Darragh placidly. "Ah, well, I suppose 'twas bound to be. I've kept my end of the bargain."

"I'd very much like to know what it was," said Alleyn.

"Didn't you guess?"

"I wondered if by chance Lord Bryonie's family had promised to keep an eye on Mr. Thringle."

"Ah, you'll end in a cocked hat with a plume in ut," said Miss Darragh, "if 'tis cocked hats they give to Chief Commissioners. That's ut, sure enough. Me poor cousin Bryonie always felt he'd been responsible for the crash. He was very indiscreet, it seems, and might have helped to patch things up if he'd kept his wits about 'um. But he didn't. He'd no head for business and he only half-suspected there was anything illegal going on. But he said he'd only learned one kind of behaviour and when it didn't fit in with finance he was entirely at sea and thought maybe he'd better hold his peace. But it wasn't in his nature not to talk and that was the downfall of 'um. The jury saw that he'd been no more than a cat's-paw, but when he got off with the lighter sentence there was a great deal of talk that 't was injustice and that his position saved him. Thringle felt so himself, and said so. Me cousin never lost his faith in Thringle, who seemed to have cast a kind of spell over 'um, though you wouldn't think ut possible, would you, to see Thringle now?

But in those days he was a fine-looking fellow. Dark as night, he was, with a small imperial, and his own teeth instead of those dreadful china falsehoods they gave 'um in prison. It's no wonder, at all, you didn't know 'um from Adam when you saw 'um. Well, the long and short of ut 'twas that, before he died, the family promised poor Bryonie they'd look after Mr. Thringle when he came out of gaol. He was on their conscience and I won't say he didn't know ut and make the most of ut. We kept in touch with 'um and he wrote from here saying he'd changed his name to Legge and that he needed money. We've not much of that to spare, but we had a family conference and, as I was planning a little sketching jaunt anyway, I said I'd take ut at Ottercombe and see for meself how the land lay. So that was what I did. Don't ask me to tell you the nature of our talks for they were in confidence and had nothing to say to the case. I wish with all me heart you could have left 'um alone, but I see 'twas impossible. He fought those two big policemen like a Kilkenny cat, silly fellow. But if it's a question of bailing him out I'll be glad to do ut."

"Thank you," said Alleyn, "I'll see that the right people are told about it. Miss Darragh, have you done any sketching along the cliffs from the tunnel to Coombe Head?"

Miss Darragh looked at him in consternation. "I have," she said.

"In the mornings?"

" 'Twas in the mornings."

"You were there on the morning Mr. Watchman arrived in Ottercombe?"

She looked steadily at him. "I was," said Miss Darragh.

"We saw where you had set up your easel. Miss Darragh, did you, from where you were working, overhear a conversation between Miss Moore and Mr. Watchman?"

Miss Darragh clasped her fat little paws together and looked dismally at Alleyn.

"Please," said Alleyn.

"I did. I could not avoid it. By the time I'd decided I'd get up and show meself above the sky-line, it had gone so far I thought I had better not."

She gave him a quick look and added hurriedly, "Please, now, don't go thinking all manner of dreadful things."

"What am I to think? Do you mean it was a love-scene?"

"Not in—no. No, the reverse."

"A quarrel?"

"It was."

"Was it of that scene you were thinking when you told me, this morning, to look further and look nearer home?"

"It was. I wasn't thinking of her. God forbid. Don't misunderstand me. I was not the only one who heard them. And that's all I'll say."

She clutched her bag firmly and stood up.

"As regards this searching," added Miss Darragh, "the Superintendent let me off. He said you'd attend to ut."

"I know," said Alleyn. "Perhaps you won't mind if Mrs. Ives goes up with you to your room."

"Not the least in the world," said Miss Darragh.

"Then I'll send for her," said Alleyn.

ii

While he waited for Harper and the chief constable, Alleyn brought his report up-to-date and discussed it with Fox, who remained weakly insubordinate, in his chair by the fire.

"It's an ill wind," said Fox, "that blows nobody any good. I take it that I've had what you might call a thorough spring-clean with the doctor's tube taking the part of a vacuum cleaner, if the idea's not too fanciful. I feel all the better for it."

Alleyn grunted.

"I don't know but what I don't fancy a pipe," continued Fox.

"You'll have another spring-clean if you do."

"Do you think so, Mr. Alleyn? In that case I'll hold off. I fancy I hear a car, sir. Coming through the tunnel, isn't it?"

Alleyn listened.

"I think so. We'll get the C.C. to fix up a warrant. Well, Br'er Fox, it's been a short, sharp go this time, hasn't it?"

"And you were looking forward to a spell in the country, sir."

"I was."

"We'll be here yet awhile, with one thing and another."

"I suppose so. Here they are."

A car drew up in the yard. The side door opened noisily, and Colonel Brammington's voice sounded in the passage. He came in, with Harper and Oates at his heels. The Colonel was dressed in a dinner suit. He wore a stiff shirt with no central stud. It curved generously away from his person and through the gaping front could be seen a vast expanse of pink chest. Evidently he had, at some earlier hour, wetted his hair and dragged a comb through it. His shoe-laces were untied and his socks unsupported. Over his dinner jacket he wore a green Tyrolese bicycling cape.

"I can't apologize enough, sir," Alleyn began, but the Chief Constable waved him aside.

"Not at all, Alleyn. A bore, but it couldn't be helped. I am distended with rich food and wines. Strong meat belongeth to them that are of full age. I freely confess I outdid the meat, outdid the frolic wine. It was, I flatter myself, a good dinner, but I shall not taunt you with a recital of its virtues."

"I am sure it was a dinner in a thousand," said Alleyn. "I hope you didn't mind coming here, sir. Fox was still—"

"By heaven!" interrupted Colonel Brammington. "This pestilent poisoner o'er-tops it, does it not? The attempt, I imagine, was upon you both. Harper has told me the whole story. When will you make an arrest, Alleyn? May we send this fellow up the ladder to bed, and that no later than the Quarter Sessions? Let him wag upon a wodden nag. A pox on him! I trust you are recovered, Fox? Sherry, wasn't it? Amontillado, I understand. Double sacrilege, by the Lord!"

Colonel Brammington hurled himself into a chair and asked for a cigarette. When this had been given him, he produced from his trousers pocket a crumpled mass of typescript which Alleyn recognized as the carbon copy of his report.

"I have been over the report, Alleyn," said Colonel Brammington, "and while you expended your energies so happily in resuscitating the poisoned Fox (and by the way, our murderer carries the blacker stigma of a fox-poisoner) I read this admirable digest. I congratulate you. A masterly presentation of facts, free from the nauseating redundancies of most bureaucratic documents. . . . I implored you to allow me to be your Watson. You consented. I come, full of my theory, ready to admit my blunders. Is there by any chance some flask of fermented liquor in this house to which cyanide has not been added? May we not open some virgin bottle?"

Alleyn went into the bar, found three sealed bottles of Treble Extra, chalked them up to himself and took them with glasses into the parlour.

"We should have a taster," said Colonel Brammington. "Some Borgian attendant at our call. What a pity the wretched Nark is not here to perform this office."

"There are times," said Alleyn, "when I could wish that Mr. Nark had been the corpse in the case. I don't think we need blench at the Treble Extra and I washed the glasses."

He broke a paper seal, drew the cork, and poured out the beer.

"Really," said Colonel Brammington, "I do feel a little timidly about it, I must say. Some fiendish device—"

"I don't think so," said Alleyn and took a pull at his beer. "It's remarkably good."

"You show no signs of stiffening limb or glassy eye. It is, as you say, good beer. Well now, Alleyn, I understand from Harper that you have all arrived at a decision. I, working independently, have also made up my mind. It would delight me to find we were in agreement and amuse me to learn that I was wrong. Will you indulge me so far to allow me to unfold the case as I see it?"

"We should be delighted, sir," said Alleyn, thinking a little of his bed.

"Excellent," said Colonel Brammington. He flattened out the crumpled report and Alleyn saw that he had made copious notes in pencil all over the typescript. "I shall relate my deductions in the order in which they came to me. I shall follow the example of all Watsons and offer blunder after blunder, inviting your compassionate scorn and remembering the observation that logic is only the art of going wrong with confidence. Are you all ready?"

"Quite ready, sir," said Alleyn.

iii

"When first this case turned up," said Colonel Brammington, "it seemed to me to be a moderately simple affair. The circumstances were macabre, the apparent weapon unlikely, but I accepted the weapon and rejoiced in the circumstances. It was an enlivening murder."

He turned his prominent eyes on Harper, who looked scandalized.

"After all," said Colonel Brammington, "I did not know the victim and I frankly confess I adore a murder. Pray, Mr. Harper, do not look at me in that fashion. I want the glib and oil art to speak and purpose not. I enjoy a murder and I enjoyed this one. It seemed to me that Legge had anointed the dart with malice aforethought and prussic acid, had prepared the ground with exhibitions of skill, and had deliberately thrown awry. He had overheard Watchman's story of his idiosyncrasy for the cyanide. He had seen Pomeroy put the bottle in the cupboard. Cyanide had been found on the dart. What more did we need? True, the motive was lacking, but when I learnt that you suspected Legge of being a gaol-bird, a sufficient motive appeared. Legge had established himself in this district in a position of trust, he handled moneys, he acquired authority. Watchman, by his bantering manner, suggested that he recognized Legge. Legge feared he would be exposed. Legge therefore murdered Watchman. That was my opinion until this afternoon."

Colonel Brammington took a prodigious swig of beer and flung himself back in his tortured chair.

"This afternoon," he said, "I was astonished at your refusal to arrest Legge, but when I took the files away and began to read them I changed my opinion. I read the statements made by the others and I saw how positive each was that Legge had no opportunity to anoint the dart. I was impressed by your own observation that his hands were clumsy, that he was incapable of what would have amounted to an essay in legerdemain. Yet cyanide was found on the dart. Who had put it there? It is a volatile poison, therefore it must have been put on the dart not long before Oates sealed it up. I wondered if after all, the whole affair was an accident, if there was some trace of poison on Abel Pomeroy's clothes or upon the bar where he unpacked the darts. It was a preposterous notion and it was smashed as squat as a flounder by the fact that the small vessel in the rat-hole had been filled up with water. I was forced to believe that the cyanide had been taken from the rat-hole immediately, or soon after, old Pomeroy put it there. Any of the suspects might have done this. But only four of the suspects had handled the darts; Legge, the Pomeroys and Parish. Only Legge controlled the flight of the darts. Watchman took them out of the board after the trial throw and gave them to Legge. Now here," said Colonel Brammington with an air of conscious modesty, "I fancy I hit on something new. Can you guess what it was?"

"I can venture to do so," Alleyn rejoined. "Did you reflect that all the darts had been thrown into the board on the trial, and then if cyanide was on any one of them it would have been effectively cleaned off?"

"Good God!" ejaculated the Chief Constable.

He was silent for some time, but at last continued with somewhat forced airiness.

"No. No, that was not my point, but by Jupiter it supports my case. I was going to say that since Watchman removed the darts and handed them to Legge, it would have been quite impossible for

Legge to know which dart was tainted. This led me to an alternative. Either all the darts were poisoned or else, or else, my dear Alleyn, the dart that wounded Watchman was tainted after, and not before, the accident." He glanced at Alleyn.

"Yes, sir," said Alleyn. "One or the other."

"You agree? You had thought of it?"

"Will Pomeroy suggested the second alternative," said Alleyn.

"Damn! However! Legge, I had decided, was not capable of anointing one, much less six, darts during the few seconds he held them in his hand before doing his trick. Legge would scarcely implicate himself by anointing the dart after he had seen Watchman die. Therefore someone had tried to implicate Legge. I was obliged to bow to your wisdom, my dear Alleyn. I dismissed Legge. I finished your report and I considered the other suspects. Who, of these seven persons, for they are seven if we include Miss Darragh and Miss Moore, could most easily have taken cyanide from the small vessel in the rat-hole? One of the Pomeroys, since their presence in or about the out-houses would not be remarked. Abel Pomeroy's fingerprints, and only his, were found on the small vessel. Who of the seven had an opportunity to smear cyanide on the dart? Abel Pomeroy, since he unpacked the darts. Who, in the first instance, had cyanide brought into the premises? Abel Pomeroy. Putting motive on one side, I felt that Abel Pomeroy was my first choice. My second fancy—and don't look so wryly upon me, Harper, a Chief Constable may have fancies as well as the next man—my second fancy fell upon Will Pomeroy. Your interview with the unspeakable Nark, my dear Alleyn, was not barren of interest. Amidst a plethora of imbecilities, Nark seemed to make one disclosure of interest. He said, or rather from your report I understood him to hint, that he had, on the occasion of Watchman's first visit to Ottercombe overheard an amorous encounter between Watchman and Miss Moore. He hinted, moreover, that as he crept farther along Apple Lane, he came upon Will Pomeroy, lurking and listening in the hedge. Now, thought I, if this were true, here is the beginning of motive; for, in the interim, the courtship between young Pomeroy and Miss Moore ripened. Suppose, on Watchman's return, that the rustic lover thought he saw a renewal of attentions? Suppose Parish or Cubitt hinted at the scene they interrupted by the furze-bushes? But ignoring motive, what of opportunity? Will Pomeroy handled the darts after they were unpacked by his father. Could he have had a phial of cyanide-solution in his pocket? Nobody watched Will Pomeroy with the close attention that they all gave to Legge. Your observation on the trial throw shatters this theory . . . Do I see another bottle of this superb beer? Thank you . . .

"On the whole I preferred Pomeroy senior. There seemed no reason to doubt young Pomeroy's violent defense of Legge. He would not have thrown suspicion on Legge and then vehemently defended him. Old Pomeroy, on the other hand, detests Legge and has, from the first, accused him of the murder. But I was determined to look with an equal eye upon the field of suspects. I turned, with, I hope, becoming reluctance, to the ladies. On Miss Darragh I need not dwell. Harper has told me of your discovery of her link with Legge and it is obvious that she merely took what may be described as a family interest in him. The family tree in this instance being unusually shady . . . Ha! But Miss Moore, if Nark is to be believed, cannot be so dismissed. There had been amorous passages between Miss Moore and Watchman. Miss Moore denied this in the course of your interview. Could love have turned into the proverbial hatred? What happened when those ambiguous heelmarks were printed in the turf behind the furze-bush? A quarrel? Was she afraid her lover would betray her to her fiancé? And opportunity? Could she have introduced poison into the glass? Who better, since she poured out the brandy? But here, as with young Pomeroy, I had to pause. Whoever poisoned Watchman took peculiar pains to implicate Legge, but ever since the investigation began, Miss Moore has been ardent to the point of rashness in her defence of Legge. She has braved everything for Legge, and there is a ring of urgency in her defence that bears the very tinct of sincerity. I dismissed Miss Moore. I turned, at last, to Sebastian Parish and Norman Cubitt. Here it was impossible to ignore motive. Motive in the form of handsome inheritances was as conspicuous as a pitchfork in Paradise. What of fact? Cubitt did not handle the darts but, on my second alternative, he could have tainted the poisoned dart after Watchman threw it down. But if the dart was a blind and didn't kill Watchman, what did? The brandy? We are told that criminals repeat the manner of their crimes and this attempt upon you and Fox supports the theory. The murderer had killed Watchman by the method of putting cyanide in his brandy? The murderer hoped to kill you by putting cyanide in your sherry? To return. The fingerprint and rathole objection applies to Cubitt and Parish, as it does to everyone but Pomeroy senior. Of course it is possible that the murderer drew the poison off with some instrument and without touching the vessel. This brings me to Parish."

Colonel Brammington darted a raffish glance at Alleyn and accepted a fresh cigarette.

"To Parish," he repeated. "And here we must not ignore a point that I feel is extremely important. Parish purchased the cyanide solution. It was he who suggested, to the certifiable Noggins, that it should be gingered up, as he put it. It was he who carried it back to the inn. Old Pomeroy said that the wretched Noggins' sealing-wax was unbroken when Parish gave him the bottle. Is it possible to substitute one drop of sealing-wax by another? And if this had been done, why the interference with the rat-hole? But suppose the wrapping and seal were intact. Suppose that Parish made sure of obtaining a strong enough poison, delivered the bottle, sealed as he had received it, and later went to the rat-hole; why, then he would be acting more wisely, he would be removing suspicion one step away from himself. His defence would be: 'If I had intended to use this damnable poison, surely I would have taken the opportunity to extract it from the bottle when it was actually in my hands.' I began to think I had got on the trail at last. I inspected the notes made by your man, Oates, when the memory of the night's events were still fresh, or as fresh as the aftermath of Courvoisier would allow. It was Parish, equally with Watchman, who suggested they should have the brandy, Parish who applauded and encouraged the suggestion that Legge should try the experiment with the darts. I began to wonder if this was an opportunity Parish had awaited, if he had the cyanide concealed about him in readiness for use. Could he have reasoned that Legge, full of brandy, was likely to make a blunder in throwing the dart, and that if he did blunder, here was Parish's opportunity to bring off his plan? This was purely conjectural, my dear Alleyn, but before long I came upon a thumping fact. Up to the moment when Miss Moore poured out the brandy that failed to restore Watchman, Parish, and only Parish, had an opportunity of putting anything in Watchman's glass. Parish knew that if Legge wounded Watchman, Watchman would turn queasy. Parish encouraged the brandy-drinking and dart throwing. Parish stood near the glass until it was used."

Colonel Brammington thumped the arm of his chair and pointed a hairy finger at Alleyn.

"Above all," he shouted, "Parish has done nothing but murmur against Legge. Suspicions, Bacon remarked, that are artificially nourished by the tales and whisperings of others, have stings. This, Parish foresaw. This he hoped would prove true. My case against Parish is that he took cyanide from the rat-hole as soon as he could after Abel Pomeroy put it there. Or, I offer it as an alternative, that he took cyanide from the original bottle, replaced the small amount with water, and contrived to re-wrap and seal the bottle, and, as a blind, upset the vessel in the rat-hole without disturbing Pomeroy's prints, and filled it with water. This suggests a subtlety of reasoning which may or may not appeal to you. But to the burden of my tale, Parish had, that very evening, heard of Watchman's idiosyncrasy for cyanide, he had been reminded of Watchman's habit of turning faint at the sight of his own blood, he had heard Watchman baiting Legge and Legge's offer to perform his trick with Watchman's hand, he had heard Watchman half-promise to let him try. The following night, when the brandy was produced and drunk, he saw his chance. He encouraged the drinking and the projected experiment. When Legge wounded Watchman and Watchman turned faint, Parish stood near the glass. He had the cyanide about him. Brandy was suggested. Parish put his poison in the glass. The lights went out. Parish groped on the floor, bumped his head against Cubitt's legs, found the dart and infected it. He then ground whatever phial he had about him into powder, together with the broken tumbler on the floor, and finding a more solid piece under his heel, threw it into the fire. And from then onwards, gentlemen, I maintain that everything the fellow did or said, is consistent with the theory that he murdered his cousin. I plump for Parish."

Colonel Brammington stared about him with an unconvincing air of modesty tinged with a hint of anxiety.

"Well," he said, "there you are. An essay in Watsoniana. Am I to be set down? Shall I perceive my mentor wafting his eyes to the contrary and falling a lip of much contempt?"

"No, indeed," said Alleyn. "I congratulate you, sir. A splendid marshalling of facts and a magnificent sequence of deductions."

If so large and red a man could be said to simper, Colonel Brammington simpered.

"Really," he said. "I have committed no atrocious blunder? My deductions march with yours?"

"Almost all the way. We shall venture to disagree on one or two points."

"I make no claim to infallibility," said the Chief Constable. "What are the points? Let us have them?"

"Well," said Alleyn apologetically, and with an uncomfortable glance at Harper and at Fox, "there's only one point of any importance. I—In our view of the case—you've—you've hit on the wrong man."

CHAPTER TWENTY

Conjecture into Fact

i

For a second or two Alleyn wondered if there would be an explosion or, worse, a retreat into heavy silence. Fearing that the expression of gloating delight upon Harper's face might turn the scales, Alleyn had placed himself between the Chief Constable and his Superintendent. But Colonel Brammington behaved admirably. He goggled for a moment, he became rather more purple in the face, and he made a convulsive movement that caused his shirt-front to crackle sharply, but finally he spoke with composure.

"Your manners, my dear Alleyn," he said, "are, as always, worthy of a Chesterfield. I am pinked on the very point of a compliment. The wrong man? Indeed? Then I must be ludicrously at fault. I have made some Gargantuan error. My entire sequence of deductions—"

"No, no, sir. Your case against Parish is supported by facts, but not by all the facts. Parish might so nearly have murdered Watchman, by either of the two methods you've described . . ."

"Then . . . Well!"

"The circumstance that excludes Parish, excludes his only means of murder. If he did it, it was by poisoning the brandy, and he couldn't tell which glass would be used. Not possibly. But we'll come to that in a minute. Our case, and I'm afraid it's a dubious one at the moment, is that there are one or two scraps of evidence that fit into the pattern only if they are allowed to point in one direction, and that is not towards Parish."

"What are they? . . . More beer, I implore you."

"To begin with," said Alleyn, filling Colonel Brammington's glass, "the two iodine bottles . . ."

"What!"

"Shall we take them, sir, as they turn up?"

"Let us, for God's sake."

"You, sir, ended with Sebastian Parish. I shall begin with him. If

Parish was a murderer, how lucky he was! How all occasions did inform against Watchman and favour Parish! It was on the evening after his decision that the brandy was produced, so *that* was pure luck. He didn't know Legge would wound Watchman, he only hoped that under the influence of brandy, he might miss his mark. When it so fell out, he had to make up his mind very rapidly and plan a series of delicate and dangerous manoeuvres. And how oddly he behaved! He risked his own immunity by handling the darts, and this, when his whole object was that Legge should seem to be the poisoner. After the accident, instead of putting cyanide in the brandy glass and moving away from it, he stood beside it, in a position that was likely to be remembered. And again, how could he tell that Miss Moore would use that glass? There were seven other glasses about the room. She might have taken a clean glass. Parish made no attempt to force that glass upon her. She chose it. More stupendous luck. Now, with the exception of Miss Moore, this objection applies to the supposition that any of them put cyanide in the brandy-glass. They couldn't be sure it would be used. Only Miss Moore could be sure of that, for she chose it."

"You surely don't . . . Go on," said Colonel Brammington.

"I entirely agree that, ruling out Legge,—and assuming that the whole arrangement of the business was an attempt to implicate Legge,—Cubitt, Miss Darragh, Will Pomeroy and Miss Moore must be counted out, since they have all declared that Legge was unable to meddle with the darts. Our case rests on a different assumption."

"Here, wait a bit," cried the Colonel. "No. All right. Go on."

"Abel Pomeroy and Parish were the only ones openly to accuse Legge. Abel Pomeroy was particularly vehement in his insistence that Legge deliberately killed Watchman. He came up to London to tell me about it."

"Old Pomeroy was my earlier choice."

"Yes, sir. To return to the brandy. For the reason I have given you, and for reasons that I hope to make clear, we are persuaded that there was no cyanide in the brandy. We are certain that cyanide was put on the dart after, and not before, it pierced Watchman's finger. Otherwise it would have been removed by the trial throw into the cork board or, if there was any trace left, possibly washed off by the blood that flowed freely from Watchman's finger and with which the dart was greatly stained. The cyanide was found on the point of the dart. Watchman, we think, was poisoned, not by the dart nor by the brandy. How, then?"

"But my dear fellow, there was no cyanide in the iodine bottle. They found the bottle. There was no cyanide."

"None. Now here, sir, we have a bit of evidence that is new to you. I feel sure that if you'd had it earlier today, it would have made a difference in your view of the case. We have found out that within a few hours of the murder, a bottle of iodine disappeared from the bathroom cupboard upstairs."

Colonel Brammington stared a little wildly at Alleyn, made as if to speak, and evidently thought better of it. He waved his hand.

"The bottle of iodine that was originally in the downstairs first-aid box," Alleyn continued, "was an entirely innocent bottle, with Abel's prints on it and only his. Legge's prints were added when he borrowed this bottle to doctor a cut on his chin. Abel gave it to him. Now that innocent and original bottle is, I consider, the one that was found under the settle. All that is left of the bottle Abel Pomeroy used, when he poured iodine into Watchman's wound, is represented, or so we believe, by the surplus amount of glass Mr. Harper swept up from the floor and by the small misshapen fragments we found in the ashes."

"Hah!" ejaculated the Colonel. "Now I have you. A lethal bottle, taken from the bathroom and infected, was substituted for the innocent bottle in the first-aid box. Only Abel Pomeroy's prints were found on the cupboard door and so on. Abel Pomeroy himself took the bottle from the box and himself poured the iodine into the wound. Splendid!"

"Exactly, sir," said Alleyn.

"Well, Alleyn, I readily abandon my second love. I return, chastened, to my first love. How will you prove it?"

"How indeed! We hope that an expert will be able to tell us that the fragments of glass are, in fact, of the same type as that used for iodine bottles. That's not much, but it's something, and we *have* got other strings to our bow."

"What's his motive?"

"Whose motive, sir?"

"Old Pomeroy's."

Alleyn looked at him apologetically.

"I'm sorry, sir. I hadn't followed you. Abel Pomeroy had no motive, as far as I know, for wishing Watchman dead."

"What the hell d'you mean."

"I didn't think Abel Pomeroy was strictly your first love, sir. May I go on? You see, once we accept the iodine theory, we must admit that the murderer knew Watchman would be wounded by the dart. Nobody knew that, sir, but Legge."

ii

It took the second half of the last bottle of Treble Extra to mollify the Chief Constable, but he was mollified in the end.

"I invited it," he said, "and I got it. In a sense, I suppose I committed the unforgivable offence of failing to lead trumps. Legge was trumps. Go on, my dear Alleyn. Expound. Is it Locke who says that it is one thing to show a man he is in error and another to convince him of the truth? You have shown me my error. Pray reveal the whole truth."

"From the first," said Alleyn, "it seemed obvious that Legge was our Man. Mr. Harper realized that, and so, sir, did you. This afternoon I told Harper that Fox and I had arrived at the same conclusion. You asked me not to give you our theory before, but before and after you came into Illington, we discussed the whole thing. Harper was for arresting him there and then, and I, mistakenly perhaps, thought that we should give him more rope. I thought that on our evidence, which rests so much upon conjecture, we would not establish a *prima-facie* case."

"What is your evidence beyond the tedious—well, go on."

"As we see it," said Alleyn, "Legge planned the whole affair to look like accident. No doubt he hoped that it would go no further than the inquest. His behaviour has been consistent with the theory of accident. He has shown us a man overwrought by the circumstance of having unwittingly killed someone. That describes his behaviour after Watchman died, at the inquest, and subsequently. He chanced everything on the accident theory. It is easy, now, to say he took an appalling risk, but he very nearly got away with it. If old Abel hadn't raised such a dust about the good name of his public house, and if Mr. Nark and others had not driven Harper, here, to fury, you might very well have got no further. Legge's motive was the one we have recognized: It harks back to the days when he was Montague Thringle and stood his trial for large-size embezzlement, and all the rest of it. At least three, of the enormous number of people he ruined, committed suicide. There was the usual pitiful list of old governesses and retired clerks. A shameful affair. Now, in defending Lord Bryonie, Watchman was able to throw almost the entire blame on Legge, or Thringle as I suppose we must learn to call him. Let him be Legge for the moment. Watchman made a savage attack on Legge, and it was in no small measure due to him that Legge got such a heavy sentence. He had an imperial and moustaches in those days, and had not turned grey. His appearance was very greatly changed when he came out of gaol. After various vicissitudes in Liverpool and London, he came down here, suffering from a weak chest and some complaint of the ear, for which he uses a lotion and a dropper. Harper found the dropper when he searched Legge's room on the morning after Watchman died. It's not there now."

"That's right," said Harper heavily.

"Legge got on well in Illington and Ottercombe. He'd got his philatelic job, and he was treasurer to a growing society. We shall inspect the books of the Coombe Left Movement. If he has not yet fallen into his old ways, on a small scale, it is, I am sure, only because the funds at his disposal are not yet large enough. All was going like clockwork until, out of a clear sky, came Watchman in his car. That collision of theirs must have given Legge an appalling shock. Watchman didn't recognize him, though, and later while Legge sat unseen in the tap-room, he overheard Watchman tell Parish of the collision and say, as Parish admitted he said, that he did not know the man who ran into him. But before Legge could go out that night, Watchman came across and tried to make friends with him. Legge doesn't seem to have been very responsive but he stuck it out. The rat-poisoning party returned and Legge's skill with darts was discussed. Legge took up Watchman's bet and won. I think it must have amused him to do that. Now, it was soon after this that Watchman began to twit Legge about his job and his political opinions. I've gone over the events of this first evening with the witnesses. Though they are a bit hazy, they agree that Watchman's manner was offensive. He ended by inviting Legge to a game of Round-the-Clock and the manner of the invitation was this: he said, 'Have you ever done time, Mr. Legge?' I think that throughout the whole evening Watchman, having recognized Legge, played cat-and-mouse with him. I knew Watchman. He has a curious feline streak of cruelty in him. I think it must have been then that Legge made up his mind Watchman had recognized him. Legge went into the public bar for a time. I believe he also went into the garage and sucked up cyanide in the little dropper he used for his lotion. Just, as they say, 'in case'!"

"Damned ingenious," said Colonel Brammington, "but conjectural."

"I know. We are only halfway through the case. It has changed its complexion with Oates's arrest of Legge for assault. We've only been here some thirty hours, you see. If we can check the time Legge appeared in the public bar with the time he left the private one, and all that dreary game, we shall be a step nearer. But dismiss all this conjecture and we still have the facts. We still know that only Legge controlled the flight of the dart."

"Yes."

"The next day was the fatal one. Legge stayed out of sight all day. Late in the afternoon, he left it as late as possible, and just before the others came in, he went down to the bar with a razor-cut on his chin and asked Abel for some iodine. Abel got the box out of the corner cupboard and gave it to Legge. Legge returned it a few minutes later. He had dabbed iodine on his chin. He had also substituted, for the iodine bottle in the box, the iodine bottle he had taken from the bathroom. This he had doctored with prussic acid from the rat-hole. By this really neat manoeuvre he got Abel to do the dirty work and accounted for any prints of his own that might afterwards be found on the bottle. In the evening Legge had a perfectly genuine appointment in Illington. At about five o'clock the storm broke, and I think that, like a good villain, Mr. Legge made plans to the tune of thunder off-stage. The storm was a fair enough reason for staying indoors. The failing lights were propitious. The Pomeroys both told him he couldn't get through the tunnel. When Will Pomeroy went up to Legge's room in the evening, he found him rather thoughtful. However, he came down and joined the party in the bar. I think he had made up his mind that, if Watchman suggested the trick should be done that night, he would wound Watchman. Abel, so keen on antisepsis, would produce the first-aid set from the cupboard. So it worked out. Two points are interesting. The first is the appearance and the consumption of the brandy. That was an unexpected development but he turned it to good account. He sat in the inglenook and appeared to get quietly and thoroughly soaked. That would account nicely for his missing with the trick. In the wood-basket beside his seat we found a newspaper into which liquid had been poured. The newspaper had been there since that night. Fox and I think we can detect a trace of the fruitful vine in the stains. But he must have watched the others anxiously. Would they be too tight to remember he had no chance to monkey with the darts? Luckily for him Will, Abel, Miss Darragh, and Miss Moore all remained sober. That brings us to the second point. Legge's great object was to provide himself with an alibi for doctoring the darts.

That was why he fell in with Abel's suggestion that he should use the new darts. Legge stood under the central light and waited for the darts to be handed to him. He was in shirt-sleeves and they were rolled back like a conjurer's. Parish, Will, Abel and Watchman all handled the darts. When Legge got them he at once threw them one by one into the board as a trial. That was his first mistake, but it would have looked odd for him not to do it. Watchman spread out his hand and the sequel followed. There were six people ready to swear Legge had done nothing to the darts."

Alleyn paused.

"I'm afraid this is heavy going," he said. "I won't be much longer. Watchman, when hit, pulled out the dart and threw it into the floor. When Oates called for the dart Legge obligingly found it on the floor behind the table, but not before Oates—who's a sharp fellow, Nick—has, as he says, spotted it alaying there. You throw those darts down as often as you like and I'll guarantee they stick in. And moreover we've statements from them all that it *did* stick in. All right. The lights had been wavering on and off throughout the evening. Before Watchman died they went off. There was a horrid interval during which Watchman made ghastly noises, everybody tramped about on broken glass, and Cubitt felt somebody's head butt against his legs. Miss Moore, she told me, heard somebody click the light to make sure it would stay off. He then dived down to find the tell-tale iodine bottle and plant the innocent one under the bench. He must, as you say, have found the bottom of the bottle hard to smash and have thrown it in the fire. You remember he called out that he would throw wood on the fire in order to get a little light. Just as he did that, the lights went on. There's a second switch in the inglenook, you know. He'd done another job of work in the dark. He'd picked up the dart and infected it with the cyanide. The dart was sticking in the floor, well away from the others. He had only to feel for the table and then find the dart. Here he made the fatal mistake of adding a fancy touch. We've proved that the dart was infected *after* the accident. Legge's fingerprints are all over it. If anyone else had pulled it out of the floor they would either have left prints of their own or smudged his. He should have left the dart alone, and we would have concluded that if it was ever poisoned the stuff was washed off by blood or had evaporated."

"I cannot conceive," said the Colonel, "why he'd wanted to anoint the dart. Why implicate himself? Why?"

"In order that we should think exactly what we did think. 'Why,' we cried, 'there was Legge, finding the dart, with every opportunity to wipe it clean, and he didn't! It couldn't be Legge!' Legge's plan, you see, depended on the theory of accident. He made it clear that he could have done nothing to the dart beforehand."

"Then," said the Colonel, "if the rest of this tarradiddle, forgive me my dear fellow, is still in the air, we yet catch him on the point of the dart."

"I think so. I explained to Harper this afternoon that I thought it better not to make an arrest at once. We realized that our case rested on a few facts and a mass of dubious conjecture. Fox and I pretended to despise conjecture and we hoped to collect many more bits of evidence before we fired point-blank. We still hope to get them before Legge comes up for assault and battery. We hope, in a word, to turn conjecture into fact. Until this evening I also hoped to get more from Legge himself, and, by George, I nearly got a dose of prussic acid. He must have slipped into the tap-room and put his last drop of poison in the decanter. He must also have had that last drop hidden away in a bottle somewhere, ever since he murdered Watchman. Not on his person for he was searched, and not in his room. Perhaps in his new room at Illington, perhaps in a *cache* somewhere outside the pub. Some time after Harper had searched his room, Legge got rid of a small glass dropper with a rubber top. If he used it to draw prussic acid from the rat-hole, he must have cleaned and filled it with his lotion, emptied it, and restored it to its place on his dressing-table. If he also used it to do his work with the decanter, he got rid of it this afternoon together with whatever vessel housed the teaspoonful of prussic acid. We'll search for them both."

Alleyn paused and looked round the circle of attentive faces. He raised a long finger.

"If we could find so much as the rubber top of that dropper," he said, "hidden away in some unlikely spot, then it would be good-bye conjecture and welcome fact!"

iii

"A needle," cried Colonel Brammington, after a long pause, "a needle in a haystack of gigantic proportions."

"It's not quite so bad as that. It rained pretty heavily during the lunch-hour. Legge hasn't changed his shoes and he hasn't been out in them. They're slightly stained and damp. He crossed the yard several times, but he didn't get off cobblestones. The paths and roads outside the pub are muddy. He's therefore either thrown the bottle and dropper from the window or got rid of them in the house or garage."

"Lavatory," said Fox gloomily.

"Possibly, Br'er Fox. We may have to resort to plumbing. His whole object would be to get rid of them immediately. He didn't know when we mightn't take a glass of sherry. Now, there's a valuable axiom which you, Colonel, have pointed out. The criminal is very prone to repetition. How did Legge get rid of the iodine bottle? He smashed if and threw the thick pieces into the fire. When he had more glass to get rid of in a hurry, wouldn't he at once think of his former method? He's a very unusual criminal if he didn't. There was no fire here, but during the afternoon he made several trips to the garage. He was packing some of his books in the car. I think our first move is to search the car and the garage. It's full of junk so it will be a delightful task."

Alleyn turned to Oates.

"Would you like to begin, Oates?"

"Yes, sir, thank you, sir."

"Search the car and garage thoroughly. I'll join you in ten minutes."

"Methodical, now," said Harper, "remember what I've told you."

"Yes, sir."

Oates went out.

"I think Mrs. Ives is still about," said Alleyn. "She works late."

"I'll see if I can find her, sir," said Fox.

"You'll stay where you are. I'll go," said Alleyn.

Mrs. Ives had gone to her room but had got no farther than her first row of curling pins. Alleyn interviewed her in Legge's room. She'd taken a cup of tea up to his room in the afternoon when he was packing his books. She couldn't say exactly when, but knew it was after three and before four o'clock. She had noticed the ear lotion and dropper on top of his dressing-table.

"Particular, I noticed it," said Mrs. Ives, "along of it being wet and marking wood. Usually, of a morning, it's all mucky with that pink stuff he puts in his ears. 'About time you washed the thing,' I said, 'and I see you've done it.' He seemed quite put-about. Well, you know—put-about, like, at my noticing."

"And did you go away soon after that, Mrs. Ives?"

"Well, sir, seeing I was not welcome," said Mrs. Ives, bridling a little, "I went. I offered to help him with his books but he seemed like he didn't fancy it. So I went on with my work upstairs. Polishing floor, I was."

"Which floor did you polish when you left Mr. Legge?"

"Passage, sir, and I might of saved myself the trouble, seeing he come and went, to and fro from yard, half a dozen times, stepping round me and dropping muck from his papers and passels."

"Did he go into the bathroom or any other room upstairs?"

Mrs. Ives blushed. "He didn't, then. He made two or three trips, and after last trip he went into private tap. The gentlemen were down there, Mr. Parish and Mr. Cubitt. You come up here soon after that to change your clothes."

Alleyn thanked her, spent an uncomfortable quarter of an hour on the roof outside Legge's window, and returned to the parlour.

"That's why he didn't fill it with lotion again and leave it. He'd just washed it when Mrs. Ives walked in, and when she noticed it, he lost his nerve and decided to get rid of it."

"The dropper," said Harper, "had a rubber top."

"It'd float," said Fox.

"He didn't go there, Br'er Fox. Mrs. Ives would have seen him. And there isn't one downstairs. It's the garage or the yard. Hullo, here's Oates!"

Oates came in. He was slightly flushed with triumph.

"Well?" said Harper.

"In accordance with instructions, sir," said Oates, "I proceeded to search the premises—"

"A truce to these vain repetitions," began Colonel Brammington with some violence.

"Never mind all that, Oates," said Harper. "Have you found anything?"

"Smashed glass, sir. Powdered to scatters and under a bit of sacking. The sacking's been newly shifted, sir."

"We'll look at it," said Alleyn. "Anything else?"

"I searched the car, sir, without success. I noted she was low in water, sir, and I took the liberty of filling her up. When she was full, sir, this come up to the top."

He opened his great hand.

Lying on the palm was a small wet India-rubber cap such as is used on a chemist's lotion-dropper, for the eye or ear.

"Good-bye conjecture," said Alleyn, "and welcome fact."

May 3, 1939
New Zealand.

Ngaio MARSH

Final Curtain

For Joan and Cecil,

with my love

CAST OF CHARACTERS

AGATHA TROY ALLEYN
KATTI BOSTOCK
NIGEL BATHGATE
SIR HENRY ANCRED, BART
CLAUDE ANCRED, his elder son (absent)
THOMAS ANCRED, his younger son
PAULINE KENTISH, his eldest daughter
PAUL KENTISH (his grandchild)
PATRICIA KENTISH (Panty) (his grandchild)
DESDEMONA ANCRED, his younger daughter
MILLAMANT ANCRED (wife to Henry Irving Ancred, deceased) his daughter-in-law
CEDRIC ANCRED, his heir presumptive (Millamant's son)
THE HONOURABLE MRS. CLAUDE ANCRED (Jenetta) his daughter-in-law (wife to Claude Ancred)
FENELLA ANCRED (her daughter)
MISS SONIA ORRINCOURT
MISS CAROLINE ABLE
BARKER, butler at Ancreton Manor
DR. WITHERS, G. P. at Ancreton
MR. JUNIPER, chemist
MR. RATTISBON, solicitor
MR. MORTIMER, OF MORTIMER & LOAME, Undertakers & Embalmers
RODERICK ALLEYN, Chief Detective-Inspector
DETECTIVE-INSPECTOR FOX
DETECTIVE-SERGEANT BAILEY
DR. CURTIS, Police Surgeon
POLICE-CONSTABLE BREAM
DETECTIVE-SERGEANT THOMPSON

CONTENTS

CHAPTER ONE

Siege of Troy

i

"CONSIDERED SEVERALLY," said Troy, coming angrily into the studio, "a carbuncle, a month's furlough and a husband returning from the antipodes don't sound like the ingredients for a hell-brew. Collectively, they amount to precisely that."

Katti Bostock stepped heavily back from her easel, screwed up her eyes, and squinting dispassionately at her work said: "Why?"

"They've telephoned from C. I. Rory's on his way. He'll probably get here in about three weeks. By which time I shall have returned, cured of my carbuncle, to the girls in the back room."

"At least," said Miss Bostock, scowling hideously at her work, "he won't have to face the carbuncle. There is that."

"It's on my hip."

"I know that, you owl."

"Well but. Katti," Troy argued, standing beside her friend, "you will allow and must admit, it's a stinker. You *are* going it," she added, squinting at Miss Bostock's canvas.

"You'll have to move into the London flat a bit earlier, that's all."

"But if only the carbuncle, and Rory and my leave had come together—well, the carbuncle a bit earlier, certainly—we'd have had a fortnight down here together. The A.C. promised us that. Rory's letters have been full of it. It *is* tough, Katti, you can't deny it. And if you so much as look like saying there are worse things in Europe—"

"All right, all right," said Miss Bostock pacifically. "I was only going to point out that it's reasonably lucky your particular back room and Roderick's job both happen to be in London. Look for the silver lining, dear," she added unkindly. "What's that letter you keep taking in and out of your pocket?"

Troy opened her thin hand and disclosed a crushed sheet of notepaper. "That?" she murmured. "Oh, yes, there's that. You never heard anything so dotty. Read it."

"It's got cadmium red all over it."

"I know. I dropped it on my palette. It's on the back, luckily."

Miss Bostock spread out the letter on her painting table, adding several cobalt finger-prints in the process. It was a single sheet of pre-war notepaper, thick, white, with an engraved heading surmounted by a crest—a cross with fluted extremities.

"Crikey!" said Miss Bostock. "Ancreton Manor. That's the Crikey!" Being one of those people who invariably read letters aloud she began to mutter:—

MISS AGATHA TROY (MRS. RODERICK ALLEYN)
TATLERS END HOUSE
BOSSICOT, BUCKS.

DEAR MADAM,

My father-in-law, Sir Henry Ancred asks me to write to you in reference to a portrait of himself in the character of Macbeth for which he would be pleased to engage your services. The picture is to hang in the entrance hall at Ancreton Manor and will occupy a space six by four feet in dimension. As he is in poor health he wishes the painting to be done here and will be pleased if you can arrange to stay with us from Saturday, November 17th until such time as the portrait is completed. He presumes this will be in about a week. He will be glad to know, by telegram, whether this arrangement will suit you and also your fee for such a commission.

I am,
Yours faithfully,
MILLAMANT ANCRED

"Well," said Miss Bostock, "of all the cheek!"

Troy grinned. "You'll notice I'm to dodge up a canvas six by four in seven days. I wonder if he expects me to throw in the three witches and the Bloody Child."

"Have you answered it?"

"Not yet," Troy mumbled.

"It was written six days ago," scolded Miss Bostock.

"I know. I must. How shall I word the telegram: 'Deeply regret am not house painter?' "

Katti Bostock paused, her square finger still planted under the crest. "I thought only peers had those things peppered about on their notepaper," she said.

"You'll notice it's a cross with ends like an anchor. Hence Ancred, one supposes."

"Oh I say!" said Katti, rubbing her nose with her blue finger. "That's funny."

"What is?"

"Didn't you do a set of designs for that production of Macbeth?"

"I did. That may have given them the idea."

"Good Lord! Do you remember," said Miss Bostock, "we saw him in the play. You and Roderick and I? The Bathgates took us. Before the war."

"Of course I do," said Troy. "He was magnificent, wasn't he?"

"What's more, he looked magnificent. *What* a head. Troy, do you remember, we said—"

"So we did. Katti," said Troy, "you're *not* by any chance going to suggest—"

"No, no, of course not. Good Lord, no! But it's rum that we did say it would be fun to have a go at him in the grand manner. Against the backcloth they did from your design; lolloping clouds and a black simplified castle form. The figure cloaked and dim."

"He wouldn't thank you for that, I daresay. The old gentleman probably wishes to appear in a flash of lightning, making faces. Well, I'd better send the telegram. Oh, damn!" Troy sighed. "I wish I could settle down to something."

Miss Bostock glowered thoughtfully at Troy. Four years of intensive work at pictorial surveys for the army, followed by similar and even more exacting work for U.N.R.R.A., had, she thought, tried her friend rather high. She was thin and a bit jumpy. She'd be better if she could do more painting, thought Katti, who did not regard the making of pictorial maps, however exquisite, as full compensation for the loss of pure art. Four years' work with little painting and no husband. "Thank God," Katti thought, "I'm different. I get along nicely."

"If he gets here in three weeks," Troy was saying, "where do you suppose he is now? He might be in New York. But he'd cable if he was in New York. The last letter was still from New Zealand, of course. And the cable."

"Why don't you get on with your work?"

"Work?" said Troy vaguely. "Oh, well. I'll send off that telegram." She wandered to the door and came back for the letter. "Six by four," she said. "Imagine it!"

ii

"Mr. Thomas Ancred?" said Troy, looking at the card in her hand. "My dear Katti, he's actually *here*, on the spot."

Katti, who had almost completed her vigorous canvas, laid down her brushes and said: "This is in answer to your telegram. He's come to badger you. Who is he?"

"A son of Sir Henry Ancred's, I fancy. Isn't he a theatrical producer? I seem to remember seeing 'Produced by Thomas Ancred' under casts of characters? Yes, of course he is. That production of *Macbeth* we were talking about at the Unicorn. He was in the picture somewhere then. Look, there's 'Unicorn Theatre' scribbled on the card. We'll have to ask him to dinner, Katti. There's not a train before nine. That'll mean opening another tin. *What* a bore."

"I don't see why he need stay. There's a pub in the village. If he chooses to come on a fool's errand!"

"I'll see what he's like."

"Aren't you going to take off that painting smock?"

"I don't suppose so," Troy said vaguely and walked up the path from her studio to her house. It was a cold afternoon. Naked trees rattled in the north wind and leaden clouds hurried across the sky. "Suppose," Troy pretended, "I was to walk in and find it was Rory. Suppose he'd kept it a secret and there he was waiting in the library. He'd have lit the fire so that it should be there for us to meet by. His face would be looking like it did the first time he stood there, a bit white with excitement. Suppose—" She had a lively imagination and she built up her fantasy quickly, warming her thoughts at it. So clear was her picture that it brought a physical reaction; her heart knocked, her hand, even, trembled a little as she opened the library door.

The man who stood before the unkindled hearth was tall and stooped a little. His hair, which had the appearance of floss, stood up thinly like a child's. He wore glasses and blinked behind them at Troy.

"Good afternoon," he said. "I'm Thomas Ancred, but of course you know that because of the card. I hope you don't mind my coming. I didn't really want to but the family insisted."

He held out his hand but didn't do anything with it when Troy took it so that she was obliged to give it a slight squeeze and let it go. "The whole thing's silly," he said. "About Papa's portrait, I mean, of course. We call him 'Papa,' you know. Some people think it sounds affected, but there it is. About Papa's portrait. I must tell you they all got a great shock when your telegram came. They rang me up. They said you couldn't have understood and I was to come and explain."

Troy lit the fire. "Do sit down," she said, "you must be frozen. What did they think I hadn't understood?"

"Well, first of all, that it was an honour to paint Papa. I told them that it would have been the other way round, if anything, supposing you'd consented. Thank you, I will sit down. It's quite a long walk from the station and I think I've blistered my heel. Do you mind if I have a look? I can feel through my sock, you know."

"Look away," said Troy.

"Yes," said Thomas after a pause, "it is a blister. I'll just keep my toe in my shoe for manners and I daresay the blister will go down. About my father. Of course you know he's the Grand Old Man of the British stage so I needn't go into all that. Do you admire his acting at all?"

"A great deal," said Troy. She was glad that the statement was truthful. This curious man, she felt, would have recognized a polite evasion.

"*Do* you?" he said. "That's nice. He is quite good, of course, though a little creaky at times, don't you feel? And then, all those mannerisms! He can't play an emotional bit, you know, without sucking in his breath rather loudly. But he really is good in a magnificent Mrs. Beeton sort of way. A recipe for everything and only the best ingredients used."

"Mr. Ancred," Troy said, "what is all this about?"

"Well, it's part of the build-up. It's supposed to make you see things in a different light. The great British actor painted by the great British artist, don't you know? And although I don't suppose you'd *like* Ancreton much it might amuse you to see it. It's very baronial. The portrait would hang under the minstrels' gallery with special lighting. He doesn't mind what he pays. It's to commemorate his seventy-fifth birthday. His own idea is that the Nation ought to have given it to him, but as the Nation doesn't seem to have thought of that he's giving it to himself. And to posterity, of course," Thomas added as an afterthought, cautiously slipping his finger inside his loosened shoe.

"If you'd like me to suggest one or two painters who might—"

"Some people prick blisters," said Thomas, "but I don't. No, thank you, they've made a second-best list. I was telling you about Ancreton. You know those steel engravings of castles and halls in Victorian books? All turrets and an owl flying across the moon?

That's Ancreton. It was built by my great-grandfather. He pulled down a nice Queen Anne house and erected Ancreton. There was a moat but people got diphtheria so it was let go and they're growing vegetables in it. The food is quite good because there are lots of vegetables and Papa cut down the Great East Spinney during the war and stored the wood so there are still fires."

Thomas smiled at his hostess. He had a tentative side-long smile. "Yes," he said, "that's Ancreton. I expect you'd hate it but you couldn't help laughing."

"As I'm not going, however," Troy began with a rising sense of panic, but Thomas continued unmoved. "And then, of course, there's the family. Well! Papa and Millamant and Pauline and Panty to begin with. Are you at all keen on the emotions?"

"I haven't an idea what you mean."

"My family is very emotional. They feel everything most deeply. The funny thing about *that*," said Thomas, "is that they really do feel deeply. They really are sensitive only people are inclined to think nobody could really be as sensitive as they seem to be so that's hard luck on the family." Thomas took off his spectacles and gazed at Troy with short-sighted innocence. "Except," he added, "that they have the satisfaction of knowing that they are so much more sensitive than anyone else. That's a point that might interest you."

"Mr. Ancred," Troy said patiently, "I am on leave because I've not been well—"

"Indeed? You look all right. What's the matter with you?"

"A carbuncle," said Troy angrily.

"Really?" said Thomas, clucking his tongue. "How sickening for you."

"And in consequence I'm not at the top of my form. A commission of the sort mentioned in your sister-in-law's letter would take at least three weeks' intensive work. The letter gives me a week."

"How long is your leave?"

Troy bit her lips. "That's not the point," she said. "The point is—"

"I had a carbuncle once. You feel better if you keep on with your job. Less depressed. Mine," said Thomas proudly, "was on my bottom. Now that *is* awkward." He looked inquiringly at Troy, who by this time, according to her custom, was sitting on the hearth-rug. "Obviously," Thomas continued, "yours—"

"It's on my hip. It's very much better—"

"Well, then—"

"—but that's not the point. Mr. Ancred, I can't accept this commission. My husband is coming home after three years' absence—"

"When?" Thomas asked instantly.

"As far as we know in three weeks," said Troy, wishing she could bring herself to lie freely to her visitor. "But one can never tell. It might be sooner."

"Well, of course Scotland Yard will let you know about that, won't they? Because, I mean, he's pretty high up, isn't he? Supposing you did go to Ancreton they could ring you up there just as well as here."

"The point is," Troy almost shouted, "I don't want to paint your father as Macbeth. I'm sorry to put it so bluntly, but I just don't."

"I told them you wouldn't," said Thomas complacently. "The Bathgates thought they knew better."

"The Bathgates? Do you mean Nigel and Angela Bathgate?"

"Who else? Nigel and I are old friends. When the family started all this business I went to see him and asked if he thought you'd do it. Nigel said he knew you were on leave and he thought it would be nice for you."

"He knows nothing whatever about it."

"He said you liked meeting queer people. He said you'd revel in Papa as a subject and gloat over his conversation. It only shows you how little we understand our friends, doesn't it?"

"Yes," said Troy. "It does."

"But I can't help wondering what you'd make of Panty."

Troy had by this time determined to ask Thomas Ancred no questions whatever and it was with a sense of impotent fury that she heard her own voice: "Did you say 'Panty?' "

"She's my niece, you know. My sister Pauline's youngest. We call her Panty because her bloomers are always coming down. She's a Difficult Child. Her school, which is a school for Difficult Children, was evacuated to Ancreton. They are quartered in the West Wing under a *very* nice person called Caroline Able. Panty is frightful."

"Oh," said Troy as he seemed to expect some comment.

"Yes, indeed. She's so awful that I rather like her. She's a little girl with two pigtails and a devilish face. This sort of thing."

Thomas put his long forefingers at right angles to his head, scowled abominably and blew out his cheeks. His eyes glittered. Much against her will Troy was suddenly confronted with the face of a bad child. She laughed shortly. Thomas rubbed his hands. "If I were to tell you," he said, "of the things that little girl does you would open your eyes. Well! A cactus, for instance, in Sonia's bed. Unfortunately she's papa's favourite, which makes control almost impossible. And of course one mustn't beat her except in anger because that's not proper child psychology."

He stared thoughtfully into the fire. "Then there's Pauline, my eldest sister, she's the important type, and Milly, my sister-in-law who perpetually laughs at nothing and housekeeps for Papa since her husband, my eldest brother, Henry Irving, died."

"Henry Irving!" Troy ejaculated, thinking with alarm: "Evidently, he's mad."

"Henry Irving Ancred, of course. Papa had a great admiration for Irving and regards himself as his spiritual successor, so he called Hal after him. And then, there's Sonia. Sonia is Papa's mistress." Thomas cleared his throat old-maidishly. "Rather a biblical situation really. You remember David and Abishag the Shulammite? They all dislike Sonia. I must say she's a *very* bad actress. Am I boring you?"

Troy, though not bored, was extremely reluctant to say so. She muttered: "Not at all" and offered Thomas a drink. He replied: "Yes, thank you, if you've got plenty." She went off to fetch it, hoping in the interim to sort out her reactions to her visitor. She found Katti Bostock in the dining-room.

"For pity's sake, Katt," said Troy, "come back with me. I've got a sort of monster in there."

"Is it staying for dinner?"

"I haven't asked it but I should think so. So we shall have to open one of Rory's tins."

"Hadn't you better go back to this bloke?"

"Do come too. I'm afraid of him. He tells me about his family, presenting each member of it in a repellent light and yet expecting me to desire nothing more than their acquaintance. And the alarming thing is, Katti, that the narrative has its horrid fascination. Important Pauline, acquisitive Sonia, dreadful little Panty, and Milly who laughs perpetually at nothing; that's Millamant, of course, who wrote the letter. And Papa, larger than life and presenting himself with his own portrait because the Nation hasn't come up to scratch—"

"You aren't going to tell me you've accepted!"

"Not I. Good Lord, no! I'd be demented. But—keep an eye on me, Katti," said Troy.

iii

Thomas accepted the invitation to dinner, expressing himself as delighted with his share of tinned New Zealand crayfish. "We've got friends in New Zealand and America too," he said, "but unfortunately tinned fish brings on an attack of Papa's gastroenteritis. If we have it he can't resist it, and so Milly doesn't let us have it. Next time I go to Ancreton she's giving me several tins to take back to my flat."

"You don't live at Ancreton?" Troy asked.

"How could I when my job's in London? I go there sometimes for week-ends to give them all an opportunity of confiding in me. Papa likes us to go. He's having quite a party for his birthday. Pauline's son, Paul, who has a wounded leg, will be there and Millamant's son, Cedric, who is a dress-designer. I don't think you'd care for Cedric. And my sister Desdemona, who is at liberty just now though she hopes to be cast for a part in a new play at the Crescent. My other sister-in-law, Jenetta, will be there too, I hope, with her daughter, Fenella. Her husband, my eldest brother Claude, is a colonel in the occupation forces and hasn't come home yet."

"Rather a large party," said Katti. "Fun for you."

"There'll be a good many rows, of course," Thomas replied. "When you get two or three Ancreds gathered together they are certain to hurt each other's feelings. That's where I come in handy because I'm the insensitive one and they talk to me about each other. And about Sonia, I needn't say. We shall all talk about Sonia. We'd hoped to unveil your portrait of Papa on this occasion," he said, looking wistfully at Troy. "Indeed, that's really what the party's for."

Troy mumbled something indistinguishable.

"Papa had a lovely time last week looking out the Macbeth clothes," Thomas continued. "I wonder if you remember his costume. Motley did it for us. It's red, a Paul Veronese-ish red, dark but clear, with a smoky overcloak. We've got a miniature theatre at Ancreton, you know. I brought down the original backdrop for one of the inset scenes and hung it. It's quite a coincidence, isn't it," Thomas went on innocently, "that you did the original designs for that production? Of course you remember the one I mean. It's very simple. A boldly distorted castle form seen in silhouette. He dressed himself and stood in front of it, resting on his claymore with his head stooped, as if listening. 'Good things of day begin to droop and drowse,' do you remember?"

Troy remembered that line very well. It was strange that he should have recalled it; for Alleyn was fond of telling her how, in the small hours of a stormy morning, a constable on night duty had once quoted it to him. Thomas speaking the line, with an actor's sense of its value, sounded like an echo of her husband and her thoughts were filled with memories of his voice.

"He's been ill off and on for some time," Thomas was saying, "and gets very depressed. But the idea of the portrait bucked him up no end and he's set his heart on you to paint it. You see you did his hated rival."

"Sir Benjamin Corporal?" Troy muttered, eyeing Katti.

"Yes. And old Ben makes a great story about how you only paint subjects that you take a fancy to—pictorially, I mean. He told us you took a great fancy to him pictorially. He said he was the only actor you'd ever wanted to paint."

"On the contrary," Troy said angrily. "It was a commission from his native town—Huddersfield. Old popinjay!"

"He told Papa he'd only be snubbed if he approached you. Actually, Papa was dressed as Macbeth when your telegram arrived. He said: 'Ah! This is propitious. Do you think, my dear, that Miss Troy—should he have said "Mrs. Alleyn"?—will care for this pose?' He was quite young-looking when he said it. And then he opened your telegram. He took it rather well, really. He just gave it to Milly and said: 'I shouldn't have put on these garments. It was always an unlucky piece. I'm a vain old fool.' And he went away and changed and had an attack of gastroenteritis, poor thing. It must almost be time I thought of walking back to the station, mustn't it?"

"I'll drive you." Troy said.

Thomas protested mildly but Troy overruled him brusquely when the time came, and went off to start her car. Thomas said good-bye politely to Katti Bostock.

"You're a clever chap, Mr. Ancred," said Katti grimly.

"Oh, do you think so?" asked Thomas, blinking modestly. "Oh, no! Clever? Me? Goodness, no. Good-night. It's been nice to meet you."

Katti waited for half an hour before she heard the sound of the returning car. Presently the door opened and Troy came in. She wore a white overcoat. A lock of her short dark hair hung over her forehead. Her hands were jammed in her pockets. She walked self-consciously down the room, looking at Katti out of the corners of her eyes.

"Got rid of your rum friend?" asked Miss Bostock.

Troy cleared her throat. "Yes. He's talked himself off."

"Well," said Miss Bostock, after a long silence. "When do you leave for Ancreton?"

"To-morrow," said Troy shortly.

CHAPTER TWO

Departure

i

TROY WISHED that Thomas Ancred would say goodbye and leave her to savour the moment of departure. She enjoyed train journeys enormously and, in these days, not a second of the precious discomfort should be left unrelished. But there stood Thomas on the Euston platform with nothing to say and filled, no doubt, with the sense of tediousness that is inseparable from these occasions. "Why doesn't he take off his hat and walk away," Troy thought fretfully. But when she caught his eye he gave her such an anxious smile that she instantly felt obliged to reassure him.

"I have been wondering," Thomas said, "if, after all, you will merely loathe my family."

"In any case, I shall be working."

"Yes," he agreed, looking immensely relieved, "there *is* that. I can't tell you how much I dislike many actors and yet when I begin to work with them, sometimes I quite love them. If they do what I tell them, of course."

"Are you working this morning?" And she thought how unreal seem the activities of people one leaves behind in railway stations.

"Yes," said Thomas, "a first rehearsal."

"Please don't wait," she said for the fourth time and for the fourth time he replied: "I'll just see you off," and looked at his watch. Doors were slammed further down the train. Troy leant out of the window. At last she was off. A man in uniform, peering frenziedly into carriage after carriage, was working his way towards her. "Nigel!" Troy shouted. "Nigel!"

"Oh, God, there you are!" cried Nigel Bathgate. "Hullo, Thomas. Here! Troy! I knew I wouldn't have time to talk so I've written." He thrust a fat envelope at her. A whistle blew. The train clunked and

Thomas said: "Well, good-bye. They *will* be pleased," raised his hat and slid out of view. Nigel walked rapidly along beside the window. "What a go! You will laugh," he said. "Is this a novel?" Troy asked, holding up the envelope. "Almost! You'll see." Nigel broke into a run. I've always wanted to—you'll see—When's Roderick—" "Soon!" Troy cried. "In three weeks!" "Good-bye! I can't run any more." He had gone.

Troy settled down. A young man appeared in the corridor. He peered in at the door and finally entered the already crowded carriage. With a slight twittering noise, he settled himself on his upturned suitcase with his back to the door and opened an illustrated paper. Troy noticed that he wore a jade ring on his first finger, a particularly bright green hat and suede shoes. The other passengers looked dull and were also preoccupied with their papers. Rows of back yards and occasional heaps of rubble would continue for some time in the world outside the window pane. She sighed luxuriously, thought how much easier it would be to wait for her husband now that she was forced to paint, fell into a brief day-dream and finally opened Nigel's letter.

Three sheets of closely typed reporter's paper fell out, together with a note written in green ink.

"13 hours, G.M.T." Nigel had written. "Troy, my dear, two hours ago Thomas Ancred, back from his visit to you, rang me up in a triumph. You're in for a party but the G.O.M. will be grand to paint. I've always died to write up the Ancreds but can't afford the inevitable libel action. So I've amused myself by dodging up the enclosed *jeu d'esprit*. It may serve to fill in your journey. N.B."

The typescript was headed: "Note on Sir Henry Ancred, Bart, and his Immediate Circle." "Do I want to read it?" Troy wondered. "It was charming of Nigel to write it but I'm in for two weeks of the Ancreds and Thomas' commentary was exhaustive." And she let the pages fall in her lap. At the same time the young man on the suitcase lowered his modish periodical, and stared fixedly at her. He impressed her disagreeably. His eyes suggested a kind of dull impertinence. Under the line of hair on his lip his mouth was too fresh and projected too far above a small white chin. Everything about him was over-elegant, Troy thought, and dismissed him as an all-too-clearly defined type. He continued to stare at her. "If he was opposite," she thought, "he would begin to ask questions about the windows. What does he want?" She lifted the sheets of Nigel's typescript and began to read.

ii

"Collectively and severally," Nigel had written, "the Ancreds, all but one, are over-emotionalized. Anyone attempting to describe or explain their behaviour must keep this characteristic firmly in mind for without it they would scarcely exist. Sir Henry Ancred is perhaps the worst of the lot but, because he is an actor, his friends accept his behaviour as part of his stock-in-trade and, apart from an occasional feeling of shyness in his presence, seldom make the mistake of worrying about him. Whether he was drawn to his wife (now deceased) by the discovery of a similar trait in her character or whether, by the phenomenon of marital acclimatization, Lady Ancred learnt to exhibit emotion with a virtuosity equal to that of her husband, cannot be discovered. It can only be recorded that she did so; and died.

"Their elder daughters, Pauline (Ancred played in *The Lady of Lyons* in '96) and Desdemona (*Othello*, 1909) and their sons Henry Irving (Ancred played a bit-part in *The Bells*) and Claude (Pauline's twin) in their several modes, have inherited or acquired the emotional habit. Only Thomas (Ancred was resting in 1904 when Thomas was born) is free of it. Thomas, indeed, is uncommonly placid. Perhaps for this reason his parent, sisters, and brothers appeal to him when they hurt each other's feelings, which they do punctually two or three times a week, and always with an air of tragic astonishment.

"Pauline, Claude, and Desdemona, in turn, followed their father's profession. Pauline joined a northern repertory company, married John Kentish, a local man of property, retired upon provincial glories more enduring than those she was likely to enjoy as an actress and gave birth to Paul and, twelve years later, Patricia (born 1936 and known as Panty). Like all Ancred's children, except Thomas, Pauline was extremely handsome and has retained her looks. She has been a widow for some time.

"Claude, her twin, drifted from Oriel into the O.U.D.S. and thence, on his father's back, into romantic juveniles. He married the Honourable Miss Jenetta Cairnes, who had a fortune but never, he is fond of saying, has understood him. She is an intelligent woman. They have one daughter, Fenella.

"Desdemona, Sir Henry's fourth child (aged thirty-six at the time of this narrative), has become a good emotional actress, difficult to place as she has a knack of cracking the seams of the brittle slickly drawn roles for which West-End managements, addled by her beauty, occasionally cast her. She has become attached to a Group and appears in pieces written by two surrealists, uttering her lines in such a heart-rendering manner that they seem, even to Desdemona herself, to be fraught with significance. She is unmarried and has suffered a great deal from two unhappy love affairs.

"The eldest son, Henry Irving Ancred, became a small part actor and married Mildred Cooper, whom his father promptly rechristened Millamant as at that time he was engaged upon a revival of *The Way of the World*. Millamant she has remained and, before her husband died, gave birth to a son, Cedric, about whom the less said the better.

"Your friend, Thomas, is unmarried. Having discovered, after two or three colourless ventures, that he was a bad actor, he set about teaching himself to become a good producer. In this, after a struggle, he succeeded and is now established as Director for Incorporated Playhouses, Limited, Unicorn Theatre. He has never been known to lose his temper at rehearsals but may sometimes be observed, alone in the stalls, rocking to and fro with his head in his hands. He lives in a bachelor's flat in Westminster.

"All these offspring, Pauline, Claude, Desdemona and Thomas, their sister-in-law, Millamant, and their children, are like details in a design, the central motive of which is Sir Henry himself. Sir Henry, known to his associates as the G.O.M. of the stage, is believed to be deeply attached to his family. That is part of his legend and the belief may be founded in fact. He sees a great deal of his family and perhaps it would be accurate to say that he loves best those particular members of it of whom, at any given moment, he sees least. His wife he presumably loved. They never quarrelled and always sided together against whichever of their young had wounded the feelings of one or the other of them. Thomas was the exception to this, as he is to most other generalities one might apply to the Ancreds.

" 'Old Tommy!' Sir Henry will say. 'Funny chap! Never quite know where you are with him. T'uh!' This scarcely articulated noise 'T'uh,' is used by all the Ancreds (except, of course, Thomas) to express a kind of disillusioned resignation. It's uttered on a high note and is particularly characteristic.

"Sir Henry is not a theatrical knight but a baronet, having inherited his title, late in life, from an enormously wealthy second cousin. It's a completely obscure baronetcy and, although perfectly genuine, difficult to believe in. Perhaps this is because he himself is so obviously impressed by it and likes to talk about Norman ancestors with names that sound as if they'd been chosen from the dramatis personae in a Lyceum programme. The Sieur'd' Ancred and so on. His crest is on everything. He looks, as his dresser is fond of saying, every inch the aristocrat—silver hair, hook nose, blue eyes. Up to a few years ago he still appeared in drawing-room comedies, giving exquisite performances of charming or irascible buffers. Sometimes he forgot his lines but, by the use of a number of famous mannerisms, diddled his audience into believing it was a lesser actor who had slipped. His last Shakesperian appearance was as Macbeth on the Bard's birthday, at the age of sixty-eight. He then developed a chronic gastric disorder and retired from the stage to his family seat, Ancreton, which in its architectural extravagances may possibly remind him of Dunsinane.

"There he remains, guarded by Millamant who, since the death of her husband, has house-kept for her father-in-law and who is supposed by the rest of her family to be feathering a nest for her son, the egregious Cedric, who is delicate. The family (excepting Thomas) is inclined to laugh with bitter emphasis when Cedric is mentioned and to criticize poor Milly's treatment of the G.O.M. Milly is a jolly woman and laughs at them. She once told Thomas that if either of his sisters cared to take on her job she'd be delighted to relinquish it. She had them there, for though they all visit Ancreton a great deal they invariably leave after a few days in a tempest of wounded feelings.

"Occasionally they close their ranks. They have done so at the moment, being at war, as a family, with Miss Sonia Orrincourt, an indifferent actress with whom, at the age of seventy-five, their father is having a fling. This astounding old man has brought the lady to Ancreton and there, it appears, she intends to remain. She is an erstwhile member of the chorus and was selected as a type to understudy a small part in a piece at the Unicorn. This was a shattering innovation. The Unicorn, in the theatre world, is as Boodles in clubland. No musical comedy artist, before Miss Orrincourt, has enlivened its stage-door. Sir Henry watched a rehearsal. In three weeks Miss Orrincourt, having proved a complete washout as an understudy, was given the sack by Thomas. She then sought out his father, wept on his waistcoat and reappeared in her present unmistakable role at Ancreton. She is a blonde. Pauline and Desdemona say that she is holding out on the Old Man with a view to matrimony. Thomas believes her to have taken the more complaisant attitude. Claude, in the Middle East, has sent a cable so guarded in its phrases that the only thing it makes clear is his rage. Claude's wife, Jenetta, a shrewd and amusing woman who maintains a detached attitude to her relations-by-marriage, has been summoned, in Claude's absence, to a conclave. It is possible that her only child, Fenella, hitherto a second favourite with Sir Henry after Pauline's child Panty, might lose ground if he married. Even jolly Millamant is shaken. Her appalling Cedric is the senior grandson and Sir Henry has of late begun to drop disconcerting hints that there is life in the old dog yet.

"This, then, is the set-up at Ancreton. My information has come by way of occasional visits and Thomas, who, as you will have discovered, is a talkative chap and doesn't know the meaning of the word reticence.

"In some such fashion as this, dear Troy, would I begin the novel that I dare not attempt. One word more. I understand you are to paint Sir Henry in the character of Macbeth. May I assure you that with Pauline's child Panty on the premises you will find yourself also furnished with a Bloody Child."

iii

Troy folded the typescript and replaced it in its envelope, across which Nigel had written her name in bold characters. The young man on the suitcase stared fixedly at the envelope. She turned it face downwards on her lap. His illustrated paper hung open across his knee. She saw, with annoyance, her own photograph.

So that was what he was up to. He'd recognized her. Probably, she thought, he potters about doing fancy little drawings. He looks like it. If the other people get out before we reach Ancreton Halt, he'll introduce himself and my lovely train journey will be ruined. Damn!

The country outside the window changed to a hurrying tapestry of hedgerows, curving downs, and naked trees. Troy watched it contentedly. Having allowed herself to be bamboozled into taking this commission, she had entered into a state of emotional suspension. It was deeply satisfactory to know that her husband would soon return. She no longer experienced moments of something like terror lest his three years' absence should drop like a curtain between their understanding of each other. The Commissioner had promised she should know two days beforehand of Alleyn's arrival and in the meantime the train carried her to a job among strangers who at least would not be commonplace. "But I hope," Troy thought, "that their family upheaval won't interfere with the old boy's sittings. That *would* be a bore."

The train drew into a junction and the other passengers, with the exception of the young man on the suitcase, began to collect themselves. Just what she'd feared, thought Troy. She opened her lunch basket and a book. "If I eat and read at him," she thought, "that may keep him off," and she remembered Guy de Maupassant's strictures upon people who eat in the train.

Now they were off again. Troy munched her sandwiches and read the opening scene of *Macbeth.* She had decided to revisit that terrible country whose only counterpart, she thought, was to be found in Emily Brontc. This fancy pleased her and she paused to transport the wraiths of Heathcliff and Cathy to the blasted heath or to follow Fleance over the moors to Wuthering Heights. But, if I am to paint Macbeth, she thought, I must read. And, as the first inflexions in the voice of a friend who is remet after a long absence instantly prepare us for tones that we are yet to hear, so with its opening phrases, the play, which she thought she had forgotten, returned wholly to her memory.

"*Do* forgive me for interrupting," said a high-pitched voice, "but I've been madly anxious to talk to you and this is such a *magical* opportunity."

The young man had slid along the seat and was now opposite. His head was tilted ingratiatingly to one side and he smiled at Troy. "*Please* don't think I'm seething with sinister intentions," he said. "Honestly, there's no need to pull the communication cord."

"I didn't for a moment suppose there was," said Troy.

"You are Agatha Troy, aren't you?" he continued anxiously. "I couldn't be mistaken. I mean it's too shatteringly coincidental, isn't it? Here I am reading my little journal and what should I see but a perfectly blissful Cecil Beaton of you. *So* exciting and so miraculously *you*. And if I'd had the weeniest doubt left, that alarming affair you're reading would have settled it."

Troy looked from her book to the young man. "Macbeth?" she said. "I'm afraid I don't understand."

"Oh, but it was too conclusive," he said. "But of course, I haven't introduced myself, have I? I'm Cedric Ancred."

"Oh," said Troy after a pause. "Oh, yes. I see."

"And then to clinch it, there was your name on that envelope. I'm afraid I peered shamelessly. But it's too exciting that you're actually going to make a picture of the Old Person in all his tats and bobs. You can't imagine what that costume is like! And the toque! Some terrifically powerful man beat it out of solid steel for him. He's my grandpa, you know. My mother is Millamant Ancred. My father—only promise you won't tell anyone—was Henry Irving Ancred. Imagine!"

Troy could think of nothing to say in reply to this recital and took another bite out of her sandwich.

"So you see I had to make myself known," he continued with an air that Troy thought of as "winsome." "I'm so burnt up always about your work and the prospect of meeting you was absolutely tonic."

"But how did you know," Troy asked, "that I was going to paint Sir Henry?"

"I rang up Uncle Thomas last night and he told me. I'd been commanded to the presence and had decided that I couldn't face it but immediately changed my plans. You see," said Cedric, with a boyish frankness which Troy found intolerable, "you see, I actually try to paint. I'm with Pont et Cie and I do the designs. Of course everything's too austerity and grim nowadays but we keep toddling."

His suit was silver grey. His shirt was pale green, his pull-over was dark green and his tie was orange. He had rather small eyes and in the middle of his soft round chin there was a dimple.

"If I may talk about your work," he was saying, "there's a quality in it that appeals to me enormously. Its—how can I describe it?—its design is always consistent with its subject matter. I mean, the actual *pattern* is not something arbitrarily imposed on the subject but an inevitable consequence of it. Such integrity, always. Or am I talking nonsense?"

He was not talking complete nonsense and Troy grudgingly admitted it. There were few people with whom she cared to discuss her work. Cedric Ancred watched her for a few seconds. She had the unpleasant feeling that he sensed her distaste for him. His next move was unexpected. He ran his fingers through his hair, which was damply blond and wavy. "God!" he said. "People! The things they say! If only one could break through, as you have. God! Why is life so perfectly bloody?"

"Oh, *dear!*" Troy thought and shut her luncheon basket. Cedric was gazing at her fixedly. Evidently she was expected to reply.

"I'm not much good," she said, "at generalities about life."

"No!" he muttered and nodded his head profoundly. "Of course not. I so agree. You are perfectly right, of course."

Troy looked furtively at her watch. "A full half-hour," she thought, "before we get to Ancreton Halt, and then he's coming too."

"I'm boring you," Cedric said loudly. "No, don't deny it. God! I'm boring you. T'uh!"

"I just don't know how to carry on this sort of conversation, that's all."

Cedric began to nod again.

"You were reading," he said. "I stopped you. One should never do that. It's an offence against the Holy Ghost."

"I never heard such nonsense," said Troy with spirit.

Cedric laughed gloomily. "Go on!" he said. "Please go on. Return to your Blasted Heath. It's an atrociously bad play, in my opinion, but go on reading it."

But it was not easy to read, knowing that a few inches away he was glaring at her over his folded arms. She turned a page. In a minute or two he began to sigh. "He sighs," thought Troy, "like the Mock Turtle and I think he must be mad." Presently he laughed shortly and, in spite of herself, Troy looked up. He was still glaring at her. He had a jade cigarette case open in his hand.

"You smoke?" he asked.

She felt certain that if she refused he would make some further peculiar scene so she took one of his cigarettes. He lit it in silence and flung himself back in his corner.

After all, Troy thought, I've got to get on with him somehow, and she said: "Don't you find it extraordinarily tricky hitting on exactly the right note in fashion drawings? When one thinks of what they used to be like! There's no doubt that commercial art—"

"Prostitution!" Cedric interrupted. "Just that. If you don't mind the initial sin it's quite amusing."

"Do you work at all for the theatre?"

"So sweet of you to take an interest," Cedric answered rather acidly. "Oh, yes. My Uncle Thomas occasionally uses me. Actually I'm madly keen on it. One would have thought that with the Old Person behind one there would have been an opening. Unfortunately he is not behind me, which is *so* sickening. I've been cut out by the Infant Monstrosity." He brightened a little. "It's some comfort to know I'm the eldest grandson, of course. In my more optimistic moments I tell myself he can't leave me *completely* out of his will. My worst nightmare is the one when I dream I've inherited Ancreton. I always wake screaming. Of course with Sonia on the tapis almost anything may happen. You've heard about Sonia?"

Troy hesitated and he went on: "She's the Old Person's little bit of nonsense. Immensely decorative. I can't make up my mind whether she's incredibly stupid or not, but I fear not. The others are all for fighting her, tooth and claw, but I rather think of ingratiating myself in case he does marry her. What do you think?"

Troy was wondering if it was a characteristic of all male Ancreds to take utter strangers into their confidence. But they couldn't all be as bad as Cedric. After all, Nigel Bathgate had said Cedric was frightful and even Thomas—she thought suddenly how nice Thomas seemed in retrospect when one compared him with his nephew.

"But *do* tell me," Cedric was saying, "how do you mean to paint him? All beetling and black? But whatever you decide it will be marvelous. You will let me creep in and see, or are you dreadfully fierce about that?"

"Rather fierce, I'm afraid," said Troy.

"I suspected so." Cedric looked out of the window and immediately clasped his forehead. "It's coming," he said. "Every time I brace myself for the encounter and every time, if there was a train to take me, I would rush screaming back to London. In a moment we shall see it. I can't bear it. God! That one should have to face such horrors."

"What in the world's the matter?"

"Look!" cried Cedric, covering his eyes. "Look! Katzenjammer Castle!"

Troy looked through the window. Some two miles away on the crest of a hill, fully displayed, stood Ancreton.

CHAPTER THREE

Ancreton

i

It was an astonishing building. A Victorian architect, fortified and encouraged by the Ancred of his day, had pulled down a Queen Anne house and, from its rubble, caused to rise up a sublimation of his most exotic daydreams. To no one style or period did Ancreton adhere. Its facade bulged impartially with Norman, Gothic, Baroque and Rococo excrescences. Turrets sprouted like wens from every corner. Towers rose up from a multiplicity of battlements. Arrow slits peered furtively at ex-ophthalmic baywindows, and out of a kaleidoscopic field of tiles, rose a forest of variegated chimney-stacks. The whole was presented, not against the sky but against a dense forest of evergreen trees, for behind Ancreton crest rose another and steeper hillside, richly planted in conifers. Perhaps the imagination of this earlier Ancred was exhausted by the begetting of his monster, for he was content to leave, almost unmolested, the terraced gardens and well-planted spinneys that had been laid out in the tradition of John Evelyn. These, maintaining their integrity, still gently led the eye of the observer towards the site of the house and had an air of blind acquiescence in its iniquities.

Intervening trees soon obliterated Troy's first view of Ancreton. In a minute or two the train paused magnanimously at the tiny station of Ancreton Halt.

"One must face these moments, of course," Cedric muttered, and they stepped out into a flood of wintry sunshine.

There were only two people on the platform: a young man in second lieutenant's uniform and a tall girl. They were a good-looking pair and somewhat alike; blue-eyed, dark and thin. They came forward, the young man limping and using his stick.

"Oh lud!" Cedric complained. "Ancreds by the shoal. Greetings, you two."

"Hullo, Cedric," they said, without much show of enthusiasm and the girl turned quickly and cordially towards Troy.

"This is my cousin, Fenella Ancred," Cedric explained languidly. "And the warrior is another cousin, Paul Kentish. Miss Agatha Troy, or should it be Mrs. Alleyn? *So* difficult."

"It's splendid that you've come," said Fenella Ancred. "Grandfather's terribly excited and easily ten years younger. Have you got lots of luggage? If so we'll either make two journeys or would you mind walking up the hill? We've only brought the governess-cart and Rozinante's a bit elderly."

"Walk?" Cedric screamed faintly. "My dear Fenella! You must be demented. Me? Rozinante (and may I say in parentheses, I consider the naming of this animal an insufferable piece of whimsy) Rozinante shall bear me up the hill though it be its last conscious act."

"I've got two suitcases and my painting gear," said Troy, "which is pretty heavy."

"We'll see what can be done about it," said Paul Kentish, eyeing Cedric with distaste, "Come on, Fen."

Troy's studio easel and heavy luggage had to be left at a cottage to be sent up to Ancreton later by carrier, but they packed her worn hand luggage and Cedric's green suede suitcases into the governess-cart and got in on top of them. The fat white pony strolled away with them down a narrow lane.

"It's a mile to the gates," Paul Kentish said, "and another mile up to the house. We'll get out at the gates, Fen."

"I should like to walk," said Troy.

"Then Cedric," said Fenella with satisfaction, "can drive."

"But I'm not a horsy boy," Cedric protested. "The creature might sit down or turn round and bite me. Don't you think you're being rather beastly?"

"Don't be an ass," said Fenella. "He'll just go on walking home."

"Who's in residence?" Cedric demanded.

"The usual," she said. "Mummy's coming for the weekend after this. I'm on leave for a fortnight. Otherwise Aunt Milly and Aunt Pauline. That's Cedric's mother and Paul's mother," Fenella explained to Troy. "I expect you'll find us rather muddling to begin with. Aunt Pauline's Mrs. Kentish and Mummy's Mrs. Claude Ancred, and Aunt Millamant's Mrs. Henry Ancred."

"Henry *Irving* Ancred, don't forget," Cedric cut in, "deceased. My papa, you know."

"That's all," said Fenella, "in our part. Of course there's Panty" (Cedric moaned), "Caroline Able and the school in the West Wing.

Aunt Pauline's helping them, you know. They're terribly short-staffed. That's all."

"All?" cried Cedric. "You don't mean to tell me Sonia's gone?"

"No, she's there. I'd forgotten her," said Fenella shortly.

"Well, Fenella, all I can say is you've an enviable faculty for forgetting. You'll be saying next that everyone's reconciled to Sonia."

"Is there any point in discussing it?" said Paul Kentish very coldly.

"It's the only topic of any interest at Ancreton," Cedric rejoined. "Personally I find it vastly intriguing. I've been telling Mrs. Alleyn all about it in the train."

"Honestly, Cedric," said Paul and Fenella together. "You *are!*"

Cedric gave a crowing laugh and they drove on in an uncomfortable silence. Feeling a little desperate, Troy at last began to talk to Paul Kentish. He was a pleasant fellow, she thought, serious-minded but friendly and ready to speak about his war service. He had been wounded in the leg during the Italian campaign and was still having treatment. Troy asked him what he was going to do when he was discharged and was surprised to see him turn rather pink.

"As a matter of fact I rather thought—well, actually I had wondered about the police," said Paul.

"My dear, how terrifying," Cedric interposed.

"Paul's the only one of us," Fenella explained, "who really doesn't want to have anything to do with the theatre."

"I would have liked to go on in the army," Paul added, "only now I'm no good for that. Perhaps, I don't know, but perhaps I'd be no good for the police either."

"You'd better talk to my husband when he comes back," Troy said, wondering if Alleyn would mind very much if he did.

"I say!" said Paul. "That would be perfectly marvelous if you really mean it."

"Well, I mean he could just tell you whether your limp would make any difference."

"How glad I am," Cedric remarked, "about my duodenal ulcer! I mean, I needn't even pretend I want to be brave or strenuous. No doubt I've inherited the Old Person's guts."

"Are you going on the stage?" Troy asked Fenella.

"I expect so, now the war's over. I've been a chauffeur for the duration."

"You will play exotic roles, Fenella, and I shall design wonderful clothes for you. It would be rather fun," Cedric went on, "when and if I inherit Ancreton, to turn it into a frightfully exclusive theatre. The only catch in that is that Sonia might be there as the dowager baronetess in which case she would insist on playing all the leading roles. Oh, dear, I *do* want some money so badly. What do you suppose is the best technique, Fenella? Shall I woo the Old Person or suck up to Sonia? Paul, you know all about the strategy of indirect approach. Advise me, my dear."

"Considering you're supposed to earn about twice as much as any of the rest of us!"

"Pure legend. A pittance, I assure you."

The white pony had sauntered into a lane that ran directly up to the gates of Ancreton, which was now displayed to its greatest advantage. A broad walk ran straight from the gates across a series of terraces and by way of flights of steps, up to a platform before the house. The carriage-drive swept away to the left and was hidden by woods. They must be an extremely rich family, Troy decided, to have kept all this going, and as if in answer to her thoughts Fenella said: "You wouldn't guess from here, how much the flower gardens have gone back, would you?"

"Are the problem children still digging for a Freudian victory?" asked Cedric.

"They're doing a jolly good job of work," Paul rejoined. "All the second terrace was down in potatoes, this year. You can see them up there now." Troy had already noticed a swarm of minute figures on the second terrace.

"The potato!" Cedric murmured. "A pregnant sublimation, I feel sure.".

"You enjoy eating them, anyway," Fenella said bluntly.

"Here we are, Mrs. Alleyn. Do you honestly feel like walking? If so, we'll go up the Middle Walk and Cedric can drive."

They climbed out. Paul opened the elaborate and becrested iron gates, explaining that the lodge was now used as a storehouse for vegetables. Cedric, holding the reins with a great show of distaste, was borne slowly off to the left. The other three began the ascent of the terraces.

The curiously metallic sound of children's singing quavered threadily in the autumn air.

Then sing a yeo-heave ho
Across the seas we'll go
There's many a girl that I know well
On the banks of the Sacramento.

As they climbed the second flight of steps a crisp woman's voice could be heard, dominating the rest.

And Down, *and* Kick, *and* Hee-ee-eeve.
And Down, *and* Kick *and* Hee-ee-vv.

On the second terrace some thirty little girls and boys were digging in time to their own singing. A red-haired young woman clad in breeches and sweater shouted the rhythmic orders. Troy was just in time to see a little boy in the back row deliberately heave a spadeful of soil down the neck of a near-by little girl. Singing shrilly, she retaliated by catching him a swinging smack across the rump with the flat of her spade.

"And *Down* and *Kick* and *Heave*. Back," shouted the young woman, waving cheerfully to Paul and Fenella.

"Come over here!" Fenella screamed. The young woman left her charges and strode towards them. The singing continued but with less vigour. She was extremely pretty. Fenella introduced her: Miss Caroline Able. She shook hands firmly with Troy, who noticed that the little girl, having downed the little boy, now sat on his face and had begun methodically to plaster his head with soil. In order to do this she had been obliged first to remove a curious white cap. Several of the other children, Troy noticed, wore similar caps.

"You're keeping them hard at it, aren't you, Carol?" said Fenella.

"We stop in five minutes. It's extraordinarily helpful, you know. They feel they're doing something constructive. Something socially worth-while," said Miss Able glowingly. "And once you can get these children, especially the introverted types, to do that, you've gone quite a bit of the way."

Fenella and Paul, who had their backs to the children, nodded gravely. The little boy having unseated the little girl was making a brave attempt to bite the calf of her left leg.

"How are their heads?" Paul asked solemnly. Miss Able shrugged her shoulders. "Taking its course," she said. "The doctor's coming again to-morrow."

Troy gave an involuntary exclamation and at the same moment the little girl screamed so piercingly that her voice rang out above the singing, which instantly stopped.

"It's—perhaps you ought to look," said Troy, and Miss Able turned in time to see the little girl attempting strenuously to kick her opponent, who nevertheless maintained his hold on her leg. "Let go, you cow," screamed the little girl.

"Patricia! David!" cried Miss Able firmly and strode towards them. The other children stopped work and listened in silence. The two principals, maintaining their hold on each other, broke into mutual accusations.

"Now, I wonder," said Miss Able brightly, and with an air of interest, "just what made you two feel you'd like to have a fight." Confused recriminations followed immediately. Miss Able seemed to understand them, and to Troy's astonishment, actually jotted down one or two notes in a little book, glancing at her watch as she did so.

"And now," she said, still more brightly, "you feel ever so much better. You were just angry, and you needed to work it off, didn't you? But you know I can think of something that would be much better fun than fighting."

"No, you can't," said the little girl, instantly, and turned savagely on her opponent. "I'll kill you," she said and fell upon him.

"Suppose," shouted Miss Able with determined gaiety above the shrieks of the contestants, "we all shoulder spades and have a jolly good marching song."

The little girl rolled clear of her opponent, scooped up a handful of earth and flung it madly and accurately at Miss Able. The little boy and several of the other children laughed very loudly at this exploit. Miss Able, after a second's pause, joined in their laughter.

"Little devil," said Paul. "Honestly Fenella, I really do think a damn good hiding . . ."

"No, no," said Fenella, "it's the method. Listen."

The ever-jolly Miss Able was saying; "Well, I expect I do look pretty funny, don't I? Now, come on, let's all have a good rowdy game. Twos and threes. Choose your partners."

The children split up into pairs and Miss Able, wiping the earth off her face, joined the three onlookers.

"How you can put up with Panty—" Paul began.

"Oh, but she really is responding splendidly," Miss Able interrupted. "That's the first fight in seven and a half hours, and David began it. He's rather a bad case of maladjustment, I'm afraid. Now Patricia," she shouted. "Into the middle with you. And David, you see if you can catch her. One tries as far as possible," she explained, "to divert the anger impulse into less emotional channels."

They left her briskly conducting the game, and continued their ascent. On the fourth terrace they encountered a tall and extremely good-looking woman dressed in tweeds and a felt hat, and wearing heavy gauntleted gloves.

"This is my mother," said Paul Kentish.

Mrs. Kentish greeted Troy rather uncertainly: "You've come to paint Father, haven't you?" she said, inclining her head in the manner of a stage dowager. "Very nice. I do hope you'll be comfortable. In these days one can't quite—" she brightened a little—"but perhaps as an artist you won't mind rather a Bohemian—" Her voice trailed away and she turned to her son. "Paul, *darling*," she said richly, "you shouldn't have walked up all those steps. Your poor leg. Fenella, dear, you shouldn't have let him."

"It's good for my leg, Mother."

Mrs. Kentish shook her head and gazed mistily at her glowering son. "Such a brave old boy," she said. Her voice, which was a warm one, shook a little and Troy saw with embarrassment that her eyes had filled with tears. "Such an old Trojan," she murmured. "Isn't he, Fenella?"

Fenella laughed uncomfortably and Paul hastily backed away. "Where are you off to?" he asked loudly.

"To remind Miss Able it's time to come in. Those poor children work so hard. I can't feel—however. I'm afraid I'm rather old-fashioned, Mrs. Alleyn. I still feel a mother knows best."

"Well, but Mother," Paul objected, "something had to be done about Panty, didn't it? I mean, she really was pretty frightful."

"Poor old Panty!" said Mrs. Kentish bitterly.

"We'd better move on, Aunt Pauline," Fenella said. "Cedric is driving up. He won't do anything about unloading if I know him."

"Cedric!" Mrs. Kentish repeated. "T'uh!"

She smiled rather grandly at Troy and left them.

"My mother," Paul said uncomfortably, "gets in a bit of a flap about things. Doesn't she, Fen?"

"Actually," said Fenella, "they all do. That generation, I mean. Daddy rather wallows in emotion and Aunt Dessy's a snorter at it. They get it from Grandfather, don't you think?"

"All except Thomas."

"Yes, all except Thomas. Don't you think," Fenella asked Troy, "that if one generation comes it rather hot and strong emotionally, the next swings very much the other way? Paul and I are as hard as nails, aren't we, Paul?"

Troy turned to the young man. He was staring fixedly at his cousin. His dark brows were knitted and his lips were pressed together. He looked preternaturally solemn and did not answer Fenella. "Why," thought Troy, "he's in love with her."

ii

The interior of Ancreton amply sustained the promise of its monstrous facade. Troy was to learn that "great" was the stock adjective at Ancreton. There was the Great West Spinney, the Great Gallery and the Great Tower. Having crossed the Great Drawbridge over the now dry and cultivated moat, Troy, Fenella, and Paul entered the Great Hall.

Here the tireless ingenuity of the architect had flirted with a number of Elizabethan conceits. There was a plethora of fancy carving, a display of stained-glass windows bearing the Ancred arms and a number of presumably collateral quarterings. Between these romped occasional mythical animals and, when mythology and heraldy had run short, the church had not been forgotten, for crosslets-ancred stood cheek-by-jowl in mild confusion with the keys of St. Peter and the Cross of St. John of Jerusalem.

Across the back of the hall, facing the entrance, ran a minstrels' gallery, energetically chiselled and hung at intervals with banners. Beneath this, on a wall whose surface was a mass of scrolls and bosses, the portrait, Fenella explained, was to hang. By day, as Troy at once noticed, it would be chequered all over with the reflected colours of stained-glass heraldry and would take on the aspect of a jig-saw puzzle. By night, according to Paul, it would be floodlit by four lamps specially installed under the gallery.

There were a good many portraits already in the hall and Troy's attention was caught by an enormous canvas above the fireplace depicting a nautical Ancred of the eighteenth century, who pointed his cutlass at a streak of forked lightning with an air of having made it himself. Underneath this work in a huge armchair, warming himself at the fire, was Cedric.

"People are seeing about the luggage," he said, struggling to his feet, "and one of the minor ancients has led away the horse. Someone has carried dearest Mrs. Alleyn's paints up to her inaccessible eyrie. *Do* sit down, Mrs. Alleyn. You must be madly exhausted. My mama is on her way. The Old Person's entrance is timed for half-past eight. We have a nice long time in which to relax. The Ancient of Days at my suggestion is about to serve drinks. In the name of my ridiculous family, in fact, welcome to Katzenjammer Castle."

"Would you like to see your room first?" asked Fenella.

"Let me warn you," Cedric added, "that the visit will entail another arduous climb and a long tramp. Where have they put her, Fenella?"

"The Siddons room."

"I couldn't sympathize more deeply, but of course the choice is appropriate. A steel engraving of that abnormally muscular actress in the role of Lady Macbeth hangs over the wash-hand stand, doesn't it, Fenella? I'm in the Garrick, which is comparatively lively, especially in the rat season. Here comes the Ancient of Days. *Do* have a stirrup-cup before you set out on your polar expedition."

An extremely old man-servant was coming across the hall with a tray of drinks. "Barker," said Cedric faintly. "You are welcome as flowers in spring."

"Thank you, Mr. Cedric," said the old man. "Sir Henry's compliments, Miss Fenella, and he hopes to have the pleasure of joining you at dinner. Sir Henry hopes Mrs. Alleyn has had a pleasant journey."

Troy said that she had and wondered if she should return a formal message. Cedric, with the nearest approach to energy that he had yet displayed, began to mix drinks. "There is one department of Katzenjammer Castle to which one can find *no* objection and that is the cellar," he said. "Thank you, Barker, from my heart. Ganymede himself couldn't foot it more featly."

"I must say, Cedric," Paul muttered when the old butler had gone, "that I don't think your line of comedy with Barker is screamingly funny."

"Dear Paul! Don't you? I'm completely shattered."

"Well, he's old," said Fenella quickly, "and he's a great friend."

Cedric darted an extraordinarily malicious glance at his cousins. "How very feudal," he said. "*Noblesse oblige*. Dear me!"

At this juncture, rather to Troy's relief, a stout smiling woman came in from one of the side doors. Behind her, Troy caught a glimpse of a vast formal drawing-room.

"This is my mama," Cedric explained, faintly waving his hand.

Mrs. Henry Ancred was a firmly built white-skinned woman. Her faded hair was scrupulously groomed into a rather wig-like coiffure. She looked, Troy thought, a little as if she managed some quiet but extremely expensive boarding-house or perhaps a school. Her voice was unusually deep, and her hands and feet unusually large. Unlike her son, she had a wide mouth but there was a resemblance to Cedric about the eyes and chin. She wore a sensible blouse, a cardigan and a dark skirt and she shook hands heartily with Troy. A capable woman.

"So glad you've decided to come," she said. "My father-in-law's quite excited. It will take him out of himself and fill in his day nicely."

Cedric gave a little shriek: "Milly *darling!*" he cried. "How you can!" He made an agonized face at Troy.

"Have I said something I shouldn't?" asked his mother. "So like me!" And she laughed heartily.

"Of course you haven't," Troy said hurriedly, ignoring Cedric. "I only hope the sittings won't tire Sir Henry."

"Oh, he'll tell you at once if he's tired," Millamant Ancred assured her, and Troy had an unpleasant picture of a canvas six by four feet to be completed in a fortnight with a sitter who had no hesitation in telling her when he felt tired.

"Well, anyway," Cedric cried shrilly. "Drinks!"

They sat round the fire, Paul and Fenella on a sofa, Troy opposite them and Millamant Ancred, squarely, on a high chair. Cedric pulled a humpty up to his mother, curled himself on it and rested an arm on her knees. Paul and Fenella glanced at him with ill-concealed distaste.

"What have you been doing, dear?" Millamant asked her son and put her square white hand on his shoulder.

"Such a lot of tiresome jobs," he sighed, rubbing his cheek on the hand. "Tell us what's going to happen here. I want something gay and exciting. A party for Mrs. Alleyn. Please! You'd like a party, wouldn't you?" he persisted, appealing to Troy. "Say you would."

"But I've come to work," said Troy and because he made her feel uncomfortable she spoke abruptly. "Damn!" she thought. "Even that sounds as if I expected her to take him seriously."

But Millamant laughed indulgently. "Mrs. Alleyn will be with us for the Birthday," she said, "and so will you, dear, if you really can stay for ten days. Can you?"

"Oh yes," he said, fretfully. "The office-place is being tatted up. I've brought my dreary work with me. But the Birthday! How abysmally depressing! Darling Milly, I don't think, really, that I can face another Birthday."

"Don't be naughty," said Millamant in her gruff voice.

"Let's have another drink," said Paul loudly.

"Is somebody talking about drink?" cried a disembodied voice in the minstrels' gallery. "Goody! Goody! Goody!"

"Oh God!" Cedric whispered. "Sonia!"

iii

It had grown dark in the hall and Troy's first impression of Miss Sonia Orrincourt was of a whitish apparition that fluttered down the stairs from the far side of the gallery. Her progress was accompanied by a number of chirruping noises. As she reached the hall and crossed it Troy saw that she wore a garment which even in the second act of a musical extravaganza would still have been remarkable. Troy supposed it was a negligee.

"Well, for Heaven's sake!" squeaked Miss Orrincourt. "Look who's here! Ceddie!" She held out both her hands and Cedric took them.

"You look too marvellous, Sonia," he cried. "Where did it come from?"

"Darling, it's a million years old. Oh, pardon me," said Miss Orrincourt, inclining towards Troy, "I didn't see—"

Millamant stonily introduced her. Fenella and Paul having moved away from the sofa, Miss Orrincourt sank into it. She extended her arms and wriggled her fingers. "Quick! Quick! Quick!" she cried babyishly. "Sonia wants a drink."

Her hair was almost white. It fell in a fringe across her forehead and in a silk curtain to her shoulders and reminded Troy vaguely of the inside of an aquarium. Her eyes were as round as saucers, with curving black lashes. When she smiled her short upper lip flattened, the corners of her mouth turned down, and the shadow of grooves-to-come ran away to her chin. Her skin was white and thick like the petals of a camellia. She was a startling young woman to look at and she made Troy feel exceedingly dumb. "But she'd probably be pretty good to paint in the nude," she reflected. "I wonder if she's ever been a model. She looks like it."

Miss Orrincourt and Cedric were conducting an extraordinarily unreal conversation. Fenella and Paul had moved away and Troy was left with Millamant Ancred, who began to talk about the difficulties of housekeeping. As she talked she stitched at an enormous piece of embroidery which hypnotized Troy by its monstrous colour-scheme and tortuous design. Intricate worms and scrolls strangled each other in Millamant's fancy work. No area was left undecorated, no motive was uninterrupted. At times she would pause and eye it with complacency. Her voice was monotonous.

"I suppose I'm lucky," she said. "I've got a cook and five maids and Barker, but they're all very old, and have been collected from different branches of the family. My sister-in-law Pauline, Mrs. John Kentish you know, gave up her own house in the evacuation time and has recently joined us with two of her maids. Desdemona did the same thing, and she makes Ancreton her headquarters now. She brought her old Nanny, Barker and the others have always been with us. But even with the West Wing turned into a school, it's difficult. In the old days of course," said Millamant with a certain air of complacency, "there was a swarm."

"Do they get on together?" Troy asked vaguely. She was watching Cedric and Miss Orrincourt. Evidently he had decided to adopt ingratiating tactics and a lively but completely synthetic flirtation had developed. They whispered together.

"Oh, no," Millamant was saying. "They fight." And most unexpectedly she added: "Like master like man, they say, don't they?" Troy looked at her. She was smiling broadly and blankly. It is a characteristic of these people, Troy reflected, that they constantly make remarks to which there is no answer.

Pauline Ancred came in and joined her son and Fenella. She did this with a certain air of determination and the smile she gave Fenella was a dismissal. "Darling," she said to Paul, "I've been looking for you." Fenella at once moved away. Pauline, using a gesture that was Congrevian in its accomplishment, raised a pair of lorgnettes and stared through them at Miss Orrincourt who now reclined at full length on the sofa. Cedric was perched on the arm at her feet."

"I'll get you a chair, Mother," said Paul hastily.

"Thank you, dear," she said, exchanging a glance with her sister-in-law. "I should like to sit down. No, *please*, Mrs. Alleyn, don't move. So sweet of you. Thank you, Paul."

"Noddy and I," said Miss Orrincourt brightly, "have been having such fun. We've been looking at some of that old jewellery." She stretched her arms above her head and yawned delicately.

"Noddy?" Troy wondered. "But who is Noddy?" Miss Orrincourt's remark was followed by a rather deadly little pause. "He's all burnt up about having his picture taken," Miss Orrincourt added. "Isn't it killing?"

Pauline Ancred, with a dignified shifting of her body, brought her sister-in-law into her field of vision. "Have you seen Papa this afternoon, Millamant?" she asked, not quite cordially but with an air of joining forces against a common enemy.

"I went up as usual at four o'clock," Millamant rejoined, "to see if there was anything I could do for him." She glanced at Miss Orrincourt. "He was engaged, however."

"T'uh!" said Pauline lightly, and she began to revolve her thumbs one round the other. Millamant gave the merest sketch of a significant laugh and turned to Troy.

"We don't quite know," she said cheerfully, "if Thomas explained about my father-in-law's portrait. He wishes to be painted in his own Little Theatre here. The backcloth has been hung and Paul knows about the lights. Papa would like to begin at eleven tomorrow morning and if he is feeling up to it he will sit for an hour every morning and afternoon."

"I thought," said Miss Orrincourt, "it would be ever so thrilling if Noddy was on a horse in the picture."

"Sir Henry," said Millamant, without looking at her, "will of course have decided on the pose."

"But Aunt Milly," said Paul, very red in the face, "Mrs. Alleyn might like—I mean—don't you think—"

"Yes, Aunt Milly," said Fenella.

"Yes, indeed, Milly," said Cedric. "I *so* agree. Please, *please* Milly and Aunt Pauline, and please Sonia, angel, *do* consider that Mrs. Alleyn is the one to—oh, my goodness," Cedric implored them, "pray *do* consider."

"I shall be very interested," said Troy, "to hear about Sir Henry's plans."

"That," said Pauline, "will be very nice. I forgot to tell you, Millamant, that I heard from Dessy. She's coming for the Birthday."

"I'm glad you let me know," said Millamant, looking rather put out.

"And so's Mummy, Aunt Milly," said Fenella. "I forgot to say."

"Well," said Millamant with a short laugh, "I *am* learning about things, aren't I?"

"Jenetta coming? Fancy!" said Pauline. "It must be two years since Jenetta was at Ancreton. I hope she'll be able to put up with our rough-and-ready ways."

"Considering she's been living in a two-roomed flat," Fenella began rather hotly and checked herself. "She asked me to say she hoped it wouldn't be too many."

"I'll move out of Bernhardt into Bracegirdle," Pauline offered. "Of course."

"You'll do nothing of the sort, Pauline," said Millamant. "Bracegirdle is piercingly cold, the ceiling leaks, and there are rats. Desdemona complained bitterly about the rats last time she was here. I asked Barker to lay poison for them but he's lost the poison. Until he finds it Bracegirdle is uninhabitable."

"Mummy could share Duse with me," said Fenella quickly. "We'd love it and it'd save fires."

"Oh, we couldn't dream of *that*," said Pauline and Millamant together.

"Mrs. Alleyn," said Fenella loudly, "I'm going up to change. Would you like to see your room?"

"Thank you," said Troy, trying not to sound too eager. "Thank you, I would."

iv

Having climbed the stairs and walked with a completely silent Fenella down an interminable picture gallery, and two long passages, followed by a breakneck ascent up a winding stair, Troy found herself at a door upon which hung a wooden plaque bearing the word "Siddons." Fenella opened the door and Troy was pleasantly welcomed by the reflection of leaping flames on white painted walls. White damask curtains with small garlands, a sheepskin rug, a low bed and there, above a Victorian wash-stand, sure enough, hung Mrs. Siddons. Troy's painting gear was stacked in a corner.

"What a nice room," said Troy.

"I'm glad you like it," said Fenella in a suppressed voice. Troy saw with astonishment that she was in a rage.

"I apologize," said Fenella shakily, "for my beastly family."

"Hullo!" said Troy. "What's all this?"

"As if they weren't damned lucky to get you! As if they wouldn't still be damned lucky if you decided to paint Grandpa standing on his head with garlic growing out of the soles of his boots. It's *such cheek*. Even that frightful twirp Cedric was ashamed."

"Good Lord!" said Troy. "That's nothing unusual. You've no conception how funny people can be about portraits."

"I hate them! And you heard how catty they were about Mummy coming. I do think old women are *foul*. And that bitch Sonia lying there lapping it all up. How they can, in front of her! Paul and I were so ashamed."

Fenella stamped, dropped on her knees in front of the fire and burst into tears. "I'm sorry," she stammered. "I'm worse than they are, but I'm so sick of it all. I wish I hadn't come to Ancreton. I loathe Ancreton. If you only knew what it's like."

"Look here," Troy said gently, "are you sure you want to talk to me like this?"

"I know it's frightful, but I can't help it. How would you feel if *your* grandfather brought a loathsome blonde into the house? How would you feel?"

Troy had a momentary vision of her grandfather, now deceased. He had been an austere and somewhat finicky don.

"Everybody's laughing at him," Fenella sobbed. "And I used to like him so much. Now he's just *silly*. A silly amorous old man. He behaves like that himself and then when I—when I went to—it doesn't matter. I'm terribly sorry. It's awful, boring you like this."

Troy sat on a low chair by the fire and looked thoughtfully at Fenella. The child really is upset, she thought, and realized that already she had begun to question the authenticity of the Ancreds' emotions. She said: "You needn't think it's awful and you're not boring me. Only don't say things you'll feel inclined to kick yourself for when you've got under way again."

"All right." Fenella got to her feet. She had the fortunate knack, Troy noticed, of looking charming when she cried. She now tossed her head, bit her lips, and gained mastery of herself. "She'll make a good actress," Troy thought and instantly checked herself. "Because," she thought, "the child manages to be so prettily distressed why should I jump to the conclusion that she's not as distressed as she seems? I'm not sympathetic enough." She touched Fenella's arm and, although it was quite foreign to her habit, returned the squeeze Fenella instantly gave to her hand.

"Come," said Troy, "I thought you said this afternoon that your generation of Ancreds was as hard as nails."

"Well, we try," Fenella said. "It's only because you're so nice that I let go. I won't again."

"Help!" Troy thought and said aloud: "I'm not much use really, I'm afraid. My husband says I shy away from emotion like a nervous mare. But let off steam if you want to."

Fenella said soberly: "This'll do for a bit I expect. You're an angel. Dinner's at half-past eight. You'll hear a warning gong." She turned at the door. "All the same," she said, "there's something pretty ghastly going on at Ancreton, just now. You'll see."

With an inherited instinct for a good exit line, Fenella stepped backwards and gracefully closed the door.

CHAPTER FOUR

Sir Henry

i

IN HER agitation Fenella had neglected to give Troy the usual hostess's tips on internal topography. Troy wondered if the nearest bathroom was at the top of another tower or at the end of some interminable corridor. Impossible to tug the embroidered bell-pull and cause one of those aged maids to climb the stairs! She decided to give up her bath in favour of Mrs. Siddons, the wash-stand and a Victorian can of warm water which had been left beside it.

She had an hour before dinner. It was pleasant, after the severely rationed fires of Tatler's End, to dress leisurely before this sumptuous blaze. She made the most of it, turning over in her mind the events of the day and sorting out her impressions of the Ancreds. Queer Thomas, she decided, was, so far, the best of the bunch though the two young things were pleasant enough. Was there an understanding between them and had Sir Henry objected? Was that the reason for Fenella's outburst? For the rest: Pauline appeared to be suffering from a general sense of personal affront, Millamant was an unknown quantity while her Cedric was frankly awful. And then, Sonia! Troy giggled. Sonia really was a bit thick.

Somewhere outside in the cold, a deep-toned clock struck eight. The fire had died down. She might as well begin her journey to the hall. Down the winding stair she went, wondering whose room lay beyond a door on the landing. Troy had no sense of direction. When she reached the first long corridor she couldn't for the life of her remember whether she should turn left or right. A perspective of dark crimson carpet stretched away on each hand and at intervals the corridor was lit by pseudo-antique candelabra. "Oh, well," thought Troy and turned to the right. She passed four doors and read their legends: "Duse" (that was Fenella's room), "Bernhardt" (Pauline's), "Terry," "Lady Bancroft," and, near the end of the passage, the despised "Bracegirdle." Troy did not remember seeing any of these names on her way up to her tower. "Blast!" she thought, "I've gone wrong." But she went on uncertainly. The corridor led at right-angles into another, at the far end of which she saw the foot of a flight of stairs like those of her own tower. Poor Troy was certain that she had looked down just such a vista on her way up. "But I suppose," she thought, "it must have been its opposite number. From outside the damn place looked as if it was built round a sort of quadrangle with a tower at the middle and ends of each wing. In that case, if I keep on turning left oughtn't I to come back to the picture gallery?"

As she hesitated, a door near the foot of the stairs opened slightly and a magnificent cat walked out into the passage.

He was white with a tabby saddle on his back, long haired and amber eyed. He paused and stared at Troy. Then, wafting his tail slightly, he paced slowly towards her. She stooped and waited for him. After some deliberation he approached, examined her hand, bestowed upon it a brief cold thrust of his nose, and continued on his way, walking in the centre of the crimson carpet and still elegantly wafting his tail.

"And one other thing," said a shrill voice beyond the open door. "If you think I'm going to hang round here like a bloody extra with your family handing me out the bird in fourteen different positions you've got another thing coming."

A deep voice rumbled unintelligibly.

"I know all about that and it makes no difference. Nobody's going to tell me I lack refinement and get away with it. They treat me as if I had one of those things in the strip ads. I kept my temper down there because I wasn't going to let them see I minded. What do they think they are? My God, do they think it's any catch living in a mausoleum with a couple of old tats and a kid that ought to be labelled Crazy Gang?"

Again the expostulatory rumble.

"I know, I know, I know. It's so merry and bright in this dump it's a wonder we don't all die of laughing. If you're as crazy as all that about me you ought to put me in a position where I'd keep my self-respect. . . . You owe it to me. . . . After all I've done for you. I'm just miserable. . . . And when I get like this, I'm warning you, Noddy, look out." The door opened a little further.

Troy, who had stood transfixed, picked up her skirts, turned back on her tracks, and fairly ran away down the long corridor.

ii

This time she reached the gallery and went downstairs. In the hall she encountered Barker, who showed her into an enormous drawing-room which looked, she thought, as if it was the setting for a scene in *Victoria Regina*. Crimson, white, and gold were the predominant colours, damask and velvet the prevailing textures. Vast canvases by Leader & MacWhirter occupied the walls. On each occasional table or cabinet stood a silver-framed photograph of Royalty or Drama. There were three of Sir Henry at different stages of his career, and there was one of Sir Henry in court dress. In this last portrait, the customary air of a man who can't help feeling he looks a bit of an ass was completely absent and for a moment Troy thought Sir Henry had been taken in yet another of his professional roles. The unmistakable authenticity of his Windsor coat undeceived her. "Golly!" she thought, staring at the photograph. "It's a good head and no mistake."

She began a tour of the room and found much to entertain her. Under the glass lid of a curio table were set out a number of orders, miniatures and decorations, several *objets d'art*, a signed programme from a command-performance, and surprisingly, a small book of antique style, bound in half-calf and heavily tooled. Troy was one of those people who, when they see a book lying apart, must handle it. The lid was unlocked. She raised it and opened the little book. The title was much faded and Troy stooped to make it out.

The Antient Arte of the Embalming of Corpes, she read, *To which is added a discourse on the Concoction of Fluids for the Purpose of Preserving Dead Bodies*. By William Hurste, Professor of Physick, London. Printed by Robert White for John Crampe at The Sign of the Three Bibles in St. Paul's Church-Yard. 1678. . . .

It was horridly explicit. Here in the first chapter, were various recipes "for the Consumation of the Arte of Preserving the Dead in perfect Verisimilitude of Life. It will be remarked," the author continued, "that in spite of their diversity the chemical of Arsenic is Common to All." There was a particularly macabre passage on the "Use of Cosmetics to Disguise the Ghastly Pallor of Death."

"But what sort of mind," Troy wondered, "could picture with equanimity, even with pleasure, these manipulations upon the body from which it must some day, perhaps soon, be parted?" And she wondered if Sir Henry Ancred had read this and if he had no imagination or too much. "And why," she thought, "do I go on reading this horrid little book?"

She heard a voice in the hall and with an illogical feeling of guilt hurriedly closed the book and the glass lid. Millamant came in, wearing a tidy but nondescript evening dress.

"I've been exploring," Troy said.

"Exploring?" Millamant repeated with her vague laugh.

"That grisly little book in the case. I can't resist a book and I'm afraid I opened the case. I do hope it's allowed."

"Oh," said Millamant. "Yes, of course." She glanced at the case. "What book is it?"

"It's about embalming, of all things. It's very old. I should think it might be rather valuable."

"Perhaps," said Millamant, "that is why Miss Orrincourt was so interested in it."

She had moved to the fireplace, looking smugly resentful.

"Miss Orrincourt?" Troy repeated.

"I found her reading a small book when I came in the other day. She put it in the case and dropped the lid. Such a bang! It's a wonder it didn't break, really. I suppose it must have been that book, mustn't it?"

"Yes," said Troy, hurriedly rearranging her already chaotic ideas of Miss Sonia Orrincourt. "I suppose it must."

"Papa," said Millamant, "is not quite at his best this evening but he's coming down. On his bad days he dines in his own rooms."

"I hope," said Troy, "that the sittings won't tire him too much."

"Well, he's so looking forward to them that I'm sure he'll try to keep them up. He's really been much better lately, only sometimes," said Millamant ambiguously, "he gets a little upset. He's very highly strung and sensitive, you know. I always think that all the Ancreds are like that. Except Thomas. My poor Cedric, unfortunately, has inherited their temperament."

Troy had nothing to say to this and was relieved when Paul Kentish and his mother came in, followed in a moment by Fenella. Barker brought a tray with sherry. Presently an extraordinarily ominous gong sounded in the hall.

"Did anyone see Cedric?" asked his mother. "I do hope he's not going to be late?"

"He was still in his bath when I tried to get in ten minutes ago," said Paul.

"Oh, dear," said Millamant.

Miss Orrincourt, amazingly dressed, and looking at once sulky, triumphant and defiant, drifted into the room. Troy heard a stifled exclamation behind her and turned to see the assembled Ancreds with their gaze riveted to Miss Orrincourt's bosom.

It was adorned with a large diamond star.

"Milly," Pauline muttered.

"Do you see what I see?" Millamant replied with a faint hiss.

Miss Orrincourt moved to the fire and laid one arm along the mantelpiece. "I hope Noddy's not going to be late," she said. "I'm starving." She looked critically at her crimson nails and touched the diamond star. "I'd like a drink," she said.

Nobody made any response to this statement though Paul uncomfortably cleared his throat. The tap of a stick sounded in the hall.

"Here *is* Papa," said Pauline nervously and they all moved slightly. "Really," thought Troy, "they might be waiting to dine with some minor Royalty. There was precisely the same air of wary expectation."

Barker opened the door and the original of all the photographs walked slowly into the room followed by the white cat.

iii

The first thing to be said about Sir Henry Ancred was that he filled his role with almost embarrassing virtuosity. He was unbelievably handsome. His hair was silver, his eyes, under the heavy brows, were fiercely blue. His nose was ducal in its prominence. Beneath it sprouted a fine snowy moustache, brushed up to lend accent to his actor's mouth. His chin jutted out squarely and was adorned with an ambassadorial tuft. He looked as if he had been specially designed for exhibition. He wore a velvet dinner-jacket, an old-fashioned collar, a wide cravat and a monocle on a broad ribbon. You could hardly believe, Troy thought, that he was true. He came in slowly, using a black silver stick but not leaning on it overmuch. It was, Troy felt, more of an adjunct than an aid. He was exceeding tall and still upright.

"Mrs. Alleyn, Papa," said Pauline.

"Ah," said Sir Henry.

Troy went to meet him. "Restraining myself," as she afterwards told Alleyn, "from curtsying, but with difficulty."

"So this is our distinguished painter?" said Sir Henry, taking her hand. "I am delighted."

He kept her hand in his and looked down at her. Behind him Troy saw in fancy a young Henry Ancred bending his gaze upon the women of his hey-day and imagined how pleasurably they must have melted before it. "Delighted," he repeated and his voice underlined adroitly his pleasure not only in her arrival but in her looks. "Hold your horses, chaps," thought Troy and removed her hand. "I hope you continue of that mind," she said politely.

Sir Henry bowed. "I believe I shall," he said. "I believe I shall." She was to learn that he had a habit of repeating himself.

Paul had moved a chair forward. Sir Henry sat in it facing the fire, with his guests and family disposed in arcs on either side of him.

He crossed his knees and rested his left forearm along the arm of his chair, letting his beautifully-kept hand dangle elegantly. It was a sort of Charles II pose, and in lieu of the traditional spaniel, the white cat leapt gracefully on his lap, kneaded it briefly and reclined there.

"Ah, Carabbas!" said Sir Henry, and stroked it, looking graciously awhile upon his family and guests. "This is pleasant," he said, including them in a beautiful gesture. For a moment his gaze rested on Miss Orrincourt's bosom. "Charming," he said. "A conversation piece. Ah! A glass of sherry."

Paul and Fenella dispensed the sherry, which was extremely good. Rather elaborate conversation was made, Sir Henry conducting it with the air of giving an audition. "But I thought," hc said, "that Cedric was to join us. Didn't you tell me, Millamant—"

"I'm so sorry he's late, Papa," said Millamant. "He had an important letter to write, I know. I think perhaps he didn't hear the gong."

"Indeed? Where have you put him?"

"In Garrick, Papa."

"Then he certainly must have heard the gong."

Barker came in and announced dinner.

"We shall not, I think, wait for Cedric," Sir Henry continued. He removed the cat, Carabbas, from his knees and rose. His family rose with him. "Mrs. Alleyn, may I have the pleasure of taking you in?" he said.

"It's a pity," Troy thought as she took the arm he curved for her, "that there isn't an orchestra." And as if she had recaptured the lines from some drawing-room comedy of her childhood, she made processional conversation as they moved towards the door. Before they reached it, however, there was a sound of running footsteps in the hall. Cedric, flushed with exertion and wearing a white flower in his dinner jacket, darted into the room.

"Dearest Grandpapa," he cried, "I creep, I grovel. So sorry, truly. Couldn't be more contrite. Find me some sackcloth and ashes somebody, quickly."

"Good evening, Cedric," said Sir Henry icily. "You must make your apologies to Mrs. Alleyn, who will perhaps be very kind and forgive you."

Troy smiled like a duchess at Cedric and inwardly grinned like a Cheshire cat at herself.

"Too heavenly of you," said Cedric quickly. He slipped in behind them. The procession had splayed out a little on his entrance. He came face to face with Miss Orrincourt. Troy heard him give a curious, half-articulate exclamation. It sounded involuntary and unaffected. This was so unusual from Cedric that Troy turned to look at him. His small mouth was open. His pale eyes stared blankly at the diamond star on Miss Orrincourt's bosom and then turned incredulously from one member of his family to another.

"But—" he stammered, "but, I say—I say."

"Cedric," whispered his mother.

"Cedric," said his grandfather imperatively.

But Cedric, still speaking in that strangely natural voice, pointed a white finger at the diamond star and said loudly: "But, my God, it's Great-Great-Grandmama Ancred's Sunburst!"

"Nice, isn't it?" said Miss Orrincourt equally loudly. "I'm ever so thrilled."

"In these unhappy times, alas!" said Sir Henry, blandly arming Troy through the door, "one may not make those gestures with which one would wish to honour a distinguished visitor. 'A poor small banquet,' as old Capulet had it. Shall we go in?"

iv

The poor small banquet was, if nothing else, a tribute to the zeal of Sir Henry's admirers in the Dominions and the United States of America. Troy had not seen its like for years. He himself, she noticed, ate a mess of something that had been put through a sieve. Conversation was general, innocuous, and sounded a little as if it had been carefully memorized beforehand. It was difficult not to look at Miss Orrincourt's diamonds. They were a sort of visual *faux pas* which no amount of blameless small talk could shout down.

Troy observed that the Ancreds themselves constantly darted furtive glances at them. Sir Henry continued bland, urbane, and, to Troy, excessively gracious. She found his compliments, which were adroit, rather hard to counter. He spoke of her work and asked if she had done a self-portrait. "Only in my student days when I couldn't afford a model," said Troy. "But that's very naughty of you," he said. "It is now that you should give us the perfect painting of the perfect subject." "Crikey!" thought Troy.

They drank Rudesheimer. When Barker hovered beside him, Sir Henry, announcing that it was a special occasion, said he would take half a glass. Millamant and Pauline looked anxiously at him.

"Papa, darling," said Pauline. "*Do* you think—" and Millamant murmured: "Yes, Papa. *Do* you think—"

"Do I think what?" he replied glaring at them."

"Wine," they murmured disjointedly. "Dr. Withers—not really advisable—however."

"Fill it up, Barker," Sir Henry commanded loudly, "fill it up."

Troy heard Pauline and Millamant sigh windily.

Dinner proceeded with circumspection, but uneasily. Paul and Fenella were silent. Cedric, on Troy's right hand, conversed in feverish spasms with anybody who would listen to him. Sir Henry's flow of compliments continued unabated through three courses and to Troy's dismay, Miss Orrincourt began to show signs of marked hostility. She was on Sir Henry's left with Paul on her other side. She began an extremely grand conversation with Paul and though he responded with every sign of discomfort she lowered her voice, cast significant glances at him and laughed immoderately at his monosyllabic replies. Troy, who was beginning to find her host very heavy weather indeed, seized an opportunity to speak to Cedric.

"Noddy," said Miss Orrincourt at once, "what are we going to do to-morrow?"

"Do?" he repeated and after a moment's hesitation became playful. "What does a little girl want to do?"

Miss Orrincourt stretched her arms above her head: "She wants things to *happen!*" she cried ecstatically. "Lovely things."

"Well, if she's very *very* good perhaps we'll let her have a tiny peep at a great big picture."

Troy heard this with dismay.

"What else?" Miss Orrincourt persisted babyishly but with an extremely unenthusiastic glance at Troy.

"We'll see," said Sir Henry uneasily.

"But Noddy—"

"Mrs. Alleyn," said Millamant from the foot of the table, "shall we—"

And she marshalled her ladies out of the dining-room.

The rest of the evening passed uneventfully. Sir Henry led Troy through the pages of three albums of theatrical photographs. This she rather enjoyed. It was strange, she thought, to see how the fashion in Elizabethan garments changed in the world of theatre. Here was a young Victorian Henry Ancred very much bepointed, beruffled, encased and furbished, in a perfect welter of velvet, ribbon and leather; here a modern elderly Henry Ancred in a stylized and simplified costume that had apparently been made of painted scenic canvas. Yet both were the Duke of Buckingham.

Miss Orrincourt joined a little fretfully in this pastime. Perched on the arm of Sir Henry's chair and disseminating an aura of black market scent she giggled tactlessly over the earlier photographs and yawned over the later ones. "My dear!" she ejaculated. "Look at you! You've got everything on but the kitchen sink!" This was in reference to a picture of Sir Henry as Richard II. Cedric tittered and immediately looked frightened. Pauline said: "I must say, Papa, I don't think anyone else has ever approached your flair for exactly the right costume."

"My dear," her father rejoined, "it's the way you wear 'em." He patted Miss Orrincourt's hand. "You do very well, my child," he said, "in your easy modern dresses. How would you manage if, like Ellen Terry, you had two feet of heavy velvet in front of you on the stage and were asked to move like a queen down a flight of stairs? You'd fall on your nice little nose."

He was obviously a vain man. It was extraordinary, Troy thought, that he remained unmoved by Miss Orrincourt's lack of reverence, and remembering Thomas's remark about David and Abishag the Shulammite, Troy was forced to the disagreeable conclusion that Sir Henry was in his dotage about Miss Orrincourt.

At ten o'clock a grog-tray was brought in. Sir Henry drank barley-water, suffered the women of his family to kiss him goodnight, nodded to Paul and Cedric and, to her intense embarrassment, kissed Troy's hand. "*A demain*" he said in his deepest voice. "We meet at eleven. I am fortunate."

He made a magnificent exit and ten minutes later, Miss Orrincourt, yawning extensively, also retired.

Her disappearance was the signal for an outbreak among the Ancreds.

"Honestly, Milly! Honestly, Aunt Pauline. Can we believe our *eyes!*" cried Cedric. "The Sunburst! I mean, *actually!*"

"Well, Millamant," said Pauline, "I now see for myself how things stand at Ancreton."

"You wouldn't believe me when I told you, Pauline," Millamant rejoined. "You've been here a month, but you wouldn't—"

"Has he *given* it to her, will somebody tell me?" Cedric demanded.

"He can't," said Pauline. "He can't. And what's more I don't believe he would. Unless—" She stopped short and turned to Paul. "If he's given it to her," she said, "he's going to marry her. That's all."

Poor Troy who had been making completely ineffectual efforts to go, seized upon the silence that followed Pauline's announcement to murmur: "If I may, I think I shall—"

"*Dear* Mrs. Alleyn," said Cedric, "I implore you not to be tactful. Do stay and listen."

"I don't see," Paul began, "why poor Mrs. Alleyn should be inflicted—"

"She knows," said Fenella. "I'm afraid I've already told her, Paul."

Pauline suddenly made a gracious dive at Troy. "Isn't it disturbing?" she said with an air of drawing Troy into her confidence. "You see how things are? Really it's too naughty of Papa. We're all so dreadfully worried. It's not what's happening so much as what might happen that terrifies one. And now the Sunburst. A little too much. In it's way it's a historic jewel."

"It was a little *cadeau d'estime* from the Regent to Great-Great-Grandma Honoria Ancred," Cedric cut in. "Not only historical but history repeating itself. And *may* I point out, Aunt Pauline, that I personally am rocked to the foundations. I've always understood that the Sunburst was to come to me."

"To your daughter," said Paul. "The point is academic."

"I'm sure I don't know why you think so," said Cedric, bridling. "Anything might happen."

Paul raised his eyebrows.

"Really, Pauline," said Millamant. "Really, Paul!"

"Paul, darling," said Pauline offensively, "Don't tease poor Cedric."

"Anyway," said Fenella, "I think Aunt Pauline's right. I think he means to marry and if he does I'm never coming to Ancreton again. Never."

"What shall you call her, Aunt Pauline," Cedric asked impertinently. "Mummy? Or a pet name?"

"There's only one thing to be done," said Pauline. "We must tackle him. I've told Jenetta and I've told Dessy. They're both coming. Thomas will have to come too. In Claude's absence he should take the lead. It's his duty."

"Do you mean, dearest Aunt Pauline, that we are to lie in ambush for the Old Person and make an altogether-boys bounce at him?"

"I propose, Cedric, that we ask him to meet us all and that we simply—we simply—"

"And a fat lot of good, if you'll forgive me for saying so, Pauline, that is likely to do," said Millamant with a chuckle.

"Not being an Ancred, Millamant, you can't be expected to feel this terrible thing as painfully as we do. How Papa, with his deep sense of pride in an old name—we go back to the Conquest, Mrs. Alleyn—how Papa can have allowed himself to be entangled! It's too humiliating."

"Not being an Ancred, as you point out, Pauline, I realize Papa as well as being blue-blooded is extremely hot-blooded. Moreover he's as obstinate and vain as a peacock. He likes the idea of himself with a dashing young wife."

"Comparatively young," said Cedric.

Pauline clasped her hands and turning from one member of her family to another said: "I've thought of something! Now, listen all of you. I'm going to be perfectly frank and impersonal about this. I know I'm the child's mother but that needn't prevent me. Panty!"

"What about Panty, Mother?" asked Paul nervously.

"Your grandfather adores the child. Now, suppose Panty were just to drop a childish hint."

"If you suggest," said Cedric, "that Panty should wind her little arms round his neck and whisper: 'Grandpapa, when will the howwid lady wun away?' I can only say I don't think she'd get into the skin of the part."

"He adores her," Pauline repeated angrily. "He's like a great big boy with her. It brings the tears into my eyes to see them together. You can't deny it, Millamant."

"I daresay it does, Pauline."

"Well, but Mother, Panty plays up to Grandpapa," said Paul bluntly.

"And in any case," Cedric pointed out, "isn't Panty as thick as thieves with Sonia?"

"I happen to know," said Millamant, "that Miss Orrincourt encouraged Panty to play a very silly trick on me last Sunday."

"What did she do?" asked Cedric.

Fenella giggled.

"She pinned a very silly notice on the back of my coat when I was going to church," said Millamant stuffily.

"What did it say, Milly darling?" Cedric asked greedily.

"Roll out the Barrel," said Fenella.

"This is getting us nowhere," said Millamant.

"And now," said Troy hurriedly, "I really think if you'll excuse me—"

This time she was able to get away. The Ancreds distractedly bade her good-night. She refused an escort to her room and left them barely waiting, she felt, for her to shut the door before they fell to again.

Only a solitary lamp burned in the hall, which was completely silent and, since the fire died out, very cold. While Troy climbed the stairs she felt as she had not felt before in this enormous house, that it had its own individuality. It stretched out on all sides of her, an undiscovered territory. It housed, as well as the eccentricities of the Ancreds, their deeper thoughts and the thoughts of their predecessors. When she reached the gallery, which was also dim, she felt that the drawing-room was now profoundly distant, a subterranean island. The rows of mediocre portraits and murky landscapes that she now passed, had a life of their own in this half-light and seemed to be indifferently aware of her progress. Here, at last, was her own passage with the tower steps at the end. She halted for a moment before them. Was it imagination or had the door, out of sight on the half-landing above her been softly closed. "Perhaps," she thought, "somebody lives in the room below me," and for some reason the notion affected her unpleasantly. "Ridiculous!" thought Troy and turned on a switch at the foot of the stairs. A lamp, out of sight beyond the first spiral, brought the curved wall rather stealthily to life.

Troy mounted briskly, hoping there would still be a fire in her white room. As she turned the spiral, she gathered up her long dress in her right hand and with her left reached out for the narrow rail.

The rail was sticky.

She snatched her hand away with some violence and looked at it. The palm and the undersurface were dark. Troy stood in the shadow of the inner wall but she now moved up into light. By the single lamp she saw that the stain on her hand was red.

Five seconds must have gone by before she realized that the stuff on her hand was paint.

CHAPTER FIVE

The Bloody Child

i

AT HALF-PAST ten the following morning Troy, hung with paint boxes and carrying a roll of canvas and stretchers, made her way to the Little Theatre. Guided by Paul and Cedric, who carried her studio easel between them, she went down a long passage that led out of the hall, turned right to a green baize door, "beyond which," Cedric panted, "the Difficult Children ravage at will," and continued towards the rear of that tortuous house. Their journey was not without incident, for as they passed the door of what, as Troy later discovered, was a small sitting-room, it was flung open and a short plumpish man appeared, his back towards them, shouting angrily: "If you've no faith in my treatment, Sir Henry, you have an obvious remedy. I shall be glad to be relieved of the thankless task of prescribing for a damned obstinate patient and his granddaughter." Troy made a valiant effort to forge ahead, but was blocked by Cedric, who stopped short, holding the easel diagonally across the passage and listening with an air of the liveliest interest. "Now, now, keep your temper," rumbled the invisible Sir Henry. "I wash my hands of you," the other proclaimed. "No, you don't. You keep a civil tongue in your head, Withers. You can't afford to lose your patients, my good Withers. You'd much better look after me and take a bit of honest criticism in the way it's intended." "This is outrageous," the visitor said but with a note of something like despair in his voice. "I formally relinquish the case. You will take this as final." There was a pause, during which Paul attempted without success to drag Cedric away. "I won't accept it," Sir Henry said at last. "Come, now, Withers, keep your temper. You ought to understand. I've a great deal to try me. A great deal. Bear with an old fellow's tantrums, won't you? You shan't regret it. See here, now. Shut that door and listen to me." Without turning, the visitor slowly shut the door.

"And *now*," Cedric whispered, "he'll tell poor Dr. Withers he's going to be remembered in the Will."

"Come on, for God's sake," said Paul and they made their way to the Little Theatre.

Half an hour later Troy had set up her easel, stretched her canvas, and prepared paper and boards for preliminary studies. The theatre was a complete little affair with a deepish stage. The Macbeth backcloth was simple and brilliantly conceived. The scenic painter had carried out Troy's original sketch very well indeed. Before it stood three-dimensional monolithic forms that composed well and broke across the cloth in the right places. She saw where she would place her figure. There would be no attempt to present the background in terms of actuality. It would be frankly a stage set. "A dangling rope would come rather nicely," she thought, "but I suppose they wouldn't like that. If only he'll stand!"

Cedric and Paul now began to show her what could be done with the lights. Troy was enjoying herself. She liked the smell of canvas and glue and the feeling that this was a place where people worked. In the Little Theatre even Cedric improved. He was knowledgeable and quickly responsive to her suggestions, checking Paul's desire to flood the set with a startling display of lighting and getting him to stand in position while he himself focused a single spot. "We must find the backcloth discreetly," he cried. "Try the ground row." And presently a luminous glow appeared, delighting Troy.

"But how are you going to *see?*" cried Cedric distractedly. "Oh, lawks! How *are* you going to see?"

"I can bring down a standard spot on an extension," Paul offered. "Or we could uncover a window."

Cedric gazed in an agony of enquiry at Troy. "But the window light would infiltrate," he said. "Or wouldn't it?"

"We could try."

At last, by an ingenious arrangement of screens, Troy was able to get daylight on her canvas and a fair view of the stage.

The clock—it was, of course, known as the Great Clock—in the central tower struck eleven. A door somewhere backstage opened and shut, and dead on his cue Sir Henry, in the character of Macbeth, walked on to the lighted set.

"Golly!" Troy whispered. "Oh, Golly!"

"Devastatingly fancy-dress," said Cedric in her ear, "but in its ridiculous way, rather exciting. Or not? Too fancy?"

"It's not too fancy for me," Troy said roundly and walked down the aisle to greet her sitter.

ii

At midday Troy drove her fingers through her hair, propped a large charcoal drawing against the front of the stage and backed away from it down the aisle. Sir Henry took off his helmet, groaned a little and moved cautiously to a chair in the wings.

"I suppose you want to stop," said Troy absently, biting her thumb and peering at her drawing.

"One grows a trifle stiff," he replied. She then noticed that he was looking more than a trifle tired. He had made-up for his sitting, painting heavy shadows round his eyes and staining his moustache and the tuft on his chin with water-dye. To this he had added long strands of crepe hair. But beneath the grease-paint and hair his face sagged a little and his head drooped.

"I must let you go," said Troy. "I hope I haven't been too exacting. One forgets."

"One also remembers," said Sir Henry. "I have been remembering my lines. I played the part first in 1904."

Troy looked up quickly, suddenly liking him.

"It's a wonderful role," he said. "Wonderful."

"I was very much moved by it when I saw you five years ago."

"I've played it six times and always to enormous business. It hasn't been an unlucky piece for me."

"I've heard about the Macbeth superstition. One mustn't quote from the play, must one?" Troy made a sudden pounce at her drawing and wiped her thumb down a too dominant line. "Do you believe it's unlucky?" she asked vaguely.

"It has been for other actors," he said, quite seriously. "There's always a heavy feeling offstage during performance. People are nervy."

"Isn't that perhaps because they remember the superstition?"

"It's there," he said. "You can't escape the feeling. But the piece has never been unlucky for me." His voice, which had sounded tired, lifted again. "If it were otherwise, should I have chosen this role for my portrait? Assuredly not. And now," he said with a return of his arch and over-gallant manner, "am I to be allowed a peep before I go?"

Troy was not very keen for him to have his peep but she took the drawing a little way down the aisle and turned it towards him. "I'm afraid it won't explain itself," she said. "It's merely a sort of plot of what I hope to do."

"Ah, yes." He put his hand in his tunic and drew out a pair of gold-rimmed pince-nez and there, in a moment, was Macbeth with glasses perched on his nose, staring solemnly at his own portrait. "Such a clever lady," he said. "Very clever!" Troy put the drawing away and he got up slowly. "Off, ye lendings!" he said. "I must change." He adjusted his cloak with a practised hand, drew himself up and, moving into the spotlight, pointed his dirk at the great naked canvas. His voice, as though husbanded for this one flourish, boomed through the empty theatre.

"Well, may you see things well done there: adieu!
Lest our old robes sit easier than our new!"

" 'God's benison go with you!' " said Troy, luckily remembering the line. He crossed himself, chuckled and strode off between the monoliths to the door behind the stage. It slammed and Troy was alone.

She had made up her mind to start at once with the laying out of her subject on the big canvas. There would be no more preliminary studies. Time pressed and she knew now what she wanted. "There is no other moment," she thought, "to compare with this, when you face the tautly stretched surface and raise your hand to make the first touch upon it." And, drawing in her breath, she swept her charcoal across the canvas. It gave a faint drum-like note of response. "We're off," thought Troy.

Fifty minutes went by and a rhythm of line and mass grew under her hand. Back and forward she walked, making sharp accents with the end of her charcoal or sweeping it flat across the grain of the canvas. All that was Troy was now poured into her thin blackened hand. At last she stood motionless, ten paces back from her work, and, after an interval, lit a cigarette, took up her duster and began to flick her drawing. Showers of charcoal fell down the surface.

"Don't you like it?" asked a sharp voice.

Troy jumped galvanically and turned. The little girl she had seen fighting on the terrace stood on the aisle, her hands jammed in the pockets of her pinafore and her feet planted apart.

"Where did you come from?" Troy demanded.

"Through the end door. I came quietly because I'm not allowed. Why are you rubbing it out? Don't you like it?"

"I'm not rubbing it out. It's still there." And indeed, the ghost of her drawing remained. "You take the surplus charcoal off," she said curtly. "Otherwise it messes the paint."

"It is going to be Noddy dressed up funny?"

Troy started at this use of a name she had imagined to be Miss Orrincourt's prerogative and invention.

"I call him Noddy," said the child, as if guessing at her thought, "and so does Sonia. She got it from me. I'm going to be like Sonia when I'm grown up."

"Oh," said Troy, opening her paint box and rummaging in it.

"Are those your paints?"

"Yes," said Troy, looking fixedly at her. "They are. Mine."

"I'm Patricia Claudia Ellen Ancred Kentish."

"So I'd gathered."

"You couldn't have gathered all of that because nobody except Miss Able ever calls me anything but Panty. Not that I care," added Panty, suddenly climbing on to the back of one of the stalls and locking her feet in the arms. "I'm double-jointed," she said, throwing herself back and hanging head downwards.

"That won't help you if you break your neck," said Troy.

Panty made an offensive gargling noise.

"As you're not allowed here," Troy continued, "hadn't you better run off?"

"No," said Panty.

Troy squeezed a fat serpent of Flake White out on her palette. "If I ignore this child," she thought, "perhaps she will get bored and go."

Now the yellows, next the reds. How beautiful was her palette!

"I'm going to paint with those paints," said Panty at her elbow.

"You haven't a hope," said Troy.

"I'm going to." She made a sudden grab at the tray of long brushes. Troy anticipated this move by a split second.

"Now, see here, Panty," she said, shutting the box and facing the child. "If you don't pipe down I shall pick you up by the slack of your breeches and carry you straight back to where you belong. You don't like people butting in on your games, do you? Well, this is my game and I can't get on with it if you butt in."

"I'll kill you," said Panty.

"Don't be an ass," said Troy mildly.

Panty scooped up a dollop of vermilion on three of her fingers and flung it wildly at Troy's face. She then burst into peals of shrill laughter.

"You can't whack me," she shrieked. "I'm being brought up on a system."

"Can't I!" Troy rejoined. "System or no system—" And indeed there was nothing she desired more at the moment than to beat Panty. The child confronted her with an expression of concentrated malevolence. Her cheeks were blown out with such determination that her nose wrinkled and turned up. Her mouth was so tightly shut that lines resembling a cat's whiskers radiated from it. She scowled hideously. Her pigtails stuck out at right angles to her head. Altogether she looked like an infuriated infant Boreas.

Troy sat down and reached for a piece of rag to clean her face. "Oh, Panty," she said, "you do look so exactly like your Uncle Thomas."

Panty drew back her arm again. "No, don't," said Troy. "Don't do any more damage with red paint, I implore you. Look here, I'll strike a bargain with you. If you'll promise not to take any more paint without asking, I'll give you a board and some brushes and let you make a proper picture."

Panty glared at her. "When?" she said warily.

"When we've asked your mother or Miss Able. I'll ask. But no more nonsense. And especially," Troy added, taking a shot in the dark, "no more going to my room and squeezing paint on the stair-rail."

Panty stared blankly at her. "I don't know what you're talking about," she said flatly. "When can I paint? I want to. Now."

"Yes, but let's get this cleared up. What did you do before dinner last night?"

"I don't know. Yes, I do. Dr. Withers came. He weighed us all. He's going to make me bald because I've got ringworm. That's why I've got this cap on. Would you like to see my ringworm?"

"No."

"I got it first. I've given it to sixteen of the others."

"Did you go up to my room and mess about with my paints?"

"No."

"Honestly, Panty?"

"Honestly what? I don't know where your room is. When can I paint?"

"Do you promise you didn't put paint—"

"You are *silly!*" said Panty furiously. "Can't you see a person's telling the truth?"

And Troy, greatly bewildered, thought that she could.

While she was still digesting this queer little scene the door at the back of the stalls opened and Cedric peered round it.

"*So* humble and timid," he lisped. "Just a mouselike squeak to tell you luncheon is almost on the table. *Panty!*" he cried shrilly, catching sight of his cousin. "You gross child! Back to the West Wing, Miss! How dare you muscle your hideous way in here?"

Panty grinned savagely at him. "Hullo, Sissy," she said.

"Wait," said Cedric, "just wait till the Old Person catches you. What he won't do to you!"

"Why?" Panty demanded.

"Why! You ask me why, Infamy! With the grease-paint fresh on your fingers?"

Both Panty and Troy gasped at this. Panty glanced at her hand. "That's her paint," she said, jerking her head at Troy. "That's not grease-paint!"

"Do you deny," Cedric pursued, shaking his finger at her, "do you deny, you toxic child, that you went into your grandfather's dressing-room while he was sitting for Mrs. Alleyn and scrawled some pot-house insult in lake-liner on his looking glass? Do you deny more-over that you painted a red moustache on the cat Carabbas?"

With an air of bewilderment that Troy could have sworn was genuine, Panty repeated her former statement. "I don't know what you're talking about. I didn't."

"Tell that," said Cedric, with relish, "to your grandpapa and see if he believes you."

"Noddy likes me," said Panty rallying. "He likes me best in the family. He thinks you're awful. He said you're a simpering popinjay."

"See here," said Troy hastily. "Let's get this straight. You say Panty's written something in grease-paint on Sir Henry's looking-glass. What's she supposed to have written?"

Cedric coughed: "Dearest Mrs. Alleyn, we mustn't allow you for a second to be disturbed—"

"I'm not disturbed," said Troy. "What was written on the glass?"

"My mama would have wiped it off. She was in his room tidying, and saw it. She hunted madly for a rag but the Old Person, at that moment, walked in and saw it. He's roaring about the house like a prophet."

"But what was it, for pity's sake?"

" 'Grandfather's a bloody old fool,' " said Cedric. Panty giggled. "There!" said Cedric. "You see? Obviously she wrote it. Obviously she made-up the cat."

"I didn't. I *didn't*." And with one of those emotional *volte-face* by which children bewilder us, Panty wrinkled up her face, kicked Cedric suddenly but half-heartedly on the shin, and burst into a storm of tears.

"You odious child!" he ejaculated, skipping out of her way.

Panty flung herself on her face, screamed industriously and beat the floor with her fists. "You all hate me," she sobbed. "Wicked beasts! I wish I was dead."

"Oh, la!" said Cedric, "how tedious! Now, she'll have a fit or something."

Upon this scene came Paul Kentish. He limped rapidly down the aisle, seized his sister by the slack of her garments and, picking her up very much as if she were a kitten, attempted to stand her on her feet. Panty drew up her legs and hung from his grasp, in some danger, Troy felt, of suffocation. "Stop it at once, Panty," he said. "You've been a very naughty girl."

"Wait a minute," said Troy, "I don't think she has, honestly. I mean, not in the way you think. There's a muddle, I'm certain of it."

Paul relinquished his hold. Panty sat on the floor, sobbing harshly, a most desolate child.

"It's all right," said Troy, "I'll explain. You didn't do it, Panty, and you shall paint if you still want to."

"She's not allowed to come out of school," said Paul. "Caroline Able will be here in a minute."

"Thank God for that," said Cedric.

Miss Able arrived almost immediately, cast a professionally breezy glance at her charge and said it was dinner time. Panty with a look at Troy which she was unable to interpret, got to her feet.

"Look here—" said Troy.

"Yes?" said Miss Able cheerfully.

"About this looking-glass business. I don't think that Panty—"

"Next time she feels like that we'll think of something much more sensible to do, won't we, Patricia?"

"Yes, but I don't think she did it."

"We're getting very good at just facing up to these funny old things we do when we're silly, aren't we, Patricia? It's best just to find out why and then forget about them."

"But—"

"Dinner!" cried Miss Able brightly and firmly. She removed the child without any great ado.

"Dearest Mrs. Alleyn," said Cedric. "Why are you so sure Panty is not the author of the insult on the Old Person's mirror?"

"Has she ever called him 'Grandfather?' "

"Well, no," said Paul. "No, actually she hasn't."

"And what's more—" Troy stopped short. Cedric had moved to her painting table. He had taken up a piece of rag and was using it to clean a finger nail. Only then did Troy realize that the first finger of the right hand he had waved at her had been stained dark crimson under the nail.

He caught her eye and dropped the rag.

"Such a Paul Pry!" he said. "Dipping my fingers in your paint."

But there had been no dark crimson laid out on her palette.

"Well," said Cedric shrilly. "Shall we lunch?"

iii

By the light of her flash-lamp Troy was examining the stair-rail in her tower. The paint had not been cleaned away and was now in the condition known as tacky. She could see clearly the mark left by her own hand. Above this, the paint was untouched. It had not been squeezed out and left, but brushed over the surface. At one point only on the stone wall above the rail, someone had left the faint red print of two fingers. "How Rory would laugh at me," she thought, peering at them. They were small, but not small enough, she thought, to have been made by a child. Could one of the maids have touched the rail and then the wall? But beyond the mark left by her own grip there were no other prints on the rail. "Rory," she thought, "would take photographs, but how could one ever get anything from these things? They're all broken up by the rough surface. I couldn't even make a drawing of them." She was about to move away when the light from her torch fell on an object that seemed to be wedged in the gap between a step and the stone wall. Looking more closely she discovered it to be one of her own brushes. She worked it out and found that the bristles were thick with half-dry rose madder.

She went down to the half-landing. There was the door that she had fancied she heard closing last night when she went to bed. It was not quite shut now and she gave it a tentative shove. It swung inwards and Troy was confronted with a Victorian bathroom.

"Well!" she thought crossly, remembering her long tramp that morning in search of a bath, "Fenella might have told me I'd got one of my own."

She had dirtied her fingers on the brush and went in to wash them. The soap in the marbled hand basin was already stained with rose madder. “This is a madhouse,” thought Troy.

iv

Sir Henry posed for an hour that afternoon. The next morning, Sunday, was marked by a massive attendance of the entire family with Troy, at Ancreton church. In the afternoon, however, he gave her an hour. Troy had decided to go straight for the head. She had laid in a general scheme for her work, an exciting affair of wet shadows and sharp accents. This could be completed without him. She was painting well. The touch of flamboyancy that she had dreaded was absent. She had returned often to the play. Its threat of horror was now a factor in her approach to her work. She was strongly aware of that sense of a directive power which comes only when all is well with painters. “With any luck,” she thought, “I’ll be able to say ‘Did the fool that is me, make this?’ ”

At the fourth sitting, Sir Henry, returning perhaps to some bygone performance, broke the silence by speaking without warning the lines she had many times read:—

Light thickens, and the crow
Makes wing to the rooky wood—

He startled Troy so much that her hand jerked and she waited motionless until he had finished the speech, resenting the genuine twist of apprehension that had shaken her. She could find nothing to say in response to this unexpected and oddly impersonal performance, but she had the feeling that the old man knew very well how much it had moved her.

After a moment she returned to her work and still it went well. Troy was a deliberate painter but the head grew with almost frightening rapidity. In an hour she knew that she must not touch it again. She was suddenly exhausted. “I think we’ll stop for to-day,” she said and again felt that he was not surprised.

Instead of going away he came down into the front of the theatre and looked at what she had done. She had that feeling of gratitude to her subject that sometimes follows a sitting that has gone well but she did not want him to speak of the portrait and began hurriedly to talk of Panty.

"She's doing a most spirited painting of red cows and a green aeroplane."

"T'uh!" said Sir Henry on a melancholy note.

"She wants to show it to you herself."

"I have been deeply hurt," said Sir Henry, "by Patricia. Deeply hurt."

"Do you mean," said Troy uncomfortably, "because of something she's supposed to have written on—on your looking-glass?"

"Supposed! The thing was flagrant. Not only that but she opened the drawers of my dressing-table and pulled out my papers. I may tell you that if she were capable of reading the two documents that she found there, she would perhaps feel some misgivings. I may tell you that they closely concerned herself and that if there are any more of these damnable tricks—" He paused and scowled portentously. "Well, we shall see. We shall see. Let her mother realize that I cannot endure for ever. And my cat! She has made a fool of my cat. There are still marks of grease-paint in his whiskers," said Sir Henry angrily. "Butter has not altogether removed them. As for the insult to me—"

"But I'm sure she didn't. I was here when they scolded her about it. Honestly, I'm sure she knew nothing whatever about it."

"T'uh!"

"No, but really—" Should she say anything about the dark red stain under Cedric's finger nail? No, she'd meddled enough. She went on quickly: "Panty brags about her naughtiness. She's told me about all her practical jokes. She never calls you grandfather and I happen to know she spells it 'farther' because she showed me a story she had written, and the word occurs frequently. I'm sure Panty's too fond of you," Troy continued, wondering if she spoke the truth, "to do anything so silly and unkind."

"I've loved that child," said Sir Henry with the appalling rich display of sentiment so readily commanded by the Ancreds, "as if she were my own. My Little Best-Beloved, I've always called her. I've never made any secret of my preference. After I'm gone," he went on to Troy's embarrassment, "she would have known—however." He sighed windily. Troy could think of nothing to say and cleaned her palette. The light from the single uncovered window had faded. Sir Henry had switched off the stage lamps and the little theatre was now filled with shadows. A draught somewhere up in the borders caused them to move uneasily and a rope-end tapped against the canvas backcloth.

"Do you know anything about embalming?" Sir Henry asked in his deepest voice. Troy jumped.

"No, indeed," she said.

"I have studied the subject," said Sir Henry, "deeply."

"Oddly enough," said Troy after a pause, "I did look at that queer little book in the drawing-room. The one in the glass case."

"Ah, yes. It belonged to my ancestor who rebuilt Ancreton. He himself was embalmed and his fathers before him. It has been the custom with the Ancreds. The family vault," he rambled on depressingly, "is remarkable for that reason. If I lie there—the Nation may have other wishes: it is not for me to speculate—but if I lie there it will be after their fashion. I have given explicit directions."

"I *do* wish," Troy thought, "*how* I do wish he wouldn't go on like this." She made a small ambiguous murmuring.

"Ah, well!" said Sir Henry heavily and began to move away. He paused before mounting the steps up to the stage. Troy thought that he was on the edge of some further confidence and hoped that it would be of a more cheerful character.

"What," said Sir Henry, "is your view on the matter of marriage between first cousins?"

"I—really, I don't know," Troy replied, furiously collecting her wits. "I fancy I've heard that modern medical opinion doesn't condemn it. But I really haven't the smallest knowledge—"

"I am against it," he said loudly. "I cannot approve. Look at Royalty. The House of Spain! The Romanoffs!" His voice died away in an inarticulate rumble.

Hoping to divert his attention Troy began: "Panty—"

"Hah!" said Sir Henry. "These doctors don't know anything. Patricia's scalp! A common childish ailment, and Withers, having pottered about with it for weeks without doing any good, is now going to dose the child with a depilatory. Disgusting! I have spoken to the child's mother but I'd have done better to hold my tongue. Who," Sir Henry demanded, "pays any attention to the old man? Nobody. Ours is an ancient house, Mrs. Alleyn. We have borne arms since my ancestor the Sieur d'Ancred fought beside the Conqueror. And before that. Before that. A proud house. Perhaps in my own humble way I have not disgraced it. But what will happen when I am gone? I look for my heir and what do I find? A Thing! An emasculated Popinjay!"

He evidently expected some reply to this pronouncement on Cedric but Troy was unable to think of one.

"The last of the Ancreds!" he said, glaring at her. "A family that came in with the Conqueror to go out a—"

"But," said Troy, "he may marry and—"

"And have kittens! P'shaw!"

"Perhaps Mr. Thomas Ancred—"

"Old Tommy! No! I've talked to old Tommy. He doesn't see it. He'll die a bachelor. And Claude's wife is past it. Well, it was my hope to know the line was secure before I went. I shan't."

"But, bless my soul," said Troy, "you're taking far too gloomy a view of all this. There's not much wrong with a man who can pose for an hour with a helmet weighing half a hundred weight on his head. You may see all sorts of exciting things happen."

It was astonishing, it was almost alarming, to see how promptly he squared his shoulders, how quickly gallantry made its reappearance. "Do you think so?" he said and Troy noticed how his hand went to his cloak, giving it an adroit hitch. "Well, perhaps, after all, you're right. Clever lady! Yes. Yes. I *may* see something exciting and what's more—" He paused and gave a very queer little giggle. "What's more, my dear, so may other people."

Troy was never to know if Sir Henry would have elaborated this strange prophecy because at that moment a side door in the auditorium was flung open and Miss Orrincourt burst into the Little Theatre.

"Noddy!" she shouted angrily. "You've got to come. Get out of that funny costume and protect me. I've had as much of your bloody family as I can stand. It's them or me. Now!"

She strode down the aisle and confronted him, her hands on her hips, a virago.

Sir Henry eyed her with more apprehension, Troy thought, than astonishment, and began a placatory rumbling.

"No you don't," she said. "Come off it and *do* something. They're in the library, sitting round a table. Plotting against *me*. I walked in and there was Pauline giving an imitation of a cat fight and telling them how I'd have to be got rid of."

"My dear, please. I can't allow. . . . Surely you're mistaken."

"Am I dopey? I tell you I *heard* her. They're all against me. I warned you before and I'm warning you again and it's the last time. They're going to frame me. I know what I'm talking about. It's a frame-up. I tell you they've got me all jittery, Noddy. I can't stand it. You can either come and tell them where they get off or it's thanks for the buggy-ride and me for town in the morning."

He looked at her disconsolately, hesitated, and took her by the elbow. Her mouth drooped, she gazed at him dolorously. "It's lonely here, Noddy," she said. "Noddy, I'm scared."

It was strange to watch the expression of extreme tenderness that this instantly evoked; strange, and to Troy, painfully touching.

"Come," Sir Henry said, stooping over her in his terrifying costume. "Come along. I'll speak to these children."

v

The Little Theatre was on the northern corner of the East Wing. When Troy had tidied up she looked out-of-doors and found a wintry sun still glinting feebly on Ancreton. She felt stuffed-up with her work. The carriage-drive, sweeping downhill through stiffly naked trees, invited her. She fetched a coat and set out bare-headed. The frosty air stung her eyes with tears, the ground rang hard under her feet. Suddenly exhilarated she began to run. Her hair lifted, cold air ran over her scalp and her ears burned icily. "How ridiculous to run and feel happy," thought Troy, breathless. And slowing down, she began to make plans. She would leave the head. In two days, perhaps it would be dry. Tomorrow, the hands and their surrounding drape and, when he had gone, another hour or so through the background. Touch after touch and for each one the mustering of thought and muscle and the inward remembrance of the scheme.

The drive curved down between banks of dead leaves, and overhead, frozen branches rattled in a brief visitation of wind and she thought: "I'm walking under the scaffolding of summer." There, beneath her, were the gates. The sun had gone and already fields of mist had begun to rise from the hollows. "As far as the gates," thought Troy, "and then back up the terraces." She heard the sound of hooves behind her in the woods and the faint rumbling of wheels. Out from the trees came the governess-cart and Rozinante, and there, gloved and furred and apparently recovered from her fury, sat Miss Orrincourt, flapping the reins.

Troy waited for her and she pulled up. "I'm going to the village," she said. "Do you want to come? Do, like a sweet, because I've got to go to the chemist and this brute might walk away if nobody watched it."

Troy got in, "Can you drive?" said Miss Orrincourt. "Do, like a ducks. I hate it." She handed the reins to Troy and at once groped among her magnificent furs for her cigarette case. "I got the willies up there," she continued. "They've all gone out to dinner at the next-door morgue. Well, next door! It's God knows how far away. Cedric and Paul and old Pauline. What a bunch. With their tails *well* down, dear. Well, I mean to say, you saw how upset I was, didn't you? So did Noddy." She giggled. "Look, dear, you should have seen him. With that tin toque on his head and everything. Made the big entrance into the library and called them for everything. 'This lady,' he says, 'is my guest and you'll be good enough to remember it.' And quite a lot more. Was I tickled! Pauline and Milly looking blue murder and poor little Cedric bleating and waving his hands. He made them apologize. Oh, well," she said with a sigh, "it was something happening anyway. That's the worst of life in this dump. Nothing ever happens. Nothing to do and all day to do it in. God, what a flop! If anybody'd told me a month ago I'd be that fed up I'd get round to crawling about the place in a prehistoric prop like this I'd have thought they'd gone haywire. Oh, well, I suppose it'd have been worse in the army."

"Were you ever in the army?"

"I'm delicate," said Miss Orrincourt with an air of satisfaction. "Bronchial asthma. I was fixed up with E.N.S.A. but my chest began a rival show. The boys in the orchestra said they couldn't hear themselves play. So I got out. I got an understudy at the Unicorn. It was that West End you barked your shins on the ice. Then," said Miss Orrincourt simply, "Noddy noticed me."

"Was that an improvement?" asked Troy.

"Wouldn't you have thought so? I mean, ask yourself. Well, you know. A man in his position. Top of the tree. Mind, I think he's sweet. I'm crazy about him: in a way. But I've got to look after myself, haven't I? If you don't look after yourself in this old world nobody's going to look after you. Well, between you and I, Mrs. Alleyn, things were a bit tricky. Till yesterday. Look, a girl doesn't stick it out in an atmosphere like this, unless there's a future in it, does she? Not if she's still conscious, she doesn't."

Miss Orrincourt inhaled deeply and then made a petulant little sound. "Well, I *am* fed up," she said as if Troy had offered some word of criticism. "I don't say he hasn't given me things. This coat's rather nice, don't you think? It belonged to a lady who was in the Wrens. I saw it advertised. She'd never worn it. Two hundred and dirt cheap, really."

They jogged on in silence broken only by the clop of Rozinante's hooves. There was the little railway halt and there, beyond a curve in the low hills, the roofs of Ancreton village.

"Well, I mean to say," said Miss Orrincourt, "when I fixed up with Noddy to come here I didn't know what I was letting myself in for. I'll say I didn't! Well, *you* know. On the surface it looked like a win. It's high up and my doctor says my chest ought to be high up and there wasn't much doing in the business. My voice isn't so hot and I haven't got the wind for dancing like I had and the 'legitimate' give me a pain in the neck. So what have you?"

Stumped for an answer as she had so often been since her arrival at Ancreton, Troy said: "I suppose the country does feel a bit queer when you're used to bricks and mortar."

"It feels, to be frank, like death warmed up. Not that I say you couldn't do something with that Jack's-come-home up there. You know. Week-end parties with the old bunch coming down and all the fun and games. And no Ancreds. Well, I wouldn't mind Ceddie. He's one-of-those, of course, but I always think they're good mixers in their own way. I've got it all worked out. Something to do, isn't it, making plans? It may come up in the lift of these days, you never know. But no Ancreds when I throw a party in the Baronial Hall. You bet no Ancreds."

"Sir Henry?" Troy ventured.

"Well," said Miss Orrincourt, "I was thinking of later on, if you know what I mean."

"Good Lord!" Troy ejaculated involuntarily.

"Mind, as I say, I'm fond of Noddy. But it's a funny old world and there you have it. I must say it's nice having someone to talk to. Someone who isn't an Ancred. I can't exactly *confide* in Ceddie because he's the heir and he mightn't quite see things my way."

"Possibly not."

"No. Although he's quite nice to me." The thin voice hardened. "And, don't you worry, I know why," Miss Orrincourt added. "He's stuck for cash, silly kid, and he wants me to use my influence. He'd got the bums on his doorstep when the jitterbugs cleaned up his place, and then he went to the money-lenders and now he doesn't know where to go. He's scared to turn up at the flat. He'll have to wait till I'm fixed up myself. Then we'll see. I don't mind much," she said, moving restlessly, "which way it goes, so long as I'm fixed up."

They faced each other across the bucket-cart. Troy looked at her companion's beautifully painted face. Behind it stood wraith-like trees, motionless, threaded with mist. It might have been a sharp mask, by a surrealist, hung on that darkling background, thought Troy.

A tiny rhythmic sound grew out of the freezing air. "I can hear a cat mewing somewhere," said Troy, pulling Rozinante up.

"That's a good one!" said Miss Orrincourt, laughing and coughing. "A cat mewing! It's my chest, dear. This damn night air's catching me. Can you hurry that brute up?"

Troy stirred him up and presently they clopped sedately down the one street of Ancreton village and pulled up outside a small chemist's shop, that seemed also to be a sort of general store.

"Shall I get whatever it is?" Troy offered.

"All right. I don't suppose there's anything worth looking at in the shop. No perfume. Thanks dear. It's the stuff for the kids' ringworm. The doctor's ordered it. It's meant to be ready."

The elderly rubicund chemist handed Troy two bottles tied together. One had an envelope attached. "For the children up at the Manor?" he said. "Quite so. And the small bottle is for Sir Henry." When she had climbed back into the governess-cart she found that he had followed her and stood blinking on the pavement. "They're labelled," he said fussily. "If you'd be good enough to point out the enclosed instructions. The dosage varies, you know. It's determined by the patient's weight. Dr. Withers particularly asked me to draw Miss Able's attention. Quite an unusual prescription, actually. Thallium acetate. Yes. Both labelled. Thank you. One should exercise care—So sorry we're out of wrapping paper. Good evening." He gave a little whooping chuckle and darted back into his shop. Troy was about to turn Rozinante when Miss Orrincourt asking her to wait, scrambled out and went into the shop, returning in a few minutes with a bulge in her pocket.

"Just something that caught my eye," she said. "Righty ho, dear. Home, John, and don't spare the horses." On their return journey she exclaimed repeatedly on the subject of the children's ringworm. She held the collar of her fur coat across her mouth and her voice sounded unreal behind it. "Is it tough, or is it tough? That poor kid Panty. All over her head, and her hair's her one beauty, you might say."

"You and Panty are rather by way of being friends, aren't you?" said Troy.

"She's a terrible kiddy, really. You know. The things she does! Well! Scribbling across Noddy's mirror with a lake-liner and such a common way to put it, whatever she thought. A few more little cracks like that and she'll cook her goose if she only knew it. The mother's wild about it, naturally. Did you know the kid's first favourite in the Will? She won't hold that role down much longer if she lets her sense of comedy run away with her. And then the way she put that paint on your bannister! I call it the limit."

Troy stared at her. "How did you know about that?"

A spasm of coughing shook her companion. "I was crazy," gasped the muffled voice, "to come out in this lousy fog. Might have known. Pardon me, like a ducks, if I don't talk."

"Did Panty tell you?" Troy persisted. "*I* haven't told anyone. Did she actually tell you she did it?"

A violent paroxysm prevented Miss Orrincourt from speaking but with her lovely and enormous eyes fixed on Troy and still clasping her fur collar over the lower part of her face, she nodded three times.

"I'd never have believed it," said Troy slowly. "Never."

Miss Orrincourt's shoulders quivered and shook. "For all the world," Troy thought suddenly, "as if she were laughing."

CHAPTER SIX

Paint

i

It was on that same night that there was an open flaring row between Paul and Fenella on the one hand and Sir Henry Ancred on the other. It occurred at the climax of a game of backgammon between Troy and Sir Henry. He had insisted upon teaching her this complicated and maddening game. She would have enjoyed it more if she hadn't discovered very early in the contest that her opponent disliked losing so intensely that her own run of beginner's luck had plunged him into the profoundest melancholy. He had attempted to explain to her the chances of the possible combinations of a pair of dice, adding, with some complacency, that he himself had completely mastered this problem. Troy had found his explanation utterly incomprehensible and began by happily moving her pieces with more regard for the pattern they made on the board than for her chances of winning the game. She met with uncanny success. Sir Henry, who had entered the game with an air of gallantry, finding pretty frequent occasions to pat Troy's fingers, became thoughtful, then pained, and at last gloomy. The members of his family, aware of his mortification, watched in nervous silence. Troy moved with reckless abandon. Sir Henry savagely rattled his dice. Greatly to her relief the tide turned. She gave herself a "blot" and looked up to find Fenella and Paul watching her with an extraordinary expression of anxiety. Sir Henry prospered and soon began to "bear." Paul and Fenella exchanged a glance. Fenella nodded and turned pale.

"Aha!" cried Sir Henry in triumph. "The winning throw, I think! The winning throw!"

He cast himself back in his chair, gazed about him and laughed delightedly. It was at this juncture that Paul, who was standing on the hearthrug with Fenella, put his arm round her and kissed her with extreme heartiness and unmistakable intention. "Fenella and I," he said loudly, "are going to be married."

There followed an electrified silence, lasting perhaps, for ten seconds.

Sir Henry then picked up the backgammon board and threw it a surprising distance across the drawing-room.

"And temper," Paul added, turning rather pale, "never got anybody anywhere."

Miss Orrincourt gave a long whistle. Millamant dropped on her knees and began to pick up backgammon pieces.

Pauline Kentish, gazing with something like terror at her son, gabbled incoherently: "No, darling! No please! No, Paul, don't be naughty. No! Fenella!"

Cedric, his mouth open, his eyes glistening, rubbed his hands and made his crowing noise. But he, too, looked frightened.

And all the Ancreds, out of the corners of their eyes, watched Sir Henry.

He was the first man Troy had ever seen completely given over to rage. She found the exhibition formidable. If he had not been an old man his passion would have been less disquieting because less pitiable. Old lips, shaking with rage, old eyes whose fierceness was glazed by rheum, old hands, that jerked in uncoordinated fury; these were intolerable manifestations of emotion.

Troy got up and attempted an inconspicuous retreat to the door.

"*Come back,*" said her host violently. Troy returned. "Hear how these people conspire to humiliate me. Come back, I say," Troy sat on the nearest chair.

"Papa!" whispered Pauline, weaving her hands together and "Papa!" Millamant echoed, fumbling with the dice. "Please! So bad for you, upsetting yourself! Please!"

He silenced them with a gesture and struggled to his feet. Paul, holding Fenella by the arm, waited until his grandfather stood before him and then said rapidly: "We're sorry to make a scene. I persuaded Fen that this was the only way to handle the business. We've discussed it with you in private, Grandfather, and you've told us what you feel about it. We don't agree. It's our show, after all, and we've made up our minds. We could have gone off and got married without saying anything about it but neither of us wanted to do that. So we thought—"

"We thought," said Fenella rather breathlessly, "we'd just make a general announcement."

"Because," Paul added, "I've sent one already to the papers and we wanted to tell you before you read it."

"But, Paul darling—" his mother faintly began.

"You damned young puppy," Sir Henry roared, "what do you mean by standing up with that goddamned conceited look on your face and talking poppycock to ME?"

"Aunt Pauline," said Fenella, "I'm sorry if you're not pleased, but—"

"Ssh!" said Pauline.

"Mother *is* pleased," said Paul. "Aren't you, Mother?"

"Ssh!" Pauline repeated distractedly.

"Be silent!" Sir Henry shouted. He was now in the centre of the hearthrug. It seemed to Troy that his first violence was being rapidly transmuted into something more histrionic and much less disturbing. He rested an elbow on his mantelpiece. He pressed two fingers and a thumb against his eyelids, removed his hand slowly, kept his eyes closed, frowned as if in pain and finally sighed deeply and opened his eyes very wide indeed.

"I'm an old fellow," he said in a broken voice. "An old fellow. It's easy to hurt me. Very easy. You have dealt me a shrewd blow. Never mind. Let me suffer. Why not? It won't be for long. Not for long, now."

"Papa, *dearest*," cried Pauline sweeping up to him and clasping her hands. "You make us utterly miserable. Don't speak like that, don't. Not for the world would my boy cause you a moment's unhappiness. Let me talk quietly to these children—Papa, I implore you."

"This," a voice whispered in Troy's ear, "is perfect Pinero." She jumped violently. Cedric had slipped round behind his agitated relations and now leant over the back of her chair. "She played the name part, you know, in a revival of *The Second Mrs. Tanqueray*."

"It's no use, Pauline. Let them go. They knew my wishes. They have chosen the cruelest way. Let them," said Sir Henry with relish, "dree their weird."

"Thank you, Grandfather," said Fenella brightly but with a shake in her voice, "it's our weird and we shall be delighted to dree it."

Sir Henry's face turned an uneven crimson. "This is insufferable," he shouted and his teeth, unable to cope with the violence of his diction, leapt precariously from their anchorage and were clamped angrily home. Fenella giggled nervously. "You are under age," Sir Henry pronounced suddenly. "Under age, both of you. Pauline, if you have the smallest regard for your old father's wishes, you will forbid this lunacy. I shall speak to your mother, Miss. I shall cable to your father."

"Mother won't mind," said Fenella.

"You know well, you know perfectly well why I cannot countenance this nonsense."

"You think, don't you, Grandfather," said Fenella, "that because we're cousins we'll have loopy young. Well, we've asked about that and it's most unlikely. Modern medical opinion—"

"Be silent! At least let some semblance of decency—"

"I *won't* be silent," said Fenella, performing with dexterity the feat known by actors as topping the other man's lines. "And if we're to talk about decency, Grandfather, I should have thought it was a damn sight more decent for two people who are young and in love, to say they're going to marry each other than for an old man to make an exhibition of himself—"

"*Fenella*" shouted Pauline and Millamant in unison.

"—doting on a peroxide blonde fifty years younger than himself, and a brazen gold-digger into the bargain."

Fenella then burst into tears and ran out of the room, followed rigidly by Paul.

Troy, who had once more determined to make her escape, heard Fenella weeping stormily outside the door and stayed where she was. The remaining Ancreds were all talking at once. Sir Henry beat his fist on the mantelpiece until the ornaments danced again and roared: "My God, I'll not have her under my roof another hour! By God!—" Millamant and Pauline, on either side of him like a distracted chorus, wrung their hands and uttered plaintive cries. Cedric chattered noisily behind the sofa where Miss Orrincourt still lay. It was she who put a stop to this ensemble by rising and confronting them with her hands on her hips.

"I am not remaining here," said Miss Orrincourt piercingly, "to be insulted. Remarks have been passed in this room that no self-respecting girl in my delicate position can be expected to endure. Noddy!"

Sir Henry, who had continued his beating of the mantelpiece during this speech, stopped short and looked at her with a kind of nervousness.

"Since announcements," said Miss Orrincourt, "are in the air, Noddy; haven't we got something to say ourselves in that line? Or," she added ominously, "haven't we?"

She looked lovely standing there. It was an entirely plastic loveliness, an affair of colour and shape, of line and texture. It was so complete in its kind, Troy thought, that to bring a consideration of character or vulgarity to bear upon it would be to labour at an irrelevant synthesis. In her kind, she was perfect. "What about it, Noddy?" she said.

Sir Henry stared at her, pulled down his waistcoat, straightened his back and took her hand. "Whenever you wish, my dear," he said, "whenever you wish."

Pauline and Millamant fell back from them, Cedric drew in his breath and touched his moustache. Troy saw, with astonishment, that his hand was shaking.

"I had intended," Sir Henry said, "to make this announcement at the Birthday. Now, however, when I realize only too bitterly that my family cares little, cares nothing for my happiness" ("*Papa!*" Pauline wailed), "I turn, in my hour of sorrow, to one who does care."

"Uh-huh!" Miss Orrincourt assented, "but keep it sunny-side-up, Petty-pie."

Sir Henry, less disconcerted than one would have thought possible by this interjection, gathered himself together.

"This lady," he said loudly, "has graciously consented to become my wife."

Considering the intensity of their emotions, Troy felt that the Ancreds really behaved with great aplomb. It was true that Pauline and Millamant were, for a moment, blankly silent, but Cedric almost immediately ran out from cover and seized his grandfather by the hand.

"Dearest Grandpapa—couldn't be more delighted—too marvelous. Sonia *darling*," he babbled, "*such* fun," and he kissed her.

"Well, Papa," said Millamant, following her son's lead but not kissing Miss Orrincourt, "we can't say that it's altogether a surprise, can we? I'm sure we all hope you'll be very happy."

Pauline was more emotional. "Dearest!" she said, taking her father's hands and gazing with wet eyes into his face. "Dearest, dearest Papa. Please, please believe my only desire is for your happiness."

Sir Henry inclined his head. Pauline made an upward pounce at his moustache. "Oh Pauline!" he said with an air of tragic resignation, "I have been wounded, Pauline. Deeply wounded."

"No," cried Pauline. "No!"

"Yes," sighed Sir Henry. "Yes."

Pauline turned blindly from him and offered her hand to Miss

Orrincourt. “Be good to him,” she said brokenly. “It’s all we ask. Be good to him.”

With an eloquent gesture, Sir Henry turned aside, crossed the room and flung himself into a hitherto unoccupied armchair.

It made a loud and extremely vulgar noise.

Sir Henry, scarlet in the face, leapt to his feet and snatched up the loose cushioned seat. He exposed a still partially inflated bladder-like object across which was printed a legend: THE RASPBERRY. MAKES YOUR PARTY GO OFF WITH A BANG. He seized it and again, through some concealed orifice, it emitted its dreadful sound. He hurled it accurately into the fire and the stench of burning rubber filled the room.

“Well, I mean to say,” said Miss Orrincourt, “fun’s fun but I think that kid’s getting common in her ways.”

Sir Henry walked in silence to the door where, inevitably, he turned to deliver an exit line. “Millamant,” he said, “in the morning you will be good enough to send for my solicitor.”

The door banged. After a minute’s complete silence Troy was at last able to escape from the drawing-room.

ii

She was not much surprised in the morning to learn that Sir Henry was too unwell to appear though he hoped, in the afternoon, to resume the usual sitting. A note on her early tea-tray informed her that Cedric would be delighted to pose in the costume if this would be of any service. Troy thought it might. There was the scarlet cloak to be attended to. She had half-expected a disintegration of the family forces, at least the disappearance, possibly in opposite directions, of Fenella and Paul. She had yet to learn of the Ancreds’ resilience in inter-tribal warfare. At breakfast they both appeared, Fenella, white and silent; Paul red and silent. Pauline arrived a little later. Her attitude to her son suggested that he was ill of some not entirely respectable disease. With Fenella she adopted an air of pained antipathy and would scarcely speak to her. Millamant presided. She was less jolly than usual but behind her anxiety, if she was indeed anxious, Troy detected a hint of complacency. There was more than a touch of condolence in her manner towards her sister-in-law and this, Troy felt, Pauline deeply resented.

“Well, Milly,” said Pauline after a long silence, “do you propose to continue your role under new management?”

"I'm always rather lost, Pauline, when you adopt theatrical figures of speech."

"Are you going to house-keep, then, for the new chatelaine?"

"I hardly expect to do so."

"Poor Milly," said Pauline. "It's going to be difficult for you, I'm afraid."

"I don't think so. Cedric and I have always thought we'd like to have a little *pied-a-terre* together in London."

"Yes," Pauline agreed much too readily. "Cedric will have to draw in his horns a bit too, one supposes."

"Perhaps Paul and Fenella would consider allowing me to house-keep for them," said Millamant with her first laugh that morning. And with an air of genuine interest she turned to them. "How *are* you going to manage, both of you?" she asked.

"Like any other husband and wife without money," said Fenella. "Paul's got his pension and I've got my profession. We'll both get jobs."

"Oh, well," said Millamant comfortably, "perhaps after all, your grandfather—"

"We don't want Grandfather to do anything, Aunt Milly," said Paul quickly. "He wouldn't anyway, of course, but we don't want him to."

"Dearest!" said his mother. "So hard! So bitter! I don't know you, Paul, when you talk like that. Something"—she glanced with extraordinary distaste at Fenella—"has changed you so dreadfully."

"Where," asked Millamant brightly, "is Panty?"

"Where should she be if not in school?" Pauline countered with dignity. "She is not in the habit of breakfasting with us, Milly."

"Well, you never know," said Millamant. "She seems to get about quite a lot, doesn't she? And, by the way, Pauline, I've a bone to pick with Panty myself. Someone has interfered with my Work. A large section of embroidery has been deliberately unpicked. I'd left it in the drawing-room—"

"Panty never goes there," cried Pauline.

"Well, I don't know about that. She must, for instance, have been in the drawing-room last evening, during dinner."

"Why?"

"Because Sonia, as I suppose we must call her, says she sat in that chair before dinner, Pauline. She says it was perfectly normal."

"I can't help that, Milly. Panty did not come in to the drawing-room last night at dinner time for the very good reason that she and the other children were given their medicine then and sent early to bed. You told me yourself, Milly, that Miss Able found the medicine in the flower-room and took it straight in for Dr. Withers to give the children."

"Oh, yes," said Millamant. "Would you believe it, the extraordinary Sonia didn't trouble to take it in to Miss Able, or to give Papa's bottle to me. She merely went to the flower-room, where it seems," said Millamant with a sniff, "orchids had been brought in for her; and dumped the lot. Miss Able hunted everywhere before she found it, and so did I."

"T'uh!" said Pauline.

"All the same," said Paul. "I don't mind betting that Panty—"

"It has yet to be proved," Pauline interrupted with spirit rather than conviction, "that Panty had anything to do with—with—"

"With the Raspberry?" said Paul, grinning. "Mother, of course she did."

"I have reason to believe—" Pauline began.

"No, really Mother. It's Panty all over. Look at her record."

"Where did she get it? I've never given her such a thing."

"Another kid, I suppose, if she didn't buy it. I've seen them in one of the village shops, haven't you, Fen? I remember thinking to myself that they ought to have been sent to a rubber dump."

"I've had a little talk with Panty," said Panty's mother obstinately, "and she promised me on her word of honour she didn't know anything about it. I know when that child is speaking the truth, Milly. A mother always knows."

"*Honestly*, Mother!" said Paul.

"I don't care what anyone says—" Pauline began but was interrupted by the entrance of Cedric, very smooth and elegant and with more than a touch of smugness in his general aspect.

"Good morning, dearest Mrs. Alleyn. Good morning, my sweets," he said. "Planning how to lay out the proverbial shilling to advantage, Paul dear? I've been so excited thinking up a scheme for a double wedding. It's a teeny bit involved. The Old Person, you see, in Uncle Claude's absence, must give Fenella away and then whisk over to the other side as First Bridegroom. I thought I might be joint Best Man and Paul could double Second Bridegroom and Sonia's papa. It's like a rather intricate ballet. Uncle Thomas is to be a page and Panty a flower girl which will give her wonderful opportunities for throwing things. And you, dearest Mama, and all the aunts shall be dowagers-in-waiting. I've invented such marvelously intimidating gowns for you."

"Don't be naughty," said Millamant.

"No, but truly," Cedric went on, bringing his plate to the table. "I *do* feel, you two, that you've managed your affairs the least bit clumsily."

"It's not given to all of us," said Paul dryly, "to be quite as nimble after the main chance as you."

"Well, I do rather flatter myself I've exhibited a pretty turn of low cunning," Cedric agreed readily. "Sonia's going to let me do her trousseau and the Old Person said that I at least showed some family feeling. But I'm afraid, dearest Auntie Pauline, that Panty has lost ground almost irretrievably. Such a very robust sense of comedy."

"I have already told your mother, Cedric, that I have reason to believe that Panty was not responsible for that incident."

"Oh, gracious!" said Cedric. "*So* touching. Such faith."

"Or for the writing on your grandfather's looking-glass."

Cedric made one of his ingratiating wriggles at Troy. "Panty has another champion," he said.

Pauline turned quickly to Troy who, with a sense of stepping from the stalls up to the stage, murmured: "I didn't think Panty wrote on the glass. I thought her protests rang true."

"There!" cried Pauline emotionally and stretched out her hand to Troy. "There, all of you! *Thank* you, Mrs. Alleyn. *Someone* has faith in *my poor old Panty*."

But Troy's faith in Panty Kentish, already slightly undermined, was to suffer a further jolt.

She went from the dining-room to the Little Theatre. Her canvas was leaning, face to the wall, where she had left it. She dragged it out, tipped it up on one corner, set it on the lowered tray of her easel and stepped back to look at it.

Across the nose and eyes of the completed head somebody had drawn in black paint an enormous pair of spectacles.

iii

For perhaps five seconds alternate lumps of ice and red-hot coal chased each other down her spine and round her stomach. She then touched the face. It was hard dry. The black spectacles were still wet. With a sense of relief so violent that it came upon her like an attack of nausea, Troy dipped a rag in oil and gingerly wiped off the addition. She then sat down and pressed her shaking hands together. Not a stain, not a blur on the bluish shadows that she had twisted under the eyes, not a trace of dirt across the strange pink veil that was the flesh under his frontal bone. "Oh Golly!" Troy whispered. "Oh Golly! Thank God. Oh Golly!"

"Good morning," said Panty, coming in by the side door. "I'm allowed to do another picture. I want some more board and lots more paint. Look, I've finished the cows and the aeroplane. Aren't they good?"

She dumped her board on the floor against the foot of the easel and, with a stocky imitation of Troy, fell back a pace and looked at it, her hands clasped behind her back. Her picture was of three vermilion cows in an emerald meadow. Above them, against a sky for which Panty had used neat new blue, flew an emerald aeroplane in the act of secreting a black bomb.

"Damn good," said Panty, "isn't it?" She tore her gaze away from her picture and allowed it to rest on Troy's.

"That's good too," she said. "It's nice. It gives me a nice feeling inside. I think you paint good pictures."

"Somebody," said Troy watching her, "thought it would be better if I put in a pair of spectacles."

"Well they must have been pretty silly," said Panty. "King's don't wear spectacles. That's a king."

"Whoever it was, painted them on the face."

"If anybody puts spectacles on my cows," Panty said. "I'll kill them."

"Who do you think could have done it?"

"I dunno," said Panty without interest. "Did Noddy?"

"I hardly think so."

"I suppose it was whoever put whatever it was on Noddy's glass. Not me, anyway. Now can I have another board and more paint? Miss Able likes me to paint."

"You may go up to my room and get yourself one of the small boards in the cupboard."

"I don't know where your room is."

Troy explained as best she could. "Oh well," said Panty, "if I can't find it I'll just yell till somebody comes."

She stumped away to the side door. "By the way," Troy called after her, "would you know a Raspberry if you saw one?"

"You bet," said Panty with interest.

"I mean a rubber thing that makes a noise if you sit on it."

"What sort of noise?"

"Never mind," said Troy wearily. "Forget about it."

"You're mad," said Panty flatly, and went out.

"If I'm not," Troy muttered, "there's somebody in this house who is."

iv

All that morning she painted solidly through the background. In the afternoon Sir Henry posed for an hour and a half with two rests. He said nothing but sighed a great deal. Troy worked at the hands, but he was restless and kept making small nervous movements so that she did little more than lay down the general tone and shape of them. Millamant came in just before the end of the sitting and, with a word of apology, went to him, and murmured something indistinguishable. "No, no," he said angrily. "It must be to-morrow. Ring up again and tell them so."

"He says it's very inconvenient."

"That be damned. Ring up again."

"Very well, Papa," said the obedient Millamant.

She went away, and Troy, seeing that he was growing still more restless, called an end to the sitting, telling him that Cedric had offered to pose for the cloak. He left with evident relief. Troy grunted disconsolately, scraped down the hands, and turned again to the background. It was a formalized picture of a picture. The rooky wood, a wet mass, rimmed with boldly stated strokes of her brush, struck sharply across a coldly luminous night sky. The monolithic forms in the middle distance were broadly set down as interlocking masses. Troy had dragged a giant brush down the canvas, each stroke the summing-up of painful thinking that suddenly resolved itself in form. The background was right and the Ancreds, she reflected, would think it very queer and unfinished. All of them except, perhaps, Cedric and Panty. She had arrived at this conclusion when on to the stage pranced Cedric himself, heavily and most unnecessarily made-up, moving with a sort of bouncing stride, and making much of his grandfather's red cloak.

"Here I am," he cried, "feeling *so* keyed up with the mantle of high tragedy across my puny shoulders. Now, what *precisely* is the pose?"

There was no need to show him, however. He swept up his drape, placed himself, and, with an expert wriggle, flung it into precisely the right sweep. Troy eyed it and with a sense of rising excitement, spread unctuous bands of brilliant colour across her palette.

Cedric was an admirable model. The drape was frozen in its

sculptured folds. Troy worked in silence for an hour, holding her breath so often that she became quite stuffy in the nose.

"Dearest Mrs. Alleyn," said a faint voice, "I have a tiny cramp in my leg."

"Lord, I'm sorry!" said Troy. "You've been wonderful. Do have a rest."

He came down into the auditorium, limping a little but still with an air, and stood before her canvas.

"It's so piercingly *right*," he said. "Too exciting! I mean it really *is* theatre and the Old Person and that devastating Bard all synthesized and made eloquent and everything. It terrifies me."

He sank into a near-by stall, first spreading his cloak over the back, and fanned himself. "I can't tell you how I've died to prattle," he went on, "all the time I was up there. This house is simply *seething* with intrigue."

Troy, who was herself rather exhausted, lit a cigarette, sat down, and eyed her work. She also listened with considerable interest to Cedric.

"First I must tell you," he began, "the Old Person has positively sent for his solicitor. Imagine! Such lobbyings and whisperings! One is reminded of Papal election in the seventeenth century. First the marriage settlement, of course. What do you suppose darling Sonia will have laid down as the minimum? I've tried *piteously* hard to wheedle it out of her but she's turned rather secretive and *grande dame*. But of course however much it is it's got to come from *somewhere*. Panty was known to be first favourite. He's left her some fabulous sum to make her a *parti* when she grows up. But we all feel her little pranks will have swept her right out of the running. So perhaps darling Sonia will have that lot. Then there's Paul and Fenella, who have undoubtedly polished themselves off. I rather *hope*," said Cedric with a modest titter and a very sharp look in his eye, "that I *may* reap something there. I *think* I'm all right but you never know. He simply detests me, really, and the entail is quite ridiculous. Somebody broke it up or something ages ago and I *may* only get this awful house and nothing whatever to keep it up with. Still, I really have got Sonia on my side."

He touched his moustache and pulled a small pellet of cosmetic off his eyelashes. "I made-up," he explained in parentheses, "because I felt it was so essential to get the feeling of the Macsoforth *seeping* through into every fold of the mantle. And partly because it's such fun painting one's face."

He hummed a little air for a moment or two and then continued:

"Thomas and Dessy and the Honourable Mrs. A. are all pouring in on Friday night. The Birthday is on Saturday, did you realize? The Old Person and the Ancient of Days will spend Sunday in bed, the one suffering from gastronomic excess, the other from his exertions as Ganymede. The family will no doubt pass the day in mutual recrimination. The general feeling is that the *piece de resistance* for the Birthday will be an announcement of the new Will."

"But, good Lord—" Troy ejaculated. Cedric talked her down.

"Almost certain, I assure you. He has always made public each new draft. He can't resist the dramatic *mise enscene*."

"But how often does he change his Will?"

"I've never kept count," Cedric confessed after a pause, "but on an average I should say once every two years, though for the last three years Panty has held firm as first favourite. While she was still doing babytalk and only came here occasionally he adored her and she, most unfortunately, was crazy about him. Pauline must curse the day when she manoeuvred the school to Ancreton. Last time I was *grossly* unpopular and down to the bare bones of the entrail. Uncle Thomas was second to Panty with the general hope that he would marry and have a son and I remain a celibate with Ancreton as a millstone round my poor little neck. *Isn't* it all too tricky?"

There was scarcely a thing that Cedric did or said of which Troy did not whole-heartedly disapprove, but it was impossible to be altogether bored by him. She found herself listening quite attentively to his recital though after a time his gloating delight in Panty's fall from grace began to irritate her.

"I still think," she said, "that Panty didn't play these tricks on her grandfather." Cedric, with extraordinary vehemence, began to protest but Troy insisted. "I've talked to her about it. Her manner, to my mind, was conclusive. Obviously she didn't know anything about last night's affair. She'd never heard of the squeaking cushion."

"That child," Cedric announced malevolently, "is incredibly, terrifying subtle. She is not an Ancred for nothing. She was acting. Depend upon it, she was acting."

"I don't believe it. And what's more she didn't know her way to my room."

Cedric, who was biting his nails, paused and stared at her. After a long pause he said: "Didn't know her way to your room? But, dearest Mrs. Alleyn, what has that got to do with it?"

It was on the tip of her tongue to relate the incident of the painted bannister. She had even begun: "Well, if you promise—" but then, catching sight of his face with its full pouting mouth and pale eyes, she suddenly changed her mind. “It doesn’t matter,” Troy said, “it wouldn’t convince you. Never mind.”

“Dearest Mrs. Alleyn,” Cedric tittered, pulling at his cloak, “you are mysterious. Anyone would suppose you didn’t trust me.”

CHAPTER SEVEN

Fiesta

i

On Friday, a week after her arrival at Ancreton, Troy dragged her canvas out of the property room where she now kept it locked up and stared at it with mixed sensations of which the predominant was one of astonishment. How in the world had she managed it? Another two days would see its completion. Tomorrow night Sir Henry would lead his warring celebrants into the little theatre and she would stand awkwardly in the background while they talked about it. Would they be very disappointed? Would they see at once that the background was not the waste before Forres Castle but a theatrical cloth presenting this, that Troy had painted, not Macbeth himself, but an old actor looking backwards into his realization of the part? Would they see that the mood was one of the relinquishment?

Well, the figure was completed. There were some further places she must attend to, a careful balancing stroke here and there. She was filled with a great desire that her husband should see it. It was satisfactory, Troy thought, that of the few people to whom she wished to show her work, her husband came first. Perhaps this was because he said so little yet was not embarrassed by his own silence.

As the end of her work drew near her restlessness increased and her fears for their reunion. She remembered phrases spoken by other women: "The first relationship is never repeated." "We were strangers again when we met." "It wasn't the same." "It felt extraordinary. We were shy and had nothing to say to each other." Would her reunion also be inarticulate? "I've no technique," Troy thought, "to see me through. I've no marital technique at all. Any native adroitness I possess has gone into my painting. But perhaps Roderick will know what to say. Shall I tell him at once about the Ancreds?"

She was cleaning her palette when Fenella ran in to say a call had come through for her from London.

It was the Assistant Commissioner at the Yard. Troy listened to him with a hammer knocking at her throat. He thought, he said with arch obscurity, that she might enjoy a run up to London on Monday. If she stayed the night the Yard might have something of interest to show her on Tuesday morning. A police car would be coming in by way of Ancreton Halt early on Monday and would be delighted to give her a lift. "Thank you," said Troy in an unrecognizable voice. "Yes, I see. Yes, of course. Yes, very exciting. Thank you."

She fled to her room, realizing as she sat breathless on her bed that she had run like a madwoman up three flights of stairs. "It's as well," she thought, "that the portrait's finished. In this frame of mind I'd be lucky if I reached Panty's form."

She began distractedly to imagine their meeting. "But I can't see his face," she thought in a panic. "I can't remember his voice. I've forgotten my husband."

She felt by turns an unreasonable urge for activity and a sense of helpless inertia. Ridiculous incidents from the Ancred repertoire flashed up in her mind. "I must remember to tell him that," she would think, and then wonder if after all the Ancreds in retrospect would sound funny. She remembered with a jolt that she must let Katti Bostock know about Tuesday. They had arranged for Alleyn's old servant to go to London and open the flat.

"I should have done it at once," she cried, and returned downstairs. While she waited, fuming, in a little telephone room near the front doors, for her call to go through, she heard wheels on the drive, the sound of voices and finally the unmistakable rumpus of arrival in the hall. A charming voice called gaily: "Milly, where are you? Come down. It's Dessy and Thomas and me. Dessy found a colonel and the colonel had a car and we've all arrived together."

"Jenetta!" Millamant's disembodied voice floated down from the gallery. Still more distantly Pauline's echoed her: "Jenetta!"

Was there an overtone of disapproval, not quite of dismay, in this greeting, Troy wondered, as she quietly shut the door?

ii

Jenetta, the Honourable Mrs. Claude Ancred, unlike Millamant, had caught none of the overtones of her relations-in-law. She was a nice-looking woman with a gay voice, good clothes, an intelligent face and an air of quietly enjoying herself. Her conversation was unstressed and crisp. If she sensed internecine warfare she gave no hint of doing so and seemed to be equally pleased with, and equally remote from, each member of that unlikely clan.

Desdemona, on the other hand was, of all the Ancreds after Sir Henry, most obviously of the theatre. She was startlingly good-looking, of voluptuous build, and had a warm ringing voice that seemed to be perpetually uttering important lines of climax from a West-End success. She ought really, Troy thought, to be surrounded by attendant figures: a secretary, an author, an agent, perhaps a doting producer. She had an aura of richness and warmth, and a knack of causing everybody else to subscribe to a larger-than-life atmosphere in which she herself moved so easily. Her colonel, after a drink, drove away to his lawful destination with Dessy's magnificent thanks no doubt ringing in his ears. Troy, emerging from the telephone room, found herself confronted by the new arrivals. She was glad to see Thomas—already she thought of him as 'old Thomas'—with his crest of faded hair and his bland smile. "Oh, hullo," he said, blinking at her, "so here you are. I hope your carbuncle is better."

"It's gone," said Troy.

"We're all talking about Papa's engagement," said Thomas. "This is my sister-in-law, Mrs. Claude Ancred, and this is my sister Desdemona. Milly and Pauline are seeing about rooms. Have you painted a nice picture?"

"Not bad. Are you producing a nice play?"

"It's quite good, thank you," said Thomas primly.

"Darling Tommy," said Desdemona, "how *can* it be quite good with that woman? What you were thinking about when you cast it!"

"Well, Dessy, I told the management you wanted the part."

"I didn't want it. I could play it, but I didn't want it, thank you."

"Then everybody ought to be pleased," said Thomas mildly. "I suppose, Jenetta," he continued, "you are anxious to see Fenella and Paul. Papa's engagement has rather swamped theirs, you may feel. Are you as angry as he is about them?"

"I'm not a bit angry," she said, catching Troy's eye and smiling at her. "I'm fond of Paul and want to talk to him."

"That's all very nice," said Dessy restlessly, "but Milly says it was Paul and Fenella who exploded the bomb."

"Oh, well," said Thomas comfortably, "I expect it would have gone off anyway. Did you know Mr. Rattisbon has been sent for to make a new Will? I suppose Papa'll tell us all about it at the

Birthday Dinner, tomorrow. Do you expect to be cut out this time, Dessy?"

"My dear," cried his sister, sinking magnificently onto the sofa and laying her arms along the back of it, "I've said so often exactly what I think of the Orrincourt that he can't possibly do anything else. I don't give a damn, Tommy. If Papa expects me to purr round congratulating them, he's never been more mistaken. I can't do it. It's been a hideous shock to me. It hurts me, *here*," she added, beating a white fist on her striking bosom. "All my respect, my love, my *ideal*—shattered." She flashed her eyes at her sister-in-law. "You think I exaggerate, Jen. You're lucky. You're not easily upset."

"Well," said Jenetta lightly, "I've yet to meet Miss Orrincourt."

"He's not your father," Dessy pointed out with emotion.

"No more he is," she agreed.

"T'uh!" said Dessy bitterly.

This conversation was interrupted by Fenella, who ran downstairs, flew across the hall and with an inarticulate cry flung herself into her mother's arms.

"Now then," said Jenetta softly, holding her daughter for a moment, "no high strikes."

"Mummy, you're not furious? Say you're not furious?"

"Do I look furious, you goat? Where's Paul?"

"In the library. Will you come? Mummy, you're Heaven. You're an angel."

"Do pipe down, darling. And what about Aunt Dessy and Uncle Thomas?"

Fenella turned to greet them. Thomas kissed her carefully. "I hope you'll be happy," he said. "It ought to be all right, really. I looked up genetics in a medical encyclopaedia after I read the announcement. The chap said the issue of first cousins was generally quite normal unless there was any marked insanity in the family which was common to both."

"Tommy!" said his sister. "Honestly, you *are!*"

"Well," said Jenetta Ancred, "with that assurance to fortify us, Fen, suppose you take me to see Paul."

They went off together. Millamant and Pauline came downstairs. "Such a nuisance," Millamant was saying. "I really don't quite know how to arrange it."

"If you're talking about rooms, Milly," said Desdemona, "I tell you flatly that unless something has been done about the rats I won't go into Bracegirdle."

"Well, but Dessy—" Pauline began.

"Has something been done about the rats?"

"Barker," said Millamant unhappily, "has lost the arsenic. I think he had it when he wanted to do Miss Orrincourt's rooms some time ago, but she objected to the use of poison, and after that the tin disappeared."

"Good God," said Thomas quietly.

"Pity he didn't put some in her tooth glass," said Desdemona vindictively.

"What about Ellen Terry?"

"I was putting Jenetta into Terry."

"Come into Bernhardt with me, Dess," Pauline suggested richly. "I'd love to have you. We can talk. Let's."

"The only thing against that," said Millamant, knitting her brows, "is that since Papa had all those large Jacobean pieces put in Bernhardt, there really isn't anywhere for a second bed. I can put one in my room, Desdemona. I wondered if you'd mind . . . Lady Bancroft, you know. Quite spacious and plenty of hanging room."

"Well, Milly, if it isn't turning you upside down."

"Not at all," said Millamant coldly.

"And you can still talk to me," said Pauline. "I'll be next door."

iii

On Friday night the weather broke and a deluge of rain beat down on the tortuous roofs of Ancreton. On Saturday morning Troy was awakened by a regular sequence of sharp percussion-like notes. *Ping, ping, ping*.

On going to her bath she nearly fell into a basin that had been placed on the landing. Into it fell a continuous progression of water drops from a spreading patch in the roof. All day it rained. At three o'clock it had grown too dark to paint in the Little Theatre but she had worked through the morning and having laid her last touch against the canvas, walked away from it and sat down. She felt that curious blankness which follows the completion of a painting. It was over. Her house was untenanted. It did not long remain so, for now, unchecked by the discipline of her work, Troy's thoughts were filled with the anticipation of reunion. "The day after to-morrow I shall be saying: 'To-morrow.' " The Ancreds and their machinations now seemed unreal. They were two-dimensional figures gesticulating on a ridiculously magnificent stage. This reaction was to colour all memories of her last two days at Ancreton, blurring their edges, lending a tinge of fantasy to commonplace events and causing her to doubt the integrity of her recollections when, in a little while, it would be imperative for her to recount them accurately.

She was to remember that Sir Henry was invisible all day, resting in preparation for his Birthday Dinner; that there was an air of anticipation in his enormous house, that his presents were set out in the library, a dark no man's land in the East Wing, and that the members of his family visited this Mecca frequently, eyeing each other's gifts with intense partiality. Troy herself in readiness for the Birthday had made a lively and diverting sketch of Panty which she had mounted and placed among the other gifts, wondering if, in view of Panty's fall from grace, it was too preposterously inept. The sketch was viewed with whole-hearted favour by Panty herself and her mother and by nobody else except Cedric, who chose to regard it as an acid comment on the child's character, which it was not.

Troy remembered afterwards how she had looked at the long dresses she had brought with her and decided that they were nothing like grand enough for the occasion. She remembered how the air of festivity had deepened as evening came and how Barker and his retinue of elderly maids were in a continuous state of controlled bustle. Most often, though still with a feeling of incredulity, would it seem to her that there had been a sense of impending climax in the house, an impression of something drawing to its close. At the time Troy said to herself: "It's because Rory's coming. It's because I've finished an intensive bit of work done at concert pitch." But in retrospect these answers sounded unconvincing and she wondered if the thoughts of one malevolent creature could have sent out a thin mist of apprehension.

Troy had cleaned her palette, shut her paint-box on ranks of depleted tubes, and washed her brushes for the last time at Ancreton. The portrait had been set up on the stage and framed in crimson velvet curtains that did their best to kill it. "If it was spring time," Troy thought, "I believe they'd have festooned it in garlands." The act drop had been lowered in front of the portrait and there it waited on a dark stage for the evening's ceremony. She couldn't glower at it. She couldn't walk in that deluge. She was unendurably restless. The dinner itself was at nine; she had three hours to fill in. Taking a book with her, she wandered uncertainly from one vast room to another and wherever she went there seemed to be two Ancreds in private conversation. Having disclosed Paul and Fenella tightly embraced in the study, disturbed Desdemona and Pauline hissing together in the drawing-room, and interrupted Millamant in what appeared to be an angry parley with Barker under the stairs, she made her way to a room next the library, known as the Great Boudoir (the Little Boudoir was upstairs). Unnerved by her previous encounters Troy paused outside the door and listened. All was still. She pushed open the door and was confronted by Cedric and Miss Orrincourt side-by-side on a sofa, doubled up in an ecstasy of silent laughter.

She was well into the room before they saw her. Their behaviour was extraordinary. They stared at her with their mouths open, the laughter drying out on their faces as if she had scotched it. Cedric turned an ugly red, Miss Orrincourt's eyes were as hard as blue glass marbles. She was the first to speak.

"Well for crying out loud," she said in a flat voice. "Look who's here."

"Dearest Mrs. Alleyn," said Cedric breathlessly. "Do come in. We've been having a dreadfully naughty giggle over everything. The Birthday, you know, and all the wheels within wheels and so on. Do join us. Or are you too grand and upright? Dear me, that sounds as if you were a piano, doesn't it?"

"It's all right," said Troy. "I won't come in, thank you; I'm on my way upstairs."

She went out, closing the door on their silence.

In the hall she found a completely strange elderly gentleman reading a newspaper before the fire. He wore London clothes, an old-fashioned wing collar and a narrow black tie. His face was thin and his hands blue-veined and knotty. When he saw Troy he dropped his newspaper, snatched off his pince-nez, and ejaculating: "M-m-m-mah!" rose nimbly to his feet.

"Are you waiting to see somebody?" Troy asked.

"Thank-yer, thank-yer, no thank-yer," said the elderly gentleman rapidly. "Made myself known. Haven't had the pleasure—Introduce myself. M-mah. Rattisbon."

"Oh, yes, of course," said Troy. "I knew you were coming. How do you do?" she introduced herself.

Mr. Rattisbon vibrated the tip of his tongue, between his lips and wrung his hands. "How d'do," he gabbled. "Delighted. Take it, fellow-guests. If I may so designate myself. Professional visit."

"So's mine," said Troy, picking the sense out of this collection of phrases. "I've been doing a job here."

He glanced at the painting smock she had not yet removed. "Surely," he clattered, "Mrs. Roderick Alleyn, nee Troy?"

"That's it."

"Pleasure of your husband's acquaintance," Mr. Rattisbon explained. "Professional association. Twice. Admirable."

"Really?" said Troy, at once delighted. "You know Roderick? Do let's sit down."

Mr. Rattisbon sucked in his breath and made a crowing sound. They sat before the fire. He crossed his knees and joined his gnarled fingers. "He's a drawing by Cruikshank," Troy thought. She began to talk to him about Alleyn and he listened exactly as if she were making a series of statements which he would presently require his clerk to come in and witness. Troy was to remember vividly this quiet encounter and how in the middle of her recital she broke off apologetically, to say: "But I don't know why I should bore you with these stories about Roderick."

"Bore?" he said. "On the contrary. Entirely so. May I add, strictly in camera, that I—ah—had contemplated this call with some misgiving as—ah—a not altogether propitious necessity. I find myself, unexpectedly, received and most charmingly so, by a lady for whose remarkable talents I have long entertained the highest regard. M-m-mah!" Mr. Rattisbon added, dipping like a sparrow towards Troy, "Entirely so."

At this juncture Pauline and Desdemona appeared in the hall and bore down rapidly upon Mr. Rattisbon.

"We are so sorry," Pauline began. "Leaving you so long. Papa's only just been told—a little upset. The great day, of course. He will be ready for you in a few minutes, dear Mr. Rattisbon. Until then Dessy and I would be so glad if you—we feel we'd like to—"

Troy was already on her way out. They were waiting for her to get out of earshot.

She heard Desdemona's voice: "Just a tiny talk, Mr. Rattisbon. Just to warn you," and Mr. Rattisbon suddenly very dry and brittle: "If you desire it, certainly."

"But," thought Troy, plodding along the passage, "they won't get much change out of Mr. Rattisbon."

iv

"It's the big scene from a film script," thought Troy looking down the table, "and I'm the bit-part lady." The analogy was unavoidable. How often had one not seen Mr. C. Aubrey Smith at the head of such a table? Where else but on the screen was such opulence to be found; where else such a welter of flowers, such sumptuously Edwardian epergnes, or such incredibly appropriate conversation? Never out of a film studio had characters been so well-typed. Even the neighbouring squire and the parson, the one lean and monocled, the other rubicund and sleek, who apparently were annual fixtures for the event; even they were carefully selected cameo parts, too like themselves to be credible. And Mr. Rattisbon? The absolute in family solicitors. As for the Ancreds themselves, to glance at them or to hear their carefully modulated laughter, their beautifully articulated small-talk, was to realize at once that this was an all-star vehicle. Troy began to make up titles. “Homage to Sir Henry.” “The Astonishing Ancreds.”

“Going quite nicely, so far, don’t you consider?” said Thomas at her left elbow. She had forgotten Thomas, although he had taken her in. Cedric, on her right hand, had directed at her and at his partner, Desdemona, a number of rather spasmodic and intensely artificial remarks, all of which sounded as if they were designed for the ears of his grandfather. Thomas, presumably, had been silent until now.

“Very nicely,” Troy agreed hurriedly.

“I mean,” Thomas continued, lowering his voice, “you wouldn’t think, if you didn’t know, how terrified everybody is about the Will, would you? Everybody except me, that is, and perhaps Cedric.”

“Ssh!” said Troy. “No, you wouldn’t.”

“It’s because we’re putting on the great Family Act, you know. It’s the same on the stage. People that hate each other’s guts make love like angels. You’d be surprised, I daresay. Outsiders think it very queer. Well,” Thomas continued, laying down his soup spoon and gazing mildly at her. “What, after all, *do* you think of Ancreton?”

“I’ve found it absorbing.”

“I’m so glad. You’ve come in for quite a set-piece, haven’t you? All the intrigues and fights. Do you know what will happen after dinner?” And without waiting for her reply he told her. “Papa will propose the King’s health and then I shall propose Papa’s. I’m the eldest son present so I shall have to, but it’s a pity. Claude would be much better. Last year Panty was brought in to do it. I coached her in the ‘business’ and she managed very nicely. Papa cried. This year, because of ringworm and the practical jokes, she hasn’t been invited. Gracious,” Thomas continued, as Troy helped herself from a dish that had appeared over her shoulder, “that’s never New Zealand crayfish! I thought Millamant had decided against it. Has Papa noticed? There’ll be trouble if he has.”

Thomas was right. Sir Henry, when offered this dish, glanced truculently at his daughter-in-law and helped himself to it. An instant silence fell upon the table and Troy, who was opposite Millamant, saw her make a helpless deprecating grimace at Pauline who, from the foot of the table, responded by raising her eyebrows.

"He insisted," Millamant whispered to Paul on her left hand.

"What?" asked Sir Henry loudly.

"Nothing, Papa," said Millamant.

"They call this," said Sir Henry, addressing himself to Mr. Rattisbon, "rock lobster. No more like a lobster than my foot. It's some antipodean shell-fish."

Furtively watched by his family he took a large mouthful and at the same time pointed to his glass and added: "One must drink something with it. I shall break my rule, Barker. Champagne."

Barker, with his lips very slightly pursed, filled the glass.

"That's a big boy," said Miss Orrincourt approvingly. The Ancreds, after a frightened second or two, burst simultaneously into feverish conversation.

"There," said Thomas with an air of sober triumph. "What did I tell you? Champagne and hot crayfish. We shall hear more of this, you may depend upon it."

"Do be careful," Troy murmured nervously, and then seeing that Sir Henry was in gallant conversation with Jenetta on his left, she added cautiously: "Is it so very bad for him?"

"I promise you," said Thomas, "disastrous. I don't think it tastes very nice anyway," he continued after a pause. "What do you think?" Troy had already come to this conclusion. The crayfish, she decided, was dubious.

"Hide it under your toast," said Thomas. "I'm going to. It's the Birthday turkey next, from the home-farm. We can fill up on that, can't we?"

But Sir Henry, Troy noticed, ate all his crayfish.

Apart from this incident the dinner continued in the same elevated key up to the moment when Sir Henry, with the air of a Field Marshal in Glorious Technicolour, rose and proposed the King.

A few minutes later Thomas, coughing modestly, embarked upon his speech.

"Well, Papa," said Thomas, "I expect you know what I'm going to say, because after all this is your Birthday Dinner and we all know it's a great occasion and how splendid it is for us to be here again as usual in spite of everything. Except Claude, of course, which is a pity because he would think of a lot of new things to say, and I can't." At this point a slight breeze of discomfort seemed to stir among the Ancreds. "So I shall only say," Thomas battled on, "how proud we are to be gathered here, remembering your past achievements and wishing you many more Birthday Dinners in the time that is to come. Yes," said Thomas, after a thoughtful pause, "that's all, I think. Oh! I almost forgot. We all, of course, hope that you will be very happy in your married life. I shall now ask everybody to drink Papa's health, please."

The guests, evidently accustomed to a very much longer speech and taken unawares by the rapidity of Thomas's peroration, hurriedly got to their feet.

"Papa," said Thomas.

"Papa," echoed Jenetta, Millamant, Pauline and Desdemona.

"Grandpapa," murmured Fenella, Cedric and Paul.

"Sir Henry," said the Rector loudly, followed by Mr. Rattisbon, the Squire and Troy.

"Noddy!" said Miss Orrincourt, shrilly. "Cheers. Oodles of juice in your tank."

Sir Henry received all this in the traditional manner. He fingered his glass, stared deeply at his plate, glanced up at Thomas, and, towards the end, raised his hand deprecatingly and let it fall. There was evidence of intense but restrained feeling. When they had all settled down he rose to reply. Troy had steeled herself for resounding periods and a great display of rhetoric. She was not prepared, in view of the current family atmosphere, for touching simplicity and poignant emotion. These, however, were the characteristics of Sir Henry's speech. It was also intensely manly. He had, he said, taken a good many calls in the course of his life as a busker and made a good many little speeches of gratitude to a good many audiences. But moving as some of these occasions had been, there was no audience as near and dear to an old fellow as his own kith and kin and his few tried and proven friends. He and his dear old Tommy were alike in this: they had few words in which to express their dearest thoughts. Perhaps they were none of the worse for it. (Pauline, Desdemona and the Rector made sounds of fervent acquiescence.) Sir Henry paused and glanced first at Paul and then at Fenella. He had intended, he said, to keep for this occasion, the announcement of the happy change he now contemplated. But domestic events had, should he say, a little forced his hand and they were now all aware of his good fortune. (Apparently the Squire and Rector were not aware of it as they had looked exceedingly startled at the end of

Thomas's toast.) There was, however, one little ceremony to be observed.

He took a small morocco box from his pocket, opened it, extracted a dazzling ring and, raising Miss Orrincourt, placed it on her engagement finger and kissed the finger. Miss Orrincourt responded by casting one practised glance at the ring and embracing him with the liveliest enthusiasm. His hearers broke into agitated applause, under cover of which Cedric muttered: "That's the Ranee's Solitaire reset, I swear it is. Stay me with flagons, playmates."

Sir Henry, with some firmness, reseated his fiancee and resumed his speech. It was, he said, a tradition in his family, that the head of it should be twice married. The Sieur d'Ancred—he rambled on genealogically for some time. Troy felt embarrassment give place to boredom. Her attention was caught, however, by a new development. It had also been the custom, Sir Henry was saying, on these occasions, for the fortunate Ancred to reveal to his family the manner in which he had set his house in order. (Mr. Rattisbon raised his eyebrows very high and made a little quavering noise in his throat.) Such frankness was perhaps out of fashion nowadays but it had an appropriate Shakespearian precedent. King Lear—but glancing at his agonized daughters Sir Henry did not pursue the analogy. He said that he proposed to uphold this traditional frankness. "I have to-day," hc said, "cxccutcd—my old friend Rattisbon will correct me if this is not the term." ("M-m-mah!" said Mr. Rattisbon confusedly.) "Thank you—executed my Will. It is a simple little document, conceived in the spirit that actuated my ancestor the Sieur d'Ancred when—" A fretful sigh eddied round the table. This time, however, Sir Henry's excursion into antiquity was comparatively brief. Clearing his throat and speaking on a note so solemn that it had an almost ecclesiastical timbre, he fired point-blank and gave them a resume of his Will.

Troy's major concern was to avoid the eyes of everybody else seated at that table. To this end she stared zealously at a detail of the epergne immediately in front of her. For the rest of her life, any mention of Sir Henry Ancred's Last Will and Testament will immediately call up for her the image of a fat silver cupid who, in a pose at once energetic and insouciant, lunged out from a central globe to which he was affixed only by his great toe, and, curving his right arm, supported on the extreme tip of his first finger a cornucopia three times his own size, dripping with orchids.

Sir Henry was speaking of legacies. Five thousand pounds to

his devoted daughter-in-law Millamant, five thousand pounds to his ewe lamb Desdemona. To his doctor and his servants, to the hunt club, to the Church, there were grand seignorial legacies. Her attention wandered, and was again arrested by a comparison he seemed to be making between himself and some pentateuchal patriarch. "Into three parts. The residue divided into three parts." This, then, was the climax. To his bride-to-be, to Thomas, and to Cedric, he would leave, severally, a life interest in a third of the residue of his estate. The capital of his fund to be held in trust and ultimately devoted to the preservation and endowment of Ancreton as a historical museum of drama to be known as The Henry Ancred Memorial.

"Tra-hippit!" Cedric murmured at her elbow. "Honestly, I exult. It might have been so much worse."

Sir Henry was now making a brief summary of the rest of the field. His son Claude, he thanked God, turning slightly towards Jenetta, had inherited a sufficient portion from his maternal grandmother and was therefore able through this and through his own talents to make provision for his wife and (he momentarily eyed Fenella), daughter. His daughter Pauline (Troy heard her make an incoherent noise) had been suitably endowed at the time of her marriage and generously provided for by her late husband. She had her own ideas in the bringing up of her children and was able to carry them out. "Which," Cedric muttered with relish, "is a particularly dirty crack at Paul and Panty, don't you feel?"

"Ssh!" said Desdemona on the other side of him.

Sir Henry drifted into a somewhat vague and ambiguous diatribe on the virtues of family unity and the impossibility, however great the temptation, of ever entirely forgetting them. For the last time her attention wandered and was jerked sharply back by the sound of her own name: "Mrs. Agatha Troy Alleyn . . . her dramatic and, if I as the subject may so call it, magnificent canvas which you are presently to see . . ."

Troy, greatly startled, learned that the portrait was to be left to the Nation.

V

"It's not the money, Milly. It's not the money, Dessy," wailed Pauline in the drawing-room. "I don't mind about the money, Jen.

It's the cruel *cruel* wound to my love. That's what hurts me, girls. That's what hurts."

"If I were you," said Millamant with her laugh, "I think I should feel a bit hipped about the money, too."

Miss Orrincourt, according to her custom, had gone away to do her face. The ladies were divided into two parties, the "haves" and the "have-nots." Dessy, a not altogether delighted legatee, had a foot in each camp. "It's damn mean," she said, "but after the things I've said about the Orrincourt I suppose I'm lucky to get anything. What do you think of her, Jen?"

"I suppose," said Jenetta Ancred thoughtfully, "she *is* real, isn't she? I mean, I catch myself wondering, quite seriously, if she could be somebody who has dressed up and is putting on the language and everything as a colossal practical joke. I didn't think people ever were so shatteringly true to type. But she's much too lovely, of course, to be a leg-pull."

"Lovely!" cried Desdemona. "Jen! Straight out of the third row of the chorus and appallingly common at that."

"I daresay, but they *are* generally rather lovely in the chorus nowadays, aren't they, Fenella?"

Fenella had withdrawn entirely from the discussion. Now, when they all turned to her, she faced them rigidly, two bright red spots burning over her cheek bones.

"I want to say," she began in a loud shaky voice, "that I'm very sorry. Aunt Pauline and Mummy, that because of Paul and me, you've been treated so disgracefully. We don't mind for ourselves. We'd neither of us, after the things he's said, touch a penny of his money. But we are sorry about you and Panty."

"Well, darling," said her mother, putting an arm through hers, "that's very handsome of you and Paul, but don't let's have any more speeches, shall we?"

"Yes, but Mummy—"

"Your two families are very anxious for both of you to be happy. It's like that, isn't it, Pauline?"

"Well, Jenetta, that, of course goes without saying, but—"

"There you are, Fen," said Jenetta. "It goes. And without saying, which is such a blessing."

Pauline, looking extremely vexed, retired into a corner with Desdemona.

Jenetta offered Troy a cigarette. "I suppose," she muttered in a friendly manner, "that was not a very good remark for me to make but, to tell you the truth, I take a pretty gloomy view of all these naked wounds. Mr. Rattisbon tells me your husband's coming back. What fun for you."

"Yes," said Troy, "it's all of that."

"Does everything else seem vague and two-dimensional? It would to me."

"It does to me, too. I find it very muddling."

"Of course the Ancreds are on the two-dimensional side anyway, if it comes to that. Especially my father-in-law. Did it make painting him easier or more difficult?"

Before Troy could answer this entertaining question Cedric, flushed and smirking, opened the door and stood against it in a romantic attitude, waving his handkerchief.

"Darlings," he said. "*Allez-houp!* The great moment. I am to bid you to the Little Theatre. Dearest Mrs. Alleyn, you and the Old Person should be jointly feted. A cloud of little doves with gilded wings should be lowered by an ingenious device from the flies and, with pretty gestures, crown you with laurels. Uncle Thomas could have arranged it. I should so adore to see Panty as an aerial coryphee. Will you all come?"

They found the men assembled in the Little Theatre. It was brilliantly lit and had an air of hopefully waiting for a much larger audience. Soft music rumbled synthetically behind the front curtain which (an inevitable detail) was emblazoned with the arms of Ancred. Troy found herself suddenly projected into a star role. Sir Henry led her up the aisle to a seat beside himself. The rest of the party settled behind them. Cedric, with a kind of consequential flutter, hurried backstage.

Sir Henry was smoking a cigar. When he inclined gallantly towards Troy she perceived that he had taken brandy. This circumstance was accompanied by a formidable internal rumbling.

"I shall," he murmured gustily, "just say a few words."

They were actually few but as usual they were intensely embarrassing. Her reluctance to undertake the portrait was playfully outlined. His own pleasure in the sittings was remorselessly sketched. Some rather naive quotations on art from *Timon of Athens* were introduced and then: "But I must not tantalize my audience any longer," said Sir Henry richly. "Curtain, my boy. Curtain!"

The house lights went down. The front drop slid upwards. Simultaneously four powerful flood-lamps poured down their beams from the flies. The scarlet tabs were drawn apart and there, in a blaze of highly unsuitable light, the portrait was revealed.

Above the sombre head and flying against a clear patch of night sky, somebody had painted an emerald green cow with vermilion wings. It was in the act of secreting an object that might or might not have been a black bomb.

CHAPTER EIGHT

Big Exit

i

THIS TIME Troy felt only a momentary sensation of panic. That particular area of background was hard-dry and almost at once she remembered the circumstance. She did, however, feel overwhelmingly irritated. Above the automatic burst of applause that greeted the unveiling and only petered out when the detail of the flying cow was observed, she heard her own voice saying loudly: "No, really, this is too much."

At the same moment Cedric, who had evidently operated the curtains, stuck his head round the proscenium, stared blindly into the front of the house, turned, saw the portrait, clapped his hand over his mouth and ejaculated: "Oh, God! Oh Dynamite!"

"Darling!" said his mother from the back row. "Ceddie, *dear!* What's the matter?"

Sir Henry, on Troy's left, breathed stertorously and contrived to let out a sort of hoarse roaring noise.

"It's all right," said Troy. "Please don't say anything. Wait."

She strode furiously down the aisle and up the steps. Sacrificing her best evening handkerchief she reduced the cow to a green smear. "I think there's a bottle of turpentine somewhere," she said loudly. "Please give it to me."

Paul ran up with it, offering his own handkerchief. Cedric flew out with a handful of rags. The blemish was removed. Meantime the auditorium rang with Miss Orrincourt's hysterical laughter and buzzed with the sound of bewildered Ancreds. Troy threw the handkerchief and rags into the wings and, with hot cheeks, returned to her seat. "I wouldn't have been so cross," she thought grimly, "if the damn thing hadn't looked funny."

"I *demand*," Sir Henry was shouting. "I *demand* to know the author of this outrage."

He was answered by a minor uproar topped by Pauline: "It was not *Panty*. I tell you, Millamant, once and for all, that Panty is in bed and has been there since five o'clock. Papa, I protest. It was *not* Panty."

"Nuts!" said Miss Orrincourt. "She's been painting green cows for days. I've seen them. Come off it, dear."

"Papa, I give you my solemn word—"

"Mother, wait a minute—"

"I shall not wait a second. Papa. I have reason to believe."

"Look here, *do* wait." Troy shouted and at once they were silent. "It's gone," she said. "No harm's been done. But there's one thing I must tell you. Just before dinner I came in here. I was worrying about the red curtains. I thought they might touch the canvas where it's still wet. It was all right then. If Panty's been in bed and is known to have been there since ten to nine, she didn't do it."

Pauline instantly began to babble. "Thank you, thank you, Mrs. Alleyn. You hear that, Papa. Send for Miss Able. I insist that Miss Able be sent for. My child shall be vindicated."

"I'll go and ask Caroline," said Thomas unexpectedly. "One doesn't send for Caroline, you know. I'll go and ask."

He went out. The Ancreds were silent. Suddenly Millamant remarked: "I thought perhaps it was just the modern style. What do they call it? Surrealism?"

"Milly!" screamed her son.

Jenetta Ancred said: "What particular symbolism, Milly, do you read into the introduction of a flying cow behaving like a rude seagull over Papa's head?"

"You never know," Millamant said, "in these days," and laughed uncertainly.

"Papa," said Desdemona, who had been bending over him, "is dreadfully upset. Papa, dearest, may I suggest—"

"I'm going to bed," said Sir Henry. "I am indeed upset. I am unwell. I am going to bed."

They all rose. He checked them with a gesture. "I am going alone," he said. "To bed."

Cedric ran to the door. Sir Henry, without a backward glance, walked down the aisle, a shadowy figure looking larger than life against the glowing stage, and passed manificently from the theatre.

The Ancreds at once began to chatter. Troy felt that she couldn't endure the inevitable revival of Panty's former misdemeanours, Pauline's indignant denials, Cedric's giggles, Millamant's stolid recital of the obvious. She was profoundly relieved when Thomas, slightly ruffled, returned with Caroline Able.

"I've asked Caroline to come," he said, "because I thought you mightn't exactly believe me. Panty's been in the sick-bay with all the other ringworms. Dr. Withers wanted them to be kept under observation because of the medicine he's given them, so Caroline has been sitting there reading, since half-past seven. So Panty, you see, didn't do it."

"Certainly, she didn't do it," said Miss Able brightly. "How could she? It's quite impossible."

"So you see," Thomas added mildly.

ii

Troy stayed behind in the Little Theatre with Paul and Fenella. Paul switched on the working lights and together they examined Troy's painting gear, which had been stacked away behind the wings.

The paint box had been opened. A dollop of emerald oxide of chromium and one of ivory black had been squeezed out on the protective under-lid that separated the paints from a compartment designed to hold sketching boards. A large brush had been used and had been dipped first in the green and then in the black.

"You know," said Paul, "this brush ought to have finger-prints on it." He looked rather shyly at Troy. "Oughtn't it?" he added.

"Well, I suppose Roderick would say so," she agreed.

"I mean, if it has and if we could get everybody's to compare, that would be pretty conclusive, wouldn't it? What's more it'd be damned interesting."

"Yes, but I've a notion finger-prints are not as easy as all that."

"I know. The hand would move about and so on. But look. There *is* some green paint smeared up the handle. I've read about it. Suppose we asked them to let us take their prints. They couldn't very well refuse."

"Oh Paul, *let's*," cried Fenella.

"What do you think, Mrs. Alleyn?"

"My dear chap, you mustn't imagine I know anything about it. But I agree it would be interesting. I *do* know more or less how they take official prints."

"I've read it up quite a bit," said Paul. "I say. Suppose we did get them to do it and suppose we kept the brush and the box intact—well—well, would—do you think—"

"I'd show them to him like a shot," said Troy.

"I say, that's perfectly splendid," said Paul. "Look here, I'll damn well put it to them in the morning. It ought to be cleared up. It's all bloody rum, the whole show, isn't it? What d'you say, Mrs. Alleyn?"

"I'm on," said Troy.

"Glory!" said Fenella. "So'm I. Let's."

"O.K.," said Paul, gingerly wrapping the brush in rags. "We'll lock up the brush and box."

"I'll take them up with me."

"Will you? That's grand."

They locked the portrait in the property room, and said good-night conspiratorially. Troy felt she could not face another session with the Ancreds, and sending her excuses, went upstairs to her room.

She could not sleep. Outside, in the night, rain drove solidly against the wall of her tower. The wind seemed to have got into the chimney and be trying uneasily to find its way out again. A bucket had replaced the basin on the landing and a maddening and irregular progression of taps compelled her attention and played like castanets on her nerves. Only one more night here, she thought, and then the comfort of familiar things in the London flat and the sharing of them with her husband. Illogically, she felt a kind of regret for the tower room and in this mood fell to revising, in their order, the eccentricities of her days and nights at Ancreton. The paint on the bannister. The spectacles on the portrait. The legend in grease-paint on Sir Henry's looking-glass. The incident of the inflated bladder. The flying cow.

If Panty was not the authoress of these inane facetiae, who was? If one person only was responsible for them all, then Panty was exonerated. But might not Panty have instituted them with the smearing of paint on the bannister and somebody else have carried them on? Undoubtedly Panty's legend and past record included many such antics. Troy wished that she knew something of modern views on child psychology. Was such behaviour characteristic of a child who wished to become a dominant figure and who felt herself to be obstructed and repressed? But Troy was positive that Panty had spoken the truth when she denied having any hand in the tricks with paint. And unless Miss Able had told a lie Panty, quite definitely, had not been the authoress of the flying cow, though she undoubtedly had a predilection for cows and bombs. Troy turned uneasily in her bed and fancied that beyond the sound of wind and rain she heard the voice of the Great Clock. Was there any significance in the fact that in each instance the additions to her canvas had been made on a dry area and so had done no harm? Which of the adults in the house would realize this? Cedric. Cedric painted, though probably in water-colours. She fancied his aesthetic fervour was, in its antic way, authentic. He would, she thought, instinctively recoil from this particular kind of vandalism. But suppose he knew that no harm would be done? And where was a motive for Cedric? He appeared to have a kind of liking for her; why should he disfigure her work? Bleakly Troy surveyed the rest of the field and one by one dismissed them until she came to Miss Orrincourt.

The robust vulgarity of these goings-on was not out of character if Miss Orrincourt was considered. Was it, Troy wondered with an uneasy grin, remotely possible that Miss Orrincourt resented the somewhat florid attentions Sir Henry had lavished upon his guest? Could she have imagined that the sittings had been made occasions for even more marked advances, more ardent pattings of the hand, closer pilotings by the elbow? "Crikey!" Troy muttered, writhing uncomfortably, "*what* an idea to get in the middle of the night!" No, it was too far-fetched. Perhaps one of the elderly maids had lost her wits and taken to this nonsense. "Or Barker," thought the now sleepy Troy. In the drumming of rain and wind about her room she began to hear fantastical things. Presently she dreamed of flying bombs that came out of the night, converging on her tower. When they were almost upon her, they changed into green cows that winked broadly and with a Cedric-like flirt dropped soft bombs, at the same time saying very distinctly: "Plop, plop, *dearest* Mrs. Alleyn."

"Mrs. Alleyn. Dearest Mrs. Alleyn, do please wake up."

Troy opened her eyes. Fenella, fully dressed, stood at her bedside. In the thin light of dawn her face looked cold and very white. Her hands opened and shut aimlessly. The corners of her mouth turned down like those of a child about to cry. "What now, for pity's sake?" cried Troy.

"I thought I'd better come and tell you. Nobody else would. They're all frantic. Paul can't leave his mother, and Mummy's trying to stop Aunt Dessy having hysterics. I feel so ghastly. I had to talk to someone."

"But why? What is it? What's happened?"

"Grandfather. When Barker went in with his tea. He found him. Lying there. Dead."

iii

There is no more wretched lot than that of the comparative stranger in a house of grief. The sense of loneliness, the feeling that one constantly trespasses on other people's sorrow, that they would thankfully be rid of one; all these circumstances reduce the unwilling intruder to a condition of perpetual apology that must remain unexpressed. If there is nothing useful to be done this misery is the more acute, and Troy was not altogether sorry that Fenella seemed to find some comfort in staying with her. She hurriedly made a fire on top of last night's embers, set Fenella, who shivered like a puppy, to blow it up while she herself bathed and dressed, and, when at last the child broke down, listened to a confused recital which harked back continually to the break between herself and her grandfather. "It's so *awful* that Paul and I should have made him miserable. We'll never be able to forgive ourselves, never," Fenella sobbed.

"Now, look here," said Troy, "that just doesn't make sense. You and Paul did what you had every right to do."

"But we did it brutally. You can't say we didn't. We grieved him frightfully. He said so."

Sir Henry had said so a great many times and with extreme emphasis. It was impossible to suggest that anger rather than grief had moved him. Troy went off on another tack. "He seemed to have got over it," she said.

"Last night!" Fenella wailed. "When I think of what we said about him last night. In the drawing-room after you'd gone up. Everybody except Mummy and Paul. Aunt Milly said he'd probably have an attack and I said I didn't care if it was fatal. Actually! And he *did* feel it. He cut Aunt Pauline and Mummy and me and Paul out of his Will because of our engagement and the way we announced it. So he did feel it deeply."

"The Will," thought Troy. "Good Heavens, yes. The Will!" She said: "He was an old man, Fenella. I don't think, do you, that the future was exactly propitious? Isn't it perhaps not so very bad that he should go now when everything seemed to him to be perfectly arranged. He'd had his splendid party."

"And look how it ended."

"Oh dear!" said Troy. "That. Well, yes."

"And it was probably the party that killed him," Fenella continued. "That hot crayfish. It's what everybody thinks. Dr. Withers had warned him. And nobody was there. He just went up to his room and died."

"Has Dr. Withers—"

"Yes. He's been. Barker got Aunt Milly and she rang up. He says it was a severe attack of gastroenteritis. He says it—it happened—it must have been—soon after he went up to bed. It's so awful when you think of all the frightful things we were saying about him, down there in the drawing-room. All of us except Cedric and he was simply gloating over us. Little beast, he's still gloating, if it comes to that."

The gong rumbled distantly. "You go down to breakfast," said Fenella. "I can't face it."

"That won't do at all. You can at least choke down some coffee."

Fenella took Troy's arm in a nervous grip. "I think I like you so much," she said, "because you're so unlike all of us. All right, I'll come."

The Ancreds in sorrow were a formidable assembly. Pauline, Desdemona and Millamant, who were already in the dining-room, had all found black dresses to wear and Troy was suddenly conscious that she had without thinking pulled on a scarlet sweater. She uttered those phrases of sympathy that are always inadequate. Desdemona silently gripped her hand and turned aside. Pauline dumbfounded her by bursting into tears and giving her an impulsive kiss. And it was strange to find an unsmiling and pallid Millamant. Thomas came in looking bewildered. "Good morning," he said to Troy. "Isn't it awful? I really can't realize it a bit, you know. Everybody else seems to realize it. They're all crying and everything, but I don't. Poor Papa." He looked at his sisters. "You're not eating anything," he said. "What can I get you, Pauline?"

Pauline said: "Oh Thomas!" and made an eloquent gesture. "I suppose," Thomas continued, "that later on, I shan't want to eat anything, but at the moment I am hungry."

He sat down beside Troy. "It's lucky you finished the portrait, isn't it?" he said. "Poor Papa!"

"*Tommy!*" breathed his sister.

"Well, but it is," he insisted gently. "Papa would have been pleased too."

Paul came in and, a moment later, Jenetta Ancred, wearing tweeds. It was a relief to Troy that, like Thomas, neither of them spoke in special voices.

Presently Millamant began to speak of the manner in which Barker had discovered Sir Henry. At eight o'clock, it appeared, he had gone in as usual with Sir Henry's cup of milk and water. As he approached the room he heard the cat Carabbas wailing inside, and when he opened the door it darted out and fled down the passage. Barker supposed that Sir Henry had forgotten to let his cat out and wondered that Carabbas had not waked him.

He entered the room. It was still very dark. Barker was short-sighted, but he could make out the figure lying across the bed. He turned on the lights and after one horrified glance, rushed down the corridor and beat on the door of Millamant's room. When she and Pauline answered together, he kept his head, remained outside, and, in an agitated whisper, asked Millamant if he might speak to her. She put on her dressing-gown and went out into the cold passage.

"And I knew," Pauline interjected at this point. "Something told me. I knew at once that something had happened."

"Naturally," said Millamant. "Barker doesn't go on like that every morning."

"I knew it was The Great Visitor," Pauline insisted firmly. "I knew."

Millamant had gone with Barker to the room. She sent Barker to rouse Thomas and herself telephoned Dr. Withers. He was out but finally arrived in about an hour. It had been, he said, a severe attack of gastroenteritis probably brought on by his indiscretions at dinner. Sir Henry's heart had been unable to survive the attack and he had collapsed and died.

"What I can't understand," said Pauline, "is why he didn't ring. He always rang if he felt ill in the night. There was a special bell in the corridor, Dessy. The cord hung beside his bed."

"He tried," said Thomas. "He must have grasped at it across the bed, we think, and fallen. It had come away from the cord. And I don't think, after all, I want very much to eat."

iv

Troy spent most of that last day between her room and the Little Theatre, lingering out her packing, which in any case was considerable. Carabbas, the cat, elected to spend the day in her room. Remembering where he had spent the night she felt a little shudder at the touch of his fur. But they had become friendly and after a time she was glad of his company. At first he watched her with some interest, occasionally sitting on such garments as she had laid out on the bed and floor. When she removed him, he purred briefly and at last, with a faint mew, touched her hand with his nose. It was hot. She noticed that his fur was staring. Was he, she wondered, actually distressed by the loss of his master? He grew restless and she opened the door. After a fixed look at her he went out, his tail drooping. She thought she heard him cry again on the stairs. She returned uneasily to her packing, broke off from time to time to wander restlessly about the room or stare out of her tower window at the rain-laced landscape. She came across a sketch-book and found herself absently making drawings of the Ancreds. Half an hour went past and there they all were, like antics on the page, for her to show her husband. Guiltily she completed her packing.

Thomas had undertaken to send by rail such heavy baggage as the Yard car could not accommodate.

She was oppressed by the sensation of unreality. She felt more strongly than ever that she was held in suspension between two phases of experience. She was out of touch, not only with her surroundings, but with herself. While her hands folded and bestowed garment after garment, her thoughts ranged aimlessly between the events of the past twenty-four hours and those that were to come. "It is I," she thought in dismay, "who will resemble the traveller who can speak of nothing but his fellow-passengers and the little events of his voyage, and it is Rory who will listen unhappily to anecdotes of these Ancreds whom he is never likely to meet."

Lunch seemed to be an uncanny extension of breakfast. There again were the Ancreds still using their special voices, still expressing so eloquently that sorrow whose authenticity Troy was not quite willing to discredit. She was half-aware of their conversation, catching only desultory pieces of information: Mr. Rattisbon had been transferred to the rectory. Thomas had been dictating obituary notices over the telephone. The funeral would be held on Tuesday. The voices murmured on. Momentarily, she was consulted, drawn in. A weekly paper had got wind of the portrait ("Nigel Bathgate," thought Troy), and would like to send down a photographer. She made suitable rejoinders and suggestions. Cedric, whose manner was fretfully subdued, brightened a little over this subject and then, unaccountably, reverted to a kind of nervous acquiescence. The conversation drifted towards Miss Orrincourt, who had expressed her inability to make a public appearance, and was having her meals in her rooms. "I saw her breakfast tray," said Millamant with a ghost of her usual laugh. "Her appetite doesn't seem to have suffered."

"T'uh!" said the Ancreds softly.

"Are we to be told," Pauline asked, "how long she proposes to—"

"I should imagine," said Desdemona, "no longer than it takes for the Will to become effective."

"Well, but I mean to say," Cedric began, and they all turned their heads towards him. "If it's not *too* inappropriate and premature, one wonders rather, or doesn't one, if darling Sonia is in *quite* the same position *unmarried* as she would have been as the Old—as dearest Grandpapa's widow? Or not?"

An attentive stillness fell upon the table. It was broken by Thomas: "Yes, well, of course," he said looking blandly about him, "won't that depend on how the Will is made out? Whether her share is left to 'Sonia Orrincourt,' you know, or to 'my wife, Sonia' and all that."

Pauline and Desdemona stared for a moment at Thomas. Cedric smoothed his hair with two unsteady fingers. Fenella and Paul looked stolidly at their plates. Millamant, with a muffled attempt at easiness, said: "There's no need to jump *that* fence, surely, till we meet it." Pauline and Desdemona exchanged glances. Millamant had used the sacred "we."

"I think it's pretty ghastly," said Fenella abruptly, "to begin talking about Grandfather's Will when he's up there—lying there—" She broke off, biting her lip. Troy saw Paul reach for her hand. Jenetta Ancred, who had been silent throughout luncheon, gave her daughter a smile, half-deprecating, half-anxious. "How she dislikes it," Troy thought, "when Fenella behaves like an Ancred."

"Darling Fen," Cedric murmured, "you of course can afford to be grand and virtuous over the Will. I mean, you are so definitely *out* of that party, aren't you?"

"That's a pretty offensive remark, Cedric," said Paul.

"Has everyone finished?" asked Pauline in a hurry, "if so, Mrs. Alleyn, shall we—"

Troy excused herself from the post-prandial gathering in the drawing-room.

As she entered the hall a car drew up outside. Barker, who seemed to have been expecting it, was already in the outer porch. He admitted three pale men, dressed in London clothes of a particular black character. They wore wide black ties. Two of them carried black cases. The third, glancing at Troy, spoke in a muted and inaudible voice.

"This way, if you please," said Barker, ushering them into a small waiting-room across the hall. "I will inform Sir Cedric."

After the newcomers had been shut away and Barker had gone on his errand, Troy stood digesting the official recognition of Cedric's ascendancy. Her glance strayed to a table where, as she had observed, the senior of the three men, with a practised modesty, suggestive, almost, of sleight-of-hand, had dropped or slid a card. He had, indeed, given it a little push with his forefinger so that it lay, partly concealed, under a book which Troy herself had brought from the library to solace her afternoon. The card was engraved in a type slightly heavier and more black than that of a normal visiting card:

MORTIMER, SON & LOAME
Undertakers . . .

Troy lifted her book, exposing the hidden corner of the card: . . . *and Embalmers*, she read.

CHAPTER NINE

Alleyn

i

BY AN alteration in the rhythm of the ship's progress, suggestive almost of a physiological change, her passengers became aware of the end of their long voyage. Her pulse died. It was replaced by sounds of blind waves washing along her sides; of gulls, of voices, of chains, and, beyond these, of movement along the wharves and in the city beyond them.

At early dawn the Port of London looked as wan and expectant as an invalid already preparing for a return to vigour. Thin mist still hung about sheds and warehouses. Muffled lights were strung like a dim necklace along the waterfront. Frost glinted on roofs and bollards and ropes. Alleyn had gripped the rail for so long that its cold had bitten through his gloves into the palms of his hands. Groups of people stood about the wharves, outward signs of a life from which the passengers were, for a rapidly diminishing period, still remote. These groups, befogged by their own breath, were composed for the main part of men.

There were three women and one wore a scarlet cap.

Inspector Fox had come out in the pilot's boat. Alleyn had not hoped for this and had been touched and delighted to meet him; but now it was impossible to talk to Fox.

"Mrs. Alleyn," said Fox, behind him, "is wearing a red cap. If you'll excuse me, Mr. Alleyn, I ought to have a word with a chap. The car's just behind the customs shed. I'll meet you there."

When Alleyn turned to thank him, he was already walking away, squarely overcoated, tidy, looking just like his job.

Now only a dark channel, a ditch, a gutter lay between the ship and the wharf. Bells rang sharply. Men moved forward to the bollards, and stared up at the ship. One raised his hand and shouted a greeting in a clear voice. Ropes were flung out and a moment later the final stop-page was felt dully throughout the ship.

That was Troy down there. She walked forward. Her hands were jammed down in the pockets of her overcoat. She looked along the deck, scowling a little, her gaze moving towards him. In these last seconds, while he waited for her to discover him, Alleyn knew that like himself she was nervous. He lifted his hand. They looked at each other and a smile of extraordinary intimacy broke across her face.

ii

"Three years, seven months and twenty-four days," said Alleyn that afternoon. "It's a hell of a time to be without your wife." He looked at Troy sitting on the hearth-rug hugging her knees. "Or rather," he added, "to be away from you, Troy. From you, who so astonishingly happen to be my wife. I've been getting myself into such a hullabaloo about it."

"Wondering," Troy asked, "if we'd run short of conversation and feel shy?"

"You too, then?"

"It does happen, they say. It might easily happen."

"I even considered the advisability of quoting Othello on his arrival at Cyprus. How would you have reacted, my darling, if I had laid hold upon you under letter A in the Customs shed and begun: 'O, my fair warrior?' "

"I should probably have made a snappy come-back with something from *Macbeth*."

"Why *Macbeth?*"

"To explain that would be to use up all the conversation I'd saved up on my own account. Rory—"

"My love?"

"I've been having a very queer time with Macbeth."

She was looking doubtfully at him from under her ruffled forelock. "You may not care to hear about it," she mumbled. "It's a long story."

"It won't be too long," Alleyn said, "if it's you who tells it."

Watching her, he thought: "That's made her shy again. We are to re-learn each other." Alleyn's habit of mind was accurate and exhaustive. He had recognized and examined in himself thoughts that another man might have preferred to ignore. During the long voyage home, he had many times asked himself if, when they met again, he and Troy might not find that the years had dropped between them a transparent barrier through which they would stare, without love, at each other. This possibility had occurred to him, strangely enough, at moments when he most desired and missed her. When she had moved forward on the quay, without at first seeing him, his physical reaction had been so sharp that it had blotted out his thoughts. It was only when she gave him the look of intimacy, which so far had not been repeated, that he knew, without question, he was to love her again.

Now, when she was before him in the room whose very familiarity was a little strange, his delight was of a virgin kind that anticipates a trial of its temper. Were Troy's thoughts at this moment comparable with his own? Could he be as certain of her as he was of himself? She had entered into an entirely different mode of life during his absence. He knew nothing of her new associates beyond the rather sparse phrases she had allowed them in her letters. Now, evidently, he was to hear a little more.

"Come over here," he said, "and tell me."

She moved into her old place, leaning against his chair, and he looked down at her with a more tranquil mind, yet with such intense pleasure, that the beginning of her story escaped him. But he had been ruthlessly trained to listen to statements and the habit asserted itself. The saga of Ancreton was unfolded.

Troy's account was at first tentative, but his interest stimulated her. She began to enjoy herself and presently hunted out her sketchbook with the drawings she had made in her tower room. Alleyn chuckled over the small lively figures with their enormous heads. "Like the old-fashioned Happy Families cards," he said, and she agreed that there was something Victorian and fantastic about the originals. After the eccentricities of the Ancreds themselves, the practical jokes turned out to be a dominant theme in her story. Alleyn heard of them with growing. concern. "Here!" he interrupted. "Did this blasted kid ruin your thing in the end or didn't she?"

"No, no. But it wasn't the blasted kid at all. Listen."

He did, with a chuckle for her deductive methods. "She might conceivably, you know, write 'grandfarther' at one moment and 'grandfather' the next but it's a point, of course."

"It was her manner more than anything. I'm quite positive she didn't do it. I know she's got a record for practical jokes—but wait till I get to the end. Don't fluster the witness."

"Why not?" said Alleyn, stooping his head.

"To continue," said Troy after a moment or two, and this time he let her go on to the end. It was an odd story. He wondered if she realized quite how odd it was.

"I don't know whether I've conveyed the general dottiness of that monstrous house," she said, "I mean, the queer little things that turned up. Like the book on embalming amongst the *objets d'art* and the missing ratsbane."

"Why do you put them together?"

"I dunno. I suppose because there's arsenic in both of them."

"You are *not* by any chance, my angel, attempting to land me with a suspected poisoning case on my return to your arms?"

"Well!" said Troy after a pause. "You would think that one up, wouldn't you?" She screwed round and looked at him. "And he's been embalmed, you know. By the Messrs. Mortimer and Loame. I met them in the hall with their black bags. The only catch in it is the impossibility of regarding any of the Ancreds in the light of a slow poisoner. But it would fit."

"A little too neatly, I fancy." With a trace of reluctance he added, "What were some of the other queer little things that happened?"

"I'd like to know what Cedric and the Orrincourt were giggling about on the sofa, and whether the Orrincourt was coughing or laughing in the governess-cart. I'd even like to know what it was she bought in the chemist's shop. And I'd like to know more about Millamant. One never knew what Millamant was thinking except that she doted perpetually on her ghastly Cedric. It would have been in her Cedric's interest, of course, to sicken Sir Henry of poor old Panty, who, by the way, has a complete alibi for the flying cow. Her alibi's a dangerous drug. For ring-worm."

"Has this odious child been taking thallium?"

"Do you know about thallium?"

"I've heard of it."

"It establishes her alibi for the flying cow," said Troy. "I'd better explain."

"Yes," Alleyn agreed when she had finished, "that lets her out for the flying cow."

"She didn't do any of them," said Troy firmly. "I wish now that Paul and Fenella and I had gone on with our experiment."

"What was that to be?"

"It involved your collaboration," said Troy looking at him out of the corners of her eyes.

"Like hell it did!"

"Yes. We wrapped up the paint brush that had been used for the flying cow and we were going to ask all of them to let us take their finger-prints for you to compare with it. Would you have minded?"

"My darling heart, I'd compare them with the Grand Cham of Tartary's if it would give you any fun."

"But we never got them. Death, as you and Mr. Fox would say, intervened. Sir Henry's death. By the way, the person who painted my bannister left finger-prints on the stone wall above it. Perhaps after a decent interval I could hint for an invitation to Ancreton and you could come down with your insufflator and black ink. But honestly, it *is* a queer story, don't you think?"

"Yes," he agreed, rubbing his nose. "It's queer enough. We heard about Ancred's death on the ship's wireless. Little did I imagine you were in at it."

"I liked him," said Troy after a pause. "He was a terrific old exhibitionist and he made one feel dreadfully shy at times but I did like him. And he was grand to paint."

"The portrait went well?"

"I think so."

"I'd like to see it."

"Well, so you shall one of these days. He said he was leaving it to the Nation. What does the Nation do under those circumstances? Hang it in a dark corner of the Tate, do you imagine? Some paper or another, I suspect Nigel Bathgate's, is going to photograph it. We might get a print."

But Alleyn was not to wait long for the photograph. It appeared that evening in Nigel's paper over a notice of Sir Henry's funeral. He had been buried in the family vault at Ancreton with as much ceremony as the times allowed.

"He hoped," said Troy, "that the Nation would wish otherwise."

"The Abbey?"

"I'm afraid so. Poor Sir Henry, I wish it had. Ah well," said Troy, dropping the newspaper. "That's the end of the Ancreds as far as I'm concerned."

"You never know," Alleyn said, vaguely. Then, suddenly impatient of the Ancreds and of anything that prolonged beyond this moment the first tentative phase of their reunion, he stretched out his hands towards Troy.

This story is concerned with Alleyn and Troy's reunion only in so far as it affected his attitude towards her account of the Ancreds. If he had heard it at any other time it is possible that, however unwillingly, he might have dwelt longer on its peculiarities. As it was he welcomed it as a kind of interlude between their first meeting and its consummation, and then dismissed it from his conscious thoughts.

They had three days together, broken only by a somewhat prolonged interview between Alleyn and his chief at the Special Branch. He was to resume, for the time being at least, his normal job at the Yard. On the Thursday morning when Troy returned to her job, he walked part of the way with her, watched her turn off and, with an odd feeling of anxiety, himself set out for the familiar room and the old associates.

It was pleasant, after all, to cross that barren back hall smelling of linoleum and coal, to re-visit an undistinguished office where the superintendent of C. I., against a background of crossed swords, commemorative photographs and a horseshoe, greeted him with unmistakable satisfaction. It was oddly pleasant to sit again at his old desk in the chief inspectors' room and contemplate the formidable task of taking up the threads of routine.

He had looked forward to a preliminary gossip with Fox, but Fox had gone out on a job somewhere in the country and would not be back before the evening. In the meantime here was an old acquaintance of Alleyn's, one Squinty Donovan, who, having survived two courts-martial, six months' confinement in Broadmoor, and a near miss from a flying bomb, had left unmistakable signs of his ingenuity upon a lock-up antique shop in Beauchamp Place, Chelsea. Alleyn set in motion the elaborate police machinery by which Squinty might be hunted home to a receiver. He then turned again to his file.

There was nothing exciting; a series of routine jobs. This pleased him. There had been enough of excursions and alarms, Lord knew, in his three years' hunting for the Special Branch. He had wanted his return to C.I. to be uneventful.

Presently Nigel Bathgate rang up: "I say," he said, "has Troy seen about the Will?"

"Whose will?"

"Old Ancred's. She told you about the Ancreds, of course."

"Of course."

"It's in this morning's *Times*. Have a look at it. It'll rock them considerably."

"What's he done?" Alleyn asked. But for some reason he was unwilling to hear more about the Ancreds.

He heard Nigel chuckling. "Well, out with it," he said. "What's he done?"

"Handed them the works."

"In what way?"

"Left the whole caboosh to the Orrincourt."

iii

Nigel's statement was an over-simplification of the facts, as Alleyn discovered when, still with that sense of reluctance, he looked up the Will. Sir Henry had cut Cedric down to the bare bones of the entail and had left a legacy of one thousand pounds to Millamant, to each of his children and to Dr. Withers. The residue he had willed to Sonia Orrincourt.

"But—what about the dinner speech and the other Will!" Troy cried when he showed her the evening paper. "Was that just a complete have, do you suppose? If so, Mr. Rattisbon must have known. Or—Rory!" she said. "I believe it was the flying cow that did it. I believe he was so utterly fed up with his family he marched upstairs, sent for Mr. Rattisbon and made a new Will there and then."

"But didn't he think the *enfant terrible* had done the flying cow? Why take it out on the whole family?"

"Thomas or somebody may have gone up and told him about Panty's alibi. He wouldn't know who to suspect and would end up by damning the whole crew."

"Not Miss Orrincourt, however."

"She'd see to that," said Troy with conviction.

She was, he saw, immensely taken up with this news and at intervals during the evening, returned to the Ancreds and their fresh dilemma. "What will Cedric do, can you imagine? Probably the entail is hopelessly below the cost of keeping up Katzenjammer Castle. That's what he called it, you know. Perhaps he'll give it to the Nation. Then they could hang my portrait in its allotted place, chequered all over with coloured lights and everybody would be satisfied. *How* the Orrincourt will gloat."

Troy's voice faded on a note of uncertainty. Alleyn saw her hands move nervously together. She caught his eye and turned away. "Let's not talk about the poor Ancreds," she said.

"What are you munching over in the back of your mind?" he asked uneasily.

"It's nothing," she said quickly. He waited, and after a moment, she came to him. "It's only that I'd like you to tell me—suppose you'd heard from somebody else, or read, about the Ancreds and all the unaccountable odds and ends—what would you think? I mean—" Troy frowned and looked at her clasped hands. "Doesn't it sound rather horridly like the beginning of a chapter in *Famous Trials?*"

"Are you really worried about this?" he said after a pause.

"Oddly enough," said Troy, "I am."

Alleyn got up and stood with his back turned to her. When he spoke again his voice had changed.

"Well," he said, "we'd better tackle it, then."

"What's the matter?" he heard Troy saying doubtfully. "What's happened?"

"Something quite ridiculous and we'll get rid of it. A fetish I nurse. I've never fancied coming home and having a nice cosy chat about the current homicide with my wife. I've never talked about such cases when they did crop up."

"I wouldn't have minded, Rory."

"It's a kind of fastidiousness. No, that's praising it. It's illogical and indefensible. If my job's not fit for you, it shouldn't be my job."

"You're being too fancy. I've got over my squeamishness."

"I didn't want you to get over it," he said. "I tell you I'm a fool about this."

She said the phrase he had hoped not to hear: "Then, do you think there's something in it? About the Ancreds?"

"Blast the Ancreds! Here, this won't do. Come on, let's tackle the thing and scotch it. You're thinking like this, aren't you? There's a book about embalming in their ghastly drawing-room. It stresses the use of arsenic. Old Ancred went about bragging that he was going to have himself mummified. Anyone might have read the book. Sonia Orrincourt was seen doing so. Arsenic, used for rat-poison, disappeared in the house. Old Ancred died immediately after altering his Will in the Orrincourt's favour. There wasn't an autopsy. If one was made now the presence of arsenic would be accounted for by the embalming. That's the colour of the nigger in the wood pile, isn't it?"

"Yes," said Troy, "that's it."

"And you've been wondering whether the practical jokes and all the rest of the fun and games can be fitted in?"

"It sounds less possible as you say it."

"Good!" he said quickly, turning to her. "That's better. Come on, then. You've wondered if the practical jokes were organized by the Orrincourt to put the old man off his favourite grandchild?"

"Yes. Or by Cedric, with the same motive. You see, Panty was hot favourite before the Raspberry and flying cow period set in."

"Yes. So, in short, you're wondering if one of the Ancreds, particularly Cedric, or Miss Orrincourt, murdered old Ancred, having, previously, in effect, hamstrung the favourite."

"This is like talking about a nightmare. It leaves off being horrid and turns silly."

"All the better," he said vigorously. "All right. Now if the lost arsenic was the lethal weapon, the murder was planned long before the party. You understood Millamant to say it had been missing for some time?"

"Yes. Unless—"

"Unless Millamant herself is a murderess and was doing an elaborate cover-up."

"Because I said one didn't know what Millamant thought about, it doesn't follow that she thought about murder."

"Of course it doesn't, bless your heart. Now, if any one of the Ancreds murdered Sir Henry, it was on the strength of the announcement made at the dinner party and without any knowledge of the effective Will made that night. If he made it that night."

"Unless one of the legatees thought they'd been cheated and did it out of pure fury."

"Or Fenella and Paul, who got nothing? Yes. There's that."

"Fenella and Paul," said Troy firmly, "are not like that."

"And if Desdemona or Thomas or Jenetta—"

"Jenetta and Thomas are out of the question—"

"—did it, the practical jokes don't fit in because they weren't there for the earlier ones."

"Which leaves the Orrincourt, Cedric, Millamant and Pauline."

"I can see it's the Orrincourt and Cedric who are really bothering you."

"More particularly," said Troy unhappily, "the Orrincourt."

"Well, darling, what's she like? Has she got the brains to think it up? Would she work out the idea from reading the book on embalming that arsenic would be found in the body anyway?"

"I shouldn't have thought," said Troy cheerfully, "that she'd make head or tail of the book. It was printed in very dim italics with the long s like an f. She's not at all the type to pore over literary curiosa unless she thought they were curious in the specialized sense."

"Feeling better?" he asked.

"Yes, thank you. I'm thinking of other things for myself. Arsenic takes effect pretty quickly, doesn't it? And tastes beastly? He couldn't have had it at dinner because, apart from being in a foul rage, he was still all right when he left the Little Theatre. And—and if Sonia Orrincourt had put it in his Ovaltine or whatever he has in his bedside thermos, could he have sipped down enough to kill him without noticing the taste?"

"Unlikely," Alleyn said. Another silence fell between them. Alleyn thought: "I've never been able to make up my mind about telepathy. Think of something else. Is she listening to my thoughts?"

"Rory," said Troy. "It is all right, isn't it?"

The telephone rang and he was glad to answer it. Inspector Fox was speaking from the Yard.

"Where have you been, you old devil!" said Alleyn and his voice held that cordiality with which we greet a rescuer.

"Good evening, Mr. Alleyn," said Fox. "I was wondering, if it would inconvenience you and Mrs. Alleyn very much if—"

"Come along!" Alleyn interrupted. "Of course it won't. Troy will be delighted, won't you, darling? It's Fox."

"Of course I shall," said Troy loudly. "Tell him to come."

"Very kind, I'm sure," Fox was saying in his deliberate way. "Perhaps I ought to explain, though. It's Yard business. You might say very unusual circumstances, really. Quite a *contretemps*."

"The accent's improving, Fox."

"I don't get the practice. About this business, though. In a manner of speaking, sir, I fancy you'll want to consult Mrs. Alleyn. She's with you, evidently."

"What is it?" Troy asked quickly. "I can hear him. What is it?"

"Well, Fox," said Alleyn after a pause, "what is it?"

"Concerning the late Sir Henry Ancred sir. I'll explain when I see you. There's been an Anonymous Letter."

iv

"Coincidence," said Fox, putting on his spectacles and flattening out a sheet of paper on his knee, "is one of the things you get accustomed to in our line of business, as I think you'll agree, sir. Look at the way one of our chaps asked for a lift in the Gutteridge case. Look at the Thompson-Bywaters case—"

"For the love of Heaven!" Alleyn cried, "let us admit coincidence without further parley. It's staring us in the face. It's a bloody quaint coincidence that my wife should have been staying in this wretched dump and there's an end of it."

He glanced at Fox's respectable, grave, and attentive face. "I'm sorry," he said. "It's no good expecting me to be reasonable over this business. Troy's had one bad enough experience of the nastiest end of our job. She'll never altogether forget it and—well, there you are. One doesn't welcome anything like a reminder."

"I'm sure it's very upsetting, Mr. Alleyn. If I could have—"

"I know, I know, I know." And looking at Fox, Alleyn felt a spasm of self-distaste.

"Fox," he said suddenly, "I'm up against a silly complexity in my own attitude to my job. I've tried to shut it off from my private life. I've adopted what I suppose the Russians would call an unrealistic approach; Troy in one compartment, the detection of crime in another. And now, by way of dotting me one on the wind, the fates have handed Troy this little affair on a platter. If there's anything in it she'll be a witness."

"There may not be anything in it, Mr. Alleyn."

"True enough. That's precisely thc remark I've been making to her for the last hour or so."

Fox opened his eyes very wide. "Oh, yes," said Alleyn, "she's already thought there was something off-colour about the festivities at Ancreton."

"Is that so?" Fox said slowly. "Is that the case?"

"It is indeed. She's left us alonc to talk it over. I can give you the story when you want it and so can she. But I'd better have your end first. What's the paper you've got there?"

Fox handed it to him. "It came in to us yesterday, went through the usual channels, and finally the Chief got on to it and sent for me this evening. You'd gone by then, sir, but he asked me to have a word with you about it. White envelope to match addressed in block capitals C.I.D. SCOTLAND YARD. LONDON. Postmark, Victoria."

Alleyn took the paper. It appeared to be a sheet from a block of faintly ruled note-paper. The lines were, unusually, a pale yellow and a margin was ruled down the side. The message it contained was flatly explicit:—

> The writer has reason to believe that Sir Henry Ancred's death was brought about by the person who has received the most benefit from it.

"Water-mark 'Crescent Script.' People write these things," said Fox. "You know yourself there may be nothing in it. But we've got to take the usual notice. Talk to the super at the local station, I suppose. And the doctor who attended the old gentleman. He may be able to put the matter beyond doubt. There's an end of it."

"He will if he can," said Alleyn grimly. "You may depend upon that."

"In the meantime, the A. C. suggested I should report to you and see about a chat with Mrs. Alleyn. He remembered Mrs. Alleyn had been at Ancreton before you came back."

"*Report* to me? If anything comes of this does he want me to take over?"

"Well, sir, I fancy he will. He mentioned, jokingly like, that it'd be quite unusual if the investigating officer got his first statement on a case from his wife."

"Facetious ass!" said Alleyn with improper emphasis.

Fox looked demurely down his nose.

"Oh, well," said Alleyn, "let's find Troy and we'll hag over the whole blasted set-up. She's in the studio. Come on."

Troy received Fox cheerfully. "I know what it's all about, Mr. Fox," she said, shaking hands with him.

"I'm sure. I'm very sorry—" Fox began.

"But you needn't be," Troy said quickly, linking her arm through Alleyn's. "Why on earth should you be? If I'm wanted, here I am. What happens?"

"We sit down," Alleyn said, "and I go over the whole story as you've told it to me. When I go wrong, you stop me and when you think of anything extra, you put it in. That's all, so far. The whole thing may be a complete wash-out, darling. Anonymous letter-writers have the same affection for the Yard that elderly naturalists have for the *Times*. Now then. Here Fox, to the best of my ability, is the Ancred saga."

He went methodically through Troy's account, correlating the events, tracing the several threads in and out of the texture of the narrative and gathering them together at the end.

"How's that?" he asked her when he had finished. He was surprised to find her staring at him as if he had brought off a feat of sleight-of-hand.

"Amazingly complete and tidy," she said.

"Well, Fox? What's it amount to?"

Fox wiped his hand over his jaw. "I've been asking myself, sir," he said, "whether you mightn't find quite a lot of circumstances behind quite a lot of sudden demises that might sound funny if you strung them together. What I mean to say, a lot of big houses keep ratsbane on the premises and a lot of people can't lay their hands on it when they want it. Things get mislaid."

"Very true, Foxkin."

"And as far as this old-fashioned book on embalming goes, Mr. Alleyn, I ask myself if perhaps somebody mightn't have picked it up since the funeral and got round to wondering about it like Mrs. Alleyn has. You say these good people weren't very keen on Miss Sonia Orrincourt and are probably feeling rather sore about the late old gentleman's Will. They seem to be a highly strung excitable lot."

"But I don't think I'm a particularly highly strung excitable lot, Mr. Fox," said Troy. "And I got the idea too."

"There!" said Fox, clicking his tongue. "Putting my foot in it as usual, aren't I, sir?"

"Tell us what else you ask yourself," said Alleyn.

"Why, whether one of these disappointed angry people hasn't let his imagination, or more likely hers, get the upper hand and written off this letter on the spur of the moment."

"But what about the practical jokes, Mr. Fox?" said Troy.

"Very silly mischievous behaviour. Committing a nuisance. If the little girl didn't do them, and it looks as if she *couldn't* have done them all, then somebody's brought off an unpleasant trick. Spiteful," Fox added severely. "Trying to prejudice the old gentleman against her, as you suggest, I daresay. But that doesn't necessarily mean murder. Why should it?"

"Why indeed!" said Alleyn, taking him by the arm. "You're exactly what we needed in this house, Br'er Fox. Let's all have a drink." He took his wife on his other arm and together they returned to the sitting-room. The telephone rang as Troy entered and she answered it. Alleyn held Fox back and they stared at each other.

"Very convincing performance, Fox. Thank you."

"Rum go, sir, all the same, don't you reckon?"

"Too bloody rum by half. Come on."

When they went into the room Troy put her hand over the mouthpiece of the telephone and turned to them. Her face was white.

"Rory," she said. "It's Thomas Ancred. He wants to come and see you. He says they've all had letters. He says he's made a discovery. He wants to come. What shall I say?"

"I'll speak to him," said Alleyn. "He can see me at the Yard in the morning, damn him."

CHAPTER TEN

Bombshell for Thomas

i

THOMAS ANCRED arrived punctually at nine o'clock, the hour Alleyn had appointed. Fox was present at the interview which took place in Alleyn's room.

Troy had the painter's trick of accurate description and she had been particularly good on Thomas. Alleyn felt he was already familiar with that crest of fine hair, those eyes wide open and palely astonished, that rather tight small mouth, and the mild meandering voice.

"Thank you very much," said Thomas, "for letting me come. I didn't much want to, of course, but it's nice of you to have me. It was knowing Mrs. Alleyn that put it into their heads."

"Whose heads?" asked Alleyn.

"Well, Pauline's and Dessy's principally. Paul and Fenella were quite keen too. I suppose Mrs. Alleyn has told you about my people?"

"I think," said Alleyn, "that it might be best if we adopt the idea that I know nothing about anybody."

"Oh dear!" said Thomas, sighing. "That means a lot of talking, doesn't it?"

"What about these letters?"

"Yes, to be sure," said Thomas, beginning to pat himself all over. "The letters. I've got them somewhere. Anonymous, you know. Of course I've had them before in the theatre from disappointed patrons and angry actresses, but this is different, really. Now, where—" He picked up one corner of his jacket, looked suspiciously at a bulging pocket, and finally pulled out a number of papers, two pencils and a box of matches. Thomas beamed at Alleyn. "And there, after all, they are," he said. In mild triumph he laid them out on the desk—eight copies of the letter Alleyn had already seen, all printed with the same type of pen on the same type of paper.

"What about the envelopes?" Alleyn asked.

"Oh," said Thomas, "we didn't keep them. I wasn't going to say anything about mine," Thomas continued after a pause, "and nor were Jenetta and Milly, but of course everybody noticed everybody else had the same sort of letter and Pauline (my sister, Pauline Kentish) made a great hullabaloo over hers and there we were, you know."

"Eight," said Alleyn. "And there are nine in the party at Ancreton?"

"Sonia didn't get one so everybody says she's the person meant."

"Do you take that view, Mr. Ancred?"

"Oh, yes," said Thomas, opening his eyes very wide. "It seems obvious, doesn't it? With the Will and everything. Sonia's meant, of course, but for my part," said Thomas, with a diffident cough, "I don't fancy she murdered Papa."

He gave Alleyn a rather anxious little smile. "It would be such a beastly thing to do, you know," he said. "Somehow one can't quite—however. Pauline actually almost leapt at the idea. Dessy, in a way, too. They're both dreadfully upset. Pauline fainted at the funeral anyway and then with these letters on top of it all she's in a great state of emotional upheaval. You can't imagine what it's like at Ancreton."

"It was Mrs. Kentish, wasn't it, who suggested you should come to the Yard?"

"And Dessy. My unmarried sister, Desdemona. We all opened our letters yesterday morning at breakfast. Can you imagine? I got down first and really—such a shock! I was going to throw it on the fire but just then Fenella came in, so I folded it up very small under the table. You can see which is mine by the creases. Paul's is the one that looks as if it had been chewed. He crunched it up, don't you know, in his agitation. Well, then I noticed that there were the same kind of envelopes in front of everybody's plate. Sonia has breakfast in her room but I asked Barker if there were any letters for her and there weren't. Well, and then everyone came straggling in. Fenella was by that time looking rather odd, having opened hers. Pauline said: 'What an extraordinary looking letter I've got. Written by a child I should think,' and Milly said: 'Panty again, perhaps' and there was a row, because Pauline and Milly don't see eye-to-eye over Panty. And then everybody said: 'I've got one too,' and then you know they opened them. Well! Pauline swooned away, of course, and Dessy said: 'O my prophetic soul' and began to get very excitable and Milly said: 'I think people who write anonymous letters are the *end*,' and Jenetta (my sister-in-law, Fenella's mother, who is married to my brother Claude), said: 'I agree, Milly.' Then the next thing was, let me see—the next thing was everybody suspecting everybody else of writing the letter, until Pauline got the idea—you must excuse me—that perhaps Mrs. Alleyn being married to—"

Alleyn, catching sight of Fox's scandalized countenance, didn't answer and Thomas, rather pink in the face, hurried on. "Of course," he said, "the rest of us pooh-poohed the notion: quite howled it down, in fact. 'The very idea,' Fenella, for instance, said, 'of Mrs. Alleyn writing anonymous letters is just *so* bloody silly that we needn't discuss it,' which led directly into another row because Pauline made the suggestion and Fenella and Paul are engaged against her wish. It ended by my nephew Cedric, who is now the head of the family, saying that he thought the letter sounded like Pauline herself. He mentioned that a favourite phrase of Pauline's is 'I have reason to believe.' Milly, Cedric's mother, you know, laughed rather pointedly, so naturally there was another row."

"Last night," Alleyn said, "you told me you had made a discovery at Ancreton. What was it?"

"Oh, yes. I was coming to that some time. Now, actually, because it happened after lunch. I really don't care at all for this part of the story. Indeed, I quite forgot myself and said I would *not* go back to Ancreton until I was assured of not having to get involved in any more goings-on."

"I'm afraid—" Alleyn began, but Thomas at once interrupted him. "You don't follow? Well, of course you wouldn't, would you, because I haven't told you. Still I suppose I'd better."

Alleyn waited without comment.

"Well," said Thomas at last. "Here, after all, we go."

ii

"All yesterday morning," Thomas said, "after reading the letters, the battle, as you might put it, raged. Nobody really on anybody else's side except Paul and Fenella and Jenetta wanting to burn the letters and Pauline and Desdemona thinking there was something in it and we ought to keep them. And by lunch time, you may depend upon it, feeling ran very high indeed. And then, you know—"

Here Thomas paused and stared meditatively at a spot on the wall somewhere behind Fox's head. He had his odd trick of stopping short in his narratives. It was as if a gramophone needle was abruptly and unreasonably lifted from the disk. It was impossible to discover whether Thomas was suddenly bereft of the right word or smitten by the intervention of a new train of thought or whether he had merely forgotten what he was talking about. Apart from a slight glazing of his eyes, his facial expression remained uncannily fixed.

"And then. . . ." Alleyn prompted after a long pause.

"Because, when you come to think of it," Thomas's voice went on, "it's the last thing one expects to find in the cheese dish. It was New Zealand cheese, of course. Papa was fortunate in his friends."

"What," Alleyn asked temperately, "is the last thing, Fox, that one would expect to find in the cheese dish?"

Before Fox could reply Thomas began again.

"It's an old piece of Devonport. Rather nice really. Blue, with white swans sailing round it. Very large. In times of plenty we used to have a whole Stilton in it but now, of course, only a tiny packet. Rather ridiculous, really, but it meant there was plenty of room."

"For what?"

"It was Cedric who lifted the lid and discovered it. He gave one of his little screams but beyond feeling rather irritated, I daresay, nobody paid much attention. Then he brought it over to the table—Did I forget to say it's always left on the side-board?—and dropped it in front of Pauline, who is in a very nervous condition anyway and nearly shrieked the place down."

"Dropped the cheese dish? Or the cheese?"

"The cheese? Good Heavens!" cried the scandalized Thomas. "What an idea! The book, to be sure."

"What book?" Alleyn said automatically.

"*The* book, you know. The one out of that glass thing in the drawing-room."

"Oh," said Alleyn after a pause. "That book. On embalming."

"And arsenic and all the rest of it. Too awkward and beastly, because, you know, Papa, by special arrangement, *was*. It upset everybody frightfully. In such very bad taste, everybody thought, and of course the cry of 'Panty' went up immediately on all sides, and there was Pauline practically in a dead faint for the second time in three days."

"Yes?"

"Yes, and then Milly remembered seeing Sonia look at the book and Sonia said she had never seen it before and then Cedric read out some rather beastly bits about arsenic and everybody began to re-member how Barker couldn't find the rat-poison when it was wanted for Bracegirdle. Then Pauline and Desdemona looked at each other in such a meaning sort of way that Sonia became quite frantic with rage and said she'd leave Ancreton there and then only she couldn't because there wasn't a train so she went out in the rain and the governess-cart and is now in bed with bronchitis to which she is subject."

"Still at Ancreton?"

"Yes, still there. Quite," said Thomas. His expression became dazed and he went off into another of his silences.

"And that," Alleyn said, "is of course the discovery you mentioned on the telephone?"

"That? Discovery? What discovery? Oh, no!" cried Thomas. "I see what you mean. Oh, no, indeed, *that* was nothing compared to what we found afterwards in her room."

"What did you find, Mr. Ancred, and in whose room?"

"Sonia's," said Thomas. "Arsenic."

iii

"It was Cedric and the girls' idea," Thomas said. "After Sonia had gone out in the governess-cart, they talked and talked. Nobody quite liked to say outright that perhaps Sonia had put rat-poison in Papa's hot drink, but even Milly remarked that Sonia had recently got into the way of making it. Papa said she made it better than any of the servants or even than Milly herself. She used to take it in and leave it at his bedside. Cedric remembered seeing Sonia with the thermos flask in her hands. He passed her in the passage on his way to bed that very night.

"It was at about this stage," Thomas continued, "that somebody, I've forgotten quite whom, said that they thought Sonia's room ought to be searched. Jenetta and Fenella and Paul jibbed at this, but Dessy and Cedric and Pauline were as keen as mustard. I had promised to lend Caroline Able a book so I went away rather gladly. Caroline Able teaches the Difficult Children including Panty and she is very worried because of Panty not going bald enough. So it might have been an hour later that I went back to our part of the house. And there was Cedric lying in wait for me. Well, he's the head of the house now so I suppose I mustn't be beastly about him. All mysterious and whispering, he was.

" 'Ssh,' he said. 'Come upstairs.' "

"He wouldn't say anything more. I felt awfully bored with all this but I followed him up."

"To Miss Orrincourt's room?" Alleyn suggested as Thomas's eye had glazed again.

"That's it. How did you guess? And there were Pauline and Milly and Dessy. I must tell you," said Thomas delicately, "that Sonia has a little sort of suite of rooms, near Papa's for convenience. It wasn't called anything because Papa had run out of famous actresses' names. So he had a new label done with 'Orrincourt' on it and that really infuriated everybody because Sonia, whatever anybody may care to say to the contrary, is a very naughty actress. Well, not an actress at all, really. Absolutely dire, you might say."

"You found your sisters and Mrs. Henry Ancred in these rooms?"

"Yes. I must tell you that Sonia's suite is in a tower. Like the tower your wife had only Sonia's tower is higher because the architect who built Ancreton believed in quaintness. So Sonia has a bedroom on top and then a bathroom and at the bottom a boudoir. The bedroom's particularly quaint with a little door and steps up into the pepper-pot roof which makes a box-room. They were milling about in this box-room and Dessy had found the rat-poison in one of Sonia's boxes. It's a preparation of arsenic. It says so on the label. Well!"

"What have you done with it?"

"So awkward!" said Thomas crossly. "They made me take it. To keep, they said, in case of evidence being needed. Cedric was very particular about it, having read detective books, and he wrapped it up in one of my handkerchiefs. So I've got it in my rooms here in London if you really want to see it."

"We'll take possession of it, I think," said Alleyn with a glance at Fox. Fox made a slight affirmative rumble. "If it's convenient, Mr. Ancred," Alleyn went on, "Fox or I will drop you at your rooms and collect this tin."

"I hope I can find it," Thomas said gloomily.

"Find it?"

"One does mislay things so. Only the other day—" Thomas fell into one of his trances and this time Alleyn waited for something to break through. "I was just thinking, you know," Thomas began rather loudly. "There we all were in her room and I looked out of the window. It was raining. And away down below, like something out of a Noah's ark, was the governess-cart, creeping up the drive and Sonia in her fur coat, flapping the reins, I suppose, in the way she has. And when you came to think of it, there, according to Pauline and Dessy and Cedric and Milly, went Papa's murderess."

"But not according to you?" said Alleyn. He was putting away the eight anonymous letters. Fox had risen and now stared down at their visitor as if Thomas was some large unopened parcel left by mistake in the room.

"*To me?*" Thomas repeated, opening his eyes very wide. "I don't know. How should I? But you wouldn't believe how uncomfortable it makes one feel."

iv

To enter Thomas's room was to walk into a sort of cross between a waste-paper basket and a workshop. Its principal feature was a large round table entirely covered with stacks of paper, paints, photographs, models for stage sets, designs for costumes, and books. In the window was an apparently unused desk. On the walls were portraits of distinguished players, chief among them Sir Henry himself.

"Sit down," invited Thomas, sweeping sheaves of papers from two chairs onto the floor. "I'll just think where—" He began to walk round his table, staring rather vacantly at it. "I came in with my suitcase, of course, and then, you know the telephone rang. It was *much* later than that when I wanted to find the letters and I had put them carefully away because of showing them to you. And I *found* them. So I must have unpacked. And I can remember thinking: 'It's poison and I'd better be careful of my handkerchief in case—' "

He walked suddenly to a wall cupboard and opened it. A great quantity of papers instantly fell out. Thomas stared indignantly at them. "I distinctly remember," he said, turning to Alleyn and Fox with his mouth slightly open, "I *distinctly* remember saying to myself—" But this sentence, also, was fated to remain unfinished for Thomas pounced unexpectedly upon some fragment from the cupboard. "I've been looking for that all over the place," he said. "I've been looking for that all over the place," he said. "It's *most* important. A cheque in fact."

He sat on the floor and began scuffling absently among the papers. Alleyn, who for some minutes had been inspecting the chaos that reigned upon the table, lifted a pile of drawings and discovered a white bundle. He loosened the knot at the top and a stained tin was disclosed. It bore a bright red label with the legend: "Rat—X—

it! Poison" and, in slightly smaller print, the antidote for arsenical poisoning.

"Here it is, Mr. Ancred," said Alleyn.

"What?" asked Thomas. He glanced up. "Oh, *that*," he said. "I *thought* I'd put it on the table."

Fox came forward with a bag. Alleyn muttering something about futile gestures, lifted the tin by the handerchief. "You don't mind," he said to Thomas, "if we take charge of this? We'll give you a receipt for it."

"Oh, will you?" asked Thomas mildly. "Thanks awfully." He watched them stow away the tin and then, seeing that they were about to go, scrambled to his feet. "You must have a drink," he said. "There's a bottle of Papa's whiskey—I think."

Alleyn and Fox managed to head him off a further search. He sat down and listened with an air of helplessness to Alleyn's parting exposition.

"Now, Mr. Ancred," Alleyn said, "I think I ought to make as clear as possible the usual procedure following the sort of information you have brought to us. Before any definite step can be taken, the police make what are known as 'further enquiries.' They do this as inconspicuously as possible since neither their original informant, nor they, enjoy the public exploration of a mare's nest. If these enquiries seem to point to a suspicion of ill-practice, the police then get permission from the Home Secretary for the next step to be taken. You know what that is, I expect?"

"I say!" said Thomas. "That *would* be beastly, wouldn't it?" A sudden thought seemed to strike him. "I say!" he repeated. "Would I have to be there?"

"We'd probably ask for formal identification by a member of his family."

"O Lor'!" Thomas whispered dismally. He pinched his lower lip between his thumb and forefinger. A gleam of consolation appeared to visit him.

"I say!" he said. "It's a good job after all isn't it, that the Nation *didn't* plump for the Abbey?"

CHAPTER ELEVEN

Alleyn at Ancreton

i

"In our game," said Fox as they drove back to the Yard, "you get some funny glimpses into what you might call human nature. I daresay I've said that before but it's a fact."

"I believe you," said Alleyn.

"Look at this chap we've just left," Fox continued with an air of controversy. "Vague! And yet he must be good at his job, wouldn't you say, sir?"

"Indisputably."

"There! Good at his job and yet to meet him you'd say he'd lose his play, and his actors, and his way to the theatre. In view of which," Fox summed up, "I ask myself if this chap's as muddle-headed as he lets on."

"A pose, you think, do you, Fox?"

"You never know with some jokers," Fox muttered, and wiping his great hand over his face, seemed by that gesture to dispose of Thomas Ancred's vagaries. "I suppose," he said, "it'll be a matter of seeing the doctor, won't it?"

"I'm afraid so. I've looked out trains. There's one in an hour. Get us there by midday. We may have to spend the night in Ancreton village. We can pick up our emergency bags at the Yard, I'll talk to the A.C. and telephone Troy. What a hell of a thing to turn up."

"It doesn't look as if we'll be able to let it alone, do you reckon, Mr. Alleyn?"

"I still have hopes. As it stands there's not a case in Thomas's story to hang a dead dog on. They lose a tin of rat-poison and find it in a garret. Somebody reads a book about embalming and thinks up an elaborate theme based on an arbitary supposition. Counsel could play skittles with it—as it stands."

"Suppose we *did* get an order for exhumation. Suppose they

found arsenic in the body. With this embalming business it'd seem as if it would prove nothing."

"On the contrary," said Alleyn, "I rather think, Fox, that if they did find arsenic in the body it would prove everything."

Fox turned slowly and looked at him. "I don't get that one, Mr. Alleyn," he said.

"I'm not at all sure that I'm right. We'll have to look it up. Here we are. I'll explain on the way down to this accursed village. Come on."

He saw his Assistant Commissioner who, with the air of a connoisseur, discussed the propriety of an investigator handling a case in which his wife might be called as a witness. "Of course, my dear Rory, if by any chance the thing should come into court and your wife be subpoenaed, we should have to reconsider our position. We've no precedent, far as I know. But for the time being I imagine it's more reasonable for you to discuss it with her than for anybody else to do so: Fox for instance. Now, you go down to this place, talk to the indigenous G.P. and come back and tell us what you think about it. Tiresome if it comes to anything. Good luck."

As they left Alleyn took from his desk the second volume of a work on medical jurisprudence. It dealt principally with poisons. In the train he commended certain passages to Fox's notice. He watched his old friend put on his spectacles, raise his eyebrows and develop the slightly catarrhal breathing that invariably accompanied his reading.

"Yes," said Fox, removing his spectacles as the train drew into Ancreton Halt, "that's different of course."

ii

Dr. Herbert Withers was a short, tolerably plump man with little of the air of well-being normally associated with plumpness. He came out into his hall as they arrived, admitting from some inner room the sound of a racing broadcast. After a glance at Alleyn's professional card, he took them to his consulting room and sat at his desk with a movement whose briskness seemed to overlie a controlled fatigue.

"What's the trouble?" he asked.

It was the conventional opening. Alleyn thought it had slipped involuntarily from Dr. Withers's lips.

"We hope there's no trouble," he said. "Would you mind if I

asked you to clear up a few points about Sir Henry Ancred's death?"

The mechanical attentiveness of Dr. Withers's glance sharpened. He made an abrupt movement and looked from Alleyn to Fox.

"Certainly," he said, "if there's any necessity. But why?" He still held Alleyn's card in his hand and he glanced at it again. "You don't mean to say—" he began and stopped short. "Well, what are these few points?"

"I think I'd better tell you exactly what's happened," Alleyn said. He took a copy of the anonymous letter from his pocket and handed it to Dr. Withers. "Mr. Thomas Ancred brought eight of these to us this morning," he said.

"Damn disgusting piffle," said Dr. Withers and handed it back.

"I hope so. But when we're shown these wretched things we have to do something about them."

"Well?"

"You signed the death certificate, Dr. Withers, and—"

"And I shouldn't have done so if I hadn't been perfectly satisfied as to the cause."

"Exactly. Now will you like a good chap help us to dispose of these letters by giving us, in nonscientific words, the cause of Sir Henry's death?"

Dr. Withers fretted a little but at last went to his files and pulled out a card.

"There you are," he said. "That's the last of his cards. I made routine calls at Ancreton. It covers about six weeks."

Alleyn looked at it. It bore the usual list of dates with appropriate notes. Much of it was illegible and almost all obscure to the lay mind. The final note however, was flatly lucid. It read: "Deceased. Between 12:30 and 2 A.M. Nov. 25."

"Yes," said Alleyn. "Thank you. Now will you translate some of this?"

"He suffered," said Dr. Withers angrily, "from gastric ulcers and degeneration of the heart. He was exceedingly indiscriminate in his diet. He'd eaten a disastrous meal, had drunk champagne and had flown into one of his rages. From the look of the room I diagnosed a severe gastric attack followed by heart failure. I may add that if I had heard about the manner in which he'd spent the evening I should have expected some such development."

"You'd have expected him to die?"

"That would be an extremely unprofessional prognostication. I would have anticipated grave trouble," said Dr. Withers stuffily.

"Was he in the habit of playing up with his diet?"

"He was. Not continuously, but in bouts."

"Yet survived?"

"The not unusual tale of 'once too often.' "

"Yes," said Alleyn, looking down the card. "Would you mind describing the room and the body?"

"Would you, in your turn, Chief Inspector, mind telling me if you have any reason for this interview beyond these utterly preposterous anonymous letters?"

"Some of the family suspect arsenical poisoning."

"Oh my God and little starfish!" Dr. Withers shouted and shook his fists above his head. "That *bloody* family!"

He appeared to wrestle obscurely with his feelings. "I'm sorry about that," he said at last. "Inexcusable outbursts. I've been busy lately and worried and there you are. The Ancreds, collectively, here tried me rather high. Why, may one ask, do they suspect arsenical poisoning?"

"It's a long story," said Alleyn carefully, "and it involves a tin of rat-poison. May I add also very unprofessionally, that I shall be enormously glad if you can tell me that the condition of the room and the body precludes the smallest likelihood of arsenical poisoning?"

"I can't tell you anything of the sort. Why? A. Because the room had been cleaned up when I got there. And B. Because the evidence as described to me and the appearance of the body were entirely consistent with a severe gastric attack and therefore *not* inconsistent with arsenical poisoning."

"Damn!" Alleyn grunted. "I thought it'd be like that."

"How the hell could the old fool have got at any rat-poison? Will you tell me that?" He jabbed a finger at Alleyn.

"They don't think," Alleyn explained, "that he got at it. They think it was introduced to him."

The well-kept hand closed so strongly that the knuckles whitened. For a moment he held it clenched and then, as if to cancel this gesture, opened the palm and examined his finger nails.

"That," he said, "is implicit in the letter, of course. Even that I can believe of the Ancreds. Who is supposed to have murdered Sir Henry? Am I, by any pleasant chance?"

"Not that I know," said Alleyn comfortably. Fox cleared his throat and added primly: "What an idea!"

"Are they going to press for an exhumation? Or are you?"

"Not without more reason than we've got at the moment," Alleyn said. "You didn't hold a post mortem?"

"One doesn't hold a P.M. on a patient who was liable to go off in precisely this fashion at any moment."

"True enough. Dr. Withers, may I make our position quite clear? We've had a queer set of circumstances placed before us and we've got to take stock of them. Contrary to popular belief the police do not, in such cases, burn to get a pile of evidence that points unavoidably to exhumation. If the whole thing turns out to be so much nonsense they are, as a general rule, delighted to write it off. Give us a sound argument against arsenical poisoning and we'll be extremely grateful to you."

Dr. Withers waved his hands. "I can't give you, at a moment's notice, absolute proof he didn't get arsenic. You couldn't do it for ninety-nine deaths out of a hundred, when there was gastric trouble with vomiting and purging and no analysis was taken of anything. As a matter of fact—"

"Yes?" Alleyn prompted as he paused.

"As a matter of fact I daresay if there'd been anything left I might have done an analysis simply as a routine measure and to satisfy a somewhat pedantic medical conscience. But the whole place had been washed up."

"By whose orders?"

"My dear man, by Barker's orders or Mrs. Kentish's or Mrs. Henry Ancred's or whoever happened to think of it. They didn't like to move him. Couldn't very well. Rigor was pretty well established, which gave me, by the way, a lead about the time of his death. When I saw him again later in the day, they'd fixed him up, of course, and a nice time Mrs. Ancred must have had of it with all of them milling about the house in an advanced condition of hysteria and Mrs. Kentish insisting on 'taking a hand in the laying-out.' "

"Good Lord!"

"Oh, they're like that. Well, as I was saying, there he was when they found him, hunched up on the bed and the room in a pretty nauseating state. When I got there two of those old housemaids were waddling off with their buckets and the whole place stank of carbolic. They'd even managed to change the bed-clothes. I didn't get there, by the way, for an hour after they telephoned. Confinement."

"About the children's ringworm—" Alleyn began.

"You know about them, do you? Yes. Worrying business. Glad to say young Panty's clearing up at last."

"I understand," Alleyn said pleasantly, "that you are bold in your use of drugs."

There was a long silence. "And how, may I ask," said Dr. Withers very quietly, "did you hear details of my treatment?"

"Why, from Thomas Ancred," said Alleyn and watched the colour return to Dr. Withers's face. "Why not?"

"I dislike gossip about my patients. As a matter of fact I wondered if you'd been talking to our local pharmacist. I'm not at all pleased with him at the moment. However—"

"Do you remember the evening the children were dosed? Monday, the nineteenth, I think it was?"

Dr. Withers stared at him. "Now why—?" he began and seemed to change his mind. "I do," he said. "Why?"

"Simply because that evening a practical joke was played on Sir Henry and the child Panty had been accused of it. It's too elaborate a story to bother you about, but I'd like to know if she was capable of it. In the physical sense. Mentally, it seems, she certainly is."

"What time?"

"During dinner. She would have visited the drawing-room."

"Out of the question. I arrived at seven-thirty—wait a moment." He searched his filing cabinet and pulled out another card. "Here! I superintended the weighing and dosing of these kids and noted the time. Panty got her quota at eight and was put to bed. I stayed on in the anteroom to their dormitory during the rest of the business and talked to Miss Able. I left her my visiting list for the next twenty-four hours so that she could get me quickly if anything cropped up. It was after nine when I left and this wretched kid certainly hadn't budged. I had a look at the lot of them. She was asleep with a normal pulse and so on."

"That settles Panty then," Alleyn muttered.

"Look here, has this any bearing on the other business?"

"I'm not sure. It's a preposterous story. If you've the time and the inclination to listen, I'll tell it to you."

"I've got," said Dr. Withers, glancing at his watch, "twenty-three minutes. Case in half an hour and I want to hear the racing results before I go out."

"I shan't be more than ten minutes."

"Go ahead, then. I should be glad to hear any story, however fantastic, that can connect a practical joke on Monday the nineteenth with the death of Sir Henry Ancred from gastro-enteritis after midnight on Saturday the twenty-fourth."

Alleyn related all the stories of the practical jokes. Dr. Withers punctuated this recital with occasional sounds of incredulity or irritation. When Alleyn reached the incident of the flying cow he interrupted him.

"The child Panty," he said, "is capable of every iniquity but as I have pointed out, she could not have perpetuated this offence with the blown-up bladder, nor could she have painted the flying cow on Mrs.—" He stopped short. "Is this lady—" he began.

"My wife, as it happens," said Alleyn, "but let it pass."

"Good Lord! Unusual that, isn't it?"

"Both unusual and bothering in this context. You were saying?"

"That the child was too seedy that night for it to be conceivable. And you tell me Miss Able (sensible girl, that) vouches for her anyway."

"Yes."

"All right. Well, some other fool, Cedric in all likelihood, performed these idiocies. I fail to see how they can possibly be linked up with Sir Henry's death."

"You have not," Alleyn said, "heard of the incident of the book on embalming, in the cheese dish."

Dr. Withers's mouth opened slightly, but he made no comment, and Alleyn completed his narrative. "You see," he added, "this final trick does bear a sort of family likeness to the others and considering the subject matter of the book, and the fact that Sir Henry was embalmed—"

"Quite so. Because the damned book talks about arsenic they jump to this imbecile conclusion—"

"Fortified, we must remember, by the discovery of a tin of arsenical rat-poison in Miss Orrincourt's luggage."

"Planted there by the practical joker," cried Dr. Withers. "I bet you. Planted!"

"That's a possibility," Alleyn agreed, "that we can't overlook."

Fox suddenly said: "Quite so."

"Well," said Dr. Withers, "I'm damned if I know what to say. No medical man enjoys the suggestion that he's been careless or made a mistake and this would be a very awkward mistake. Mind, I don't for a split second believe there's a fragment of truth in the tale, but if the whole boiling of Ancreds are going to talk arsenic—Here! Have you seen the embalmers?"

"Not yet. We shall do so, of course."

"I don't know anything about embalming," Dr. Withers muttered. "This fossil of a book may not amount to a row of beans."

"Taylor," said Alleyn, "has a note on it. He says that in such manipulations of a body, antiseptic substances are used (commonly arsenic), and might prevent the detection of poison as the cause of death."

"So if we have an exhumation, where are we? Precisely nowhere."

"I'm not sure of my ground," said Alleyn, "but I fancy that an exhumation should definitely show whether or not Sir Ancred was poisoned. I'll explain. . . ."

iii

Fox and Alleyn lunched at the Ancreton Arms, on jugged hare, well cooked, and a tankard each of the local draught beer. It was a pleasant enough little pub and the landlady, on Alleyn's enquiry, said she could, if requested, put them up for the night.

"I'm not at all sure we shan't be taking her at her word," said Alleyn as they walked out into the village street. It was thinly bright with winter sunshine and contained beside the pub and Dr. Withers's house, a post-office-shop, a chapel, a draper's, a stationer's, a meeting hall, a chemist-cum-fancy-goods shop, and a row of cottages. Over the brow of intervening hills, the gothic windows, multiple towers and indefatigably varied chimney-pots, of Ancreton Manor glinted against their background of conifers, and brooded, with an air of grand-seigneury, faintly bogus, over the little village.

"And here," said Alleyn, pausing at the chemist's window, "is Mr. Juniper's pharmacy. That's a pleasant name, Fox. E. M. Juniper. This is where Troy and Miss Orrincourt came in their governess-cart on a misty evening. Let's call on Mr. Juniper, shall we?"

But he seemed to be in no hurry to go in and began to mutter to himself before the side window. "A tidy window, Fox. I like the old-fashioned coloured bottles, don't you? Writing paper, you see, and combs and ink (that brand went off the market in the war) cheek-by-jowl with cough lozenges and trusses in their modest boxes. Even some children's card games. Happy Families. That's how Troy drew the Ancreds. Let's give them a pack. Mr. Juniper the chemist's window. Come on."

He led the way in. The shop was divided into two sections. One counter was devoted to fancy goods and one, severe and isolated, to Mr. Juniper's professional activities. Alleyn rang a little bell, a door opened, and Mr. Juniper, fresh and rosy in his white coat, came out together with the cleanly smell of drugs.

"*Yes*, sir?" Mr. Juniper enquired, placing himself behind his professional counter.

"Good morning," said Alleyn. "I wonder if by any chance you've got anything to amuse a small girl who's on the sick-list?"

Mr. Juniper removed to the fancy-goods department. "Happy Families? Loto? Bubble blowing?" he suggested.

"Actually," Alleyn lied pleasantly, "I've been told I must bring back some form of practical joke. Designed, I'm afraid, for Dr. Withers."

"Really? T't. Ha-ha!" said Mr. Juniper. "Well, now. I'm afraid we haven't anything much in that line. There were some dummy ink spots but I'm afraid—No. I know exactly the type of thing you mean, mind, but I'm just afraid—"

"Somebody said something about a thing you blow up and sit on," Alleyn murmured vaguely. "It sounded disgusting."

"Ah! The Raspberry?"

"That's it."

Mr. Juniper shook his head sadly and made a gesture of resignation.

"I thought," said Alleyn, "I saw a box in your window that looked—"

"Empty!" Mr. Juniper sighed. "The customer didn't require the box so I'm afraid I've just left it there. Now isn't that a pity," Mr. Juniper lamented. "Only last week, or would it be a fortnight ago, I sold the last of that little line to a customer for exactly the same purpose. A sick little girl. Yes. One would almost think," he hazarded, "that the same little lady—"

"I expect so. Patricia Kentish," said Alleyn.

"Ah, quite so. So the customer said! Up at the Manor. Quite a little stinker," said Mr. Juniper. "Well, sir, I think you'll find that Miss Pant—Miss Pat—has already got a Raspberry."

"In that case," said Alleyn, "I'll take a Happy Families. You want some tooth-paste, don't you, Fox?"

"Happy Families," said Mr. Juniper, snatching a packet from the shelf. "Dentifrice? Any particular make, sir?"

"For a plate," said Fox stolidly.

"For the denture. Quite," said Mr. Juniper, and darted into the professional side of his shop.

"I wouldn't mind betting," said Alleyn cheerfully to Fox, "that it was Sonia Orrincourt who got in first with that thing."

"Ah," said Fox. Mr. Juniper smiled archly. "Well now," he said, "I oughtn't to give the young lady away, ought I? Professional secrets. Ha-ha!"

"Ha-ha!" Alleyn agreed, putting Happy Families in his pocket. "Thank you, Mr. Juniper."

"Thank *you*, sir. All well up at the Manor, I hope? Great loss, that. Loss to the Nation, you might say. Little trouble with the children clearing up, I hope?"

"On its way. Lovely afternoon, isn't it? Good-bye."

"I didn't want any tooth-paste," said Fox, as they continued up the street.

"I didn't see why I should make all the purchases and you were looking altogether too portentous. Put it down to expenses. It was worth it."

"I don't say it wasn't that," Fox agreed. "Now, sir, if this woman Orrincourt took the Raspberry I suppose we look to her for all the other pranks, don't we?"

"I hardly think so, Fox. Not all. We know at least, that this ghastly kid tied a notice to the tail of her Aunt Millamant's coat. She's got a reputation for practical jokes. On the other hand she definitely, it seems, did not perpetrate the Raspberry and the flying cow, and my wife is convinced she's innocent of the spectacles, the painted stair-rail and the rude writing on Sir Henry's looking-glass. As for the book in the cheese dish, I don't think either Panty or Miss Orrincourt is guilty of that flight of fancy."

"So that if you count out the little girl for anything that matters, we've got Miss Orrincourt and another."

"That's the cry."

"And this other is trying to fix something on Miss Orrincourt in the way of arsenic and the old gentleman?"

"It's a reasonable thesis but Lord knows."

"Where are we going, Mr. Alleyn?"

"Are you good for a two-mile walk? I think we'll call on the Ancreds."

iv

"It isn't," said Alleyn as they toiled up the second flight of terraces, "as if we can hope to keep ourselves dark, supposing that were advisable. Thomas will have rung up his family and told them that we have at least taken notice. We may as well announce ourselves and see what we can see. More especially, this wretched old fellow's bedroom."

"By this time," said Fox sourly, "they'll probably have had it repapered."

"I wonder if Paul Kentish is handy with electrical gadgets. I'll wager Cedric Ancred isn't."

"What's that?" Fox demanded.

"What's what?"

"I can hear something. A child crying, isn't it, sir?"

They had reached the second terrace. At each end of this terrace, between the potato fields and the woods, were shrubberies and young copses. From the bushes on their left hand came a thin intermittent wailing; very dolorous. They paused uncertainly, staring at each other. The wailing stopped and into the silence welled the accustomed sounds of the countryside; the wintry chittering of birds and the faint click of naked branches.

"Would it be some kind of bird, should you say?" Fox speculated.

"No bird!" Alleyn began and stopped short. "There it is again."

It was a thin piping sound, waving and irregular and the effect of it was extraordinarily distressing. Without further speculation they set off across the rough and still frost-encrusted ground. As they drew nearer to it the sound became, not articulate, but more complex, and presently, when they had drawn quite close, developed a new character.

"It's mixed up," Fox whispered, "with a kind of singing."

Good-bye poor pussy your coat was so warm.
And even if you did moult you did me no harm.
Good-bye poor pussy for ever and ever
And make me a good girl, amen.
For ever and ever . . .

the thin voice repeated and drifted off again into its former desolate wail. As they brushed against the first low bushes, it ceased and there followed a wary silence disrupted by harsh sobbing.

Between the bushes and the copse they came upon a little girl in a white cap, sitting by a newly-turned mound of earth. A child's spade was beside her. Stuck irregularly in the mound of earth were a few heads of geraniums. A piece of paper threaded on a twig stood crookedly at the head of the mound. The little girl's hands were earthy and she had knuckled her eyes so that black streaks ran down her face. She crouched there scowling at them rather like an animal that flattens itself near the ground, unable to obey its own instinct for flight.

"Hullo," said Alleyn. "This is a bad job." And unable to think of a more satisfactory opening he heard himself repeating Dr. Withers's phrase. "What's the trouble?" he asked.

The little girl was convulsed, briefly, by a sob. Alleyn squatted beside her and examined the writing on the paper. It had been executed in large shaky capitals.

KARABAS
R.S.V.P.
LOVE FROM PANTY

"Was Carabbas," Alleyn ventured, "your own cat?"

Panty glared at him and slowly shook her head.

Alleyn said quickly, "How stupid of me, he was your grandfather's cat, wasn't he?"

"He loved me," said Panty, on a high note. "Better than he loved Noddy. He loved me better than he loved anybody. I was his friend." Her voice rose piercingly like the whistle of a small engine. "And I didn't," she screamed. "I didn't, I didn't, I didn't give him the ringworms. I hate my Auntie Milly. I wish she was dead. I wish they were all dead. I'll kill my Auntie Milly." She beat on the ground with her fists, and catching sight of Fox screamed at him: "Get out of here, will you. This is my place."

Fox stepped back hastily.

"I've heard," said Alleyn, cautiously, "about Carabbas, and about you. You paint pictures, don't you? Have you painted any more pictures lately?"

"I don't want to paint any more pictures," said Panty.

"That's a pity, because we rather thought of sending you a box of paints for yourself from London."

Panty sobbed dryly. "Who did?" she said.

"Troy Alleyn," said Alleyn. "Mrs. Alleyn, you know. She's my wife."

"If I painted a picture of my Auntie Milly," said Panty, "I'd give her pig's whiskers, and she'd look like Judas Iscariot. They said my cat Carabbas had the ringworms, and they said I'd given them to him, and they're all, *all* liars. He hadn't, and I didn't. It was only his poor fur coming out."

With the abandon which Troy had witnessed in the Little Theatre, Panty flung herself face forward on the ground and kicked.

Tentatively Alleyn bent over her, and after a moment's hesitation, picked her up. For a moment or two she fought violently, but suddenly, with an air of desolation, let her arms fall and hung limply in his hands.

"Never mind, Panty," Alleyn muttered helplessly. "Here, let's mop up your face." He felt in his pocket and his fingers closed round a hard object. "Look here," he said. "Look what I've got," and pulled out a small packet. "Do you ever play Happy Families?" he said. He pushed the box of cards into her hands and not very successfully mopped her face with his handkerchief. "Let's move on," he said to Fox.

He carried the now inert Panty across to the third flight of steps. Here she began to wriggle, and he put her down.

"I want to play Happy Families," said Panty thickly. "Here," she added. She squatted down and, still interrupting herself from time to time with a hiccoughing sob, opened her pack of picture cards and with filthy fingers began to deal them into three heaps.

"Sit down, Fox," said Alleyn. "You're going to play Happy Families."

Fox sat uneasily on the second step.

Panty was a slow dealer, principally because she examined the face of each card before she put it down.

"Do you know the rules?" Alleyn asked Fox.

"I can't say I do," he replied, putting on his spectacles. "Would it be anything like euchre?"

"Not much, but you'll pick it up. The object is to collect a family. Would you be good enough," he said turning to Panty, "to oblige me with Mrs. Snips, the Tailor's Wife?"

"You didn't say 'Please' so it's my turn," said Panty. "Give me Mr. Snips, the Tailor, and Master Snips and Miss Snips. Please."

"Damn," said Alleyn. "Here you are," and handed over the cards, each with its cut of an antic who might have walked out of a Victorian volume of Punch.

Panty pushed these cards underneath her and sat on them. Her bloomers, true to her legend, were conspicuous. "Now," she said, turning a bleary glance on Fox. "You give me—"

"Don't I get a turn?" asked Fox.

"Not unless she goes wrong," said Alleyn. "You'll learn."

"Give me," said Panty, "Master Grit, the Grocer's Son."

"Doesn't she have to say 'please'?"

"Please," yelled Panty. "I said 'please.' Please."

Fox handed over the card.

"And Mrs. Grit," Panty went on.

"It beats me," said Fox, "how she knows."

"She knows," said Alleyn, "because she looked."

Panty laughed raucously. "And you give me Mr. Bull, the Butcher," she demanded, turning on Alleyn. "Please."

"Not at home," said Alleyn, triumphantly. "And now you see, Fox, it's my turn."

"The game seems crooked to me," said Fox, gloomily.

"Master Bun," Panty remarked presently, "is azzakerly like my Uncle Thomas." Alleyn in imagination changed the grotesque faces on all the cards to those of the Ancreds as Troy had drawn them in her note book. "So he is," he said. "And now I know you've got him. Please give me Master Ancred, the Actor's Son." This sally afforded Panty exquisite amusement. With primitive guffaws she began to demand cards under the names of her immediate relations and to the utter confusion of the game.

"There now," said Alleyn at last, in a voice that struck him as being odiously complacent. "That was a lovely game. Suppose you take us up to see the—ah."

"The Happy Family," Fox prompted in a wooden voice.

"Certainly," said Alleyn.

"Why?" Panty demanded.

"That's what we've come for."

Panty stood squarely facing him. Upon her stained face there grew, almost furtively, a strange expression. It was compounded, he thought, of the look of a normal child about to impart a secret and of something less familiar, more disquieting.

"Here!" she said. "I want to tell you something. Not him. You."

She drew Alleyn away and with a sidelong glance, pulled him down until she could hook her arm about his neck. He waited, feeling her breath uncomfortably in his ear.

"What is it?"

The whispering was disembodied but unexpectedly clear. "We've got," it said, "a murderer in our family."

When he drew back and looked at her she was smiling nervously.

CHAPTER TWELVE

The Bell and the Book

i

So ACCURATE and lively were Troy's drawings that Alleyn recognized Desdemona Ancred as soon as she appeared on the top step of the third terrace and looked down upon the group—doubtless a curious one—made by himself, Panty and Fox. Indeed, as she paused, she struck precisely the attitude, histrionic and grandiose, with which Troy had invested her caricature.

"Ah!" said Dessy richly. "Panty! At last!"

She held out her hand towards Panty and at the same time looked frankly at Alleyn. "How do you do?" she said. "Are you on your way up? Has this terrible young person waylaid you? Shall I introduce myself?"

"Miss Ancred?" Alleyn said.

"He's Mrs. Alleyn's husband," Panty said. "We don't much want you, thank you, Aunt Dessy."

Dessy was in the act of advancing with poise, down the steps. Her smile remained fixed on her face. Perhaps she halted for a fraction of time in her stride. The next second her hand was in his and she was gazing with embarrassing intensity into his eyes.

"I'm so glad you've come," she said in her deepest voice. "So glad! We are terribly, terribly distressed. My brother has told you, I know." She pressed his hand, released it, and looked at Fox.

"Inspector Fox," said Alleyn. Desdemona was tragically gracious.

They turned to climb the steps. Panty gave a threatening wail.

"You," said her aunt, "had better run home as fast as you can. Miss Able's been looking everywhere for you. What *have* you been doing, Panty? You're covered in earth."

Immediately they were confronted with another scene. Panty repeated her former performance, roaring out strange threats against her family, lamenting the cat Carabbas and protesting that she had not infected him.

"Really, it's *too* ridiculous," Dessy said in a loud aside to Alleyn. "Not that we didn't all feel it. Poor Carabbas! And my father so attached always. But honestly it was a menace to all our healths. Ringworm, beyond a shadow of doubt. Fur coming out in handfuls. Obviously it had given them the disease in the first instance. We did perfectly right to have it destroyed. Come *on*, Panty."

By this time they had reached the top terrace with Panty waddling lamentably behind them. Here they were met by Miss Caroline Able, who brightly ejaculated: "Goodness, what a noise!" cast a clear sensible glance at Alleyn and Fox, and removed her still bellowing charge.

"I'm so distressed," Desdemona cried, "that you should have had this reception. Honestly, poor Panty is simply beyond everything. Nobody loves children more than I do, but she's got such a *difficult* nature. And in a house of tragedy, when one's nerves and emotions are lacerated—"

She gazed into his eyes, made a small helpless gesture and finally ushered them into the hall. Alleyn glanced quickly at the space under the gallery, but it was still untenanted.

"I'll tell my sister and my sister-in-law," Dessy began, but Alleyn interrupted her. "If we might just have a word with you, first," he said. And by Dessy's manner, at once portentous and dignified, he knew that this suggestion was not unpleasing to her. She led them to the small sitting-room where Troy had found Sonia Orrincourt and Cedric giggling together on the sofa. Desdemona placed herself on this sofa. She sat down, Alleyn noticed, quite beautifully; not glancing at her objective but sinking on it in one movement and then elegantly disposing her arms.

"I expect," he began, "that your brother has explained the official attitude to this kind of situation. We're obliged to make all sorts of enquiries before we can take any further action."

"I see," said Desdemona nodding owlishly. "Yes, I see. Go on."

"To put it baldly, do you yourself think there is any truth in the suggestion made by the anonymous letter-writer?"

Desdemona pressed the palms of her hands carefully against her eyes. "If I *could* dismiss it," she cried, "if I could!"

"You have no idea, I suppose, who could have written the letters?" She shook her head. Alleyn wondered if she had glanced at him through her fingers.

"Have any of you been up to London since your father's funeral?"

"How frightful!" she said, dropping her hands and gazing at him. "I was afraid of this. How frightful!"

"What?"

"You think one of us wrote the letter? Someone at Ancreton?"

"Well, really," said Alleyn, stifling his exasperation, "it's not a preposterous conjecture, is it?"

"No, no. I suppose not. But what a disturbing thought."

"Well, did any of you go to London—"

"Let me think. Let me think," Desdemona muttered, again covering her eyes. "In the evening. After we had—had—after Papa's funeral, and after Mr. Rattisbon had—" She made another little helpless gesture.

"—had read the Will?" Alleyn suggested.

"Yes. That evening, by the seven-thirty. Thomas, and Jenetta (my sister-in-law), and Fenella (her daughter), and Paul (my nephew, Paul Kentish), all went up to London."

"And returned? When?"

"Not at all. Jenetta doesn't live here and Fenella and Paul because of— However! Fenella has joined her mother in a flat and I think Paul's staying with them. My brother, Thomas, as you know, lives in London."

"And nobody else has left Ancreton?"

Yes, it seemed that the following day Millamant and Cedric and Desdemona herself had gone up to London by the early morning train. There was a certain amount of business to be done. They returned in the evening. It was by that evening's post, the Wednesday's, Alleyn reflected, that the anonymous letter reached the Yard. He found by dint of cautious questioning that they had all separated in London and gone their several ways to meet in the evening train.

"And Miss Orrincourt?" Alleyn asked.

"I'm afraid," said Desdemona grandly, "that I've really no knowledge at all of Miss Orrincourt's movements. She was away all day yesterday; I imagine in London."

"She's staying on here?"

"You may well look astonished," said Desdemona, though Alleyn, to his belief, had looked nothing of the sort. "After everything, Mr. Alleyn. After working against us with Papa! After humiliating and wounding us in every possible way. In the teeth, you might say, of the Family's feelings, she stays on. T'uh!"

"Does Sir Cedric—"

"Cedric," said Desdemona, "is now head of the family, but I have no hesitation in saying that I think his attitude to a good many things inexplicable and revolting. Particularly where Sonia Orrincourt (you'll never get me to believe she was born Orrincourt) is concerned. What he's up to, what both of them—However!"

Alleyn did not press for an exposition of Cedric's behaviour. At the moment he was fascinated by Desdemona's. On the wall opposite her, hung a looking-glass in a Georgian frame. He saw that Desdemona was keeping an eye on herself. Even as she moved her palms from before her eyes, her fingers touched her hair and she slightly turned her head while her abstracted yet watchful gaze noted, he thought, the effect. And as often as she directed her melting glance upon him, so often did it return to the mirror to affirm with a satisfaction barely veiled, its own limpid quality. He felt as if he were interviewing a mannequin.

"I understand," he said, "that it was you who found the tin of ratsbane in Miss Orrincourt's suitcase?"

"Wasn't it awful? Well, it was all four of us, actually. My sister Pauline (Mrs. Kentish), my sister-in-law, and Cedric and I. In her box-room, you know. A very common-looking suitcase smothered in Number Three Company touring labels. As I've pointed out to Thomas a thousand times, the woman is simply a squalid little ham actress. Well, *not* an actress. All eyes and teeth in the third row of the chorus when she's lucky."

"Did you yourself handle it?"

"Oh, we all handled it. Naturally. Cedric tried to prise up the lid, but it wouldn't come. So he tapped the tin and said he could tell from the sound that it wasn't full." She lowered her voice. "Only half-full, he said. And Milly (sister-in-law, Mrs. Henry Ancred) said—" She paused.

"Yes?" Alleyn prompted, tired of these genealogical parentheses. "Mrs. Henry Ancred said?"

"She said that to the best of her knowledge it had never been used." She changed her position a little and added: "I don't understand Milly. She's so off-hand. Of course I know she's frightfully capable but—well, she's not an Ancred and doesn't feel this as we do. She's—well, let's face it, she's a bit M.C. Do you know?"

Alleyn did not respond to this appeal from blue blood to blue blood. He said: "Was the suitcase locked?"

"We wouldn't have broken anything open, Mr. Alleyn."

"Wouldn't you?" he said vaguely. Desdemona glanced in the mirror. "Well—Pauline might," she admitted after a pause.

Alleyn waited for a moment, caught Fox's eye, and stood up. He said: "Now, Miss Ancred, I wonder if we may see your father's room?"

"Papa's *room?*"

"If we may."

"I couldn't—you won't mind if I—I'll ask Barker—"

"If he'd just show us the general direction we could find our own way."

Desdemona stretched out her hands impulsively. "You *do* understand," she said. "You do understand how one feels. Thank you."

Alleyn smiled vaguely, dodged the outstretched hands and made for the door. "Perhaps, Barker," he suggested, "could show us the room."

Desdemona swept to the bell-push and in a moment or two Barker came in. With enormous aplomb she explained what he was to do. She contrived to turn Barker into the very quintessence of family retainers. The atmosphere in the little sitting-room grew more and more feudal. "These gentlemen," she ended, "have come to help us, Barker. We, in our turn, must help them, mustn't we? You will help them, won't you?"

"Certainly, Miss," said Barker. "If you would come this way, sir?"

How well Troy had described the great stairs and the gallery and the yards and yards of dead canvas in heavy frames. And the smell. The Victorian smell of varnish, carpet, wax and, mysteriously, paste. A yellow smell, she had said. Here was the first long corridor and there, branching from it, the passage to Troy's tower. This was where she had lost herself that first night and these were the rooms with their ridiculous names. On his right, Bancroft and Bernhardt; on his left Terry and Bracegirdle; then an open linen closet and bathrooms. Barker's coattails jigged steadily ahead of them. His head was stooped and one saw only a thin fringe of grey hair, and a little dandruff on his black collar. Here was the cross-corridor, corresponding with the picture gallery and facing them a closed door with the legend, in Gothic lettering, "Irving."

"This is the room, sir," said Barker's faded and breathless voice.

"We'll go in, if you please."

The door opened on darkness and the smell of disinfectant. A momentary fumbling and then a bedside lamp threw a pool of light upon a table and a crimson counterpane. With a clatter of rings Barker pulled aside the window curtains and then let up the blinds.

The aspect of the room that struck Alleyn most forcibly was the extraordinary number of prints and photographs upon the walls. They were so lavishly distributed that almost all the paper, a red flock powdered with stars, was concealed by them. Next he noted the heavy richness of the appointments; the enormous looking-glass, the brocades and velvets, the massive and forbidding furniture.

Suspended above the bed was a long cord. He saw that it ended, not in a bell-push, but in raw strands of wire.

"Will that be all, sir?" said Barker, behind him.

"Stop for a minute, will you?" Alleyn said. "I want you to help us, Barker."

ii

He was indeed very old. His eyes were filmy and expressed nothing but a remote sadness. His hands seemed to have shrunk away from their own empurpled veins, and were tremulous. But all these witnesses of age were in part disguised by a lifetime's habit of attentiveness to other people's wants. There was the shadow of alacrity still about Barker.

"I don't think," Alleyn said, "that Miss Ancred quite explained why we are here. It's at Mr. Thomas Ancred's suggestion. He wants us to make fuller enquiries into the cause of Sir Henry's death."

"Indeed, sir?"

"Some of his family believe that the diagnosis was too hastily given."

"Quite so, sir."

"Had you any such misgivings yourself?"

Barker closed and unclosed his hands. "I can't say I had, sir. Not at first."

"Not at first?"

"Knowing what he took to eat and drink at dinner, sir, and the way he was worked up, and had been over and over again. Dr. Withers had warned him of it, sir."

"But later? After the funeral? And now?"

"I really can't say, sir. What with Mrs. Kentish, and Mrs. Henry and Miss Desdemona asking me over and over again about a certain missing article and what with us all being very put about in the servants' hall, I can't really say."

"A tin of ratsbane was the missing article?"

"Yes, sir. I understand they've found it now."

"And the question they want settled is whether it was an opened or unopened tin before it was lost. Is that it?"

"I understand that's it, sir. But we've had that stuff on the premises these last ten years and more. Two tins there were, sir, in one of the outside store-rooms and there was one opened and used up and thrown out. That I do know. And this one that's turned up, I can't say. Mrs. Henry Ancred recollects, sir, that it was there about a year ago unopened and Mrs. Bullivant, the cook, says it's been partly used since then, and Mrs. Henry doesn't fancy so, and that's all I can say, sir."

"Do you know if rat-poison has ever been used in Miss Orrincourt's room?"

Barker's manner became glazed with displeasure.

"Never to my knowledge, sir," he said.

"Are there no rats there?"

"The lady in question complained of them, I understand, to one of the housemaids who set traps and caught several. I believe the lady said she didn't fancy the idea of poison and for that reason it was not employed."

"I see. Now, Barker, if you will, I should like you to tell me exactly what this room looked like when you entered it on the morning after Sir Henry's death."

Barker's sunken hand moved to his lips and covered their trembling. A film of tears spread over his eyes.

"I know it's distressing for you," Alleyn said, "and I'm sorry. Sit down. No, please sit down."

Barker stooped his head a little and sat on the only high chair in the room.

"I'm sure," Alleyn said, "that if there was anything gravely amiss you'd want to see it remedied."

Barker seemed to struggle between his professional reticence and his personal distress. Finally, in a sudden flood of garrulity, he produced the classical reaction: "I wouldn't want to see this house mixed up in anything scandalous, sir. My father was butler here to the former baronet, Sir Henry's second cousin—Sir William Ancred—that was—I was knife-boy and then footman under him. He was not," said Barker, "anything to do with theatricals, sir, the old gentleman wasn't. This would have been a great blow to him."

"You mean the manner of Sir Henry's death?"

"I mean—" Barker tightened his unsteady lips. "I mean the way things were conducted lately."

"Miss Orrincourt?"

"T'uh!" said Barker and thus established his lifelong service to the Ancreds.

"Look here," Alleyn said suddenly. "Do you know what the family have got into their heads about this business?"

There was a long pause before the old voice whispered: "I don't like to think. I don't encourage gossip below stairs, sir, and I don't take part in it myself."

"Well," Alleyn suggested, "suppose you tell me about this room."

It was, after all, only a slow enlargement of what he had already heard from Troy. The darkened room, the figure hunched on the bed, "As if," Barker said fearfully, "he'd been trying to crawl down to the floor," the stench and disorder and the broken bell-cord.

"Where was the end?" Alleyn asked. "The bell-push itself?"

"In his hand, sir. Tight clenched round it, his hands was. We didn't discover it at first."

"Have you still got it?"

"It's in his dressing-table drawer, sir. I put it there, meaning to get it mended."

"Did you unscrew it or examine it in any way?"

"Oh, no, sir. No. I just put it away and disconnected the circuit on the board."

"Right. And now, Barker, about the night before, when Sir Henry went to bed. Did you see anything of him?"

"Oh, yes indeed, sir. He rang for me as usual. It was midnight when the bell went and I came up to his room. I'd valeted him sir, since his own man left."

"Did he ring his room bell?"

"No, sir. He always rang the bell in the hall as he went through. By the time he reached his room, you see, I had gone up the servants' stairs and was waiting for him."

"How did he seem?"

"Terrible. In one of his tantrums and talking very wild and angry."

"Against his family?"

"Very hot against them."

"Go on."

"I got him into his pyjamas and gown and him raging all the while and troubled with his indigestion pain as well. I put out the medicine he took for it. He said he wouldn't take it just then so I left the bottle and glass by his bed. I was offering to help him into bed when he says he must see Mr. Rattisbon. He's the family solicitor, sir, and always comes to us for the Birthday. Well, sir, I tried to put Sir Henry off, seeing he was tired and upset, but he wouldn't hear of it. When I took him by the arm he got quite violent. I was alarmed and tried to hold him but he broke away."

Alleyn had a sudden vision of the two old men struggling together in this grandiose bedroom.

"Seeing there was nothing for it," Barker went on, "I did as he ordered and took Mr. Rattisbon up to his room. He called me back and told me to find the two extra helps we always get in for the Birthday. A Mr. and Mrs. Candy, sir, formerly on the staff here and now in a small business in the village. I understood from what Sir Henry said that he wished them to witness his Will. I showed them up and he then told me to inform Miss Orrincourt that he would be ready for his hot drink in half an hour. He said he would not require me again. So I left him."

"And went to give this message?"

"After I had switched over the mechanism of his bell, sir, so that if he required anything in the night it would sound in the passage outside Mrs. Henry's door. It has been specially arranged like this, in case of an emergency. And of course, sir, it must have broke off in his hand before it sounded, because even if Mrs. Henry had slept through it, Miss Dessy was sharing her room and must have heard. Miss Dessy sleeps very light, I understand."

"Isn't it strange that he didn't call out?"

"He wouldn't be heard, sir. The walls in this part of the house are very thick, being part of the original outer walls. The previous baronet, sir, added this wing to Ancreton."

"I see. At this time where was Miss Orrincourt?"

"She had left the company, sir. They had all moved into the drawing-room."

"*All* of them?"

"Yes, sir. Except her and Mr. Rattisbon. And Mrs. Alleyn, who was a guest. They were all there. Mrs. Kentish said the young lady had gone to her rooms and that's where I found her. Mr. Rattisbon was in the hall."

"What was the business with the hot drink?"

The old man described it carefully. Until the rise of Sonia Orrincourt, Millamant had always prepared the drink. Miss Orrincourt had taken over this routine. The milk and ingredients were left in her room by the housemaid who turned down her bed. She brewed the drink over a heater, put it in a thermos flask and, half an hour after he had retired, took it to his room. He slept badly and sometimes would not drink it until much later in the night.

"What happened to the thermos flask and the cup and saucer?"

"They were taken away and washed up, sir. They've been in use since."

"Had he drunk any of it?"

"It had been poured into the cup, sir, at all events and into the saucer for that cat, as was always done, and the saucer set on the floor. But the cup and the flask and the medicine bottle had been overturned and there was milk and medicine soaked into the carpet."

"Had he taken his medicine?"

"The glass was dirty. It had fallen into the saucer."

"And has of course been washed," said Alleyn. "What about the bottle?"

"It had been knocked over, sir, as I mentioned. It was a new bottle. I was very much put out, sir, but I tried to tidy the room a bit, not knowing exactly what I was doing. I remember I took the dirty china and the bottle and thermos downstairs with me. The bottle was thrown out, and the other things cleared up. The medicine cupboard has been cleaned out thoroughly. It's in the bathroom, sir, through that door. The whole suite," said Barker conscientiously, "has been turned out and cleaned."

Fox mumbled inarticulately.

"Well," said Alleyn. "To go back to the message you took to Miss Orrincourt that night. Did you actually see her?"

"No, sir. I tapped on the door and she answered." He moved uneasily.

"Was there anything else?"

"It was a queer thing—" His voice faded.

"What was a queer thing?"

"She must have been alone," Barker mused, "because as I've said, sir, the others were downstairs and afterwards, *just* afterwards, when I took in the grog tray, there they all were. But before I knocked on her door, sir, I could have sworn that she was laughing."

iii

When Barker had gone, Fox sighed gustily, put on his spectacles and looked quizzically through them at the naked end of the bell cord.

"Yes, Br'er Fox, exactly," said Alleyn and went to the dressing-table. "That'll be the lady," he said.

A huge photograph of Sonia Orrincourt stood in the middle of the dressing-table.

Fox joined Alleyn. "Very taking," he said. "Funny you know, Mr. Alleyn. That's what they call a pin-up girl. Plenty of teeth and hair and limbs. Sir Henry put it in a silver frame, but that, you might say, is the only difference. Very taking."

Alleyn opened the top drawer on the left.

"First pop," Fox remarked.

Alleyn pulled on a glove and gingerly took out a pear-shaped wooden bell-push. "One takes these pathetic precautions," he said, "and a hell of a lot of use they are. Now then." He unscrewed the end of the bell-push and looked into it.

"See here, Fox. Look at the two points. Nothing broken. One of the holding screws and its washer are tight. No bits of wire. The other screw and washer are loose. Got your lens? Have a look at that cord again."

Fox took out a pocket lens, and returned to the bed. "One of the wires is unbroken," he said presently. "No shiny end and its blackened like they do get with time. The other's different though. Been dragged through and scraped, I'd say. That's what must have happened. He put his weight on it and they pulled through."

"In that case," Alleyn said, "why is one of the screws so tight? And only one wire shiny? We'll keep this bell-push, Fox."

He had wrapped his handkerchief round it and dropped it in his pocket when the door was opened and Sonia Orrincourt walked in.

iv

She was dressed in black, but so dashingly, that mourning was not much suggested. Her curtain of ashen hair and her heavy fringe were glossy, her eyelids were blue, her lashes incredible and her skin sleek. She wore a diamond clasp and bracelet and earrings. She stood just inside the room.

"Pardon the intrusion," she said. "But am I addressing the police?"

"You are," said Alleyn. "Miss Orrincourt?"

"That's the name."

"How do you do. This is Inspector Fox."

"Now listen!" said Miss Orrincourt, advancing upon them with a professional gait. "I want to know what's cooking in this icehouse. I've got my rights to look after, same as anybody else, haven't I?"

"Undoubtedly."

"Thank you. Very kind, I'm sure. Then perhaps you'll tell me who asked you into my late fiance's room and just what you're doing now you've got there."

"We were asked by his family and we're doing a job of work."

"*Work?* What sort of work? Don't tell me the answer to that one," said Miss Orrincourt angrily. "I seem to know it. They're trying to swing something across me. Is that right? Trying to pack me up. *What is it?* That's what I want to know. Come on. *What is it?*"

"Will you first of all tell me how you knew we were here and why you thought we were police officers?"

She sat on the bed, leaning back on her hands, her hair falling vertically from her scalp. Behind her was spread the crimson counterpane. Alleyn wondered why she had ever attempted to be an actress while there were magazine artists who needed models. She looked in a leisurely manner at Fox's feet. "How do I know you're police? That's a scream! Take a look at your boy friend's boots."

"Yours, partner," Alleyn murmured, catching Fox's eye.

Fox cleared his throat. "Er—*touche*," he said carefully. "Not much good me trying to get by with a sharp-eyed young lady, is it, sir?"

"Well, come on," Miss Orrincourt demanded. "What's the big idea? Are they trying to make out there's something funny in the Will? Or what? What are you doing, opening my late fiance's drawers? Come on!"

"I'm afraid," said Alleyn, "you've got this situation the wrong way round. We're on a job and part of that job is asking questions. And since you're here, Miss Orrincourt, I wonder if you'd mind answering one or two?"

She looked at him, he thought, as an animal or a completely unself-conscious child might look at a stranger. It was difficult to expect anything but perfect sounds from her. He experienced a shock each time he heard the cockney voice with its bronchial overtones, and the phrases whose very idiom seemed shoddy, as if she had abandoned her native dialect for something she had half-digested at the cinema.

"All upstage and county!" she said. "Fancy! And what were you wanting to know?"

"About the Will, for instance."

"The Will's all right," she said quickly. "You can turn the place inside out. Crawl up the chimney if you like. You won't find another Will. I'm telling you and I know."

"Why are you so positive?"

She had slipped back until she rested easily on her forearm. "I don't mind," she said. "I'll tell you. When I came in here last thing that night, my fiance showed it to me. He'd had old Ratsbane up and a couple of witnesses and he'd signed it. He showed me. The ink was still wet. He'd burnt the old one in the fireplace there."

"I see."

"And he couldn't have written another one even if he'd wanted to. Because he was tired and his pain was bad and he said he was going to take his medicine and go to sleep."

"He was in bed when you visited him?"

"Yes." She waited for a moment, looking at her enamelled finger nails. "People seem to think I've got no feelings, but I've been very upset. Honestly. Well, he was sweet. And when a girl's going to be married and everything's marvellous it's a terrible thing for this to happen, I don't care what anyone says."

"Did he seem very ill?"

"That's what everybody keeps asking. The doctor and old Pauline and Milly. On and on. Honestly, I could scream. He just had one of his turns and he felt queer. And with the way he'd eaten and thrown a temperament on top of it, no wonder. I gave him his hot drink and kissed him nighty-nighty and he seemed all right and that's all I know."

"He drank his hot milk while you were with him?"

She swung over a little with a luxurious movement and looked at him through narrowed eyes. "That's right," she said. "Drank it and liked it."

"And his medicine?"

"He poured that out for himself. I told him to drink up like a good boy, but he said he'd wait a bit and see if his tummy wouldn't settle down without it. So I went."

"Right. Now, Miss Orrincourt," said Alleyn, facing her with his hands in his pockets, "you've been very frank. I shall follow your example. You want to know what we're doing here. I'll tell you. Our job, or a major part of it, is to find out why you played a string of rather infantile practical jokes on Sir Henry Ancred and let it be thought that his grand-daughter was responsible."

She was on her feet so quickly that he actually felt his nerves jump. She was close to him now; her under lip jutted out and her brows, thin hairy lines, were drawn together in a scowl. She resembled some drawing in a man's magazine of an infuriated baggage in a bedroom. One almost expected some dubious caption to issue in a balloon from her lips.

"Who says I did it?" she demanded.

"I do, at the moment," Alleyn said. "Come now. Let's start at Mr. Juniper's shop. You bought the Raspberry there, you know."

"The dirty little so-and-so," she said meditatively. "What a pal! *And* what a gentleman, I don't suppose."

Alleyn ignored these strictures upon Mr. Juniper. "Then," he said, "there's that business about the paint on the bannisters."

Obviously this astonished her. Her face was suddenly bereft of expression, a mask with slightly dilated eyes. "Wait a bit," she said. "That's funny!"

Alleyn waited.

"Here!" she said. "Have you been talking to young Ceddie?"

"No."

"That's what you say," she muttered and turned on Fox. "What about you, then?"

"No, Miss Orrincourt," said Fox blandly. "Not me or the Chief Inspector."

"Chief Inspector?" she said. "Coo!"

Alleyn saw that she was looking at him with a new interest and had a premonition of what was to come.

"That'd be one of the high-ups, wouldn't it? Chief Inspector who? I don't seem to have caught the name."

Any hopes he may have entertained that his connection with Troy was unknown to her, vanished when she repeated his name, clapped her hand over her mouth and ejaculating "Coo! That's a good one," burst into fits of uncontrollable laughter.

"Pardon me," she said presently, "but when you come to think of it it's funny. You can't get away from it you know, it's funny. Seeing it was her that— Well of course! That's how you knew about the paint on the bannisters."

"And what," Alleyn asked, "is the connection between Sir Cedric Ancred, and the paint on the bannisters?"

"I'm not going to put myself away," said Miss Orrincourt, "nor Ceddie either, if it comes to that. Ceddie's pretty well up the spout anyway. If he's let me down he's crazy. There's a whole lot of things I want to know first. What's all this stuff about a book? What's the idea? Is it me, or is it everybody else in this dump that's gone haywire? Look. Somebody puts a dirty little book in a cheese dish and serves it up for lunch. And when they find it, what do these half-wits do? Look at me as if I was the original whodunit. Well, I mean to say, it's silly. And what a book! Written by somebody with a lisp and what about? Keeping people fresh after they're dead. Give you the willies. And when I say I never put it in the cheese dish what do they do? Pauline starts tearing herself to shreds and Dessy says 'Wc'rc not so foolish as to suppose you'd want to run your head in a noose,' and Milly says she happens to know I've read it and they all go out as if I was something the cat brought in, and I sit there wondering if it's me or all of them who ought to be locked up."

"And had you ever seen the book before?"

"I seem to remember," she began, and then looking from Alleyn to Fox with a new wariness, she said sharply: "Not to notice. Not to know what it was about." And after a pause she added dully: "I'm not much of a one for reading."

Alleyn said, "Miss Orrincourt, will you without prejudice tell me if you personally were responsible for any of the practical jokes other than the ones already under discussion?"

"I'm not answering any questions. I don't know what's going on here. A girl's got to look after herself. I thought I had one friend in this crazy gang, now I'm beginning to think *he's* let me down."

"I suppose," said Alleyn, wearily, "you mean Sir Cedric Ancred?"

"*Sir* Cedric Ancred," Miss Orrincourt repeated with a shrill laugh. "The bloody little baronet. Excuse my smile, but honestly it's a scream." She turned her back on them and walked out, leaving the door open.

They could still hear her laughing with unconvincing virtuosity as she walked away down the corridor.

V

"Have we," Fox asked blandly, "got anywhere with that young lady? Or have we not?"

"Not very far, if anywhere at all," Alleyn said, morosely. "I don't know about you, Fox, but I found her performance tolerably convincing. Not that impressions of that sort amount to very much. Suppose she did put arsenic in the old man's hot milk, wouldn't this be the only line she could reasonably take? And at this stage of the proceedings when I still have a very faint hope that we may come across something that blows their damn' suspicions to smithereens, I couldn't very well insist on anything. We'll just have to go mousing along."

"Where to?" Fox asked.

"For the moment, in different directions. I've been carrying you about like a broody hen, Foxkin, and it's time you brought forth. Down you go and exercise the famous technique on Barker and his retinue of elderly maids. Find out all about the milk, trace its whole insipid history from cow to thermos. Inspire gossip. Prattle. Seek out the paper dump, the bottle dump, the mops and the pails. Let us go clanking back to London like a dry canteen. Salvage the thermos flask. We'll have to try for an analysis, but what a hope! Get along with you, Fox. Do your stuff."

"And where may I ask, Mr. Alleyn, are you going?"

"Oh," said Alleyn, "I'm a snob. I'm going to see the baronet."

Fox paused at the doorway. "Taking it by and large, sir," he said, "and on the face of it as it stands, do you reckon there'll be an exhumation?"

"There'll be one exhumation at all events. To-morrow, if Dr. Curtis can manage it."

"To-morrow?" said Fox, startled. "Dr. Curtis? Sir Henry Ancred?"

"No," Alleyn said, "the cat Carabbas."

CHAPTER THIRTEEN

Spotlight on Cedric

i

ALLEYN INTERVIEWED Cedric in the library. It was a place without character or life. Rows of uniform editions stood coldly behind glass doors. There was no smell of tobacco, or memory of fires, only the dankness of an unused room.

Cedric's manner was both effusive and uneasy. He made a little dart at Alleyn and flapped at his hand. He began at once to talk about Troy. "She was too marvelous, a perfect darling. So thrilling to watch her at work: that *magical* directness, almost intimidating, one felt. You must be madly proud of her, of course."

His mouth opened and shut, his teeth glinted, his pale eyes stared and his voice gabbled on and on. He was restless too, and wandered about the room aimlessly, lifting lids of empty cigarette boxes and moving ornaments. He recalled acquaintance with Alleyn's nephews with whom, he said, he had been at school. He professed a passionate interest in Alleyn's work. He returned again to Troy, suggesting that he alone among the Philistines had spoken her language. There was a disquieting element in all this and Alleyn, when an opportunity came, cut across it.

"One moment," he said. "Our visit is an official one. I'm sure you will agree that we should keep it so. May we simply think the fact of my wife having been commissioned to paint Sir Henry a sort of freakish coincidence and nothing to do with the matter in hand? Except, of course, in so far as her job may turn out to have any bearing on the circumstances."

Cedric's mouth had remained slightly open. He turned pink, touched his hair and said: "Of course if you feel like that about it. I merely thought that a friendly atmosphere—"

"That was extremely kind," said Alleyn.

"Unless your somewhat muscular sense of the official proprieties forbids it," Cedric suggested acidly, "shall we at least sit down?"

"Thank you," said Alleyn tranquilly, "that would be much more comfortable."

He sat in a vast arm-chair, crossed his knees, joined his hands and, with what Troy called his donnish manner, prepared to tackle Cedric.

"Mr. Thomas Ancred tells me you share the feeling that further enquiries should be made into the circumstances of Sir Henry's death."

"Well, I suppose I do," Cedric agreed fretfully. "I mean it's all pretty vexing, isn't it? Well, I mean one would like to know. All sorts of things depend—And yet again it's not very delicious—Of course, when one considers that I'm the one who's most involved . . . Well, *look* at me. *Incarcerated*, in this frightful house! And the entail a pittance. All those taxes too, and *rapacious* death duties. Never, never will anybody be found mad enough to rent it, and as for schools, Carol Able does nothing but exclaim how inconvenient and how damp. And now the war's over the problem children will be hurtled away. One will be left to wander in rags down whispering corridors. So that you see," he added, waving his hands, "one does rather wonder—"

"Quite so."

"And they *will* keep talking about me as Head of the Family. Before I know where I am I shall have turned into another Old Person."

"There are one or two points," Alleyn began, and immediately Cedric leant forward with an ineffable air of concentration, "that we'd like to clear up. The first is the authorship of these anonymous letters."

"Well, I didn't write them."

"Have you any idea who did?"

"Personally I favour my Aunt Pauline."

"Really? Why?"

"She prefaces almost every remark she makes with the phrase: 'I have reason to believe.' "

"Have you asked Mrs. Kentish if she wrote the letters?"

"Yes, indeed. She denies it hotly. Then there's Aunt Dessy. Quite capable, in a way, but more likely, one would have thought, to tell us flatly what she suspected. I mean, why go in for all this hush-hush letter-writing? That leaves my cousins Paul and Fenella who are, one imagines, too pleasurably engrossed in their amorous martyrdom for any outside activities; my mama, who is much too commonsensical; my aunt-in-law Jenetta, who is too grand; and all the servants led by the Ancient of Days. That, as they say in sporting circles, is the field. Unless you feel inclined to take in the squire and the parson and dear old Rattlebones himself. It couldn't be more baffling. No, on the whole I plump for Pauline. She's about somewhere. Have you encountered her? Since the Tragedy she is almost indistinguishable from Lady Macduff. Or perhaps that frightful Shakespearian dowager who curses her way up hill and down dale through one of the historical dramas. Constance? Yes, Pauline is now all compact of tragedy. Dessy's pretty bad but wait till you meet Pauline."

"Do you know if there's any paper in the house of the kind used for these letters?"

"Gracious, no! Exercise-book paper! The servants wouldn't have had it at any price. By the way, talking of exercise-books, *do* you think Caroline Able might have done it? I mean she's so wrapped up in ids and isms and tracing everything back to the Oedipus Complex. Might it perhaps have all snapped back at her and made her a weeny bit odd? It's only an idea, of course. I merely throw it out for what it's worth."

"About this tin of ratsbane," Alleyn began. Cedric interrupted him with a shrill cry.

"My dear, what a party! Imagine! Milly, the complete *Hausfrau* (my mama, you know)"—Cedric added the inevitable parentheses—"and Dessy, steaming up the stairs and Pauline tramping at her heels like one of the Fates, and poor little me panting in the rear. We didn't know what we were looking for, really. Partly rat-poison and partly they thought there might be compromising papers somewhere because Sonia's quite lovely, don't you think, and *really*—the Old Person! *Hardly* adequate, one couldn't help feeling. I pointed out that, constant or flighty, a Will was a Will, but nothing would stay them. I said in fun: 'You don't expect, darlings, to find phials of poison in her luggage, do you?' and that put the idea of luggage into their heads. So up into the box-room they hounded me, and there, to use the language of the chase, we 'found.' "

"You yourself took the tin out of the suitcase?"

"Yes, indeed. I was petrified."

"What was it like?"

"Like? But didn't dear Uncle Tom give it to you?"

"Was it clean or dirty?"

"My dear, *filthy*. They wanted me to prise open the lid and such a struggle as I had. Little bits of ratsbane flying up and hitting me. I was terrified. And then it wouldn't come out."

"Who first suggested this search?"

"Now, that *is* difficult. Did we, thinking of that beastly little brochure in the cheese dish (and there, I must tell you, I see the hand of Panty), did we with one accord cry 'ratsbane' and let loose the dogs of war? I fancy Pauline, after coining the phrase 'no smoke (or is it reek?) without heat,' said: 'But where would she get any arsenic?' and that Milly (my mama), or it might have been me, remembered the missing ratsbane. Anyway no sooner was it mentioned than Pauline and Dessy were in full cry for the guilty apartment. If you could see it, too. Darling Sonia! Well, 'darling' with reservations. The bed-chamber a welter of piercing pink frills and tortured satin and dolls peering from behind cushions or squatting on telephones, do you know?"

"I would be very glad," said Alleyn, "if the suitcase could be produced."

"Really? You wish, no doubt, to explore it for fingerprints? But, of course, you shall have it. Unbeknown, I suppose, to darling Sonia?"

"If possible."

"I'll trip upstairs and get it myself. If she's there I'll tell her there's a telephone call."

"Thank you."

"Shall I go now?"

"One moment, Sir Cedric," Alleyn began and again Cedric, with that winsome trick of anxiety, leant towards him. "Why did you, with Miss Sonia Orrincourt, plan a series of practical jokes on your grandfather?"

It was not pleasant to watch the blood sink from Cedric's face. The process left his eyelids and the pouches under his eyes mauvish. Small grooves appeared beside his nostrils. His colourless lips pouted and then widened into an unlovely smile.

"Well, really!" he tittered, "that just shows you, doesn't it? So darling Sonia has confided in you." And after a moment's hesitation he added: "As far as I'm concerned, dear Mr. Alleyn, that's the end of darling Sonia."

ii

"Perhaps I should explain," Alleyn said after a pause, "that Miss Orrincourt has not made any statement about the practical jokes."

"She *hasn't?*" The ejaculation was so incisive that it was difficult to believe Cedric had uttered it. He now lowered his head and appeared to look at the carpet between his feet. Alleyn saw his hands slide over each other. "How perfectly futile," Cedric's voice said. "Such a *very* old gag. Such an ancient wheeze! I didn't know, but you've just told me! And in I go, as they say, boots and all." He raised his face. Its pinkness had returned and its expression suggested a kind of boyish ruefulness. "Now *do* promise you won't be lividly angry. It sounds too childish, I know. But I implore you, dear Mr. Alleyn, to look about you. Observe the peculiar flavour of Katzenjammer Castle. The facade now. The utterly unnerving inequalities of the facade. The terrifying Victoriana within. The gloom. Note particularly the gloom."

"I'm afraid," Alleyn said, "that I don't follow this. Unless you're going to tell me you hoped to enliven the architecture and *decor* of Ancreton by painting spectacles and flying cows on your grandfather's portrait."

"But I didn't!" Cedric protested shrilly. "That *miraculous* portrait! No, believe me, I didn't."

"And the paint on the bannister?"

"I didn't do that either, darling Mr. Alleyn! I wouldn't have dreamed of it."

"But at least you seem to have known about it."

"I didn't do it," he repeated.

"The message written in grease-paint on the mirror? And the grease-paint on the cat?"

Cedric gave a nervous giggle. "Well—"

"Come," said Alleyn. "You had dark red grease-paint under your finger nail, you know."

"*What* sharp eyes!" cried Cedric. "Dearest Mrs. Alleyn! *Such* a help she must be to you."

"You did, in fact—"

"The Old Person," Cedric interrupted, "had been particularly rococo. I couldn't resist. The cat, too. It was a kind of practical pun. The cat's whiskers!"

"And had you anything to do with the squeaking cushion in his chair?"

"Wasn't it too robust and Rabelaisian? Sonia bought it and I—I can't deny it—I placed it there. But why not? If I might make a tiny squeak of protest, dear Mr. Alleyn, *has* all this got *anything* to do with the business in hand?"

"I think it might well have been designed to influence Sir

Henry's Will and with both his Wills we are, as I think you'll agree, very definitely concerned."

"This is too subtle for my poor wits, I'm afraid."

"It was common knowledge, wasn't it, that his youngest granddaughter was, at this time, his principal heir?"

"But one never knew. We bounced in and out of favour from day to day."

"If this is true, wouldn't these tricks, if attributed to her, very much affect her position?" Alleyn waited but was given no answer. "Why, in fact, did you allow him to believe she was the culprit?"

"That devilish child," Cedric said, "gets away with innumerable hideous offences. A sense of injured innocence must have been quite a change for her."

"You see," Alleyn went on steadily. "The flying cow was the last trick of five and, as far as we know was the final reason for Sir Henry's changing his Will that night. It was fairly conclusively proved to him that Panty did not do it and it's possible that Sir Henry, not knowing which of his family to suspect, took his revenge on all."

"Yes but—"

"Now whoever was a party to these tricks—"

"At least you'll admit that I wouldn't be very likely to try and cut myself out of the Will—"

"I think that result was unforeseen. You hoped perhaps, to return to your former position with Panty out of the picture. To something, in fact, on the lines of the Will rcad at the dinner party, but rather better. You have told me that you and Miss Orrincourt were partners in one of these practical jokes. Indeed you've suggested to me that you at least had knowledge of them all."

Cedric began to speak very rapidly. "I resent all this talk of partnership. I resent the implication and deny it. You force me into an intolerable position with your hints and mysteries. I suppose there's nothing left but for me to admit I knew what she was doing and why she did it. It amused me and it enlivened the ghastly boredom of these wretched festivities. Panty, I consider an abomination and I don't in the least regret that she was suspected or that she was cut out of the Will. She probably wallowed in her borrowed glory. There!"

"Thank you," said Alleyn. "That clears up quite a lot of the fog. And now, Sir Cedric, are you quite sure you don't know who wrote the letters?"

"Absolutely."

"And are you equally sure you didn't put the book on embalming in the cheese dish?"

Cedric gaped at him. "I?" he said. "Why should I? Oh, no! I don't want Sonia to turn out to be a murderess. Or I didn't, then. I'd rather thought—I—we'd—it doesn't matter. But I must say I'd like to *know*."

Looking at him, Alleyn was visited by a notion so extravagant that he found himself incapable of pressing Cedric any further on the subject of his relationship with Miss Orrincourt.

He was, in any case, prevented from doing so by the entrance of Pauline Kentish.

Pauline entered weeping; not loudly but with the suggestion of welling tears held bravely back. She seemed to Alleyn to be an older and woollier version of her sister Desdemona. She took the uncomfortable line of expressing thankfulness that Alleyn was his wife's husband. "Like having a *friend* to help us." Italicized words and even phrases surged about in her conversation. There was much talk of Panty. Alleyn had been so kind, the child had taken a tremendous fancy to him. "And I always think," Pauline said gazing at him, "that they KNOW." From here they were soon involved in Panty's misdoings. Pauline, if he had now wanted them, supplied good enough alibis for the practical jokes. "How could she when the poor child was being watched; closely, anxiously watched? Dr. Withers had given explicit orders."

"And much good they've done, by the way!" Cedric interrupted. "Look at Panty!"

"Dr. Withers is extremely clever, Cedric. It's not his fault if Juniper's drugs have deteriorated. Your grandfather's medicines were always a great help to him."

"Including ratsbane?"

"That," said Pauline in her deepest voice, "was not prescribed, Cedric, by Dr. Withers."

Cedric giggled.

Pauline ignored him and turned appealingly to Alleyn. "Mr. Alleyn, what are we to think? Isn't it all too tragically dreadful? The suspense! The haunting suspicion! The feeling that here in our midst—What are we to do?"

Alleyn asked her about the events following Sir Henry's exit from the Little Theatre on the night of his death. It appeared that Pauline herself had led the way to the drawing-room, leaving Troy, Paul and Fenella behind. Miss Orrincourt had only remained a very short time in the drawing-room where, Alleyn gathered, a lively discussion had taken place as to the authorship of the flying cow. To this family wrangle the three guests had listened uncomfortably until Barker arrived, with Sir Henry's summons for Mr. Rattisbon. The squire and the rector seized upon this opportunity to make their escape. Paul and Fenella came in on their way to bed. Troy had already gone upstairs. After a little more desultory haggling the Birthday party broke up.

Pauline, Millamant and Desdemona had fore-gathered in Pauline's room, Bernhardt, and had talked exhaustively. They went together to the bathrooms at the end of the passage and encountered Mr. Rattisbon, who had evidently come out of Sir Henry's rooms. Alleyn, who knew him, guessed that Mr. Rattisbon skipped, with late Victorian coyness, past the three ladies in their dressing-gowns and hurried down the passage to his own wing. The ladies performed their nightly rites together and together returned to their adjacent rooms. At this juncture Pauline began to look martyred.

"Originally," she said, "Bernhardt and Bancroft were one large room, a nursery I think. The wall between is the merest partition. Milly and Dessy shared Bancroft. Of course, I knew there was a great deal to be talked about and for a time I joined in. Milly's bed was just through the wall from mine, and Dessy's quite close. But it had been a long day and one was *exhausted*. They went on and on. I became quite frantic with sleeplessness. Really it *was* thoughtless."

"Dearest Aunt Pauline, why didn't you beat on the wall and scream at them?" Cedric asked, with some show of interest.

"I wasn't going to do that," Pauline rejoined with grandeur and immediately contradicted herself. "As a matter of fact I did at last tap. I said wasn't it getting rather late. Dessy asked what time it was and Milly said it couldn't be more than one. There was quite an argument and at last Dessy said, 'Well, if you're so certain, Pauline, look at your watch and see.' And in the end I did and it was five minutes to three. So at last they stopped and then it was only to snore. Your mother snores, Cedric."

"I'm so sorry."

"And to *think* that only a little way away, while Dessy and Milly gossiped and snored, a frightful tragedy was being enacted. To think that if only I had obeyed my instinct to go to Papa and tell him—"

"Tell him what, Aunt Pauline?"

Pauline shook her head slowly from side to side and boggled a little. "Everything was so sad and dreadful. One seemed to see him rushing to his doom."

"One also saw Paul and Panty rushing to theirs, didn't one?" Cedric put in. "You could have pleaded with him for them, perhaps?"

"I cannot expect, Cedric, that you would understand or sympathize with disinterested impulses."

"No," Cedric agreed with perfect candour. "I don't think they exist."

"T'uh!"

"And if Mr. Alleyn has no further absorbing questions to ask me I think I should like to leave the library. I find the atmosphere of unread silent friends in half-morocco exceedingly gloomy. Mr. Alleyn?"

"No, thank you, Sir Cedric," Alleyn said cheerfully. "No more questions. If I may go ahead with my job?"

"Oh, do. Please consider this house your own. Perhaps you would like to buy it. In any case I do hope you'll stay to dinner. And your own particular silent friend. What is his name?"

"Thank you so much, but Fox and I," Alleyn said, "are dining out."

"Then in that case," Cedric murmured sidling towards the door, "I shall leave Aunt Pauline to divert you with tales of Panty's innocence, in the matter of cheese dishes, and her own incapability of writing anonymous letters."

He was prevented from getting to the door by Pauline. With a movement of whose swiftness Alleyn would have thought her incapable, she got there first and there she stood in a splendid attitude, the palms of her hands against the door, her head thrown back. "Wait!" she said breathlessly. "Wait!"

Cedric turned with a smile to Alleyn. "As I hinted," he said, "Lady Macduff. With all her pretty chickens concentrated in the persons of Panty and Paul. The hen (or isn't it oddly enough 'dam'?) at bay."

"Mr. Alleyn," said Pauline, "I was going to say nothing of this to anybody. We are an ancient family—"

"On my knees," said Cedric, "on my knees, Aunt Pauline, not the Sieur d'Ancred."

"—and perhaps wrongly, we take some pride in our antiquity. Until to-day no breath of dishonour has ever smirched our name. Cedric is now Head of the Family. For that reason and for the sake of my father's memory I would have spared him. But now, when he does nothing but hurt and insult me and try to throw suspicion on my child, now when I have no one to protect me—" Pauline stopped as if for some important peroration. But something happened to her. Her face crinkled and reminded Alleyn instantly of her daughter's. Tears gathered in her eyes. "I have reason to believe," she began and stopped short, looking terrified. "I don't care," she said and her voice cracked piteously. "I never could bear people to be unkind to me." She nodded her head at Cedric. "Ask him," she said, "what he was doing in Sonia Orrincourt's rooms that night. Ask him."

She burst into tears and stumbled out of the room.

"Oh *bloody* hell!" Cedric ejaculated shrilly and darted after her.

iii

Alleyn, left alone, whistled disconsolately and after wandering about the cold and darkening room went to the windows and there made a series of notes in his pocket-book. He was still at this employment when Fox came in.

"They said I'd find you here," Fox said. "Have you done any good, Mr. Alleyn?"

"If stirring up a hive and finding foul-brood can be called good. What about you?"

"I've got the medicine bottle and three of the envelopes. I've had a cup of tea in Mr. Barker's room."

"That's more than I've had in the library."

"The cook and the maids came in and we had quite a nice little chat. Elderly party, it was. Mary, Isabel and Muriel, the maids are. The cook's Mrs. Bullivant."

"And what did you and Mary and Isabel and Muriel talk about?"

"We passed the time of day and listened to the wireless. Mrs. Bullivant showed me photographs of her nephews in the fighting forces."

"Come *on*, Fox," said Alleyn grinning.

"By gradual degrees," said Fox, enjoying himself, "we got round to the late baronet. He must have been a card, the late old gentleman."

"I believe you."

"Yes. The maids wouldn't say much while Mr. Barker was there but he went out after a bit and then it was, as you might say, plain sailing."

"You and your methods!"

"Well we were quite cosy. Naturally, they were dead against Miss Orrincourt, except Isabel, and she said you couldn't blame the old gentleman for wanting a change from his family. It came as a bit of a surprise from Isabel, who's the oldest of the maids, I should say. She's the one who looks after Miss Orrincourt's rooms and it seems Miss Orrincourt got quite friendly with her. Indiscreet, really, but you know the type."

"It's evident, at least, that you do."

"They seemed to be as thick as thieves. Miss O. and Isabel, and yet, you know, Isabel didn't mind repeating most of it. The garrulous sort, she is, and Mrs. Bullivant egging her on."

"Did you get anywhere with the history of the milk?"

"Isabel took it out of a jug in the refrigerator and left it in Miss Orrincourt's room. The rest of the milk in the jug was used for general purposes next day. Miss O. was in her room and undressing when Isabel brought it. It couldn't have been more than ten minutes or so later that Miss O. took it to the old gentleman. It was heated by Isabel in the kitchen and some patent food put in. The old gentleman fancied Miss O. did it and said nobody else could make it to suit him. It was quite a joke between Isabel and Miss O."

"So there's no chance of anybody having got at it?"

"Only if they doped the tin of patent food and I've got that."

"Good."

"And I don't know if you're thinking she might have tampered with the medicine, sir, but it doesn't seem likely. The old gentleman never let anybody touch the bottle on account of Miss Desdemona Ancred having once given him embrocation in error. It was a new bottle, Isabel says. I've got it from the dump. Cork gone, but there's enough left for analysis."

"Another job for Dr. Curtis. What about the thermos?"

"Nicely washed and sterilized and put away. I've taken it but there's not a chance."

"And the same goes, I imagine, for the pails and cloths?"

"The pails are no good, but I found some tag-ends of rag."

"Where have you put these delicious exhibits?"

"Isabel," said Fox primly, "hunted out a case. I told her I had to buy pyjamas in the village, being obliged unexpectedly to stay the night, and I mentioned that a man doesn't like to be seen carrying parcels. I've promised to return it."

"Didn't they spot you taking these things?"

"Only the patent food. I let on that the police were a bit suspicious about the makers and it might have disagreed. I daresay they didn't believe me. Owing to the behaviour of the family I think they know what's up."

"They'd be pretty dumb if they didn't."

"Two other points came out that might be useful," said Fox.

Alleyn had a clear picture of the tea-party. Fox no doubt, had sipped and complimented, had joked and sympathized, had scarcely asked a question, yet had continually received answers. He was a past-master at the game. He indulged his hostesses with a few innocuous hints and was rewarded with a spate of gossip.

"It seems, Mr. Alleyn, that the lady was, as Isabel put it, leading Sir Henry on and no more."

"D'you mean—"

"Relationship," said Fox sedately, "according to Isabel, had not taken place. It was matrimony or nothing."

"I see."

"Isabel reckons that before this business with the letters came out, there was quite an understanding between Miss O. and Sir Cedric."

"What sort of understanding, in the name of decency?"

"Well, sir, from hints Miss O. dropped, Isabel works it out that after a discreet time had clapsed Miss O. would have turned into Lady A., after all. So that what she lost on the swings she would, in a manner of speaking, have picked up on the roundabouts."

"Good Lord!" said Alleyn. " 'What a piece of work is man'! That, if it's true, would explain quite a number of the young and unlovely baronet's antics."

"Supposing Miss Orrincourt did monkey with the thermos, Mr. Alleyn, we might have to consider whether Sir Cedric knew what she was up to."

"We might indeed."

"I know it's silly," Fox went on, rubbing his nose, "but when a case gets to this stage I always seem to get round to asking myself whether such-and-such a character is a likely type for homicide. I know it's silly because there isn't a type, but I ask myself the question just the same."

"And at the moment you ask it about Sonia Orrincourt?"

"That's right, sir."

"I don't see why you shouldn't. It's quite true, that beyond the quality of conceit, nobody's found a nice handy trait common to all murderers. But I'm not so sure that you should sniff at yourself for saying: 'That man or woman seems to me to have characteristics that are inconceivable in a murderer!' They needn't be admirable characteristics either."

"D'you remember what Mr. Barker said about the rats in Miss Orrincourt's rooms?"

"I do."

"He mentioned that Miss Orrincourt was quite put-about by the idea of using poison, and refused to have it at any price. Now, sir, would a young woman who was at least, as you might say, toying with the idea of poison, behave like that? Would she? She wouldn't do it by accident. She might do it to suggest she had a dread of poison though that'd be a very far-fetched kind of notion, too. And would she have owned up as readily to those practical jokes? Mind, you caught her nicely, but she gave me the impression she was upset more on account of being found out for these pranks themselves, than because she thought they'd lead us to suspect something else."

"She was more worried about the Will than anything else," Alleyn said. "She and Master Cedric planned those damned stunts with the object of setting the old man against Panty. I fancy she was responsible for the portrait vandalism, Cedric having possibly told her to confine her daubs to dry canvas. We know she bought the Raspberry, and he admits he placed it. I *think* she started the ball rolling by painting the bannister. They plotted the whole thing together. He practically admitted as much. Now, all that worries her may be merely an idea that the publication of these goings-on could upset the Will."

"And yet—"

"I know, I know. That damn bell-push. All right, Fox. Good work. And now, I suppose we'd better see Mrs. Henry Ancred."

iv

Millamant was at least a change from her relations-by-marriage in that she was not histrionic, answered his questions directly, and stuck to the point. She received them in the drawing-room. In her sensible blouse and skirt she was an incongruous figure there. While she talked she stitched that same hideously involved piece of embroidery which Troy had noticed with horror and which Panty had been accused of unpicking. Alleyn heard nothing either to contradict or greatly to substantiate the evidence they had already collected.

"I wish," he said, after a minute or two, "that you would tell me your own opinion about this business."

"About my father-in-law's death? I thought at first that he died as a result of his dinner and his temperament."

"And what did you think when these letters arrived?"

"I didn't know what to think. I don't now. And I must say that with everybody so excited and foolish about it one can't think very clearly."

"About the book that turned up in the cheese dish—" he began.

Millamant jerked her head in the direction of the glass case. "It's over there. Someone replaced it."

He walked over to the case and raised the lid. "If you don't mind, I'll take charge of it presently. You saw Miss Orrincourt reading it?"

"Looking at it. It was one evening before dinner. Some weeks ago, I think."

"Can you describe her position and behaviour? Was she alone?"

"Yes. I came in and she was standing as you are now, with the lid open. She seemed to be turning over the leaves of the book as it lay there. When she saw me she let the lid fall. I was afraid it might have smashed but it hadn't."

Alleyn moved away to the cold hearth, his hands in his pockets.

"I wonder," said Milly, "if you'd mind putting a match to the fire. We light it at four-thirty, always."

Glad of the fire, for the crimson and white room was piercingly cold, and faintly amused by her air of domesticity, he did as she asked. She moved, with her embroidery, to a chair before the hearth. Alleyn and Fox sat one on each side of her.

"Mrs. Ancred," Alleyn said. "Do you think anyone in the house knew about this second Will?"

"She knew. She says he showed it to her that night."

"Apart from Miss Orrincourt?"

"They were all afraid he might do something of the sort. He was always changing his Will. But I don't think any of them knew he'd done it."

"I wondered if Sir Cedric—"

The impression that with Millamant all would be plain-speaking was immediately dispelled. Her short hands closed on her work like traps. She said harshly: "My son knew nothing about it. Nothing."

"I thought that as Sir Henry's successor—"

"If he had known he would have told me. He knew nothing. It was a great shock to both of us. My son," Millamant added, looking straight before her, "tells me everything. Everything."

"Splendid," murmured Alleyn after a pause. Her truculent silence appeared to demand comment. "It's only that I should like to know whether this second Will was made that night when Sir Henry went to his room. Mr. Rattisbon, of course, can tell us."

"I suppose so," said Millamant, selecting a strand of mustard-coloured silk.

"Who discovered the writing on Sir Henry's looking-glass?"

"I did. I'd gone in to see that his room was properly done. He was very particular and the maids are old and forget things. I saw it at once. Before I could wipe it away he came in. I don't think," she said meditatively, "that I'd ever before seen him so angry. For a moment it seemed to me he actually thought I'd done it, and then, of course, he realized it was Panty."

"It was not Panty," Alleyn said.

He and Fox had once agreed that if, after twenty years of experience, an investigating officer has learned to recognize any one manifestation, it is that of genuine astonishment. He recognized it now in Millamant Ancred.

"What are you suggesting?" she said at last. "Do you mean—"

"Sir Cedric has told me he was involved in one of the other practical jokes that were played on Sir Henry, and knew about all of them. He's responsible for this one."

She took up her embroidery again. "He's trying to shield somebody," she said. "Panty, I suppose."

"I think not."

"It was very naughty of him," she said in her dull voice. "If he played one of these jokes, and I don't believe he did, it was naughty. But I can't see—I may be very stupid but I can't see why you, Mr. Alleyn, should concern yourself with any of these rather foolish tricks."

"Believe me we shouldn't do so if we thought they were irrelevant."

"No doubt," she said and after a pause, "you've been influenced by your wife. She would have it that Panty was all innocence."

"I'm influenced," Alleyn said, "by what Sir Cedric and Miss Orrincourt have told me."

She turned to look at him, moving stiffly. For the first time her alarm, if she felt alarm, coloured her voice. "Cedric? And that woman? Why do you speak of them together like that?"

"It appears that they planned the practical jokes together."

"I don't believe it. She's told you that. I can see it, now," said Millamant on a rising note. "I've been a fool."

"What can you see, Mrs. Ancred?"

"She planned it all. Of course she did. She knew Panty was his favourite. She planned it and when he'd altered the Will she killed him. She's trying to drag my boy down with her. I've watched her. She's a diabolical scheming woman, and she's trying to entrap my boy. He's generous and unsuspecting and kind. He's been too kind. He's at her mercy," she cried sharply and twisted her hands together.

Confronted by this violence and with the memory of Cedric fresh in his mind, Alleyn was hard put to it to answer her. Before he could frame a sentence she had recovered something of her composure. "That settles it," she said woodenly. "I've kept out of all this, as far as one can keep out of their perpetual scenes and idiotic chattering. I've thought all along that they were probably right but I left it to them. I've even felt sorry for her. Now, I hope she suffers. If I can tell you anything that will help you, I'll do so. Gladly."

"Oh, damn!" thought Alleyn. "Oh, Freud! Oh, hell!" And he said: "There may still be no case, you know. Have you any theory as to the writer of the anonymous letters?"

"Certainly," she said with unexpected alacrity.

"You have?"

"They're written on the paper those children use for their work. She asked me some time ago to re-order it for them when I was in the village. I recognized it at once. Caroline Able wrote the letters."

And while Alleyn was still digesting this, she added, "Or Thomas. They're very thick. He spent half his time in the school wing."

CHAPTER FOURTEEN

Psychiatry and a Churchyard

i

THERE WAS something firmly coarse about Milly Ancred. After performances by Pauline, Desdemona and Cedric, this quality was inescapable. It was incorporate in her solid body, her short hands, the dullness of her voice and her choice of phrase. Alleyn wondered if the late Henry Irving Ancred, surfeited with ancestry, fine feeling and sensibility had chosen his wife for her lack of these qualities; for her normality. Yet was Milly, with her adoration of an impossible son, normal? "But there is no norm," he thought, "in human behaviour. Who should know this better than Fox and I?"

He began to ask her routine questions; the set of questions that crop up in every case and of which the investigating officer grows tired. The history of the hot drink was traced again with no amendments, but with clear evidence that Milly had resented her dethronement in favour of Miss Orrincourt. He went on to the medicine. It was a fresh bottle. Dr. Withers had suggested an alteration and had left the prescription at the chemist. Miss Orrincourt had picked it up at Mr. Juniper's on the day she collected the children's medicine, and Milly herself had sent Isabel with it to Sir Henry's room. He was only to use it in the event of a severe attack, and until that night had not done so.

"She wouldn't put it in that," said Milly. "She wouldn't be sure of his taking a dose. He hated taking medicine and only used it when he was really very bad. It doesn't seem to have been much good, anyway. I've no faith in Dr. Withers."

"No?"

"I think he's careless. I thought at the time he ought to have asked more questions about my father-in-law's death. He's too much wrapped up in his horse-racing and bridge and not interested enough in his patients. However," she added with a short laugh, "my father-in-law liked him well enough to leave more to him than to some of his own flesh and blood."

"About the medicine—" Alleyn prompted.

"She wouldn't have interfered with it. Why should she use it when she had the thermos in her own hands?"

"Have you any idea where she could have found the tin of ratsbane?"

"She complained of rats when she first came here. I asked Barker to set poison and told him there was a tin in the store-room. She made a great outcry and said she had a horror of poison."

Alleyn glanced at Fox, who instantly looked extremely bland.

"So," Milly went on, "I told Barker to set traps. When we wanted ratsbane, weeks afterwards, for Bracegirdle, the tin had gone. It was an unopened tin to the best of my knowledge. It had been in the store-room for years."

"It must have been an old brand," Alleyn agreed. "I don't think arsenical ratsbane is much used nowadays."

He stood up and Fox rose with him. "I think that's all," he said.

"No," said Millamant strongly. "It's not all. I want to know what that woman has said about my son."

"She suggested they were partners in the practical jokes and he admitted it."

"I warn you," she said, and for the first time, her voice was unsteady, "I warn you, she's trying to victimize him. She's worked on his kindness and good-nature and his love of fun. I warn you—"

The door at the far end of the room opened and Cedric looked in. His mother's back was turned to him and, unconscious of his presence, she went on talking. Her shaking voice repeated over and over again that he had been victimized. Cedric's gaze moved from her to Alleyn, who was watching him. He sketched a brief grimace; deprecating, rueful, but his lips were colourless and the effect was of a distortion. He came in and shut the door with great delicacy. He carried a much belabelled suitcase, presumably Miss Orrincourt's, which, after a further grimace at Alleyn, he placed behind a chair. He then minced across the carpet.

"Darling Milly," he said, and his hands closed on his mother's shoulders. She gave a startled cry. "There, now! I made you jump. *So* sorry."

Millamant covered his hands with her own. He waited for a moment, submissive to her restless and possessive touch. "What is it, Milly?" he asked. "Who's been victimizing Little Me? Is it Sonia?"

"Ceddie?"

"I've been such a goose, you can't think. I've come to 'fess up,' like a good boy," he said nauseatingly and slid round to his familiar position on the floor, leaning against her knees. She held him there, strongly.

"Mr. Alleyn," Cedric began, opening his eyes very wide, "I couldn't be more sorry about rushing away just now after Aunt Paulinc. Really, it was too stupid. But one does like to tell people things in one's own way and there she was huffing and puffing and going on as if I'd been trying to conceal some dire skeleton in my, I assure you, too drearily barren cupboard."

Alleyn waited.

"You see (Milly, my sweet, this is going to be a faint shock to you, but never mind), you see, Mr. Alleyn, there's been a—what shall I call it?—a—well, an *understanding*, of sorts, between Sonia and me. It only really developed quite lately. After dearest Mrs. Alleyn came here. She seems to have noticed quite a number of things; perhaps she noticed that."

"If I understand you," Alleyn said, "she, I am sure, did not."

"Really?"

"Are you trying to tell me why you visited Miss Orrincourt's rooms on the night of your grandfather's death?"

"Well," Cedric muttered petulantly, "after Aunt Pauline's announcement—and, by the way, she gleaned her information through a noctural visit to the *archaic* offices at the end of the passage—after and that there seems to be nothing for it but an elaborate cleaning of the breast, does there?"

"Cedric," Millamant said, "what has this woman done to you?"

"My sweet, nothing, thank God. I'm trying to tell you. She really is too beautiful, Mr. Alleyn, don't you think? I know you didn't like her, Milly dear, and how right you seem to have been. But I really was quite intrigued and she was so bored and it was only the teeniest flutter, truly. I merely popped in on my way to bed and had a good giggle with her about the *frightful* doings down below."

"Incidentally," Alleyn suggested, "you may have hoped to hear the latest news about Sir Henry's Will."

"Well, that among other things. You see I did rather wonder if the flying cow hadn't been sort of once too often, as it were. Sonia did it before dinner, you know. And then at the Dinner the Old Person announced a Will that was really quite satisfactory from both our points of view and with the insufferable Panty not even a starter, one rather wished Sonia had left well alone."

"Cedric," said his mother suddenly, "I don't think, dear, you should go on. Mr. Alleyn won't understand. Stop."

"But, Milly, my sweet, don't you see dear old Pauline has already planted a horrid little seed of suspicion and one simply must tweak it up before it sprouts. Mustn't one, Mr. Alleyn?"

"I think," Alleyn said, "you'll be well advised to make a complete statement."

"There! Now, where was I? Oh, yes. Now, all would have been well if Carol Able, who is so scientific and 'un*thing*' that she's a sort of monster, hadn't made out a watertight alibi for that septic child. This, of course, turned the Old Person's suspicious glare upon all of us equally and so he wrote the second Will and so we were all done in the eye except Sonia. And to be *quite* frank, Milly and Mr. Alleyn, I should so like to have it settled whether she's a murderess or not, rather quickly."

"Of course she is," Millamant said.

"Yes, but are you *positive?* It really is of mountainous significance to me."

"What do you mean? Cedric. I don't understand—"

"Well— Well, never mind."

"I think I know what Sir Cedric means," Alleyn said. "Isn't it a question of marriage, at some time in the future, with Miss Orrincourt?"

Millamant, with a tightening of her hold on Cedric's shoulder, said "No!" loudly and flatly.

"Oh, Milly darling," he protested, wriggling under her hand, "please let's be civilized."

"It's all nonsense," she said. "Tell him it's all nonsense. A disgusting idea! Tell him."

"What's the use when Sonia will certainly tell him something else?" He appealed to Alleyn. "You do understand, don't you? I mean one can't deny she's decorative and in a way it would have been quite fun. Don't you think it would have worked, Mr. Alleyn? I do."

His mother again began to protest. He freed himself with ugly petulance and scrambled to his feet. "You're idiotic, Milly. What's the good of hiding things?"

"You'll do yourself harm."

"What harm? I'm in the same position, after all, as you. I don't know the truth about Sonia but I want to find out." He turned to Alleyn with a smile. "When I saw her that night she told me about the new Will. I knew then that if he died I'd be practically ruined.

There's no collaboration where I'm concerned, Mr. Alleyn. I didn't murder the Old Person. *Pas si bete!*"

ii

"Pas si bete," Fox quoted as they made their way to the school wing. "Meaning, 'Not such a fool.' I shouldn't say he was, either, would you, Mr. Alleyn?"

"Oh, no. There are no flies on Cedric. But what a cold-blooded little worm it is, Fox! Grandpapa dies, leaving him encumbered with a large unwanted estate and an insufficient income to keep it up. Grandpapa, on the other hand, dies leaving his extremely dubious fiancee a fortune. What more simple than for the financially embarrassed Cedric to marry the opulent Miss O.? I could kick that young man," said Alleyn thoughtfully, "in fourteen completely different positions and still feel half-starved."

"I reckon," said Fox, "it's going to be a case for the Home Secretary."

"Oh, yes, yes, I'm afraid you're right. Down this passage, didn't they say? And there's the green baize door. I think we'll separate here, Fox. You to collect your unconsidered trifles in Isabel's case and by the way, you might take charge of Miss Orrincourt's. Here it is. Then, secretly, Foxkin, exhume Carabbas, deceased, and enclose him in a boot-box. By the way, do we know who destroyed poor Carabbas?"

"Mr. Barker," said Fox, "got Mr. Juniper to come up and give him an injection. Strychnine, I fancy."

"I hope, whatever it was, it doesn't interfere with the autopsy. I'll meet you on the second terrace."

Beyond the green baize door the whole atmosphere of Ancreton was changed. Coir runners replaced the heavy carpets, passages were draughty and smelt of disinfectant, and where Victorian prints may have hung there were pictures of determined modernity that had been executed with a bright disdain for comfortable, but doubtless undesirable, prettiness.

Led by a terrific rumpus, Alleyn found his way to a large room where Miss Able's charges were assembled, with building games, with modelling-clay, with paints, hammers, sheets of paper, scissors and paste. Panty, he saw, was conducting a game with scales, weights and bags of sand and appeared to be in hot dispute with a small boy. When she saw Alleyn she flung herself into a strange attitude and screamed with affected laughter. He waved to her and she at once did a comedy fall to the floor, where she remained, aping violent astonishment.

Miss Caroline Able detached herself from a distant group and came towards him.

"We're rather noisy in here," she said crisply. "Shall we go to my office? Miss Watson, will you carry on?"

"Certainly, Miss Able," said an older lady, rising from behind a mass of children.

"Come along, then," said Caroline Able.

Her office was near at hand and was hung with charts and diagrams. She seated herself behind an orderly desk upon which he at once noticed a pile of essays written on paper with yellow lines and a ruled margin.

"I suppose you know what all this is about," he said.

Miss Able replied cheerfully that she thought she did. "I see," she said frankly, "quite a lot of Thomas Ancred and he's told me about all the trouble. It's been a pretty balanced account, as a matter of fact. He's fairly well-adjusted and has been able to deal with it quite satisfactorily, so far."

Alleyn understood this to be a professional opinion on Thomas and wondered if a courtship had developed and if it was conducted on these lines. Miss Able was pretty. She had a clear skin, large eyes and good teeth. She also had an intimidating air of utter sanity.

"I'd like to know," he said, "what you think about it all."

"It's impossible to give an opinion that's worth much," she replied, "without a pretty thorough analysis of one if not all of them. Obviously the relationship with their father was unsatisfactory. I should have liked to know about his marriage. One suspected, of course, that there was a fear of impotency, not altogether sublimated. The daughters' violent antagonism to his proposed second marriage suggests a rather bad father-fixation."

"Does it? But it wasn't a particularly suitable alliance from—from the ordinary point of view, was it?"

"If the relationship with the father," Miss Able said firmly, "had been properly adjusted, the children should not have been profoundly disturbed."

"Not even," Alleyn ventured, "by the prospect of Miss O. as a mother-in-law and principal beneficiary in the Will?"

"Those may have been the reasons advanced to explain their antagonism. They may represent an attempt to rationalize a basic and essentially sexual repulsion."

"Oh, dear!"

"But, as I said before," she added with a candid laugh, "one shouldn't pronounce on mere observation. Deep analysis might lead to a much more complex state of affairs."

"You know," Alleyn said, taking out his pipe and nursing it in his palm, "you and I, Miss Able, represent two aspects of investigation. Your professional training teaches you that behaviour is a sort of code or cryptogram disguising the pathological truth from the uninformed, but revealing it to the expert. Mine teaches me to regard behaviour as something infinitely variable *after* the fact and often at complete loggerheads with the fact. A policeman watches behaviour, of course, but his deductions would seem completely superficial to you." He opened his hand. "I see a man turning a dead pipe about in his hand and I think that, perhaps unconsciously, he's longing to smoke it. May he?"

"Do," said Miss Able. "It's a good illustration. I see a man caressing his pipe and I recognize a very familiar piece of fetishism."

"Well, don't tell me what it is," Alleyn said hurriedly.

Miss Able gave a short professional laugh.

"Now, look here," he said. "How do you account for these anonymous letters we're all so tired of? What sort of being perpetuated them and why?"

"They probably represent an attempt to make an effect and are done by someone whose normal creative impulses have taken the wrong turning. The desire to be mysterious and omnipotent may be an additional factor. In Patricia's case, for instance—"

"Patricia? Oh, I see. That's Panty, of course."

"We don't use her nickname over here. We don't think it a good idea. We think nicknames can have a very definite effect, particularly when they are of a rather humiliating character."

"I see. Well, then, in Patricia's case?"

"She formed the habit of perpetrating rather silly jokes on people. This was an attempt to command attention. She used to let her performances remain anonymous. Now she usually brags about them. That, of course, is a good sign."

"It's an indication, at least, that she's not the author of the more recent practical jokes on her grandfather."

"I agree."

"Or the author of the anonymous letters."

"That, I should have thought," said Miss Able patiently, "was perfectly obvious."

"Who do you think is responsible for the letters?"

"I've told you, I can't make snap decisions or guesses."

"Couldn't you just unbend far enough to have one little pot-shot?" he said persuasively. Miss Able opened her mouth, shut it again, looked at him with somewhat diminished composure and finally blushed. "Come!" he thought, "she hasn't analyzed herself into an iceberg, at least." And he said aloud: "Without prejudice, now, who among the grown-ups would you back as the letter-writer?" He leant forward smiling at her and thought, "Troy would grin if she saw this exhibition." As Miss Able still hesitated, he repeated, "Come on. Who would you back?"

"You're very silly," Miss Able said and her manner, if not coy, was at least very much less impersonal.

"Would you say," Alleyn went on, "that the person who wrote them is by any chance the practical joker?"

"Quite possible."

He reached a long arm over the desk and touched the top sheet of the exercises. "They were written," he said, "on this paper."

Her face was crimson. With a curious and unexpected gesture she covered the paper with her hands. "I don't believe you," she said.

"Will you let me look at it?" He drew the sheet out from under her hands and held it to the light. "Yes," he said. "Rather an unusual type with a margin. It's the same water-mark."

"He didn't do it."

"He?"

"Tom," she said and the diminutive cast a new light upon Thomas. "He's incapable of it."

"Good," Alleyn said. "Then why bring him up?"

"Patricia," said Miss Able, turning a deeper red, "must have taken some of this exercise paper over to the other side. Or—" she paused, frowning.

"Yes?"

"Her mother comes over here a great deal. Too often, I sometimes think. She's not very wise with children."

"Where is the paper kept?"

"In that cupboard. The top one. Out of reach of the children."

"Do you keep it locked?"

She turned on him quickly. "You're not going to suggest that I would write anonymous letters? I?"

"But you do keep it locked, don't you?" said Alleyn.

"Certainly. I haven't denied that."

"And the key?"

"On my ring and in my pocket."

"Has the cupboard been left open at all? Or the keys left out of your pocket?"

"Never."

"The paper comes from a village shop, doesn't it?"

"Of course it does. Anyone could buy it."

"So they could," he agreed cheerfully, "and we can find out if they have. There's no need, you see, to fly into a huff with me."

"I do not," said Miss Able mulishly, "fly into huffs."

"Splendid. Now look here. About this medicine your kids had. I want to trace its travels. Not inside the wretched kids, but *en route* to them."

"I really don't see why—"

"Of course you don't and I'll tell you. A bottle of medicine for Sir Henry came up at the same time and its history is therefore bound up with theirs. Now, as the pudding said to the shop-assistant: Can you help me, Moddom?"

This laborious pun was not immediately absorbed by Miss Able. She looked at him with wonder but finally produced a tolerably indulgent smile.

"I suppose I can. Miss Orrincourt and Mrs. Alleyn—"

Here came the now familiar pause and its inevitable explanation. "Fancy!" said Miss Able. "I know," said Alleyn. "About the medicine?"

"I was really very annoyed with Miss Orrincourt. It seems that she asked Mrs. Alleyn to drive the trap round to the stable and she herself brought in the medicine. Instead of leaving it in the hall or, as you would think she might have done, bringing it in here to me, she simply dumped the whole lot in the flower-room. It seems that Sir Henry had given her some flowers out of the conservatory and she'd left them there. She's abnormally egocentric, of course. I waited and waited and finally, at about seven o'clock, went over to the other side to ask about it. Mrs. Ancred and I hunted everywhere. Finally, it was Fenella who told us where they were."

"Was Sir Henry's medicine with theirs?"

"Oh, yes. Mrs. Ancred sent it up at once."

"Were the bottles alike?"

"We made no mistake, if that's what you're wondering. They were the same sort of bottles but ours was much larger and they were both clearly labelled. Ours had the instructions attached. Unnecessarily, as it turned out, because Dr. Withers came up himself that evening and he weighed the children again and measured out their doses himself. It was odd because he'd left it that I should give the medicine and I could have managed perfectly well; but evidently," said Miss Able with a short laugh, "he'd decided I was not to be trusted."

"It's a fault on the right side, I suppose," Alleyn said, vaguely. "They have to be careful."

Miss Able looked unconvinced. "No doubt," she said. "But I still can't understand why he wanted to come up to Ancreton, when he was supposed to be so busy. And after all that fuss, we've had to go back to the ointment."

"By the way," Alleyn asked. "Did you happen to see the cat Carabbas before it died?"

Instantly she was away on her professional hobbyhorse. He listened to an exposition on Panty's fondness for the cat, and the strange deductions which Miss Able drew, with perfect virtuosity, from this not unusual relationship.

"At this stage of her development it was really a bad disturbance when the link was broken."

"But," Alleyn ventured, "if the cat had ringworm—"

"It wasn't ringworm," said Miss Able firmly. "I ought to know. It might have been mange."

Upon that pronouncement he left her, apparently in two minds about himself. She shook hands with an air of finality but when he reached the door he thought he heard an indeterminate sound, and turned to find her looking anxiously at him.

"Is there anything else?" he asked.

"It's only that I'm worried about Tom Ancred. They're dragging him in and making him do all their dirty work. He's quite different. He's too good for them. I'm afraid this will upset him."

And then with a rather strenuous resumption of her professional manner: "Psychologically, I mean," said Miss Able.

"I quite understand," said Alleyn, and left her.

He found Fox waiting for him on the second terrace. Fox was sitting on the steps with his greatcoat drawn closely round him and his spectacles on his nose. He was reading from the manual on poisons which Alleyn had lent him in the train. By his side were two suitcases. One of these Alleyn recognized as Miss Orrincourt's. The other he presumed was Isabel's. Near by was a boot-box tied up with string. As Alleyn bent over Fox he noticed an unpleasant smell.

"Carabbas?" he asked, edging the box away with his foot.

Fox nodded. "I've been asking myself," he said, and placed a square finger under a line of print. Alleyn read over his shoulder. "Arsenic. Symptoms. Manifested as progressive cachexia and loss of flesh; falling out of hair . . ."

Fox glanced up and jerked a thumb at the boot-box.

"Falling out of hair," he said. "Wait till you've had a look at Carabbas deceased."

iii

"You know, Fox," Alleyn said as they walked back to the village, "if Thomas Ancred can stand having his lightest caress implacably laid at the door of some infantile impropriety, he and Miss Able will probably get along together very nicely. Obviously, she's in love with him or should I say that obviously she finds herself adjusted to a condition of rationalized eroticism in relation to poor old Thomas?"

"Courting, do you reckon?"

"I think so. Fox, I think we've had Ancreton for the moment, but I'm going to ask you to stay behind and warn the parson about an exhumation. Return to Katzenjammer Castle in the morning and ask the inmates if they've any objection to having their prints taken. They won't have any if they're not completely dotty. Bailey can come down by the morning train and work round the house for the stuff we want there. Get him to check prints on any relevant surfaces. It'll all be utterly useless, no doubt, but it had better be done. I'll go back to the Yard. I want to learn Messrs. Mortimer and Loame's receipt for tasteful embalming. As soon as we get the exhumation order through we'll come down and meet you here. There's a train this evening. Let's have a meal at the pub and then I'll catch it. I was going to see Dr. Withers again but I fancy that particular interview had better wait. I want to get the medicine bottle and poor old Carabbas up to London."

"What's the betting, Mr. Alleyn? Arsenic in the medicine or not?"

"I'm betting *not*."

"Routine job. It'll be a nuisance if they don't find anything, though. Not a hope with the thermos."

"No, damn it."

They walked in silence. Frost tingled in the dusk and hardened the ground under their feet. A pleasant smell of burning wood laced the air and from Ancreton woods came the sound of wings.

"What a job!" Alleyn said suddenly.

"Ours, sir?"

"Yes, ours. Walking down a country lane with a dead cat in a boot-box and working out procedure for disentombing the body of an old man."

"Somebody's got to do it."

"Certainly. But the details are unlovely."

"Not much doubt about it, sir, is there? Homicide?"

"Not much doubt, old thing. No."

"Well," said Fox, after a pause, "as it stands the evidence all points one way. It's not one of those funny affairs where you have to clear up half a dozen suspects."

"But *why* kill him? She knew the Will was in her favour. She wanted to be Lady Ancred. She knew he wasn't likely to live much longer. Why incur the appalling risk? When all she had to do was marry him and wait?"

"He was always changing his Will. Perhaps she thought he might do it again."

"She seems to have had him pretty well where she wanted him."

"Might she be all that keen on the present baronet?"

"Not she," said Alleyn. "Not she."

"Hard to imagine, I must say. Suppose, though, that Miss O. is not the party we'll be after, and suppose we know the old gentleman was done away with. Who's left? Not Sir Cedric, because he knew about the second Will."

"Unless," said Alleyn, "hc gambled on marrying the heiress."

"By gum, yes, there's that, but what a gamble! With that fortune she would have hoped for better, wouldn't you say?"

"She could hardly hope for worse, in my opinion."

"Well then," Fox reasoned, "suppose we count those two out. Look at the rest of the field."

"I do so without enthusiasm. They all thought the Will announced at the Birthday Dinner was valid. Desdemona, Millamant, Dr. Withers and the servants expected to do moderately well; Thomas's expectations were handsome. The Kentish family, and the Claude Ancreds got damn all. In the 'haves' the only motive is cupidity, in the 'have-nots,' revenge."

"Opportunity?" Fox speculated.

"If an analysis of the medicine bottle proves negative, we're left with the thermos flask, now sterilized, and as far as we can see, Miss O. Unless you entertain a notion of delayed action, with Barker inserting arsenic in the crayfish."

"You will have your joke, Mr. Alleyn."

"You should have heard me trifling with Miss Able," Alleyn grunted. "That was pretty ghastly, if you like."

"And the exhumation's *on*," Fox ruminated after another long silence. "When?"

"As soon as we've got the order and Dr. Curtis can manage it. By the way, Ancreton Church is above the village over there. We'll have a look at the churchyard while the light still holds."

And presently they climbed a gentle lane now deep in shadow and pushed open a lych-gate into the churchyard of St. Stephens, Ancreton.

It was pleasant after the dubious grandeurs of the manor house to encircle this church, tranquil, ancient, and steadfastly built. Their feet crunched loudly on the gravelled path and from the hedges came a faint stir of sleepy birds. The grass was well kept. When they came upon a quiet company of headstones and crosses they found that the mounds and plots before them also were carefully tended. It was possible in the fading light to read inscriptions. "Susan Gascoigne of this parish. Here rests one who in her life rested not in well-doing." "To the Memory of Miles Chitty Bream who for fifty years tended this churchyard and now sleeps with those he faithfully served." Presently they came upon Ancred graves. "Henry Gaisbrook Ancreton Ancred, fourth baronet, and Margaret Mirabel, his wife." "Percival Gaisbrook Ancred" and many others, decently and properly bestowed. But such plain harbourage was not for the later generations, and towering over this sober company of stone rose a marble tomb topped by three angels. Here, immortalized in gold inscriptions, rested Sir Henry's predecessor, wife, his son, Henry Irving Ancred, and himself. The tomb, Alleyn read, had been erected by Sir Henry. It had a teak and iron door, emblazoned in the Ancred arms, and with a great keyhole.

"It'll be one of these affairs with shelves," Fox speculated. "Not room enough for the doctor, and no light. It'll have to be a canvas enclosure, don't you reckon, Mr. Alleyn?"

"Yes."

The lid of Fox's large silver watch clicked. "It's five o'clock, sir," he said. "Time we moved on if you're to have tea at the pub and catch that train."

"Come along, then," said Alleyn quietly, and they retraced their steps to the village.

CHAPTER FIFTEEN

New System

i

As Troy waited for Alleyn's return her thoughts moved back through the brief period of their reunion. She examined one event, then another; a phrase, a gesture, an emotion. She was astonished by the simplicity of her happiness; amused to find herself expectant, even a little sleek. She was desired, she was loved, and she loved again. That there were hazards ahead, she made no doubt, but for the moment all was well; she could relax and find a perspective.

Yet, like a rough strand in the texture of her happiness, there was an imperfection, and her thoughts, questing fingers, continually and reluctantly sought it out. This was Alleyn's refusal to allow his work a place in their relationship. It was founded, she knew, in her own attitude during their earliest encounters which had taken place against a terrible background; in her shrinking from the part he played at that time and in her expressed horror of capital punishment.

Troy knew very well that Alleyn accepted these reactions as fundamental and implicit in her nature. She knew he did not believe that for her, in love, an ethic unrelated to that love could not impede it. It seemed to him that if his work occasionally brought murderers to execution then surely, to her, he must at those times, be of the same company as the hangman. Only by some miracle of love, he thought, did she overcome her repulsion.

But the bald truth, she told herself helplessly, was that her ideas were remote from her emotions. "I'm less sensitive than he thinks," she said. "What he does is of no importance. I love him." And although she disliked such generalities, she added: "I am a woman."

It seemed to her that while this withdrawal existed they could not be completely happy. "Perhaps," she thought, "this business with the Ancreds will, after all, change everything. Perhaps it's a kind of beastly object lesson. I'm in it. He can't keep me out. I'm in on a homicide case." And with a sensation of panic, she realized that she had been taking it for granted that the old man she had painted was murdered.

As soon as Alleyn came in and stood before her she knew that she had made no mistake. "Well, Rory," she said going to him, "we're for it, aren't we, darling?"

"It looks a bit like it." He walked past her, saying quickly, "I'll see the A.C. in the morning. He'll let me hand over to someone else. Much better."

"No," Troy said, and he turned quickly and looked at her. She was aware, as if she had never before fully appreciated it, of the difference in their heights. She thought: "That's how he looks when he's taking statements," and became nervous.

"No?" he said. "Why not?"

"Because it would be highfalutin. Because it would make me feel an ass."

"I'm sorry."

"I look upon this case," Troy said and wished her voice would sound more normal, "as a sort of test. Perhaps it's been sent to larn us, like Acts of God; only I must say I always think it's so unfair to call earthquakes and tidal waves Acts of God and not bumper harvests and people like Leonardo and Cezanne."

"What the devil," Alleyn asked in a mild voice, "are you talking about?"

"Don't snap at me," said Troy. He made a quick movement towards her. "No. Please listen. I want, I really do want you to take this case as long as the A.C. lets you. I really want you to keep me with you this time. We've got in a muddle about me and your job. When I say I don't mind your job you think I'm not telling the truth and if I ask you questions about these kinds of cases you think I'm being a brave little woman and biting on the bullet."

She saw his mouth twist in an involuntary smile.

"Whereas," she hurried on, "I'm not. I know I didn't relish having our courtship all muddled up with murder on the premises, and I know I don't think people ought to hang other people. But you do and you're the policeman, not me. And it doesn't do any good trying to pretend you're dodging out to pinch a petty larcener when I know jolly well what you are up to and, to be perfectly honest, am often dying to hear about it."

"That's not quite true, is it? The last bit?"

"I'd infinitely rather talk about it. I'd infinitely rather feel honestly shocked and upset with you, than vaguely worried all by myself."

He held out a hand and she went to him. "That's why I said I think this case has been sent to larn you."

"Troy," Alleyn said, "do you know what they say to their best girls in the antipodes?"

"No."

"You'll do me."

"Oh."

"You'll do me, Troy."

"I thought perhaps you'd prefer me to remain a shrinking violet."

"The truth is I've been a bloody fool and never did and never will deserve you."

"Don't," said Troy, "let's talk about deserving."

"I've only one excuse and logically you'll say it's no excuse. Books about C.I.D. men will tell you that running a murderer to earth is just a job to us, as copping a pick-pocket is to the ordinary P.C. It's not. Because of its termination it's unlike any other job in existence. When I was twenty-two I faced its implications and took it on, but I don't think I fully realized them for another fifteen years and that was when I fell most deeply in love, my love, with you."

"I've faced its implications, too, and once for all, over this Ancred business. Before you came in I even decided that it would be good for both of us if, by some freak, it turned out that I had a piece of information somewhere in the back of my memory that's of virtual importance."

"You'd got as far as that?"

"Yes. And the queer thing is," Troy said, driving her fingers through her hair, "I've got the most extraordinary conviction that somewhere in the back of my memory, it is there, waiting to come out."

ii

"I want you," Alleyn said, "to tell me again, as fully as you possibly can, about your conversation with Sir Henry after he'd found the writing on the looking-glass and the grease-paint on the cat's whiskers. If you've forgotten how it went at any particular stage, say so. But for the love of Mike, darling, don't elaborate. Can you remember?"

"I think so. Quite a lot, anyway. He was furious with Panty, of course."

"He hadn't a suspicion of Cedric?"

"None. Did Cedric—"

"He did. He's lisped out an admission."

"Little devil," said Troy. "So it *was* grease-paint on his finger nail."

"And Sir Henry—"

"He just went on and on about how much he'd doted on Panty and how she'd grieved him. I tried to persuade him she hadn't done it, but he only made their family noise at me: 'T'uh!' you know?"

"Yes, indeed."

"Then he started to talk about marriages between first cousins and how he disapproved of them and this got mixed up in no time with a most depressing account of how he was—" Troy swallowed and went on quickly "—was going to be embalmed. We actually mentioned the book. Then I think he sniffed a bit at Cedric as his heir and said he'd never have children and that poor Thomas wouldn't marry."

"He was wrong there, I fancy."

"No! Who?"

"The psychiatrist or should it be 'psychiatriste?' "

"Miss Able?"

"She thinks he's quite satisfactorily sublimated his libido or something."

"Oh, good. Well, and then as he would keep talking about when he was gone, I tried to buck him up a bit and had quite a success. He turned mysterious and talked about there being surprises in store for everybody. And upon that Sonia Orrincourt burst in and said they were all plotting against her and she was frightened."

"And that's all?" Alleyn said after a pause.

"No. No, it isn't. There was something else he said. Rory, I can't remember what it was, but there was something else."

"That was on Saturday the seventeenth, wasn't it?"

"Let me see. I got there on the sixteenth. Yes. No, it was on Monday. But I wish," Troy said slowly, "I do wish I could remember the other thing he talked about."

"Don't try. It may come back suddenly."

"Perhaps Miss Able could screw it out of me," said Troy with a grin.

"In any case we'll call it a day."

As they moved away she linked her arm through his. "First installment of the new system," she said. "It's gone off tolerably quietly, hasn't it?"

"It has, my love. Thank you."

"One of the things I like about you," Troy said, "is your nice manners."

iii

The next day was a busy one. The Assistant Commissioner, after a brisk interview with Alleyn, decided to apply for an exhumation order. "Sooner the better, I suppose. I was talking to the Home Secretary yesterday and told him we might be on his tracks. You'd better go right ahead."

"To-morrow then, sir, if possible," Alleyn said. "I'll see Dr. Curtis."

"Do." And as Alleyn turned away: "By the way, Rory, if it's at all difficult for Mrs. Alleyn—"

"Thank you very much, sir, but at the moment she's taking it in her stride."

"Splendid. Damn' rum go, what?"

"Damn' rum," Alleyn agreed politely and went to call on Mr. Rattisbon.

Mr. Rattisbon's offices in the Strand had survived the pressure of the years, the blitz and the flying bomb. They were as Alleyn remembered them on the occasion of his first official visit before the war, a discreetly active memorial to the style of Charles Dickens, with the character of Mr. Rattisbon himself written across them like an inscription. Here was the same clerk with his trick of slowly raising his head and looking dimly at the enquirer, the same break-neck stairs, the same dark smell of antiquity. And here, at last, shrined in leather, varnish and age was Mr. Rattisbon, that elderly legal bird, perched at his desk.

"Ah, yes, Chief Inspector," Mr. Rattisbon gabbled, extending a claw at a modish angle, "come in, come in, sit down, sit down. Glad to see yer. M-m-maah!" And when Alleyn was seated Mr. Rattisbon darted the old glance at him, sharp as the point of a fine nib. "No trouble, I hope?" he said.

"The truth is," Alleyn rejoined, "my visits only arise, I'm afraid, out of some sort of trouble."

Mr. Rattisbon instantly hunched himself, placed his elbows on his desk and joined his finger tips in front of his chin.

"I've come to ask about certain circumstances that relate to the late Sir Henry Ancred's Will. Or Wills."

Mr. Rattisbon vibrated the tip of his tongue between his lips, rather as if he had scalded it and hoped in this manner to cool it off. He said nothing.

"Without more ado," Alleyn went on, "I must tell you that we are going to ask for an exhumation."

After a considerable pause Mr. Rattisbon said: "This is exceedingly perturbing."

"May I, before we go any further, say I do think that instead of coming to us with the story I'm about to relate, Sir Henry's successors might have seen fit to consult their solicitor."

"Thank yer."

"I don't know, sir, of course, how you would have advised them but I believe that this visit must sooner or later have taken place. Here is the story."

Twenty minutes later Mr. Rattisbon tipped himself back in his chair and gave a preparatory bay at the ceiling.

"M-m-ah!" he said. "Extraordinary. Disquieting. Very."

"You will see that all this rigmarole seems to turn about two factors. A. It was common knowledge in his household that Sir Henry Ancred was to be embalmed. B. He repeatedly altered his Will and on the eve of his death appears to have done so in favour of his intended wife, largely to the exclusion of his family and in direct contradiction to an announcement he made a couple of hours earlier. It's here I hope, Mr. Rattisbon, that you can help us."

"I am," said Mr. Rattisbon, "in an unusual, not to say equivocal position. Um. As you have very properly noted, Chief Inspector, the correct procedure on the part of the family, particularly on the part of Sir Cedric Gaisbrook Percival Ancred, would have been to consult this office. He has elected not to do so. In the event of a criminal action he will scarcely be able to avoid doing so. It appears that the general intention of the family is to discredit the position of the chief beneficiary and, further, to suggest that there is a case for a criminal charge against her. I refer, of course, to Miss Gladys Clark."

"To *whom?*"

"—known professionally as Miss Sonia Orrincourt."

" 'Gladys Clark,' " Alleyn said thoughtfully. "Well!"

"Now as the solicitor for the estate, I am concerned in the matter. On consideration, I find no objection to giving you such information as you require. Indeed I conceive it to be my professional duty to do so."

"I'm extremely glad," said Alleyn, who had known perfectly well that Mr. Rattisbon, given time, would arrive at precisely this decision. "Our principal concern at the moment is to discover whether Sir Henry Ancred actually concocted his last Will after he left the party on the eve of his death."

"Emphatically, no. It was drawn up, in this office, on Sir Henry's instruction, on Thursday, the twenty-second of November of this year, together with a second document which was the one quoted by Sir Henry as his Last Will and Testament at his Birthday Dinner."

"This all sounds rather erratic."

Mr. Rattisbon rapidly scratched his nose with the nail of his first finger. "The procedure," he said, "was extraordinary. I ventured to say so at the time. Let me take these events in their order. On Tuesday, the twentieth of November, Mrs. Henry Irving Ancred telephoned this office to the effect that Sir Henry Ancred wished me to call upon him immediately. It was most inconvenient but the following day I went down to Ancreton. I found him in a state of considerable agitation and clothed—m-m-m-ah—in a theatrical costume. I understood that he had been posing for his portrait. May I add, in parentheses," said Mr. Rattisbon with a bird-like dip of his head, "that although your wife was at Ancreton I had not the pleasure of meeting her on that occasion. I enjoyed this privilege upon my later visit."

"Troy told me."

"It was the greatest pleasure. To return. On this first visit of Wednesday the twenty-first of November, Sir Henry Ancred showed me his rough drafts of two Wills. One moment."

With darting movements, Mr. Rattisbon drew from his filing cabinet two sheaves of paper covered in a somewhat flamboyant script. He handed them to Alleyn. A glance showed him their nature. "Those are the drafts," said Mr. Rattisbon. "He required me to engross two separate Wills based on these notes. I remarked that this procedure was unusual. He put it to me that he was unable to come to a decision regarding the—ah—the merits of his immediate relatives and was, at the same time, contemplating a second marriage. His previous Will, in my opinion a reasonable disposition, he had already destroyed. He instructed me to bring these two new documents to Ancreton when I returned for the annual Birthday observances. The first was the Will witnessed and signed before the Dinner and quoted by Sir Henry *at* dinner as his Last Will and

Testament. It was destroyed late that evening. The second is the document upon which we are at present empowered to act. It was signed and witnessed in Sir Henry Ancred's bedroom at twelve-thirty that night. Against, may I add, *against* my most earnest representations."

"Two Wills," Alleyn said, "in readiness for a final decision."

"Precisely. He believed that his health was precarious. Without making any specific accusations he suggested that certain members of his family were acting separately or in collusion against him. I believe, in view of your own exceedingly lucid account," Mr. Rattisbon dipped his head again, "that he referred, in fact, to these practical jokes. Mrs. Alleyn will have described fully the extraordinary incident of the portrait. An admirable likeness if I may say so. She will have related how Sir Henry left the theatre in anger."

"Yes."

"Subsequently the butler came to me with a request from Sir Henry that I should wait upon him in his room. I found him still greatly perturbed. In my presence, and with considerable violence, he tore up the, as I considered, more reasonable of the two drafts and, in short, threw it on the fire. A Mr. and Mrs. Candy were shown in and witnessed his signature to the second document. Sir Henry then informed me that he proposed to marry Miss Clark in a week's time and would require my services in the drawing-up of a marriage settlement. I persuaded him to postpone this matter until the morning and left him, still agitated and inflamed. That, in effect, is all I can tell you."

"It's been enormously helpful," Alleyn said. "One other point if you don't mind. Sir Henry's two drafts are not dated. He didn't by any chance tell you when he wrote them?"

"No. His behaviour and manner on this point were curious. He stated that he would enjoy no moment's peace until both Wills had been drawn up in my office. But, no. Except that the drafts were made before Tuesday the twentieth, I cannot help you here."

"I'd be grateful if they might be put away and left untouched."

"Of course," said Mr. Rattisbon, greatly flustered. "By all means."

Alleyn placed the papers between two clean sheets and returned them to their drawer.

That done he rose and Mr. Rattisbon at once became very lively. He escorted Alleyn to the door, shook hands and uttered a string of valedictory phrases. "Quite so, quite so," he gabbled. "Disquieting. Trust no foundation but nevertheless disquieting. Always depend upon your discretion. Extraordinary. In many ways, I fear, an unpredictable family. No doubt if counsel is required—well, goodbye. Thank yer. Kindly remember me to Mrs. Alleyn. Thank yer."

But as Alleyn moved away Mr. Rattisbon laid a claw on his arm. "I shall always remember him that night," he said. "He stopped me as I reached the door and I turned and saw him, sitting upright in bed with his gown spread about him. He was a fine-looking old fellow. I was quite arrested by his appearance. He made an unaccountable remark, too, I recollect. He said: 'I expect to be very well attended, in future, Rattisbon. Opposition to my marriage may not be as strong in some quarters as you anticipate. Good-night.' That was all. It was, of course, the last time I ever saw him."

iv

The Honourable Mrs. Claude Ancred had a small flat in Chelsea. As a dwelling-place it presented a startling antithesis to Ancreton. Here all was lightness and simplicity. Alleyn was shown into a white drawing-room, modern in treatment, its end wall one huge window overlooking the river. The curtains were pale yellow powdered with silver stars, and this colour with accents of clear cerise appeared throughout the room. There were three pictures, a Matisse, a Christopher Wood and, to his pleasure, an Agatha Troy. "So you still stick around, do you?" he said winking at it and at that moment Jenetta Ancred came in.

An intelligent-looking woman, he thought. She greeted him as if he was a normal visitor and, with a glance at the painting, said: "You see that we've got a friend in common," and began to talk to him about Troy and their meeting at Ancreton.

He noticed that her manner was faintly and recurrently ironic. Nothing, she seemed to say, must be insisted upon or underlined. Nothing really matters very much. Overstatement is stupid and uncomfortable. This impression was conveyed by the crispness of her voice, its avoidance of stresses, and by her eyes and lips which constantly erected little smiling barriers that half-discredited the frankness of her conversation. She talked intelligently about painting but always with an air of self-deprecation. He had a notion she was warding off the interview for which he had asked.

At last he said: "You've guessed, of course, why I wanted you to let me come?"

"Thomas came in last night and told me he'd seen you and that you'd gone down to Ancreton. This is an extremely unpleasant development, isn't it?"

"I'd very much like to hear your views."

"Mine?" she said with an air of distaste. "They can't possibly be the smallest help, I'm afraid. I'm always a complete onlooker at Ancreton. And please don't tell me the onlooker sees most of the game. In this instance, she sees as little as possible."

"Well," said Alleyn cheerfully, "what does she think?"

She waited for a moment, looking past him to the great window. "I think," she murmured, "that it's almost certain to be a tarradiddle. The whole story."

"Convince us of that," Alleyn said, "and we're your slaves for ever in the C.I.D."

"No but, really. They're so absurd, you know; my in-laws. I'm very attached to them but you can't imagine how absurd they can be." Her voice died away. After a moment's reflection she said: "But Mrs. Alleyn saw them. She must have told you."

"A little."

"At one time it was fifth columnists. Pauline suspected such a nice little Austrian doctor who's since taken a very important job at a big clinic. At that time he was helping with the children. She said something told her . . . And then it was poor Miss Able who was supposed to be undermining her influence with Panty. I wonder if, having left the stage, Pauline's obliged to find some channel for her histrionic instincts. They all do it. Naturally, they resented Miss Orrincourt, and resentment and suspicion are inseparable with the Ancreds."

"What did you think of Miss Orrincourt?"

"I? She's too lovely, isn't she? In her way, quite flawless."

"Apart from her beauty?"

"There didn't seem to be anything else. Except a very robust vulgarity."

"But does she really think as objectively as all that?" Alleyn wondered. "Her daughter stood to lose a good deal through Sonia Orrincourt. Could she have achieved such complete detachment?" He said: "You were there, weren't you, when the book on embalming appeared in the cheese dish?"

She made a slight grimace. "Oh, yes."

"Have you any idea who could have put it there?"

"I'm afraid I rather suspected Cedric. Though why— For no reason except that I can't believe any of the others would do it. It was quite horrible."

"And the anonymous letters?"

"I feel it must have been the same person. I can't imagine how any of the Ancreds—after all they're not— However."

She had a trick of letting her voice fade out as if she had lost faith in the virtue of her sentences. Alleyn felt that she pushed the suggestion of murder away from her, with both hands, not so much for its dreadfulness as for its offence against taste.

"You think, then," he said, "that their suspicion of Miss Orrincourt is unfounded and that Sir Henry died naturally?"

"That's it. I'm quite sure it's all a make-up. They think it's true. They've just got one of their 'things' about it."

"That explanation doesn't quite cover the discovery of a tin of ratsbane in her suitcase, does it?"

"Then there must be some other explanation."

"The only one that occurs to me," Alleyn said, "is that the tin was deliberately planted and if you accept that you accept something equally serious: an attempt to place suspicion of murder upon an innocent person. That in itself constitutes—"

"No, no," she cried out. "No, you don't understand the Ancreds. They plunge into fantasies of their own making without thinking of the consequences. This wretched tin must have been put in the suitcase by a maid or have got there by some other freakish accident. It may have been in the attic for years. None of their alarms ever means anything. Mr. Alleyn, may I implore you to dismiss the whole thing as nonsense. Dangerous and idiotic nonsense but, believe me, utter nonsense."

She had leant forward, and her hands were pressed together. There was a vehemence and an intensity in her manner that had not appeared before.

"If it's nonsense," he said, "it's malevolent nonsense."

"Stupid," she insisted, "spiteful, too, perhaps, but only childishly so."

"I shall be very glad if it turns out to be no more."

"Yes, but you don't think it will."

"I'm wide open to conviction," he said lightly.

"If I could convince you!"

"You can at least help by filling in some of the gaps. For instance you can tell me anything about the party in the drawing-room when you all returned from the Little Theatre? What happened?"

Instead of answering him directly she said, with a return to her earlier manner, "Please forgive me for being so insistent. It's silly to try and ram one's convictions down other people's throats. They merely feel that one protests too much. But you see, I know my Ancreds."

"And I'm learning mine. About the aftermath of the Birthday Party?"

"Well, two of our visitors, the rector and a local squire, said good-night in the hall. Very thankfully, poor darlings, I'm sure. Miss Orrincourt had already gone up. Mrs. Alleyn had stayed behind in the theatre with Paul and Fenella. The rest of us went into the drawing-room and there the usual family arguments started, this time on the subject of that abominable disfigurement of the portrait. Paul and Fenella came in and told us that no damage had been done. Naturally they were very angry. I may tell you that my daughter, who has not quite grown out of the hero-worship state of affairs, admires your wife enormously. These two children planned what they fondly imagined to be a piece of detective work. Did Mrs. Alleyn tell you?"

Troy had told Alleyn, but he listened again to the tale of the paint-brush and finger-prints. She dwelt at some length on this, inviting his laughter, making, he thought, a little too much of a slight incident. When he asked her for further details of the discussion in the drawing-room, she became vague. They had talked about Sir Henry's fury, about his indiscretions at dinner. Mr. Rattisbon had been sent for by Sir Henry. "It was just one more of their interminable emotional parties," she said. "Everyone, except Cedric and Milly, terrifically hurt and grand because of the Will he told us about at dinner."

"Everyone? Your daughter and Mr. Paul Kentish too?"

She said much too lightly: "My poor Fen does go in a little for the Ancred temperament but not, I'm glad to say, to excess. Paul, thank goodness, seems to have escaped it, which is such a very good thing as it appears he's to be my son-in-law."

"Would you say that during this discussion any of them displayed singular vindictiveness against Miss Orrincourt?"

"They were all perfectly livid about her. Except Cedric. But they're lividly angry with somebody or another a dozen times a month. It means nothing."

"Mrs. Ancred," Alleyn said, "if you've been suddenly done out of a very pretty fortune your anger isn't altogether meaningless. You yourself must surely have resented, a little, your daughter's position."

"No," she said quickly. "I knew as soon as she told me of her engagement to Paul, that her grandfather would disapprove. Marriage between cousins was one of his bugbears. I knew he'd take it out of them both. He was a vindictive old man. And Fen hadn't bothered to hide her dislike of Miss Orrincourt. She'd said—" She stopped short. He saw her hands move convulsively.

"Yes?"

"She was perfectly frank. The association offended her taste. That was all."

"What are her views of all this business? The letters and so on?"

"She agrees with me."

"That the whole story is simply a flight of fancy, on the part of the more imaginative members of the family?"

"Yes."

"I should like to see her if I may."

The silence that fell between them was momentary, a brief check in the even flow of their voices, but he found it illuminating. It was as if she winced from an expected hurt, and poised herself to counter it. She leant forward and with an air of great frankness, made a direct appeal.

"Mr. Alleyn," she said, "I'm going to ask a favour. Please let Fenella off. She's highly strung and sensitive. Really sensitive. It's not the rather bogus Ancred sensibility. All the unhappy wrangling over her engagement and the shock of her grandfather's death and then—this horrid and really dreadful business; it's fussed her rather badly. She overheard me speaking to you when you rang up for this talk and even that upset her. I've sent them both out. Please, will you be very understanding and let her off?"

He hesitated, wondering how to frame his refusal, and if her anxiety was based on some much graver reason than the one she gave him.

"Believe me," she said, "Fenella can be of no help to you."

Before he could reply Fenella herself walked in, followed by Paul.

"I'm sorry, Mummy," she said rapidly and in a high voice. "I know you didn't want me to come. I had to. There's something Mr. Alleyn doesn't know and I've got to tell him."

CHAPTER SIXTEEN

Positively the Last Appearance of Sir Henry Ancred

i

AFTERWARDS, when he told Troy about Fenella's entrance, Alleyn said the thing that struck him most at the time was Jenetta Ancred's command of *savoir faire*. Obviously this was a development she had not foreseen and one which filled her with dismay. Yet her quiet assurance never wavered, nor did she neglect the tinge of irony that was implicit in her good manners.

She said: "Darling, how dramatic and alarming. This is my girl, Fenella, Mr. Alleyn. And this is my nephew, Paul Kentish."

"I'm sorry to burst in," said Fenella. "How do you do? Please may we talk to you?" She held out her hand.

"*Not* just at this moment," said her mother. "Mr. Alleyn and I really are rather busy. Do you mind, darling?"

Fenella's grip on his hand had been urgent and nervous. She had whispered, "Please." Alleyn said: "May we just hear what this is about, Mrs. Ancred?"

"Mummy, it's important. Really."

"Paul," said her mother, "can't you manage this firebrand of yours?"

"I think it's important too, Aunt Jen."

"My dearest children, I honestly don't think you know—"

"But Aunt Jen, we do. We've talked it over quite cold bloodedly. We know that what we've got to say may bring a lot of publicity and scandal on the family," said Paul, with something very like relish. "We don't enjoy the prospect but we think any other course would be dishonest."

"We accept the protection of the law," said Fenella rather loudly. "It'd be illogical and dishonest to try and circumvent justice to save the family face. We know we're up against something pretty horrible. We accept the responsibility, don't we, Paul?"

"Yes," said Paul. "We don't like it, but we do it."

"Oh!" Jenetta cried out vehemently, "for pity's sake don't be so heroic. Ancreds, Ancreds, both of you!"

"Mummy, we're *not*. You don't even know what we're going to say. This isn't a matter of theatre, it's a matter of principle and, if you like, of sacrifice."

"And you both see yourselves being sacrificial and high-principled. Mr. Alleyn," Jenetta said (and it was as if she added: "after all we speak the same language, you and I"), "I do most earnestly beg you to take whatever these ridiculous children have to say with a colossal pinch of salt."

"Mummy, it's important."

"Then," said Alleyn, "let's have it."

She gave in, as he had expected, lightly and with grace. "Well then, if we must be interrupted— Do at least sit down, both of you, and let poor Mr. Alleyn sit down too."

Fenella obeyed with the charm of movement that was characteristic of all the female Ancreds. She was, as Troy had told him, a vivid girl. Her mother's spareness was joined in Fenella with the spectacular Ancred beauty and lent it a delicacy. "Nevertheless," Alleyn thought, "she can make an entrance with the best of them."

"Paul and I," she began at once, speaking very rapidly, "have talked and talked about it. Ever since those letters came. We said at first that we wouldn't have anything to do with it. We thought people who wrote that kind of letter were beyond everything and it made us feel perfectly beastly to think there was anyone in the house who could do such a thing. We were absolutely certain that what the letter said was an odious, malicious lie."

"Which is precisely," her mother said without emphasis, "what I have been telling Mr. Alleyn. I really do think, darling—"

"Yes, but that's not all," Fenella interrupted vehemently. "You can't just shrug your shoulders and say it's horrid. If you don't mind my saying so, Mummy dear, that's your generation all over. It's muddled thinking. In its way it's the kind of attitude that leads to wars. That's what Paul and I think, anyway. Don't we, Paul?"

Paul with a red determined face, said: "What Fen means, I think, Aunt Jenetta, is that one can't just say 'Jolly bad form and all ballyhoo,' and let it go at that. Because of the implications. If Sonia Orrincourt didn't poison Grandfather, there's somebody in the house who's trying to get her hanged for something she didn't do, and that's as much as to say there's somebody in the house who's as good as a murderer." He turned to Alleyn: "Isn't that right, sir?"

"Not necessarily right," Alleyn said. "A false accusation may be made in good faith."

"Not," Fenella objected, "by the kind of person who writes anonymous letters. And anyway even if it was in good faith we know it's a false accusation and the realistic thing to do is to say so and, and—" She stumbled, shook her head angrily and ended with childish lameness, "and jolly well make them admit it and pay the penalty."

"Let's take things in their order," Alleyn suggested. "You say you know the suggestion made in the letters is untrue. How do you know this?"

Fenella glanced at Paul with an air of achievement and then turned to Alleyn and eagerly poured out her story.

"It was that evening when she and Mrs. Alleyn drove down to the chemist's and brought back the children's medicine. Cedric and Paul and Aunt Pauline were dining out, I'd got a cold and cried off. I'd been doing the drawing-room flowers for Aunt Milly and I was tidying up in a sinkroom where the vases were kept. It's down some steps off the passage from the hall to the library. Grandfather had had some orchids sent for Sonia and she came to get them. I must say she looked lovely. Sort of sparkling with furs pulled up round her face. She swept in and asked in that ghastly voice for what she called her 'bokay' and when she saw it was a spray of absolutely heavenly orchids she said: 'Quite small, isn't it? Not reely much like flowers, are they?' Everything she'd done and everything she meant at Ancreton seemed to sort of ooze out of her and everything I felt about her suddenly boiled over in me. I'd got a cold and was feeling pretty ghastly, anyway. I absolutely blazed. I said some pretty frightful things about even a common little gold-digger having the decency to be grateful. I said I thought her presence in the house was an insult to all of us and I supposed that when she'd bamboozled Grandfather into marrying her she'd amuse herself with her frightful boy-friends until he was obliging enough to die and leave her his money. Yes, Mummy, I know it was awful, but it just *steamed* out of me and I couldn't stop it."

"O, my poor Fen!" Jenetta Ancred murmured.

"It's the way she took it that's important," Fenella continued, still gazing at Alleyn. "I must admit she took it pretty well. She said, quite calmly, that it was all very fine for me to talk but I didn't know what it was like to be on my beam ends with no chance of getting anything in my job. She said she knew she wasn't any good for the stage except as a show-girl and that didn't last long. I can remember the actual words she used. Fifth-rate theatrical slang. She said: 'I know what you all think. You think I'm playing Noddy up for what I can get out of him. You think that when we're married I'll begin to work in some of the funny business. Look, I've had all that and I reckon I'll be as good a judge as anybody of what's due to my position. And then she said she'd always thought she was the Cinderella type. She said she didn't expect me to understand what a kick she'd get out of being Lady Ancred. She was extraordinarily frank and completely childish about it. She told me she used to lie in bed imagining how she'd give her name and address to people in shops, and what it would sound like when they called her M'lady. 'Gee,' she said, 'will that sound good! Boy, oh boy!' I really think she'd almost forgotten I was there, and the queer thing is that I didn't feel angry with her any longer. She asked me all sorts of questions about precedence; about whether at a dinner party she'd go in before Lady Baumstein. Benny Baumstein is the frightful little man who owns the Sunshine Circuit shows. She was in one of his No. 3 companies. When I said she would, she said 'Yip-ee' like a cow-girl. It was frightful, of course, but it was so completely real that in a way I respected it. She actually said she knew what she called her 'ac-cent' wasn't so hot, but she was going to ask 'Noddy' to teach her to speak more refined."

Fenella looked from her mother to Paul and shook her head helplessly: "It was no good," she said. "I just succumbed. It was awful, and it was funny, and most of all it was somehow genuinely pathetic." She turned back to Alleyn: "I don't know if you can believe that," she said.

"Very easily," Alleyn returned. "She was on the defensive and angry when I saw her, but I noticed something of the same quality myself. Toughness, naivete, and candour all rolled into one. Always very disarming. One meets it occasionally in pickpockets."

"But in a funny sort of way," Fenella said, "I felt that she was honest and had got standards. And much as I loathed the thought of her marriage to Grandfather, I felt sure that according to her lights she'd play fair. And most important of all I felt that the title meant much more to her than the money. She was grateful and affectionate because he was going to give her the title, and never would she have done anything to prevent him doing so. While I was still gaping at her she took my arm and believe it or not we went upstairs together like a couple of schoolgirls. She asked me into her frightful rooms, and I actually sat on the bed while she drenched herself in pre-war scent, repainted her face and dressed for dinner. Then she came along to my room and sat on my bed while I changed. She never left off talking, and I suffered it all in a trance. It really was most peculiar. Down we went, together still, and there was Aunt Milly, howling for the kids' and Grandfather's medicine. We'd left it, of course, in the flower-room, and the queerest thing of all," Fenella slowly wound up, "was that although I still took the gloomiest possible view of her relationship with Grandfather, I simply could *not* continue to loathe her guts. And, Mr. Alleyn, I swear she never did anything to harm him. Do you believe me? Is all this as important as Paul and I think it is?"

Alleyn, who had been watching Jenetta Ancred's hands relax and the colour return to her face, roused himself and said: "It may be of enormous importance. I think you may have tidied up a very messy corner."

"A messy corner," she repeated. "Do you mean—"

"Is there anything else?"

"The next part really belongs to Paul. Go on, Paul."

"Darling," said Jenetta Ancred, and the two syllables, in her deepish voice sounded like a reiterated warning. "Don't you think you've made your point? Must we?"

"Yes, Mummy, we must. Now then, Paul."

Paul began rather stiffly and with a deprecatory air. "I'm afraid, sir, that all this is going to sound extremely obvious and perhaps a bit highfalutin, but Fen and I have talked it over pretty thoroughly and we've come to a definite conclusion. Of course it was obvious from the beginning that the letters meant Sonia Orrincourt. She was the only person who didn't get one and she's the one who benefited most by Grandfather's death. But those letters were written before they found the ratsbane in her suitcase, and, in fact, before there was a shred of evidence against her. So that if she's innocent, and I agree with Fenella that she is, it means one of two things. Either the letter writer knew something that he or she genuinely thought suspicious, and none of us did know anything of the sort; or the letter was written out of pure spite, and not to mince matters, with the intention of getting her hanged. If that's so, it seems to me that the tin of ratsbane was deliberately planted. And it seems to me—to Fen and me—that the same person put that book on embalming in the cheese dish because he was afraid nobody would ever remember it, and was shoving it under our noses in the most startling form he could think of."

He paused and glanced nervously at Alleyn, who said: "That sounds like perfectly sound reasoning to me."

"Well then, sir," said Paul quickly, "I think you'll agree that the next point is important. It's about this same damn' silly business with the book in the cheese dish, and I may as well say at the outset, it casts a pretty murky light on my cousin Cedric. In fact, if we're right, we've got to face the responsibility of practically accusing Cedric of attempted murder."

"Paul!"

"I'm sorry, Aunt Jen, but we've decided."

"If you're right, and I'm sure you're wrong, have you thought of the sequel? The newspapers. The beastliness. Have you thought of poor Milly, who dotes on the little wretch?"

"We're sorry," Paul repeated stubbornly.

"You're inhuman," cried his aunt and threw up her hands.

"Well," said Alleyn peaceably, "let's tackle this luncheon party while we're at it. What was everybody doing before the book on embalming made its appearance?"

This seemed to nonplus them. Fenella said impatiently: "Just sitting. Waiting for someone to break it up. Aunt Milly does hostess at Ancreton but Aunt Pauline (Paul's mother) rather feels she ought to when in residence. She—you don't mind my mentioning it, Paul darling?—she huffs and puffs about it a bit and makes a point of waiting for Aunt Milly to give the imperceptible signal to rise. I rather fancied Aunt Milly kept us sitting for pure devilment. Anyway, there we stuck."

"Sonia fidgeted," said Paul, "and sort of groaned."

"Aunt Dessy said she thought it would be nice if we could escape having luncheon dishes that looked like the village pond when the floods had subsided. That was maddening for Aunt Milly. She said, with a short laugh, that Dessy wasn't obliged to stay on at Ancreton."

"And Dessy," Paul continued, "said that to her certain knowledge Milly and Pauline were holding back some tins of white-bait."

"Everybody began talking at once and Sonia said: 'Pardon me, but how does the chorus go?' Cedric tittered and got up and wandered to the sideboard."

"And this is our point, sir," Paul cut in with determination. "The cheese was found by my cousin Cedric. He went to the sideboard and came back with a book and dropped it over my mother's shoulder on to her plate. It gave her a shock, as you can imagine."

"She gave a screech and fainted, actually," Fenella added.

"My mama," said Paul unhappily, "was a bit wrought-up by the funeral and so on. She really fainted, Aunt Jen."

"My dear boy, I'm sure she did."

"It gave her a fright."

"Naturally," Alleyn murmured. "Books on embalming don't fall out of cheese dishes every day in the week."

"We'd all," Paul went on, "just about *had* Cedric. Nobody paid any attention to the book itself. We merely suggested that it wasn't amazingly funny to frighten people and that anyway he stank."

"I was watching Cedric, then," Fenella said. "There was something queer about him. He never took his eyes off Sonia. And then, just as we were all herding Aunt Pauline out of the room, he gave one of his yelps and said he'd remembered something in the book. He ran to the door and began reading out of it about arsenic."

"And then somebody remembered that Sonia had been seen looking at the book."

"And I'll swear," Fenella cut in, "she didn't know what he was driving at. I don't believe she ever really understood. Aunt Dessy did her stuff and wailed and said: 'No, no, don't go on! I can't bear it!' and Cedric purred: 'But Dessy, my sweet, what have I said? Why shouldn't darling Sonia read about her fiance's coming embalmment?' and Sonia burst into tears and said we were all plotting against her and rushed out of the room."

"The point is, sir, if Cedric hadn't behaved as he did, nobody would have thought of connecting the book with the suggestion in the letters. You see?"

Alleyn said: "It's a point."

"There's something else," Paul added, again with that tinge of satisfaction in his voice. "*Why* did Cedric look in the cheese dish?"

"Presumably because he wanted some cheese?"

"No!" Paul cried triumphantly. "That's just where we've got him, sir. He never touches cheese. He detests it."

"So you see," said Fenella.

ii

When Alleyn left, Paul showed him into the hall and, after some hesitation, asked if he might walk with him a little way. They went together, head-down against a blustering wind, along Cheyne Walk. Ragged clouds scurried across the sky, and the sounds of river traffic were blown intermittently against their chilled ears. Paul, using his stick, limped along at a round pace, and for some minutes in silence.

At last he said: "I suppose it's true that you can't escape your heredity." And as Alleyn turned his head to look at him, he went on slowly: "I meant to tell you that story quite differently. Without any build-up, Fen did too. But somehow when we got going something happened to us. Perhaps it was Aunt Jen's opposition. Or perhaps when there's anything like a crisis we can't escape a sense of audience. I heard myself doing the same sort of thing over there." He jerked his head vaguely towards the east. "The gay young officer rallying his men. It went down quite well with them, too, but it makes me feel pretty hot under the collar when I think about it now. And about the way we strutted our stuff back there at Aunt Jen's."

"You made your points very neatly," said Alleyn.

"A damn' sight too neatly," Paul rejoined, grimly. "That's why I think I'd like to try and say without any flourishes that we do honestly believe that all this stuff about poison has simply been concocted by Cedric to try and upset the Will. And we think it would be a pretty poor show to let him get away with it. On all counts."

Alleyn didn't reply immediately, and Paul said, nervously: "I suppose it'd be quite out of order for me to ask whether you think we're right."

"Ethically," said Alleyn, "yes. But I don't think you realized the implications. Your aunt did."

"I know, Aunt Jen's very fastidious. It's the dirty linen in public that she hates."

"And with reason," said Alleyn.

"Well, we'll all have to lump it. But what I meant, really, was, were we right in our deductions?"

"I ought to return an official and ambiguous answer to that," Alleyn said. "But I won't. I may be wrong, but on the evidence that we've got up to date I should say your deductions were ingenious and almost entirely wrong."

A sharp gust carried away the sound of his voice.

"What?" said Paul, distantly and without emphasis. "I didn't quite hear—"

"Wrong," Alleyn repeated, strongly. "As far as I can judge, you know, quite wrong."

Paul stopped short, and dipping his head to meet the wind stared at Alleyn with an expression not of dismay but of doubt, as if he still thought he must have misunderstood.

"But I don't see . . . we thought . . . it all hangs together—"

"As an isolated group of facts, perhaps it does."

They resumed their walk and Alleyn heard him say fretfully: "I wish you'd explain." And after another pause, he peered rather anxiously at Alleyn. "Perhaps it wouldn't do though," he added.

Alleyn thought for a moment, and then taking Paul by the elbow, steered him into the shelter of a side street. "We can't go on bawling at each other in a gale," he said, "but I don't see that it can do any harm to explain this much. It's quite possible that if all this dust had not been raised after your grandfather's death, Miss Orrincourt might still have become Lady Ancred."

Paul's jaw dropped. "I don't get that."

"You don't?"

"Good God!" Paul roared out suddenly. "You can't mean Cedric?"

"Sir Cedric," said Alleyn, dryly, "is my authority. He tells me he has seriously considered marrying her."

After a long silence, Paul said slowly: "They're as thick as thieves, of course. But I never guessed . . . No, it'd be too much. . . . I'm sorry, sir, but you're sure—"

"Unless he invented the story."

"To cover up his tracks," said Paul instantly.

"Extremely elaborate and she could deny it. As a matter of fact her manner suggested some sort of understanding between them."

Paul raised his clasped hands to his mouth and thoughtfully blew into them. "Suppose," he said, "he suspected her, and wanted to make sure?"

"That would be an entirely different story."

"Is that your theory, sir?"

"Theory?" Alleyn repeated vaguely. "I haven't got a theory. I haven't sorted things out. Mustn't keep you standing here in the cold." He held out his hand. Paul's was like ice. "Good-bye," said Alleyn.

"One minute, sir. Will you tell me this? I give you my word it'll go no further. Was my grandfather murdered?"

"Oh, yes," said Alleyn. "Yes. I'm afraid we may be sure of that. He was murdered." He walked down the street, leaving Paul, still blowing on his frozen knuckles, to stare after him.

iii

The canvas walls were faintly luminous. They were laced to their poles with ropes and glowed in the darkness. Blobs of light from hurricane lanterns suspended within, formed a globular pattern across the surface. One of these lanterns must have been touching the wall, for the village constable on duty outside could clearly make out shadows of wire and the precise source of light.

He glanced uneasily at the motionless figure of his companion, a police-officer from London, wearing a short cape. "Bitter cold," he said.

"That's right."

"Be long, d'yew reckon?"

"Can't say."

The constable would have enjoyed a talk. He was a moralist and a philosopher, well known in Ancreton for his pronouncements upon the conduct of politicians and for his independent views in the matter of religion. But his companion's taciturnity and the uncomfortable knowledge that anything he said would be audible on the other side of the canvas, put a damper on conversation. He stamped once or twice, finding reassurance in the crunch of gravel under his feet. There were noises within the enclosure: voices, soft thumps. At the far end and high above them, as if suspended in the night, and lit theatrically from below, knelt three angels. "Through the long night watches," the constable said to himself, "may thine angels spread their white wings above me, watching round my head."

Within the enclosure but close behind him, the voice of the Chief Inspector from the Yard said: "Are we ready, Curtis?" His shadowy figure suddenly loomed up inside the canvas wall. "Quite ready," somebody else said. "Then if I may have the key, Mr. Ancred?" "Oh—oh, er—yes." That was poor Mr. Thomas Ancred.

The constable listened, yet desired not to listen, to the next too-lucid train of sounds. He had heard them before, on the day of the funeral, when he came down early to have a look while his cousin, the sexton, got things fixed up. Very heavy lock. They'd had to give it a drop of oil. Seldom used. His flesh leapt on his bones as a screech rent the cold air. "Them ruddy hinges," he thought. The blobs of light were withdrawn and the voices with them. He could still hear them, however, though now they sounded hollow. Beyond the hedge a match flared up in the dark. That would be the driver of the long black car, of course, waiting in the lane. The constable wouldn't have minded a pipe himself.

The Chief Inspector's voice, reflected from stone walls, said distantly: "Get those acetylene lamps going, Bailey." "Yes, sir," someone answered, so close to the constable that he jumped again. With a hissing noise, a new brilliance sprang up behind the canvas.

Strange distorted shadows flickered among the trees about the cemetery.

Now came sounds to which he had looked forward with squeamish relish. A drag of wood on stone followed by the uneven scuffle of boots and heavy breathing. He cleared his throat and glanced stealthily at his companion.

The enclosure was again full of invisible men. "Straight down on the trestles. Right." The squeak of wood and then silence.

The constable drove his hands deep into his pockets and looked up at the three angels and at the shape of St. Stephen's spire against the stars. "Bats in that belfry," he thought. "Funny how a chap'll say it, not thinking." An owl hooted up in Ancreton woods.

Beyond the canvas there was movement. A light voice said jerkily: "I think, if it doesn't make any difference, I'd like to wait outside. I won't go away. You can call me, you know."

"Yes, of course."

A canvas flap was pulled aside, letting out a triangle of light on the grass. A man came out. He wore a heavy overcoat and muffler and his hat was pulled over his face but the constable had recognized his voice and shifted uneasily.

"Oh, it's you, Bream," said Thomas Ancred.

"Yes, Mr. Thomas."

"Cold, isn't it?"

"Hard frost before dawn, sir."

Above them the church clock gave a preparatory whirr and with a sweet voice told two in the morning.

"I don't like this much, Bream."

"Very upsetting, sir, I'm sure."

"Terribly upsetting, yes."

"And yet, sir," said Bream with a didactic air, "I been thinking: this here poor remains beant a matter to scare a chap, if rightly considered. It beant your respected father hisself as you might put it, sir. He's well away receiving his reward by now, and what you are called to look upon is a harmless enough affair. No more, if you'll excuse me, than a left-off garment. As has been preached at us souls regular in this very church."

"I daresay," said Thomas. "Nevertheless— Well, thank you."

He moved away down the gravel path. The London officer turned to watch him. Thomas did not move quite out of range of the veiled light. He stood, with his head bent, near the dim shape of a gravestone and seemed to be rubbing his hands together.

"Cold and nervous, poor chap," Bream said to himself.

"Before we go any further" (that was Chief Inspector Alleyn again), "will you make a formal examination, Mr. Mortimer? We'd like your identification of the nameplate and your assurance that everything is as it was at the time of the funeral."

A clearing of the throat, a pause and then a muffled voice. "Perfectly in order. Our own workmanship, Mr. Alleyn. Casket and plate."

"Thank you. All right, Thompson."

The click of metal and the faint grind of disengaging screws. This seemed to Bream to continue an unconscionable time. Nobody spoke. From his mouth and nostrils and those of the London constable, little jets of breath drifted out and condensed on the frozen air. The London man switched on his flash-lamp. It's beam illuminated Thomas Ancred, who looked up and blinked. "I'm just waiting," he said, "I won't go away."

"Quite all right, sir."

"Now," ordered the voice in the enclosure. "Everything free? Right."

"Just ease a little, it's a precision fit. That's right. Slide."

"Oh, cripes!" Bream said to himself.

Wood whispered along wood. This sound was followed by complete silence. Thomas Ancred turned away from grass to gravel path and walked aimlessly to and fro.

"Curtis? Will you and Dr. Withers—"

"Yes. Thanks. Move that light a little this way, Thompson. Will you come here, Dr. Withers?"

"The—ah—the process is quite satisfactory, don't you consider, Doctor? Only a short time, of course, but I can assure you there would be no deterioration."

"Indeed? Remarkable."

"One is gratified."

"I think we'll have that bandage taken away, if you please. Fox, will you tell Mr. Ancred we're ready for him?"

Bream watched the thick-set Inspector Fox emerge and walk over towards Thomas. Before he had gone more than a few paces there was a sudden and violent ejaculation inside the enclosure. *"Good God, look at that."* Inspector Fox paused. The Chief Inspector's voice said, very sharply, "Quiet, Dr. Withers, please," and there followed a rapid whispering.

Inspector Fox moved away and joined Thomas Ancred. "If you'll come this way, Mr. Ancred." "Oh! Yes, of course. Very good. Right ho!" said Thomas in a high voice and followed him back to the enclosure. "If I moved a bit," Bream thought, "when they opened the flaps, I'd see in." But he did not move. The London constable held the doorway open, glancing impassively into the tent before he let the canvas fall. The voices began again.

"Now, this is not going to be a very big ordeal, Mr. Ancred."

"Oh, isn't it? Oh, good."

"Will you—"

Bream heard Thomas move. "There, you see. Quite peaceful."

"I—yes—I identify him."

"That's all right, then. Thank you."

"No," said Thomas and his voice rose hysterically. "It's not all right. There's something all wrong, in fact. Papa had a fine head of hair. Hadn't he, Dr. Withers? He was very proud of it, wasn't he? And his moustache. This is bald. *What have they done with his hair?*"

"Steady! Put your head down. You'll be all right. Give me that brandy, Fox, will you. Damn, he's fainted."

iv

"Well, Curtis," Alleyn said as the car slid between rows of sleeping houses, "I hope you'll be able to give us something definite."

"Hope so," said Dr. Curtis, stifling a heavy yawn.

"I'd like to ask you, Doctor," said Fox, "whether you'd expect one fatal dose of arsenic to have that effect."

"What effect? Oh, the hair. No, I wouldn't. It's more often a symptom of chronic poisoning."

"In for one of those messes, are we?" Fox grumbled. "That will be nice. Field of suspects opened up wide, with the possibility of Miss O. being framed."

"There are objections to chronic poisoning, Br'er Fox," Alleyn said. "He might die when he'd concocted a Will unfavourable to the poisoner. And moreover you'd expect a progressive loss of hair, not a sudden post-mortem moult. Is that right, Curtis?"

"Certainly."

"Well then," Fox persisted heavily, "how about the embalming process? Would that account for it?"

"Emphatically not," Mr. Mortimer interjected. "I've given the Chief Inspector our own formula. An unusual step but in the circumstances, desirable. No doubt, Doctor, he has made you conversant—"

"Oh, yes," sighed Dr. Curtis. "Formalin. Glycerin. Bòric acid. Menthol. Potassium nitrate. Sodium citrate. Oil of cloves. Water."

"Precisely."

"Hey!" said Fox. "No arsenic?"

"You're two days late with the news, Br'er Fox. Things have moved while you were at Ancreton. Arsenic went out some time ago, didn't it, Mr. Mortimer?"

"Formalin," Mr. Mortimer agreed with hauteur, "is infinitely superior."

"There now," Fox rumbled with great satisfaction. "That does clear things up a bit, doesn't it, Mr. Alleyn? If arsenic's found it's got no business to be there. That's something definite. And what's more, any individual who banked on its being used by the embalmer made the mistake of her life. Nothing for counsel to muddle the jury with, either. Mr. Mortimer's evidence would settle that. Well."

Alleyn said, "Mr. Mortimer, had Sir Henry any notion of the method used?"

In a voice so drowsy that it reminded Alleyn of the dormouse's, Mr. Mortimer said: "It's very curious, Chief Inspector, that you should ask that question. Oh, very curious. Because, between you and I, the deceased gentleman showed quite an unusual interest. He sent for me and discussed the arrangements for the interment. Two years ago, that was."

"Good Lord!"

"That is not so unusual in itself. Gentlemen of his position do occasionally give detailed instructions. But the deceased was so very particular. He—well, reely," Mr. Mortimer said, coughing slightly, "he quite read me a little lecture on embalming. He had a little book. Yes," said Mr. Mortimer, swallowing a yawn, "rather a quaint little book. Very old. It seemed an ancestor of his had been embalmed by the method, *quate* outdated, I may say, outlined in his tainy tome. Sir Henry wished to ascertain if our method was similar. When I ventured to suggest the book was somewhat demode, he became—well, *so* annoyed that it was rather awkward. Very awkward, in fact. He was insistent that we should use the same process on—ah—for—ah—himself. He quate *ordered* me to do it."

"But you didn't consent?"

"I must confess, Chief Inspector, I—I—the situation was most awkward. I feared he would upset himself seriously. I must confess that I compromaysed. In point of fact, I—"

"You consented?"

"I would have gladly refused the commission altogether but he would take no refusal. He forced me to take the book away with me. I returned it with compliments, and without comment through the registered post. He replied that when the time came I was to understand my instructions. The—ah—the time came and—and—"

"You followed your own method? And said nothing to anybody?"

"It seemed the only thing to do. Anything else was impossible from the point of view of technique. Ridiculous in fact. Such preposterous ingredients! You can't imagine."

"Well," said Fox, "as long as you can testify there was no arsenic. Eh, Mr. Alleyn?"

"I must say," said Mr. Mortimer, "I don't at all care for the idea of giving evidence in an affair of this sort. Ours is a delicate and you might say exclusive profession, Chief Inspector. Publicity of this kind is most undesirable."

"You may not be subpoenaed, after all," said Alleyn.

"Not? But I understood Inspector Fox to say—"

"You never know. Cheer up, Mr. Mortimer."

Mr. Mortimer muttered to himself disconsolately and fell into a doze.

"What about the cat?" Fox asked. "And the bottle of medicine?"

"No report yet."

"We've been busy," Dr. Curtis complained. "You and your cats! The report should be in some time today. What's all this about a cat anyway?"

"Never you mind," Alleyn grunted, "you do your Marsh-Berzelius tests with a nice open mind. And your Fresenius process later on, I shouldn't wonder."

Dr. Curtis paused in the act of lighting his pipe. "*Fresenius* process?" he said.

"Yes, and your ammonium chloride and your potassium iodide and your Bunsen flame and your platinum wire. And look for the pretty green line, blast you."

After a long silence, Dr. Curtis said: "It's like that is it?" and glanced at Mr. Mortimer.

"It may be like that."

"Having regard to the general lay-out?"

"That's the burden of our song."

Fox said suddenly: "Was he bald when they laid him out?"

"Not he. Mrs. Henry Ancred and Mrs. Kentish were both

present. They'd have noticed. Besides, the hair was there, Fox. We collected it while you were ministering to Thomas."

"Oh." Fox ruminated for a time and then said loudly, "Mr. Mortimer. Mr. Mortimer."

"Wha—"

"Did you notice Sir Henry's hair when you were working on him?"

"Eh? Oh, yes," said Mr. Mortimer, hurriedly but in a voice slurred with sleep. "Yes, indeed. We all remarked on it. A magnificent head of hair." He yawned hideously. "A magnificent head of hair," he repeated.

Alleyn looked at Dr. Curtis. "Consistent?" he asked.

"With your green line? Yes."

"Pardon?" said Mr. Mortimer anxiously.

"All right, Mr. Mortimer. Nothing. We're in London. You'll be in bed by daybreak."

CHAPTER SEVENTEEN

Escape of Miss O.

i

AT BREAKFAST Alleyn said: "This case of ours is doing the usual snowball business, Troy."

"Gathering up complications as it goes?"

"A mass of murky stuff in this instance. Grubby stuff and a lot of waste matter. Do you want an interim report?"

"Only if you feel like making one. And is there enough time?"

"Actually there's not. I can answer a crisp question or two, though, if you care to rap them out at me."

"You know, I expect, what they'll be."

"Was Ancred murdered? I think so. Did Sonia Orrincourt do it? I don't know. I shall know, I believe, when the analyst sends in his report."

"If he finds arsenic?"

"If he finds it in one place, then I'm afraid it's Sonia Orrincourt. If he finds it in three places, it's Sonia Orrincourt or one other. If he doesn't find it at all then I *think* it's that other. I'm not positive."

"And—the one other?"

"I suppose it's no more unpleasant for you to speculate about one than about several."

"I'd rather know, if it's all right to tell me."

"Very well," Alleyn said and told her.

After a long silence she said: "But it seems completely unreal. I can't possibly believe it."

"Didn't everything they did at Ancreton seem a bit unreal?"

"Yes, of course. But to imagine that underneath all the showings-off and temperaments *this* could be happening—I can't. Of all of them—that one!"

"Remember, I may be wrong."

"You've a habit of not being wrong, though, haven't you?"

"The Yard," said Alleyn, "is littered with my blunders. Ask Fox. Troy, is this very beastly for you?"

"No," said Troy. "It's mostly bewildering. I didn't form any attachments at Ancreton. I can't give it a personal application."

"Thank God for that," he said and went to the Yard.

Here he found Fox in waiting with the tin of ratsbane. "I haven't had a chance to hear your further adventures at Ancreton, Foxkin. The presence of Mr. Mortimer rather cramped our style last night. How did you get on?"

"Quite nicely, sir. No trouble really about getting the prints. Well, when I say no trouble, there was quite a bit of high-striking in some quarters as was to be expected in that family. Miss O. made trouble and, for a while, stuck out she wouldn't have it, but I talked her round. Nobody else actually objected though you'd have thought Mrs. Kentish and Miss Desdemona Ancred were being asked to walk into the condemned cell, the way they carried on. Bailey got down by the early train in the morning and worked through the prints you asked for. We found a good enough impression in paint on the wall of Mrs. Alleyn's tower. Miss O. all right. *And* her prints are in the book. Lots of others too, of course. Prints all over the cover, from when they looked at it after it turned up in the cheese dish, no doubt. I've checked up on the letters but there's nothing in it. They handed them round and there you are. Same thing in the flower-room. Regular mess of prints and some odds and ends where they'd missed sweeping. Coloured tape off florists' boxes, leaves and stalks, scraps of sealing wax, fancy paper and so on. I've kept all of it in case there was anything. I took a chance to slip into Miss O.'s room. Nothing beyond some skittish literature and a few letters from men written before Sir Henry's day. One, more recent, from a young lady. I memorized it. 'Dear S. Good for you, kid, stick to it and don't forget your old pals when you're Lady A. Think the boyfriend'd do anything for me in the business? God knows I'm not so hot on this Shakespeare, but he must know other managements. Does he wear bed-socks? Regards Clarrie.' "

"No mention of the egregious Cedric?"

"Not a word. We looked at Miss Able's cupboard. Only her own prints. I called in at Mr. Juniper's. He says the last lot of that paper was taken up with some other stuff for the rest of the house a fortnight ago. Two sets of prints on the bell-push from Sir Henry's room. His own and old Barker's. Looks as if Sir Henry had grabbed at it, tried to use it and dragged it off."

"As we thought."

"Mr. Juniper got in a great way when I started asking questions. I went very easy with him but he made me a regular speech about how careful he is and showed me his books. He reckons he always double-checks everything he makes up. He's particularly careful, he says, because of Dr. Withers being uncommonly fussy. It seems they had a bit of a row. The doctor reckoned the kids' medicine wasn't right and Juniper took it for an insult. He says the doctor must have made the mistake himself and tried to save his face by turning round on him. He let on the doctor's a bit of a lad and a great betting man and he thinks he'd been losing pretty solidly and was worried and made a mistake weighing the kids or something. But that wouldn't apply to Sir Henry's medicine because it was the mixture as before. And I found out that at the time he made it up he was out of arsenic and hasn't got any yet."

"Good for Mr. Juniper," said Alleyn dryly.

"Which brings us," Fox continued, "to this tin." He laid his great hands beside it on the desk. "Bailey's gone over it for dabs. And here we have got something, Mr. Alleyn, and about time too, you'll be thinking. Now, this tin has got the usual set of prints. Some of the search party's, in fact. Latent, but Bailey brought them up and got some good photographs. There's Mrs. Kentish's. She must have just touched it. Miss Desdemona Ancred seems to have picked it up by the edge. Mr. Thomas Ancred grasped it more solidly round the sides and handled it again when he took it out of his bag. Mrs. Henry Ancred held it firmly towards the bottom. Sir Cedric's prints are all over it, and there, you'll notice, are the marks round the lid where he had a shot at opening it."

"Not a very determined shot."

"No. Probably scared of getting ratsbane on his manicure," said Fox. "But the point is, you see—"

"No Orrincourt?"

"Not a sign of her. Not a sign of glove marks either. It was a dusty affair and the dust, except for the prints we got, wasn't disturbed."

"It's a point. Well, Fox, now Bailey's finished with it we can open it."

The lid was firm and it took a penny and considerable force to prise it up. An accretion of the contents had sealed it. The tin was three parts full and the greyish paste bore traces of the implement that had been used to scoop it out.

"We'll have a photo-micrograph of this," Alleyn said.

"If Orrincourt's our bird, sir, it looks as if we'll have to hand the tin over to the defence, doesn't it?"

"We'll have to get an expert's opinion, Fox. Curtis's boys can speak up when they've finished the job in hand. Pray continue with, as the Immortal used to say, your most interesting narrative."

"There's not much more. I took a little peep at the young baronet's room, too. Dunning letters, lawyer's letters, letters from his stockbroker. I should say he was in deep. I've made a note of the principal creditors."

"For an officer without a search warrant you seem to have got on very comfortably."

"Isabel helped. She's taken quite a fancy for investigation. She kept a look-out in the passage."

"With parlour-maids," Alleyn said, "you're not on your own. A masterly technique."

"I called on Dr. Withers yesterday afternoon and told him you'd decided on the exhumation."

"How did he take it?"

"He didn't say much but he went a queer colour. Well, naturally. They never like it. Reflection on their professional standing and so on. He thought a bit and then said he'd prefer to be present. I said we'd expect that, anyway. I was just going when he called me back. 'Here!' he said, kind of hurriedly and as if he wasn't sure he might not be making a fool of himself; 'you don't want to pay too much attention to anything that idiot Juniper may have told you, the man's an ass.' As soon as I was out of the house," said Fox, "I made a note of that to be sure the words were correct. The maid was showing me out at the time."

"Curtis asked him last night, after we'd tidied up in the cemetery, if he'd like to come up and watch the analysis. He agreed. He's sticking to it that the embalmers must have used something that caused the hair to fall out. Mr. Mortimer was touched to the professional quick, of course."

"It's a line defending counsel may fancy," said Fox gloomily.

The telephone rang and Fox answered it.

"It's Mr. Mortimer," he said.

"Oh Lord! You take it, Fox."

"He's engaged at the moment, Mr. Mortimer. Can I help you?"

The telephone cackled lengthily and Fox looked at Alleyn with bland astonishment. "Just a moment," he said into the receiver. "I don't follow this. Mr. Alleyn hasn't got a secretary."

"What's all this?" said Alleyn sharply.

Fox clapped his hand over the receiver. "He says your secretary rang up their office half an hour ago and asked them to repeat the formula for embalming. His partner, Mr. Loame, answered. He wants to know if it was all right."

"Did Loame give the formula?"

"Yes."

"Bloody fool," Alleyn said violently. "Tell him it's all wrong and ring off."

"I'll let Mr. Alleyn know," said Fox and hung up the receiver. Alleyn reached for it and pulled the telephone towards him.

"Ancreton, 2A," he said. "Priority. Quick as you can." And while he waited: "We may want a car at once, Fox. Ring down, will you? We'll take Thompson with us. And we'll need a search warrant." Fox went into the next room and telephoned. When he returned Alleyn was speaking. "Hello. May I speak to Miss Orrincourt? Out? When will she be in? I see. Get me Miss Able, Barker, will you? It's Scotland Yard here." He looked round at Fox. "We'll be going," he said. "She came up to London last night and is expected back for lunch. Damn! Why the hell doesn't the Home Office come to light with that report? We need it now, and badly. What's the time?"

"Ten to twelve, sir."

"Her train gets in at twelve. We haven't an earthly.— Hullo. Hullo, is that you, Miss Able? Alleyn here. Don't answer anything but yes or no, please. I want you to do something that is urgent and important. Miss Orrincourt is returning by the train that arrives at midday. Please find out if anyone has left to meet her. If not make some excuse for going yourself in the pony cart. If it's too late for that, meet it when it arrives at the house. Take Miss Orrincourt into your part of the house and keep her there. Tell her I said so and take no refusal. It's urgent. She's not to go into the other part of the house. Got that? Sure? Right. Splendid. Good-bye."

He rang off and found Fox waiting with his overcoat and hat. "Wait a bit," he said. "That's not good enough," and turned back to the telephone. "Get me Camber Cross police station. They're the nearest to Ancreton, aren't they, Fox?"

"Three miles. The local P.C. lives in Ancreton parish, though. On duty last night."

"That's the chap. Bream. Hullo. Chief Inspector Alleyn, Scotland Yard. Is your chap Bream in the station? Can you find him? Good. The Ancreton pub. I'd be much obliged if you'd ring through. Tell him to go at once to Ancreton Halt. A Miss Orrincourt will get off the midday train. She'll be met from the Manor house. He's to let the trap go away without her, take her to the pub, and wait there for me. Right. Thanks."

"Will he make it?" Fox asked.

"He has his dinner at the pub and he's got a bike. It's no more than a mile and a half. Here we go, Fox. If, in the ripeness of time, Mr. Loame is embalmed by his own firm I hope they make a mess of him. What precisely did this bogus secretary say?"

"Just that you'd told him to get a confirmation of the formula. It was a toll-call but of course Loame thought you were back at Ancreton."

"And so he tells poor old Ancred's killer that there was no arsenic used in the embalming and blows our smoke screen to hell. As Miss O. would say, what a pal! Where's my bag? Come on."

But as they reached the door the telephone rang again.

"I'll go," Alleyn said. "With any luck it's Curtis."

It was Dr. Curtis. "I don't know whether you'll like this," he said. "It's the Home Office report on the cat, the medicine and the deceased. First analysis completed. No arsenic anywhere."

"Good!" said Alleyn. "Now tell them to try for thallium acetate and ring me at Ancreton when they've found it."

ii

They were to encounter yet another interruption. As they went out to the waiting car, they found Thomas, very white and pinched, on the bottom step.

"Oh, hullo," he said. "I was coming to see you. I want to see you awfully."

"Important?" Alleyn said.

"To me," Thomas rejoined with his air of innocence, "it's as important as anything. You see I came in by the morning train on purpose. I felt I had to. I'm going back this evening."

"We're on our way to Ancreton now."

"Really? Then I suppose you wouldn't—or shouldn't one suggest it?"

"We can take you with us. Certainly," said Alleyn after a fractional pause.

"Isn't that lucky?" said Thomas wistfully and got into the back seat with them. Detective-Sergeant Thompson was already seated by the driver. They drove away in a silence lasting so long that Alleyn began to wonder if Thomas, after all, had nothing to say. At last, however, he plunged into conversation with an abruptness that startled his hearers.

"First of all," said Thomas loudly, "I want to apologize for my behaviour last night. Fainting! Well! I thought I left that kind of thing to Pauline. Everybody was so nice, too. The doctors and you," he said smiling wanly at Fox, "driving me home and everything. I couldn't be more sorry."

"Very understandable, I'm sure," said Fox comfortably. "You'd had a nasty shock."

"Well, I had. Frightful, really. And the worst of it is, you know, I can't shake it off. When I *did* go to sleep it was so beastly. The dreams. And this morning with the family asking questions."

"You said nothing, of course," said Alleyn.

"You'd asked me not to so I didn't, but they took it awfully badly. Cedric was quite furious and Pauline said I was siding against the family. The point is, Alleyn, I honestly don't think I can stand any more. It's unlike me," said Thomas. "I must have a temperament after all. Fancy!"

"What exactly do you want to see us about?"

"I want to know. It's the uncertainty. I want to know why Papa's hair had fallen out. I want to know if he was poisoned and if you think Sonia did it. I'm quite discreet, really, and if you tell me I'll give you my solemn word of honour not to say anything. Not even to Caroline Able though I daresay she could explain why I feel so peculiar. I want to know."

"Everything from the beginning?"

"Yes, if you don't mind. Everything."

"That's a tall order. We don't know everything. We're trying, very laboriously, to piece things together and we've got, I think, almost the whole pattern. We believe your father was poisoned."

Thomas rubbed the palms of his hands across the back of the driver's seat. "Are you certain? That's horrible."

"The bell-push in his room had been manipulated in such a way that it wouldn't ring. One of the wires had been released. The bell-push hung by the other wire and when he grasped it the wooden end came away in his hand. We started from there."

"That seems a simple little thing."

"There are lots of more complicated things. Your father made two Wills and signed neither of them until the day of his Birthday Party. The first he signed, as I think he told you, before the dinner. The second and valid one he signed late that night. We believe that Miss Orrincourt and your nephew Cedric were the only two people, apart from his solicitor, who knew of this action. She benefited greatly by the valid Will. He lost heavily."

"Then why bring him into the picture?" Thomas asked instantly.

"He won't stay out. He hovers. For one thing, he and Miss Orrincourt planned all the practical jokes."

"Goodness! But Papa's death wasn't a practical joke. Or was it?"

"Indirectly, it's just possible that it was caused by one. The final practical joke, the flying cow on the picture, probably caused Sir Henry to fix on the second draft."

"I don't know anything about all that," Thomas said dismally. "I don't understand. I hoped you'd just tell me if Sonia did it."

"We're still waiting for one bit of the pattern. Without it we can't be positive. It would be against one of our most stringent rules for me to name a suspect to an interested person when the case is still incomplete."

"Well, couldn't you behave like they do in books? Give me a pointer or two?"

Alleyn raised an eyebrow and glanced at Fox. "I'm afraid," he said, "that without a full knowledge of the information our pointers wouldn't mean very much."

"Oh, dear. Still I may as well hear them. Anything's better than this awful blank worrying. I'm not quite such a fool," Thomas added, "as I daresay I seem. I'm a good producer of plays. I'm used to analyzing character and I've got a great eye for a situation. When I read the script of a murder play I always know who did it."

"Well," Alleyn said dubiously, "here, for what they're worth, are some relative bits of fact. The bell-push. The children's ringworm. The fact that the anonymous letters were written on the children's school paper. The fact that only Sir Cedric and Miss Orrincourt knew your father signed the second Will. The book on embalming. The nature of arsenical poisoning and the fact that none has been found in his body, his medicine, or in the body of his cat."

"Carabbas? Does he come in? That *is* surprising. Go on."

"His fur fell out, he was suspected of ringworm and destroyed. He had not got ringworm. The children had. They were dosed with a medicine that acts as a depilatory and their fur did *not* fall out. The cat was in your father's room on the night of his death."

"And Papa gave him some hot milk as usual. I see."

"The milk was cleared away and the thermos scalded out and used afterwards. No chemical analysis was possible. Now, for the tin of ratsbane. It was sealed with an accretion of its content and had not been opened for a very long time."

"So Sonia didn't put arsenic in the thermos?"

"Not out of the tin, at any rate."

"Not at all, if it wasn't—if—"

"Not at all, it seems."

"And you think that somehow or another he took the Dr. Withers ringworm poison."

"If he did, analysis will show it. We've yet to find out if it does."

"But," said Thomas, "Sonia brought it back from the chemist's. I remember hearing something about that."

"She brought it, yes, together with Sir Henry's medicine. She put the bottles in the flower-room. Miss Fenella Ancred was there and left the room with her."

"And Dr. Withers," Thomas went on rather in the manner of a child continuing a narrative, "came up that night and gave the children the medicine. Caroline was rather annoyed because he'd said she could do it. She felt," Thomas said thoughtfully, "that it rather reflected on her capability. But he quite insisted and wouldn't let her touch it. And then, you know, it didn't work. They should have been as bald as eggs, but they were not. As bald as eggs," Thomas repeated with a shudder. "Oh, yes, I see. Papa *was*, of course."

He remained sitting very upright with his hands on his knees, for some twenty minutes. The car had left London behind and slipped through a frozen landscape. Alleyn, with a deliberate effort, retraced the history of the case: Troy's long and detailed account, the turgid statements of the Ancreds, the visit to Dr. Withers, the scene in the churchyard. What could it have been that Troy knew she had forgotten and believed to be important?

Thomas, with that disconcerting air of switching himself on, broke the long silence.

"Then I suppose," he said very abruptly and in a high voice, "that you think either Sonia gave him the children's medicine or one of us did. But we are not at all murderous people. But I suppose you'll say that lots of murderers have been otherwise quite nice people like the Dusseldorf Monster. But what about motive? You say Cedric knew Papa had signed the will that cut him out of almost everything, so Cedric wouldn't. On the other hand Milly didn't know he'd signed a second Will and she was quite pleased about the first one, really, so *she* wouldn't. And that goes for Dessy too. She wasn't best pleased but she wasn't much surprised or worried. And I hope you don't think— However," Thomas hurried on, "we come to Pauline. Pauline might have been very hurt about Paul and Panty and herself but it was quite true, what Papa said. Her husband left her very nicely off and she's not at all revengeful. It's not as if Dessy and Milly or I *wanted* money desperately and it's not as if Pauline or Panty or Fenella (I'd forgotten Fenella and Jen) are vindictive slayers. They just aren't. And Cedric thought he was all right. And *honestly*," Thomas ended, "you can't suspect Barker and the maids."

"No," said Alleyn. "We don't."

"So it seems you must suspect a person who wanted money very badly and was left some in the first Will. And, of course, didn't much care for Papa. And Cedric, who's the only one who fits, won't do."

He turned, after making this profound understatement, to fix upon Alleyn a most troubled and searching gaze.

"I think that's a pretty accurate summing-up," Alleyn said.

"Who could it be?" Thomas mused distractedly and added, with a sidelong glance, "But then, you've picked up all sorts of information which you haven't mentioned."

"Which I haven't time to mention," Alleyn rejoined. "There are Ancreton woods above that hill. We'll stop at the pub."

P.C. Bream was standing outside the pub and stepped forward to open the door of the car. He was scarlet in the face.

"Well, Bream," Alleyn said. "Carried out your job?"

"In a manner of speaking, sir," said Bream. "No. Good afternoon, Mr. Thomas."

Alleyn stopped short in the act of getting out. "What? Isn't she there?"

"Circumstances," Bream said indistinctly, "over which I 'ad no control, intervened, sir." He waved an arm at a bicycle leaning against the pub. The front tyre hung in a deflated festoon about the axle. "Rubber being not of the best—"

"Where is she?"

"On my arrival, having run one mile and a quarter—"

"Where is she?"

"Hup," said Bream miserably, "at the 'ouse."

"Get in here and tell us on the way."

Bream wedged himself into one of the tip-up seats and the driver turned the car. "Quick as you can," Alleyn said. "Now, Bream."

"Having received instructions, sir, by telephone, from the Super at Camber Cross, me having my dinner at the pub, I proceeded upon my bicycle in the direction of Ancreton 'Alt at 11.50 A.M."

"All right, all right," said Fox. "And your tyre blew out."

"At 11.51, sir, she blew on me. I inspected the damage and

formed the opinion it was impossible to proceed on my bicycle. Accordingly, I ran."

"You didn't run fast enough, seemingly. Don't you know you're supposed to keep yourself fit in the force?" said Fox severely.

"I ran, sir," Bream rejoined with dignity, "at the rate of one mile in ten minutes and arrived at the 'alt at 12.04, the train 'aving departed at 12.01 and the ladies in the pony carriage being still in view on the road to the Manor."

"The ladies?" said Alleyn.

"There was two of them. I attempted to attract their attention by raising my voice but without success. I then returned to the pub, picking up that there cantankerous bike ong rowt."

Fox muttered to himself.

"I reported by 'phone to the Super. He give me a blast and said he would ring the Manor and request the lady in question to return. She 'as not done so."

"No," Alleyn said. "I imagine she'd see him damned first."

The car turned in at the great entrance and climbed through the woods. Half way up the drive they met what appeared to be the entire school, marching and singing under the leadership of Miss Caroline Able's assistant. They stood aside to let the car pass. Alleyn could not see Panty among them.

"Not their usual time for a walk," said Thomas.

The car drew up at last into the shadow of the enormous house.

"If nothing else has gone cock-eyed," Alleyn said, "she'll be in the school."

Thomas cried out in alarm: "Are you talking about Caroline Able?"

"No. See here, Ancred. We're going into the school. There's a separate entrance back there, and we'll use it. Will you go in to this part of the house and please say nothing about our arrival?"

"Well, all right," said Thomas, "though I must say I don't quite see—"

"It's all very confusing. Away you go."

They watched Thomas walk slowly up the steps, push open the great door and pause for a second in the shadowy lobby. Then he turned and the door closed between them.

"Now, Fox," Alleyn said, "you and I will go into the school. I think the best thing we can do is to ask her to come back with us to London and make a statement. Awkward if she refuses, but if she does we'll have to take the next step. Drive back to the end of the building, there."

The car was turned and stopped again at a smaller door in the West Wing. "Thompson, you and Bream wait back there in the car. If we want you, we'll get you. Come on, Fox."

They got out. The car moved away. They had turned to the doorway when Alleyn heard his name called. Thomas was coming down the steps from the main entrance. He ran towards them, his coat flapping, and waved his arm.

"Alleyn! *Alleyn!* Stop."

"*Now* what?" Alleyn said.

Thomas was breathless when he reached them. He laid his hands on the lapels of Alleyn's coat. His face was colourless and his lips shook. "You've got to come," he said. "It's frightful. Something frightful's happened. Sonia's in there, horribly ill. Withers says she's been poisoned. He says she's going to die."

CHAPTER EIGHTEEN

Last Appearance of Miss O.

i

THEY HAD carried her into a small bedroom in the school.

When Alleyn and Fox, accompanied as far as the door by Thomas, walked unheralded into the room, they found Dr. Withers in the act of turning Pauline and Desdemona out of it. Pauline appeared to be in an advanced state of hysteria.

"*Out*, both of you. At once, please. Mrs. Ancred and I can do all that is necessary. And Miss Able."

"A curse. That's what I feel. There's a curse upon this house. That's what it is, Dessy."

"Out, I say. Miss Ancred, take this note. I've written it clearly. Ring up my surgery and tell them to send the things up immediately the car arrives. Can your brother drive my car? Very well."

"There's a man and a car outside," Alleyn said. "Fox, take the note, will you?"

Pauline and Desdemona who had backed before the doctor to the door, turned at the sound of Alleyn's voice, uttered incoherent cries and darted past him into the passage. Fox, having secured the note, followed them.

"What the hell are you doing here!" Dr. Withers demanded. "Get out." He glared at Alleyn and turned back to the bed. Millamant Ancred and Caroline Able were stooped above it, working, it seemed, with difficulty, over something that struggled and made harsh inhuman noises. A heavy stench hung in the air.

"Get the clothes away, but put that other thing on her. Keep her covered as far as possible. That's right. Take my coat, Mrs. Ancred, please, I can't do with it. Now, we'll try the emetic again. Careful! Don't let her break the glass."

Miss Able moved away with an armful of clothes. Millamant

stood back a little, holding the doctor's jacket, her hands working nervously.

There, on a child's bed with a gay counterpane, Sonia Orrincourt strained and agonized, the grace of her body distorted by revolt and the beauty of her face obliterated in pain. As Alleyn looked at her, she arched herself and seemed to stare at him. Her eyes were bloodshot; one lid drooped and fluttered and winked. One arm, like that of a mechanical toy, repeatedly jerked up its hand to her forehead in a reiterated salaam.

He waited, at the end of the room, and watched. Dr. Withers seemed to have forgotten him. The two women after a startled glance turned again to their task. The harsh cries, the straining and agonizing, rose in an intolerable crescendo.

"I'm going to give a second injection. Keep the arm still, if you can. Very well, then, get that thing out of the way. Now."

The door opened a fraction. Alleyn moved to it, saw Fox and slipped through.

"Our chap ought to be back any minute with the doctor's gear," Fox muttered.

"Have you rung for Dr. Curtis & Co.?"

"They're on the way."

"Thompson and Bream still on the premises?"

"Yes, sir."

"Bring them in. Keep the servants in their own quarters. Shut up any rooms she'd been in since she got here. Herd the family together and keep them together."

"That's all been fixed, Mr. Alleyn. They're in the drawing-room."

"Good. I don't want to leave here yet."

Fox jerked his thumb. "Any chance of a statement?"

"None at the moment, far as I can see. Have you got anything, Fox?"

Fox moved closer to him and in a toneless bass began to mutter rapidly: "She and the doctor and Miss Able had tea together in Miss Able's room. He'd come up to see the kids. She sent the little Kentish girl through to order it. Didn't fancy schoolroom tea. Tea set out for the rest of the family in the dining-room. Second tray brought from the pantry by Barker with tea for one. Second pot brewed by Mrs. Kentish in the dining-room. Miss Desdemona put some biscuits on the tray. It was handed over to Miss Panty by Mrs. Ancred. Miss Panty brought it back here. Miss O. was taken bad straight away before the other two had touched anything. The little girl was there and noticed everything."

"Got the tea things?"

"Thompson's got them. Mrs. Ancred kept her head and said they ought to be locked up but, in the fluster of getting the patient out, the tray was knocked over. She left Mrs. Kentish to carry on but Mrs. Kentish took hysterics and Isabel swept it up in the finish. Tea and hot water and broken china all over the shop. We ought to get a trace, though, somewhere, if there's anything. That little girl's sharp, by gum she is."

Alleyn laid his hand swiftly on Fox's arm. In the room the broken sounds changed into a loud and rapid babbling: "Ba-ba-ba-ba," and stopped abruptly. At the same moment the uniformed driver appeared at the far end of the passage, carrying a small case. Alleyn met him, took the case, and motioning Fox to come after, re-entered the room.

"Here's your case, Dr. Withers."

"All right. Put it down. When you go out tell those women to get in touch with her people if she's got any. If they want to see her, they'll have to be quick."

"Fox, will you—"

Fox slipped away.

"I said, when you go out," Dr. Withers repeated angrily.

"I'm afraid I must stay. This is a police matter, Dr. Withers."

"I'm perfectly well aware of what's happened. My duty is to my patient and I insist on the room being cleared."

"If she should become unconscious—" Alleyn began, looking at the terrible face with its half-open eyes and mouth.

"If she regains consciousness, which she won't, I'll inform you." Dr. Withers opened the case, glanced up at Alleyn and said fiercely: "If you don't clear out I'll take the matter up with the Chief Constable."

Alleyn said briskly: "That won't do at all, you know. We're both on duty here and here we both stay. Your patient's been given thallium acetate. I suggest that you carry on with the treatment, Dr. Withers."

There was a violent ejaculation from Caroline Able. Millamant said: "That's the ringworm stuff! What nonsense!"

"How the hell—" Dr. Withers began and then: "Very well. Very well. Sorry. I'm worried. Now, Mrs. Ancred, I'll want your help here. Lay the patient—"

Forty minutes later, without regaining consciousness, Sonia Orrincourt died.

ii

"The room," Alleyn said, "will be left exactly as it is. The police surgeon is on his way and will take charge. In the meantime, you'll all please join the others in the drawing-room. Mrs. Ancred, will you and Miss Able go ahead with Inspector Fox?"

"At least, Alleyn," said Dr. Withers, struggling into his jacket, "you'll allow us to wash up."

"Certainly. I'll come with you."

Millamant and Caroline Able, after exchanging glances, raised a subdued outcry. "You must see—" Dr. Withers protested.

"If you'll come out, I'll explain."

He led the way and they followed in silence. Fox came out last and nodded severely to Bream, who was in the passage. Bream moved forward and stationed himself before the door.

Alleyn said: "It's perfectly clear, I'm sure, to all of you that this is a police matter. She was poisoned and we've no reason to suppose she poisoned herself. I may be obliged to make a search of the house (here is the warrant) and I must have a search of the persons in it. Until this has been done none of you may be alone. There is a wardress coming by car from London and you may, of course, wait for her if you wish."

He looked at the three faces, all of them marked by the same signs of exhaustion, all turned resentfully towards him. There was a long silence.

"Well," Millamant said at last, with an echo of her old short laugh, "you can search me. The thing I want to do most is sit down. I'm tired."

"I must say," Caroline Able began, "I don't quite—"

"Here!" Dr. Withers cut in. "Will this suit you? I'm these ladies' medical man. Search me and then let them search each other in my presence. Any good?"

"That will do admirably. This room here is vacant, I see. Fox, will you take Dr. Withers in?" Without further ado, Dr. Withers turned on his heel and made for the open door. Fox followed him in and shut it.

Alleyn turned to the two women: "We shan't keep you long," he said, "but if, in the meantime, you would like to join the others I can take you to them."

"Where are they?" Millamant demanded.

"In the drawing-room."

"Personally," she said, "I'm beyond minding who searches me and who looks on." Bream gave a self-conscious cough. "If you and Miss Able like to take me into the children's play-room, which I believe is vacant, I shall be glad to get it over."

"Well, really—" said Miss Able, "well, of course, that is an extremely sane point of view, Mrs. Ancred. Well, if *you* don't object."

"Good," Alleyn said. "Shall we go?"

There was a screen with Italian primitives pasted over it, in the play-room. The two women, at Alleyn's suggestion, retired behind it. First Millamant's extremely sensible garments were thrown out one by one, examined by Alleyn, collected again by Miss Able and then, after an interval, the process was reversed. Nothing was discovered, and Alleyn, walking between them, escorted the two ladies to the bathroom and finally through the green baize door and across the hall to the drawing-room.

Here they found Desdemona, Pauline, Panty, Thomas and Cedric, assembled under the eye of Detective-Sergeant Thompson. Pauline and Desdemona were in tears. Pauline's tears were real and ugly. They had left little traces, like those of a snail, down her carefully restrained make-up. Her eyes were red and swollen and she looked frightened. Desdemona, however, was misty, tragic and still beautiful. Thomas sat with his eyebrows raised to their limit and his hair ruffled, gazing in alarm at nothing in particular. Cedric, white and startled, seemed to be checked, by Alleyn's arrival, in a restless prowl round the room. A paper knife fell from his hands and clattered on the glass top of the curio cabinet.

Panty said: "Hullo. Is Sonia dead? Why?"

"Ssh, darling! Darling, ssh!" Pauline moaned and attempted vainly to clasp her daughter in her arms. Panty advanced into the centre of the room and faced Alleyn squarely: "Cedric," she said loudly, "says Sonia's been murdered. Has she? Has she, Miss Able?"

"Goodness!" said Caroline Able in an uneven voice. "I call that rather a stupid thing to say, Patricia, don't you?"

Thomas suddenly walked up to her and put his arm about her shoulders.

"Has she, Mr. Alleyn?" Panty insisted.

"You cut off and don't worry about it," Alleyn said. "Are you at all hungry?"

"You bet."

"Well, ask Barker from me to give you something rather special, and then put your coat on and see if you can meet the others coming home. Is that all right, Mrs. Kentish?"

Pauline waved her hand and he turned to Caroline Able.

"An excellent idea," she said more firmly. Thomas's hand still rested on her shoulder.

Alleyn led Panty to the door. "I won't go," she announced, "unless you tell me if Sonia's dead."

"All right, old girl, she is." A multiple ejaculation sounded behind him.

"Like Carabbas?"

"No!" said her Aunt Millamant strongly and added: "Pauline, must your child behave like this?"

"They've both gone away," Alleyn said. "Now cut along and don't worry about it."

"I'm not worrying," Panty said, "particularly. I daresay they're in Heaven and Mummy says I can have a kitten. But a person likes to know." She went out.

Alleyn turned and found himself face to face with Thomas. Behind Thomas he saw Caroline Able stooping over Millamant, who sat fetching her breath in dry sobs while Cedric bit his nails and looked on. "I'm sorry," Millamant stammered, "it's just reaction I suppose. Thank you, Miss Able."

"You've been perfectly splendid, Mrs. Ancred."

"Oh, Milly, Milly!" wailed Pauline. "Even you! Even your iron reserve. Oh, Milly!"

"O *God!*" Cedric muttered savagely. "I'm so *sick* of all this."

"You," Desdemona said, and laughed with professional bitterness. "In less tragic circumstances, Cedric, that would be funny."

"Please, all of you *stop*."

Thomas's voice rang out with authority, and the dolorous buzz of reproach and impatience was instantly hushed.

"I daresay you're all upset," he said. "So are other people. Caroline is and I am. Who wouldn't be? But you can't go on flinging temperaments right and left. It's very trying for other people and it gets us nowhere. So I'm afraid I'm going to ask you all to shut up because I've got something to say to Alleyn and if I'm right, and he says I'm right, you can all have hysterics and get on with the big scene. But I've got to know."

He paused, still facing Alleyn squarely, and in his voice and his manner Alleyn heard an echo of Panty: "A person likes to know," Panty had said.

"Caroline's just told me," Thomas said, "that you think somebody gave Sonia the medicine Dr. Withers prescribed for those kids. She says Sonia had tea with her. Well, it seems to me, that means somebody's got to look after Caroline and I'm the person to do it because I'm going to marry her. I daresay that's a surprise to all of you but I am, so that's that, and nobody need bother to say anything, please."

With his back still turned to his dumbfounded family, Thomas, looking at once astonished and determined, grasped himself by the lapels of his coat and continued. "You've told me you think Papa was poisoned with this stuff and I suppose you think the same person killed Sonia. Well, there's one person who ordered the stuff for the kids and wouldn't let Caroline touch it and who ordered the medicine for Papa, and who is pretty well known to be in debt, and who was left quite a lot of money by Papa, and who had tea with Sonia. He's not in the room now," said Thomas, "and I want to know where he is and whether he's a murderer. That's all."

Before Alleyn could answer, there was a tap on the door and Thompson came in. "A call from London, for you, sir," he said. "Will you take it out here?"

Alleyn went out, leaving Thompson on guard and the Ancreds still gaping. He found the small telephone room across the hall and, expecting a voice from the Yard, was astonished to hear Troy's.

"I wouldn't have done this if it mightn't be important," said Troy's voice, miles away. "I telephoned the Yard and they told me you were at Ancreton."

"Nothing wrong?"

"Not here. It's just that I've remembered what Sir Henry said that morning. When he'd found the writing on his looking-glass."

"Bless you. What was it?"

"He said he was particularly angry because Panty, he insisted it was Panty, had disturbed two important documents that were on his dressing-table. He said that if she'd been able to understand them she would have realized they concerned her very closely. That's all. Is it anything?"

"It's almost everything."

"I'm sorry I didn't remember before, Rory."

"It wouldn't have fitted before. I'll be home tonight. I love you very much."

"Good-bye."

"Good-bye."

When Alleyn came out in the hall Fox was there waiting for them.

"I've been having a bit of a time with the doctor," Fox said, "Bream and our chap are with him now. I thought I'd better let you know, Mr. Alleyn."

"What happened?"

"When I searched him I found this in his left-hand side pocket."

Fox laid his handkerchief on the hall table and opened it out, disclosing a very small bottle with a screw top. It was almost empty. A little colourless fluid lay at the bottom.

"He swears," said Fox, "that he's never seen it before, but it was on him all right."

Alleyn stood looking at the little phial for a long moment. Then he said: "I think this settles it, Fox. I think we'll have to take a risk."

"Ask a certain party to come up to the Yard?"

"Yes. And hold a certain party while this stuff is analyzed. But there's no doubt in my mind about it, Fox. It'll be thallium acetate."

"I'll be glad to make this arrest," said Fox heavily, "and that's a fact."

Alleyn did not answer and after another pause Fox jerked his head at the drawing-room door.

"Shall I—"

"Yes."

Fox went away and Alleyn waited alone in the hall. Behind the great expanse of stained-glass windows, there was sunlight. A patchwork of primary colours lay across the wall where Henry Ancred's portrait was to have hung. The staircase mounted into shadows, and out of sight, on the landing, a clock ticked. Above the enormous fireplace, the fifth baronet pointed his sword complacently at a perpetual cloud-burst. A smouldering log settled with a whisper on the hearth and somewhere, away in the servants' quarters, a voice was raised and placidly answered.

The drawing-room door opened and with a firm step and a faint meaningless smile on her lips, Millamant Ancred came out and crossed to the hall to Alleyn.

"I believe you wanted me," she said.

CHAPTER NINETEEN

Final Curtain

i

"IT WAS the mass of detail," Troy said slowly, "that muddled me at first. I kept trying to fit the practical jokes into the pattern and they wouldn't go."

"They fit," Alleyn rejoined, "but only because she used them after the event."

"I'd be glad if you'd sort out the essentials, Rory."

"I'll try. It's a case of maternal obsession. A cold, hard woman with a son for whom she had a morbid adoration. Miss Able would tell you all about that. The son is heavily in debt, loves luxury and is intensely unpopular with his relations. She hates them for that. One day, in the ordinary course of her duties, she goes up to her father-in-law's room. The drafts of two Wills are lying on the dressing-table. One of them leaves her son, who is his heir, more than generous means to support his title and property. The other cuts him down to the bare bones of the entailed estate. Across the looking-glass someone has scrawled: "Grandfather is a bloody old fool." As she stands there, and before she can rearrange the papers, her father-in-law walks in. He immediately supposes, and you may be sure she shares and encourages the belief, that his small granddaughter, with a reputation for practical jokes, is responsible for the insulting legend. She may even have picked out her own embroidery, though it sounds like something Panty might have done. Millamant is a familiar figure in his room, and he has no cause to suspect her of such an idiotic prank. Still less does he suspect the real perpetrator, her son, Cedric Ancred, who has since admitted that this was one of a series of stunts designed by himself and Sonia Orrincourt to set the old man against Panty, hitherto his favourite.

"Millamant Ancred leaves the room with the memory of those two drafts rankling in her extremely tortuous mind. She knows the old man changes his Will as often as he loses his temper. Already

Cedric is unpopular. Some time during the next few days, perhaps gradually, perhaps in an abrupt access of resentment, an idea is born to Millamant. The Will is to be made public at the Birthday Dinner. Suppose the one that is favourable to Cedric is read, how fortunate if Sir Henry should die before he changes his mind! And if the dinner is rich and he, as is most probable, eats and drinks unwisely, what more likely that he should have one of his attacks and die that very night? If, for instance, there was tinned crayfish? She orders tinned crayfish."

"Just—hoping?"

"Perhaps no more than that. What do you think, Fox?"

Fox, who was sitting by the fire with his hands on his knees, said: "Isabel reckons she ordered it on the previous Sunday when they talked over the dinner."

"The day after the looking-glass incident. And on the following Monday evening, the Monday before the Birthday, when Cedric and Paul and his mother were all out, Millamant Ancred went into the flower-room and found a large bottle of medicine marked Poison for the school children, and another smaller bottle for Sir Henry. The bottles had been left on the bench by Sonia Orrincourt, who had joined Fenella Ancred there and had gone upstairs with her and had never been alone in the flower-room."

"And I," Troy said, "was putting the trap away and coming in by the East Wing door. If— Suppose I'd let Sonia do that and taken the medicine into the school "

"If you'll excuse my interrupting you, Mrs. Alleyn," Fox said, "it's our experience that when a woman makes up her mind to turn poisoner, nothing will stop her."

"He's right, Troy."

"Well," said Troy. "Go on."

"She had to chip away the chemist's sealing-wax before she got the corks out and Fox found bits of it on the floor and some burnt matches. She had to find another bottle for her purpose. She emptied Sir Henry's bottle, filled it up with thallium and, in case of failure, poured the remainder into her own small phial. Then she filled the children's bottle with water and recorked and resealed both Mr. Juniper's bottles. When Miss Able came in for the children's medicine she and Millamant hunted everywhere for it. It was not found until Fenella came downstairs, and who was more astonished than Millamant to learn that Sonia had so carelessly left the medicine in the flower-room?"

"But suppose," Troy said, "he'd wanted the medicine before she knew about the Will?"

"There was the old bottle with a dose still in it. I fancy she removed that one some time during the Birthday at the same time that she loosened the wire of the bell-push. If a Will unfavourable to Cedric had been made public that bottle would have been replaced and the other kept for a more propitious occasion. As it was, she saw to it that she was never alone from dinner until the next morning, when Barker beat on the door of the room she shared with Desdemona. She had talked to Desdemona, you remember, until three o'clock—well after the time of Sir Henry's death. She built herself up a sort of emergency alibi with the same elaborate attention which she gives to that aimless embroidery of hers. In a way, this led to her downfall. If she'd risked a solitary trip along those passages, that night, to Cedric's room, she would have heard, no doubt, that Sir Henry had signed the second Will and she would have made a desperate attempt to stop him taking his medicine."

"Then she didn't mean at that time to throw suspicion on Sonia?"

"No, indeed. His death would appear to be the natural result of rash eating and pure temper. It was only when the terms of his last Will were made known that she got her second idea."

"An atrocious idea."

"It was all of that. It was also completely in character—tortuous and elaborate. Sonia had come between Cedric and the money. Very well, Sonia must go and the second Will be set aside. She remembered the book on embalming. She remembered that she had found Sonia reading it. She remembered the ratsbane with its printed antidote to arsenical poisoning. So, the anonymous letters, printed on the kids' paper she herself fetched from the village, appeared on the breakfast table. A little later, as nobody seemed to have caught on to the right idea, the book on embalming appeared on the cheese dish, and finally the tin of ratsbane appeared in Sonia's suitcase. At about this time, she got a horrible jolt."

"The cat," said Fox.

"Carabbas!" Troy ejaculated.

"Carabbas had been in Sir Henry's room. Sir Henry had poured out milk for him. But the medicine glass had overturned into the saucer and presently Carabbas began to lose his fur. No wonder. He'd lapped up thallium acetate, poor chap. Millamant couldn't stand the sight of him about the house; he was one too much for her iron nerve. Accusing him of ringworm, and with the hearty consent of everyone but Panty, she had him destroyed.

"She sat back awaiting events and unobtrusively jogging them along. She put the tin of arsenical ratsbane in Sonia Orrincourt's suitcase and joined in the search for it. She declared that it had been a full tin but the servants disagreed. She forgot, however, to ease the lid which was cemented in with the accretion of years."

"But to risk everything and plan everything on the chance that arsenic was used by the embalmers!" Troy exclaimed.

"It didn't seem like a chance. Sir Henry had ordered Mortimer and Loame to use it and Mr. Mortimer had let him suppose they would do so. Her nerve went a bit, though, after the exhumation. She rang up the embalmers, using no doubt the deepest notes of her masculine voice, and said she was my secretary. Loame, the unspeakable ass, gave her their formula. That must have been a bitter moment for Millamant. Cedric's only means of avoiding financial ruin was by marrying the woman she loathed and against whom she had plotted; and now she knew that the frame-up against Sonia Orrincourt was no go. She didn't know, however, that we considered thallium acetate a possible agent and would look for it. She'd kept the surplus from the amount she could get into Sir Henry's bottle and she waited her chance. Sonia could still be disposed of; Cedric could still get the money."

"She must be mad."

"They're like that, Mrs. Alleyn," Fox said. "Female poisoners behave like that. Always come at it a second time and a third and fourth, too, if they get the chance."

"Her last idea," Alleyn said, "was to throw suspicion on Dr. Withers, who's a considerable beneficiary in both Wills. She put thallium in the milk when the tea-tray was sent in to Miss Able, knowing Withers and Sonia Orrincourt were there and knowing Sonia was the only one who took milk. A little later she slipped the bottle into Withers's jacket. With Sonia dead, she thought, the money would revert after all, to Cedric."

"Very nasty, you know," Fox said mildly. "Very nasty case indeed, wouldn't you say?"

"Horrible," Troy said under her breath.

"And yet, you know," Fox went on, "it's a guinea to a gooseberry she only gets a lifer. What do you reckon, sir?"

"Oh, yes," Alleyn said, looking at Troy. "It'll be that if it's not acquittal."

"But surely—" Troy began.

"We haven't got an eye-witness, Mrs. Alleyn, to a single action that would clinch the case. Not one." Fox got up slowly. "Well, if you'll excuse me. It's been a long day."

Alleyn saw him out. When he returned, Troy was in her accustomed place on the hearth-rug. He sat down and after a moment she leant towards him, resting her arm across his knees.

"Nothing is clear-cut," she said, "when it comes to one's views. Nothing." He waited. "But we're together," she said. "Quite together, now. Aren't we?"

"Quite together," Alleyn said.